Praise for
The Monarchies of God

"Paul Kearney's *Monarchies of God* is simply the best fantasy series I've read in years and years."
– Steven Erikson

"One of the best fantasy works in ages... Tough, muscular realism... Kearney paints the gore, the sex, and the lust for power in vivid colour."
– *SFX*

"Impressive for its human insights, its unusual take on the use of magic and its fine blending of historical elements with sheer invention."
– *Locus*

"I found it more or less impossible to put down the books... I can honestly say that I have not enjoyed a fantasy series this much in a long time."
– *Fantasy Freaks*

"Action-packed, fast-paced fantasy adventure."
– *SF Site*

"A bold, strong new voice in fantasy."
– Robert Silverberg

Other Books by Paul Kearney

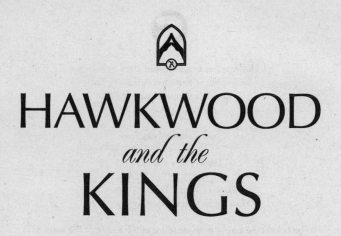

HAWKWOOD
and the
KINGS

PAUL KEARNEY

SOLARIS

This omnibus first published 2010 by Solaris
an imprint of Rebellion Publishing Ltd,
Riverside House, Osney Mead,
Oxford, OX1 0ES, UK

www.solarisbooks.com

ISBN: 978 1 906735 71 5

Hawkwood's Voyage © Paul Kearney 1995
The Heretic Kings © Paul Kearney 1996

The right of the author to be identified as the author of this work has
been asserted in accordance with the Copyright,
Designs and Patents Act 1988.

10 9 8 7 6 5 4 3 2 1

A CIP catalogue record for this book is available from the
British Library.

Designed & typeset by Rebellion Publishing

Printed in the US

HAWKWOOD'S VOYAGE

They that go down to the sea in ships,
that do business in great waters;
these see the works of the Lord, and
his wonders in the deep.

– Psalm 107:23-24

For the Museum Road bunch:
John, Dave, Sharon, Felix and Helen;
and for Dr. Marie Cahir,
partner in everything.

PROLOGUE

A SHIP OF the dead, it coasted in on the northwest breeze, topsails still set but the yards braced for a long-lost wind on the open ocean. The yawlsmen sighted it first, on the eve of St. Beynac's Day. It was heeling heavily, even on the slight swell, and what was left of its canvas shuddered and flapped when the breeze fell.

It was a day of perfect blueness – sea and sky vast, even reflections of one another. A few gulls flapped expectantly round the silver-filled nets the yawl crews were hauling in hand over fist, and a school of gleaming oyvips were sporting off to port: an unlucky omen. Within each, it was said, howled the soul of a drowned man. But the wind was kind, and the shoal was large – it could be seen as a broad shadow under the hull, twinkling now and then with the bright flank of a twisting fish – and the fishermen had been here since the forenoon watch, filling their nets with the sea's uncertain bounty, the dark line of the Hebrionese coast a mere guess off behind their right shoulders.

The skipper of one yawl shaded his eyes, paused and peered out to sea, blue stone glinting out from rippled leather, his chin bristling with hairs as pale as those on the stem of a nettle.

Water shadow writhed luminously in the hollows of his eye-sockets.

"There's a sight," he muttered.

"What is it, Fader?"

"A carrack, lad, a high-seas ship by the looks of her. But the canvas is hanging in strips off her yards – there's a brace flying free. And she's made a ton of water, if I'm any judge.

She's taken a pounding, all right. And what of the crew? Un-handy lubbers."

"Maybe they're dead, or wore out," his son said eagerly.

"Maybe. Or maybe sick of the plague as I hears ravages them eastern lands. The curse o' God on unbelievers."

The other men in the yawl paused at that, staring darkly out at the oncoming vessel. The wind veered a point – they felt it shift out of one eye – and the strange ship lost way. She was hull up, her battered masts black against that uncertain band of horizon that is either sea or sky. Water dripped from the men's hands; the fish flapped feebly in the nets, forgotten and dying. Droplets of sweat gathered on noses and stung their eyes: salt in everything, even the body's own water. They looked at their skipper.

"It's salvage, if the crew's all dead," one man said.

"It's an unlucky ship that coasts in from the empty west and no sign of life aboard," another muttered. "There's naught out there but a thousand score leagues of unsailed sea, and beyond that the very rim of the earth."

"There may be men alive aboard her in need of help," the skipper said sternly. His son gazed at him with round eyes. For a moment, the stares of all his crew were fixed on his face. He felt them like he did the warmth of the sun, but his seamed visage revealed nothing as he made his decision.

"We'll close with her. Jakob, set the forecourse, brace her round. Gorm, get these nets in and hail the other boats. They should stay. There's a good shoal here, too good to let by."

The crew leapt to their tasks, some sullen, some excited.

The yawl was two-masted, the mizzen stepped abaft the rudder head. She would have to beat into the landward breeze to board the carrack. Men on the other boats paused in the hauling of their catch to watch as the yawl closed on her goal. The bigger vessel was broadside on to the swell, listing to starboard as the waves broke on her windward side. As the yawl drew close, her crew broke out sweeps and strained at the heavy oars whilst the skipper and a few others stood poised on the gunwale, ready to make the perilous leap on to the side of the carrack.

She towered darkly above them now, a looming giant, her running rigging flying free, the lateen yard on her mizzen a mere stump and the thick wales that lined her side smashed and splintered as though she had squeezed through a narrow place. There was no sign of life, no reply to the skipper's hail. Surreptitiously, men at the sweeps paused in their labour to make the Sign of the Saint at their breasts.

The skipper leapt, grunted at the impact as he hit the carrack's side, hauled himself over her rail and stood panting. The others followed, two with their dirks in their teeth as if they expected to fight their way aboard. And then the yawl drew off, her mate putting her about on the port tack. She would heave to, keep the wind on her weather bow and ride out the breeze. The skipper waved at her as she eased away.

The carrack was wallowing low in the water and the wind was working on her high fore- and sterncastles. There was no sound but the hiss and lap of the sea, the creak of wood and rigging, the thump of a staved cask that rolled back and forth in the scuppers. The skipper raised his head as he caught the whiff of corruption. He met the knowing gaze of old Jakob. They nodded at each other. There was death aboard, corpses rotting somewhere.

"The Blessed Ramusio preserve us, let it not be the plague," one man said hoarsely, and the skipper scowled.

"Hold your tongue, Kresten. You and Daniel see what you can do to put her before the wind. It's my belief her seams are working in this swell. We'll see if we can't get her into Abrusio before she spews her oakum and sinks her bow."

"You're going to bring her in?" Jakob asked.

"If I can. We'll have to look below though, see if she's anywhere near settling." The roll of the ship made him lurch a little. "Wind's picking up. That's all to the good if we can get her head round. Come, Jakob."

He pushed open one of the doors in the sterncastle and entered the darkness beyond. The bright blue day was cut off. He could hear Jakob padding barefoot and breathing heavily behind him in the sudden gloom. He stopped. The ship heaved like a dying thing under his feet – that smell of putrefaction, stronger now, rising even over the familiar sea smells of salt and tar and hemp. He gagged as his hands, groping, found another door.

"Sweet Saint!" he breathed, and pushed it open.

Sunlight, bright and blazing, flooding through shattered stern windows. A wide cabin, a long table, the gleam of falchions crossed on a bulkhead, and a dead man sitting watching him.

The skipper made himself move forward.

There was water underfoot, sloshing about with the heave of the ship. It looked as though a following sea had swamped the windows; at the forward end of the cabin was a tangle of clothing, weapons, charts, and a small brassbound chest, much battered. But the dead man sat upright in his chair with his back to the stern windows and the brown skin stretched tight as parchment over the lines of his skull. His hands were shrunken claws. The rats had gnawed him. His chair was fixed in wooden runners to the deck, and he was tied into the chair by line after line of sodden cordage. It looked as though he had bound himself; the arms were free. A tattered scrap of paper was clenched in one decaying fist.

"Jakob, what is this we see?"

"I know not, Captain. There has been devilry at work in this ship. This man was the master – see the charts? – and there is a broken cross-staff here too. But what happened to him that he did this?"

"There is no explaining it – not yet. We must go below. See if you can find a lantern here, or a candle. I must have a look at her hold."

"The hold?" The old man sounded doubtful.

"Yes, Jakob. We must see how fast she is making water, and what her cargo is."

The light left the windows and the motion of the ship grew easier as the men on deck put her before the wind. Jakob and his captain gave a last look at the dead master and his skull face, and left. Neither told the other what he was thinking: the dead man had ended his tenure of the world with his face distorted by terror.

BRIGHT SUNLIGHT AGAIN, the clean spray of the sea. The other boarders were busy with the lifts and braces, moving yards far heavier than they were used to. The skipper barked a few orders. They would need canvas and fresh cordage. The mainmast shrouds were ripped to shreds on the port side; a wonder she had not rolled out the mast.

"No storm ever did this to a ship," Jakob said, and ran his horny hands along the ship's rail. The wood was torn, punctured. Bitten, the skipper thought, and he felt a cold worm of fear coil in his stomach.

But he shut his face to Jakob's look of enquiry.

"We are mariners, not philosophers. Our task is to make the ship swim. Now are you coming with me or shall I ask one of the youngsters?"

They had sailed the Hebrionese coast for more than two-score years together, weathered more storms than they could remember, hauled in a million fish. Jakob nodded mutely, anger burning away his fear.

The tarpaulins over the hatchways were flapping and torn.

It was dark there, in the very bowels of the ship, and they lowered themselves down with care. One of the others had found and lit a lantern. It was passed down into the dark and by its beam they found themselves surrounded by crates, casks and sacks. There was a musty smell in the air, and again the faint stink of corruption. They could hear the swirl and gurgle of water deeper in the hold, the rolling rumble of loose cargo, the creak of the ship's overworked hull. The stink of the bilge, usually overpowering in a large ship, had been overwhelmed by incoming seawater.

They made their slow way along an avenue between the cargo, the lantern beam swinging shadows in chaotic directions. They found the remains of rats half eaten, but none alive. And there was no sign of the crew. The master in his cabin above might have been piloting the ship alone and unaided until his death.

Another hatch, and a companion ladder leading down, deep into utter blackness. The ship creaked and groaned under their feet. They could no longer hear the voices of their shipmates above, in that other world of salt air and spray. There was only this hole opening on nothingness, and beyond the wooden walls that surrounded them nothing but the drowning sea.

"Water down there, deep enough too," Jakob said, lowering the lantern through the hatch. "I see it moving, but there's no spume. If it's a leak, it's slow."

They paused, peering down into a place neither of them wanted to see. But they were mariners, as the skipper had said, and no man bred to the sea could stand idle and watch a ship die.

The skipper made as if to start down, but Jakob stopped him with an odd smile and went first, the breath rattling audibly in his throat. The skipper saw the light break and splinter on multifaceted water, things bobbing in it, a splash amid the chiaroscuro of shadow and flame.

"Bodies here." Jakob's voice came up, distorted, far away. "I think I've found the crew. Oh sweet God, his blessed Saints –"

There was a snarling, and Jakob screamed. The lantern went out and in the blackness something thrashed the water into a fury. The skipper glimpsed the yellow gleam of an eye, like a ravening fire far off on a pitch-dark night. His lips formed Jakob's name but no sound came out; his tongue had turned to sand. He backed away and bumped into the sharp corner of a crate. *Run*, some part of his mind shrieked at him, but his marrow had become like granite within his very bones.

Then the thing was swarming up the companion towards him, and he had not even the time to mouth a prayer before it was rending his flesh, and the yellow eyes were witness to his soul's flight.

PART ONE

The FALL of AEKIR

One

THE CITY OF God was burning...

Long plumes of fire sailed up from the streets like windcoiled banners, detaching to consume themselves and become lost in the grim thunderheads of impenetrable smoke that lowered above the flames. For miles along the Ostian river the city burned and the buildings crumbled, their collapse lost in the all-encompassing roar of the fire. Even the continuing noise of battle by the western gates, where the rearguard was still fighting, was swallowed up by the bellowing inferno.

The cathedral of Carcasson, greatest in the world, stood stark and black against the flames, a solitary sentinel horned with steeples, nippled with domes. The massive granite shrugged off the heat but the lead on the roof was melting in rivulets and the timber beams were blazing all along their length. The bodies of priests littered the steps; the Blessed Ramusio gazed down sorrowfully with a horde of the lesser saints in attendance, their eyes cracking open, the bronze staffs they held buckling in the inferno. Here and there a gargoyle, outlined in scarlet, grinned malevolently down.

The palace of the High Pontiff was full of looting troops.

The Merduks had ripped down tapestries, hacked apart relics for the precious stones that adorned them, and now they were drinking wine out of the Holy Vessels whilst they waited their turn with captured women. Truly, Ahrimuz had been good to them today.

Further westwards within the city, the streets were clogged with fleeing people and the troops who had been stationed here to guard them. Hundreds were trampled underfoot in the panic, children abandoned, the old and slow kicked

aside. More than once a collapsing house would bury a
score of them in a fury of blazing masonry, but the rest
would spare hardly a glance. Westwards they forged, west
towards the gates still held by Ramusian troops, the last
remnant of John Mogen's Torunnans, once the most feared
soldiers in all the west. These were a desperate rabble now,
their valour bled away by the siege and the six assaults
which had preceded the last. And John Mogen was dead.
Even now, the Merduks were crucifying his body above the
eastern gate where he had fallen, cursing them to the last.

The Merduks poured through the city like a tide of
cockroaches, glinting and barbed in the light of the fires,
their faces shining, sword arms bloody to the elbows. It had
been a long siege and a good fight, and at last the greatest
city of the west was theirs for the taking. Shahr Baraz had
promised to let them loose once the city had fallen and they
were intent on plunder. It was not they who were burning
the city, but the retreating western troops. Sibastion Lejer,
lieutenant of Mogen, had sworn to let not one building fall
intact into the hands of the heathens and he and a remnant
of men still under orders were methodically burning the
palaces and arsenals, the storehouses and pleasure theatres
and churches of Aekir, and slaughtering anyone, Merduk or
Ramusian, who tried to stop them.

CORFE WATCHED THE tall curtains of flame shift against the
darkened sky. The smoke of the burning had brought about
a premature twilight, the end of a long day for the defenders
of Aekir; for many thousands, the last day.

He was on a flat rooftop, apart from the maelstrom of
screaming people below. The sound of them carried up in a
solid wave. Fear, anger, desperation. It was as though Aekir
itself were screaming, the tormented city in the midst of
its death throes, the fire incinerating its vitals. The smoke
stung Corfe's eyes and he wiped them clear. He could feel
ashes settling on his brow like a black snow.

A tatterdemalion figure, no longer the dapper ensign, he
was scorched, ragged and bloodied. He had cast aside his
half-armour in the flight from the walls, and wore only his

doublet and the heavy sabre that was the mark of Mogen's men. He was short, lithe, deep-eyed. In his gaze alternated murder and despair.

His wife was somewhere down there, enjoying the attentions of the Merduks or trampled underfoot in some cobbled alley, or a burnt corpse in the wreck of a house.

He wiped his eyes again. Damn smoke.

"*Aekir cannot fall,*" Mogen had told them. "*It is impregnable, and the men on its walls are the best soldiers in the world. But that is not all. It is the Holy City of God, first home of the Blessed Ramusio. It cannot fall.*" And they had cheered.

A quarter of a million Merduks had proved otherwise.

The soldier in him wondered briefly how many of the garrison had or would escape. Mogen's bodyguards had fought to the death after he had gone down, and that had started the flight. Thirty-five thousand men had garrisoned Aekir. If a tenth of them made it through to the Ormann line they would be lucky.

"*I can't leave you, Corfe. You are my life. My place is here.*" So she had said with that heartbreakingly lopsided smile of hers, the hair as dark as a raven's feather across her face. And he, fool, fool, fool, had listened to her, and to John Mogen.

Impossible to find her. Their home, such as it was, had been in the shadow of the eastern bastion, the first place to fall. He had tried to get through three times before giving up. No man lived there now who did not worship Ahrimuz, and the women who survived were already being rounded up. Handmaidens of Ahrimuz they would become, inmates of the Merduk field brothels.

Damned stupid bitch. He had told her a hundred times to move, to get out before the siege lines began to cut the city off.

He looked out to the west. The crowds pulsed that way like sluggish blood in the arteries of a felled giant. It was rumoured that the Ormann road was still open all the way to the River Searil, where the Torunnans had built their second fortified line in twenty years. The Merduks had left that one slim way out deliberately, it was said, to tempt the garrison into evacuation. The population would be choking it up for twenty leagues. Corfe had seen it before, in the score of battles that had followed after the Merduks had first crossed the Jafrar Mountains.

Was she dead? He would never know. Oh, Heria.

His sword arm ached. He had never before been a part of such slaughter. It seemed to him that he had been fighting for ever, and yet the siege had lasted only three months. It had not, in fact, been a siege as *The Military Manual* knew one. The Merduks had isolated Aekir and then had commenced to pound it into the ground. There had been no attempt to starve the city into submission. They had merely kept on attacking with reckless abandon, losing five men for every defender who fell, until the final assault this morning. It had been pure savagery on the walls, a to and fro of carnage, until the critical moment had been reached, the cup finally brimming over, and the Torunnans had begun the trickle off the ramparts which had turned into a rout. Old John had roared at them, before a Merduk scimitar cut him down. There had been near panic after that. No thought of a second line, a fighting retreat. The bitter tension of the siege, the multiple assaults, had left them too worn, as brittle as a rust-eaten blade. The memory made Corfe ashamed. Aekir's walls had not even been breached; they had simply been abandoned.

Was that why he had paused, was standing here now like some spectator at an apocalypse? To make up for his flight, perhaps.

Or to lose himself in it. *My wife. Down there somewhere, alive or dead.*

Rumbling booms, concussions that shook the smoke-thick air. Sibastion was touching off the magazines. Crackles of arquebus fire. Someone was making a stand. Let them. It was time to abandon the city, and those he had loved here. Those fools who chose to fight on would leave their corpses in its gutters.

Corfe started down off the roof, wiping his eyes angrily. He probed the stairway before him with his sabre like a blind man tapping his stick.

It was suffocatingly hot as he came out on the street, and the acrid air made his throat ache. The raw sound of the crowds hit him like a moving wall, and then he was in amongst them, being carried along like a swimmer lost in a millrace. They stank of terror and ashes and their faces seemed hardly human to him in the hellish light. He could see unconscious men and women being held upright by the closeness of the throng, small children crawling upon the serried heads as though they were a carpet. Men were being crushed at the edges of the street as they were smeared along the sides of the confining walls. He could feel the bodies of others under his feet as he was propelled along. His heel slid on the face of a child. The sabre was lost, levered out of his hand in the press. He tilted his face to the shrouded sky, the flaming buildings, and fought for his share of the reeking air.

Lord God, he thought, *I am in Hell.*

AURUNGZEB THE GOLDEN, third Sultan of Ostrabar, was dallying with the pert breasts of his latest concubine when a eunuch paddled through the curtains at the end of the chamber and bowed deeply, his bald pate shining in the light of the lamps.

"Highness."

Aurungzeb glared, his black eyes boring into the temerarious intruder, who remained bowed and trembling.

"What is it?"

"A messenger, Highness, from Shahr Baraz before Aekir. He says he has news from the army that will not wait."

"Oh, won't it?" Aurungzeb leapt up, hurling aside his pouting companion. "Am I at the beck and call, then, of every hairless eunuch and private soldier in the palace?" He kicked the eunuch sprawling. The glabrous face twisted silently.

Aurungzeb paused. "From the army, you say? Is it good news or bad? Is the siege broken? Has that dog Mogen routed my troops?"

The eunuch hauled himself to his hands and knees and wheezed at the fantastically coloured carpet. "He would not say, Highness. He will only relay the news to you personally. I told him this was very irregular but –" Another kick silenced him again.

"Send him in, and if he has bad news then I'll make a eunuch of him too."

A jerk of his head sent the concubine scurrying into the corner. From a jewelled chest the Sultan took a plain dagger with a worn hilt. It had seen much use, but had been put away as though it were something hugely precious. Aurungzeb tucked it into his waist sash, then clapped his hands.

The messenger was a Kolchuk, a race the Merduks had long ago conquered in their march west. The Kolchuks ate reindeer and made love to their sisters. Moreover, this man stood tall before Aurungzeb despite the hissings of the eunuch. He had somehow bypassed the Vizier and the Chamberlain of the Harem to come this far. It must be news indeed. If it was bad tidings Aurungzeb would make him less tall by a head.

"Well?"

The man had the unknowable eyes of the Kolchuks; flat stones behind slits in his expressionless face. But there was something of a glow about him, despite the fact that he swayed slightly as he stood. He smelt of dust and lathered horse, and Aurungzeb noticed with interest that there was a gout of dried blood blackening the gut of his armour.

Now the man did fall to one knee, but his face remained tilted upwards, shining.

"The compliments of Shahr Baraz, Commander in Chief of the Second Army of Ostrabar, Highness. He begs leave to report that, should it please your Excellency, he has taken possession of the infidel city of Aekir and is even now cleansing it of the last of the western rabble. The army is at your disposal."

Aekir has fallen.

The Vizier burst in, followed by a pair of tulwar-wielding guards. He shouted something, and they grasped the kneeling Kolchuk by the shoulders. But Aurungzeb held up a hand.

"Aekir has fallen?"

The Kolchuk nodded, and for a second the inscrutable soldier and the silk-clad Sultan smiled at each other, men sharing a triumph only they could appreciate. Then Aurungzeb pursed his lips. It would not do to press the man for information; that would smack of eagerness, even gracelessness.

"Akran," he barked at his glowering, uncertain Vizier. "Quarter this man in the palace. See that he is fed, bathed, and has whatever he wishes."

"But Highness, a common soldier –"

"Do it, Akran. This common soldier could have been an assassin, but you let him slip past you into the very harem. Had it not been for Serrim" – here the eunuch coloured and simpered – "I would have been taken totally by surprise. I thought my father had taught you better, Akran."

The Vizier looked bent and old. The guards shifted uneasily, contaminated with his guilt.

"Now go, all of you. No, wait. Your name, soldier. What is it and with whom do you serve?"

The Kolchuk gazed at him, remote once more. "I am Harafeng, Lord. I am one of the Shahr's bodyguard."

Aurungzeb raised an eyebrow. "Then, Harafeng, when you have eaten and washed, the Vizier will bring you back to me and we will discuss the fall of Aekir. You have my leave to go, all of you."

The Kolchuk nodded curtly, which made Akran splutter with indignation, but Aurungzeb smiled. As soon as he was alone in the chamber his smile turned into a grin which split his beard, and it was possible to see the general of men that he had briefly been in his youth.

Aekir has fallen.

Ostrabar was counted third in might of the Seven Sultanates, coming after Hardukh and ancient Nalbeni, but this feat of arms, this glorious victory, would propel it into the first rank of the Merduk sultanates, and Aurungzeb at its head. Centuries hence they would talk of the sultan who had taken the holiest and most populous city of the Ramusians, who had broken the army of John Mogen.

The way lay open to Torunn itself now; there remained only the line of the River Searil and the fortress of Ormann Dyke. Once they fell there was no line of defence until the Cimbric Mountains, four hundred miles further west.

"Ahrimuz, all praise to thee!" the Sultan whispered through his grin, and then said sharply, "Gheg."

A homunculus sidled from behind one of the embroidered curtains, flapped its leathery little wings and perched on a nearby table.

"Gheg," it said in a tiny, dry voice, its face a picture in cunning malevolence.

"I wish to speak to your keeper, Gheg. Summon him for me."

The homunculus, no larger than a pigeon, yawned, showing white needle-teeth in a red mouth. One clawed hand scratched its crotch negligently.

"Gheg hungry," it said, disgruntled.

Aurungzeb's nostrils flared. "You were fed last night, as fine a babe as you could wish. Now get me your keeper, hellspawn."

The homunculus glowered at him, then shrugged its tiny shoulders. "Gheg tired. Head hurts."

"Do as I say or I'll spit you like a quail."

The homunculus smiled: a hideous sight. Then a different light came into its glowing eyes. In a deep, human tone it said, "I am here, Sultan."

"Your pet is somewhat sullen of late, Orkh – one of the reasons I use him so seldom nowadays."

"My apologies, Highness. He is getting old. I shall consign him to the jar soon and send you a new one... What is your wish?"

"Where are you?" It was odd to hear petulance from such a big, hirsute figure.

"It is no matter. I am close enough. Have you a boon you would ask of me?"

Aurungzeb struggled visibly to control his temper.

"I would have you look south, to Aekir. Tell me what transpires there. I have had news. I wish to see it substantiated."

"Of course." There was a pause. "I see Carcasson afire. I see siege towers along the inner walls. There is a great burning, the howls of Ramusians. I congratulate you, Highness. Your troops run amok through the city."

"Shahr Baraz. What of him?"

Another moment's silence. When the voice came again it held mild surprise.

"He views the crucified body of John Mogen. He weeps, Sultan. In the midst of victory, he weeps."

"He is of the old *Hraib*. He mourns his enemy, the romantic fool. The city burns, you say?"

"Yes. The streets are crawling with unbelievers. They fire the city as they go."

"That will be Lejer, the dastard. He will leave us nothing but ashes. A curse on him and his children. I'll have him crucified, if he is taken. Is the Ormann road open?"

The homunculus had come out in beads of shining sweat. It trembled and its wing tips drooped. The voice which came out of it did not change, however.

"Yes, Highness. It is clogged with carts and bodies, a veritable migration. The House of Ostrabar reigns supreme."

Eighty years before the House of Ostrabar had consisted solely of Aurungzeb's grandfather and a trio of hardy concubines. Generalship, not lineage, had reared it up out of the eastern steppes. If the Ostrabars could not win battles themselves, they hired someone who could. Hence Shahr Baraz, who had been Khedive to Aurungzeb's father. Aurungzeb had commanded troops competently in his youth, but he could not inspire them in the same way. It was a lack he had never ceased to resent. Shahr Baraz, though originally an outsider, a nomad chief from far Kambaksk, had served three generations of Ostrabars honestly and ably. He was now in his eighties, a terrible old man much given to prayer and poetry. It was well that Aekir had fallen when it did; Shahr Baraz's long life was near its close, and with it would go the last link between the Sultans and the horse-borne chieftains of the steppes who had preceded them.

Shahr Baraz had recommended that the Ormann road be left open. The influx of refugees would weaken and demoralize the men who manned the line of the Searil river, he said. Aurungzeb had wondered if some outdated chivalry had had a hand in the decision also. No matter.

"Tell the –" he began, and stopped. The homunculus was melting before his eyes, glaring at him reproachfully as it bubbled into a foul-smelling pool.

"Orkh! Tell the Khedive to push on to the Searil!"

The homunculus's mouth moved but made no sound. It dissolved, steaming and reeking. In the nauseous puddle it became it was possible to make out the decaying foetus of a child, the wing-bones of a bird, the tail of a lizard. Aurungzeb gagged and clapped his hands for the eunuchs. Gheg had outlived its usefulness, but no doubt Orkh would send him another of the creatures soon. He had other messengers – not so swift, perhaps, but just as sure.

Aekir has fallen.

He began to laugh.

Two

"Sweet God!" Hawkwood said. "What is happening?"

"Vast heaving there!" the boatswain roared, eyeing a flapping sail. "Brace round that foretopsail, you God-damned eunuchs. Where do you think you are, a two-copper curiosity show?"

The *Grace of God*, a square-rigged caravel, slid quietly into Abrusio at six bells in the forenoon watch, the water a calm blue shimmer along her sides dotted with the filth of the port. Where the sun struck the sea there was a white glitter, painful to look at. A faint north-west breeze – the Hebrionese trade – enabled her to waft in like a swan, with hardly a rope to be touched by the staring crew despite the outrage of the boatswain.

Abrusio. They had heard the bells of its cathedral all through the last two turns of the glass, a ghostly echo of piety drifting out to sea.

Abrusio, capital of Hebrion and greatest port of the Five Kingdoms. It was a beautiful sight to behold when coming home from even a short coasting voyage such as the *Grace*'s crew had just completed; an uneasy cruise along the Macassar coast, haggling with the Sea-Rovers over tolls, one hand to their dirks and the slow-match burning alongside the culverins all the while. But profitable, despite the heat, the flies, the pitch melting in the seams and the marauding river lizards. Despite the feast drums at night along the bonfire-studded coast and the lateen-winged feluccas with their cargoes of grinning corsairs. Safe in the hold were three tons of ivory from the skeletons of great marmorills, and fragrant Limian spice by the hundredweight. And they had lost only one man, a clumsy first-voyager who had leaned too far out over the rail as a shallowshark passed by.

Now they were back among the Monarchies of God, where men made the Sign of the Saint over their viands and the Blessed Ramusio's likeness stared down upon every crossroads and market place.

Abrusio was home port for almost half of them, and contained the shipyard where the *Grace*'s keel had been laid down thirty years before.

Two things struck the seaward observer about Abrusio: the forest and the mountain.

The forest sprouted out of the glassy bay below the city, a vast tangle of masts and spars and yards, like the limbs of a leafless wood, perfect in their geometry, interconnected with a million rigging lines. Vessels of every nationality, tonnage, rig, complement and calling were anchored in the bay of Abrusio by the hundred, from coastal hoys and yawls with their decks asprawl with nets and shining fish to ocean-going carracks bedecked with proud pennants. And the Navy of Hebrion had its yards here also, so there were tall war-carracks, galleys and galleasses by the score, the wink of breastplate and helmet on quarterdecks and poops, the slow flap of the heavy Royal standards on mainmasts, the pendants of admirals on mizzens.

Two more things about this floating forest, this waterborne city: the noise and the smell. There were hoys offloading their catches, merchantmen at the quays with their hatches open and gangs hauling on tackles to bring forth from their bellies the very life's blood of trade. Wool from Almark, amber from Forlassen, furs from Fimbria, iron from Astarac, timber from the tall woods of Gabrion, best in the world for the building of ships. The men that worked the vessels of the port and the countless waggons on the wharves set up a rumbling murmur of sound, a clatter, a squeal of trucks, a creak of wood and hemp that carried for half a mile out to sea, the very essence of a living port.

And they stank. Further out to sea on such a still day drifted the smell of unwashed humanity in its tens of thousands, of fish rotting in the burnished sunlight, of offal tossed into the water to be quarrelled over by hordes of gulls, of pitch from the shipyards, ammonia from the tanneries; and underlying it all a heady mixture, like a glimpse of foreign lands, a concoction of spices and new timber, salt air and seaweed, an elixir of the sea.

That was the bay. The mountain, also, was not what it seemed. From afar it looked to be a blend of dust and ochre stone, pyramidal in shape, hazed with blue smoke. Closer inshore an approaching mariner would see that a hill reared up from the teeming waterfront and built upon it, row upon row, street upon narrow, crowded street, was the city itself, the house walls whitewashed and thick with dust, the roofs of faded red clay from the inland tile works of Feramuno. Here and there a church thrust head and lofty shoulders above the throng of humbler dwellings, its spire a spike reaching for blue, unclouded heaven. And here and there was the stonebuilt massiveness of a prosperous merchant's house – for Abrusio was a city of merchants as well as of mariners. Indeed, some said that a Hebrian must be one of three things at birth: a mariner, a merchant or a monk.

Towards the summit of the low hill, making it higher than it truly was and giving it the aspect of a steep-sided mountain, was the citadel and palace of the King, Abeleyn IV, monarch of Hebrion and Imerdon, admiral of half a thousand ships.

The dark granite walls of his fortress-palace had been reared up by Fimbrian artificers four centuries before, and over their high walls could be glimpsed the tallest of the King's cypresses, the jewels of his pleasure gardens. (A fifth of the city's water consumption, it was rumoured, went on keeping those gardens green.) They had been planted by the King's forebears when the first Hebrion shrugged off the decaying Fimbrian yoke. They flickered now in the awful heat, and the palace swam like a mirage of the Calmari desert.

Beside the King's palace and pleasure gardens the monastery of the Inceptine Order shimmered also. So-called because they were the first religious order founded after the visions of the Blessed Ramusio brought light to the darkness of the idol-worshipping west (indeed, some would have folk believe that Ramusio himself founded them), the Inceptines were the religious watchdogs of the Ramusian kingdoms.

Palace and monastery, they frowned down together over the sprawling, stinking, vibrant city of Abrusio. A quarter of a million souls toiled and bargained and revelled beneath them, natives of the greatest port in the known world.

"Sweet God," Richard Hawkwood had said. "What is happening?"

He had reason to speculate, for over the upper half of Abrusio a black smoke hung in the limpid air, and a worse stink was wafting over the crowded port towards his ship. Burning flesh. The gibbets of the Inceptines were crowded with sticklike shapes and a pall of scorched meat hung sickeningly far out to sea, more greasy and unclean than the foulest odour of the sewers.

"They're sending heretics to the pyre," the boatswain said, disgusted and awed. "God's Ravens are at it again. The Saints preserve us!"

Old Julius, the first mate, an easterner with a face as black as pitch, looked at his captain with wide eyes, his dusky countenance almost grey. Then he bent over the rail and hailed a bumboat close by, packed to the gills with fruit, its pilot a broad hideous fellow who lacked an eye.

"Ho! What's in the air, friend? We're back from a monthlong cruise down in the Rovers' kingdoms and our tongues are hanging out for news."

"What's in the air? Cannot your nostrils take in the stink of it? Four days it's been hanging over the city, honest old Abrusio. We're a haven of sorcerers and unbelievers it seems, every one of them in the pay of the sultans. God's Ravens are ridding us of them, in their kindness." He spat over the gunwale into water becoming thick with the detritus of the port. "And I'd watch where you go with that dark face, friend. But wait – you've been out a month, you say. Have you heard the news from the east? Surely to God you know?"

"Know what, fellow?" Julius cried out impatiently.

The bumboat was being left behind. Already it was half a cable abaft the port beam. The one-eyed man turned to shout:

"We are lost, my friends! Aekir has fallen!"

The port captain was waiting for them as one of Abrusio's tugs, her crew straining at the oars, towed them to a free wharf. The breeze had failed entirely and the brassy heat beat down unrelentingly on the maze of ships and men and docks, shortening tempers and loosening rigging. And all the while the slick stench of the pyres hung in the air.

Once the dock-hands had moored them to bollards fore and aft, Hawkwood collected his papers and stepped ashore first, reeling as his sea-accustomed legs hit the unyielding stone of the wharf. Julius and Velasca, the boatswain, would see that the offloading was conducted correctly. The men would be paid and no doubt would scatter throughout the city seeking sailors' pleasures, though they would find little pleasure tonight, Hawkwood thought. The city was busying along at something like its normal, frenetic pace, but it seemed subdued. He could see sullen looks, even open fear on the faces of the dock-hands who stood ready to help with the offloading; and they regarded the *Grace*'s crew, at least half of whom were foreigners out of one port or another, with some suspicion. Hawkwood felt the heat, the bustle and the uneasiness working him up into a black mood, which was strange considering that only hours before he had been looking forward to the voyage's end. He shook hands with Galliardo Ponera, the port captain whom he knew well, and the two fell into step as they wove their way to the port offices.

"Ricardo," the port captain said hurriedly, "I must tell you –"

"I know, lord God I know! Aekir has fallen at last and the Ravens are seeking scapegoats, hence the stink." The "Inceptines' incense" it was sometimes called, that bleary reek which marked the end of heretics.

"No, it is not that. It is the orders of the Prelate. I could do nothing – the King himself can do nothing."

"What are you prattling about, Galliardo?" The port captain was a short man, like Hawkwood himself, and once a fine seaman. A native of the Hebrionese, his skin was burnt as dark as mahogany, making for brilliant smiles. But he was not smiling now.

"You have returned from Macassar, the Malacar Islands?"

"So?"

"There is a new law, an emergency measure the Inceptines have badgered the King into drawing up. I would have got you word, warned you to divert to another port –"

But Hawkwood had halted in his tracks. Marching down the wharf towards them was a demi-tercio of Hebriate

Marines, and at their head a brother of the Inceptines in rich black, the "A" sign that was the symbol of the Saint swinging from a golden chain at his breast, glinting painfully in the sun. He was youngish, apoplectic-looking in his heavy robes and the blaring heat, but his face was shining with self-importance. He halted before Hawkwood and Galliardo and the marines crashed to attention behind him. Hawkwood pitied them in their armour. Their sergeant met his eyes and raised his own a fraction towards heaven. Hawkwood smiled despite himself, then bowed and kissed the brother's hand, as was expected.

"What can we do for you, Brother?" he asked brightly, though his heart was sinking fast.

"I am on God's business," the brother said. Sweat dripped from his nose. "It is my duty to inform you, Captain, that in his infinite wisdom the Prelate of Hebrion has come to a painful but necessary decision under God, to whit, foreigners who are not of the Five Ramusian Kingdoms of the West, or of states in vassalage to the above, are to be denied entry to their kingdoms, lest they with their unholy beliefs contaminate still further the sorry souls of our peoples and bring further calamities upon their heads."

Hawkwood stood rigid with anger, but the brother went on in a rushed monotone, as if he had said the words many times before:

"I am therefore bound to search your ship, and on finding any persons on board who come under the writ of the Prelate, am to escort them from this place to a place of security, there to retain them until our spiritual guides at the head of the august order of which I am a minuscule part have decided what is to be their fate." The brother wiped his brow and appeared slightly relieved.

Hawkwood spat with feeling over the side of the wharf into the oily water. The Inceptine did not seem offended. Sailors, soldiers and others of the lower orders often expressed themselves similarly.

"So if you will stand aside, Captain..."

Hawkwood drew himself up. He was not tall – the brother topped him by half a head – but he was as broad as a door with the arms of a longshoreman. Something cold in the sea-grey of his eyes halted the Inceptine in his tracks.

Behind the cleric the marines broiled silently.

"I am Gabrionese, Brother," Hawkwood said in a quiet voice.

"I have been made aware of that. Special dispensation has been granted to your countrymen in recognition of their gallant efforts at Azbakir. You need not worry, Captain. You are exempt."

Hawkwood felt Galliardo's hand on his arm.

"What I am saying, Brother, is that many of my crew, though not of the kingdoms or even of the no-doubt-worthy vassal states of the kings, are fine seamen, honest citizens, and worthy comrades. Some of them I have sailed with all my life, and one even took part in the battle of which you speak, a battle which saved southern Normannia from the Sea-Merduks."

He spoke hotly, thinking with rage of Julius Albak, a secret worshipper of Ahrimuz but who as a boy, a mere child out of Ridawan, had stood on the deck of a Gabrionese war-carrack as three Merduk galleys rammed and boarded, one after the other. That was at Azbakir. The Gabrionese, consummate sea-men but proud, wilful and stubborn, had stood alone that day and turned aside the fleets of the Sea-Merduks off the Calmaric coast as they sought to invade southern Astarac and Candelaria, the soft underbelly of the west.

"What were you at the time of Azbakir, Brother? A seed in your father's loins? Or were you out in the world and still shitting yellow?"

The Inceptine flushed dark, and behind him Hawkwood saw the marine sergeant's face struggling to maintain a wooden blankness.

"I should have expected no more from a Gabrionese corsair. Your time will come, Captain, and that of all your stiff-necked countrymen. Now stand aside or you will share the fate of the unbelievers in our midst a little early."

And when Hawkwood did not move: "Sergeant, shift me this impious dog!"

The sergeant hesitated. He met Hawkwood's eyes for a second. It was almost as if they had made an agreement on something. Hawkwood stood aside, hand on dirk.

"Were it not for your calling, Priest, I would spit you like the black, liverless fowl you are," he said, his voice icy as spindrift off the northern sea.

The Inceptine quailed. "Sergeant!" he screeched.

The marine moved forward purposefully, but Hawkwood let him and his fellows clank past him towards his ship, closely followed by the cleric. The brother turned once they were past.

"I know your name, Gabrionese. The Prelate will soon know it also, I promise you."

"Flap away, Raven," Hawkwood jeered, but Galliardo pulled him along.

"For the Saint's sake, Ricardo, come away. We can do nothing here but make things worse. Do you want to end up on a gibbet?"

Hawkwood moved stiffly, a sea creature out of its element. The blood had filled his face.

"Come to my offices. We will discuss this. Maybe we can do something."

The marines were boarding the Grace. Hawkwood could hear the official drone of the Inceptine's voice again.

Then there was a splash, and one of the crew had leapt over the side and was swimming with no visible destination in mind. The Inceptine shouted and Hawkwood, as if in a nightmare, saw a marine level his arquebus.

A sharp report that seemed to stun the port into silence for a moment, a heavy globe of smoke that obscured the ship's rail, and then the man was no longer swimming but was a dead, bobbing thing in the filthy water.

"Holy God!" Galliardo said, shocked, staring. Around the wharves work ceased as men paused to look on. The marine sergeant's voice could be heard bellowing angrily.

"May God curse them," Hawkwood said slowly, his voice thick with grief and hatred. "May He curse all black-robed Ravens that practice such foulness in His name."

The dead man had been Julius Albak.

Galliardo pulled him away by main strength, the sweat pulsing down his dark face in shining beads. Hawkwood let himself be dragged from the wharf, but stumbled like an old man, his eyes blind with tears.

ABELEYN IV, KING of Hebrion, was not happy either. Though
he knelt in the required manner to kiss the Prelate's ring,
there was a stiffness, a certain reluctance about his gesture
that betrayed his feelings. The Prelate laid a hand on his
dark circleted head.

"You wish to speak to me, my son."

Abeleyn was a proud young man in the prime of life.
More, he was a king, one of the Five Kings of the West;
and yet this old man never failed to treat him like an erring,
wilful but ultimately amiable child. And it never failed to
irritate him.

"Yes, Holy Father." He straightened. They were in the
Prelate's own apartments. High, massive stone walls and
the vaulted ceiling kept out the worst of the heat. Far off,
Abeleyn could hear the brothers singing Prime, preparing
for their midday meal. He had misjudged the timing of
his visit: the Prelate would be impatient for his lunch, no
doubt. Well, let him be.

Tapestries depicting scenes from the life of the Blessed
Ramusio relieved the austere grandeur of the chamber. There
was good carpet underfoot, sweet oil burning in censers,
the glint of gold in the hanging lamps, a tickle of incense in
the nostrils. On either side of the Prelate an Inceptine sat on
a velvet-covered stool. One had pen and parchment, for all
conversations were recorded here. Behind him Abeleyn could
hear the boots of his bodyguards clumping softly as they
knelt also. Their swords had been left at the door: not even
a king came armed into the Prelate's presence. Since Aekir,
and the disappearance of the High Pontiff in the wreck of
the city's fall, the five Prelates of the Kingdoms were God's
direct representatives on earth. Abeleyn's mouth twitched.
It was rumoured that the High Pontiff, Macrobius IV, had
wished to leave Aekir early on in the siege to preserve the Holy
Person, but John Mogen and his Torunnans had convinced
him otherwise, saying that for the Pontiff to flee the city would
be to acknowledge defeat. It was said that Macrobius had had
to be locked in a storeroom of his own palace to convince him.

Abeleyn's mood soured. The west would need men like
Mogen in the times to come. He had been worth half a
dozen kings.

As Abeleyn rose, a low stool was brought for him, and he sat at the Prelate's feet, for all the world like an apprentice at the foot of his master. Abeleyn swallowed anger and made his voice as even as silk.

"We have spoken about this edict concerning the heretics and foreigners of the city, and we have agreed that it is necessary to root out the disloyal, the unbelieving, the treacherous..."

The Prelate inclined his head, smiling graciously. With his large nose and keen eyes he looked like a liver-spotted eagle nodding on a perch.

"...but, Father, I noticed you have included in the wording of the edict the cantrimers, the mindrhymers, the petty Dweomer-users of the kingdom – the folk who possess any kind of theurgical ability. Already my soldiers, under the leadership of your brothers, are rounding up these people. What for? Surely you cannot mean to consign them to the flames?"

The Prelate continued to smile. "Oh, but I do, my son." Abeleyn's mouth became a scar in his face, as though a bitter fruit had been placed therein.

"But that would mean hunting out every old wife who cures warts, every herbalist who spells his wares, every –"

"Sorcery is sorcery, my son. All theurgy comes from the same source. The Evil One." The Prelate was like a saintly tutor humouring a dull-witted pupil. One of Abeleyn's bodyguards stirred angrily, but a glance from one of the Inceptines quelled him.

"Father, in doing this you could send thousands to the pyre, even members of my own court. Golophin the Mage, one of my own advisers –"

"God's work is never easy. We live in trialling times, as you should know better than anyone, my lord King," Abeleyn, interrupted twice in as many minutes, struggled to keep his voice from rising. He felt an urge to pick up the Prelate and dash his brains out against a convenient wall.

He smiled in his turn. "But surely you must at least recognize the practical difficulties involved in fulfilling such an edict, especially at a time like this. The Torunnans are crying out for reinforcements to halt the Merduk push and hold the Searil line. I am not sure" – here Abeleyn's smile took on a particular sweetness – "I am not sure I can spare you the men to carry out your edict."

The Prelate beamed back. "Your concern does you credit, my son. I know that the temporal cares of the moment lie heavy on your shoulders, but do not fear. God's will shall be done. I have asked for a contingent of the Knights Militant to be dispatched from the home of our order at Charibon. They will relieve you somewhat of the burden you bear. Your soldiers will be freed for service elsewhere, in the defence of the Ramusian kingdoms and the True Faith."

Abeleyn went white, and at his look even the Prelate seemed to shrink.

"I do what I can for the good of the kingdom, my lord King."

"Indeed." The Prelate was playing for higher stakes than Abeleyn had thought. Whilst his own soldiers were off on the frontier helping the Torunnans, the Knights Militant – the military arm of the Church – would have free rein in Abrusio. His spies should have informed him of this before today, but it was notoriously difficult to eavesdrop on the doings of the Inceptines. They were as tightly knit as chainmail. Abeleyn beat down the simmering fury and chose his words with care.

"Far be it for me, Father, to point out to you, one of the lords of the Church, what may or may not be necessary or desirable in God's eyes. But I do feel bound to say that your edict – our edict – has not been well received among the populace. Abrusio, as you are well aware, is a port, the most important in the west. It survives on trade, trade with other kingdoms, other nations and other peoples. Therefore in the way of things a certain number of foreigners filter through and make lives for themselves here in Hebrion. And there are Hebrians living in a dozen other countries of Normannia – even in Calmar and distant Ridawan."

The Prelate said nothing. His eyes were like seapolished shards of jet. Abeleyn ground on.

"Trade lives on goodwill, on accommodation, and on compromise. It has been represented to me that this latest edict could do much towards strangling our trade with the southern kingdoms and the city-states of the Levangore –

Merduk lands, yes, but they have not lifted a finger against us since Azbakir, forty years ago, and their galleys help us keep the Malacar Straits free of the corsairs."

"My son," the Prelate said, his smile as warm as flint, "it grieves me to hear you speak thus, as though your concerns were those of a common merchant rather than those of a Ramusian king."

There was a sudden, dead silence in the chamber. The scribe's quill described an inky screech across his parchment. No one spoke thus to a king in his own kingdom.

"It is unfortunate," Abeleyn said into the hush, "but I feel I cannot send to Torunna the reinforcements which are so needed there. I feel, Holy Father, that the True Faith can be safeguarded here by my men as well as on the frontier. As you have so ably made clear to me, threats to the crown can come from any quarter, within and without its borders. I think it prudent that my troops continue their work in conjunction with the Church here, in Abrusio; and though you have not, in your graciousness, rebuked me, I feel I have not taken a responsible enough role in these matters until now. Henceforth the lists of the suspects, the heretics, the foreigners – and the sorcerers, of course – will be brought to me so that I may confirm them. I will then pass them on to you. As you say, these are trialling times. It grieves me to think that a man of your piety and advanced years should have the twilight of his life disturbed by such distasteful matters. I will endeavour to lift some of your burden. It is the least I can do."

The Prelate, a vigorous man in his fifties, inclined his head, but not before Abeleyn had glimpsed the fire in his cold eyes. They had both revealed their weapons, had put their pieces on the board and shifted them in the opening moves. Now the real negotiations would have to begin, the haggling for advantage that men called diplomacy. And Abeleyn had the upper hand. The Prelate had revealed his strategy too soon.

So I must debate with this old man, Abeleyn thought darkly, manoeuvre for advantage in my own kingdom. *And the Torunnans; they will have to stand alone for a while longer because this grasping cleric chooses to see how far he can flex his muscles with me.*

THREE

BARDOLIN'S IMP WAS restless. It was the heat. The little creature darted from inkwell to table lantern, its green tongue lolling. Finally it collapsed in a heap atop the parchment the wizard had been working on and scratched behind one hairy ear with the nub of an old quill, covering itself with ink.

Bardolin chuckled and lifted it gently up to the shelf. Then he smoothed the parchment and continued to write.

The Prelate of Abrusio is not, of course, an evil man, but he is an ambitious one, and with the fall of Macrobius there is a certain hiatus. All five of the Prelates will be watching events along the Searil with an interest that goes beyond the mere outcome of siege and battle. Will Macrobius surface again? That is the question. It is rumoured that eight thousand of the Knights Militant have already been set aside for policing duties within the borders of the five Kingdoms. Eight thousand! And yet they are to send only five thousand to the Searil defences. This is a war within a war. These holy men will see the Merduk at their altars ere they will lift a finger to help another of their rank. It is the Inceptine disease, this empire-building. It may yet bring the west to its knees.

He paused. It was late, and the stars were hanging bright and heavy over the humid, sleeping city. Now and then he would catch the cry of a night watchman or one of the city patrol. A dog barked and there was a sudden burst of laughter from some revellers leaving an all-night tavern. The offshore breeze had not yet picked up, and the reek of the burning hung over the city like a shroud.

I tell you, Saffarac: leave Cartigella while there is time. This madness will spread, I am sure of it. Today it is Hebrion, tomorrow it will be Astarac. These holy men will not be happy until they have burnt half the west in their zeal to outdo one another in piety. A city is not a safe place to be.

Again, he stopped. Would it revert to the way it had been in the beginning? The Dweomer-folk reduced to petty oldwifery, the doctoring of dry cows in some mountain village. There would be a welcome in such a place, at least. The country-folk understood these things better. Some of them still worshipped the Horned One in nights of moon up in the Hebros.

He dipped his quill in the inkwell but the pen remained unmoving in his fingers. A drop of ink slipped down the nib and drip, dripped on to the parchment, like a raven tear. The imp watched Bardolin from its shelf, chirruping quietly to itself. It could sense his grief.

He knuckled his bloodshot eyes, grimaced at the blotted page, and then wrote on.

They took away my apprentice today. I have made protests, enquiries, even bribes; but nothing will answer. The Inceptines have begun to whip up fear, and with the news from the east that is no hard task. When it started, the soldiers would sometimes look the other way: now they also have the sniff of fanaticism about them. It is rumoured, though, that King Abeleyn disapproves of the scale of the purge and keeps the Prelate from even worse excesses. They burned forty today, and they hold half a thousand in the catacombs for want of space in the palace cells. God forgive them.

He halted a third time. He could write no more, but it would have to be finished tonight for there might not be time in the morning. He sighed and continued.

You are high in the councils of King Mark. I beg you, Saffarac, use your influence with him. This hysteria must be halted before it sweeps all the Ramusian states. But if you see no hope, you must get some of our folk out. Gabrion will take them, I am sure, and if not Gabrion then the Sea-Merduks.

Desperate times, to suggest such remedies. Take care, my friend. May God's light shine ever on your path.

He signed and sealed the letter, and his eyes stung with tiredness. He felt worn and old. A dispatch-runner would take it on the morning tide, if this calm lifted and the north-west breeze struck up again.

His imp was asleep. He smiled at the little creature, the last in a long line of familiars. They would come for him tomorrow as they had come today for young Orquil, his apprentice. A promising lad, he had been, already at home in cantrimy and beginning to learn the way of mindrhyming, perhaps the least understood of the Seven Disciplines.

He knew why they had not taken him today.

Bardolin had been a soldier once upon a time. He had served with one of the tercios which currently garrisoned Abrusio and he knew their commanding officer well. His... abilities had begun to manifest themselves on a campaign against bandits in the Hebros. They had saved lives. The ensign had recommended him for promotion, but he had left to study thaumaturgics under Golophin, a great name, even then.

That had been thirty years ago, but Bardolin still had the carriage of a soldier. He kept his hair brutally short and his broken nose gave him the appearance of a prize fighter. He did not look like a wizard, a master of at least four of the Realms of Dweomer. He looked more like the hard-bitten sergeant of arquebusiers that he had once been, the tell-tale scars at his temples speaking of long years wearing the iron helmet of the Hebriate soldiery.

That's why they left me, he thought. *But they'll be back tomorrow, no doubt, with one of the Ravens prodding them on.*

A distant tumult outside. A rattle of hard voices, feet spattering on the cobbles.

Had they come for him already?

He stood up. The imp sprang awake, its eyes glowing.

The feet pattered past, the shouts faded. Bardolin relaxed, chiding himself for his hammering heart.

An arquebus shot. It ripped the night quiet apart. Another,

and then a ragged volley. There was a huge animal howling, and men began to scream.

Bardolin leapt to the window.

Dark streets, the sliver of a moon shining faintly off cobbles. Here and there a yellow light flickering. If he leaned out far enough he could see the glitter of moonlight on the Western Sea. Abrusio slept like a tired old libertine made weary by his excesses.

Where, then?

"Go, my friend; be my eyes for me."

The imp's eyes dulled. The useless wings on its back flapped feebly. It darted out of the window and appeared to leap into empty space, though the air was so warm and thick it seemed a different element, capable of buoying the tiny body up like a leaf.

Now, yes. Bardolin was seeing in the spectrum of the imp's vision. A lantern at a window was a green flare, too bright to look at. A rat made a small luminosity and the imp changed its swift scamper in pursuit, but Bardolin held it to his will again, reproved it gently and sent it on its way.

A leap between two roofs, an unbelievably quick series of gymnastic movements and the imp was in the street scurrying along in the gutter, ignoring the rats now. There was a confused glow up ahead, green figures dancing. But one towered over the rest, and shone as brightly as a bonfire. The heat from it was a palpable thing on the imp's clammy skin.

A shifter cornered by the city patrol! And it was already badly wounded. Bardolin noted the three corpses which lay in fragments around the street. The shifter was giving a good account of itself, but that last volley had caught it at pointblank range and even its immense vitality was waning. The lead balls had ripped through the great chest and out of the muscles of the back. Already the wounds were repairing themselves, but the arquebusiers were reloading with panicked haste, not daring to go near the dying creature. The darkened street was sickening with the reek of gore and slow-match and powder smoke.

"Damn you all," the shifter said clearly, despite its beast's mouth. "You and all black-robed carrion. You have no right –"

A bang. One fellow, reloading faster than the rest, fired his weapon at the huge, long-eared skull. The shifter's head bounced back to hit the wall behind it. The jaws opened, roaring, and the black tongue lolled wetly.

Others fired. Bardolin's imp whimpered but remained at its station, impelled by its master's will. It shut its sensitive eyes to the flashes of the volley, poked tiny fingers in its ears and cowered, appalled, as the patrol fired ball after ball into the massive beast. Pieces of flesh, dark-furred, were blasted off to litter the cobbles. One of the luminous yellow eyes went dark.

People began coming out of their houses. The entire district was waking to what sounded like a small battle being fought in their midst. Lantern light spilled out in pools and wands on the cobbles. The stouter-hearted ventured close to the inferno of noise and light that was the firing patrol, saw what they were aiming at and hurried back into their homes, barring their doors.

The noise stopped. The street was an opaque fog of powder smoke and the patrolmen shouted to one another reassuringly in the midst of it. They had used all their charges, but the beast was dead – sure to be after having thirty rounds blasted into it.

"Ho, Harlan, where are you? Can't see a thing in this powder brew!"

"I claim its paw, Ellon. It's the biggest I've ever seen."

"Where in the name of the Saint is it?"

There was a silence, heavy with fear. The powder smoke refused to clear; in fact if anything it was growing thicker by the moment. The arquebusiers blundered around, terrified, sure that the shifter had somehow called up a fog and was still alive in the midst of it, biding its time.

"Sorcery!" one wailed. "The beast lives! It'll be at our throats in a moment. This is no gunpowder smoke!"

Their sergeant tried to rally them, but they made off, some dropping their weapons, seeking only to get away from the unnatural smoke. They scattered, shouting, whilst the folk who lived on the street shuttered their windows despite the heat of the night and knelt behind locked doors, quaking.

SLOWLY, MY LITTLE comrade, slowly. Look into him. Can you see the heat? Is that the radiance of his heart, beating yet? Yes! See how the bright bloodlines clot and heal themselves, the darker holes knit together and close. And there is the eye rebuilding itself, pushing out again like an air-filled bladder.

Bardolin was trembling with strain. Casting was difficult enough at the best of times without having to relay it through his familiar. And now the creature was edging out of his control, like a tool slipping in sweat-blurred hands. It wanted to come home to its safe, quiet shelf, but Bardolin was making it approach the great body that lay seemingly inert on the ground with its blood a thick sticky pool around it.

A hairy piece of meat slithered across the stones and reattached itself to the shifter.

Bardolin was lucky in the powder smoke. All he had had to do was thicken it, and the still, humid air of the night had done the rest. But now he was attempting something more difficult. Mindrhyming, through the minute skull of the imp. The familiar acted as a buffer, a cut-off, but a frail one. Its heart would fail if it suffered much more stress this night, but there was not much time. The fog was thinning, and the patrol would soon return with reinforcements.

Shifter, can you hear me? Are you listening?

Pain agony light blooming in my skull the muzzles pointing at me rend them tear them drink sweet blood dying. Dying.

Shifter! Listen to me. I am a friend. Look at me. See the imp before you.

The yellow eyes blazed, shot with blood. "I see you. Whose are you?"

The imp spoke with its master's voice, quivering with relief. Its brain was near overload. "Bardolin. I am the mage Bardolin. Follow the imp and it will lead you to me."

The huge muzzle worked. The words came out as a growl. "Why should you help me?"

"We are brothers, Shifter. They are after us all."

The shifter raised its blood-mired head off the cobbles and seemed to sigh. "You have the right of it there. Lead on, then, but go slow – and no crevices or cracks. I am no imp that can crawl through keyholes."

They moved out, the imp scampering ahead, its eyes two green lights shining in the dark, the shifter a hulking, shattered shape behind it. After them the cadenced step of the city patrol came echoing up the street.

THE IMP WAS barely conscious by the time it returned, and Bardolin immediately popped it into a rejuvenating jar.

The shifter entered the room warily, the candlelight shining on the broken places in its body that had not yet mended. Its heat was overwhelming; a by-product of the sorcery which kept its form stable. Hunched with pain though it was, it towered over Bardolin like some black, spiked monolith, the saffron-bright eyes slitted like a cat's, its horn-like ears scraped the ceiling.

"I thirst."

The mage nodded and sank a gourd dipper in the pail he had prepared. The shifter took it and drank greedily, water running down the fur of the bull-thick neck. Then it slumped to the floor.

"Can you shift back yet?" Bardolin asked.

The creature shook its great head. "My injuries would kill me. I must remain in this form until they are healed... I am called Tabard, Griella Tabard. I thank you for my life."

Bardolin waved a hand. "They took away my apprentice today. Tomorrow they will take away me. I have brought you a momentary respite, no more."

"Nevertheless I am in your debt. I will kill them tomorrow when they come for you, hold them off so you may escape."

"Escape? To where? The soldiery have Abrusio sealed off tighter than a virago's bustle. There is no escape for the likes of us, my friend."

"Then why did you aid me?"

Bardolin shrugged. "I do not like wanton slaughter."

The shifter laughed, a hideous sound in the beast's mouth.

"You say that to the likes of me, a sufferer of the black disease? Wanton slaughter is half my nature." The creature sounded bitter.

"And yet, you do not kill me."

"I... I would not harm a friend. Like a fool I came down out of the Hebros, seeking a cure for my affliction, and arrived here in the midst of a purge. I killed my father, Mage."

"Why?"

"We are a simple folk, we mountain dwellers. He tried to force me."

Bardolin was puzzled, and the beast laughed again. "No matter. You will understand in the morning maybe. For now, I am hurt and weary. I would sleep here if you'll let me."

"For tonight you will be my guest. Is there anything I can do for your hurts?"

"No. They heal themselves. It takes a lot to kill a full-blooded shape-shifter, though no doubt your magicks could do so in a trice. Those stinking militia thought to use me for their sport, and before I could stop myself the change was upon me. Then the hue and cry began. Six of them at least I slew. I was fortunate. Some of them have taken to using iron balls in their arquebuses. That would have been my end."

Bardolin nodded. Iron and silver were the only things which disrupted the magical regenerative powers of a shifter. Golophin had presented a paper on the subject to the Mages' Guild only the year before, little knowing it would soon be put to use.

Bardolin yawned. His imp stared dreamily at him from the liquid depths of its jar. He tapped the glass, and the little mouth smiled vaguely. It would be recovered in the morning. Some mages, it was rumoured, had bigger jars made for themselves to rejuvenate their ailing bodies, but there was the cautionary tale of the treacherous apprentice who had not followed instructions and had left his master in the jar to smile dreamily for all eternity.

"I'm for bed," he told his monstrous guest. "You are safe here tonight; the imp made sure you were not followed. But it will be dawn in less than four hours. If you wish to make good your escape before then you are welcome."

"I will be here when you wake," the shifter insisted.

"If you will. The soldiers usually come midmorning, after a hearty breakfast and a tot of rum."

The shifter grinned horribly. "They will have need of their rum if they are to take us."

Us? Bardolin thought. But his bed was calling him.

Perhaps tomorrow night he would be sharing a pallet of bare stone with Orquil in the catacombs.

"Goodnight, then." He tottered off to bed, an old man in need of rest. The Dweomer always did that to him, and working through the imp had been doubly exhausting.

HE WOKE UP, though, in the dark hour before the dawn with a name going through his head.

Griella?

And when he crept downstairs, instead of the monstrous, bloodied beast, he saw sleeping on his floor the pale shape of a nude young woman.

FOUR

THE FIRE WAS brightening as evening drew on. The storm had blown itself out and the sky was a washed-out blue with rags of sunset-tinted clouds scudding off along the darkening horizon. Northward the Thurian Mountains loomed, dark and tall, and to the south-east the sunset was rivalled by another red glow that gave way to a black smoke cloud like the thunderhead of an approaching tempest. Aekir, still ablaze even now.

Closer by, a constellation of winking lights littered the earth for as far as a tired man might care to look. The campfires of a defeated army, and the multitude of refugees that clung to it. A teeming throng, enough to populate half a dozen minor cities, sat under the light of the first stars and the waning moon, cooking what food they had gleaned from the famished countryside, or sitting blank-eyed with their stares anchored in the flames.

As Corfe was sitting.

Perhaps a dozen of them squatted round the wind-ruffled campfire, their faces black with soot and filth and encrusted blood. Aekir was ten leagues back, but the red glimmer of its dying had followed them for the past five days. It would follow them for ever, Corfe thought, fastening on their minds like a succubus.

Heria.

He poked at the blackened turnips in the fire with a stick and finally managed to lever one out of the ashes. The others at the fire eyed it hungrily, but knew better than to ask for some. They knew enough not to cross this silent soldier of Mogen's.

Corfe did not wince as the turnip burnt his fingers. He wiped off the ash and then ate mechanically. A sabre lay in its scabbard at his side. He had taken it off a dead trooper to replace the one he had lost in the flight from the city. It and his tattered uniform commanded respect from his fellow fugitives. There were men who went about the displaced horde in ragamuffin bands, killing for food and gold and horses, anything which would speed their journey west, to safety. Corfe had slain four of them, appropriating their meagre spoils for himself. Thus he was the richer by three turnips.

Merduk cavalry had shadowed the mass of moving people ever since they had left Aekir's flaming gates, but had not closed. They were monitoring the progress of the fleeing hordes, channelling them along the Searil road like so many sheep. Leagues to the rear, it was said, Sibastion Lejer and eight thousand of the surviving garrison were fighting a hopeless rearguard battle against twelve times their number. The Merduk would let the noncombatants escape, it seemed, but not what was left of the Torunnan army.

Which makes me an absconder, a deserter, Corfe thought calmly. *I should be back there dying with the others, making an end worth a song.*

The thought raised a sneer on his face. He bit into the wood-hard turnip.

Children crying in the gathering darkness, a woman keening softly nearby. Corfe wondered what they would find when they got to the Searil line, and shook his head when he considered the enormity of the task awaiting its defenders. Like as not the Merduk would strike when the confusion of the refugee influx was at its height. That was why Lejer and his men were making their stand, to buy time for the Searil forces.

And what will I do when I reach the river? he wondered. *Offer my services to the nearest tercio?*

No. He would trek on west. Torunna was done for. Best to keep going, across the Cimbric Mountains, perhaps, and into Perigraine. Or even further west, to Fimbria. He could sell his services to the highest bidder. All the kingdoms were crying out for fighting men these days, even men who had run with their tails between their legs.

That would be giving up any dream of ever finding his wife again.

She is dead, Corfe, an empty-eyed corpse in a gutter of Aekir.
He prayed it was so.

There was a commotion in the firelit gloom, movement. His hand strayed to his sabre as a long line of mounted shapes came looming up. Cavalry, all light and shadow as they wound through the dotted campfires. People raised hands to them as they passed. It was a half-troop heading east, joining Lejer's embattled command, no doubt. They would have a devil of a time fighting their way through the Merduk screen.

Something in Corfe stirred. He wanted momentarily to be riding east with them, seeking a hero's oblivion. But the feeling passed as quickly as the shadowed horsemen. He gnawed on his turnip and glared at those who peered too closely at his tattered livery. Let the fools ride east. There was nothing there but death or slavery and the burning ruins of an empty city.

"THERE IS A rutter, a chart-book, that will confirm the man's story," Murad told the King.

"Rutters can be forged," Abeleyn said.

"Not this one, Majesty. It is over a century old, and most of it details the everyday passages of an everyday oceangoer. It contains bearings and soundings, moon changes and tides for half a hundred ports from Rovenan of the corsairs to Skarma Sound in far Hardukh, or Ferdiac as it was known then. It is authentic."

The King grunted noncommittally. They were seated on a wooden bench in his pleasure garden, but even this high above the city it was possible to catch the reek of the pyre. The sun beat down relentlessly, but they were in the dappled shade of a stand of mighty cypresses. Acacia and juniper made a curtain about them. The grass was green and short, a lawn tended by a small army of gardeners and nourished with a stupefying volume of water diverted from the city aqueducts.

Abeleyn popped an olive into his mouth, sipped his cold wine and turned the crackling pages of the old chart-book with delicate care.

"So this western voyage is authentic also, this landfall made in the uttermost west?"

"I believe so."

"Let us say you are right, cousin. What would you have me do about it?"

Murad smiled. His smile was humourless, wry. It twisted his narrow face into an expression of knowing ruefulness.

"Why, help me outfit a voyage to test its veracity."

Abeleyn slammed the ancient book shut, sending little flakes of powder-dry paper into the air. He set one long-fingered hand atop the salt-stained cover. Sweat beaded his temples, coiling his dark hair into tiny, dripping tails.

"Do you know, cousin, what kind of a week I've had?"

"I –"

"First I have this God-cursed – may the Saints forgive me – holy Prelate with his putrefactive intrigues in search of more authority; I have the worthy merchants of the city crying on my shoulder about his – no, our – edict's resultant damage to trade; then I have old Golophin avoiding me – and who can blame him? – just at the time when I need his counsel most; I have this blasted burning every God-given hour of the day in the one month of the year when the trade wind has fallen, so that we wallow in it like peasants in a chimneyless hut; and finally I have the Torunnan king screaming for troops at the one time when I cannot afford to give them to him – so up in more smoke goes the Torunnan monopoly trade. And now you say I should outfit an expedition into the unknown, presumably so that I may rid myself of the burden of a few good ships and the crack-brained notions of a sun-struck kinsman."

Murad sipped wine. "I did not say that you should provide the ships, Majesty."

"Oh, they'll spring out of the yards fully rigged, will they?"

"I could, with your authority, commandeer some civilian ships – four would suffice – and command them as your viceroy. A detachment of marines is all I would have to ask you for, and I would have volunteers aplenty from my own tercio."

"And supplies, provisions, equipment?"

"There is any amount of that locked up in warehouses all along the wharves – the confiscated property of arrested merchants and captains. And I know for a fact that I could crew half a flotilla from the foreign seamen currently languishing in the palace catacombs."

Abeleyn was silent. He stared at his kinsman closely. "You come here with some interesting notions under your scalp along with the tomfoolery, cousin," he said at last. "Maybe you will overreach yourself yet."

Murad's pale countenance became a shade whiter. He was a long, lean nobleman with lank dark hair and a nose any peregrine would have been proud of. The eyes suited the nose: grey as a fish's flank, and with something of the same brightness when they caught the light. One cheek was ridged with a long scar, the legacy of a fight with one of the corsairs. It was a surpassingly ugly, even sinister face, and yet Murad had never lacked the companionship of the fairer sex. There was a magnetic quality about him that drew them like moths to a candle flame until, burnt, they limped away again. Several of their outraged husbands, fathers and brothers had challenged Murad to duels. None had survived.

"Tell me again how you came by this document," Abeleyn said softly.

Murad sighed. "One of my new recruits was telling tall tales. His family were inshore fishermen, and his great-grandfather had a story of a crewless ship that came up out of the west one day when he and his father were out on the herrin run. His father boarded with three others, but a shifter was on board, the only thing living, and it killed them. The ship – it was a high-seas carrack bound out of Abrusio half a year before – was settling slowly and the yawlsmen drew off. But the shifter jumped overboard and swam for shore. They reboarded to collect their dead and the boy, as he was then, found the rutter in the stern cabin along with the corpse of the master and took it as a sort of were-gild for his father's life."

"How old is this man?" Abeleyn demanded.

Murad shifted uncomfortably. "He died some fifteen years ago. This is a tale kept by the family."

"The mutterings of an old man garbled by the passage of time and the exaggerations of peasant storytelling."

"The rutter bears the story out, Majesty," Murad protested. "The Western Continent exists, and what is more the voyage there is practicable."

Abeleyn bent his head in thought. His thick, curly hair was hardly touched by grey as yet. A young king fighting against encroachments on his authority from the Church, the guilds, other monarchs. His father had had no such problems, but then his father had not lived to see the fall of Aekir.

We live in trialling times, he thought, and smiled unpleasantly.

"I do not have the time to pore over an ancient rutter, Murad. I will take what you have told me on trust. How many ships did you say you would need?"

The scarred nobleman's face blazed with triumph, but he kept his voice casual.

"As I said, four, maybe five. Enough men and stores to start a viable colony."

Abeleyn's head snapped up. "A colony, sanctioned by the Hebriate crown, must needs have someone of sufficient rank to be its governor. Who do you have in mind, cousin?"

Murad coloured. "I thought... it had occurred to me that –"

Abeleyn grinned and raised a hand. "You are the King's cousin. That is rank enough." His grin faded swiftly. "I cannot, however, let you commandeer the ships of those who have been caught up in these heresy trials. Men would say that I was profiting from them, and some of the odium that the Prelate is unfortunately collecting for himself would be dumped at my door. A king must not be *seen* to benefit from the misfortune of his subjects."

Murad caught the slight emphasis and watched his monarch narrowly.

"However, what stores and cordage and spare yards and provisions and suchlike that are currently piling up in the warehouses might conceivably be moved elsewhere, for the sake of storage, you understand. These things, Murad, would not be missed. Ships are a different thing. We Hebrionese have a sentimental attachment to them. For their masters they are like wives. I know of your reputation in the wife-netting field, but if this is to be a crown-sponsored expedition it must start off on a wholesome note. Do you understand me?"

"Perfectly, Majesty."

"Excellent. No ships, then, will be confiscated, but I will give you a letter of Royal credit for the purpose of hiring out and outfitting two ships."

"Two ships! But, Majesty –"

"Kings do not relish being interrupted, Murad. As I have said, two ships, both out of Abrusio, and they must be ships whose masters have lately lost a large number of crewmen to the Inceptines. You will represent to their masters that they will regain their full crews for the voyage, which, if they undertake it, will be considered a form of amnesty. If they choose not to avail themselves of the crown's generosity then you must make it clear that they are liable to be investigated for having so many heretics and foreigners in their complement in the first place."

Murad began to grin.

"The letters of credit, I take it, Majesty, will be redeemed on the safe return of the ships to Abrusio."

The King inclined his head. "Even so. I will also let you take a demi-tercio of marines from your own command and will confer on you the governorship – under certain conditions – of whatever colony you choose to set up in this Western Continent. But to set up a colony you will need colonists."

Here the King looked so pleased with himself that Murad became wary.

"I will find you colonists, never fear," the King continued. "I have a body of people in mind at this very moment. Is all this agreeable to you, cousin? Are you still willing to undertake the expedition?"

"I will, of course, be able to vet the potential colonists for myself."

"You will not," Abeleyn said sharply. And in a softer tone:

"You will be far too busy to interview each and every passenger. My people will look after that end of things."

Murad nodded. His wings had been well and truly clipped. Instead of a small fleet sailing out under his command to set up an almost independent fiefdom, he would be transporting a horde of undesirables into the unknown in two – *two* – crowded vessels.

"I beseech you, Majesty, let me have more ships. If the colony is to succeed –"

"We do not yet know for sure if there is land for the colony to be founded upon," the King said. "I will not hazard more than I have to on what is to all intents a doubtful scheme. It is only my affection for you and trust in your abilities, cousin, that prompts me to do anything."

Murad bowed. *That,* he told himself, *and the fact that my idea can be worked into your own plans.*

But he had to admire Abeleyn. Only five years on the throne, and the Hebrian monarch had already established himself as one of the most formidable of the western rulers.

I must work with what I am given, Murad thought, *and be grateful for it.*

Abeleyn poured out more wine for them both. It was losing its chill, even in the shade of the cypresses.

"Come, cousin, you must see that we all act under certain constraints, even those of us who are kings. The world is a place of compromise. Unless, of course, you happen to be an Inceptine."

They laughed together, and clinked glasses. Murad could see a trio of Royal secretaries hovering in the trees, their arms full of papers, inkwells hanging from their buttonholes. Abeleyn followed his gaze, and sighed.

"Damned paperwork follows me everywhere. You know, Murad, I almost wish I were coming with you, leaving the cares of a kingdom behind. I remember my voyage on the *Blithe Spirit* when I was a prince, a snotty-nosed youngster full of himself. The first time I felt the blow of a rope's end I wanted the boatswain hung, drawn and quartered." He took a gulp of wine. "Those were the days, following the coast round to the easternmost of the Hebrionese, and then across the Fimbrian Gulf to Narbosk. There is something about the sea that is in our blood, we Hebrians. Maybe we do not have veritable saltwater running in our veins like the Gabrionese, but the tilt of a deck under our feet is always in the manner of a homecoming."

He stared into his wine.

"I will see this land the greatest sea-power on the earth ere I die, Murad – if I am spared, and if grasping clerics do not finish me before my time."

"Your reign will be a long and glorious one, Majesty. People will look back on it in later years and wonder what men were like who lived then, what giants they were."

The king looked up and laughed, seeming like a boy as he threw back his head. "I put on my breeches one leg at a time the same as everyone else, kinsman. No, it is the glow of history, the mist of the intervening years that confers glory on a man. It may be that I will be remembered solely because the Holy City fell in my reign, and my troops stayed home chasing witches instead of joining the defence of the west. Posterity is a fickle thing. Look at my father."

Murad said nothing. Bleyn II had been a tyrannical ruler and a fanatically pious man. It was rumoured that the current purge had been first suggested by him a dozen years before, but the old Mage Golophin had talked him out of it. Now the Inceptines were portraying him as the ideal of a saintly king, and his son was described in a hundred pulpits as a wild young man, good-hearted but wayward and totally lacking in respect for the representatives of the Blessed Saint on earth. Relations between crown and Church did not seem destined to improve.

And yet the navy and the army worshipped Abeleyn, and in the pikes of the soldiers and the culverins of the ships rested the power behind the throne. So the Inceptines trod warily, and hastened to bring their own swords, the Knights Militant, into the city.

"I have heard that none of the Aekir garrison escaped," Murad said sombrely, following his own train of thought. "Thirty-five thousand men."

"You heard wrong," the King told him. "Sibastion Lejer brought almost ten thousand men out of the city and is fighting a rearguard action on the Searil road."

Murad wanted to ask his king how he knew, how news travelled so swiftly over seven hundred leagues, but stopped himself. Golophin would have his ways and means. But if Golophin was avoiding Abeleyn...

"Duty calls," Abeleyn said. "I must meet another delegation from the guilds this afternoon. Thanks to you, Murad, I may have a crumb of comfort for the Thaumaturgists' Guild. Golophin may even begin talking to me again. Just as well. There is the Conclave of Kings to prepare for in a month's time."

"Is it still going ahead?" Murad asked, surprised.

"Now more than ever. Lofantyr of Torunn will be shrieking for more troops, of course, and Skarpathin of Finnmark will be convinced that the next blow is to fall upon him. I foresee a trying time, especially as the Synod meets a short while before, so we will have their worthy resolutions to debate also. I tell you, Murad, you are lucky in only having to worry about a hazardous voyage into the unknown. The shoals between palaces are more difficult to navigate."

Murad rose, and bowed deeply. "With your permission I will leave you to your navigating, Majesty."

As he left the shade of the cypresses the punishing sunlight bore down on him, and he saw the cluster of secretaries gather round their monarch like flies feeding off a corpse. The image was an unlucky one, and Murad banished it from his mind. He would have his ships, and his men, and he would have his city in the west.

He had not told the King that there was a log accompanying the rutter which detailed that voyage to the west of a century ago, and he was glad that he had kept the knowledge to himself. If the King had read the tattered pages he would most likely have found nothing. Murad himself had had a hard time deciphering the scrawled writing and stained parchment of the document, and the entries were hard to find – but they were there.

They referred to the very first expedition to the west, three centuries before the master of the *Faulcon* had made his ill-fated voyage. It was a venture that had ended, as far as Murad could make out, in slaughter and madness.

But that had been a long time ago. Such things became garbled and fantastic with every passing year. There would be nothing in the west that Hebrian arquebuses and pikes could not face down.

Time enough to worry about such things when the fabled Western Continent was looming off his bow with its secrets, its dangers and its unknown riches. It would be too late then for anyone to turn back.

FIVE

RICHARD HAWKWOOD OPENED the ornate grille that enclosed the balcony and stood naked, sipping his wine.

There was no breeze. It was unheard of for the Hebrian trade to fail so early in the year. He could look down the steep, teeming roofs to the harbour and see the Outer Roads crowded with caravels and carracks, galeots and luggers, all harbourbound by lack of wind. The only seamen doing a good trade were the masters of oar-powered galleys and galleasses, the swift dispatch runners of the crown who would sometimes condescend to transport compact cargoes for a small fortune.

He could see the *Grace* in the inner yards, still being refitted. Seaworms had riddled her hull in the voyage to the Malacars and she was having her outer planking replaced. Somewhat further out was his other ship, a tall carrack named the *Gabrian Osprey*. She had crawled in two days ago, labouring under sweeps, and was now at anchor waiting for a free berth. Her crew were being kept under hatches until Hawkwood could devise some way of slipping them past the Inceptines. A longboat perhaps, at night. Or he could hire a smack to stand off and let them swim out to it. No, that would never do.

He rubbed his forehead wearily. His torso shone with sweat and the stink of the pyres seemed to grease it like some foul second skin. He closed the grille as a woman's voice said: "Richard, are you coming back to bed?"

"A moment."

But she had risen, a sheet draped about her shoulders, and was padding over the cool marble floor toward him. Her arms encircled him from behind and he felt the heat of her through the crumpled linen.

"My poor captain who has so much to occupy his mind. Are you thinking of Julius?"

"No." Julius Albak's body had been retrieved and burnt by the Inceptines. There was no family to speak of, save the sea-going one that was Richard's crew. A dozen of them were in chains in the catacombs awaiting a hearing. No, Julius Albak had gone to the long rest at last. There was nothing more to be done about that.

The woman's hand drifted down to caress his manhood but he was unresponsive.

"I'm not in the mood, Jem."

"I noticed. Usually when you return from a voyage we never even make it as far as the bed."

"I have a lot on my mind. I'm sorry."

She left him and went back to the bed and the tall decanter that stood beside it. The room was quite cool, thick-walled, faced with marble and white-painted plaster. The ceiling rose up far beyond Hawkwood's head to be lost in a maze of arches and buttresses of dark cedar. The enclosed balcony stretched along the whole of one wall, and the bed occupied another. There were elegant chairs, a dressing table, hangings heavy with gilt. Over all were thrown a pretty tumble of women's clothes and head-dresses. High in a corner a tiny monkey stared down from a golden cage with wide, unblinking eyes. Richard had brought it to her from far Calmar half a dozen years ago.

The sound of the city drifted in as a distant surf of noise. This far up the hill one was removed from the narrow filth of the streets, the shocking heat, the stinking open sewers, the noisy vitality of Abrusio. This was how the nobility lived.

"Have you seen your wife yet?" Jemilla asked him tartly, and he winced.

"No. You know I haven't."

"You've been back three days, Richard. Shouldn't you pay her a visit, at least for form's sake?"

He turned to look at her. Whereas his body was burnt a deep brown by sun and wind and seaspray, hers was as white as alabaster, which made the heavy mane of dark hair all the more striking. Her eyes were as black and bright as pitch bubbles on a tropic-heated deck, wonderfully mobile brows arching over them like two black birds rising and falling in tune with her moods. She was a passionate, almost a savage lover, and he often came away from her covered with scratches and bites. And yet he had seen her on her way to the palace in a barouche, hair coiled on her head, robes stiff with brocade, a linen ruff encircling her face making it seem that of a porcelain doll.

She had other lovers: noble, or humble like himself. He could not expect her to be faithful, she always protested, when he was away two-thirds of the year. But she was careful. A virtuous noble widow she appeared to be, and was believed to be by most people at court, but the servants knew differently, as did Hawkwood. He had procured a misbirth for her not two years ago – at her insistence. An oldwife in the lower city had done it in a cramped little back room. She would never tell him if the child had been his or not. Perhaps she did not know herself. He thought about it sometimes.

"My wife understands that I have many things to clear up when I finish a voyage," he said coldly.

She laughed, water rippling in a silver ewer, and reached out a slender hand. "Oh, don't be so stiff and proper, Richard. Come here to me. You look like a mahogany statue."

He joined her on the bed.

"It is Julius and your crew, I know. I have tried, Richard. There is nothing anyone can do, perhaps not even Abeleyn himself. He is not happy about it either."

"He discusses policy with you, then, as you lie together."

She flushed. "I don't know what you mean."

"Only that you should be more careful, Jem. I've been back three days, but already I know who the King's new bedfellow is."

One eyebrow soared up her forehead disdainfully. "Rumour and truth have a large gap between them."

"The King does not like his lovers to bruit his affairs in public. He has made a policy of bachelorhood. If you are not careful you may wake up one morning aboard a Merduk slave transport."

"Do you presume to tell me how to regulate my affairs, Captain? I suppose your voyaging from one louse-ridden port to another makes you qualified to discuss the doings at court."

He turned away. She loved throwing his humble birth in his face. Perhaps it gave their lovemaking an added spice for her. And yet they were as close as lovers ever got. Sometimes they argued as though they were married.

He finished his wine and stood up. "I must go. You are right. I should visit Estrella."

"No!" She pulled him back down on the bed, eyes blazing. He had to smile. For all her bedhopping, she was still jealous if he went to someone else.

"Stay, Richard. We have things to talk about."

"Such as?"

"Well... news. Don't you wish to catch up on what has happened since you left?"

"I know what has been happening, and so does my crew."

"Oh, that silly edict. Everyone knows that the Prelate put Abeleyn up to it. The King is not the sort to think up a thing like that, though his father was. No, Abeleyn is more one of your sort. A soldier's man, the sailor's darling. He and the Prelate have had a contretemps, and all Abrusio is on the side of the King, except those whose wits are addled by religion, may God forgive me." She made the Sign of the Saint against her bare breasts. For some reason Hawkwood found the gesture arousing.

"The Prelate is on his way to the Synod in Charibon, and do you know, the moment he was out of the city gates the burnings lessened? Two days ago they were consuming forty unfortunates every afternoon. Today six were sent to the pyre. Abeleyn has his officers accompanying the Inceptines on their rounds and the lists go straight to him. Just as well. My maid was becoming hysterical. She's from Nalbeni."

Hawkwood stroked her smooth thigh. "I know."

"And Golophin. Some say he has organized a kind of underground escape route for the Dweomer-folk of the city. He's never at court any more. The King went in person to the old bird's tower to seek him out, but the door was barred! To the King! Abeleyn's father would have had the place razed to the ground, but not our young monarch. He's biding his time."

Hawkwood's fingers were caressing the curly hair at the crux of her legs, but she appeared not to notice.

"And the streets are a terror at night. There are shifters abroad, seeking revenge for the execution of their kinfolk. Only last night one of them slaughtered a dozen of the city patrol and then slipped away..." She moaned as Hawkwood's fingers worked on her.

"Murad has been stalking around the palace with a smug grin on his face. I don't like him... Oh, Richard!"

She lay back on the bed with her legs asprawl and began to touch herself where he had been touching her. Hawkwood watched her with the fascination of the mouse eyeing the cat.

"Is this not better than the rump of some cabin boy?" she asked.

Hawkwood became very still, and she smiled teasingly. "Oh come on, Richard. I know what pressures are on you seamen on a long voyage, with never a woman aboard to relieve your... stress. Everyone knows what you get up to. In the hold, perhaps, in a dark corner with the rats skipping round you? Does the boy squeal, Richard, as you take him? My fine Captain, were you even taken yourself by some hairy master's mate when you first began your voyaging?"

As she saw his face flood with anger she laughed her tinkling laugh and worked ever more busily on herself.

"Will you deny it to my face? Will you say it's not true? I can read it in your eyes, Richard. Is that why you have been unable to please me on this return? Are you pining after some smooth-chinned boy with lice in his hair?"

He set his hand about her white throat. His skin looked as dark as leather against hers. As his fingers tightened, hers became busier. Her back arched slightly.

"Am I not enough for you?" she moaned. "Or am I too much for you?"

With one swift movement he spun her on her stomach. The blood of fury and shame and arousal was beating a rigid tattoo in his every vein. He set his weight atop her, crushing her into the bed. She cried out, flailing behind her with her arms. He caught the thin wrists and imprisoned them.

She screamed into the pillow and bit the linen fiercely as he forced inside her. It did not take long. He withdrew, feeling sickened and exultant at the same time.

She rolled on to her back. Her body was mottled with the rush of blood. Her wrists were red. She bruised so easily, he thought. He could not meet her eyes.

"Poor Richard. So easily goaded, so easily outraged." She extended a hand and pulled him down beside her.

He was baffled, confused. "Why do you say such things?"

She stroked his face. "You are an odd mix, my love. Sometimes as unapproachable as a closed oak door, sometimes all your nerves in the open, to be played on like the strings of a lute."

"I'm sorry, Jem."

"Oh, don't be absurd, Richard. Don't you know that you never do anything unless I want you to?"

ELSEWHERE IN ABRUSIO, the day passed and the soldiers did not come. The girl Griella, who had been a beast, dressed herself in some of Bardolin's cast-off robes and sat at his table looking absurdly young and vulnerable.

They sipped cellar-cool water and ate bread with olives and a bowl of pistachios, which she loved. The imp stirred restlessly and watched them from its jar; it was almost recovered from its ordeal of the night before.

Why had they not come? Bardolin did not know; but instead of relieving him, their non-appearance made him more uneasy and this was compounded by the face of the slim young girl sitting across the table from him, swinging her bare feet as she ate.

She had a peasant face, which was to say it was browned and freckled by hours and days out in the sun. Her hair was cut short and it gave back a bronze tint to the sunlight, as though some smith had hammered it out on his anvil that morning. Her eyes were as brown as the neck of a thrush and her skin where the ingrained dust had been washed off had a tawny bloom. She was not more than fifteen years old.

Bardolin had helped her wash the clotted blood from her hands and mouth.

After lunch they sat by the great window in the wall of Bardolin's tower that looked out to the west, down over the city to the sea and the crowded harbour with its tangle of masts. Out on the horizon ships were becalmed by the fallen trade. Their boats were hauling them in, oarstroke by agonizing oarstroke under the torrid examination of the sun.

"Can you see them?" Griella asked him. "I've heard that wizards can look further than any other men, can even watch the flames that flicker in the bosoms of the stars."

"I could cast a farseeing cantrip. With my own eyes I would not be much good to you, I am afraid."

She digested this. "When I am a beast, I can see the light of men's hearts in their breasts. I can see the heat of their eyes and bowels in the dark, and I can smell the fear that comes out of them. But I cannot see their faces, whether they are afraid or brave, surprised or astonished. They are no longer men then. That is the way the beast thinks when I am inside it instead of it being inside me." She looked at her fingers, clean now, the nails bitten down to the quick.

"I can feel their life give out under my hands, and it is a joyous thing. It does not matter whether they are my enemies or not."

"Not everyone is your enemy, child."

"Oh, I know. But I do not know of anyone who is my friend. Except you, of course." She smiled so brightly at him that he felt both touched and disturbed.

"Why did they not come?" she asked. "You said they would try to take you away today."

"I don't know." He would have liked to send the imp out into the city to nose around, but he doubted if it were up to that yet. And with Griella here, he did not like to go out himself. Though he had barely admitted it even to himself, he knew he would not let her slaughter any more men, even those who were taking the pair of them to their deaths. If the soldiers came he would smite her with a spell of unconsciousness. They might even leave her alone, believing her to be just another street urchin. If she changed into her beast form again, she would surely be killed.

"No, don't touch that."

She was tapping the imp's jar and exchanging grins with the little creature.

"Why not? I think it likes me."

"Nothing must disturb it when it is rejuvenating, else it might metamorphose into something different to what it should be."

"I don't understand. Explain."

"The liquid in the jar is Ur-blood, a thaumaturgical fluid. It is the basis for many experiments, and is difficult to create. But once it has been made, it is... malleable. I can adjust it to the needs of the moment. At the moment it is a balm for the tiredness of the imp, like wet plaster being pasted over the cracks in the facade of a house. The imp was grown out of Ur-blood, helped along by various spells and the power of my own mind."

"Can you grow me one? What a pet it would make!"

Bardolin smiled. "They take months to grow, and the procedure is exhausting, consuming some of the essence of the caster himself. If the imp dies, some of me dies also. There are quicker ways of breeding familiars, but they are abhorrent and the creatures thus engendered, called homunculi, are wayward and difficult to control. And their appetites are foul."

"I thought that a true mage would be able to whistle up anything he pleased in a trice."

"The Dweomer is not like that. It extracts a price for every gift it gives. Nothing is had for nothing."

"You sound like a philosopher, one of those old men who hold forth in Speakers' Square."

"There is a philosophy, or rather a law, to the Dweomer. When I was an apprentice I did not learn a single cantrip for the first eight months, though my powers had already manifested themselves. I was put to learning the ethics of spell weaving."

"Ethics!" She seemed annoyed. "I partake of this Dweomer also, do I not?"

"Yes. Shape-shifting is one of the Seven Disciplines, though perhaps the least understood."

She brightened. "Could I become a mage, then?"

"To be a mage you must master four of the Seven, and shape-shifters are rarely able to master any discipline other than shifting. There was a debate in the Guild some years ago which contended that shifting was not a discipline at all but a deviancy, a disease as the common folk believe. The motion failed. You and I both have magic in our blood, child."

"The black disease, they call it, or sometimes just 'The Change,'" Griella said quietly. Her eyes were huge and dark.

"Yes, but despite the superstitions it is not infectious. And it can be controlled, made into a true discipline."

She shook her head. Her eyes had filled with tears. "Nothing can control it," she whispered.

He set a hand on her shoulder. "I can help you control it, if you'll let me."

She buried her head in his barrel-like chest. Someone hammered on the door downstairs.

Her head snapped up. "They're here! They've come for you!"

Under his appalled stare, her eyes flooded with yellow light and the pupils became elongated, cat-like slits. He felt her slight body shift and change under his hands. A beast's growl issued from her throat.

While she is changing. Before it is too late.

He had had the construction of the spell memorized all morning. Now it left him like a swift exhalation of breath and swooped into her.

There was a savage conflict as the birthing beast fought him and the girl writhed, agonized, caught between two forms. But he beat the thing down. It retreated and underneath it he could sense her mind – human, unharmed, but utterly alien. The revelation shocked him. He had never looked into the soul of a shifter before. In the split second before the spell took hold he saw the beast spliced to the girl in an unholy marriage, each feeding off the other. Then she was limp in his arms, breathing easily. He shuddered. The beast had been strong, even in the moment of its birthing. He knew that if it ever became fully formed he would not be able to control it. He would have to destroy it.

Sweat was rolling down into his eyes. He set the girl down, still trembling.

"Prettily done, my friend," a voice said.

Standing in the room's doorway was a tall old man who looked as thin as a tinker's purse. His doublet, though expensive, hung on him like a sack and his broad-brimmed hat was wider than his shoulders. Behind him a frightened-looking young man bobbed up and down, crushing his own hat between his hands.

"Master," said Bardolin, a swell of relief rushing through him.

Golophin took his arm. "I must apologize for the rowdiness of our entrance. Blame young Pherio here. He does not like me walking the streets in these times, and he sees an Inceptine on every corner. Pherio, the girl."

The young man stared at Griella as though she were a species of particularly poisonous snake. "Master?"

"Put her on a couch somewhere, Pherio. You need not worry. She will not rip your head off. And hunt up some wine – no, Fimbrian brandy. Bardolin always has a stock in his cellar. Run now."

The boy staggered off carrying Griella. Golophin helped Bardolin into a chair.

"Well, Bard, what's this? Consorting with nubile young shifters, eh?"

Bardolin held up a hand. "No jokes if you please, Golophin. It was too close, and it has wearied me."

"Worth a paper in the Guild's records, I think. If this is in the nature of research, Bard, then you are certainly on the cutting edge." He chuckled and swept off his preposterous hat, revealing a scalp as bald as an egg.

"We were expecting soldiers with an Inceptine at their head," said Bardolin.

"Ah." Golophin's bright humour darkened.

"They took Orquil away yesterday. I had thought today they would take me."

When Pherio came back with the brandy Golophin poured two glasses and he and his one-time apprentice drank together.

"You bring me to the reason for my visit, Bard: these atrocities that the Inceptines practice in the name of piety."

"What about them? In the name of the Saints, Golophin, they can't be after *you*. You've been the adviser to three kings. You had Abeleyn sitting on your knee when he was too young to wipe his own arse –"

"Which is why I am the one man the Prelate *must* bring down. Without me the King has no disinterested advisers –

nor any who can tell him what is going on halfway across the world at the drop of a hat, I might add. Abeleyn knows this too, as I hoped he would. With the Prelate on his way to the Synod at Charibon he has a breathing space. Already the burnings have abated, which is why you are here today, my friend. Only the hopelessly heretical are going to the pyre at the moment, but the catacombs are still filling. By the time the Prelate returns there will be thousands there awaiting his pleasure, and if the Synod approves his actions here then there will be nothing Abeleyn can do, unless he wants to be excommunicated. Worse, the Prelate of Abrusio will no doubt try to persuade the other Prelates of the Kingdoms to instigate similar purges in their own vicariates."

"I have already written to Saffarac in Cartigella, warning him."

"So have I. He can speak to King Mark. But there is another thing. Macrobius has not reappeared. He must be dead, so they will have to elect a new High Pontiff, a man who shows by his actions that he is not afraid to incur the ill-will of kings in the struggle to fulfil God's plans, a man who has the good of the Kingdoms at heart, who is willing to purify them with the fire."

"Holy Saints! You're not telling me that maniac of ours has a chance?"

"More than a chance. The damned fool cannot see further than his own crooked nose. He will bring down the west, Bard, if he has his way."

"Surely the other Prelates will see this also."

"Of course they will, but what can they say? They are each striving to outdo one another in zealousness. None of them will dare denounce our Prelate's actions in common-sense terms. He might face excommunication himself. There is a hysteria abroad with the fall of Aekir. The Church is like an old woman who's had her purse snatched. She longs to strike out, to convince herself that she is still all of a piece. And do not forget that almost twelve thousand of the Knights Militant went up in smoke along with the Holy City, so the Church's secular arm is crippled also. These clerics are afraid that their privileges are going to be swept away in the aftermath of the disaster in the east, so they make the first move to remind the monarchies that they are a force to be reckoned with. Oh, the other Prelates will jump at the chance to do something, I assure you."

"So where does that leave us, the Dweomer-folk?" Bardolin asked.

"In the shit, Bard. But here in Abrusio at least there is a slim ray of hope. I talked with Abeleyn last night. Officially we never see one another these days, but we have our ways and means. He has intimated that there may be an escape route for some of our folk. He is hiring ships to transport a few fortunates away from these shores to a safe place."

"Where?"

"He would not tell me. I have to trust him, he says, the whelp. But he does not want our sort fleeing wholesale into the hands of the Merduk, as you can imagine."

"Gabrion?" Bardolin said doubtfully. "Narbosk maybe? Not the Hardian Provinces, surely. Where else is there that is not under the thumb of the Church?"

"I don't know, I tell you. But I believe him. He is twice the man his father was. What I am saying, Bard, is would you be willing to take ship in one of these vessels?"

Bardolin sipped his brandy. "Have you put this to the Guild?"

"No. The news would be out on the streets in half an hour. I am approaching people I trust, personally."

"And what about the rest? Is it just we mages who are to be offered this way out, Golophin? What about the humbler of our folk, the herbalists, the oldwives – even shifters like poor Griella there? Have they a choice?"

"I must do what I can, Bard. I will not be going. I stay here to save as many of them as I can. Abeleyn will hide me, if it comes to that, and there are others of the nobility with sons and daughters in training with the Guild who are, naturally, sympathetic to our cause. It may be that we will be able to evacuate a shipload from time to time and sail them out to whatever bucolic utopia you will have carved out of the wilderness. This thing will blow over once the true extent of the Merduk threat is realized." He paused. "After Ormann Dyke falls there will be less of this nonsense. The clerics will be brushed aside, and the soldiers will come into their own. We have only to ride out the storm."

"After Ormann Dyke falls? What makes you think it will? Golophin, that would be a disaster to rival the taking of Aekir."

"There is little hope that it will stand," Golophin said firmly.

"Lejer's men were overwhelmed this morning, and soon the Searil line will be fatally disorganized by the refugees streaming west. Shahr Baraz's army will surely move once more."

"You're positive?"

Golophin smiled. "You have your imp, I have my gyrfalcon. I can see the earth spread out beneath me. The mobs of fugitives on the western roads, the blackened ruins of Aekir, the lines of Ramusian slaves trekking north under the lash, may God help them. And I can see the columns of Merduk heavy cavalry fanning out from where Lejer's men fought their last stand. I can see Shahr Baraz, a magnificent old man with the soul of a poet. I would like to talk to him some day. He has served kings as I have."

Golophin rubbed his eyes. "Abeleyn knows this. It has helped convince him. I will not be going with him to the Conclave of Kings next month, though. I am needed here, and I must be discreet these days. It will be Abeleyn's job to try and convince the other monarchs of the knife-edge we teeter on. It may be that he will even save the dyke; who knows?"

He stood up and retrieved his hat. "What about it, Bardolin? Will you take ship? Your little shifter can come along if you've a mind to continue your research, but I can do nothing for poor Orquil, I'm afraid. He must make his peace with God."

Bardolin looked around at the rooms which had been his home for twenty years. He missed the breezy exuberance of young Orquil, and it was a shattering blow to realize the boy was beyond saving. The knowledge left him feeling very old, obsolete. But even his battered old nose could sniff the hint of burning flesh that hung on the air. The city would be a long time getting free of it. And Bardolin was sick of it.

He raised his glass.

"To foreign shores," he said.

SIX

A TERRACE SHADED by a canopy of stickreed stems, the earthen water jars hanging from every corner to add some moisture to the arid air. In the shade the heat was bearable, and Hawkwood had his hands about a flagon of cold beer as though he were warming them.

The quayside tavern was busy both inside and out. It was an up-market sort of place, not a sailor's haunt, more the kind of place a landsman would imagine a sailor to frequent. Periodically men watered the street in front of the tables so that patrons would not be sullied by the rising dust as the waggons and carts and mules and oxen and peasants and sailors and soldiers sauntered past.

But the beer was good, straight up from a cold subterranean taproom below the street, and there was a fine view of the harbour. Hawkwood could just pick out the tall mainmast of the *Osprey*, berthed at long last, her hatches open and men hauling on tackles to bring the precious cargo out into the white sunlight. Galliardo had assured him that the Inceptines no longer came down to the wharves to check the ship crews for foreigners. Things had relaxed somewhat, but Hawkwood had still left orders that none of the *Osprey*'s crew who were not native-born Hebrionese were to be allowed ashore. The men had not protested: news of Julius Albak's fate had raced through the port like fire. Yawlsmen on the herrin run reported that Abrusio-bound ships were diverting to Cherrieros and even Pontifidad. The madness could not last. If it did, trade would be ruined.

Hawkwood sipped his beer and picked at his bread. He could hardly hear himself think with the noise of the tavern and the wharves surrounding it. He wished the wind would pick up. He felt almost marooned by the unmoving air, though many a time he had cursed the Hebrian trade as it blew in his teeth and he beat up into it, tack upon tack, trying to clear the headland beyond the harbour.

He must promote himself a new first mate, take on more hands. Would Billerand relish promotion?

For some reason he thought of his wife, delicate little Estrella. He had been back five days and still he had not been home. He hated her tears, her hysterics, her protestations of love. She was like some nervous little bird when he was around, forever darting about and cocking one eye to look at him for approval. It drove him mad. He would far rather be clawed and abused by that high-born bitch, Jemilla.

I love Jemilla, a whisper inside him said, but he hunted the thought quickly out of his mind.

A nobleman on a black destrier clove a path down the crowded street like a crag breaking a wave. He was thin to the point of emaciation, and he wore sable riding leathers, even in the heat. His face was long, narrow, marred by a badly puckered scar, and his hair hung in sweaty strings to his shoulders. A basket-hilted rapier was scabbarded by his side. He reined in and dismounted as the keeper of the tavern rushed out, clucking solicitously and brushing the dust from his shoulders. He batted the man from him, caressed the destrier's muzzle as a liveryman led it away, and then stalked over to Hawkwood's table, his spurs jingling. Hawkwood rose.

"My lord Murad of Galiapeno. You are late."

Murad said nothing, but sat and slapped dust from his thighs with a doeskin gauntlet. The tavern keeper set a decanter of wine and two glasses on the table, and bowed as he retreated. Hawkwood chuckled.

"Something amuses you?" Murad asked, pouring the wine. He somehow managed to give an aura of world-weary contempt that immediately set Hawkwood's teeth on edge.

"You said you wanted this meeting to be discreet."

"That does not mean we must tryst in some stinking pothouse. Do not worry, Captain; the people I must be discreet for would never come so far down into the city."

Hawkwood sampled the wine. It was a Gaderian red, one of the finest he had ever tasted, and yet when Murad sipped his he grimaced as though it were vinegar.

"You said in your missive that you might have need of my ships. Do you have a cargo you wish to transport?"

Murad smiled. His lips were as thin as blood-starved leeches. "A cargo. Yes, I suppose so. I wish to commission you, Captain, and both your vessels, to undertake a voyage with myself and several others as passengers."

"To where?"

"West."

"The Hebrionese, the Brenn Isles?" Hawkwood was puzzled. Hebrion was the westernmost kingdom in the world.

"No." Murad's voice lowered suddenly, became almost conspiratorial.

"I mean to sail across the Western Ocean, to a continent that exists on the other side."

Hawkwood blinked for a moment, and finally found his voice. "There is no such continent."

"And if I were to tell you that you are mistaken, and that I know where it lies and how to get there?"

Hawkwood hesitated. His first impulse was to tell this nobleman that he was either a liar or a fool – or both – but something in the man's manner stopped him.

"I would need convincing."

Murad leaned back, satisfied. "Of course you would. No sane captain would risk his ships on a foolhardy venture without some manner of surety." He leaned forward again until Hawkwood could smell the wine and garlic on his breath.

"I have the rutter of a ship which accomplished the voyage to the west and returned safely. I can tell you, Captain, that the crossing of the Western Ocean took this vessel some two and a half months, with favourable winds, and that it was bound out of this very port. One has but to keep on a certain latitude for some twelve hundred leagues, and the same landfall can be made."

"I have never heard of this ship, or this voyage," said Hawkwood, "and my family has been at sea for five generations. Why is this discovery not better known?"

"The master died soon after the return voyage, and the voyage itself took place a century ago. The Hebrian crown has kept the information to itself until now, for reasons of state, you understand. But the time is ripe at last for this information to be exploited."

"The crown, you say. Then the King himself is behind this?"

"I am the King's kinsman. I speak for him in this also."

A crown-sponsored voyage. Hawkwood experienced mixed feelings. The Hebrian crown had sponsored several expeditions down the years, and the captains of some had become rich, even ennobled as a result. But many others had lost their ships, their lives and their reputations.

"How do I know you come from the King?" he asked at last.

Wordlessly, Murad reached into his belt pouch and produced two rolls of parchment weighed down with heavy seals. Hawkwood unrolled them with sweating hands. One was a Royal letter of credit for the hiring and provisioning of two ships of between eighty and two hundred tons, and the other was a letter of authorization conferring upon Lord Murad of Galiapeno the governorship of the new colony to be founded in the west with the powers of viceroy. A list of conditions followed. Hawkwood let the parchments spring back in on themselves.

"They seem genuine enough." In truth, he was shocked. He felt as though he were cruising in through shoaling water without a leadsman in the bows.

"Why me?" he asked. "There are many captains in Abrusio, and the crown owns many ships. Why hire a small independent who is not even Hebrionese?"

"You fulfil certain... conditions. I want two ships owned by the same man; that way it is easier to keep a track of things. You are a skilled seaman, not afraid to sail the lonelier sea lanes beyond sight of land. It is amazing, the number of so-called sea captains who do not feel comfortable unless they have a coastline within spitting distance of their hull."

"And?"

"And, I have something you want."

"What?"

"Your crew, Hawkwood, those men of yours currently interned in the catacombs. Take on this commission and they will be returned to you the same day."

Hawkwood met the cold eyes and scimitar smile, and knew he was being manipulated by the same forces which governed kingdoms.

"What if I refuse the commission?"

Murad's smile did not waver. "Six of them are marked down for the pyre tomorrow. I would be sorry to see such worthy men go to the flames."

"It may be that I value my own skin over theirs," Hawkwood blustered.

"There is that, of course. But there is also the fact that certain captains with a large proportion of foreigners and heretics in their crew are open to investigation themselves, especially since some of those captains are not even Hebrionese to begin with."

So there it was: the sword hanging over his head. He had expected something like this from the moment he had seen the Royal letters. He uncurled his fist from around the wine glass lest it break.

"Come now, Captain, think about what is being offered you. The lives of your crew, a chance to make history, to join the ranks of the great in this world. The riches of a new world beyond the bend of the seas."

"What concessions can I expect, always assuming that this venture works out as you have planned it?"

Murad watched him for a moment, gauging.

"The man who sails me to my governorship can expect certain prerequisites. Monopolies, Captain. If you wish, the only ships which sail from our new colony will be constructed in your yards. A modest tariff on incoming and outgoing cargoes will finance whatever ambitions you have. There may" – and here Murad could not stop himself from sneering – "even be a title in it for you. Think of passing that down to your sons."

Estrella was barren. There would never be any sons for Hawkwood. He wondered if Murad somehow knew that, and felt like flinging his glass in the sneering aristocrat's face.

Yet again the agonized question: had it been his child that Jemilla had aborted?

Hawkwood stood up. He felt soiled and filthy. He wanted a living deck under his feet, a sea wind in his hair.

"I will think over your proposition."

Murad looked surprised, then shrugged. "As you will. But do not take too long, Captain. I must know by tomorrow morning if your men are to be spared their ordeal."

"I will think over your proposition," Hawkwood repeated.

He tossed some small, greasy coins on the table and then walked away, losing himself in the lifestream of the port. He was going to find some stinking pothouse and drink himself into oblivion, and in the morning he would send word to this aristocratic serpent accepting his offer.

"THAT, LORD, WAS the Street of the Silversmiths. Already our men have recovered half a ton of the metal, melted by the heat of the burning. It is the only thing which survived."

The horses of the entourage picked their way gingerly in between the broken masonry, the charred wood – some beams still had tiny flames licking at them – and the scattered bricks. The corpses had been hauled from their path and the way cleared a little, but Shahr Baraz could see objects which seemed to be thick lengths of burnt logs inside the ruins on either side. Bodies, immolated until they were nothing but the stumps of torsos. They had been so thoroughly burned that they presented no threat of disease. The reek of ash and smoke was the only smell in the air. Shahr Baraz nodded approvingly. The clean-up crews had done their work well.

For as far as the eye could see the desolation extended. The shells of buildings towered in abject ruin, burnt black, gutted, half fallen. Their remains were as bare as gravestones, the foundations buried in rubble, like black crags standing in the breakers of a grey sea. Aekir had become a ghostly place. Already it seemed like a monument, the ruin of a long-dead civilization.

Jaffan was jovially pointing out other landmarks gleaned from books and maps. Even the more stolid of his staff, Shahr Baraz thought, seemed a bit drunk, as though the victory were a potent spirit still singing in the blood five days after the event. The enormity of the thing they had achieved had been slow in sinking home in the aftermath of reorganization and the crushing of the last resistance. Now, as they rode unhindered through what had been the greatest and holiest city of the unbelievers in the world, they were at last savouring the taste of triumph.

For Shahr Baraz, the triumph had a bitter aftertaste. Aekir had been burned to the ground. The day after the city's fall, he had been forced to order its evacuation by all troops and let the fires burn themselves out. The huge walls still stood, as did the more robust buildings, including the palaces of the High Pontiff, the cathedral and other public buildings. But the poor brick of much of the city had collapsed in the intense heat of the burning and vast expanses of the space within the walls were levelled plains of dust, rubble and ash.

The rubble and the ash had cost his army almost fifty thousand men to win.

Three leagues to the east of the city, the female prisoners covered almost nine acres. A good proportion of those would remain with the army. His men had earned them. And trundling back to Orkhan was a train of waggons two leagues long; the spoils of Aekir sent back to the Sultan Aurungzeb. The richest city in the world should have yielded more in the way of plunder, but most of it had gone up in smoke ere his troops were able to come to it. The men were restless as a result. Well, that restlessness would be put to good use.

Aekir was a shell. It would require the labour of several lifetimes to rebuild it, but Shahr Baraz did not doubt that it would be done. Aurungzeb wanted Aekir to be his capital some day. Aurungabar he had said he would rename it, but he had been drunk at the time.

A cat darted out of a cleft between the stones and sped across the street, startling the lead horses. The staff officers fought the excited animals into submission. Shahr Baraz's own mount laid back his ears, but the old general talked to him softly and he remained quiet. The young men were too impatient with horses these days. They treated them like tools instead of companions. He would have a word with the cavalry-quartermaster when they returned to camp.

Jaffan had regained his composure. He was pointing

out something else... ah, yes. The spires of Carcasson.
They loomed through the smoke haze like the horns of
some huge, crouching beast. What would they do with
that place? Baraz wondered. It was his own ambition to
found a university in Aekir before he died, and Carcasson –
what a library it would make! And in the centre, where the
Ramusians had worshipped their idols, would be the prayer
mats of Ahrimuz.

Baraz's thoughts darkened. The retreating Torunnans had
fired the library of Gadorian Hagus as they retreated. Two
hundred thousand books and scrolls, some of them dating
back into the dim history before the days of the Fimbrian
Hegemony. All of them had been lost. Horb, Shahr Baraz's
secretary, had been in tears at the news.

John Mogen would not have done that. He would have
known that the Merduks would have preserved the library
and would have left it intact behind him. But this Lejer
fellow, he was a barbarian. He deserved the fate which
awaited him.

They were riding to view his crucifixion.

The cavalcade turned left, into the afternoon sun. The
buildings, or their remnants, receded on either side and all
of a sudden there was a space before them, a square fully
a sixth of a league wide. This was the Square of Victories,
built by the Fimbrian Elector Myrnius Kuln himself. It was
the largest square in the world, and drawn up in it to meet
their general were a hundred and twenty thousand Merduk
troops in full battle array.

The cavalcade halted before that sea of faces. Rank
on rank of soldiers with their pikes held upright in salute,
the slow-match of the *Hraibadar* arquebusiers drifting in
blue streamers down the breeze, the drawn tulwars of the
Subadars and Jefadars and Imrahins catching the faint
sunlight in serried glitters. The cavalry was there, regiment
by regiment, the tall headdresses of the horses nodding and
waving, their riders stock-still. Beyond them the elephants
stood in long lines, so fantastically caparisoned so as to
seem like animals out of some fabled bestiary. In the towers
that perched on their broad backs their crews swayed as the
beasts shifted from foot to foot; they did not like the feel of

the grit underfoot. Notoriously footsore creatures, elephants. Dozens had been crippled by caltrops in the last assault.

Shahr Baraz's staff took up their places behind him in a momentary stillness. The old Khedive was helmetless and the wind swayed the long white hair of his topknot, the two ends of his drooping moustache. His face seemed hardly lined despite his age, and his eyes were almost invisible within their slits. He sat his steed as easily as a young man, in black and gold lacquered armour, his scimitar sheathed at one thigh. His horse, a tall grey gelding, bore a black chamfron and a tall yellow crest, and its tail was bound up with white ribbons.

Shahr Baraz tightened his knees, and his mount started forward into the square at an easy canter.

There was a murmur of sound from the assembled army. As the old Khedive approached the centre of the square it swelled into a roar. The army was cheering him, three sides of the gargantuan space erupting as the thousands upon thousands of throats joined in an air-shaking storm of noise. Then it began to form words, a phrase repeated over and over again:

"Hor-la Kadhar, Hor-la Khadar!"

Glory to God they were chanting, thanking their creator for this moment of triumph, this spectacle of their greatness. And their cheers were directed at Shahr Baraz on his horse near the heart of their formations. Glory to God for this evidence of His love for them, this victory of victories.

"Hor-la Kadhar," Shahr Baraz whispered, his eyes stinging with tears that he would not let fall. He whipped out his scimitar so that it was a white flash in the sunlight, and the cheering redoubled. They would hear it for leagues, he thought. They would hear the Merduk army giving praise to the One True God, and they would tremble, those unbelievers, knowing at last that the time of the Saint had ended and the time of the Prophet was beginning.

Shahr Baraz sheathed his scimitar. The blood was racing through him like a spring tide, making him young again. The gelding caught his mood and began to dance beneath him. The pair continued on their way to the scaffold that had been set up in the square where the statue of Myrnius Kuln stood looking on with granite eyes, as he had looked on for six centuries in this city he had founded. The Khedive's staff caught up with him, their silk surcoats flapping like banners, the battle fanions streaming like brightly coloured serpents above their heads.

The cheering abated like a retreating gale, became a murmur again and then a silence, so that the hooves of the Khedive's entourage were loud on the flagged surface of the square.

When Shahr Baraz reached the scaffold he halted and donned his war-helm. It was black with a long neck guard and full cheekpieces that made the wearer's face into a mask. Set atop it was a representation of a crescent moon, a curving horn two feet across encased in silver. It was the badge of the Baraz clan.

At the foot of the scaffold Sibastion Lejer stood in tattered rags, a hooded Merduk soldier on either side of him. His dark eyes glowed with hatred.

The last stand of the Torunnans had ended a few leagues outside the city, on a low hillock beside the Searil road. There the remnants of John Mogen's once great army had turned at bay, to be annihilated by the massed Merduk forces. Only a handful had survived the last savage hand-to-hand struggle, and these, having refused service in the Merduk army, were already on their way eastwards in chains so that the people of Ostrabar might have a look at the soldiers who had defied them for sixty years, since the crossing of the Jafrar Mountains and the first battles between Merduk and Ramusian.

But Lejer – for him a different fate was reserved.

It would be good for the army to watch his death. He had baulked them of a fortune in loot, and left them masters of a dead city. Now they would see their general make him pay for it, and know that he shared their anger.

Shahr Baraz spoke, his voice hollowed by the tall-crested helm.

"I had thought to have you killed by the elephants, like the criminal you are," he told Lejer matter-of-factly. "You destroyed the jewel of the world out of sheer malice. My people would have made the Aekir you knew into an even more wondrous place, a fit capital for the greatest of the Seven Sultans.

"And yet this I could have forgiven, it being the act of a desperate mind in its greatest extremity. It may be that had your men been knocking on the gates of Orkhan, my own city, I would have burned it rather than see unbelievers trample the prayer mats in the Temple of Ahrimuz.

"And your conduct in the last fight was admirable. You Torunnans will be long remembered by us as the noblest enemy we ever had, and in John Mogen I had a worthy adversary. I would that he had survived, so that we might speak of the future together. The Prophet tells us that all men take different roads to the same place. For men such as us the roads lead to a soldier's death. We have that in common.

"But you destroyed one thing that cannot be replaced. You took the wisdom of the past ages, the voices of great men, the accumulated knowledge of centuries, and you wantonly burned it, removing it for ever from the earth and ensuring that your people and mine could never enjoy it again. For that you have earned death, and you will die like the traitor to later generations that you are. You will be crucified. Have you anything to say, Sibastion Lejer?"

The man in rags straightened to his full height.

"Only this, Merduk. You will never conquer the west. There are too many men there who love their freedom and their faith. Your God is but a shadow cast by ours, and in the end the Blessed Saint will prevail. Kill me and have done with it. I weary of your philosophizing."

Shahr Baraz nodded, and gestured to the hooded soldiers.

Lejer was forced on to his back and his rags torn away. Other Merduks came, also hooded, bearing mallets and iron spikes. The Torunnan's arms were stretched out across a stout beam of wood and the spikes poised over his wrists.

The kettledrums of the elephants began a low, thunderous roll.

The spikes were hammered in, blood jetting bright in the sunshine. Then Lejer was hauled to his feet, attached to the heavy beam.

A pair of ropes snaked down and were swiftly tied to the two ends of the beam. Men behind the scaffold began to haul, and Lejer was hoisted up on to it. For the first time his mouth opened in a scream, but it was drowned out by the roar of the kettledrums.

They fastened him to the scaffold, the hooded men clambering up after him. Finally they hammered a last spike through both his ankles before climbing down.

The drums stopped. Lejer's eyes were wide and white in his filthy face. A ribbon of blood trickled down over his chin where he was biting through his lower lip, but he made no sound. Shahr Baraz nodded approvingly, then twitched his reins and began his stately progress back across the square. His aides and staff officers streamed after him.

"What now, Khedive?" Jaffan, his adjutant, asked.

"I want the men redeployed, Jaffan, as soon as is practicable. We must start planning our next move. You will send the quartermaster-general to me after lunch and we will discuss a new supply route."

"We are advancing on the Searil, then?" Jaffan asked, his eyes shining.

"Yes. It will take time, of course; time to reorganize and to consolidate, but we are advancing on the Searil. May Ahrimuz continue to bless our arms as he has done in this place. I will call an indaba of general officers this evening to discuss things in detail."

"Yes, Khedive!"

"Oh, and Jaffan –"

"Khedive?"

"Make sure that Lejer is dead within the hour. With all his faults, he is a brave man. I do not like to see brave men hanging on gibbets."

SEVEN

Further west, along the Searil road.

The rain was falling steadily, mourning, perhaps, the fall of the City of God. The Thurians were hidden behind its diffuse, livid veil; the moisture beaded the air in a mother-of-pearl dimness so all Corfe could see were shapes moving off on every side, occasionally becoming darker and clearer as they staggered nearer then, wraithlike, fading again.

His boots sank calf-deep in the clutching mud, and water rolled down his face as though it were the sweat of his toil. He was tired, chilled to the marrow, numb as a stone.

The fleeing hordes had been passing this way for days. They had scoured a scar across the very face of the earth, a long snake of churned mud almost a third of a league wide obscuring the original slim track that had been the route west. The rain was filling up the broken soil, turning it into something near liquid glue. Along it bodies lay partly submerged every few yards: the ranks were beginning to thin. Folk who had fled Aekir with nothing more than the tunics on their backs were shivering and shuddering as they trudged towards the dubious sanctuary of the Torunnan lines. The very old and the very young were the first to falter; most of the bodies Corfe had passed were those of children and the elderly.

Here and there was the angular shape of a cart askew, sinking in the mud, the carcass of a mule or a pair of oxen sprawled between its shafts. People had already been at the flesh, stripping the bodies clean so that bones glinted palely in the unending rain.

There was shouting away in the rain mist. A fight up ahead by the sound of it. Corfe heard an old man's voice cry out in pain, the sound of blows. He did not quicken his pace, but slogged wearily along. He had seen a score of such encounters since Aekir; they were as unremarkable as the falling rain.

But suddenly he was in the midst of it. An elderly man, his clothes black with mud and his face hideously scarred, came blundering out of the mist with one hand stretched before him as though feeling his way through the damp air. His other hand clutched something at his breast. There were half a dozen shapes in pursuit, snarling and shouting to one another.

The old man tripped and fell full length in the mud. For a second he lay as if struck down; then he began moving feebly. As he lifted his head Corfe saw that his eyes had been gouged out. They were dark, scabbed pits filled with mud and rain.

The pursuers became more visible, a rag-tag crowd of wild-eyed men. They carried cudgels and poniards. One bore a pike with a broken shaft. He poked the old man with the splintered end.

"Come on, grandfather, let us have the pretty bauble and perhaps we will let you live. It's little good to you anyway. You'll never see it glitter no more."

The old man tried to struggle to his knees, but the mud held him fast. His breath was coming in hoarse whines.

"I beg you, my sons," he bleated, "in the name of the Blessed Saint, let me be." Corfe could see now that dangling from a chain around his wizened neck was the A-shaped symbol of the praying hands, the badge of a Ramusian cleric. It was smeared with mud, but the yellow gleam of gold and precious stones could be made out through the filth.

"Have it your own way then, you God-damned Raven." The men closed in on the prone figure like vultures moving in on a carcass. The old man's body began jerking up and down as they tried to wrest the chain off his neck.

Corfe was level with the scuffle. He could either step off to one side and continue on his way or walk right through the middle of them. He stopped, hesitating, furious with himself for even caring.

There was a squawk of anguish from the old man as the chain broke free. The men laughed, one holding it aloft like a trophy.

"You accursed priests," he said, and kicked the old man in the ribs. "Your sort always have gold about you, even if all around is ruin and wreckage."

"Cut his saintly throat, Pardal," one of the men said. "He should have stayed to burn in his precious holy city."

The man named Pardal bent with a steel glitter in his fist. The old man groaned helplessly.

"That's enough, lads," Corfe heard himself say, for all the world as though he were back in barracks breaking up a brawl.

The men paused. Their victim blinked withered eyelids on bleeding holes. One side of his face was as black as a Merduk's with the mud.

"Who's that?"

"Just a traveller, like yourselves. Has not there been enough murder done these past days, without you adding to it? Leave the old crow alone. You have what you want."

The men peered at him, curious and wary.

"What are you, a Knight Militant?" one asked.

"Nay," another said. "See his sabre? That's the weapon of Mogen's men. He's a Torunnan."

The man called Pardal straightened. "The Torunnans died with Mogen or with Lejer. He's got that pig-sticker off a corpse."

"What else do you think he's got?" another asked greedily. The men growled and moved into a line confronting Corfe. Six of them.

Corfe drew out the heavy sabre in one fluid movement.

"Who'll be first to test whether I be one of Mogen's men or no?" he asked. The sabre danced in his hand. He loosened his feet in the gripping muck.

The men stared at him doubtfully, then one said: "What's that in your pouch, fellow?"

Corfe tapped his bulging belt pouch, smiling, and said truthfully: "Half a turnip."

"Throw it over here, and maybe we won't cut off your prick."

"Come and get it, you long streak of yellow shit."

The six paused, greed and fear fighting a curious battle on their countenances.

Then: "Take him!" one of them bellowed, and they were lurching towards Corfe with their weapons upraised.

He moved aside. They bunched on him, which was what he had hoped for. A jab of the sabre point made one throw himself backwards, to slip and tumble in the slithery mud. As he brought the blade back Corfe smashed the heavy basket hilt into another of their faces. The short spike on the hilt ripped up the man's nostril with a spray of dark blood, and he turned aside with a cry.

Corfe whirled – too slowly. A cudgel caught him just above the ear, grazing his skull and tearing the skin and hair. He hardly felt the blow, but ducked low and swung at the man's knee, feeling the crunch of bone and cartilage up his forearm as the keen blade destroyed the joint.

He tore the sabre free and the man fell, tripping up another.

Corfe swung at the nape of the tripped man's neck, saw the flesh slice apart and again felt the familiar jar as the sabre broke through the bone.

No more of them came at him. He stood with the sword held at the ready position, hardly panting. His head was ringing and he could feel the burning swell of the blow that had landed there, but he felt as light as thistledown. There was laughter fluttering in his throat like some manic, trapped bird.

One man lay dead, his head attached to his body only by the clammy gleam of the windpipe. Another was sitting holding his mangled knee, groaning. A third had both hands clutched to the hole in his face. The other three looked at Corfe darkly.

"The bastard is a Torunnan after all," one said with disgust. "Aren't you?" he asked Corfe.

Corfe nodded.

"We'll leave you to your Raven then, Torunnan. May you have joy of each other."

They helped up the crippled man and stumbled off into the curtain of the rain, joining the other anonymous shapes who were staggering westwards. The dead man's blood darkened the mud, rain-stippled. Corfe felt strangely let down. With a flash of insight he realized he had been hoping to die and leave his own corpse on the churned ground. The knowledge sapped his strength. His shoulders sagged, and he sheathed the sabre without cleaning it. There was only himself again, and the rain and the mud and the shadows passing by.

Someone else was stumbling towards him: a robed shape bent over as if burdened with pain. It was a young monk, his tonsure a white circle in the gloom. He splashed to his knees beside the old, eyeless man who lay forgotten on the ground.

"Master," he sobbed. "Master, they have killed you." There was a black bar of blood striping the young monk's face. Corfe joined him, kneeling in the mud like a penitent.

The terrible face on the ground twitched. The mouth moved, and Corfe heard the old man say in a whisper of escaping breath:

"God has forsaken us. We are alone in a darkening land. Sweet Saint, forgive us."

The monk cradled his master's head in his lap, weeping. Corfe stared at the pair dull-eyed, still somewhat blasted at finding himself yet living. But there was something here at least – something for him to do.

"Come," he said, tugging at the monk's arm. "We'll find us some shelter, a space out of the rain. I have food I'm willing to share."

The young man stared at him. His face was swollen grotesquely on one side and Corfe thought there were bones broken there.

"Who are you, that has saved my master's life?" he asked. "What blessed angel sent you to watch over us?"

"I'm just a soldier," Corfe told him irritably. "A deserter fleeing west like the rest of the world. No angel sent me." The young man's piety soured his humour further. He had seen too many horrors lately to give it credence.

"Well, soldier," the monk said with absurd formality, "we are in your debt. I am Ribeiro, a novice of the Antillian Order." He paused, almost as if he were weighing something up in his mind. Then he looked down at the wreck of a man whose savaged head was pillowed on his knees. "And this is His Holiness the High Pontiff of the Five Monarchies, Macrobius the Third."

THE RAIN HAD stopped with the rising of the moon, and it looked as though the night sky would clear. Already Corfe could see the long curve of Coranada's Scythe twinkling around the North Star.

He threw another piece of wood on the fire, relishing the heat. His back was sodden and cold; but his face was aglow. The saturated leather of his boots was steaming and beginning to split, what with the heat and the rough usage. Mud was dropping in hard scales from his drying garments.

He shook his head testily. The blood pooled in his ear had dried to a black crust, affecting his hearing. He would see about that when dawn came.

He was huddled under an ox-waggon, burning the spokes of its shattered wheels for fuel. Ribeiro was asleep but the old man – Macrobius – was awake. It was somehow awful to see him blink like that, the eyelids sunken and wrinkled over the pits which had once housed his sight. Corfe could see now that he wore the black habit of the Inceptines, and that once the garment had been rich and full. It was a mosaic of mud and blood and broken threads now, and the old man shivered within it despite the warmth of the flames.

"You do not believe us," the old priest said. "You do not believe that I am who I say I am."

Corfe stabbed a stick into the fire's glowing heart and said nothing.

"It is true, though. I am – or was – Macrobius, head of the Ramusian Faith, guardian of the Holy City of Aekir."

"John Mogen was its guardian, and the men who died there with him," Corfe said roughly.

"And were you, my son, one of Mogen's men?"

It was eerie, having a conversation with an eyeless man. Corfe's glare went unheeded.

"I heard those brigands talk. They called you a Torunnan. Were you one of the garrison?"

"You talk too much, old man."

For a second the man's face changed; the saintly look fled and something like a snarl passed over it. That too faded, though, and the old man laughed ruefully.

"I ask your pardon, soldier. I am not much used to blunt speech, even yet. It must be that God is chastising me for my pride. 'The Proud shall be humbled, and the Meek shall be raised above them.'"

"There aren't many meek folk abroad tonight," Corfe retorted. "It surprises me that the pair of you got so far without getting your holy throats slit." As he spoke, he saw again the place where the old man's eyes had been and cursed himself for his clumsiness.

"I'm sorry," he grated. "We have all suffered."

Macrobius's fingers touched the ragged pits in his face gingerly. "'And those who do not see me, though they have eyes, yet they will be blind,'" he whispered. He bent his head, and Corfe thought he would have wept had he been able.

"The Merduks found me cowering in a storeroom in the palace. They gouged out my sight with glass from the windows. They would have slain me, but the building was in flames and they were in haste. They thought me just another priest, and left me for dead as they had left a thousand others. It was Ribeiro who found me." Macrobius laughed again, the sound more like the croak of a crow. "Even he did not know at first who I was. Perhaps that is my fate now, to become someone else. To atone for what I did and did not do."

Corfe stared closely at him. He had seen the High Pontiff before, conducting the ritual blessings of the troops and sometimes at High Table when he had been commanding the guard for the night, but it had been at a distance. There was only the vague impression of a grey-haired head, a thin face. *How much we need the eyes*, he thought, *to truly know someone, to give them an identity*.

It was true that Mogen had purportedly made the High Pontiff a prisoner in his own palace to keep him from fleeing the city – the Knights Militant in the garrison had almost created an internal war when they had heard – but surely it was impossible that this wreck, this decrepit flotsam of war, was the religious leader of the entire western world?

No. Impossible.

Corfe poked the blackened turnip out of the fire and nudged the old man beside him, who seemed lost in some interior wilderness.

"Here. Eat."

"Thank you, my son, but I cannot. My stomach is closed. Another penance, perhaps." He bent over the young monk who was sleeping to one side and shook his shoulder gently.

Ribeiro woke with a start, his eyes brimming with nightmares. His mouth opened and for an instant Corfe thought he would scream, but then he seemed to shiver and, scrubbing at one eye with a grubby knuckle, he sat up. His face was a dark purple bruise, and the cheekbone on one side had swollen out to close the eye and stretch the skin to a shiny drum tightness.

"The soldier has food here, Ribeiro. Eat and keep up your strength," Macrobius said.

The young monk smiled. "I cannot, Master. I cannot chew. There is nothing left of my teeth but shards. But I am not so hungry anyway. You must have sustenance – you are the important one."

Corfe stared towards the starlit heaven, stifling his exasperation. The smell of the charred turnip brought the water running round his tongue. He wondered what ridiculous impulse had made him risk his life to save these two pious fools.

But he knew the answer to that. It was the darkest impulse of all.

He almost laughed. A soldier, a monk and a blind lunatic who believed himself Pontiff sitting under an ox-cart arguing over who should eat a burnt turnip, whilst behind them burned the greatest city in the world. It might have been a comedy written by one of the playwrights of Aekir, a sketch to keep the mob happy when bread was scarce.

But then he thought of his wife, his sweet Heria, and the thin, bitter humour ran cold. He sat and stared into the flames of the fire as though they were the conflagration that blazed at the heart of his very soul.

IT TOOK AN hour of soaking in the big copper bath for Hawkwood to lose the stink and filth of the catacombs, even with the perfumes he had poured into the water.

He could see them in his mind's eye: the low arched ceilings of rounded brick, the torches in the hands of the jailers guttering blue with the stench and the lack of air. And the countless figures lying as still as corpses in row on row with heavy irons at their wrists and ankles. A white face would flash as one looked up, but the rest remained prone, or sitting with their backs to the streaming damp of the walls. Hundreds of men and women and even children sprawled together. There was blood here and there where they had fought amongst themselves, and a woman keened softly because of some violation. Hawkwood had been in sties where the pigs were fifty times better looked after. But these, of course, were dead meat already. They were destined for the pyre.

"Radisson!" he had called out. "Radisson of Ibnir! It is the Captain, Hawkwood, come to free you!"

Someone reared up, snarling, and one of the turnkeys beat him down savagely, his arm with its club descending again and again until the man lay still, a broken place shining in his skull. The other prisoners stirred restlessly. There were more faces turned to Hawkwood, ovals of white flesh in the gloom with holes for eyes.

"Lasso! Lasso of Calidar! Stand up, damn you!" An unwise order. Though Hawkwood was short himself, he had to crouch under the low vaulted ceiling. The turnkeys seemed permanently bent, as though warped by their ghastly labour.

"I am here for the crew of the *Grace of God*. Where are you, shipmates? I am to take you out of here!"

"Take me, take me!" a woman screamed. "Take my child, sir, for pity's sake!"

"Take me!" another shouted. And suddenly there was a cacophony of shouting and screaming that seemed to echo and re-echo off the walls, pounding Hawkwood's brain.

"Take me, Captain! Take me! Save me from the flames in the name of God!"

HE POURED MORE water over himself and relaxed in the rose-scented steam. He did not like the perfumes Estrella used. They were too sickly for his tastes, but today he had poured vial after vial of them into the water to wash away the stink.

He had his men – most of them, at any rate. One had died, beaten to death by his fellow prisoners for the blackness of his face, but the rest were back on board ship, no doubt being scrubbed down in sea water by Billerand, the new first mate, if Billerand had time for such niceties in the chaos of outfitting for the voyage.

The voyage. He had not yet told his wife that he was leaving again within two sennights. He knew only too well the scene that would provoke.

The door to the bathing chamber swung open and his wife walked in, averting her eyes from Hawkwood's nakedness. She carried clean clothes and woollen towels in her arms, and bent to set them down on the bench that lined one wall.

She was wearing brocade, even in the heat. Her tiny fingers were covered with rings, like so many gilded knuckles, and the steam in the air made the tong-curled frizz of her hair wilt.

"I burned the other things, Ricardo," she said. "They were fit for nothing, not even the street beggars... There is cold ale waiting in the dining chamber, and some sweetmeats."

Hawkwood stood up, wiping the water out of his eyes. The air in the room seemed scarcely cooler than the liquid in the tub. Estrella's eyes rested on his nakedness for a second and then darted away. She coloured and reached for a towel for him, her eyes still averted. He smiled sourly as he took it from her. His wife and he only saw each other nude when in the bed chamber, and even then she insisted on there being no light. He knew her body only by moonlight and starlight, and by the touch of his hard-palmed hands. It was thin and spare, like a boy's, with tiny, dark-nippled breasts and a thick fleece of hair down in her secret part. Absurdly, she reminded Hawkwood of Mateo, the ship's boy who had shared his bunk a few times on that last long voyage to the Kardian Sea. He wondered what his wife would make of that comparison, and his smile soured further.

He stepped out of the bath, wrapping the towel about himself. Ricardo. Like Galliardo, she had always used the Hebrionese rendering of his name instead of his native version. It irked him to hear it, though he had heard it ten thousand times before.

Estrella had been a good marriage. She was a scion of one of the lesser noble houses of Hebrion, the Calochins. His father had arranged the match, terrible old Johann Hawkwood who had wanted a toe in the door in Abrusio, even in his day the fastest-growing port in the west. Johann had convinced the Calochins that the Hawkwood family was a noble Gabrionese house when in fact it was nothing of the sort. Johann had been given a set of arms by Duke Simeon of Gabrion for his services at the battle of Azbakir. Before that he had been merely a first mate on board a Gabrionese dispatch-runner with no pedigree, no lineage, no money, but a vast store of ambition.

He would be pleased if he could see me, Hawkwood thought wryly, *consorting with the emissaries of kings and with a Royal victualling warrant in my pouch*.

Hawkwood dressed, his wife leaving the room before the towel fell from his waist. His hair and beard dripped water but the arid air would soon put paid to that. He padded barefoot into the high-ceilinged room that was at the centre of his house. Louvred windows far above his head let in slats of light that blazed on the flagged floor. When his bare foot rested on one of the sun-warmed stones he felt the pain and the heat of it. Abrusio without the trade wind was like a desert without an oasis.

High-backed chairs, as stiffly upright as his wife's slender backbone, a long table of dark wood, various hangings as limp as dead flowers against the whitewashed plaster of the walls – they seemed unfamiliar to him because he had had no part in choosing them – and the balcony with its wooden screens, closed now, dimming the light in the room. *The place is like a church*, Hawkwood thought, *or a nunnery*.

He stepped to the balcony screens and wrenched them aside, letting in the golden glare and heat and dust and noise of the city. The balcony faced west, so he could see the bay and the Inner and the Outer Roads, as the two approaches to the harbour were called; the quays, the wharves, the seaward defence towers and the watch beacons on the massive mole of the harbour wall. He noted half a dozen vessels standing out to sea, their sails flaccid as empty sacks, their crews hauling them in with longboats. He listened to the clatter of wheels on cobbles, the shouts of hawkers and laughter from a nearby tavern.

Not for him the isolation of a nobleman's villa on the higher slopes of Abrusio Hill. He was looking out from one of the lower quarters, where the houses of the merchants clung to the slopes like tiers of sand martins' nests and it was possible to sniff bad fish and tar and salt air, a reek more welcome to him than any perfume.

"The ale will get warm," Estrella said hesitantly.

He did not reply, but stood drinking in the life of Abrusio – the sight of the flawless sea, as calm as milk. When would the trade start up again? He did not want to begin the voyage with his ships being towed out of the bay, searching for a puff of air on the open ocean.

That thought made him feel guilty, and he turned back into the room. It was full of light now, the early afternoon sun pouring down to flood the stone and touch off the gilt thread in the tapestries, bring out a warmer glow from the dark wood of the furniture.

He sat and ate and drank, whilst Estrella hovered like a humming-bird unable to settle upon a flower. There was a sheen of sweat on her collar-bone, gathering like a jewel in the hollow of her throat before sliding gently below the ruff and down into her bodice.

"How long have you been back, Ricardo? Domna Ponera says her husband spoke to you days ago, when there was that shooting in the harbour... I have been waiting, Ricardo."

"I had business to attend to, lady, a new venture that involves the nobility. You know what the nobility are like."

"Yes, I know what they are like," she said bitterly, and he wondered if court gossip about Jemilla had come this far down from the Noble Quarter. Or perhaps she was just reminding him of her own origins. It mattered not, he told himself, though again the remorse edged into his mind, making him defensive.

"Half my crew were taken away by the Ravens when we docked. That is why I stank like a privy when I arrived. I have been in the catacombs trying to get them released."

"Oh." Her face slumped, some of the energy going out of her. He noted with satisfaction that not even she could find fault with such a virtuous cause. She loved virtuous causes.

She sat down on one of the high-backed chairs and clapped her small hands together with a snap. A servant appeared at once and bowed low.

"Bring me wine, and see it is cold," she said.

"At once, my lady." The servant hurried away.

She could order the common folk like a true noble at any rate, Hawkwood reflected. Let her try that tone of voice once with me and we'll see how that narrow rump of hers likes a seaman's belt across it.

"Berio, was that?" he asked, slugging thirstily at his ale.

"Berio is gone. He was slovenly. This new one is named Haziz."

"Haziz? That's a Merduk name!"

Her eyes widened a little. He could see the pulse beat in her neck. "He is from the Malacars. His father was Hebrionese. He was afraid of the burnings, so I gave him a position."

"I see." Another stray dog. Estrella was a strange mixture of the petulant and the soft-hearted. She might take in a man off the street out of pity and throw him out again a week later because he was slow in serving dinner. Jemilla at least was unrelentingly hard on her attendants.

And her lovers, Hawkwood added to himself.

The wine came, borne by the ill-favoured Haziz who had the look of a seaman about him despite the fine doublet Estrella had procured for him. He looked at Hawkwood as though Richard were about to strike him.

They sat in silence, the husband and wife, drinking their tepid drinks slowly. As he sat there, Hawkwood had an overwhelming longing to be at sea again, away from the torrid heat, the crowds, the reek of the pyres. Away from Estrella and the silences in his home. He called it his home, though he had spent more time in either of his two ships and felt more at ease in them.

Estrella cleared her throat. "Domna Ponera was also saying today that your ships are being outfitted for a new voyage in great haste, and that all the port is buzzing with talk of the issue of a Royal warrant."

Hawkwood silently cursed Domna Ponera. Galliardo's wife was a huge woman with a moist moustache and the appetite of a goat for both food and information. As wife to the port captain she was in a fine position to acquire the latter, and her mine of information obtained her invitations to households where ordinarily she would not have been countenanced. Hawkwood knew that Galliardo had upbraided her many times for being too free with her tongue, but he was as much to blame. He could not, he had once told Hawkwood with a sigh, keep his tongue from wagging in the marriage bed, and he so loved the marriage bed. Hawkwood preferred not to dwell on that. His friend was an admirable fellow in many respects, but his unbridled lust for his enormous wife was inexplicable.

It was Domna Ponera who took the bribes, and then bullied her husband into carrying out her promises. A convenient berth, a vacant warehouse, an extra gang of longshoremen, or an eye turned aside for a special cargo. There were many ways a port captain might be of service to the high and the low of Abrusio; but though it made Galliardo rich, it did not make him happy, even if it did make his wife gratifyingly agile in the afore-mentioned bed. Sometimes though, Hawkwood thought that Galliardo would give it all up to be master of a swift caravel again, plying the trade-routes of the Five Seas and raising a riot in every port he put into to wet his throat.

As for Domna Ponera's Royal warrant, Hawkwood had already seen it. The scarred nobleman, Murad of Galiapeno, was in possession of it, and had sent the victualling documents to Hawkwood as soon as he had received Richard's agreement on the proposed voyage. Hence his visits to the catacombs this morning. Some other poor devils had gone to the pyre today, but not Hawkwood's crew. There was that to be thankful for.

"Do you know anything about this warrant?" Estrella asked him. She was trembling. She probably hated the silences even more than he did.

"Yes," he said heavily at last. "I know about it."

"Perhaps you would be so good as to tell your wife then, before she hears about it from someone else."

"Estrella, I would have told you today in any case. The commission is for my ships. I have been hired to undertake a voyage by the nobility, and ultimately by the King himself."

"Where to? What is the cargo?"

"There is no cargo as such. I am carrying... passengers. I cannot tell you where, because I am not yet entirely sure myself." He hoped she would recognize the element of truth in that statement.

"You do not know how long it is to be for, then?"

"No, lady, I do not." Then he added, out of some belated sense of decency, "But it is likely to be a long time."

"I see."

She was trembling again and he could see the tears coming. Why did she cry? He had never worked it out. They took little pleasure in each other's company, in bed or at board, and yet she always hated to see him go. He could not decipher it.

"You would not have told me – not until you had to," she said, her voice breaking.

He stood up and padded barefoot out to the balcony. "I knew you would not like it."

"Does it matter greatly to you what I like and do not like?"

He did not reply, but stared out at the crescent of the teeming harbour and its forest of masts and, further out, the blue of the horizon where it met the sky in the uttermost west. What lay out there? A new land ready for the taking, or nothing but the rim of the earth as the old sailors had believed, where the Western Ocean tipped away eternally into the gulf wherein circled the very stars?

He heard the swish of her heavy robe as she left the room behind him, the gulp of breath as she swallowed a sob. For a second he hated himself. It might have been different had she borne him a son – but then he could imagine the scenes when first the father took the son to sea with him. No, they were too far apart from each other ever to find some middle ground.

And did it matter? It had been a political marriage, though the Hawkwoods had done better out of it than the Calochins. Estrella's dowry had bought the *Osprey*. He forgot that sometimes.

I'd as lief have the ship, he thought, *without the wife*.

He was the last of his line; after Richard Hawkwood the name would disappear. The last chance to perpetuate it had died with the abortion he had procured for Jemilla, unless by chance there was a whore in some port who had borne his progeny in a moment of carelessness.

He wiped his eyes. The dry heat had baked the bath water out of his hair and now he stank of roses. He would go down to the yards and see how the outfitting was coming along. He would regain the smell of cordage and salt and sweat that was his proper scent, and he would ready his ships for the voyage ahead.

EIGHT

DOWN NEAR THE Guilds' Quarter of the city the streets were quieter than at the rowdy waterfront. Here the merchants rented or owned the stoutest warehouses for the most expensive of their commodities. It was a district of clean alleyways and bland shopfronts, with privately hired guards at most corners and the odd, cramped little tavern where men of business might meet in peace without being disturbed by the drunken antics of paid-off sailors or off-duty marines.

Most of the guilds of Abrusio owned property here, from the humble Potters' Guild to the mighty Guild of Shipmasters. The Thaumaturgists' Guild owned towers and mansions further up the hillside, near the courts as befitted their role. But those towers were closed now, by order of the Prelate of Abrusio, and Golophin the Mage, Adviser to King Abeleyn of Hebrion, was waiting patiently in a tiny tavern tucked behind one of the warehouses built of stone or the storage of ship timber. His wide-brimmed hat was pulled down to shade his eyes, though the lights were low in the place, as if to encourage conspiracy. He smoked a long pipe of pale clay whilst a flagon of barley beer grew ever warmer on the table in front of him.

The door of the inn opened and three men entered, all cloaked despite the closeness of the night. They ordered ale, and two took theirs to a table on the other side of the inn while the third sat down opposite Golophin. He threw back his hood and raised his flagon to the old wizard, grinning.

"Well met, my friend."

Golophin's narrow, lined face cracked into a smile. "You might order me another beer, lad. This one is as flat as an old crone's tit."

A fresh flagon came, and Golophin drank from its moisture-beaded pewter gratefully.

"The landlord seems singularly incurious about the nature of his customers," King Abeleyn of Hebrion said.

"It is his business. This will not be the first whispered discussion he will have seen in his tavern. In places such as this the commerce of Abrusio is directed and misdirected."

Abeleyn raised one dark eyebrow. "So? And not in the court or the throne room then?"

"There as well, of course, sire," said Golophin with mock sincerity.

"I do not see why you could not have made your way into the palace invisibly or suchlike. This trysting in corners smacks of fear, Golophin. I don't like it."

"It is for the best, sire. It may seem to complicate things, but in fact it keeps life a lot simpler. Our friend the Prelate may be out of the city, but he has spies aplenty to do his watching for him. It were best you were not seen in my company while this current purge lasts."

"It is you he aims at, Golophin."

"Oh, I know. He wants my hide nailed to a tree, to halt what he sees as the Guild's meddling in the affairs of state. He would rather the clergy did the meddling. The Prelate has a whole host of issues he means to address, sire, and this edict he badgered you into signing is one way of getting to the heart of several of them."

"I know it only too well, but I cannot risk excommunication. With Macrobius gone there is no voice of reason left among the senior Church leaders, except possibly Merion of Astarac. By the way, how is the Synod coming together? What have you seen in your sorcerous travels?"

"They are still gathering. Our worthy Prelate had a good passage once he was out of the calms around these coasts. His vessel is currently crossing the Gulf of Almark, south of Alsten Island. He will be in Charibon in ten days, if the weather holds."

"Who is there already?"

"The Prelates of Almark, Perigraine and Torunna have preceded him. Their colleague, Merion of Astarac, had a longer journey to make than any of the others, and the

Malvennor Mountains to cross. It will be two weeks, I fear, before the Synod is convened, sire."

"The longer the better, if it keeps that tonsured wolf from my door. I will soon be setting off myself for the Conclave of Kings at Vol Ephrir. Can you keep me informed about the doings here while I am away, Golophin?"

The old mage sucked deeply on his pipe, and then shrugged with a twitch of his bony shoulders.

"It will not be easy. I will have to cast through my familiar, something no mage likes to do at any time, but I will do my best, sire. It will mean losing our eye on the east, though."

"Why? I thought all you wizards had to do was gaze into a crystal and see what you wanted to see."

"If only it were that simple. No, if my gyrfalcon accompanies you I will be able to send you news from here through it, but do not expect regular bulletins. The process is exhausting and dangerous."

Abeleyn looked troubled. "I would not ask, except —"

"No, you have a right to ask, and it is a thing which must be done. Let us speak no more of it."

No one else could have spoken thus to the King of Hebrion, but Golophin had been one of Abeleyn's tutors when he had been a runny-nosed little miscreant, and the young prince had felt the back of the wizard's hand many times. Abeleyn's father, Bleyn the Pious, had believed in a stern upbringing laden with religious instruction, but Abeleyn had always hated the Inceptine tutors, dry men whose imagination was a thing of dust, a storehouse of past aphorisms and never-to-be-questioned rules. It was Golophin who had saved him, who had defused the incipient rebellion in the youngster and coaxed him into an appearance at least of dutiful submission. The wizard's closeness to the King's son had been one of the things which had protected him from the malice of the Inceptines when they had tried to rid the court of all vestiges of unorthodoxy and sorcery. The irony was that with the wizard's pupil at last on the throne, they had finally succeeded. Aekir's fall, Golophin thought with real bitterness, had been a Godsend to them.

"Speaking of the east," Abeleyn said conversationally, "how are the Torunnans holding out?"

Golophin tapped his long pipe out delicately on the table. He preferred leaf imported from Ridawan flavoured with cinnamon. The smoking pile of ashes smelled like an essence of the east itself. Abeleyn wondered if there were a tinct of kobhang in the leaf, the mild euphoric that easterners chewed or smoked to fight tiredness and clear their thinking. Golophin made patterns in the ashes with one long, white finger.

"I have been working the bird hard lately. He is tired, and when he is tired he begins to slip away from me, and I receive pictures of the stoop, the kill, blood and feathers drifting in the air. It is said that a tired or a despairing mage will sometimes let his self slip wholly into his familiar and become one with it, leaving his body an empty husk behind him. He glories thereafter in the animal emotions of the creature, and eventually forgets what he once was."

Golophin smiled thinly.

"My familiar sleeps on a withered tree not far from Ormann Dyke. Today he has seen a hundred thousand people go by, dragging their feet through the mud towards the last Torunnan fortress before the mountains. They have left thousands on the road behind them, and on their flanks the Merduk light cavalry prowl like ghouls. Ormann Dyke itself is in chaos. Half its defenders are taken up with dealing with the refugees, and the land to the west of the dyke resembles an enormous shanty town. The poor folk of Aekir can walk no more. Perhaps they will squat in the rain and await the outcome of another battle before they will have the strength to trek further west. But after Ormann Dyke, where can they go?"

"You believe the dyke will fall," Abeleyn said.

"I believe the dyke will fall, but more importantly so do its defenders. They feel forsaken by God, and King Lofantyr of Torunna they believe has abandoned them. He has drawn off men of the garrison to defend the capital."

Abeleyn thumped a fist down on the table, making the beer jump in the flagons. "The damned fool! He should be concentrating all he has at the dyke."

"He is afraid he will lose all he has," Golophin said calmly. "There are less than eighteen thousand men left

in the garrison, and the Knights Militant have been riding
away to the west in large bodies for days. If Shahr Baraz
finds more than twelve thousand manning the defences
when he arrives I will be surprised. And even leaving
troops to garrison Aekir and their supply lines, the
Merduk can still put a hundred thousand men before the
dyke, probably more."

"How long do we have before the assault?" Abeleyn
asked.

"More time than you might imagine. Sibastion Lejer's
fighting rearguard badly mangled the *Hraibadar*, the
shock-troops of Shahr Baraz's forces. He will wait for them
to come up before launching a serious assault, and with the
Western Road in a shambles and the weather showing no
sign of changing, his transport will have difficulties moving
with the troops. The River Searil is swollen. Once the
Torunnans cut the bridges, the Merduks will have to force
a river crossing under fire; but the Torunnans will not cut
the bridges whilst there are refugees on the eastern bank.
If I were the Khedive, I'd wait until the roads improved
before I advanced. The refugees are still pouring west, so
for the moment time is on his side. That is not to say that
his cavalry will not attack the dyke first, before the main
body comes up, but the dyke will hold them for a little
while. Its defenders are Torunnans, after all."

Abeleyn nodded absently. "I begin to see that Ormann
Dyke is not solely a Torunnan affair. Lofantyr needs troops,
needs them desperately. But what do I have to give him, and
how could they get there in time? An army would take five
or six months to march to the dyke."

"By sea it might take five weeks, with fair winds or the
aid of a weather-worker," Golophin said.

"By sea?" Abeleyn shook his head. "The navy has
its hands full patrolling the Malacar Straits against the
corsairs; and then there is Calmar to consider. A western
armament sailing into the Levangore would have to contend
with the Calmaric Sea-Merduks. They have been quiet
since Azbakir, but they would not tolerate an incursion
of that size. It would be Azbakir all over again, save we'd
be fighting it with transports instead of war-carracks. No,

Golophin, unless you can magically spirit a few thousand men halfway across the world there is nothing we can do about the dyke. Lofantyr will love hearing that when I meet him at the conclave. Already he thinks the other monarchies have abandoned Torunna."

"Perhaps he is right," the mage said sharply. "There were seven great Kingdoms after the Fimbrian Hegemony ended; now the Merduks have reduced it to five. Will you sit in Abrusio until their elephants come tramping over the Hebros?"

"What would you have me do, teacher?"

Golophin paused, looking suddenly weary. "Teachers do not always know the answers."

"Nor do kings." Abeleyn set his brown fingers atop the old mage's lean wrist and smiled.

Golophin laughed. "What a jest it is to sit and try to put the world to rights. The earth was a flawed place ere man arrived to skew it further; we shall never set it straight upon its foundations. Only God can do that, or the 'Lord of Victories,'" as the Merduks call Him."

"We will do our best, nonetheless," Abeleyn said.

"Now, my King, you are beginning to sound like your father."

"God forbid that I should ever sound like that sanctimonious, cold-eyed old warhorse."

"Do not be so hard on his memory. He loved you in his own way, and everything he did was for the good of his people. I do not believe he ever committed one act which could be attributed to personal motives."

"That much is certainly true," Abeleyn said tartly.

"Were he Torunna's king, sire, I'll guarantee you that Aekir would be standing and the Merduks would be breaking their heads against its walls as they have done for the past sixty years. And the Knights Militant would be there in number also, instead of carrying out purges up and down the continent. It is hard to argue with a man of perfect convictions."

"That I know."

"John Mogen was such a man, but he was too abrasive. He inspired either love or hate, and alienated those who should have been his allies in Aekir's defence. A king must appear to be as solid as a stone in his beliefs, lad, but he must bend like a willow when the gale blows."

"And bend invisibly," Abeleyn pointed out.

"Even so. There is a vast difference between blinkered intolerance and the ability to compromise without being seen to compromise."

"Ironic, Golophin, isn't it, that the best soldiers in the world, the Torunnans, are ruled by a king who has never seen battle, a young man who knows nothing of war?"

"The old monarchs are gone or going, sire. There is you, Lofantyr, King Mark of Astarac and Skarpathin of Finnmark – young men only a few years on the throne. The older kings who remember the earlier struggles with the Merduk are on their way out. The fate of Normannia rests on the shoulders of a new generation. I pray they will prove equal to the burden."

"Thank you for your confidence, Golophin," the King said dryly.

"You have it, sire, insofar as any man can have it. But I worry. The Ramusians have stood off the Merduk threat so long because they were united, strong, and of one faith. Now the holy men of the west seem intent on splitting each kingdom apart in the search for – what? Piety or earthly authority? I cannot yet say, but it worries me. Perhaps it is time there was a change. Perhaps Macrobius's downfall and the loss of Aekir is a new beginning – or the beginning of the end. I am no seer; I do not know."

Abeleyn stared into the cloudy heart of his beer. The tavern around them was quiet. There were a few murmuring knots of men in the corners, and the landlord stood at the bar smoking a short, foul-smelling pipe and whittling a piece of wood. Only Abeleyn's bodyguards, across the dim room, were looking about them, ever alert for the safety of their king.

"I need something, Golophin," Abeleyn said in a low voice. "Some morsel to take with me to the Conclave of Kings, some means of raising hope."

"And of staving off requests for troops," Golophin told him.

"That too. But I cannot think of anything."

"You just spoke of the Torunnans, sire, and how they were the best soldiers in the world. That was not always true."

"I don't follow you."

"Think, lad. Who once held all of Normannia in their fist? Whose tercios marched from the shores of the Western Ocean to the black heights of the Jafrar in the east? The Fimbrians, whose hegemony lasted two hundred years before they tore themselves apart in their endless civil wars. The Fimbrians, whose hands built Aekir and laid the foundations of Ormann Dyke, who broke the power of the Cimbric tribes and founded the Kingdom of Torunna itself."

"What about them?"

"They are still there, aren't they? They have not disappeared."

"They have shut themselves off in their electorates for this past century and more, endlessly quarrelling amongst themselves. They are no longer interested in empire, or in any events east of the Malvennor Mountains."

"They have fine armies, though. *There* is something you can take to your meeting of kings, Abeleyn. The west needs troops? There are untold tens of thousands of them in Fimbria contributing nothing to the defence of the continent."

"The Five Kingdoms distrust Fimbria; men have long memories. I am not sure even Torunna would welcome Fimbrian troops on its soil, despite the urgency of its needs – and even if we could persuade the Fimbrians to send them. They are an isolationist power, Golophin. They are not even sending a representative to the conclave."

Golophin leaned back from the table and flapped a hand in exasperation. "So be it then. Let the men of the west keep their fears and prejudices. They will no doubt still possess them when the hordes of Ahrimuz have cast the shadow of their scimitars over all the Ramusian kingdoms."

Abeleyn scowled, feeling as though he were the pupil again and Golophin the teacher who had just received the wrong answer.

"All right then, blast you! I'll see what can be done. It can do no harm, after all. I'll send envoys to the four

Fimbrian Electorates, and I'll bring the whole thing up at the conclave. Much good it will do me."

"That's my boy," Golophin said, knowing how much that phrase irritated the King. "But there is one thing you might remember when dealing with the Fimbrians, sire."

"Yes?"

"Do not be proud. They hoard memories of empire, even if they say they no longer hanker after it. You must make yourself into a supplicant, no matter if it galls your pride."

"I must be a willow, eh, bending in the wind?"

Golophin grinned. "Exactly – but not, of course, seen to be bending. You are a king, after all."

They clinked flagons like men sealing a bargain or toasting a birth. The King drank deeply, and then pinched foam from his upper lip.

"There is one last thing tonight, something near to your heart, perhaps."

Golophin cocked an eyebrow.

"The list. The list we drew up of those of your own kind who might be saved from the pyre." The King did not meet the old wizard's eyes as he spoke. He seemed oddly abashed. "Murad tells me he will be ready to sail within two sennights. He takes a demi-tercio with him, fifty Hebrian arquebusiers and sword-and-buckler men. Counting the crews, that leaves space for some hundred and forty passengers."

"Less than we had hoped," Golophin said tersely.

"I know, but he is convinced he will need the soldiers once landfall is made."

"To deal with the wild natives he may meet, or with the passengers he must travel with?"

Abeleyn shrugged helplessly. "I have hamstrung his scheme enough as it is, Golophin. If I prune away at it any further he may throw it all up, and then we are back where we started. A man like Murad needs some kind of incentive."

"The viceroyship of a new colony."

"Yes. He has few superstitious prejudices against the Dweomer-folk, He should treat them fairly. They could be said to be the backbone of his ambitions."

"And your ambitions, sire. How do the Dweomer-folk fit into those?"

The King coloured. "Let us say that Murad's expedition eases my conscience and –"

"So many fewer innocents consigned to the flames."

"I do not relish being interrupted, Golophin, not even by you."

The old mage bowed in his seat.

"As you have said, it is a means of putting these folk beyond the reach of the Church, but you know also that there are other motives involved."

"As always."

"If there is a Western Continent, it must be claimed by Hebrion – must be. We are the westernmost seafaring power in the world. It is our right to expand in that direction whilst Gabrion and Astarac look to the Levangore for trade and influence. Think of it, Golophin. A new world, an empty world free of monopolies or corsairs. A virgin continent waiting for us."

"And if the continent is not virgin?"

"What do you mean?"

"What if this fabled western land is inhabited?"

"I cannot imagine that it is, or at least that they have a civilization comparable to ours. And I am certain that they will not possess gunpowder. That is something we ourselves have had for only a century and a half."

"So Murad will slaughter his way to a Hebrian hegemony on the shores of this primitive land, and the sorcerers who are his cargo will be the living artillery which backs him up?"

"Yes. It was the only way, Golophin. The colonists must be hardy, talented, able to defend themselves. What better way to ensure that they survive than to make every one a sorcerer, a herbalist, a weather-worker, or even a true thaumaturgist?"

Or a shifter, Golophin thought to himself, remembering Bardolin's new ward. But he said nothing of that.

"A king's motives are never simple," he intoned at last. "I should have remembered that."

"I do my best with what God sees fit to give me."

"God, and Murad of Galiapeno. I would you had found another man to lead this expedition. He has a face I do not like. There is murder written in it and as for the ambition of which you spoke I do not think even he has yet plumbed the depths of it."

"It was his discovery, his idea. I could not take it away from him without making an enemy."

"Then tie him to you. Make sure he knows how long the arm of the Hebrian crown can be."

"You are beginning to sound like an old woman, Golophin."

"Maybe I am, but there is wisdom in the words of old women too, you know."

Abeleyn grinned, looking boyish in the dim tavern light. "Come, will you not return to the court and assume your rightful place?"

"What, crouching behind your throne and whispering in your ear?"

It was the popular Inceptine image of the King's wizardly advisor.

"No, sire," Golophin went on. "It is too early yet. Let us see how the Synod goes, and this conclave of yours. I have a feeling, like the ache in an old wound before a storm. I think the worst is yet to come; and not all of it is drawing in from the east."

"You were ever free with prophecies of doom, despite the fact that you are no seer," Abeleyn said. His good humour had thinned. The boy had disappeared. It was a man who stood up and held out a strong hand to the old mage. "I must go. Tongues wag in the court. They think I have a woman down near the waterfront."

"An old woman?" Golophin asked, with one eye closed.

"A friend, Golophin. Even kings need those."

"Kings most of all, my lord."

THE NIGHT WAS as close as ever. Abeleyn and his bodyguards strolled up the street as nonchalantly as if they were three night-watchmen. The closed carriage was in a courtyard at the top, the horses standing stock-still, patient as graven images. The bodyguards clambered up behind whilst Abeleyn let himself inside.

There was a scratch of steel, a shower of sparks, then a glow. As the candle lantern took the flame, the interior of the curtained coach flickered with glowing gold. The carriage lurched into motion, the hooves of the horses clicking on the cobbles.

"Well met, my lord," the lady Jemilla said, her white face olive-coloured in the swaying candlelight.

"Indeed, my lady. I am sorry to have kept you waiting for so long."

"The wait was no trouble. It sharpens the anticipation."

"Indeed? Then I must make sure to keep you waiting more often." The King's tone seemed casual, but there was a tenseness about him that he had not evidenced whilst in the tavern with Golophin.

Jemilla threw off her dark, hooded cloak. Underneath she wore one of the tight-fitting dresses of the court. It emphasized the perfect lines of her collar-bones, the smoothness of the skin on her breastbone.

"I hope, my lord, that you have not been squandering yourself on one of the lower-city doxies. That would grieve me extremely."

She was ten years older than the King. Abeleyn felt the difference now as he met the dancing darkness of her eyes. He was no longer the ruler of a kingdom, the commander of armies. He was a young man on the brink of some glorious dispensation. It had always been this way with her. He half resented it. And yet it was the reason he was here.

The lady Jemilla unfastened the laces of her bodice whilst Abeleyn watched, fascinated. He saw the high, dark-nippled breasts spring out, red-marked where the tight clothing had imprisoned them.

Their quiet noises were hidden by the creak of leather and wood, the rattle of the iron-bound wheels, the clatter of the horses' progress. The carriage wound its leisurely way up Abrusio Hill towards the Noble quarter, whilst down on the waterfront the gaudy riot of the pothouses and brothels continued to paint the hot night in hues of flesh and scarlet, and in the harbour the quiet ships floated stark and silent at their moorings.

The high clouds shifted; the stars wheeled overhead in the nightly dance of heaven. Men sitting on the sea walls in the reek of fish and weed with bottles at their feet paused in their low talk to sniff the air and feel its sudden caress as it moved against their faces. Canvas flapped idly once, twice; then it bellied out as the moving air took it. The glassy sea, a mirror for the shining stars, broke up in swell on swell as the clouds rose higher out on the Western Ocean. Finally the men on the sea wall could feel it in their hair, and they looked at one another as if they had experienced some common revelation.

The breeze grew, freshening and veering until it was blowing steadily from the north-west, in off the sea. It swayed the countless ships at their moorings until the mooring ropes creaked, raised smokes of dust off the parched streets of the city and stirred the branches of the King's cypresses, moving inland to refresh sweat-soaked sleepers. The Hebrian trade wind had started up again at last.

NINE

BARDOLIN STARED IMPASSIVELY at the wreckage of his home. The tower's massive walls had shrugged off the fury of the mob, but the interior had been gutted. The walls were black with soot, the floor inches deep in it. Someone had smashed the jar of Ur-blood and it had gelled into a slithering, gelatinous, slug-like creature, incorporating the ashes and the fragments of scale and bone that were all that was left of his specimen collection. It was the Ur-creature that had finally frightened them off, he guessed. He stared at it as its pseudopodia blindly touched the air, trying to make sense out of this new world it had been so violently born into.

For a second Bardolin felt like reshaping it, adding the crocodile skull that lay mouldering in a corner, giving it the sabre-cat claws he had picked up on a trip to Macassar, and then launching the finished, unholy beast into the streets to wreak his revenge. But he settled for unbinding the Ur-blood from its gathered organic fragments and letting it sink, mere liquid again, into the scorched floor.

All gone – everything. His books, some of which dated back to before the Fimbrian Hegemony, his spell grimoires, his references, his collections of birdskins and insects, even his clothes.

The imp tiptoed across the ravaged chamber with wide, bewildered eyes. It clambered up Bardolin's shoulder and nestled in the hollow of his neck, seeking reassurance. He could feel the fear and confusion in its mind. Thank God he had removed it from the rejuvenating jar before he had left and had taken it with him, hidden in the bosom of his robe. Otherwise it would be one more rotting mess amid the littered debris.

There were things here which disturbed him, unanswered questions amid the ruin of his home which hinted at larger answers; but he was too blasted and bewildered to tackle them now. How had they forced the mage bolt on the door? How had they known he was not at home, but was away watching poor Orquil burn?

Orquil. He shut his eyes. Despite the cool sea breeze that washed over the city like a blessing, he could still smell burnt flesh. Not in the air, but off his own clothes. He had stood at the foot of the boy's pyre looking up into his apprentice's pitifully young face, as pale as chalk, but smiling somehow; and he had smote him with a bullet of pure thaumaturgy as potent as his grief and rage could make. The boy had been dead before the first flames began to lick round his shins. The first life Bardolin had ever taken with magic, though he had taken many more with blade and arquebus ball.

There will be more taken by magic before I am done, he promised himself, the bitter anger rising in him. He wondered if Griella felt like this when the black change was upon her. That unfocused hatred, the mounting fury craving outlet in some act of extreme violence.

But that was not the mage way. Anger did no one any good. And besides, if Bardolin were truly honest with himself, he would have to admit that it was guilt that fuelled his rage as much as grief. The fact that he himself had not burned.

Griella entered the blasted room. She had a sack slung over one slim shoulder and her hands were black with ash.

"I tried to salvage some things, but there's not much left."

She smiled as the imp chirruped at her, but then her face went flat again. "If you had let me stay, I would have stopped it," she said.

Bardolin did not look at her.

"How? By slaughtering them like cattle? And then the city guard would have been swarming over this place like flies around summer dung."

"I don't think so. I think they would not have come here whatever happened. I think they were told to stay away."

Bardolin did look at her now, startled by the depth of her reasoning.

"Something does not smell right, it is true," he admitted.

"Golophin has ensured our safety, by order of the King himself; but someone else is determined to hurt us ere we take ship for the West."

"Well, we've less to pack at any rate," Griella said brightly. Her smile eventually drew an answering one from him. The heavy sun pouring through the splintered windows gave her hair the aspect of beaten bronze. Her very skin seemed golden.

"You are still sure you want to take ship with me, then?" Bardolin asked.

"Of course! I shall become your new apprentice, to replace the one they burned today. And I shall keep you safe. Not even when the change is upon me would I hurt you, I think."

Bardolin said nothing. When she had come round from the spell of unconsciousness she had been both furious and fascinated. She had never dreamed there could be a power to knock out a full-blooded shifter in the midst of the change. She had been a little in awe of him afterwards. But she was young, and she was not apt for an apprenticeship in the Seven Disciplines; shifters never were. And there was an aspect of her he had glimpsed whilst wrestling the beast down into' oblivion, a hunger that was not part of the werewolf she became, but that was buried in her human soul. He had seen it only briefly, flickering as if in the depths of a long abyss, but it gave him doubts as to the wisdom of letting her accompany him on the voyage.

But what alternative was there for her here in Abrusio? She had been abused before; it would happen again, and then she would become the beast once more, and she would be hunted down. They would cut off the beast's head with a silver knife and stick it on a spear in the market place. In a few hours the head would change, and it would be her brown eyes staring down, that bronze helmet of shining hair atop the ragged stump of the neck. He had seen it before. He could not allow it to happen to her, and he would not yet allow himself to ask why.

He rose to his feet. He had only a leather satchel to carry; they had saved pitifully little. His magicks would be crude for a while, and reduced in power, for his memory was not up to the task of remembering all the subtleties and nuances of casting that were necessary to make a piece of thaumaturgy perfect. He hoped that some of his fellow passengers on the voyage would be able to help him regain his lost knowledge.

The imp crawled into the bosom of his robe, not minding the smell of the pyre. New clothes; he must have new clothes, and get rid of this reek.

"Let us leave this place," he said. "We have things to do. I would like to see these ships that are to bear us, and perhaps buy a few things to make the voyage more tolerable."

"Salt beef and wormy bread are what sailors eat," Griella informed him. "And unwatered wine. They wash in seawater, when they wash at all, and they use each other in the way a man uses a woman."

"Enough," Bardolin said, uncomfortable with hearing such things from such a young mouth. "To the harbour, then. Let's take a look at these terrible seafarers."

There was one thing he could still do, though. As they left through the shattered doorway of his burned-out tower, Bardolin traced in the stone lintel a glyph of warding. It flamed briefly as his fingers brushed the stone, then died into invisibility. If anyone came after, picking around the bones of his home, the glyph would burst into an inferno and mayhap burn the bastards while they rummaged.

To a LANDSMAN, the Great Harbour of Abrusio was a vast and labyrinthine place. Now that the Hebrian trade had started up again, ships that had lain becalmed beyond the curve of the horizon were working in under all the canvas they could bear. The place was a stinking chaos of shouting men, squealing trucks and pulleys, creaking rope and thundering noise as a convoy of caravels out of Cartigella disgorged their cargoes of wine tuns on the quays and the enormous barrels were rolled up into waiting waggons which in turn would transport them to the public cellars.

On another wharf a beast transport had her square hull doors open wide, letting out a stench of animal excrement as the frightened cattle within were prodded and cursed down the ramps, scattering dung and straw as they went.

Bardolin and Griella paused to watch a Royal dispatch-runner, a lateen-rigged galleass, come sweeping into the harbour like some precisely rhythmed sea insect, the oars soaring up and out of the water at the same moment and the crew backing the mizzen to heave her to within yards of a free berth. These were the famous deep-water berths of Abrusio, hollowed out by the Fimbrians in past centuries using forced Hebrian labour. Abrusio could accommodate a thousand fully rigged ships at her wharves, it was said, and still have space for more.

Here were boxes of fish and sea squid shining in the hard sunlight, sacks of pepper from Punt or Ridawan, gleaming piles of marmorill tusks from the jungles of Macassar and stumbling, chained lines of slaves bought from the Rovenan corsairs to work the estates of the Hebrian nobility.

Sailors, fishermen, marines, merchants, vintners and longshoremen. They worked without pause in the unrelenting heat with the sweat shining on their faces and limbs – unable, it seemed, to communicate in anything less than a bellow. Bardolin and Griella found themselves holding hands in the crush to avoid being separated, for all the world like father and daughter. The heat glued their palms together with slick perspiration, and inside Bardolin's robe the imp whimpered with the noise and the smells and the jostling press of it.

They stopped half a dozen times to ask for the Hawkwood vessels, but each time were regarded pityingly, like imbeciles abroad by mistake, and then the throng pushed them along again. Finally they found themselves inside the tall, stone-built harbour offices, and there were told by a harried clerk to go to the twenty-sixth outfitting berth and ask for the *Grace of God* or the *Gabrian Osprey*, Ricardo Hawkwood, Master. They would find them easily, they were told. A ship-rigged caravel of one hundred tons, and a low-fo'c'sled carrack twice that tonnage with a mouldy looking bird for a figurehead.

They left the place only slightly less bewildered than when they had entered. This was a different world, down here by the water's edge. This was the world of the sea, with its own rules, laws, and even language. They felt like travellers in a foreign country as they pushed past ship after ship, wharf after wharf, and passed men of every land and faith and colour as they went. Since the easing of the edict in the wake of the Prelate of Abrusio's departure for the Charibon Synod, foreign ships had been putting into Abrusio without let-up. It was as though they were trying to make up for the time they had lost – or would lose again once the Prelate returned and foreigners were once more hauled off their ships and into the catacombs by the hundred.

"There," Bardolin said at last. "I think that's them. See the bird figurehead? It's a sea osprey from the Levangore. One knows from the speckles on its breast."

They stood before a wide stone dock dotted with mooring bollards and littered with guano. Snug in the berth behind the dock were two ships, their bowsprits projecting out over Bardolin's head and their masts tall, rope-tangled edifices towering up into the blue sky.

There were men everywhere it seemed, clinging to every piece of rigging and every rail. Some were out on the hulls on stages, painting the sea-battered wood with what looked like white lead. Others were knotting and splicing furiously in the shrouds. A gang of them were heaving on the windlass, and Bardolin saw that they were replacing a topmast. He knew little of ships, but he knew it was unusual, not to say revolutionary, to have masts in several pieces instead of one long, massive yard. This Hawkwood seemed to take his calling seriously.

Yet more men were on the dock, hauling on tackles attached to the mainyard, lifting net-wrapped bundles of casks and crates up over the ships' sides and on to the decks. On the decks themselves the hatches were wide open and gaping to receive the dangling goods, and Bardolin was astonished to see sheep, goats and cages of chickens go up in the air along with the wine barrels and boxes of salt meat and ship's biscuit. He noted with approval a huge sack of lemons being loaded also. It was thought by many that they combated the killer disease of scurvy, though many others believed the condition was caused by the unsanitary conditions aboard any ship.

"Who are we to talk to?" Griella asked wide-eyed. Her grip on the wizard's hand had not relaxed one whit.

Bardolin pointed to a burly, ornately mustachioed figure on the larger of the two ships. He was standing at the back – the quarterdeck? – and shouting furiously at a group of men down in the waist of the ship. He had a long, eastern water-pipe in one hand and he shook it at the men as though it were a weapon. His hair was cut so short that the sunlight made his scalp gleam through the bristle.

"I would say he is in charge," Bardolin decided.

"Is he this Hawkwood man?"

"I don't know, child. We'll have to ask."

He and Griella made their tortuous way through the piled provisions and cordage and timber on the wharf to where a gangway with raised planks for steps had been thrown down from the waist of the larger ship. Some of the sailors stopped to stare at the hard-faced, soldierly looking man and the shining-haired girl on his arm. There was an appreciative whistle and ribald chatter in a language even Bardolin did not recognize; but the meaning and the gesture that accompanied it were obvious.

Griella spun round on the obscenely capering seamen. With the sunlight in her eyes it seemed they had a yellow glow, and the lips drew back from her white teeth in a snarl.

Bardolin tugged her on, leaving the sailors staring after the pair. One man hurriedly made the Sign of the Saint.

They laboured up the precarious gangplank, which seemed designed for the agility of apes rather than that of men. Once on deck, Bardolin raised a hand to the furious mustachioed man and shouted in his best sergeant of arquebusiers voice:

"Ho there, Captain! Might we have a word with you?"

The man yanked his water-pipe out of his mouth as though it had bitten him and glared at the pair.

"Who in the name of the Prophet's Arse are *you*?"

"Someone who is to take ship with you in a short while. May we speak to you?"

The man's eyes rolled in his head. "A warlock I shouldn't wonder, and his doxy with him too. Sweet Saints, what a trip this is promising to be!"

He turned away from the quarterdeck rail, muttering to himself. Bardolin and Griella looked at one another, and

then clambered up towards him, feeling two dozen baleful
stares on their backs as they went. It was like intruding on
the territory of some alien, primitive tribe.

The quarterdeck was littered with coiled ropes and light
spars of timber. Everywhere lines of the running rigging came
down to be hitched about fiferails. A brass bell glittered,
painfully bright in the sun, and the huge tiller that steered the
ship from the half-deck below had been unshipped and lay to
one side. The man was leaning on the taffrail and puffing on
his gurgling pipe. His eyes were slits of suspicion.

"Well, what do you want? We're outfitting for a blue-
water voyage and we're short of men. I have things to do, and
passing the time of day with landsmen is not one of them."

"I am Bardolin of Carreirida and this is my ward, Griella
Tabard. We have been told we are to be passengers on one
of the vessels of Ricardo Hawkwood, and we wanted to
see them and ask for advice on preparing for the coming
voyage."

The man looked as though he were about to give a sneering
answer, but something in Bardolin's eye stopped him.

"You've been a soldier," he said instead. "I can see the
helm scar. You don't look like a wizard." He paused, staring
into the glass-sided bubble of his pipe for a second, then
grudgingly said: "I am Billerand, first mate of the *Osprey*,
so don't call me captain, not yet at least. Richard is up in
the city wrestling with the provisioners and moneylenders.
I don't know when he'll be back."

The imp squirmed in Bardolin's bosom, making Billerand
gape.

"Might we talk below?" Bardolin asked. "There are
many sets of ears up here."

"All right."

The mate led them down a companionway in the deck and
they blinked in the gloom, startling after the harsh brightness
of the day. It was close down here; the heat seemed to hang
like a tangible thing in their throats. They could smell the
wood of the ship, the pitch that caulked the seams, soft and
bitter-smelling, and the faint stink of the bilge, like filth and
water left to lie stagnant in a warm place. They could hear,
too, the thumps and shouts of men off in the ship's hold. It

sounded like a fight going on in the adjacent room of a large house, muffled but somehow very near.

They went through a door, stepping over a high storm sill, and found themselves in the Master's cabin. One side of it was taken up by the long stern windows. They could look out and see the harbour sunlit and framed by the curving lines of the interior bulkheads, like a backlit painting of sharp brilliance.

There were two small culverins on either side of the cabin, lashed up tight against their closed gunports. Billerand sat down behind the table that ran athwartships, the scene of the harbour behind him.

"Is that a familiar you have there?" he asked, pointing to the wriggling movement in the breast of Bardolin's robe.

"Aye, an imp."

The mate's face seemed to lighten somewhat. "They're lucky things to have on a ship, imps. They keep the rats down. The men will be pleased with that at least. Let him out, if you please."

Bardolin let the imp crawl out of the neck of his robe. The tiny creature blinked its eyes, its ears moving and quivering on either side of its head. Bardolin could feel its fear and fascination.

Billerand's fierce face relaxed into a smile. "Here, little one. See what I have for you?" He produced a small quid of tobacco from a neck pouch and held it out. The imp looked at Bardolin, and then leapt on to the table and sniffed at the tobacco. It took it delicately in one minute, clawed hand and then began to gnaw on it like a squirrel working at a nut. Billerand scratched it gently behind the ear and his smile widened into a grin.

"As I said, the hands will be pleased." He leaned back again. "What would you have me tell you then, Bardolin of Carreirida?"

"What do you know of this voyage we are to undertake?"

"Very little. Only that it is to the west. The Brenn Isles, maybe. And we are not taking cargo, only passengers and some Hebrian soldiery. We'll be packed in these two ships tighter than a couple on their honeymoon night."

"And the nature of the other passengers, besides the soldiers?"

"Dweomer-folk, like yourself. The hands do not know it yet, and I'd as soon leave it that way for the moment."

"Do you know who is sponsoring the voyage?"

"There is talk of a nobleman, and even of a Royal warrant. Richard has yet to brief his officers."

"What kind of a man is this Hawkwood?"

"A good seaman, even a great one. He has redesigned his ships according to his own lights, despite the grumbling of the older hands. They'll make less leeway than any vessel in this port, I'll promise you. And they're drier than any other ships of their class. I've been in this carrack in a tearing gale off the Malacar Straits with a lee shore a scant league away and a south-easter roaring in off the starboard quarter, but she weathered it. Many another ship, under many another captain, would have been driven on to the shoals and broken."

"Is he a Hebrian native?"

"No, and neither are most of his crews. Nay, our Richard is Gabrionese, one of the mariner race, though he has made his home in Abrusio these twenty years, ever since his marriage to one of the Calochins."

"Is he a... pious man?"

Billerand roared with laughter, and a spit of fluid sparked out of the brim of his pipe. The imp jumped, afraid, but he soothed it with the caress of one callused hand.

"Easy, little fellow, it's all right. No, wizard, he is not particularly pious. Do you think he'd take your sort as supercargo if he was? Why, I've seen him make a sacrifice to Ran the god of storms to placate the tribesmen among the crew. If the Inceptines had heard of that he'd have been burnt flesh a long time ago. You need not fear; he loves the Ravens even less than the next man. They had Julius Albak, the first mate before me and a damned good shipmate, shot in front of our eyes and then they hauled half the crew of the *Grace* off to the catacombs to await the pyre – but our Richard got them back, God knows how."

"Which lands do your seamen come from?" Bardolin asked with interest, perching on a seachest that rested against the forward bulkhead.

Billerand sucked a moment on his gurgling pipe.

"What are these questions in aid of, wizard? You

wouldn't be a spy of the Inceptines yourself, would you?"

"Far from it." Bardolin's face changed, going as white as marble, but his eyes flashed. "A friend of mine they burned today, sailor, a boy who was like a son to me. They have wrecked my home and the researches of thirty years. I am about to be exiled because of them. I have no love for the Ravens."

Billerand nodded. "I believe you. And I'll tell you that our crews are from every kingdom and sultanate in Normannia. We've men from Nalbeni and Ridawan, Kashdan and Ibnir. Men of Gabrion who sailed under Richard's father; Northmen from far Hardalen, and even one from the jungles of Punt, though he don't speak much on account of the Merduks cutting out his tongue. We have tribesmen from the Cimbrics captured by the Torunnans and sold as slaves. They were oarsmen in a Macassian galley which we took last year. Richard is their headman now. They have blue faces, with the tattooing.

"Myself, I'm from Narbosk, the Fimbrian electorate that broke off from the empire and went its own way back in my great-grandfather's time. I've served my stint in the Fimbrian tercios, but it's a boring life fighting the same battles on the Gaderian river every year. I tired of it, and took to the sea. Which army did you serve with?"

"The Hebrian. I was a sword-and-buckler man, and later an arquebusier. We fought the Fimbrians at Himerio, and they trounced us up and down. They pulled out of Imerdon, though, and thus it now belongs to the Hebrian crown."

"Ah, the Fimbrians," Billerand said, his eyes shining. Abruptly he reached under the table and produced a wide-bottomed bottle of dark glass. "Have a taste of *Nabuksina* with me, in memory of battling Fimbrians," he said, his smile baring teeth as square and yellow as those of a horse.

They shared the fiery Fimbrian root spirit, slugging in turn from the bottle. The imp watched, grinning from ear to long, pointed ear, the tobacco a bulge in one cheek. Griella stirred restlessly. She was bored with this talk of battles and armies. When Bardolin noticed, he wiped his mouth on his sleeve, as he had not done in years, and held up a hand when the bottle was proffered to him again.

"Some other time, perhaps, my friend. I have other questions for you."

"Question away," Billerand said expansively, curling one end of his luxurious moustache on a finger.

"Why are the soldiers taking ship with us? Is that usual?"

Billerand belched. "If a king's warrant is involved, why then yes."

"How many are coming?"

"We've been told to provision for fifty – a demi-tercio."

"That's a lot of fighting men for two vessels such as these."

"Indeed. Perhaps they're to keep the Dweomer-folk from magicking us when we've put to sea. We've to provide berths for half a dozen nags, too, both mares and stallions, so the nobles don't wear out their boots when we make landfall."

"And you're sure you don't know where that landfall will be?"

"Upon mine honour as a soldier, no. Richard is keeping that nugget to himself. He does that sometimes if we're putting to sea in search of a prize, so that word will not get out over the harbour. Sailors can be like a bunch of gossiping old women when they choose, and they dearly love a prize."

"This ship is a privateer also, then?"

"It is anything it has to be to make a little money; but we don't like that too widely known in Hebrion. Our good captain has contacts with the sea-rovers, the corsairs of Rovenan, or Macassar as they call it now. Our culverins and falconets are not for decoration alone."

"I'm sure," Bardolin said, standing up. "Can you tell me when you expect to sail?"

Billerand shook his head mournfully. The drink was beginning to trickle into place behind his eyes, making them as glassy as wet marbles. "We weigh anchor some time in the next fortnight, that's all I know. I doubt if even Richard himself knows the exact date yet. A lot depends on these nobles."

"Then we'll see you again, Billerand. Let us hope the voyage will be a prosperous one."

Billerand winked one eye slowly, showing them his square-toothed grin again.

BACK OUT ON the dock Bardolin strolled along lost in thought, the imp fast asleep in his bosom. Griella had to jog beside him to keep up.

"Well?" she demanded.

"Well what?"

"What have you learned?"

"You were there – you heard what was said."

"But you've guessed something. You're not telling me everything."

Bardolin stopped and gazed down at her. Her lower lip was caught up between her teeth. She looked absurdly fetching, and incredibly young.

"It is the presence of so many soldiers, and the nobles who command them. And the horses."

"What about them?"

"We cannot be sailing to any port in any of the civilized kingdoms or principalities; their authorities would not readily permit so many foreign soldiery to put ashore. And the horses. Billerand said they were mares and stallions. Warhorses are geldings. Those horses are for breeding. And did you see the sheep being taken on board? I'll wager they are for the same purpose."

"What does it all mean?"

"That we are going somewhere where there are no sheep and no horses; where there is no recognized authority. We truly are sailing into the unknown."

"But where?" Griella insisted, growing petulant.

Bardolin stared out across the maze of docks and ships and labouring men, out to where the flawless sky came down and merged with the brim of the horizon.

"West, we were told; maybe the Brenn Isles. But I reckon our worthy first mate was not telling us everything he knows. I think our course is set beyond them. I believe we are to sail further than any ship ever has before."

"And what are we supposed to find?" Griella asked him irritably.

Bardolin smiled and put an arm about her slim shoulders. "Who knows? A new beginning, perhaps."

TEN

OUTSIDE, THE TRAMP of cadenced feet and the bark of orders were filling up the afternoon. Little zephyrs of dust swirled in the doorway to curl up on the floor. A lizard clung motionless to the whitewashed wall.

Lord Murad of Galiapeno sipped wine, his eyes running down the muster lists. Unlike many nobles of the old breed, he could read and write perfectly and did not consider it beneath him. The older generation had cooks to feed them, grooms to care for their horses and scribes to read or write their books and letters. Murad, like King Abeleyn, had never thought that a prudent state of affairs. He liked to decipher evidence with his own wits without having to rely on a commoner. And there were some things which he liked to reserve for his eyes alone.

Fifty-two men, including two sergeants and two ensigns. They were the best in the Abrusio garrison, and Murad had commanded the bulk of them himself for more than two years. No cavalry, alas. The only horses they were taking were breeding stock. There were arquebuses for every man, though not all of them were yet trained in their use; and Hawkwood's crews – they were familiar with firearms. Many of them were no better than pirates.

Murad dipped his quilt in the inkwell and did some calculations. Then he leaned back, gnawing the end of the goose feather with his teeth. Two hundred and sixty-two souls all told, in two ships. Of that total perhaps a hundred and twenty were able to bear arms, plus an unknown quantity of these God-cursed sorcerers. They might well be more useful than field guns if their powers were as great as rumour made them, but it was best not to expect too much. They would know nothing of discipline, and would have to be herded like the cattle they were.

His eye fell on another list, and he examined it carefully. Of the passengers on the ships, some sixty were women. That was good. His men would need recreation, to say nothing of himself. He would look them over ere they sailed and pick out a couple of the comeliest for his servants.

Murad put down his pen and stretched, the new leather of his doublet creaking. There was a shadow in the doorway, backlit by the glaring sunlight.

"Come."

Ensign Valdan di Souza entered, ducking his head a little. He snapped to attention before his superior officer, his armour clinking. He seemed half broiled, his face a mask of dust save where the sweat had cut long runnels down it. There was sweat dripping off his nose also, Murad noted with distaste. The man smelled like a Calmaric bathing room.

"Well, Valdan?"

"My men have drawn all weapons and equipment, sir, and I have quartered them apart from the others as you ordered. Sergeant Mensurado is inspecting them now, prior to your own inspection."

"Good." Mensurado was the best sergeant in the city, a filthy beast of a man and an inveterate whoremonger, but a born soldier. "Sit down, Valdan. Loosen your harness, for the sake of the Saint. Have some wine."

Valdan sat gratefully and plucked at his armour straps. He was a big, lanky youth with straw-yellow hair, unusual in Hebrion. His father was a prosperous merchant who had paid for his son to be adopted by one of the lesser noble houses, the Souzas. That was the way noble blood was watered down these days. Nobles without money sold their names to commoners with it. A century previously it would have been much different, but times were changing.

Still, di Souza was a good officer and the men liked him – perhaps, Murad thought wryly, because he was on their level. He was one of the two junior officers who would be accompanying him on the voyage. The other was Ensign Hernan Sequero, a member of the noblest family in the kingdom save for the Royal line of the Hibrusios. He might even be a closer relation to the King than Murad himself. But however blue his blood, he was late.

Sequero eventually arrived as Ensign di Souza was gulping down his second glass of the chilled wine. Murad looked him up and down coolly as he stood at attention. He smelled of Perigrainian perfume. His forehead shone with the heat, yet he somehow contrived to appear completely at ease despite his heavy half-armour.

"Sit." Sequero did so, flashing a glance of contempt at the gasping di Souza.

"The horses, Hernan. Have you seen to them?" Murad drawled.

"Yes, sir. They are to be loaded on to the ships the day before we sail. Two stallions and six mares."

"That's two more than this fellow Hawkwood bargained for, but no doubt he will find room for them somewhere. We need the wider range of brood mares for a healthy line."

"Indeed, sir," Sequero said. Horse-breeding was a passion of his. He had selected the stock himself from his father's studs.

"What about their feed?"

"Being loaded tomorrow: hay and best barley grain. I hope, sir, that there will be good pasture at our landfall. The horses will need fresh grass to get back into condition."

"There will be," Murad said confidently, although he did not know for sure himself.

There was a silence. They could hear cicadas singing in the trees that bordered the parched parade ground. Here, on the eastern side of Abrusio hill, the landward breeze was blocked and the country was as dry as a desert. Still, it was moving into autumn and rain could not be far away.

Where will autumn find us? Murad thought momentarily. *Somewhere on the face of an unexplored ocean, or maybe a league below it.*

He stood up and began pacing back and forth in the small room. It was stone-floored and thick-walled to keep out the worst of the heat. There was a bunk in one corner, a tall wall cupboard and a table covered in papers with his rapier lying across it. The two ensigns sat uncomfortably by the small desk. The window had been shuttered, and the place was dim save where the afternoon light flooded in through the open door. Murad's quarters were monk-like in their austerity, but he made up for it when he had time to spend in the city. His conquests were almost as legendary as the duels they engendered.

"You know, gentlemen," he said, continuing to pace, "that we are to undertake a voyage in a few days' time. That we are taking the best of the garrison and enough stock to breed us a new line of warhorses. Thus far, that is all you have known."

The two ensigns leaned forward in their chairs. Murad's black eyes swept over them both balefully.

"What I am about to tell you will not leave this room, not until the day and very hour we sail. You will not repeat it to the sergeants, to the men, to your sweethearts or your families. Is that understood?"

The two younger men nodded readily.

"Very good. The fact is, gentlemen, that we are taking ship with a Gabrian sea captain and a crew of black-faced easterners, so I want you to watch the men once we are aboard. Any fighting when we are at sea will not be tolerated. No man of any piety likes having veritable Sea-Merduks as travelling companions, but we make do the best we can with what God sees fit to give us. On that note, you had best be aware that we are not the only passengers on these ships. Some one hundred and forty other folk will be sailing with us, as... colonists. These people are, to put it bluntly, sorcerers who are fleeing the purges in Abrusio. Our king has seen fit to allow them to take ship for a place of sanctuary, and they will be the citizens of the state we intend to found in the west."

Hernan Sequero's face had darkened at the mention of sorcerers, but now it took on a narrow-eyed intensity at Murad's last word.

"West, sir? Where in the west?"

"On the as yet undiscovered Western Continent, Hernan."

"Is there such a place?" di Souza asked, shocked out of his respectful silence.

"Yes, Valdan, there is. I have proof of it, and I am to be the viceroy of a new Hebrian province we will establish there."

Murad could see that his officers' minds were working furiously, and he had to smile. They were the only other Hebrians of any rank who would be on the voyage; they were busy calculating what that meant in terms of personal position and prestige.

"As viceroy," Sequero said at last. "You are not expected to command troops, but to be the administrative head of the province. Is that not true, sir?"

Trust Sequero to work it out first. "Yes, Hernan."

"Then someone will have to be appointed overall commander of the military part of the expedition once it reaches this Western Continent."

"Eventually, yes."

Di Souza and Sequero were looking at one another sidelong and Murad had to make an effort not to laugh. He had planned it well. Now they would be striving like titans to gain his favour in the hopes of promotion. And there would be no conspiring behind his back, either. They would trust each other too little for that.

"But that is in the future," he said smoothly. "For the moment, I want you both to begin drawing up guard rosters and training routines with the assistance of your sergeants. I want the men well drilled while we are at sea, and they must be proficient with arquebuses by the time we make landfall. That includes the officers."

He saw Sequero wrinkle up his nose at the thought. Nobles disliked firearms, considering them the weapons of commoners. Swords and lances were the only arms a man of any quality should have to know how to use. Murad had had to overcome that prejudice himself. Di Souza, who was closer to his troops, already knew how to use an arquebus and how to read and write, whereas Sequero, though quicker witted, was of the old school. He was illiterate and fought with sword alone. It would be interesting to see how they both developed in the voyage west. Murad was pleased with his choice of subordinates. They complemented each other.

"Sir," Sequero asked, "do you expect any kind of resistance in the west? Is the continent inhabited?"

"I am not entirely sure," Murad said. "But it is always best to be prepared. I am positive, though, that we will meet nothing which can overcome a demi-tercio of Hebrian soldiers."

"These sorcerers we are sailing with," di Souza said. "Are they convicts being deported, sir, or are they passengers embarking of their own free will? The Prelate of Abrusio –"

"Let me worry about the Prelate of Abrusio," Murad snapped. "It is true that we could choose better stuff to form the seed of a new province, but I do as the King wills. And besides, their abilities could prove useful."

"I take it, then, that we will not be embarking a priest, sir?" Sequero asked.

Murad glared blackly at him. Sequero sometimes liked to walk a narrower line than most.

"Probably not, Hernan."

"But sir –" di Souza began to protest.

"Enough. As I said, we are all subject to the will of higher authorities. There is no cleric in our complement, nor to be honest would I expect one to take ship with such fellow travellers. The new province will have to do without spiritual guidance until the first ships make the return voyage."

Di Souza was obviously troubled and Murad cursed himself. He had forgotten how God-damned pious some of the lower classes could be. They needed religion like the nobility needed wine.

"The men will not be happy, sir," di Souza said, almost sullenly. "You know how they like to have a priest on hand ere they go into battle."

"The men will follow orders, as they always do. It is too late now to do any differently. We sail, gentlemen, in eight days. You may inform your sergeants of the timing two days before departure – no sooner. Are there any other questions?"

Both ensigns were silent. Both looked thoughtful, but that was as it should be. Murad had given them a lot to think about.

"Good. Then, gentlemen, you are dismissed to your duties." The two rose, saluted, and then left. There was a charming pause at the doorway as they silently wrangled over who should precede whom. In the end di Souza exited first, and Sequero followed him smiling unpleasantly.

Murad sat at his desk once more and steepled his fingers together. He did not like di Souza's emphasis on the priest. That was the last thing the King wanted – a cleric accompanying the ships westward to send back reports to the Prelate of Hebrion. It would seem odd, though, to the men not to have one.

He shook his head angrily. He felt like a warhorse beset by horseflies. It would be better once they were at sea and he had his own little kingdom to rule. And the Saints protect anyone who tried to gainsay him.

He opened the locked drawer of the desk and heaved out an ancient-looking book, much battered and stained. Hawkwood had sent him a letter, in his insolence, asking for a perusal of it. It was the rutter of the *Cartigellan Faulcon*'s master, the ship which had returned an empty and leaking hulk to the shores of Hebrion over a century before, with nothing living on board save a werewolf.

He flipped through the worn tome, squinting sometimes at the spidery scrawl of the entries. Finally he lit a candle, shut the door and sat peering at page after page in the yellow light as though it were the middle of the night. The parade-ground noises faded. In the sour salt and water smell of the rutter it seemed he was transported to another age, and heard instead the slap and rush of waves against a wooden hull, the creak of timbers working, the flap of canvas.

On leaving Abrusio, steer west-south-west with the wind on the starboard bow. With the Hebrian trade, it is 240 turns of the glass or five kennings to North Cape in the Hebrionese. Half a kenning from the shore the lead will find white sand at 40 fathoms. Change course to due west and keep on the latitude of North Cape for 42 days more of good sailing. Thereafter the trade veers to north-north-west. With the wind on the starboard bow it is 36 days more on that latitude before sounding will find a shelving shore from 100 fathoms and shallowing. At 80 fathoms there will be shells and white clay, and land will be a kenning and a half away. Keep a good lookout and at 30 fathoms there will be sighted green hills and a white strand. There is a bay there one league north of the latitude of North Cape. Behind it stands a mountain with two summits, clothed in trees. Stand off and let go anchor in fifteen fathoms. Low surf, high water when moon is north-north-west and south-south-east. A sixth of a league inland there is a sweet spring. Greenstuff is to be found all along the

*shore, and fruit. Winds freshen coming on to late autumn.
Use the best bow and a stern anchor or else she is liable to
drag in the soft ground.*

These instructions had I from the rutter of the Godspeed's
*master, gone to his rest these three hundred years and
eleven, the Lord God rest his soul. I am –*

Tyrenius Cobrian
Master, Cartigellan Faulcon
St. Mateo's Eve
Year of the Blessed Saint, 421

Murad knuckled his eyes irritably. So much of what was
written in the rutter seemed to him utterly incomprehensible,
though no doubt to a sailor it would make perfect sense.
He was not going to let Hawkwood see this, though. No,
he would give the good captain as much information as it
suited him to give.

Conjoined to the rutter was the log of the *Faulcon*, and
it made better reading though there were still long lines of
boring entries.

*16th day of Enmian, 421. Wind NNW, fresh. Course due
west. 206 leagues out of Abrusio by dead-reckoning. Four
knots with courses and topsails. Killed the last pig, weight
123lbs. Body of Jann Toft of Hebriero, seaman, this day
committed to the deep. May the Lord God have mercy on his
soul. Hands employed about the ship. Recaulked the cutter.*

It was the record of an uneventful voyage westwards. The
health of the crew seemed good apart from a few minor
accidents, and there was only one major storm.

*14th day of Forlion 421. Wind NNW backing to NW.
Running before the wind under bare poles. Three foot of
water in the hold. Preventer-stays aloft and eight men on
the tiller. Estimate we are making over eight knots, and
have been blown some fifteen leagues to SE.*

*15th day of Forlion 421. Wind NW, slacking. Course
due west under unbonneted topsails. Speed three knots.*

Hands employed pumping ship and knotting and splicing rigging. Small cutter carried away. Seaman Gabriel Timian unaccounted for when all hands called in the forenoon watch. Ship searched from tops to bilge, but no sign. Presumed lost overboard, may God have mercy on him.

From here the log began to grow more interesting.

22nd day of Forlion 421. Wind NNW, moderate breeze. Course WNW, wind on starboard bow. Four knots, under topsails and mizzen course. Estimate we are three leagues south of North Cape latitude. 37 days out of Abrusio.

The first mate has reported to me that three casks of salt meat have been broken in the hold and their contents half gone. Hands restless at being so long out of sight of land. Gave speech in first dog-watch to encourage hands. Isreel Hobin, bosun's mate, stated our voyage was cursed. Had him put in irons in the bilge.

23rd day of Forlion 421. Wind NNW. Course due west. Four knots under unbonneted courses and topsails. By cross-staff reckoning we are back on North Cape latitude.

Isreel Hobin found dead in irons this day. Hands frightened. First mate, John Maze of Gabrir, reported privately to me that Hobin's throat had been torn out. Doubled the men on the night watches at their own request. The hands believe something haunts the ship.

24th day of Forlion 421. Wind NNW. Course due west. Six knots under courses and topsails. 215 leagues due west of Abrusio by dead-reckoning.

This day committed the body of Isreel Hobin, bosun's mate, to the deep. May the Lord have mercy on his soul. All hands engaged in carrying out search of the ship, but nothing found. Passengers worried and hands uneasy. May the Blessed Saint watch over us all, and give me the strength to take us across this accursed ocean.

The Blessed Saint must indeed have been watching over Tyrenius, for the *Faulcon* made landfall five and a half weeks later, dropping anchor in a sheltered bay on the Western Continent. By that time three more crewmen had disappeared without trace, presumed lost overboard, and the crew were refusing to venture down into the deeper, darker parts of the ship below the hold.

Murad poured himself more wine. There was no sound from the parade ground outside; it must have been near time for the men's evening meal. He sat and stared at page after page of the century-old log, his puckered scar twitching as he went over the entries one by one.

Something had been aboard the ship with them, that much was clear. But had it been the shifter which was the *Faulcon*'s sole occupant on its arrival back off the shore of Hebrion, or was there something else? In any case, the men had been glad to leave the ship on making landfall. Tyrenius could not even prevail upon them to mount an anchor watch. They had all slept ashore, save one.

The master had stayed with his vessel, had slept alone on board whilst the crew threw up shelters on the shore. A brave man, this Tyrenius, to face down his own fear and stick by his duty. Murad drank a silent toast to him.

8th day of Endorion 421. Wind NNW, veering to north, light breeze. One foot swell. At anchor.

This day I named the bay in which we rest Essequibo Bay after our good king of Astarac, whose humble subject I am. Crew on shore gathering provisions and preparing with certain of the passengers to mount an expedition into the interior. I remain aboard alone, for no man will stand with me in this hour.

Here the clipped, precise nature of the entry slipped and the jagged uprightness of Tyrenius's handwriting became more ragged. The pen-strokes began flying both higher and lower along the line, and tiny spatters of ink here and there spoke of the force he was exerting on his quill. He had been drinking, Murad guessed, trying to swallow his fear.

It is the last glass of the middle watch, and only I remain on the ship to turn the glass and keep the time which we have kept faithfully since leaving Abrusio. I hear the ship moving on the swell, and I think of the faces of the men whose lives this voyage has claimed. In the last First Watch one of the men swore he saw a pair of eyes staring up out of the open hatchway at him. Bright eyes, glowing in the night. After that no one would remain on board save me. But Sweet Blessed Saints forgive me, I do not remain on this ship out of duty alone. Fear also keeps me at my post.

Half a glass ago I was on deck, watching the fires of the men on the shore burning in the night, and something came up out of the main hatch, something monstrous. It padded across the deck whilst I remained on the quarterdeck above, and then it slipped over the rail and into the sea with never a splash to mark its passing. I saw it once, the dark head of it breasting the swell as it struck out for shore, and then it was gone. I sit here now and know that whatever unholy thing it was that took ship with us is gone. It is ashore, among the men on the beaches – whilst they sleep on under the trees, believing themselves safe. May God forgive me, I cannot leave the ship. I must sit and wait, and watch for the return of my men and whatever stories of horror they may bring with them. I would to God that we had a priest with us in this God-forsaken land, if only to give the last blessing which our frail souls crave before the final closing of death's curtain.

There were pages missing from the log, ripped out. Some of them Murad had removed himself, lest the King see them in his brief perusal of the volume; but others had been removed long before. Murad found himself staring at one page which seemed to have been spattered with thick, black ink. It was blood, old blood, and it had soaked through several pages, gluing them irrevocably together.

He sat back, trying to clear his head of the mouldy parchment smell, breathing in instead the dry heat of Hebrion in late summer.

Tyrenius's passengers – who had they been? And had they remained there in the west, or had they taken ship back with him to the Kingdoms of God? Whatever they had done, not one had survived to tell his story; all that was left of it was housed in the fragments of the document that was now before Murad.

It had to be a shifter, the same that had jumped from the ship on its return to Hebrion; but its behaviour tallied with nothing that Murad knew about the beasts. And why had it taken ship with the *Faulcon* in the first place? Had it signed on as a crew member in human form, or had it stowed away as a beast? The former was far more likely.

Murad flipped back to the rutter, turning page after page with a frown until he found what he was looking for. There.

Sailing directions for the western route as per the rutter of the Godspeed, *bound out of Abrusio in the year of the Saint 109, Pinarro Albayero Master. Given to me by Tobias of Garmidalan, Duke of East Astarac, this 14th day of Miderialon 421 on the understanding that the rutter be destroyed after the relevant parts are copied. Witnessed by Ahern Abbas, Mage to the Court of King Essequibos of Astarac.*

That reference to an earlier voyage was not unique; there were others throughout the rutter. It seemed that high-ranking men from both Hebrion and Astarac had sailed into the west three centuries before the *Faulcon*'s ill-fated voyage. Tyrenius had been able to draw from their experience in his own journey, which meant they must have sent a ship back at some point. If so, what had happened to them, out in the west? There was no reference to finding them or their descendants in the *Faulcon*'s log. If they had not come back in the returning ship then they must have died there and left nothing but their bones for posterity.

It was hard to be sure, though. So much of Tyrenius's log had been removed. There were cryptic references to the earlier expedition, talk of sorcery and madness; a fever that struck down men and destroyed their reason. Darker still were veiled references to theurgical experiments carried out by the members of the first expedition – experiments that had gone badly awry.

What it added up to, Murad thought, was that there had been two previous expeditions to the west, the first sponsored by what seemed to be a group of high-born mages, the second by the government – or at least some of the nobility – of Astarac. Both had ended in disaster; but had the first disaster somehow contributed to the second?

Murad stared moodily into the candlelit depths of his wine. Here he was, again sailing into the west, again with a crowd of sorcerers on board. But the earlier voyages had not had Hebrian soldiery as part of their complement. *Or Murad of Galiapeno*, he added to himself.

He looked again over the part of Tyrenius's log that detailed the anchorage he called Essequibo Bay. From the description, the Western Continent seemed rich, heavily vegetated, and uninhabited.

He flipped the pages. More of the crew had died in Essequibo Bay, and the expedition into the interior had been abandoned. They had reprovisioned and sailed away leaving nothing behind.

Nothing at all, for the beast had been back on board ship by the time they had weighed anchor. Two weeks out to sea, and the first disappearances had begun. The return voyage had been a nightmare. A dwindling ship's company, contrary winds, and terror down in the hold.

The last pages of the log were missing. There was no word of how Tyrenius had met his end, or how he had managed to pilot his ship to the very coasts he had left six months before. The writing was hard to decipher. It shook and scratched as though written in haste or terrible apprehension. Murad was surprised to find that he pitied long-dead Tyrenius and his haunted crew. They had found Hell within the wooden walls of a ship, and had carried it with them across half the world and back again.

There was a knock on the door and he started, spilling his wine. He cursed and snapped: "Who is it?"

"Renaldo, my lord, come with your supper."

"Enter."

His servant eased the door open and entered bearing a wooden tray. He cleared a space on the large table and began to set out a place. Murad put away the log and rutter and sat down before a plate of sliced roast boar and wild mushrooms, fresh-baked bread and olives, and a chunk of gleaming goat's cheese.

"Will that be all, sir?" Renaldo asked.

Murad was still screwing up his eyes against the flood of light that the open door admitted. He was surprised to see it, for he had thought it later in the day. But he liked to eat early; it gave him a chance to ride up to the city afterwards if he felt in need of amusement.

"Yes. You are dismissed."

The servant left, and Murad paused a moment in his tearing of the fragrant bread. They were sailing in eight days. There was time enough to call off the voyage.

He shook his head incredulously, wondering what had prompted that thought. This was the chance he had been waiting for all his life, the chance to carve out a principality for himself. He could not throw it away.

As he ate, though, not tasting the food, he could see in his mind's eyes the picture of a deserted ship sailing across an endless ocean with a dead man's hand on the tiller. And the eyes of a beast burning as bright as candles in the depths of its hold.

ELEVEN

IT HAD BEEN a busy time, but now the worst was over. Hawkwood's two ships had been towed out of their berths by sweating harbourmen and were anchored in the Inner Roads, yards crossed and the last of the water completed. They were ready for sea, and rose and fell slowly on the swell that the trade wind had brushed up in the bay. Even this small distance from the land, it was cooler. There was no dust hanging in the throat out here, only the tang of the ocean and the shipboard smells that to Richard Hawkwood had always been the aroma of home.

The deck of the *Gabrian Osprey*, Hawkwood's flagship, was a scene of utter chaos. Billerand could be seen down in the waist of the ship bellowing and shoving along with a pair of bosun's matés. The goats were bleating madly in their pen aft of the main hatch and at least threescore of the passengers and soldiers who were aboard were lining the lee bulwark and peering up at Abrusio hill as it towered over the shining expanse of the bay.

The ship was dangerously overcrowded, and when sailing as close to the wind as they would need to in order to clear the bay itself, Hawkwood would have to make sure that the passengers manned the weather side of the ship to stiffen her against the breeze. A beam wind – not the *Osprey*'s best point of sailing, not by a long chalk. Richard had lost count of the times he had beaten out of this port with the north-west trade in his right eye. It was an ordeal every sailor leaving Hebrion had to undergo, except in the hottest of the summer months when the trade might fail altogether, or veer a point and make it necessary to tack out of the bay, for there was not enough sea room here for wearing. Old salts had a saying that Abrusio loved to welcome ships, but hated to let them go.

"Take your hands off me!" a shrill voice cried. A girl down in the waist, her hair a dark golden bob. One of the crew was lifting her bodily from the ship's side to get at the fiferail. But then, unaccountably, the sailor was lying clear across the other side of the ship, looking dazed, and the girl was standing with her hands on her slim hips, eyes aflame. The rest of the crew roared with laughter, loving it. Eventually an older man, who looked like a soldier or a prize fighter, calmed her down and led her away. The dazed seaman had to endure the derision of his comrades, but he went back to his work readily enough.

Hawkwood frowned. Women on board ship, and in such numbers. And soldiers, too. That was a potentially explosive mixture. He must have a formal meeting with Murad and his officers as soon as possible and lay down a few ground rules.

Billerand was restoring some sort of order to the deck in his rough way. The passengers were being hustled below, the last of the goats lowered down through the main hatch by a gang of men with tackles, and the soldiers were being patiently ushered up to the forecastle, their armour clinking and glittering in the bright air.

The breeze was freshening. Over an hour still to the evening tide. But it was a long pull to the Inner Roads with the trade blowing, half a league at least. Hawkwood hoped Murad would not cut it too fine.

The scar-faced nobleman was in Abrusio tying up some last matters of his own, and the *Osprey*'s longboat, along with eight good oarsmen, was waiting for him at the harbour wall.

The past week had been a nightmare in every way possible. Hawkwood swore to himself that he would never allow himself to be threatened or cajoled into a joint expedition again. It was the old story of soldier versus sailor, noble versus commoner. At times he had almost believed that Murad was throwing obstacles in his path and disregarding his arrangements for the sheer satisfaction of seeing him rant.

Billerand joined him on the quarterdeck, sweating and red-faced. His fantastic moustache seemed to bristle with suppressed fury.

"God-damned landsmen!" was all he could utter for several moments. Hawkwood grinned. He was glad he had kept Billerand here with him on the *Osprey* instead of giving him command of the *Grace*. He looked across at the smaller vessel. The rigging of the caravel was black with men. They were just finishing the job of rerigging her with the long lateen yards; she carried them on all three masts now. They would serve her well in the beam wind they would be sailing on. Haukal of Hardalen, the master of the *Grace*, had been brought up on the square-rigged, snakelike ships of the far north, but he had soon picked up the nuances of sailing with lateen yards. Hawkwood could see him, a tall, immensely bearded man who habitually carried a hand axe slung at his waist. He was standing on the *Grace*'s tiny quarterdeck waving his arms about. He and Billerand were close friends; their exploits in the brothels and taverns of half a hundred ports had become the stuff of legend.

The *Grace*'s decks were also crowded with soldiers and passengers, hampering the work of the sailors. It was to be expected; this would be the last real sight of land they would have for many days. For most of them, Hawkwood supposed, it was probably their last ever sight of Hebrion and gaudy old Abrusio. Their fates were set in the west, now.

"How is the supercargo settling in?" he asked the fuming Billerand.

"We've hammocks slung fore and aft the length of the gundeck, but God help us if we're brought to action, Captain. We'll have to cram the whole miserable crowd of them down with the cargo or in the bilge." That thought made his face brighten a little. "Still, the soldiers will be useful."

Billerand had time for soldiers; he had been one himself. For Hawkwood, they were just another nuisance. He had thirty-five of them here on the *Osprey*, the rest on the caravel. Two-thirds of the expedition travelled in the carrack, including Murad and both his junior officers. Hawkwood had had to partition the great cabin with an extra bulkhead so the nobility might sail in the style it was accustomed to. The sailors were berthed in the forecastle, the soldiers in the forward part of the gundeck. They would be living cheek by jowl for the next few months. And they had so many stores on board for the setting up of the colony, to say nothing of provisions for the voyage, that both ships sat low in the water and were sluggish answering the tiller. It would take very little to put the tall-sterned *Osprey* in irons or make her miss stays. Hawkwood was not happy about it. It was like mounting a normally fiery horse and finding it lame.

"Longboat on the larboard beam!" the lookout called from the foretop.

"Our tardy nobleman, at last," Billerand muttered. "At least he will not make us miss our tide."

"What have you heard of this Murad fellow?" Hawkwood asked him.

"Only what you already know, Captain. That he has an eye for the ladies, and is as swift as a viper with that rapier of his. A good soldier, according to his sergeants, though he's overfond of flogging."

"What nobleman is not?"

"I've been meaning to tell you, Captain. This Murad is to bring no valet on board with him. Instead he has selected a pair of girls from among the passengers as his cabin servants."

"So?"

"I've heard the soldiers talking. He'll have them as bed-mates and the soldiers intend to try and follow his example. We have forty women on the carrack alone, married most of them, or someone's daughter."

"I hear you, Billerand. I'll talk to him about it."

"Good. We don't want the mariners feeling left out. There's enough friction as it is, and raping a sorcerer's wife or daughter is no light matter. Why, I saw a man once –"

"I said I'd talk to him."

"Aye, sir. Well, I'd best see to the windlass. We'll weigh as soon as the tide is on the ebb?"

"Aye, Billerand." Hawkwood slapped his first mate on the shoulder, and the man left the quarterdeck, sensing his captain wanted to be alone.

Or as alone as it is possible to be in a ship thirty yards long with ninescore souls on board, Hawkwood thought. He peered out towards the land and saw the longboat skimming along like a sea-snake half a mile away. Murad was standing in the stern, straight as a flagstaff. His long hair was flying free in the wind. He looked as though he were coming to lay claim to the ships and all in them.

Hawkwood moved over to the weather side of the deck, pausing to shout down through the connecting hatch to the tillerdeck below.

"Relieving tackles all shipped there?"

"Aye, sir," a muffled voice answered. "Course west-sou'-west by north as soon as we weigh."

The men knew their job. Hawkwood was fidgeting, anxious to get started, but they needed the ebb of the tide to help pull them out of the bay. There was a while to wait yet.

He had said his farewells, for what they were worth. He and Galliardo had drunk a bottle of good Gaderian and chewed half a dozen pellets of *kobhang* so they might talk the night through. The port captain would look after his affairs while he was gone, and call in on Estrella occasionally.

Estrella. Saying farewell to her had been like ridding one's hands of fresh pitch. She knew this was no common voyage – no coasting trip, or ordinary cruise after a prize. He could still feel her thin arms about his waist as she knelt before him, sobbing, the tears streaking kohl down her cheeks.

And then Jemilla. What was it she had said?

"I'll look for you in the spring, Richard. I'll look out over the harbour. I'd know that absurd carrack of yours anywhere."

She had been naked, lying on the wide bed with her head resting on one hand, watching him with those feline eyes of hers. Her thighs had been slick with the aftermath of their loving and his back was smarting from where she had clawed him.

"Will you still be the King's favourite when I return?" he had asked, lightly enough.

That smile of hers, infuriating him.

"Who knows? Favourites come and go. I live in the present, Richard. This time next year we could all be under the Merduks."

"In which case you would no doubt be chief concubine in the Sultan's harem. Still spinning your webs."

"Oh, Richard," she said, feigning hurt, "you wrong me." But then her face had changed at seeing the anger on his.

The dark eyes had sparked in the way that never failed to raise the hair on his nape. She opened her legs so he could see the pink flesh amid the dark fur at her crotch, and then she spread herself wide there with shining fingers so that it seemed he was looking at some carnivorous flower from the southern sultanates.

"You have your ships, your culverins, your crews. I only have this, the one weapon all women have possessed since time began. You would prate to me of love, fidelity – I can see it in your great sad eyes. You who have a wife weeping the night away at home. The sea is your real mistress, Richard Hawkwood. I am only your whore, so let me pursue the same aims in life as you, in my own way. If that means bedding every noble in the kingdom, I will do it. Soon enough my charms will be taken from me. My skin will wither and my hair will grey, while your God-cursed sea will always be there, always the same. So let me play what games I can while I can."

He had felt like a child groping for an adult's comprehension. It was true that he had been about to tell her that he loved her. In her own way, he thought she returned his love – if it was in her to love any man at all. And he realized that, in her own way, she hated his leaving as much as Estrella did, and resented it similarly.

They had loved again, after that. But this time there was no hectic passion; they had coupled like two people grown old together, savouring every moment. And Hawkwood had known somehow that it was the last time. Like a ship, she had slipped her cables and was drifting away, letting the wind take her further on her voyage. He had been discarded.

"Longboat alongside!" someone shouted, and there was a commotion on deck, a glittering clatter as a file of soldiers shouldered arms and Murad of Galiapeno hauled himself up the carrack's sloping side.

Murad sketched a salute to his officers and went below without further ceremony. He had a small chest under one arm. Hawkwood saw his face as a pale, sneering flash before the lean nobleman had stepped into the companionway and disappeared.

"Sir, shall we stow the longboat on the booms?" Billerand shouted.

"No, we'll tow her. The waist is crowded enough as it is."
Hawkwood had a momentary, silent argument with himself,
and then left the quarterdeck. He went below, following in
Murad's footsteps, and knocked on the new door the ship's
carpenter had wrought in the bulkhead next to his own.

"Come."

He went in. At the back of his mind he was counting off
the minutes before they weighed anchor, but it was best to
do this now, to get it over with. Billerand would manage if
he were detained.

Murad had his back to him when he entered. He was
studying something on the long table that spanned the
cabin. He locked it away, whatever it was, in the chest he
had brought aboard, before turning round with a smile.

"Well, Captain. To what do I owe the pleasure?"

"I would have a word with you, if I may."

"I am entirely at your disposal. Speak freely." Murad
leaned back against the table and folded his arms.
Hawkwood stood awkwardly before him as though he
had been summoned to the cabin. He noted with some
satisfaction, however, that the nobleman was finding the
slight roll and pitch of the ship awkward. He swung like a
reed in a thin breeze, whereas to Richard the deck was solid
and steady under his feet.

Wait until the bastard gets his first taste of seasickness, he
thought malevolently.

"It is about your men. It has been brought to my attention
that they seem to think they can have the pick of the women
on board."

Murad frowned. "So?"

"They cannot."

Murad straightened, his arms coming down by his sides.
"*Cannot?*"

"No. There will be no women molested on my ships, not
by my men and not by yours. These are not strumpets from
the back alleys of Abrusio we have embarked. They are
decent women, with families."

"They are Dweomer-folk –"

"They are passengers and thus my responsibility. I have
no wish to challenge your authority with your own men,

especially in public; but if I hear of a rape, I'll give the man involved the strappado, be he seaman or soldier. I'd as lief have you order it, though. It would help relations between the services."

Murad stared silently at Hawkwood as though he were seeing him for the first time. Then, very softly, he said:

"And I? If I choose to take a woman, Captain, will you give me the strappado?"

"Rules are different for the nobility – you know that. I cannot touch you. But I beg you to consider what such an example would do for the men. There is also the fact that the passengers are, as you have said, Dweomer-folk. They are not defenceless. I've no wish to have my vessel blown out of the water."

Murad nodded curtly, as if finally accepting the justice of this. "We must get along as best we may, then," he said pleasantly. "Perhaps your crews can persuade my men to follow their example and fuck each other's arses as sailors are wont to do, I am told."

Hawkwood felt the blood rising into his face and his sight darkened with fury. He bit back the words that were forming in his mouth, however, and when he spoke again his tone was as civil as Murad's.

"There is another thing."

"Of course. What is it?"

"The rutter. I need it if I am to plot a proper course. So far you have told me to set sail for North Cape in the Hebrionese, but after that I am wholly in the dark. That is no way for the master of a ship to be. I need the rutter."

"Don't you mariners ever use the proper form of address, Hawkwood?"

"I am Captain Hawkwood to you, Lord Murad. What about the rutter?"

"I cannot give it to you." Murad held up a hand as Hawkwood was about to speak again. "But I can give you a set of sailing instructions copied out of it word for word." He snatched up a sheaf of papers from the table behind him. "Will that suffice?"

Hawkwood hesitated. The rutter of a true seaman, an open-ocean navigator, was a rare and wonderful thing.

Shipmasters guarded their rutters with their lives, and the knowledge that this ignorant landsman had in his possession such a document – and containing the details of such a voyage – was maddening. Perhaps he even had a log as well. So much information would be there, information any captain in Hebrion would give an arm for, and this ignorant swine kept it to himself where it was useless. What was he afraid that Hawkwood might see? What was out there in the west that had to be kept so secret?

He snatched the papers greedily out of Murad's hand but forced himself not to look at them. There would be a better time. He would lay his hands on the rutter yet. He had to, if he was to be responsible for his ships.

"Thank you," he said stiffly, stuffing the papers in his bosom as though they were of little account.

Murad nodded. "There! You see, Captain, we can work together if we've a mind to. Now will you sit with me and have some wine?"

They would be weighing anchor soon, but Hawkwood took a chair, feeling that the scarred nobleman had somehow outfoxed him. Murad rang a little handbell that sat on the table.

The cabin door opened and a girl's voice said, "Yes?"

Hawkwood turned in his chair, and found himself staring at a young woman with olive-coloured skin, green eyes and a mane of tawny, shining hair that was cropped short just below her ears. She wore the breeches of a boy, and could almost have passed for one were it not for the subtle delicacy of her features and the undeniable curves of her slim figure. He saw her hand on the door handle: brown fingers with close-bitten nails. A peasant girl, then. And he remembered – she was the one the sailor had tussled with up on deck.

"Wine, Griella, if you please," Murad drawled, his eyes drinking in the girl as he spoke. She nodded and left without another word, eyes blazing.

"Marvellous, eh, Captain? Such spirit! She hates me already, but that is only to be expected. She will grow used to me, and her comrade also. It promises to be a pleasant tussle of wills."

The girl came in with a tray, a decanter and two glasses. She set them on the table and exited again. She met Hawkwood's stare as she went, and her eyes made him sit very still. He was silent as Murad poured the wine. Something in the eyes was not right; it reminded Hawkwood of the mad eyes of a rabid dog, windows into some unfathomable viciousness. He thought of saying something, but then shrugged to himself. Perhaps Murad liked them that way, but he had best be wary when bedding such a one.

"Drink, Captain." The nobleman's normally sinister face was creased with a smile: the sight of a girl seemed to have quickened his humour. Hawkwood knew that he had called her in for a reason, to make a point. He sipped at his glass, face flat.

A good wine, perhaps the best he had ever tasted. He savoured it a moment.

"Candelarian," Murad told him. "Laid down by my grandfather. They call it the wine of ships, for it is said that it takes a sea voyage to age it properly, a little rolling in the cask. I have half a dozen barrels below, thank the Saints."

Hawkwood knew that. It had meant carrying six fewer casks of water. But he said nothing. He had come to realize that he could do little about the whims of the nobleman whilst Hebrion was in sight. Once they were on the open ocean, though – then it would be different.

"So tell me, Captain," Murad went on, "why the delay? We are all aboard, everything is ready, so why do we sit at anchor? Aren't we wasting time?"

"We are waiting for the tide to turn," Hawkwood said patiently. "Once it reverses its flow and begins pulling out of the bay, then we'll up anchor and have the current to aid us when we're trying to get past the headland. A beam wind – one that hits the ship on the side – is not the best for speed. With the *Osprey* I'd sooner have one from the quarter, that is coming up at an angle from aft of amidships."

Murad laughed. "What a language you sailors have among yourselves!"

"Once we clear Abrusio Head we'll be steering a more southerly course and we'll have that quartering wind; but it'll be pushing us towards a lee shore so I'll be taking the ships further out to gain sea room."

"Surely it would be quicker to remain inshore."

"Yes, but if the wind picks up, and with the leeway the ships make, we could find ourselves being pushed on the shore itself, embayed or run aground. A good mariner likes to have deep water under him and a few leagues of sea room to his lee."

Murad waved a hand, growing bored. "Whatever. You are the expert in this matter."

"When we hit the latitude of North Cape," Hawkwood went on relentlessly, "if we sail due west we'll have that beam wind again. Only the rutter of the *Cartigellan Faulcon*'s master can tell me if we can expect to have the Hebrian trade with us out into the Western Ocean, or if we pick up a different set of winds at some point. It is important; it will dictate the length of the voyage."

"It is there in the sheets I copied for you," Murad said sharply. His scar rippled on his face like a pale leech.

"You may not know what should be copied and what should not. You may not have given me everything I need to navigate this enterprise with any safety."

"Then you will have to come back to me, Captain. There will be no more discussion of the matter."

Hawkwood was about to retort when he heard a cry beyond the cabin.

"*Osprey* ahoy! Ahoy the carrack there! We've a passenger for you. You left him behind, it seems."

Hawkwood glanced at Murad, but the nobleman seemed as puzzled as himself. They rose as one and left the cabin, stepping along the passage to the waist of the ship. Billerand and a crowd of others were leaning over the side.

"What is it? Who is this?" Murad demanded, but Billerand ignored him.

"Seems we left someone behind, Captain. They've an extra passenger for us, brought out in the harbour scow."

Hawkwood looked down the sloping ship's side. The scow crew had hooked on to the carrack's main chains and a figure was clambering up the side of the ship, his robe billowing in the sea breeze. He laboured over the ship's rail and stood on deck, his tonsured head shining with effort.

"The peace of God on this ship and all in her," he said, panting.

He was an Inceptine cleric.

"What foolishness is this?" Murad shouted. "By whose orders are you come aboard? You there, in the boat – take this man off again!" But the scow had already unhooked and her crew were pulling away from the carrack, one waving as they went.

"Damnation! Who are you, sir? On whose authority do you take ship with this company?" Murad was livid, furious, but the Inceptine was calm and collected. He was an oldish man, white-haired, but ruddy and spare of feature. His shoulders were rounded under the habit and he had the stocky build of a longshoreman. The Saint symbol glinted at his breast.

"Please, my son, no blasphemy on the eve of so great an undertaking as this."

For a moment Hawkwood thought that Murad was going to draw his sword and run the priest through. Then he spun on his heel and left the deck, disappearing down the companionway.

"Are you the master of this vessel?" the Inceptine asked Hawkwood.

"I am Richard Hawkwood, yes."

"Ah, the Gabrian. Then, sir, might I ask you to find me some quarters? I have little in the way of belongings with me. All I need is a space to lay my head."

Men were gathering in the waist, soldiers and sailors both. The sailors looked uneasy, even hostile, but the soldiers seemed pleased.

"Give us a blessing, Father!" one of them cried. "Call God and the Saints to watch over us!"

His cry was taken up by a score of his comrades. The Inceptine beamed and held up an open hand. "Very well, my sons. Kneel and receive the blessing of the Holy Church upon your enterprise."

There was a mass movement as the soldiers knelt on the deck. A pause, and then most of the sailors joined them. The ship creaked and rolled on the swell, and there was almost a silence. The Inceptine opened his mouth to speak.

In the quiet came the four, distinct, lovely notes of the ship's bell marking the end of the second dog-watch, and the turn of the tide.

"All hands!" Hawkwood roared instantly. "All hands to weigh anchor!"

The sailors leapt up, and the waist became a massive confusion of figures. Billerand began shouting; some of the kneeling soldiers were knocked sprawling.

A series of orders were bandied back and forth as the seamen hurried to their duties. There were casks, crates, boxes and chests everywhere on the deck and they, along with the bewildered soldiers, impeded the working of the ship, but there was no help for it; the hold was filled to capacity already. Hawkwood and Billerand shouted and shoved the crew to their well-known stations, whilst the cleric was left with his hand hanging impotently in the air, his face filling with blood.

In a twinkling, the crew were in position. Some were standing by at the windlass and the hawse-holes ready to begin winding in the thick cables that connected the ship to the anchors. More were busy on the yards, preparing to flash out the courses and topsails as soon as the anchor was weighed. The sailmaker and his mates were bringing up sail bonnets from belowdecks so they would be handy when the time came for lashing them to the courses for a greater area of sail.

"Brace them round!" Hawkwood shouted. "Brace them right round, lads. We've a beam wind to work with. I don't want to spill any of it!"

He felt the ship tilt under his feet, like a horse gathering its legs under it for a spring. The ebb was flowing out of the bay.

"Weigh anchor! Start her there, at the windlass. Stand by at the tiller!"

The anchor ropes began to come aboard, mud-slimed and foul-smelling. They were like thick-bodied serpents that slithered down the hatches to be coiled in the top tiers by men below.

"Up and down!" a sweating master's mate cried.

"Tie her off," Hawkwood told him. "On the yards there – courses and topsails. Bonnet on the main course!"

The crackling and booming expanses of creamy canvas were let loose, billowing and filling against the blue sky. The carrack staggered as the breeze hit her. Hawkwood ran up to the quarterdeck. The ship had canted to larboard as the sails took the wind.

"Brace her, brace her there, damn you!"

The men hauled on the braces – ropes which angled the yards at the best attitude to the wind. The carrack began to move. Her bow dipped and cut through the rising swell, coming up again with the grace of a swan. Spray flew round her bows, and Hawkwood could feel the tremor of her keel as it gathered way. He looked across at the *Grace* and saw that she was pulling ahead, her great lateen sails like the wings of some monstrous, beautiful bird. Haukal was on her quarterdeck, waving and grinning through his beard like a maniac. Hawkwood waved back.

"Let loose the pennants!"

Men on the topmasts shimmied up the shrouds and pulled loose the long, tapering flags so that they sprang free at the mastheads, snapping and writhing in the wind. They were of shimmering Nalbeni silk, the dark blue device of the Hawkwoods at the main and the scarlet of Hebrion on the mizzen.

"Light along the log to the forechains there! Let's see what she's doing."

Men ran along the decks with the log and rope that would let them know the speed of the carrack once she had fully taken the wind. Hawkwood bent down to the tiller hatch.

"Helm there, west-sou'-west by north."

"Aye, sir. West-sou'-west by north it is."

The larboard heel of the carrack became more pronounced. Hawkwood hooked an arm about the mizzen backstay as the ship rose and dipped, cleaving the waves like a spearhead, her timbers groaning and the rigging creaking as the strain rose on it. She would make a deal of water until the timber of her upper hull became wet and swollen again, but she was moving more easily than he had dared hope, even with the heavy load. It must be the ebb tide, pushing her out to sea along with the blessed wind.

The soldiers had mostly been cleared from the decks, and the Inceptine had vanished below, his blessing unsaid. Some of the passengers were in sight, though, being shunted about by sailors intent on their work. Hawkwood saw Murad's cabin servant, the girl Griella. She was on the forecastle, her hair flying and the spray exploding about her. She looked beautiful and happy and alive, her eyes alight. He was glad for her.

He stared back over the taffrail. Hebrion and Abrusio were sliding swiftly astern. He guessed they must be doing six knots. He wondered if Jemilla were on her balcony, watching the carrack and the caravel grow smaller and smaller as they forged further out to sea.

The *Osprey* rose and fell, rose and fell, breasting the waves with an easy rhythm. The sails were drum-taut; Hawkwood could feel the strain on the mast through the twanging-tight backstay. If he looked up all he could see were towering expanses of canvas criss-crossed with the running rigging, and beyond the hard unclouded blue of heaven. He grinned fiercely as the ship came to life under his feet. He knew her as well as he knew the curves of his wife's body; he knew how the masts were creaking and the timbers stretching as his ship answered his demands, like a willing horse catching fire from his own spirit. No landsman could ever feel this, and those who spent their time politicking on land would never know the exhilaration, the freedom of a fine ship answering the wind.

This, he thought, *is life; this is living. Maybe it is even prayer.*

The two ships sailed steadily on as the afternoon waned, leaving the land in their wake until Abrusio hill was a mere dark smudge on the rim of the world behind them. They crested the rising swell of the coastal sea and touched upon the darker, purer colour of the open ocean. They left the fishing boats and the screaming gulls behind, carving their own solitary course to the horizon and setting their bows toward a gathering wrack and fire of cloud in the west, a flame-tinted arch which housed the gleam of the sinking sun.

PART TWO

In DEFENCE

of the WEST

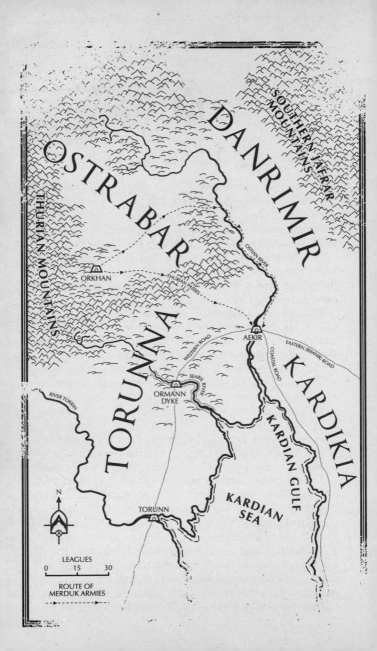

TWELVE

THEY HAD BEEN three weeks on the road, this giant convoy, this rolling city. They had fought against slime and snow and marauding wolves to force the waggons over the narrow passes of the Thurian Mountains before beginning the long, downward haul to the green plains of Ostrabar beyond.

The Sultanate of Ostrabar, now first in the ranks of the Seven Sultanates, its head, Aurungzeb the Golden, one of the richest men in the world – or he would be when this caravan reached him.

This had been a Ramusian country once, a settled land of tilled fields and coppiced woods with a church in every village and a castle on every hill. Ostiber had been its name, and its king had been one of the Seven Monarchs of Normannia.

That had changed with the advent of the Merduks sixty years ago. They had poured over the inadequately defended passes of the terrible Jafrar Mountains to the east, crossed the headwaters of the Ostian river and had overrun Ostiber in less than a year, exposing the city of Aekir's northern flank and coming to a halt only when faced with the defended heights of the Thurians manned by grim Torunnans who included in their ranks a youthful John Mogen. Ostiber had become Ostrabar, and the wild steppe chieftain who had conquered this country took that as his family name. The captain of his guard had been Shahr Baraz, who would in time rise to command all his armies. And his sons, when they had finished poisoning one another, became sultan after him. Thus was the Kingdom of Ostiber lost to the west, its Royal line extinguished, its people enslaved, tortured, ravished and pillaged and, worst of all, forced to change their faith so their eternal souls were lost to the Company of the Saints for ever.

Thus were the children of the Western Kingdoms taught.

To them the Merduk were a teeming tribe of savages, held at bay only by the valour of the Ramusian armies and the swift terror of horse and sword and arquebus.

For the folk living in Ostrabar now it was different. True, they must needs pray to Ahrimuz every day in one of the domed temples that had been erected throughout the land, and they yielded yearly tribute to the Sirdars and Beys who now inhabited the hilltop castles; but there had always been nobles in the castles exacting tribute, and they had always prayed. The terror of the first invasion was long past, and many descendants of those who had fought in Ramusian armies six decades before wielded tulwar and scimitar in the ranks of Aurungzeb's regiments.

For some, indeed, life had improved under the Merduk yoke. Wizards and thaumaturgists and alchemists were tolerated under the new regime, not persecuted as they occasionally had been when the Knights Militant roved the land. Many, in fact, had wealthy patrons, for the Merduk nobility treasured learning above all things save, perhaps, the profession of arms and the breeding of horses.

So for those among the long train of waggons who had expected to see a nightmarish, unholy land upon their descent from the heights of the Thurians, there was a shock. They saw the same countryside, the same houses, and in the main the same people whom they had encountered every day in Aekir before its fall. The only differences were the domes of the temples glittering across the peaceful landscape, and the fantastical shapes of elephants working in the woods and along the well-kept roads. Those and the flashing silk finery of the Merduk nobility who gathered to see the train that held the spoils of Aekir.

Six miles long, it straggled out of the high land to the south. Over nine hundred waggons hauled by patient oxen, their tarred covers ragged and flapping in the wind. Trudging beside them in long lines were thousands upon thousands of captives who had been brought back as trophies for Aurungzeb to view. Most were women destined for harems and brothels, or the kitchen. Others were Torunnan soldiers, bitter-faced and savage. For them crucifixion awaited; they were to be made an example of, and were too dangerous to be allowed to live. And there were the children: young boys who would be made into eunuchs for the courts or the more specialized of the pleasure houses, young girls who would serve the same ends as the women, despite their age. There were all tastes and persuasions among the nobles of Ostrabar.

Along the flanks of the train rode bodies of Merduk light cavalry. During the crossing of the mountains they had been muffled in furs and cloaks, spattered with mud and haggard with exhaustion, but before nearing the country of their homes they had spruced themselves up, grooming their mounts and donning coloured silk surcoats over their chainmail. Pennons snapped and danced in the wind, and decorations glittered on the breasts of the horses. They made a fine sight as they stepped out, regiment by regiment, the very picture of a victorious army escorting a beaten foe.

In the better covered of the waggons the occupants shuddered as they listened to the thunder of hooves and the voices shouting gaily in the harsh Merduk tongue. Not for these select ones the killing labour of marching and scrambling in the rutted path of the train; they were to be kept apart, and spared the ordeal of the journey. They knelt in chains and rags, hardly looking at one another, whilst the waggons bounced and jolted under them, carrying them closer to their fate by the hour.

They were the pick of the spoils, the choicest treasures that Aekir had to offer. Two hundred of the most beautiful women in the city, rounded up like cattle to await the appraising eye of the Grand Vizier and in turn the perusal of Aurungzeb himself. The lucky ones would be taken into the harem to join the numerous ranks of the Sultan's concubines. The rest would be shared out amongst court officials and senior officers – rewards for men of ability and loyalty in this happy time.

The woman named Heria pulled her rags closer about her, the chains on her wrists clinking as she moved. Her bruises were fading. As they had begun to near their destination the soldiers had left the women in the waggons alone; they had to reach the capital looking relatively unabused. At night she and her sister slaves had huddled under the canopy and listened to the screams of the less fortunate outside, and the laughter of the soldiers.

Corfe, she thought yet again. *Do you live? Did you get away, or did they kill you like the others?*

There was a red memory in her mind, the picture of the city's fall and the fury that had followed. Merduks everywhere, looting, killing, running. And the flames of Aekir's burning rising as high as hills into the smoke-black night beyond.

She had been caught whilst trying to flee towards the western gate. A grinning devil with a face as black as leather had seized her and dragged her into the ruin of a burning building. There she had been raped.

As he had worked busily upon her the blade of his sword had rested against her throat, already bloody, and sparks had come sailing down out of the air to land on his back and gleam like little leering eyes on his armour. She remembered staring at them and watching them go dark one by one to be replaced by others. Not feeling anything much.

His breastplate had bruised her and her back had been cut by the glass and broken stones on the floor. Then the officer had come, his horsehair plume nodding above his helm and his eyes as greedy as a child's. He had taken her, despite the first soldier's protests, and hauled her to the city wall where she had been raped again. Finally she had joined the thousands of others herded into the pens on the hillsides beyond the city, all weeping, all bloody and terrified and ashamed like herself. That had been the first stage in her journey.

For days the terrified masses had shivered on the hills and watched the ruin of the City of God. They had seen the Merduks withdraw in the face of the flames and then had been witness to the final conflagration, a holocaust that seemed caused by the hand of God, so immense was the scale of it. In the morning the ashes had covered the ground like a grey snow, and the sun had been shrouded so that the land about was in twilight. It had seemed like the end of the world.

And, in a way, it was.

They had started north on the eighth day after her capture, herded by hordes of Merduk soldiers. The entire country had seemed covered with moving people, soldiers, horses and elephants, and untold hundreds of waggons bumping and lurching in the mud. And all the while the rain had poured down, numbing their very souls.

But the worst thing had been the sight of hundreds of Ramusian soldiers, the much-vaunted Torunnans of John Mogen, trudging north with their arms in capture yokes. From stolen conversations and whispered words the women learned that Sibastion Lejer was dead, his command annihilated; Lejer himself had been crucified in the square of Myrnius Kuln. The garrison of Aekir no longer existed, and the inhabitants of the city were fleeing westwards to Ormann Dyke, blackening the very face of the earth with the vastness of their exodus.

The train had laboured north at a snail's pace, the bodies of the weak and injured littering the land in its wake. They had passed the enormous camps of the Merduk army, cities of canvas and silk flags sprawled out across the blasted countryside. They had seen the wrecked churches, the gutted castles and burned villages of the north of the country. And the Thurians had loomed closer and closer on the horizon, and ice had begun to collect on the muzzles of the oxen.

A hard, timeless nightmare of mud and snow and savage faces. The wind had come down from the north like an avenging angel, ripping the covers from the waggons and making the horses scream. There had been brief snowstorms, snap freezes that had given the mud the consistency of wood. The Merduks had dined on horseflesh, their captives occasionally on each other.

A few of the Torunnans had tried to escape, and the Merduks had shot them full of arrows, perhaps wary even now of coming to grips with them.

They had lost waggons by the score. Heria had seen ancient tapestries trampled into the mud, incense sticks scattered across the snow, little children wide-eyed and dead, their faces grey with frost. The Merduks had been brutal in their haste, striving to get the train over the high passes before the first heavy snows of autumn. And somehow they had done it, though fully two thousand of the prisoners were left dead in the drifts of the mountains.

Heria had been one of the lucky ones. A Merduk officer had taken her out of the long line of chained women on seeing her face, and put her in one of the waggons and given her a blanket. That night he had taken her against a waggonwheel watched by a laughing score of his fellows, but had stopped the rest from following suit. From then on he had visited the waggon from time to time, to bring her morsels of food – even wine once – and to take her again. But he had stopped coming once the Thurians were behind them. Perhaps he too lay dead in the snows.

So she had remained alive, for what it was worth. The rutted quagmires of the mountain roads had given way to good paved highways, and the air had become warmer. There was food again, though never enough to banish hunger entirely. And she had been left in peace at night.

Ceasing to think, to wonder or to hope, she had crouched in the waggon, feeling the lice move in her hair, and had stared at the blank canvas, rocking with the movement of the vehicle as though she were in a ship at sea. A thousand fantasies had glimmered in her mind, dreams of rescue, images of scarlet carnage. But they had burned down to black ash now. Corfe was dead and she was glad, for she was no longer fit to be his wife. The body she had kept for him alone was an item of property to be bartered for a crust of bread, and the looks she had been so secretly proud of had gone. Her eyes were as dull as slate, her heavy mane of raven hair matted and infested, her body covered with bites and sores, and her ribs saw-toothed ridges down her sides.

I am carrion, she thought.

Thirty-six days out of Aekir, though, something pricked her apathy. There was a shout at the head of the train, men cheering and horses neighing. The women in the waggon shifted and looked at one another fearfully. What was it now? What devilish torment had the Merduks contrived for them?

Suddenly there was a ripping sound, and the entire canopy of the waggon was peeled off and torn away. A pair of horsemen rode off with it flapping between them, grinning like apes.

Sunlight, blinding and searingly painful to their shadow-accustomed eyes. The women covered their faces and tried to pull their rags about them. There were hoots of laughter, and the world was a chaos of galloping shapes, half-glimpsed dark faces, capering horses. Then they cleared away, leaving the women staring.

The land before them dipped in a great shallow bowl leagues across. At its bottom was the sword-blade glitter of a large river, lightning-bright in the sun. All around were broken and rolling hills, green or gold with crops or dotted with grazing herds. They stretched to every horizon, gilded by the sunshine and ruffled to glimmering waves by the northern breeze.

As the expanse rose up to meet the blue shadows of the mountains in the north, so the watchers saw a wider hill there. It was a city, white-walled and towered, the smoke of its hearths rising to haze the cerulean arch of the cloudless sky. Everywhere amid the clotted disorder of its streets minarets and cupolas caught the sun, and at the height of the hill gleamed the massive dome of the Temple of Ahrimuz, the biggest in the world after its older rival in Nalbeni.

There were palaces there, in the shadow of the temple. The women could see parks amid the city, the ripple of water in tended gardens. And even at this distance they could hear the chanters in the towers calling the faithful to prayer. Their oddly harmonious wails drifted down the wind, and the Merduk escort bowed their heads for a moment in acknowledgement.

"Where are we? What is this place?" one of the women demanded in a panic-shrill whisper.

But one of the escort had heard her. He bent from his horse into the waggon and gripped the woman's jaw with one brown hand.

"We are home," he said distinctly. "This is *Orkhan*, home for me and you. This is the city of Ostrabar. *Horla Kadhar, Ahrimuzim-al kohla ab imuzir...*" He trailed off into his own language as if he were reciting something, then turned to the women in the waggon again.

"You go to Sultan's bed!" And he laughed uproariously before touching spurs to his horse's belly and cantering off.

"Lord God in heaven!" someone murmured. Others began sobbing quietly. Heria bent her head until her filthy hair covered her face.

Can you remember him? How he was when he had that devil-may-care grin on his face, his eyes alight? Can you remember?

A LONG SUMMER'S day, the sun hanging in a cobalt sky and the Thurians mere guesses of shadow at the edge of the world. They were in the hills above the city, watching the huge length of Aekir sprawl out along the shining length of the Ostian river. Far enough to view the whole of the city walls but near enough to hear the bells of Carcasson tolling the hour, the sound drifting up into the hills along with a faint rush of noise; the echo of a distant throng.

Wine they had had, and white bread from the city bakeries. Apples from last year's crop, wrinkled but still sweet and moist. If they looked out to the south, beyond the city, they could see where the Ostian river widened in its estuary before opening out into the Kardian Sea. Sometimes when the wind was from the south, the gulls wheeled and cried in the very streets of the city itself and the salt tang was in the air so that Aekir might have been a harbour city on the rim of an ocean. Heria had always loved to come into the hills and see the Kardian glittering on the horizon. It was like seeing the promise of tomorrow, a doorway into a wider world. She had often wondered what it would be like to have a ship, to ply the sea routes of the wide world, sleep beneath a wooden deck and hear the waves lapping at her ear.

Corfe had laughed at her fantasies, but never tired of hearing them. He had been wearing his ensign's uniform that day – Torunnan black edged with scarlet. Blood and bruises, they called it. His sabre had lain scabbarded at his side.

She could not remember what they had said, only that they had been content. It seemed to her now that they had never thought how lucky they might be to have each other, the sun flooding down on the grass-covered hillside, Aekir spread out on the earth below them like a brilliantly coloured cloak let slip upon the world and the sea glimmering at the limit of vision, full of possibilities. Everything had been possible; though even then, in that last, glorious summer, the Merduk host had already been on the move. Their fates had been fixed, and their snatched seconds were trickling away like sand in an hourglass.

The train of booty and prizes lurched and trundled downhill towards Orkhan, capital of the Northern Merduks, whilst in the waggons the women sat stark and silent and the Merduk horsemen sang their songs of victory all around.

THE RAIN HAD held off and a weak sun was pouring down over the blasted expanse of the land. Corfe helped the old man up the muddy slope, using his sabre as a staff. Ribeiro came behind them, his face swathed in filthy rags, one eye invisible with the awful swelling.

They reached the top of the hill and stood panting. Macrobius leaned on Corfe with his head bent, his bony chest sucking in and out. Corfe looked down the western slope and suddenly went very still. Macrobius tensed at once, his liver-spotted fingers gripping Corfe's arm.

"What is it? What do you see?"

"We're there, old man, there at last. Ormann Dyke."

The land levelled out west of where they stood. It dipped down into a broad valley in which the wide expanse of the Searil river foamed and churned, full after the recent rains. There was a bridge there, spanning the current. On the western bank it was constructed of weather-beaten stone, but here on the eastern side the supports were of fresh timber.

On the eastern side of the Searil great works of earth and stone had been thrown up, revetments and trenches and stockades. The smoke of burning slow-match drifted down the breeze along with the cooking fires, and above the fortifications the black and scarlet Torunnan flag flapped. Corfe felt a strange ache in his breast at the sight of it.

The eastern fortifications extended maybe half a mile on either side of the bridge. Corfe could see culverins gleaming with brass behind gabion-strengthened emplacements, soldiers walking up and down, a knot of cavalry here and there. But the entire rear of the position seemed choked with people. There were thousands there in the spaces behind the battlements, some obviously cooking, others sleeping in the mud and more trudging purposefully towards the river.

The bridge was clogged with them. All along its length it was jammed with handcarts, animals, people on foot and in waggons. Torunnan troopers were trying to direct the traffic. There was nothing panicked about it. It was more like a sullen retreat, as though the crowds of refugees were too exhausted to feel fear.

Corfe peered further west, across the river. The land rose there in two ridges running parallel to the Searil. The ridges themselves were steep and rocky, and their summits were dotted with watchtowers and signal stations. But there was a gap close to where the bridge arched out from the western bank, and in this gap, maybe a league wide, the fortress of Ormann Dyke proper stood.

The walls were sixty feet high and wide enough for a waggon to drive along. Every cable or so their length was interrupted by a tower which jutted up to a hundred feet, guns glinting in the embrasures. There were odd kinks in the layout of the walls, and the sides of the towers met at strange angles. These were recent innovations, designed to concentrate the gunfire of the defenders so that anyone approaching the dyke would be caught in a deadly crossfire.

At the southern end of the Long Walls was the citadel. It was built on a steep-sided spur that jutted out from the main line of the ridges. Its guns would dominate the whole frontage of the dyke itself.

In front of the walls, and constructed at least six centuries before them, was a vast ditch, carved out of the very bones of the land. It was forty feet deep and at least two hundred wide, a work of unimaginable labour built by the Fimbrians when Ormann Dyke had marked the limits of their empire, before the first ships sailed up the Ostian river to found the trading post that would eventually become Aekir. This ditch extended for fully three miles in front of the walls, like a second river to mirror the brown flow of the Searil. It, too, was full of muddy water, and its sides were constructed of slick, close-joined brick. Corfe knew that under the water were entanglements, impaling caltrops, and all manner of devilry designed to rip out the bottoms of any boats foolish enough to try and cross. He knew also that once there had been charges of gunpowder placed in waterproof caches along the ditch, with underground fuse tunnels connecting them to the main fortress. These had fallen into disrepair within the past few years, but he did not doubt that the dyke's defenders had remedied that by now.

The garrison of Ormann Dyke usually numbered some twenty thousand men. It was one of the three great Torunnan armies. The others were stationed at Aekir and Torunn itself. The Aekir army no longer existed, and the Torunn force was some thirty thousand strong. Corfe was sure that most of the capital's garrison were here at the dyke now. The Torunnan king would concentrate his forces here, at the Gateway to the West.

"It still stands then, the dyke?" Macrobius asked querulously.

"It stands," Corfe told him, "though it looks as though half the world is trekking westwards through it."

Ribeiro joined them at the hilltop and stared down at the teeming fortress, the river, the bristling ridges beyond.

"God be praised!" he said thickly. He knelt and kissed Macrobius's knuckle. "We will find someone who will recognize you for who you really are, Your Holiness. Your sojourn in the wilderness is ended. You are come back into your kingdom."

Macrobius shook his head, smiling slightly.

"I have no kingdom. I never had, unless it be in the souls of men. Always I was a mere cipher, a figurehead. Perhaps my hand helped guide the tiller a little, but that is all. I know that now, and I do not know if I would greatly care to be such a figure again."

"But you must! Holiness –"

"Patrol coming," Corfe said brusquely, wearying of this pious raving. "Torunnan heavy horse – cuirassiers by the look of them."

The cavalry troop was forcing a way out of the clogged gate of the eastern defences. They parted the flow of refugees like a rock splitting a wave, and then their mounts were stepping through the broken mud of the hillside below Corfe and his companions. Corfe did not move. He doubted that, what with the filth and wear of the past days, his clothing was recognizable as a Torunnan uniform. There was no reason for the horsemen to note three more ragged refugees.

But Ribeiro was sliding and tumbling down the sodden hillside, waving his arms and shouting. His habit billowed out above his thin limbs like the wings of an ungainly bird. The lead horsemen reined in. Corfe swore rabidly.

"What is he doing?" Macrobius asked. There was real fear in his voice.

"The damn fool is... ach, they'll think he's merely mad."

Ribeiro was talking to the halted cavalry. Corfe could not make out what he was saying, but he could guess.

"He's probably trying to convince them that you're the Pontiff."

Macrobius shook his head as if in pain. "But I am not – not any more. That man died in Aekir. There is no Macrobius any more."

Corfe looked at him quickly. Something in the tone of the old man's voice, some note of loss and resignation, struck a painful chord in his own breast. For the first time he wondered if this Macrobius might indeed be whom he said he was.

"Easy, Father. They'll put his claims down to the ravings of a demented cleric, no more."

Macrobius sank to his knees in the mud. "Let them leave me alone. I am in darkness, and always will be. I am no longer even sure of the faith which once sustained me. I am a coward, soldier of Mogen. You fought to save the City of God whilst I cowered in a storeroom, imprisoned in my own palace lest I flee and take the heart of the city with me."

"We are all cowards, in one way or another," Corfe said with rough gentleness. "Were I a braver man, I'd be lying dead before Aekir myself, along with my wife."

The old man raised his head at that. "You left your wife in Aekir? I am sorry, my friend, very sorry."

The horsemen rode on, leaving Ribeiro behind them. The young monk shook his fist at them, and then his whole frame seemed to sag. Corfe helped Macrobius to his feet.

"Come on, Father. We'll see if we can't get you a roof over your head tonight, and something warm in your belly. Let the great ones argue over the fate of the west. It is our concern no more."

"Oh, but it is, my son, it is. If it is not the concern of us all, then we may as well lie down here on the ground and wait for death to take us."

"We'll think about that another time. Come. Ho! Ribeiro! Give me a hand with the old man!"

But Ribeiro seemed not to have heard. He was standing

with one hand over the eye he could still see out of, and his lips were moving silently.

They joined the straggling crowds of ragged and wild-eyed people who were disappearing into the eastern gate of the dyke. They sank calf-deep in mud – what was left of the Western Road – and were shoved and jostled as they went. Eventually, though, the darkness of the barbican was around them, and then they were within the walls of the last Ramusian outpost east of the Searil river.

There was chaos within the defences.

People everywhere, in all states of filth and desperation. They stood in huddles around fires on the very drill ground and the interior walls of the fortifications were lined with primitive shelters and lean-tos that had been thrown up to combat the rain. Some enterprising souls had set up market stalls of sorts, selling whatever they had brought with them out of the wreck of Aekir. Corfe saw a mule being butchered, people hanging round the carcass like gore-crows. There were women, pathetically haggard, who were offering themselves to passers-by for food or money, and here and there some callous souls were playing dice on a cloak thrown over the mud.

Corfe glimpsed violence, also. There were groups of men with long knives extorting anything of value from fellow refugees, once the Torunnans had passed by. He wondered if Pardal's comrades had made it this far.

What he saw disturbed him. There seemed to be little order within the fortress, no organization or authority. True, men in Torunnan black were on the battlements, their armour gleaming darkly, but they appeared thin on the ground, as though the garrison were not up to strength. And no effort had been made, it seemed, to bring the mob of fleeing civilians under control. If Corfe were in command here, he'd have them herded west, well clear of the dyke, and then perhaps try and rig up provisions for them and police the camps with what men he could spare. But this – this was mere anarchy. Was Martellus still in command, or had there been some reshuffle which had engendered this chaos?

He found a spot to stop in the shadow of one of the eastern revetments, kicking a couple of sullen young men from the space. They left after a hard stare at the sabre and the ragged remnants of the uniform, but Corfe was too weary and troubled to care. He collected pieces of wood – there were plenty lying about, and he guessed that the refugees had demolished some of the inner stockades and catwalks – and got a fire going with the greatest difficulty. By that time the light was beginning to fail, and across the open ground within the fortress campfires were flickering into life like lambent stars, whilst if he stood up he could see across the Searil river to where the lights of the dyke burned by the thousand. People were crossing the bridge by torchlight in an unending procession and the eastern gates remained open despite the dimming light, which seemed to Corfe to be the merest madness: in the dark, Merduks might mingle with the swarm of civilians entering the fortress and gain access to the interior. Who was in command here? What kind of fool?

Ribeiro was uncommunicative and seemed shaken by the fact that Macrobius had not immediately been recognized. He sat with his swollen head in his hands and stared into the flames of Corfe's fire as though he were looking for some revelation.

Macrobius, however, was almost serene. He sat on the wet ground, the firelight making a hideous mask out of his savaged face, and nodded to himself. Corfe had seen that look before, on men about to go into battle. It meant they no longer feared death.

Could this crazy old man really be the High Pontiff?

His stomach rumbled. They had eaten nothing in the past day and a half, and precious little in the days before that. In fact, the last time he had eaten a solid meal...

The last time, it had been Heria who had prepared it, and brought it to him at his post on the wall of Aekir. It had been dark then, as it was now. They had stood together on the catwalk looking out at the campfires of the Merduk thousands, smelling the tar and smoke of the siege engines, the stench of death that hung over the city continually. He had begged her to go once more, but she would not leave him. That had been the last time he had ever seen his wife; that heartbreaking smile, one corner of her mouth quirking upwards, one eyebrow lifting. He remembered her going down the steps from the wall, the torchlight shining on her hair.

Two hours later the final assault had begun, and then his world had been utterly destroyed.

He felt a hand on his arm and started. It was wholly dark but for the fire. The open ground within the fortress was a flame-stitched blueness in which shadows moved aimlessly.

"She is gone to God's rest, my son. You no longer have to fear for her," Macrobius said softly.

"How did you – ?"

"You had relaxed, as though in a dream, and then I felt your muscles go as rigid as wood. I am good, I find, at recognizing suffering in others these days. She is with Ramusio in the company of the Saints of heaven. Nothing more can touch her."

"I hope so, old man. I hope so."

He could not voice, even to himself, the fear that Heria might yet be alive and suffering torment at the hands of those eastern animals. And so he prayed that his wife was dead.

He stood up abruptly, shaking off the priest's hand.

"Food. We have to eat if we're to be good for anything. Ribeiro, look after the old man."

The young monk nodded. His face was shiny and discoloured, like a bruised fruit, and he kept spitting out bits of teeth. Privately Corfe did not give much for his chances.

He strode off between the fires, stepping over exhausted bodies lying unconscious on the sodden ground, brushing aside two women who tried to solicit him. It was only in extremity that the true depths and heights of human nature were visible. Folk who had been civilized, upright, even downright saintly in Aekir before its fall were now whores and thieves and murderers.

And cowards, he added to himself. *Let us not forget cowards.*

No man could truly say what he was until he had been pushed to the edge of things with the precipice of his own ruin staring up at him. Things changed that close to the brink, and people changed too. Rarely, Corfe believed, for the better.

He turned aside at the approach of two Torunnan troopers, twitching his sabre behind his body so it would not be seen. He was not sure what his position might be with the army, whether he was a deserter or a mere straggler, but he felt guilty enough in his own mind not to want to find out.

He had not been afraid on abandoning Aekir. He had seen most of the men he commanded slaughtered on the walls, and had been caught up in the headlong retreat that followed. After that, knowing Heria was lost to him, one way or another, he had merely wanted to leave the blood and the smoke behind. It had been a bitter thing, but he could not remember being afraid. He could not remember feeling anything much. The events in which he had been caught up had seemed too vast for human emotion.

But away from the roaring chaos of that day, he was not so sure. *Had* it been fear? At any rate, his duty would have been to stay with Lejer's rearguard and fight on. He would be dead by now in that case, or marching east under a Merduk capture yoke.

"You there!" a voice barked. "Halt where you are. What's that you're carrying?"

Two fellow Torunnans. They had noticed the sabre after all. Corfe contemplated running for a second, but then smiled at the absurdity of the idea. He had nowhere else to go.

The Torunnans were in black and scarlet, their half-armour lacquered so that it was like shining ebony. Sabres that were the twin of Corfe's hung by their sides and they wore the light helms with beak-like nose guards that were typical of their race. One also carried an arquebus over his shoulder, but the slow-match was not lit.

"Where did you get that weapon?" the one without the arquebus demanded.

"From a dead Torunnan," Corfe said carelessly.

The man's breath hissed through his teeth. "You God-damned vulture, I'll stick you like a pig –" But then his companion stopped him.

"Wait, Han. What's that he's wearing?"

They both stared, and Corfe could almost have laughed at the dawning comprehension on their faces.

"Yes, I am Torunnan also. John Mogen was my general, and I saw him die on the eastern wall of Aekir. Any other questions?"

It puzzled Corfe that he was being taken so seriously. He paced the stone floor of the anteroom, listening to the voices rising and falling on the other side of the door. The two troopers had brought him here at once, across the crowded Searil bridge to the dyke and into the very heart of the fortress on the western bank.

Here the chaos had been even greater than it was across the river. The refugees had set up a kind of shanty town of sticks and canvas and whatever else they could find within the fortress, and it spilled beyond the towering walls out into the surrounding countryside. Everywhere fires glittered in the night, stretching far across the land and roughly following the line of the Western Road. Everywhere there was the hubbub and stink of an enormous camp.

It troubled Corfe to see Ormann Dyke in this state. He had always thought of it as impregnable, but then he had thought the same about Aekir in the months before its fall. He had a hollow feeling in the pit of his stomach as he waited to be called in by General Pieter Martellus, the commanding officer. He had seen the long lines of waggons waiting in the drill yards piled high with supplies, and he had seen the activity along the horse lines, the blacksmiths working through the night, their forges like little Hell-lit caverns. He had a feeling the dyke was being abandoned without a battle, and despite the detachment he affected the knowledge shook him to the core. If the dyke fell, what hope was there for Torunn itself?

He was called in at last, and found himself in a high-ceilinged room built entirely of stone but for black beams as thick as his waist criss-crossing near the roof. A fire burned in a deep brazier and there was a long table covered with maps and papers, and so many quills that it seemed a flock of birds had just been startled into flight from there. A group of men stood or sat around the table, some smoking pipes. They stared at him as he entered.

He saluted, acutely conscious of his wretched appearance and the mud that was falling from his boots to clod the floor.

One man, whom Corfe recognized as Martellus, stood up, throwing aside a quill as though it were a dart.

The troops called him "the Lion," not without reason. He had a mane and beard of shaggy black hair shot through with grey and russet tints, and his eyebrows shadowed his cavernous sockets. He was a huge man, but surprisingly slim-waisted – quite unlike the barrel-chested firebrand that had been John Mogen. He had been Mogen's lieutenant for ten years and had a reputation for cold-blooded severity. There were also barrack rumours that he was a wizard of sorts. His pale eyes regarded Corfe unblinkingly.

"We are told you were at Aekir," he said, and his voice was as deep as the splash of a coin at a well's bottom. "Is this so?"

"Yes, sir."

"You were one of Mogen's command?"

"I was."

"Why did you not join Lejer in his rearguard?"

Corfe's heart hammered as the officers watched him intently, some with their pipes halfway to their mouths. They were Torunnans like himself, the much-vaunted warrior race. It had been the Torunnans who had first thrown off the Fimbrian yoke, Torunnans who had beaten back the first of the Merduk invasions. That tradition seemed to hang heavy in the room now, along with the unfamiliar taste of defeat. Mogen had been their best, and they knew it. The garrison of Aekir had been widely recognized as the finest army in the world. No one had ever contemplated its defeat – especially these men, the generals of the last fortress of the west. But none of them had been at Aekir: how could they know?

"There was no time. After the eastern bastion fell – after Mogen died – there was a rout. My men were all dead. I got cut off..." His voice trailed away. He remembered the flames, the panic of the mobs, the falling buildings. He remembered his wife's face.

Martellus continued to stare at him.

"I'd had enough of the killing," he said, his words grating out unwillingly. "I wanted to look for my wife. When I failed to find her it was too late to join Lejer. I got caught up in the crowd. I –" He hesitated, then went on, his gaze never leaving Martellus's cold eyes: "I fled with the rest into the countryside."

"You deserted," someone said, and there was a murmur round the table.

"Maybe I did," Corfe said, surprising himself with his calmness. "Aekir was burning. There was nothing left in the city to fight for. Nothing I cared about. Yes, I deserted. I ran away. Do with me what you will. I am tired, and have come a long way."

One man thumped the table angrily at this, but Martellus held up a hand then stood with his hands behind his back, the red light from the brazier making his face seem more than ever like that of a feline predator.

"Easy, gentlemen. We did not bring this man here to judge him, but to gain information. What is your name, Ensign?"

"Corfe. Corfe Cear-Inaf. My father served under Mogen also."

"Inaf, yes. I know the name. Well, Corfe, I have to tell you that you are the first Torunnan soldier we have seen who came out of Aekir alive. The best field army of the Five Monarchies is no more. You may be its last survivor."

Corfe gaped, unable to believe it. "There have been no more? None?"

"Not one. The Merduks took many hundreds prisoner after Lejer's last battle, that much we know. They are destined for crucifixion in the east. No others have got this far."

Corfe bowed his head. He was alive, then, when every other Torunnan who had fought under Mogen was dead or captured. The shame of it made his face burn. Small wonder the men around the table seemed so hostile. In all the thousands of men who had been part of that army, only Corfe had fled and saved his own skin. The knowledge staggered him.

"Take a seat," Martellus said, not unkindly. "You look as though you need it."

He fumbled for a chair and sat down, his head in his hands.

"What do you want of me?" he whispered.

"As I said, information. I want to know the composition of the Merduk army. I want to know how badly Mogen's men damaged it before the end. And I want to know why Aekir fell."

Corfe looked up. "Are you going to stay here, to fight the Merduk again?"

"Yes."

"It doesn't seem that way to me."

The men at the table stirred at his words. Martellus glared at them to silence them, then nodded. "Some of the garrison have been transferred west, to Torunn. Thus we are shorthanded."

"How many? On whose orders?"

"On the orders of King Lofantyr himself. Twelve thousand will be left here for the defence of the dyke, no more."

"Then the dyke will fall."

"I do not intend to let it fall, Ensign."

"You have refugees crawling all over the fortress. If the Merduks chanced upon this place it would not last an hour."

"There has been confusion, what with the transfers to the west. It is coming under control." Martellus appeared faintly irritated. "Our scouts inform us that the Merduk main body is still in Aekir, though they have light troops out skirmishing a scant league away from here. We have time and to spare; it will be weeks yet ere the main enemy body begins to move. My orders are to get as many of Aekir's refugees away to the west as possible before cutting the bridges. Now, tell me. What is the enemy strength?"

Corfe hesitated. "Since the siege, they may be left with some hundred and fifty thousand."

The officers glanced at one another. Such an army had never been seen before, never imagined.

"How many did they have before the siege began?" one asked harshly.

"A quarter of a million, maybe. We cut them down like straw, but they kept coming. I know that many were also sent back to guard the supply routes over the mountains, but the first snows will be in the passes of the Thurians now. I cannot see how they will keep supplied through the winter."

"I can," Martellus said. "Duke Comorin of Kardikia says they are building boats by the hundred on the Ostian river. That will be their new supply route, and it will remain open through the winter. Their advance will continue."

Martellus bent over the table and examined a map of the land between the Searil and the Ostian rivers.

"Show me the line of their advance," he said to Corfe.

Corfe got up, but then something occurred to him. "Has Macrobius been seen yet, or his body found?"

"The High Pontiff? Why, no. He died in Aekir."

"Are you sure? Did anyone see him killed?"

"His palace burned, and just about every priest who was in the city was put to the sword. I have it from civilians and clerics who were there. I do not think the Merduks could have overlooked someone of his eminence."

"But Mogen had him locked in a storeroom in the palace to stop him fleeing the city."

Martellus stared, incredulous. "Are you serious?"

"It was a rumour in the city just before its fall. The Knights Militant almost left Mogen's command over it. Would you know the High Pontiff if you saw him?"

Martellus became exasperated. "I suppose so. I have supped at the same table as him a few times. Why?"

"Then you must send men over to the eastern bank. You will find an old man there near the barbican who lacks eyes, and a young monk with an injured face."

"What about them?"

"I think the old man may be Macrobius."

THIRTEEN

CHARIBON.

The oldest monastery in the world, home of the Inceptine Order.

It stood on the shores of the Sea of Tor in the north-west foothills of the wild Cimbric Mountains. Surrounded by the Kingdom of Almark, it was nevertheless autonomous, as Aekir had been, and was governed by the elders of the Church and their head, the High Pontiff.

Some seven thousand clerics lived and worked here, the majority of them in Inceptine black though there were some in the brown of the Antillians and others in the warm saffron of the Mercurians. Very few indeed were robed in the ordinary, undyed wool of the ascetic missionaries, the Friars Mendicant.

Here resided the greatest libraries in Normannia, now those in Aekir were no more, and here were the chief barracks and training grounds of the Knights Militant. They had a citadel of their own higher up in the hills beside Charibon, and there some eight thousand of them were quartered. Usually there were several times that number on hand, but most of them were in the east or had been dispatched to the various Ramusian monarchies to aid in the struggle against heresy. Two thousand were even now riding west, to Hebrion.

Down in the complex of the monastery itself there were the famed Long Cloisters of Charibon, walked by fifteen generations of clerics, roofed over by cedar imported from the Levangore and floored with basalt blocks hewn out of the once-volcanic Cimbrics.

Radiating out from the square of the cloisters and the rich gardens they enclosed were the other structures of the monastery, built in massive stone and roofed with slate from the quarries in the nearby Narian Hills. No humble thatch here.

But the Cathedral of the Saint towered over and dominated the rest. Its outline defined the skyline of Charibon, made it recognizable from leagues away in the hills. A huge, three-sided tower with a horn of granite at each corner formed the apex of the triangle that was the rest of the cathedral. It was the classic Ramusian shape, reminiscent of the Praying Hands but on a scale vaster than anyone had ever envisaged. Only Aekirians might sniff at the cathedral of Charibon, comparing it to their own Carcasson, of which it was a copy.

But Carcasson was no more.

The monastery sprawled out from the twin foci of cloisters and cathedral, the original pure design of the place lost in a welter of later building. There were schools and dormitories, cells of contemplation, gardens restful on the eye and conducive to contemplative thought. Most of the theories which had shaped the Ramusian religion had sprung from here as their authors looked out on the fountain-rich gardens or the green hills beyond.

There were also kitchens and workshops, smithies and tanneries, and, of course, the famed printing presses of the Inceptines. Charibon had its own lands and herds and crops, for there was a secular side to it as well as the spiritual. A town had sprung up around the swelling monastery complexes and a fishing village on the lake's western shores kept the monks supplied with freshwater halibut, mackerel and even turtle on fast days. Charibon was a self-sufficient little kingdom whose chief exports were the books that the presses ceaselessly turned out and the faith that the Inceptines promulgated and the Knights Militant enforced.

The monastery had been sacked a hundred and fifty years before by a confederation of the savage Cimbric tribes. There had been a war then, with troops from Almark and Torunna sending expeditions into the mountains' interior along with contingents of the Knights. The tribes had eventually been crushed and brought into the Ramusian fold, finally completing the task which the Fimbrians had attempted and failed to accomplish some four centuries earlier. Since then, a dozen tercios of Almarkan troops had also been stationed at Charibon, even as the Torunnans had garrisoned Aekir further east. Charibon was a jewel, a light to be kept burning no matter how dark the night – especially as the brightness that had been Aekir was now extinguished.

ALBREC SQUINTED INTO the cold, eye-watering wind, looking for all the world like a short-sighted vole peering from its burrow at the close of winter. This high in the hills the winters were bitter, snow lying for four months in the cloisters and the inland sea growing fringes of ice along its shores. His cell then would be like a small cube of gelid air in the mornings, and he would have to break the ice in his washing bowl before spluttering at the coldness of the water on his pointed face.

He wore a habit of Antillian brown, much worn, and the Saint symbol at his breast was of mere wood, carved by himself in the dim, candlelit nights. Though all were clerics alike here in Charibon, some were of a higher order than others. Some indeed were of aristocratic background, the younger sons of noble families whose fathers had nothing to give in the way of inheritance. So they became Inceptines, a different kind of noble. For the commoners, however, there was only the Antillians, the Mercurians, or if one was of a zealous turn of mind, and hardy to boot, the Friars Mendicant.

Albrec's father had been a fisherman from the shores of northern Almark. A dour man, from a hard country. He had never quite forgiven his son's fear of the open sea, or his ineptness with the nets and the tiller. Albrec had attached himself to a small monastery of Antillians from a nearby village, and found a place where he was not reviled or beaten, where the work was hard but not frightening as the days on an open boat had been frightening. And where his natural curiosity and inherent stubbornness could be put to good use.

He worked in the library of St. Garaso, his hand not being apt for the rigour of the presses or the finer of the illustrating that went on in the scriptorium. He lived in a dusty, half-subterranean world of books and manuscripts, old scrolls and parchment and vellum. He loved it, and could lay his hands on any tome in the entire library within a few minutes.

It was because of his labyrinthine knowledge of the shelves and chests and stacks that he was kept on as assistant librarian, and in return he was allowed to read anything he chose, which for him was a reward beyond price. There were levels to the library which were rarely visited, ancient archives and forgotten cupboards, their contents mouldering away in dust and silence. Albrec made it his mission in life to explore them all.

He had been here for thirteen years, his eyesight progressively worsening and his shoulders becoming more bowed with every book he squinted over. And yet he knew he had not yet unearthed one-tenth of the riches contained in the library.

There were scrolls there from the time of the Fimbrian Hegemony, works which he spent days coaxing open with sweet oil and a blunt knife. Most of them were dismissed by Brother Commodius, the senior librarian, as secular rubbish, or even heresy. Some had been burned, horrifying Albrec. After that he had shown no more of his unearthed treasures to the other brothers, but had hoarded them secretly. Books should not be burned, he believed, no matter what they contained. To him all books were sacred, fragments of the minds of the past, thoughts from men long gone to their graves. Such things should be preserved.

And so Albrec hid the more controversial of his finds, thus unintentionally beginning a private library of his own, a library of works which, had his spiritual superiors discovered them, would have consigned him to the flames in their company.

THIS MORNING HE was staring out of one of the library's rare windows to the hills beyond. His Excellency the Prelate of Hebrion was expected to arrive today to join the three other Prelates who were lodged in Charibon already. The entire monastery was abuzz with gossip and speculation. There were rumours that since Macrobius was dead, God have mercy on his soul, the Prelates were meeting to choose a new High Pontiff. Others said there was heresy brewing in the western kingdoms, sorcerers willing to take advantage of the confused state of the Ramusian monarchies in the wake of Aekir's fall. This synod would be the beginnings of a crusade, it was said, a holy war to rid the west both of its enemies within and the Merduks who bayed at the gate.

Momentous times, Albrec thought a little nervously. He had always considered Charibon as a retreat of sorts, isolated as it was up here in the hills; but he saw now that it was becoming one of the hubs upon which the world turned. He was not sure if the feeling thrilled or frightened him. All he asked for was the peace to continue his reading undisturbed, to remain in his dusty, candlelit kingdom in the depths of the library.

"Gathering wool again, Brother?" a voice drawled casually. Albrec backed away from the window hurriedly. His addresser was in rich Inceptine black, and the symbol clinking at his breast shone with gold.

"Oh, it's you, Avila. Don't do that! I thought you were Commodius."

The other cleric, a handsome young man with the pale, spare visage of a nobleman, laughed.

"Don't worry, Albrec. He's closeted with the rest of the worthies in the Vicar-General's quarters. I doubt if you'll be seeing him today."

Albrec blinked. He had an armful of books which he was cradling as tenderly as a young mother might her first child. They shifted in his grasp and he gave a grunt of dismay as they began to topple. But Avila caught them and set them to rights.

"Come, Albrec. Lay down those dead tomes for a while. Walk in the cloisters with me and watch the arrival of Himerius of Hebrion."

"He's here, then?"

"A patrol has reported his party to be approaching. You can lock the library after you – no one will be needing it for the next few hours. I think half of Charibon is outside indulging their curiosity."

"All right."

It was true that the library was deserted. The cavernous place resounded to their voices and the patient dripping of the ancient water-clock in a corner. They turned the triple locks of the massive door behind them – it was always a source of pride to Albrec, a pride that he immediately chastised himself for, that he carried on his person the keys to one of the great libraries of the world – and, tucking their hands in their habits, they journeyed out into the cold clearness of the day.

"What is it about this Hebrian Prelate that has the monastery in such a fuss?" Albrec asked irritably. The broad corridors they traversed were crammed with fast-walking, gabbling monks. Everyone, from novices to friars, seemed to be on the move today, and twice they had to stop and bow to an Inceptine monsignore.

"Don't you know, Albrec? By the Saints, you spend so much time with your head buried in the spines of books that you let the events of the real world roll over you like water."

"Books are real, too," Albrec said obstinately. It was an old argument. "They tell of what happened in the world, its history and its composition. That is real."

"But this is happening *now*, Albrec, and we are part of it. Great events are afoot, and we are lucky enough to be alive to see them happen."

Avila's eyes were shining, and Albrec looked at him with a curious mixture of affection, exasperation and awe. Avila was a younger son of the Dampiers of Perigraine. He had gone into the Inceptines as a matter of course, and no doubt his rise in the order would be meteoric. He had charisma, energy and was devastatingly attractive. Albrec was never sure how the two of them had become friends. It had something to do with the ideas they pummelled each other with, the arguments that they flung back and forth like balls between them. Half a dozen novices were hopelessly in love with Avila, but Albrec was sure that the young noble was not even aware of them. There was a curious innocence about him which had survived the rough and tumble of his first years here. On the other hand, no one could play the Inceptine game better than he. Albrec could not help but feel that his friend was wasted here. Avila should have been a leader of men, an officer in his country's army, instead of a cleric tucked away in the hills.

"Tell me, then, what I should know in my ignorance," Albrec said.

"This Himerius is the champion of the Inceptines at the moment. Hebrion has a young and irreligious king on the throne, one who has scant respect for the Church, I am told, and who regularly consorts with wizards. Abrusio has become a haven for all sorts of heretics, foreigners and sorcerers. Himerius has instigated a purge of the city and is coming here to try to persuade the other Prelates to do likewise."

Albrec screwed up his pointed nose. "I don't like it. Everyone is panicked after Aekir. It smells like politics to me."

"Of course it does! My dear fellow, the Church is leaderless. Macrobius is dead and we no longer have a High Pontiff. This Himerius is establishing his credentials as soon as he can, putting himself forward as the sort of strong leader that the Church needs at a time like this – one not afraid to cross swords with kings. Everyone is already talking of him as Macrobius's successor."

"Everyone except his fellow Prelates, I take it."

"Oh, naturally! There will be deals done, though, with the Vicar-General brokering the whole thing. He is barred of course from the Pontiffship by virtue of his present office, but I do not doubt that he will have another Inceptine at the Church's head in a short while."

"Over a century, it has been, since we have had a non-Inceptine High Pontiff," Albrec said, stroking his brown Antillian habit reflectively. "And of all the Prelates, only Merion of Astarac is not an Inceptine, but an Antillian like myself."

"The Ravens have always run things their way," Avila said cheerfully. "It'll never be any different."

They walked out of the cloisters and began toiling up the cobbled streets of the town that formed the fringes of the monastery. The buildings here were tall, leaning over the road, and the streets were clean. The entire place had been tidied up for the Synod on the orders of the Vicar-General.

Clerics clogged the streets, climbing higher so as to be the first to catch sight of the man who was favourite for the Pontiffship. Avila helped Albrec along as the little monk puffed and sweated up the hill. Their breath clouded around them in the cold air, and they could see the snow on the higher slopes above them.

"There," Avila said, satisfied.

They stood on the ridge that curled protectively about the south-west of Charibon. The slope around them was black with people, religious and lay alike. They could stare down and see the entire, beautiful profile of Charibon with its towers and spires kindled by the autumn sunlight, and the inland sea of Tor glittering off to their right.

"I see him," Avila said.

Albrec squinted. "Where?"

"Not there, you ninny, along the northern road. He's coming by way of Almark, remember. See the escort of Knights? There must be close on two hundred of them. Himerius will be in the second coach, the one flying the scarlet Hebrian flag. They're certainly putting on a show for him. I'd say he had the Pontiffship in the palm of his hand already."

One of their neighbours, a hard-faced priest in the plain robe of a Friar Mendicant, turned at Avila's words.

"What's that you say? Himerius as Pontiff?"

"Why yes, Brother. That seems to me to be the way of it."

"And you have looked deeply into these matters, have you?"

Avila's face seemed to stiffen. It was with his full aristocratic hauteur that he replied, "I have a mind. I can examine the evidence and form an opinion as well as the next man."

The Friar Mendicant smiled, then nodded to the approaching cavalcade. "If yon Prelate assumes the High Pontiffship you may no longer be permitted the luxury of an opinion, lad. And many innocent folk will no longer possess the luxury of life. I doubt if that was the way of the Blessed Ramusio when he was on this earth, but it is the way of your brother Inceptines these days, with their Knights Militant, their purges and their pyres. Where in the *Book of Deeds* does it say you must murder your fellow man if he differs from you? Inceptines! You are God's gorecrows, flapping round the pyres you have created."

The grey-clad Friar turned at that and stumped off, elbowing his way roughly through the gathering throng. Avila and Albrec stared after him, speechless.

"He's mad," Albrec said at last. "The Friars are always an eccentric lot, but he's lost his mind entirely."

Avila stared down the hillside to where the Prelate of Hebrion's retinue was thundering along the muddy northern road, raising a spray of water as it came.

"Is he? I cannot ever remember a tale of Ramusio destroying someone who did not believe in him. Maybe he is right."

"He struck down the demon-possessed women of Gebrar," Albrec pointed out.

"Yes," Avila said absently, "there is that." Then he grinned suddenly with his accustomed good humour. "Which is another reason why clerics do not marry. Women have too many demons in them! I believe all clerics have mothers, though."

"Hush, Avila. Someone will hear."

"Someone will hear, yes. And what if they do, Albrec? What would happen? What if they chanced upon that cache of books you have saved? Do you ever wonder what would happen if they did? We had a mage on my father's staff when I was a boy. He used to do tricks with light and water, and no one could heal a broken limb faster than he. He became my tutor. Is that the sort of man the Church wants to destroy? Why?"

"For the sake of the Saint, Avila, will you be quiet? You'll get us into all manner of trouble."

"But what manner?" Avila asked. "What manner, Albrec? When does a conversation, an idea, lead to the pyre? What must one do to earn such a death?"

"Oh shut up, Avila. I won't argue with you, not here and now." Albrec looked round with increasing nervousness. Some of the nearby clerics were turning to listen to Avila's voice.

Avila smiled again. "All right, Brother. We'll chase this hare later. Maybe Brother Mensio can help us out."

Albrec said nothing. Avila loved to carry a conversation to the edge of things – to the limits of orthodoxy. It was worrying. Albrec sometimes thought that the gap between what Avila believed and what he said was widening and even he, the nobleman's friend, could not say for sure just how deep was the gulf between what appeared to be and what was in the younger man's mind.

The Prelate's cavalcade splashed by, one pale hand waving graciously from the depths of the coach at the assembled crowd. Then it was gone. There was a feeling of anticlimax.

"He could at least have got out and given us his blessing," a monk next to them grumbled.

Avila slapped the man on the back. "That was his blessing, Brother! Didn't you see his fingers tracing the Sign of the Saint as he galloped past? A swift blessing, it's true, but none the worse for that."

The monk, an Inceptine novice with the white hood of a first-year student, beamed broadly.

"So I've been blessed by the future Pontiff of the world. Thanks, Brother. I'd never have noticed. You have good eyes."

"And a lively imagination," Albrec muttered while he and Avila made their way back down into Charibon. The bells of the cathedral were tolling the third hour and the flocks of monks were returning to their respective colleges for the morning meal. Albrec's stomach gave a premonitory twinge at the thought.

"Why do you do such things?" he asked his friend.

"You are strangely snappish this morning, Brother. Why do I do it? Because it pleases me, and it brightened that novice's day. By tomorrow the tale will be round his college how Himerius endowed them with his personal blessing, much good may it do them."

"Avila, I do believe you are in danger of becoming a cynic."

"Maybe. Sometimes I think that every man who wears this black habit must be either a pious fanatic or a cold-blooded schemer."

"Or a nobleman's younger son. There are a lot of those, don't forget."

Avila grinned at his diminutive friend. "Come, Antillian. Will you dine with the noblemen's sons this morning? If anyone points a finger at your mud-coloured habit I'll say you're a scholar come to use our library. And our refectory is renowned, as you well know."

"I know. All right. So long as you fend off the antics of the novices. I'm in no mood for a bread fight this morning."

The two of them picked a path down the cobbled streets into the monastery proper, the tall Inceptine and the plump little Antillian. No one looking at the unlikely pair could have guessed that between them they would one day change the course of the world.

THE BELLS OF the cathedral tolled the hours of Charibon away. The inhabitants of the monastery-city said their devotions, ate their meals and read their offices in fast mumbles, but in the splendidly appointed quarters of the Vicar-General a more select company sat at their ease and sipped the Candelarian wine that had come with the meal. They had pushed their chairs back from the long table, said their thanks to God for the bounty which had presented itself before them and were now enjoying the fire burning in the huge hearth to one side.

Five men, the most powerful religious leaders in the world.

At the head of the table sat the Vicar-General of the Inceptine Order, Betanza of Astarac, formerly a duke of that kingdom. He had found his vocation late in life, helped, some said, by the sea-rovers who had destroyed his fief in a lightning raid one summer thirty years ago. He was a big, powerful man edging into corpulence, with a ruddy face and a pate that would have been bald even had it not been tonsured. The Saint symbol that hung from his neck was of white gold inset with pearls and tiny rubies. He was fingering it absently as he stared into the candlelit depths of his wine.

The other men represented four kingdoms. Merion of Astarac was not yet present, delayed, it was believed, by early snowstorms in the passes of the Malvennor Mountains, but Heyn of Torunna was there, as were Escriban of Perigraine and Marat of Almark. And seated at the foot of the table, delicately drinking the last of his wine, was Himerius of Hebrion whose arrival this morning had caused such commotion throughout the monastery.

All the men present were Inceptines and all had served their novitiate in this very monastery. For all except Betanza, it was the home of their youth and held fond memories, but their faces were grave now, even disgruntled.

"I cannot let go any more of the Knights," Betanza said with the weary air of a man repeating himself. "They are needed where they are."

"You have thousands of them on the hill, sitting on their hands," Heyn of Torunna said. He was a thin, black-bearded man. He looked ill, so dark were the circles under his eyes and the hollows at his temples.

"They are our only reserve. Charibon cannot be left defenceless. What if the tribes grow restive?"

"The tribes!" Heyn scoffed. "They did not stop you sending two thousand men to Hebrion to do Brother Himerius's policing for him. Are there *tribes* in Hebrion, or Merduks at the gate?"

The Hebrian Prelate raised his eyebrows slightly at that, but otherwise maintained an aloof, patrician air that irritated his colleagues intensely.

"Lofantyr needs men, needs them desperately. Even five thousand would be a boon at this time," Heyn went on doggedly.

"And yet he is withdrawing troops from Ormann Dyke," Himerius said mildly. "Is he so confident in the dyke's impregnability?"

"Torunn must be adequately garrisoned in case the dyke falls," Heyn said.

"God forbid!" said Marat of Almark.

"Really, Brothers," Betanza said. "We are not here to argue politics, but to debate the spiritual needs of the time that is upon us. It is for the kings of the world to be the buckler of the faith. We are merely guides."

"But –" Heyn began.

"And the resources of the Church surely should be reserved for the needs of the Church. We have been free enough with our help so far. How many thousands of the Knights perished in Aekir? No, there are other issues at hand here which are every bit as important as the defence of the western fortresses."

Escriban of Perigraine, a long, languid man who would have looked more at home in court brocade than a monk's habit, laughed shortly.

"My dear Betanza, if you are referring to the High Pontiffship, then surely there is nothing to decide. If the acclaim of your own monks is anything to go by, then our esteemed Brother Himerius already has the position in his lap."

The men around the table scowled. Even Himerius had the grace to look embarrassed.

"The High Pontiffship is decided by the votes of the five Prelates of the Ramusian monarchies and the Colleges of Bishops under them. Nothing else," Betanza said, his red face growing redder. "We will discuss it at the proper time, and pray for God's guidance in this, the most important of decisions. Besides, our number is not complete. Brother Merion of Astarac has yet to join us."

"Your countryman, the Antillian – of course. I meant no offence," Escriban said smoothly. "What way will he vote, do you think?"

Betanza glowered. "Brother Escriban, as referee and overseer of these proceedings I advise you to take a more responsible tone."

"What proceedings? My dear friend, we are only colleagues in the Church talking over dinner. The Synod is not even convened as yet."

The men around the table knew that. They also knew that the real business of the Synod would probably be resolved before it even began. Merion was a nonentity, a non-Inceptine, but if the Prelates were evenly divided his vote would be decisive. He could not be ignored.

"How did he ever become a Prelate anyway?" Marat muttered. "A man of no family and from another order."

"King Mark thinks the world of him. He was the only Astaran candidate put forward," Betanza said. "The College of Bishops had little choice."

"They order these things better in Almark," Marat said. He was stockily built, with a huge white beard that coursed down over his broad chest and belly. His homeland, Almark, had been the last land to be conquered by the Fimbrians before their Hegemony ended, yet it was widely seen as the most conservative of the Five Kingdoms.

"What of these purges our learned colleague has instigated in Hebrion?" Heyn asked, rubbing his sunken temples with bone-white fingers. "Are we to make them a continent-wide phenomenon, or are they merely a local problem?"

Himerius was studying his crystal goblet, his bird-of-prey features revealing nothing. He knew they were waiting for his word. For all their bluster and confidence, he realized that they looked to him at the moment; he was the only one among them who had dared to cross the wishes of his king.

He put down the glass and paused to make sure he had their attention.

"The situation in Hebrion is grave, Brothers. In its way it is every bit as grave as the crisis in the east." The firelight flickered off his wonderfully aquiline nose. He had the features of a Fimbrian emperor, and knew it.

"Abrusio is a colourful city, perched as it is on the edge of the Western Ocean. Ships call there from every part of Normannia, both Ramusian and Merduk. The population of the place is a hybrid, a conglomeration of the dregs of a hundred other cities. And in such a soil, Brothers, heresy takes root easily.

"The King of Hebrion is a young man. He had a great father, Bleyn the Pious whose name you all know, but the son is not hewn out of the same wood. He had a wizard as a tutor in his youth, scorning the wisdom of his Inceptine teachers, and as a result he lacks a certain... respect for the authority and the traditions of the Church."

Escriban of Perigraine grinned. "You mean he's his own man."

"I mean nothing of the sort," Himerius snapped, suddenly peevish. "I mean that if he is left to do as he will the Church's influence in Hebrion may be irrevocably damaged, and then the Saint knows what flotsam and jetsam from the corners of the world will take root in Abrusio. I have acted to prevent this, seeking to cleanse the city and eventually the kingdom, but my sources tell me that the moment I left the place the scale of the purge was reduced, no doubt on the orders of the King."

"Nothing like a few burnings to bring them flocking to the Church on their knees," Marat of Almark said gruffly. "You did right, Brother."

"Thank you. At any rate, dear colleagues, I mean to bring the whole affair up at the Synod once it is convened. Abeleyn of Hebrion must be taught not to flout the authority of the Church."

"What do you mean to do, excommunicate him?" Heyn of Torunna asked incredulously.

"Let us say that the threat of excommunication is sometimes as effective as the act itself."

"You forget one thing, Brother," Betanza said, his fingers playing restlessly with his Saint symbol. "Only the High Pontiff has the authority to excommunicate – or otherwise chastise – an anointed Ramusian king. As mere Prelate, you cannot touch him."

"All the more reason for choosing the new Pontiff as soon as possible," Himerius said, unperturbed.

There was a silence as the others digested this.

"Is this really the time to be picking arguments with kings?" Heyn asked at last. "Are there not enough crises facing the west without adding more?"

"This is the best time," Himerius said. "The prestige of the Church has been badly damaged by the fall of Macrobius, of Aekir and the loss of the army of Knights Militant there. We must regain the initiative, use our influence as a coherent body and prove to the west that we are still the ultimate authority on the continent."

"Do we let Ormann Dyke fall, then, in order to prove how powerful we are?" Escriban asked.

"If we do, then later generations will abhor our names – and rightly so," Heyn said hotly.

"There is no reason that the dyke should fall," Himerius said, "but it is the responsibility of Torunna, not of the Church."

Heyn stood up at that, scraping back his chair. His black habit flapped around his thin form as he put his back to the fire, his eyes smouldering like the gledes at its heart.

"This talk of *responsibility*... the west has a responsibility to aid Torunna at this time. If the Merduks take the dyke, then Torunn itself will almost certainly fall and the heathens will have no other barrier to their advance save the heights of the Cimbrics. And what if they turn north, skirting the mountains? Then it will be our precious Charibon next in line. Will it be our responsibility then to defend it – or should we wait until the Merduk tide is lapping at the gates of Abrusio?"

"You are excited, Brother," Betanza said soothingly. "And with reason. It cannot be easy for you."

"Yes. I'll bet Lofantyr has all but got the thumbscrews on you, Heyn," Escriban said. "What did you promise him before you came here? An army of the Knights? The Lancers of Perigraine? Or perhaps the Cuirassiers of Almark."

Heyn scowled. His face was like a bearded skull in the firelight.

"Not all of us see life as one big joke, Escriban," he said venomously.

Betanza thumped a large hand on the table, setting the glasses dancing and startling them all.

"*Enough!* We did not assemble here to trade insults with one another. We are the elders of the Church, the inheritors of the tradition of Ramusio himself. There will be no pettiness. We cannot afford the time for it."

"Agreed," old Marat said into his white beard. "It seems to me there are two issues confronting us at this time, Brothers. First, the High Pontiffship. It must be decided before anything else, for it affects everything. And secondly, these purges which our Hebrian brother has instigated and wishes to see extended. Do we want to see them across the Five Kingdoms? Personally, I'm in favour of them. The common folk of the world are like cattle; they need to feel the drover's stick once in a while."

"Merion of Astarac is one of your cattle, Marat," said Escriban. "He will not vote for a continent-wide pogrom, I'll tell you now."

"He is only one man, and there are five of us." Marat glanced about the table, and then smiled. He looked like a benevolent patriarch, but his eyes held no humour. "Good," he said.

Heyn remained by the fire, isolated. At last he said:

"Torunna has not the resources to undertake a purge at the moment. We will need outside help."

Betanza nodded, his, bald head shining. "But of course, Brother. I am sure I can let you have a sizeable contingent of the Knights to aid God's work in your beleaguered prelacy."

"Six thousand?"

"Five."

"Very well."

Himerius drained the last of his wine, looking like a hawk which had just stooped on a fat pigeon. "It is good to have these things out in the open, to talk them over with friends, amicably, without rancour." His eyes met Betanza's. He nodded imperceptibly.

Escriban of Perigraine chuckled.

"What about the Pontiffship?" Betanza asked. "Who here wishes to stand?"

"Oh, please, Brother Betanza," Escriban said with feigned shock. "Must you be so blunt?"

Another silence, more profound this time. In accepting Himerius's proposals the decision had more or less been made, but no one wanted to voice what they all knew.

"I will stand, if God will grant me the strength," Himerius said at last, a little annoyed that no one had publicly urged him to.

Betanza sighed. "So be it. This is entirely informal, of course, but I must ask you, Brothers, if there are any objections to Brother Himerius's candidature."

Still, no one spoke. Heyn turned away to face the fire. "Will no one else put themselves forward?" Betanza waited a moment and then shrugged. "Well, we have a candidate to put to the Synod. It remains to be seen what the College of Bishops makes of it."

But they all knew that the Bishops voted with their respective Prelates. The High Pontiffship of the western world had effectively been decided: by five men in a firelit room over dinner.

FOURTEEN

AUTUMN IN THE Malvennor Mountains. Already the snow had begun to block the higher passes, and from the vast peaks streamers and banners of white were being billowed out by the freshening wind.

Abeleyn pulled the fur of his collar tighter around his throat and stared up at the high land to the east and north. The Malvennors were fifteen thousand feet above sea level, and even here, on the snow-pocked hills at their knees, the air was sharp and thin and the guides had warned the party of the dangers of mountain sickness and snow blindness.

He was five weeks out of Abrusio, on his way to the Conclave of Kings at Vol Ephrir in Perigraine. His ship had made a rapid passage across the Fimbrian Gulf, docking at the breakaway Fimbrian city of Narbukir, then he had gone aboard a river boat for the laborious journey up the Arcolm river, taking to horses when the Arcolm was no longer navigable. He could see the river now, a narrow stream running and foaming through the icicle-dripping rocks off to one side. Further up in the mountains it was said that a man might bestride it if he had long legs. Hard to believe that down on the gulf its mouth formed an estuary fully three leagues wide.

The rest of the party were still below, labouring up the steep slopes towards him. He had a tolerably large escort: two hundred Hebrian arquebusiers and swordsmen and eighty heavy cavalry armed with lances and paired matchlock pistols. Then there were the muleteers of the pack-train, the cooks, the grooms, the smiths and the score of other servants who made up his travelling household. All told, some four hundred men accompanied the King of Hebrion across the Malvennor Mountains; a modest enough show. Only a king would ever be allowed to take such a force into a foreign country. It was part and parcel of the dignity of monarchs.

"We'll camp here, and attempt the pass in the morning," the King said to his chief steward.

The man bowed in the saddle and then wrenched his horse around to begin the job of setting up camp.

The King sat relaxed in the saddle and watched the ungainly straggling groups of men and animals gradually coalesce on the slope below him. The horses were finding it heavy going. If the snow grew much deeper – and it would – then they would all be afoot, hauling their mounts behind them. The snows had come early this year, and there was a bitter wind winnowing the high peaks. The baking heat of Abrusio seemed like a dream.

"Is it here you hope to meet up with King Mark, sire?" a woman's voice asked.

"Hereabouts." The King turned to regard the hooded lady who sat her palfrey behind him. The fine-stepping horse was feeling the cold; it was not the best of mounts for a journey such as this. "I hope you have good walking boots with you, lady. That nag of yours will drop in its tracks ere we've put another ten leagues behind us."

The lady Jemilla threw back her hood. Her dark hair was bound up in circled braids around her head, held in place with pearl-topped pins. Two larger pearls shone like little moons in her earlobes. Her eyes sparkled in the snow-light.

"The walk will do me good. I am putting on weight." Abeleyn grinned. If so, he had not noticed. He looked down the hillside. His staff were erecting the huge hide tents, and he could see the dull flicker of a fire. His toes were numb in his fur-lined boots and his breath was whipped away from his lips, but he did not immediately ride down to the warmth of the fires. Rather he gazed south, along the line of the mountains to where Astarac loomed blue with distance on the southern side of the Arcolm river. If truth be told, they were in Astarac now, for the Arcolm had always been the traditional boundary between Astarac and Fimbria. But up in the mountains such technicalities were irrelevant. Shepherds herded their goats from one kingdom to another without formalities, as they always had. Up here the niceties

of borders and diplomacy seemed like a faraway farce to be
played out in the palaces of the world.

"When will he arrive, do you think?" Jemilla asked.

She was becoming a little familiar of late. He must watch
that.

"Soon I hope, lady, soon. But he will be here no quicker
for our watching. Come, let us warm ourselves and give our
poor mounts a rest." He kicked his horse into motion down
the icy slope.

Jemilla did not follow him at once. She sat her shivering
steed and stared at the King's retreating back. One gloved
hand felt her stomach tentatively, and for a moment her
face became as hard as glass. Then she followed her king
and lover down to the growing bustle of the camp, and the
fires that were burning orange and yellow against the snow.

THE WIND HAD blown up into a gale. Abeleyn held his
hands out to the glowing brazier – they would be running
out of coal soon – and listened to the snowstorm that had
come upon them with the swooping in of night. Perhaps
he should have taken the sea route, south-east through the
Malacar Straits, but then he would have needed a small
fleet as escort. To the corsairs, a Hebrian king would have
been too tempting a target to let by unmolested, despite –
or perhaps because of – the long standing accommodations
they had had with the Hebrian crown.

And besides, he needed this chance to talk openly with King
Mark before the intrigue of the conclave swallowed them all.

Something struck the side of the tent, seemingly propelled
by the wind. It scrabbled there for a moment, and the
steward came in from the adjoining extension. There was
the clatter of plates from in there; they were clearing the
remains of dinner.

"Was there something, sire? I thought I heard –"

"It was nothing, Cabran. Dismiss the servants, will you?
They can finish in the morning."

The steward bowed, then left for the spacious extension,
clapping his hands at the serving maids. Abeleyn rose and
let slip the heavy hide curtain that shut out their noise.

"Sire." It was the bodyguard at the entrance. "We've something here. It struck the tent, and you told us to look out for –"

"Yes," Abeleyn snapped. "Bring it here, and then let no others enter."

The tent flap was thrown back and a heavily cloaked and armoured man thrust his way in, admitting a gust of snow and chill air. He had something in his hands, which he left on the low cot at a nod from Abeleyn.

"Thank you, Merco. Have you men a decent fire out there?"

"Good enough, sire. We switch round every hour." The man's voice was muffled in the folds of cloak he had wrapped round his face.

"Very well. That will be all, then."

The man bowed and left. The snow he had let in began to melt on the thick hide of the tent's floor.

"Well, Golophin?" Abeleyn said. He bent over the ice-encrusted gyrfalcon that crouched on the furs of the cot and gently wiped its feathers. The yellow inhuman eyes glared at him. The beak opened, and the voice of the old wizard said:

"Well met, my lord."

"Is the bird drunk, that he crashes into my tent?"

"The bird is exhausted, lad. This damn snowstorm almost put paid to him for good. You will have a fine time forcing the pass if this keeps up."

"I know. What word of King Mark?"

"He is only hours away. He travels with a smaller party than you. Perhaps his ideas as to the dignity of kings differ."

Abeleyn smiled, stroking the bird's feathers. "Perhaps. Well, old man, what news have you for me this time?"

"Momentous news, my boy. I have had the bird monitor Charibon as you requested. He has just come from there. I thought the flight over the mountains would kill him, but he had the east wind on his tail so he made good time in the end.

"You have to know, I suppose. The Synod convened eight days ago. Our good Himerius has been elected High Pontiff of the Five Kingdoms."

Abeleyn's hand went very still on the water-beaded plumage of the savage bird. "So they did it. They actually elected that slaughter-mongering wolf-livered bastard."

"Guard your words, sire. You speak of the spiritual head of the Ramusian world."

"By the blood of the Saints! Did no one object, Golophin?"

"Merion did, but he's an Antillian of low birth, and thus an outsider. I had thought Heyn of Torunna would also, but he must have been bought off somehow. No doubt Himerius is even now doling out rewards to the faithful who voted him into office."

"And the purges. I take it they will be extended continent-wide."

"Yes, lad. A Pontifical bull is expected within a few weeks. It is a black day for the Dweomer-folk, and for the west."

Abeleyn's face was as white as bone in the scarlet shadow of the tent.

"I will not allow it. The kings will not allow it. I will put it to the conclave that we can not tolerate this interference in the day-to-day running of the state. These people are our subjects; whether the Church considers them heretics or no."

"Careful, lad. There is talk of excommunication in the air at Charibon, and Himerius has the power to issue a bull against you. A heretic king has no right to rule in the eyes of the world."

"Damn them," Abeleyn said through clenched teeth. "Is there nothing an anointed king can do in his kingdom without these God-cursed Ravens meddling in it?"

"It is the Inceptine game, sire. They have been playing it for centuries."

"I will speak to Mark of it. He is a moderate like me. We may not sway Lofantyr of Torunna, for he needs the Knights Militant too badly at the moment, or Haukir of Almark – he is too old, too set in his ways. Cadamost of Perigraine, though. He may be open to reason; he has always struck me as an amenable sort of fellow. What news from the dyke, Golophin? Does it hold?"

"Shahr Baraz's army is finding the passage of the Western Road difficult. The main body has begun to move at last and there is skirmishing at the dyke itself, but so far there has been no major assault. This is old news, sire, gleaned from a colleague of mine. The bird has been too busy in Charibon to have a closer look at the east."

"Of course."

"There is a rumour, though, from Ormann Dyke."

"What? What of it?"

"It is rumoured that Macrobius was not slain in Aekir's fall, that he is alive. As I say, it is a rumour, no more."

"Macrobius alive? No, it's impossible, Golophin! Torunnan wishful thinking."

"Do you want me to look into it, sire?"

Abeleyn paused. "No. I need your feathered alter ego back at Charibon. I must be up to date with developments there when the conclave is assembled. There is no time to chase will-o'-the-wisps in the east."

"Very well, sire."

There was a silence. The gyrfalcon struggled to its taloned feet and shook its wings, spraying water over Abeleyn.

"Will the bird stay here tonight, Golophin?"

"If you please, sire. He needs a rest, and King Mark is on the right route to find you in the morning. I congratulate you on your navigating."

"I spend my life navigating, Golophin, trying to keep the ship of state from foundering."

"Then beware of shoals, my King. They are approaching by the score. Have you heard anything from Fimbria?"

Abeleyn rubbed his eyes, suddenly weary. "Yes. Narbukir is sending an envoy to the conclave. He travels with us, though he wants to remain as low-key as possible. From Fimbria proper there has been no reply to my emissary as yet. I do not honestly expect one, Golophin."

"Do not give up hope, sire. The Fimbrians may yet be the answer to some of our problems. They have never loved the Church; they blame it for their downfall. They would be a powerful ally if the worst happened and Hebrion went its own way."

"You mean if its king were excommunicated and it became an outlawed kingdom, beyond the pale of the Ramusian monarchies?"

"That is a picture I would not care to regard too closely, sire."

"Nor I. I am tired, Golophin, and your magnificent bird seems a little the worse for wear. Maybe we'll both sleep now. I have a perch ready, if it does not object to roosting on the end of a king's bed."

"He – and I – would be honoured, sire."

"My lord King." It was the steward's voice, coming from the other side of the hide partition.

"Yes, Cabran, what is it?"

"The lady Jemilla wonders if you would receive her, sire."

Abeleyn frowned. "No, Cabran. Tell her I am not to be disturbed until morning."

"Yes, sire."

"And Cabran – I am to be wakened the moment King Mark's party is sighted."

"As you wish, sire. Good night."

Some kings and princes had body servants to undress them and prepare them for bed, but Abeleyn preferred to perform those functions himself. He reached under the low cot for the chamber-pot and pissed into it gratefully.

"You brought Jemilla, then," the gyrfalcon said. Odd to hear Golophin's deep tones issue out of the harsh beak, as though the bird had the lips and lungs of a man.

. Abeleyn shoved the steaming pot back under the cot. "Yes. What of it?"

"She has ambitions, that one."

"She will never be my queen, if that's what you're afraid of. She's much too old, and she was married before."

"I think she hopes, sire, in the way women do. Be careful of her. I do not think she is the kind of lady to be discarded lightly."

"*I* will worry about that, Golophin."

"And it is high time you were married yourself. You must be the most eligible bachelor in the Five Kingdoms."

"You sound like a mother goose fussing over her brood, Golophin. You know why I have not married. If I ally myself with one of the other monarchies through a state marriage then I alienate the others –"

"And Hebrion depends on the goodwill of all the kings for the trade that sustains her. I know the arguments, sire, but there is a new one now. You must bind Hebrion to another state if you intend to flout the holy writ of our new Pontiff; you cannot afford to let yourself be isolated. It is something you might bring up with King Mark when you meet."

"What schemes are you hatching now, Golophin?"

"Think of it, sire. An alliance between Astarac and Hebrion, and in between them the neutral state of Fimbria. That would be a bloc that even the Church would think twice before provoking. If you wish to shake free of the Church's authority then you should be thinking of the part of the continent that lies west of the Malvennor Mountains. The western states have always had a reputation for going their own way."

"If certain clerics heard your words, Golophin, you would be a heap of ashes at the foot of a blackened stake."

"If certain clerics saw this talking bird my end would be the same. I no longer have anything to lose and nor have you, sire. Think about what I have said, and if you have to bend a little to avoid becoming a heretic king, then so be it – but make sure that if you cannot bend far enough Hebrion is not left to stand alone."

Abeleyn yawned. "All right, I am convinced. Ah, this mountain air! It makes a man sleepy. Your bird looks shattered, Golophin."

"We both are. The powers of mages are not all they are rumoured to be. This night I feel as old and brittle as a dried leaf. This will be the last you hear from me in a while, Abeleyn. The old man needs his rest."

"So does the King," Abeleyn said, yawning again. "I'd best get some ere King Mark turns up on our doorstep." He lay back on the cot and the falcon flapped and hopped, screaming softly, until it perched on the wooden frame at his feet.

Abeleyn stared at the roof of the heavy tent. The whole structure was swaying and creaking in the wind that was blasting down from the mountains.

"Do you remember the *Blithe Spirit*, Golophin?"

The bird was silent. Abeleyn smiled, putting his hands behind his head.

"I remember the green depths of the Hebrian Sea, and the master pointing out over the ship's rail to where the water turned deeper; that colour, as dark as an old wine. The Great Western Ocean that marks the end of the world.

"We were putting about to steer a course for the Fimbrian Gulf, back to the world of men. I remember the loom of the

Hebros Mountains, like a thin line at the edge of sight. And the coast of Astarac with the shadows of the Malvennors. I remember the smell, Golophin. There is no other smell on earth like it. The smell of the open ocean, and the ship smells.

"Sometimes I wish I could have been a master mariner, carving my own road upon the surface of the world and leaving nothing but a wake of white water behind me. And nothing but a plank of Gabrionese oak between my soul and eternity..."

Abeleyn's eyes were closed. His breathing slowed.

"I wonder if Murad has found his fabled land in the west..." he murmured. His head tilted to one side.

The King slept.

KING MARK OF Astarac and his entourage arrived just before dawn, having travelled through the night in the blinding snowstorm. When the Astaran monarch was shown into Abeleyn's tent his face was grey beneath its mask of ice and frozen snow, and his young man's beard had been frosted white.

Abeleyn had had to struggle up from a great depth, a lightless pit of slumber, but he shrugged off his tiredness and shouted commands at his retinue. Mark had barely two hundred men in his party, and they were taken into the Hebrian tents to save them the labour of erecting their own in the snow-thick gale that still howled about the peaks of the mountains. Servants ran to and fro like men possessed, lighting extra braziers and heaving around platters of food and drink for the cold-blasted men of Astarac. King Mark's bodyguards joined Abeleyn's at the tent entrance, the two groups eyeing each other somewhat askance until some enlightened soul produced a skin of barley spirit and passed it round.

Dressed in dry clothes and seated in front of a glaring brazier, King Mark's face became slowly human again. There was little ceremony between him and Abeleyn; the two men had spent much time together as boys, skylarking at past conclaves whilst their fathers helped decide the fate of the world. Mark had a white gap in one eyebrow where Abeleyn had split his forehead open with a lead-bladed sword. They had shared wenches and wine and were much of an age. Now they sat in Abeleyn's tent companionably enough, and sipped mulled ale and listened to the gradually dying hubbub that the arrival of the Astarans had produced in the Hebrian camp.

Mark nodded to the gyrfalcon that perched with closed eyes on the end of Abeleyn's cot.

"That Golophin's, is it?"

"Aye. Both he and his master are sleeping. He'll be full of life later, no doubt."

Mark grinned, showing strong, even teeth in his square face. "Saffarac has an owl as his familiar. An owl – I ask you! And of course he has it flying in the daytime with never a thought, and the common folk who see it making the sign of the Saint at the bad omen."

They laughed together, and Abeleyn poured out more of the steaming ale for them both.

"You and your men seem to be in a degree of haste, cousin," he said. He and Mark were not related, but kings often used the term, implying that all royalty were somehow akin to each other.

"Indeed, and I'll tell you why. Do you travel with any clerics in your entourage, Abeleyn?"

Abeleyn sipped his ale, grimacing at the heat of it. "Nary a one. I refused every Raven I was offered."

"I thought as much. I'd best warn you then that I have one here clinging to my coattails. He was foisted on me by the College of Bishops, who were outraged at the thought of an Astaran king travelling without a priest to shrive him of his sins every so often."

"An Inceptine?"

"Of course. Just because I was able to get Merion the Antillian elected Prelate doesn't mean I get my way in all affairs ecclesiastical. No, he's a spy, no doubt about it. It's as well that Golophin is not with you, but I wouldn't let anyone catch you talking to your bird if I were you, cousin. What used to be seen as honest thaumaturgy is being transformed into something entirely different in the eyes of the Church."

"This doesn't explain your haste."

"Doesn't it? We've been pushing as hard as this ever since

we left Cartigella; the old crow is near to dropping. With a little luck he'll lose himself in a snowdrift once we get into the mountains proper, and we'll be well rid of his prying beak."

They both roared with laughter.

"Has Saffarac's owl brought you any word of what is going on in the east?" Abeleyn asked when the mirth had faded. Mark's face grew sombre.

"Some word, yes. The Merduk army has stalled, it seems, bogged down by the weather, and Martellus has been sending out reconnaissances in force under the old cavalryman, Ranafast. There has been a good deal of skirmishing, but the Torunnans cannot commit themselves to any large-scale action beyond the Searil. They have not the men. Lofantyr has drawn off all but twelve thousand of the dyke's garrison, the Saints know why."

"He is afraid for his capital. Are there no generals left in Torunna to advise him?"

"The best one, Mogen, died at Aekir and Martellus commands the dyke. There is no one else at that level left in the country. Torunna is bled almost dry."

"Aye, they've been the bulwark of the west for too long, perhaps. Have you heard anything of a rumour concerning Macrobius?"

"That he is alive? Yes, I've heard. My guess is it's a tale set about by Martellus to put some heart into his men. As far as I know there's nothing behind it, but I do know that an old blind man has been paraded before the garrison as the High Pontiff. What the worthies in Charibon will make of that I cannot say. Martellus may be running a fine line on one side of excommunication with his holy impostor."

"Unless –" Abeleyn began.

Mark glanced at him. "No, I cannot believe it. Not one Ramusian of any rank escaped the wreck of Aekir. I cannot conceive that they somehow missed the most important man of all. He would have been the first they would have sought out."

"Of course, of course. What a blessing it would be for the west, though..."

"I take it you're not happy with your fellow Hebrian as High Pontiff."

"He means to excommunicate me, I think, if he cannot geld me first. This is one of the reasons I have asked you to meet me here, cousin."

Mark sat back on his camp chair looking satisfied.

"Aha! I wondered when you'd get round to it."

Abeleyn stared into the steam-wreathed depths of his ale flagon, his dark brows drawn together.

"Golophin's falcon was giving me the old man's advice last night, and it concurred with what I was thinking myself. This is a bad time, Mark – like the chaos of the world when the empire of the Fimbrians began to fall apart, or when the Merduks first invaded, or in the Religious Wars when Ramusio's faith was spread through the west with fire and sword. And I think this time may be the worst of the lot.

"It is not just the Merduks. Theirs is an outside threat, which I believe the west can see off if we cease our squabbling. No, it runs deeper than that. It is the very faith we all believe in, and the men who are the custodians of that faith. They have become princes in their own right, and they are hankering after kingdoms to rule. I tell you – I truly believe, and Golophin does too – that the Inceptines are intent on ruling, and if we let them they will make the monarchs of Normannia into mere ciphers, and they will write their rule in letters of fire and blood clear across the continent."

King Mark was listening intently, but he had an uneasy expression on his face. Abeleyn continued:

"The Inceptines need their wings clipped, and it must be done now or in the very near future. They have trodden on the authority of the rightful rulers of the kingdoms, and they have reduced the other Ramusian religious orders to the level of servants. With Aekir's fall, they have become not less powerful but more so, because of the fear the city's fall has generated in the west. Macrobius was a moderate, Inceptine though he was, but Himerius of Hebrion is a fanatic. He is determined to harness that fear, to be a priest-emperor."

"Oh come now, Abeleyn –"

But the Hebrian King held up a hand. "The contest has already begun. There are two thousand Knights Militant riding towards Hebrion even as we speak. When they arrive, they will instigate a purge the likes of which the west has not seen for centuries. And they wish to do the same in Astarac, in Perigraine, in Almark, even in besieged Torunna. Himerius's insanities are now Church policy, and we can either stand back and let the Ravens do as they will in our kingdoms, or we can stop them."

"And how do we stop them? Do you wish to be excommunicated, Abeleyn, Hebrion labelled a heretic kingdom, shunned by the other monarchies of the west?"

"Hebrion may not have to stand alone," Abeleyn said quietly.

Mark stared at him for a moment, then laughed shortly and stood up. He threw his flagon aside and started pacing up and down on the soft tent floor.

"I know what you are asking, and I tell you I want no part of it."

"Will you hear me out before you start refusing me?" Abeleyn asked irritably.

"What is it you envisage? Astarac and Hebrion standing alone outside the Ramusian world, cut off from the other kingdoms, ostracized? The rest of the Ramusian lands would have to mount a crusade to bring us back within the fold – and this in the midst of an eastern war which may be the climax to Merduk expansion. You are mad, Abeleyn. Such a plan would rip the west apart. I will have no part of it."

"For the Saint's sake, sit down, will you? And listen. Astarac and Hebrion would not be alone."

Mark sat, still visibly sceptical.

"Think, man. What is to the east of Hebrion and the north of Astarac? Fimbria. Fimbria, whose empire fell largely because of the Ramusian religion and the conversions of the Inceptines. The Fimbrians may be believers in the Saint now, but they have no love for the Church. And no alliance would lightly seek to force an armament through their electorates; it would be the one thing guaranteed to reunite them and have the Fimbrian tercios at war again."

"So we have Fimbria as a buffer. But there is always the sea route, Abeleyn. You of all people should know that."

"The four major sea powers of the world are Hebrion, Astarac, Gabrion and the Sea-Merduks."

"And the Macassian corsairs."

"True. And none of them has any love for the Church either. A crusading fleet would have to sail through the Malacar Straits, or detour to the south of Gabrion. The Sea-Merduks would attack any Ramusian naval armament in their waters, as would the corsairs. The Gabrionese would not be happy either. And what was left of it after those nations had mauled it could easily be taken care of by our combined navies."

Mark shook his head. "Ramusian versus Ramusian on a huge scale. I don't like it. It is not right, especially at this time."

"It won't happen, for the reasons I have outlined to you and for others besides."

"Tell me the others, then," Mark said wearily.

"I believe that if we can reinforce Torunna sufficiently then we will nullify Lofantyr's reliance on the Knights Militant. Perigraine may well follow the lead of Torunna and Almark will then be isolated, even if it has the support of Finnmark and the northern duchies. What will the Church do – excommunicate half the monarchs of Normannia? I think not. The power of the Inceptines will be broken, and we can promote another order in their place. The Antillians, perhaps."

Mark chuckled. "Divide and conquer? But what you are advocating could very well lead to a religious schism of the west. Almark is virtually governed by the Inceptines, and their influence runs deep in Perigraine also. Those bastions will not be easy to reduce."

Abeleyn flapped a hand casually. "Haukir of Almark is an old man. He will not last for ever. And Cadamost of Perigraine is a lightweight, easily swayed."

Mark was silent for a moment, then said: "How much of this do you intend to outline to the other kings at the conclave?"

"Very little. But I do want to go to the conclave with one or two weapons in my belt."

"Such as?" asked Mark, though he already knew.

"Such as a formal alliance between Hebrion and Astarac."

"And how do you propose to formalize it?"

"By marrying your sister."

The two kings stared at one another, wary, gauging. Finally a grin broke out on Mark's broad face.

"So the mighty tree is felled at last. Abeleyn the Bachelor King will finally consent to share his bed with a wife. She is not pretty, my sister."

"If she brings the friendship of a kingdom with her she can be as plain as a frog for all I care. What say you, Mark?"

The Astaran king shook his head ruefully. "You are a cunning dog, Abeleyn, to sweeten the bitterness of your pill thus. You know that half the kings in the west seek an alliance with Hebrion for the trade privileges it would bring, and now you throw it in my lap. But at what a cost!"

"I also have a certain influence with the corsairs who infest your southern coast," Abeleyn remarked.

"Oh, I know! Many's the Astaran cargo that has ended up on the wharves of Abrusio. You'd help curtail their depredations on your brother-in-law's ships, then?"

"Perhaps."

"An alliance. Where would it end, Abeleyn? I can see what you are doing – forming a trading block in the west of the continent that can remain self-supporting even if it becomes outcast from the rest of the Five Kingdoms. Even if it means increased trade with the Sea-Merduks. And you will hold this over the heads of the other kings like a cleaver over the neck of a lamb. Yet it is not lambs we are dealing with, cousin, but wolves."

"Which is why we must move quickly, and with sufficient might to force the issue. If you and I can go to the conclave already allied and say to the other kings, 'Look, this is the way things will be,' they should be startled enough to pay some attention to our ideas. And if you can promise help to Torunna also, why then I think we have them."

"If I can promise help?"

"Why, yes. You are closer to the dyke than I. You could have the place reinforced within two months by land or half that by sea, if you had a mind to."

"And if the place is still standing by that time."

"True. But the gesture is everything. Lofantyr will be grateful, and will not have to be so reliant on the soldiery of the Church. He will be his own man again."

"You mean he will be our man."

Abeleyn smiled. "Perhaps," he said again.

"My sister's dowry may yet cost me my throne," Mark muttered.

"Will you agree, then? Think of the opportunities, Mark! Our combined fleets would be irresistible. We might even clear Macassar of the corsairs entirely and make it into Rovenan again, your lost province."

"Don't seek to convince me with pipe dreams, Abeleyn. I must think about this."

"Do not take too long."

"My advisers will throw themselves into fits when the news gets back to the court."

"Not necessarily. All they need to know is that you have finally succeeded in wooing Hebrion. There should be no trouble from that quarter so long as they do not know the whole story."

Mark contemplated Abeleyn's face. "We have been friends for a long time, you and I, insofar as monarchs can ever be friends. I pray to the Saints that I do not let that friendship cloud my thinking now. I like you, Abeleyn. It is our mutual esteem that has brought an end to the endless raiding and rivalry that plagued our two kingdoms from time immemorial. But I tell you this as Astarac's king: if you play me false, or if I find that you intend to use Astarac as Hebrion's workhorse, then I will annul our alliance in the blink of an eye, and I will be in the first rank of those who bay for your blood."

"I would do likewise, were I Astarac's king," Abeleyn said gently.

"So be it." Mark stood up and held out a brawny hand. Abeleyn rose also and took it, face grave. Mark topped him by half a head, but he did not feel the smaller man.

"Come," said Mark. "Let us sniff the air. My head is full of the fumes of ale and coal."

They slipped out of the tent together, the bodyguards at the entrance snapping to attention as they appeared. Their fire had burned down low and the men were stamping their feet and flapping their arms. Mark and Abeleyn dismissed them and stood alone. As one, they walked out to the edge of the camp where the ground fell away in a gentle curve of white to the lower land below. They trudged through knee-deep snow, bound by some mutual arrangement, until they could hear the tiny rill and trickle of water. The Arcolm river. When they found it, they each stood on one side: one man in Astarac, the other in Narboskan Fimbria.

The sun was beginning to top the mountains so the Malvennors were a huge soundless silhouette of shadow. Behind them the sky was brightening and glowing a delicate lilac, whilst over the highest of the peaks wisps of cloud caught fire from the sun and blazed in a glory of saffron and gold.

"Our path will be a hard one," Mark said quietly.

"Aye. But men have trod it before, and no doubt will again. And these mountains will see other sunrises, other kings making bargains in their shadow. It is the way of the world."

"Abeleyn, the Philosopher King," Mark said with gentle mockery.

Abeleyn grinned, but when he spoke again his voice was serious.

"We have the luck or the misfortune to be part of the forces which shape the fate of the world, Mark. We have a conversation over a flagon of ale and lo! History is changed. Sometimes I think about it."

He fumbled in his fur-lined robes and produced a small silver flask. He unscrewed the top, which transformed into two tiny, gleaming cups.

"Here. We'll seal our history shaping with a little wine."

"I hope it's good," Mark said. "We must toast the alliance of Astarac and Hebrion in the finest you possess."

"Good enough."

They raised their cups to each other and drank, two kings sealing a bargain, whilst above them the sun broke out over the peaks of the mountains and bathed them both in blood.

FIFTEEN

28TH DAY OF Forlion, Year of the Saint 551.

Wind NNW, backing. Light airs. Course due west with the wind on the starboard bow. Two knots.

Sighted North Cape at two bells in the first dog-watch on this, the seventh day out of Abrusio harbour. At three bells the lead found white sand at forty fathoms. Changed course to due west, remaining on the same latitude. Bespoke a Brenn Isle herrin yawl and purchased three hundredweight of fish. Hands employed about the ship. Brother Ortelius preached a sermon in the afternoon watch and afterward the soldiers had small-arms practice. First Mate Billerand ran out the guns in the last dog-watch and called all hands for gunnery practice. Gunner reported to me that number two larboard gun is honeycombed.

Hawkwood laid down his quill and stretched his arms behind him until the muscles cracked. If he looked up he could see out of the stern windows to where the wake of the ship was faintly phosphorescent in the dimming light of the evening. There was very little swell; they had been plagued by light winds since leaving Hebrion and had not made good time, but he was pleased with the performance of the crew and of the ship herself. Though inclined to be sluggish with the extra cargo on board, the *Osprey* could still eat the wind out of any other carrack of her tonnage. Hawkwood was convinced it was because of her peculiar design, which he had supervised himself. Her fore- and sterncastles were lower than in other ships of her class, which meant they took less of the wind, and they were structures built as an integral part of the main hull, not tacked on afterwards. There were drawbacks, of course. There was less space on board, and she might be more vulnerable to boarding; but his crews knew their gunnery. The ship's culverins would riddle any enemy vessel long before she drew close enough to board.

The *Grace* was a different matter. Haukal had had to take in canvas to avoid outpacing the carrack entirely, though Hawkwood knew he chafed at the slow progress and longed to break out his whole store of lateen sails and plough ahead. At this moment the caravel was under main course alone, bobbing along some four cables to starboard. This beam wind suited her admirably, though she had yards enough down in her hold to transform her into a square-rigged ship should the wind veer round and come from right aft.

Little chance of that. They would be sailing close to the wind in more ways than one for nearly all of this voyage, if the word of long-dead Tyrenius Cobrian was to be believed.

Well, they had hit upon North Cape, as pretty a sighting as could be wished for. All Hawkwood had to do in theory was steer due west until he bumped into the Western Continent. It sounded simple, but there were the winds to take into account, ocean currents, storms or doldrums. He and Haukal both took sightings of the North Star every night with their cross-staffs and compared notes afterwards, but Hawkwood still felt that the ships were sailing in the dark. True, he had the baldly summarized sailing instructions that Murad had copied out of the old rutter for him, but he needed more. He needed to read the account of the *Cartigellan Faulcon*'s crossing. He admitted to himself that he needed reassurance, the account of another seaman's accomplishment of what he was attempting to do. He also knew that Murad was concealing something, something to do with the fate of the earlier voyage. The knowledge maddened him.

He stood up from his desk, long accustomed to the slight roll and pitch of the ship, and extinguished the single candle which lit his cabin. Fire was one of the most dreaded accidents aboard ship, and the use of naked flame was carefully regulated. Only in the galley was any cooking permitted, and only on the forecastle could the soldiers and sailors smoke their pipes. There were sea lanterns hanging in serried rows in the crowded filth of the gundeck for the passengers' comfort, but these were the responsibility of the master-at-arms and his mates. The kegs which contained the powder both for the ship's guns and the soldiers' arquebuses were stored below the waterline in a tin-lined room so that the rats might not gnaw at them, and no naked light was permitted in there. A tiny pane of double glass allowed the powder store to be illuminated from outside, and only the gunner had access to the interior.

And what a hullabaloo that had caused! Soldiers! They had moaned and bitched about not being able to get at their ammunition quickly enough, about not being able to smoke their pipes in the comfort of their hammocks, about not being able to prepare their own food in their own messes as they were used to. And Murad had not helped. He had insisted that his food and that of his officers be prepared separately from the men's and served at a different time, doubling the workload of the ship's cook. And the delicacies he had laid in by way of private stores! There were fully two tons of foodstuff in the hold that were for the exclusive consumption of Murad and his two officers. It beggared belief. And those damn horses! One was dead already, having gone mad in its cramped stall and thrashed about until it had broken its leg. That aristocratic young ensign, Sequero, had almost been in tears as he had cut its throat. The sailors had jointed the animal and salted down the meat despite the protestations of the soldiers. The cooper had barrelled it and placed it in the hold. Those same soldiers might be glad of it ere they saw land again.

Hawkwood made his unlit way out of his cabin, stepping over the storm sill with the grace of habit and exiting the companionway to enter the fresh air of the evening. He ran up the ladder to the quarterdeck where Velasca, the second mate, had the watch. The hourglass ran out, the ship's boy turned it, then stepped forward to the break of the deck and rang the ship's bell twice. Two bells in the last dog-watch, or the seventh hour after the zenith to a landsman.

"All quiet, Velasca?"

"Aye, sir. There are a few souls puking over the larboard rail, but most of 'em are below preparing for dinner."

Hawkwood nodded. Even in the failing light he could make out the wisps of smoke from the galley chimney drifting off to leeward.

Velasca cleared his throat. "I've had a deputation from the soldiers come to see me this watch, sir."

"Another one? What did they want this time?"

"They don't like the idea of a priest berthing in the forecastle with the common sailors, sir. They think he should be aft with the officers."

"There's no room aft, unless he cares to sling his hammock in my chartroom. No, we didn't ask for a Raven on board so he must make the best of it. Trust an Inceptine to put the common soldiers up to intercede for him."

"Oh, they say he hasn't said a word, sir. He seems to be a kindly enough sort of fellow for one of his order. They took it upon themselves to ask."

"Well they can take it upon themselves to keep their mouths shut, or go through their own officers. The running of the ship is difficult enough as it is without playing runaround with the assigned quarters."

"Yes, sir."

"How's the wind?"

"Light as a baby's fart, sir. Still nor'-nor'-west, though it's showing signs of backing to nor'-west."

"I hope not. We're close-hauled enough as it is. I'll take the watch now if you like, Velasca. I'm as restless as a springtime bear. Get yourself below and grab some food."

"Aye, sir, thanks. Shall I have the cook send something up?"

"No, I'll survive."

Velasca left the deck, Hawkwood having relieved him an hour early.

The carrack sailed on as the first stars came out to brighten the sky. There would be a moon later on; it was near the full, but the wind was fitful and wayward. The *Osprey* was under courses and topsails, the courses bonneted, but Hawkwood guessed she was making less than three knots. A peaceful evening, though. He could hear the growing hubbub from belowdecks as the passengers assembled for the evening meal, and light poured out in shafts from the gunports. They kept them open most of the time these nights, for ventilation.

He heard the clink of glass and laughter from the officers' cabins below his feet: Murad entertaining again. The scar-faced nobleman had even invited Ortelius, the last-minute Inceptine, to dinner a few times. Primarily, Hawkwood thought, to interrogate him as to his reasons for joining the ship. Someone high up in the Inceptines of Abrusio had ordered him to, that was clear, but so far Ortelius had deflected all Murad's enquiries.

He was being watched. Turning, Hawkwood caught Mateo, the ship's boy, staring at him. He frowned and Mateo looked away hurriedly. The boy's voice was breaking; soon he would be a man. He no longer held any temptation for Hawkwood, not with the sneering Murad and an Inceptine on board. No doubt the lad was hurt by Hawkwood's curt treatment of him, but he would get over it.

Unwillingly Hawkwood found himself thinking of Jemilla, her white skin and raven-dark hair, her wildcat passions. She was a king's plaything now, not for the likes of himself any more. He wondered if King Abeleyn of Hebrion had scratches on his back under his regal robes. The world was a strange place sometimes.

He paced his way to the weather rail, and stood there gazing out on the even swell of the quiet sea whilst the breeze fanned his face and pushed at the towering canvas above his head.

"YOU'RE NOT WAITING on the high table tonight, then?" Bardolin asked as Griella joined him at the swaying, rope-suspended table.

The girl sat on the sea chest next to him. Her colour was up, and her coppery hair clung to her forehead in wires and tails.

"No. Mara said she would do it for me. I can't stick the thought of it tonight."

Bardolin said nothing. Around them the hubbub of the gundeck was like a curtain of noise. In between the dull gleam of the long guns, hanging tables had been let down from the ceiling (what was the nautical term, deckhead?) and around each of these a motley crowd of figures jostled and elbowed for space. Each table seated six, and one person from each took it in turns to bring the food for the table down the length of the deck from the steaming galley.

This was the first night Bardolin had seen it as full as this; most of the passengers seemed to be getting over their sea-sickness, especially as the weather was mild and the ship's movement not too severe. They were an odd mix. He could see men in fine robes, some of whom he recognized as figures at the Hebrian court, and ladies in brocade and linen – even here clinging to their past status – but the majority looked like well-to-do merchants or small artisans with nothing remarkable about them. There had as yet been no manifestation of power, and he did not know if there might be a weather-worker on board to speed the passage of the ships. Probably the presence of the Inceptine had put the captain off from enquiring.

Neither did he know if there was another full-blooded mage on board, for he had as yet seen no other familiars in evidence and his own imp was asleep in the bosom of his robe. He and Golophin were not, of course, the only mages in Abrusio; Bardolin was personally acquainted with another half-dozen. But he saw none that he knew here, and wondered if Golophin had had other plans for them.

The air was heavy and thick, hanging around the brutal great guns and the laden tables. Bardolin could smell the aroma of the cooking pork, heavy with grease and salt, and around that the sweat of close-packed humanity. Underlying these was a faint stink of vomit and ordure. Not all the passengers possessed the necessary spirit to crouch out on the beakhead of the ship and perform their necessary functions there, with the warm sea lapping at their arse. And there had been those who had surrendered to seasickness a mite more violently than they had expected. The deck would have to be washed out, or swabbed down, but that was the sailors' job.

Oh, such a rich web woven by unknown forces! They were not a ship sailing serenely across a placid ocean, they were a fly caught quivering in a vast spider's web. And that nobleman, Murad, he was one of the spinners of the web, along with Golophin and the King of Hebrion.

But not Hawkwood, the captain. He and Murad loathed each other, that was plain. Bardolin got the impression that their good captain was about as enthusiastic for the voyage as the majority of his passengers were. He must know their destination; it might be worth talking to him, or to Billerand.

"HE HAS INVITED that Raven to his table yet again," Griella was saying between gulped mouthfuls of the tough pork and hard biscuit.

"Who, Murad?" Bardolin marshalled his thoughts hurriedly.

Griella had a light in her eye that he did not like. He had already cursed himself a score of times for bringing her with him on this voyage. And yet – and yet...

"Yes. He means to ply him with brandy once more and find out who ordered him to take ship with us. But Ortelius is as slippery as an eel. He smiles and smiles and says nothing of import, just mouths saintly platitudes that no one can disagree with. There is something about him I truly do not like."

"Naturally enough. He's an Inceptine, child. There is nothing strange about your dislike of him."

"No, it is something more. I feel I know him, but I cannot think how."

Bardolin sighed. He was no longer hungry. His stomach had been used to such rough fare in his youth; it had grown dainty with age. And this was the good stuff. Later in the voyage their meat would be wormy and their bread full of weevils, while the water would be as thick as soup. He had endured it once before, on a Hebrian troop transport. He was not looking forward to undergoing such a diet again.

I've become soft, he thought.

"Don't worry about the damned Inceptine, girl," he said. "He cannot touch you here, unless he means to take on all the passengers of the ship by himself."

But Griella was not listening. Her fingers had curled into claws around her meat knife.

"Murad will ask for me again tonight, Bardolin. I cannot put him off much longer without – without something happening."

She was staring into her wooden platter as though its contents were the stuff of an augury. Bardolin leaned close to her.

"I beg you, Griella, commit no violence aboard this ship. Do not. Do not let your emotions overcome your reason, and do not lift a finger against him. He is a nobleman. He would be within his rights to slay you out of hand."

Griella grinned without humour. Her teeth were strong and very white, the lips almost purple against them.

"He might find that difficult."

"You might kill him." Bardolin's voice had dropped. It was almost inaudible in the clatter about them. "But even with the change upon you, you would find it hard to kill all the soldiers on this ship, and the sailors, and the passengers who would stand against you. And once your nature is revealed, Griella, you are lost, so for the Saint's sake rein in your temper, no matter what happens."

She kissed him on the mouth without warning, so hard that he felt the imprint of the teeth behind her lips. He felt his face flush with blood and the immediate stir of warmth in his groin. The imp moved restlessly in the breast of his robe.

"Why did you do that?" he asked her when she drew back. He was uncomfortably aware of the erection throbbing in his breeches.

"Because you wanted me to. You have wanted me to this long time, even if you did not know it."

He could not answer her.

"It's all right, Bardolin. I don't mind. I love you, you see. You are like a father and a brother and a friend to me."

She stroked the stubble of his ruddy cheek.

"You are right, though. Everyone knows you are my guardian. Were I to refuse him, I might be damning you along with myself and I would never do that." She smiled as sunnily as a child. Only her eyes mocked the image. He could see the beast in them, forever biding its time.

Bardolin took her hand, heedless of the stares they were attracting from their neighbours at the table.

"Hold fast, Griella, no matter what happens. Hold fast to that part of yourself that is not the animal; then you can beat it down; you can defeat it."

She blinked. "Why would I want to do that?" Then she flashed a feral grin at him and rose, her hand slipping out from under his. "I must go. Mara expects me to help her clear up. Dear Bardolin, don't look so worried! I know what I have to do – for your sake as well as mine."

Bardolin watched her slim, straight back as it moved down the gundeck and was finally lost in the crowd. His face was profoundly troubled, and the imp was trembling like a leaf against the slick sweat on his chest.

"MORE BRANDY FOR the good cleric there, girl. Don't be shy with the stuff!"

Murad was smiling, his scar a wriggling pink furrow down one side of his face. When the girl Mara bent to pour the brandy he slid a hand under her robe, up the satin-smooth back of her leg. She twitched like a horse with a fly settling on it, but did not move away. He tweaked the soft flesh where the buttock swelled out at the top of her thigh. Then she straightened as if nothing were amiss and moved away. Di Souza was red in the face with glee, but Sequero looked merely disdainful. Murad smiled at him and raised his glass so the aristocratic young man had to follow suit.

The four of them were seated around a table which ran fore and aft along the line of the keel. At Murad's back were the stern windows which he shared with the captain's cabin on the other side of the thin bulkhead. The eastern sky was black, but there was a glimmer from the ship's wake as it foamed and churned behind them. They could see the level of wine in the decanters arrayed about the table tilt slightly with the carrack's roll, but it was so slight as to be hardly noticeable.

Sequero was still out of sorts at the death of one of his beloved broodmares. A good thing they had shipped two more than originally planned. He was not a natural shipboard companion, was Ensign Hernan Sequero. He hated the cheek-by-jowl promiscuity, the awkward hammocks, the continual stench, and especially the stubborn independence of the mariners, who looked to their own officers alone and obeyed the order of no soldier. It was an inversion of the natural order of things. His plight had provided Murad with endless private amusement in the week they had been at sea.

Di Souza, on the other hand, seemed to relish the entire experience. His prowess with an arquebus had won him the respect of soldiers and sailors alike, and his low birth seemed to have inured him to the indignities of life aboard ship. He could laugh when shitting from the ship's head, whilst Murad suspected that Sequero performed his own functions in the depths of the hold rather than let his men see their officer hanging bare-arsed over the sea. Murad himself had a pot, emptied daily by one of his two cabin servants.

He studied the amber depths of his brandy in the light of the table lanterns. Fimbrian, casked in the time of his great-grandfather. And here he was wasting it on a low-born buffoon, a cleric and a tight-arsed minor noble. Well, it oiled the tongues. It let the evening slip along pleasantly enough. But it did not help loosen the lips of the damned Raven, Ortelius.

The girl, Mara, retrieved the dinner dishes and the silver cutlery that glittered the length of the table. They had dined on potted meat, freshly killed chicken, fish caught that morning and fruit from the orchards of Galiapeno. Now they sipped their brandy, cracked walnuts and popped black olives into their mouths. There was little conversation. The two junior officers did not like to speak without being spoken to first whilst at their superior officer's table, and the Inceptine seemed to value silence as much as his own discretion.

Murad would have to invite Hawkwood to dinner one night along with the Raven, and then watch the sparks fly. By the looks of things there would be little else in the way of amusement this voyage, and he would have to be inventive if he were not to expire of boredom before they made landfall in the west.

He caught the girl looking at him and stared back blandly until her eyes darted away. She had a pleasant peasant-brown face surrounded by a mass of dark curls, and her body was stocky and strong but not overly exciting. She had shared his hanging cot ever since leaving Abrusio, but she was not the one he was truly hungering for. That short-haired, snapping-eyed wench named Griella; she was the one he wanted. It would be diverting to break her in, and he was curious to see what kind of shape hid under those boyish clothes she wore. She hated him too, which was even better. Where was she tonight? Her absence irritated him, which was one of the reasons for the fear in the other girl's eyes.

"A capital brandy," Ortelius said in the silence. "You keep a good cellar even while afloat, Lord Murad."

Murad inclined his head. "There are certain luxuries which are not in fact luxuries, but more... accessories of rank. We may not need them, but they serve to remind us of who we are."

Ortelius nodded gravely. "Just so long as we do not find we cannot do without them."

"You have precious few luxuries with you on this voyage, I fear," Murad said sympathetically, though inwardly he was seething at the cleric's implication.

"Yes. I came aboard in some haste, I am afraid. But it is no matter. I may not have the austere habits of a Friar Mendicant, but it will do me no harm to forgo some of the prerequisites of my rank for a time. Such things bring us closer to God." He tossed back the last of his brandy.

"Of course, admirable," Murad said absently. He was searching for an opening, a chink in the Inceptine's bland manner. He saw Sequero and di Souza exchange glances; they knew the nightly game had started again.

"Well, we are in your spiritual charge, Father Ortelius. I am sure I speak for all the soldiers and mariners and common folk aboard when I say we shall rest easier knowing that you are here to shrive us of our sins and to watch over our moral welfare. But tell me what do you think of the worthy crews who maintain these ships, or indeed of the passengers with whom you have taken ship?"

Ortelius looked at him, his normally urbane countenance twisting with what seemed like a spot of wariness.

"I'm not sure I follow you, my son."

"Oh come now, Father! Surely you must have noticed that half of Hawkwood's crew have faces as black as apes. They are heathens – Merduks!"

"Are you sure, my son?" Ortelius had stopped playing with his empty glass and was watching Murad closely, like a fencer waiting for the change of balance that heralded a thrust.

"Why, yes! Some of them are black worshippers of the evil prophet Ahrimuz."

"Then I must do my humble best to show them the true and righteous path to the Company of the Saints," Ortelius said sweetly.

But Murad went on as if the priest had not spoken.

"And the passengers, Father. Do you know who they are? I'll tell you. They are the dregs of our society. They are sorcerers, herbalists, oldwives and even, God save us, mages. Didn't you know?"

"I – I may have heard something to that effect."

"Indeed, the very type of folk that the Inceptines have so industriously been ridding Abrusio of for these past weeks. Yet now you take ship with them, you sleep in their midst, and you minister to their so-called spiritual needs. Forgive me for saying so, Father, but I find it difficult to comprehend why a man like you should have taken it upon himself to associate with such fellow travellers. We know the vocation of the Friars Mendicant is to proselytize and convert, to spread the news of the Visions of the First Saint, but surely the Inceptines are rather loftier in the Church's hierarchy."

Murad let the unspoken question hang in the air.

"We go where we are sent, Lord Murad. We are all servants, we wearers of the black robe."

"Ah, so you were *sent* to join us?"

"No. I have used that word clumsily. You must excuse me."

"Either you were sent or you were not, Father. Do have some more brandy, by the way."

Murad poured the cleric more of the Fimbrian whilst his two ensigns looked on like spectators at a gladiatorial contest. Sequero seemed amused and fascinated, but Murad was surprised to see a look of downright terror on di Souza's face.

"Are you all right, Valdan?" he asked at once. "A touch of seasickness, perhaps?"

The straw-haired officer shook his head. He was like a man going to the gallows.

"As I was saying," Murad said smoothly, turning to the cleric, "either you were *sent*, Father, or you came of your own accord. Or someone asked you to join our company."

Here he stared back at di Souza, reading the young man's suffused face and letting his last sentence hang in the air.

"I asked him to come!" di Souza blurted out. "It was me, sir – my idea alone. The soldiers wanted a chaplain. I asked Father Ortelius. I thought I did right, sir, upon mine honour!"

Murad glanced around the table. Ortelius was delicately wiping his lips with a napkin, eyes cast down and countenance serene once again. Sequero's face was wooden, as if he feared to be associated with di Souza's guilt by his proximity to his brother officer.

Murad laughed. "Well, why did you not say so?" He stood up. "I am sorry to have tried your patience thus these last few days, Father. Please forgive me." And he bent to kiss the priest's knuckle.

Ortelius beamed. "That is quite all right, my son."

"And with this revelation I am afraid I must end our delightful evening, gentlemen. I would like to retire. Good night, Father. I hope you have a pleasant sleep. Sequero, good evening. You will see Father Ortelius to his hammock, I am sure. Ensign di Souza, stay behind a moment, if you please."

When the other two had left di Souza sat stiffly in his chair with his hands in his lap.

"Talk to me, Ensign," Murad said softly.

The younger man's slab-like face was shining with sweat. His skin was red with wine and heat, contrasting vividly with his yellow hair.

"The men did not like the idea of sailing without a chaplain, as I said once before to you sir, I think."

"Did Mensurado put you up to this?" Murad interrupted.

"No, sir! It was my idea alone." Had di Souza placed the blame on his sergeant, Mensurado, Murad would have been forced to have the man strappadoed, or perhaps shot. And Mensurado was the most experienced soldier on the ship.

"How well do you know this Ortelius?"

Di Souza's eyes flickered up and met Murad's steady glare for a second. He seemed to shrink in his chair.

"Not well, sir. I know he was once on the staff of the Prelate of Hebrion, and is well thought of in the order."

"And why should such a distinguished cleric take ship with an expedition into the unknown and with such travelling companions, eh?"

Di Souza shrugged helplessly. "He is a priest. It is his job. When he shrove me before we took ship he seemed to know about the voyage. He asked if I was at ease at the thought of undertaking it with no spiritual guide. I was not, sir – I tell the truth. He volunteered to come, but I thought he was only trying to comfort my wretched soul. I did not think he truly meant what he said."

"You have a lot to learn, Valdan," Murad said. "Ortelius is a spy in the pay of Himerius the Prelate of Hebrion. He has come along to see what the King is up to, commissioning this expedition, and with such passengers. But no matter. I know him now for what he is, and can deal with him accordingly."

"Sir! You're not going to –"

"Shut up, Valdan. You are a stupid young fool. I could have you stripped of rank and put in irons for the rest of the voyage for what you have taken upon yourself to do. But I need you. I will tell you one thing you had best remember, though."

Murad leaned close until he could smell the brandy on his subordinate's breath.

"Your loyalty will be to *me*, and no one else. Not to the Church, not to a priest, not to your own mother. You will look to me for everything. If you do not your career is over, and mayhap your life as well. Do I make myself clear?"

"Yes," di Souza croaked.

Murad smiled. "I am glad you understand. You are dismissed."

The ensign got up out of his chair like an arthritic man, saluted and then bolted out of the door. Murad sat down in his own chair and propped his feet on the table. He turned his head to stare out aft at the ship's wake. No sign of land. The Hebrionese were already out of sight, which meant they were at last truly in the Great Western Ocean.

And no one can touch us, Murad thought. *Not kings, not priests, not the machinations of government. Until one of these ships returns, we are alone and no one can find us.*

He remembered the log of Tyrenius Cobrian, the dark story of slaughter and madness that it told, and felt a chill of unease.

"Wine!" he called loudly.

When he turned back from his contemplation of the stern windows he found that the wine was already on the table, glowing as red as blood in its decanter with one remaining table lantern burning behind it.

The girl, Griella. She stood in the shadows. He knew her by the absurd breeches she wore, the bob of hair. And the peculiar shine of her eyes which always reminded him of a beast's seen by torchlight.

Murad was momentarily startled by her silent presence; he had not heard a sound. He poured himself some of the luminous wine.

"Come into the light, girl. I won't bite you."

She moved forward, and her eyes became human again. She regarded him with a detached interest that never failed to infuriate him. He had to bed her, impress his presence and superiority upon her. Her skin had a kind of light about it, emphasized by the lantern. In the neck of her shirt he could see the swell of one slight breast, that curve of light and shadow.

"Take off my boots," he said brusquely.

She did as she was bidden, kneeling before him and slipping the long sea boots off his legs with a strength that surprised him. He could see down the neck of her shirt. He sipped wine steadily.

"You will share my bed tonight," he said.

She stared at him.

"There will be no excuses. The blood will have stopped by now, and if it has not I care not. Stand up."

She did so.

"Why do you not speak? Have you nothing to say? A few nights ago you were as livid as a cat. Have you reconciled yourself to your newfound station? Speak to me!"

Griella watched him, a small smile turning up one corner of her mouth.

"You are a noble," she said. "On this ship your word is the law. I have no choice."

"That's right," he sneered. "Has your ageing guardian been talking some sense into your pretty little head, then?"

"Yes, he has."

"A wise man, obviously." Why did he feel that she was getting the better of him, that she was secretly laughing at him? He wanted to kiss that smile off her ripe young mouth, bruise it away with his teeth.

"Remove your clothes," he said. He drank more wine. His heartbeat was beginning to become an audible thing, hammering in his temples.

She slipped her shirt off over her head, then unfastened her belt and let her breeches slip to the deck. As she stood before him naked he distinctly heard the ship's bell being struck eight times. Eight bells in the first watch. Midnight. It was like a warning.

Murad stood up, towering over her. She was golden in the lantern light before his shadow covered her. He brushed her nipples and heard the breath sucked down her throat. He grinned, happy at having punctured her weird composure. Then he bent his head and crushed his mouth on hers.

AFTERWARDS, HE REMEMBERED how slight she had seemed in his arms, how slim and hard and alive. She was taut with muscle, every nerve jumping on the surface of her skin.

She had been virgin, too, but had not cried out as he entered her, merely flinching for a second. He remembered the hot, liquid sensation, the way he pressed her down into the blankets and bit at her neck and shoulder, her breasts. She had lain quiet under him until something kindled her. Unwillingly she had moved and begun to make small sounds. Then the coupling had transformed into a battle, a fight for mastery. Joined together, their bodies had struggled against one another until her scream had rung out and she had scissored her legs about him and wept furiously in the darkness. They had slept after that, spent, their bodies glued together by sweat and the fluid of their exertions. It had been strangely peaceful, like the truce after two armies had battled each other into exhaustion.

He had woken in the dark hour before the dawn – or thought he had. He could not breathe. He was suffocating in a baking, furnace heat and his lungs were being constricted by a crippling weight. Something huge and heavy was lying atop him, pinioning his limbs. He had opened his eyes, feeling hot breath on his face, and had seen two yellow lights regarding him from six inches away. The cold gleam of teeth. A vague impression of two horn-like ears arcing up from a broad, black-furred skull. And the paralysing heat and weight of it on his body.

He had passed out, or the dream had faded. He woke later, after sunrise, with a scream on his lips – but found himself alone in the gently swaying cot, sunlight streaming in the stern windows, a patch of blood on the blankets. He drew in shuddering breaths. A dream or nightmare, nothing more. It could be nothing more.

He swung off the cot on to rubber legs. The ship was rolling more heavily, the bow rising and falling. He could see white-topped waves breaking in the swell beyond the windows.

It took the last pint in the wine decanter to quell the trembling in his hands, to wipe out the horror of the dream. When it had faded all he could remember was the taut joy of her under him, the unwilling surrender. Strangely, he did not feel triumphant at the memory, but quickened, somehow invigorated.

By the time he had broken his fast, he had forgotten the vision of the night entirely. Too much brandy and wine, perhaps. All he could think of was the slim girl and her bright eyes, the taut joy of her under him.

He hungered for more.

SIXTEEN

THE MERDUK ARMY was on the move.

It had taken time; far too much time, Shahr Baraz thought. Aekir had damaged them more than they had cared to admit at the time, but now many of their losses had been made good. Fresh troops had been sent through the Thurian passes before the snows closed them for the winter, and Maghreb, Sultan of Danrimir, had sent fifty elephants and eight thousand of his personal guard to join the taking of Ormann Dyke. It was a gesture as much as anything else, with the inevitable political ramifications behind it. The other sultans had sat up quickly when Aekir had fallen, and soon the scramble for the spoils would begin. Shahr Baraz had heard camp rumours that ancient Nalbeni, not to be outdone by its northern rival, had commissioned a fleet of troop transports to cross the Kardian Sea and fall on the southern coastal cities of Torunna. That snippet made him smile. With luck, it had already reached the ears of the Torunnan king and might make him detach troops from the north.

Shahr Baraz had no illusions as to the difficulty of the task before him. He had maps of the fortress complex, made by the troopers of the countless armed reconnaissances he had sent west. The Fimbrians had first built the dyke, and as with everything they constructed it had been built to last. His distant ancestors had attacked it once, way back in the mists of tribal memory when it had marked the boundary of the Fimbrian Empire. They had died in their screaming thousands, it was said, and their bodies had filled to the brim the dyke itself.

But that was then. This was now. One of the reasons the Merduk advance had been so slow to recommence after the fall of Aekir was because he had had his engineers at work day and night. The results of their labour had been dismantled and loaded on to gargantuan waggons, each pulled by four elephants. Now he had everything he needed: siege-towers, catapults, ballistae. And boats. Many boats.

He sat on his horse on a low muddy hill with a gaggle of staff officers about him and his bodyguard in silent ranks on the slope below. He watched his army trudging past.

Outriders on the flanks, squadrons of light cavalry armed with lances and wearing only leather *cuir boulli*, something they had picked up from the Ramusians. Then the main vanguard, a picked force of the *Hraibadar*, the shock-troops who specialized in assaults, breachings and, if necessary, last stands. Their ranks were thinner than they had been – so many had fallen at Aekir that he was pressed to field more than ten regiments of them, scarcely twelve thousand men.

Trundling through their ranks were the dotted bulk of elephants. Only a score of them travelled with the van, and each pulled a train of light waggons loaded with provisions. The vanguard was Shahr Baraz's most mobile force, and his most hard-hitting. It would spearhead the final assault, once he had softened the dyke up a little.

At the rear of the van, a brigade of heavy cavalry, what the Ramusians called *cuirassiers*. They were known as *Ferinai* to his own people, who had specialized in their use for generations. They wore chainmail reinforced with glittering plates of steel, and their faces were covered by tall helms. In addition to their swords they each carried a pair of matchlock pistols, a recent innovation that the *Ferinai* had accepted only with much grumbling. These were the best troops that Shahr Baraz possessed; his own bodyguard had been picked mainly from their ranks. They were professional soldiers, unlike the majority of the army, and their general was as niggardly with them as a miser with his gold.

The van passed by, almost twenty thousand strong, and as Shahr Baraz calmed his restless horse, the main body came up. Here the discipline was not so rigid. Men waved and cheered at him as they marched past and he nodded curtly in reply. These were the *Minhraib*, the common footsoldiers who when not at war were small farmers, tradesmen, peasants or labourers. A hundred thousand strong, they marched in a column whose head was fifty men wide, and it extended for over three and a half miles. It would take an hour and a half at least for them to pass by their general in their entirety. The sight of them made Shahr Baraz stiffen, and he raised his old eyes to heaven in a moment's prayer, thanking his God and his Prophet that he had been given the chance to see this, to command this: the largest army ever fielded by an eastern sultanate. Its like had not been seen on the continent since the terrible wars of the Ramusians, when they had fought among themselves to bring down the Fimbrian Hegemony.

He would not wait to view the rearguard or the siege train; they were seven miles down the road. When the van went into camp that night, the rearguard would be ten miles behind them. Such was the logistical nightmare of moving an army this size across country.

Still, he had the Ostian river now. Already the first barges had come downstream from Ostrabar and the supplies were building up on the burnt wharves of Aekir's riverfront. Incredible, the amount of supplies an army of this size needed. The elephants alone required eighty tons of forage daily.

"Have you spoken to the chief of engineers about the road?" he asked an aide crisply.

The aide started in the saddle. The old man's eyes had seemed so vacant, so far away, that he had thought his general was in some sort of tired daze.

"Yes, Khedive. The materials are already on the road. Once the army is in position about the dyke, the work will go on apace. We have rounded up some thirty thousand head of labour from the countryside. The new road will, the engineer tells me, be finished in sixteen days. And it will bear the elephant waggons."

"Excellent," Shahr Baraz said, and stroked the silver-white moustache that fell past his chin in two tusk-like lengths. His black eyes glittered between their almond-shaped lids.

"Read me again that dispatch from Jaffan at the dyke." The aide fumbled in a saddlebag and produced a piece of parchment. He squinted at it intently for a moment, making the old man's eyes narrow with humour. Officers had to learn to read and write before being seconded to his staff. For many it was an arcane chore that did not come naturally.

"He says," the aide reported haltingly, "that... that the refugees are all across the river and encamped about the fortress, but the – the bridges have not yet been cut. Ramusian forces are making sorties east of the river, harrying his troops. He wants more men." Finished, the aide blinked rapidly, relief on his face.

"He will have sixscore thousand of them in his lap soon enough," Shahr Baraz said casually, his eyes still fixed on the unending files of men and horses and waggons that were moving west. "I want another dispatch sent to Jaffan," he went on, ignoring the sudden rustle of paper and scratch of quill. "The usual greetings, et cetera.

"Your orders are changed. You are to cease the harrying of Ramusian forces east of the river and concentrate on reconnaissance of the enemy position. You will send squadrons to north and south of the dyke looking for fords or possible bridging points. The eastern bank will be reconnoitred for at least ten leagues on either side of the dyke. At the same time you will, using whatever means necessary, ascertain the strength of the fortress garrison and find out how many men have been detached for service further west. You will also confirm or deny the constant rumour I have been hearing that the head of the Ramusian Church did not die in Aekir but is alive and well in Ormann Dyke.

"May the Prophet Ahrimuz watch over you in your endeavours and the enlightenment of the true faith constantly illuminate your path. I and my forces will relieve you within a week. Shahr Baraz, High Khedive of the Armies of the Sultanate of Ostrabar. Et cetera... Did you get that, Ormun?"

The aide was scribbling frantically, using his broad pommel as a writing desk.

"Yes, Khedive."

"Good. Get it off to the dyke at once."

Ormun galloped away as soon as Shahr Baraz had inscribed his flowing signature on the parchment with elaborate flourishes of the quill.

"An enthusiastic young man," he noted to Mughal, one of his senior officers.

The other man nodded, the horsehair plume atop his helm bobbing as he did. "You are a legend of sorts to them, the young men."

"Surely not."

"But yes, old friend. They call you *the terrible old man*, even at court."

Shahr Baraz allowed himself one of his rare grins. "Am I so terrible?"

"Only to your enemies."

"I have seen eighty-three winters upon the face of the world, Mughal. This will be my last campaign. If I am spared, I will make a pilgrimage to the land of my fathers and see the open steppes of Kambaksk one last time ere I die."

"The Khedive of Ostrabar, mightiest warleader the east has ever seen, in a felt hut eating yoghurt. Those days are done, Ibim Baraz." Mughal used the general's personal name as he was entitled to, being a close friend.

"Yes, they are done. And the old *Hraib*, the warrior's code of conduct, is gone too. Who out of this current generation remembers it? A different code rules our lives: the code of expediency. I believe that if I conclude this campaign successfully and do not step down, I may be forced to."

"Who by? Who would do – ?"

"Our Sultan, of course, may the Prophet watch over him. He thinks me too soft on the Ramusians."

"He should have been at Aekir," Mughal said grimly.

"Yes, but he thinks I let the refugees escape out of chivalry, some outmoded sense of the *Hraib*'s rules of conduct. Which I did. But there were sound tactical reasons also."

"I know that. Any soldier with sense can see it," Mughal said.

"Yes, but he is not a true soldier – he never has been, at heart. He is a ruler, a far more subtle thing. And he resents my popularity with the army. It might be best for me were I to quietly disappear once Ormann Dyke falls. I have no wish to taste poison in my bread, or be knifed in my sleep."

Mughal shook his head wonderingly. "The world is a strange place, Khedive."

"Only as strange as the hearts of men make it," Shahr Baraz retorted. "I am constantly harried by orders from Orkhan. I must advance, advance, advance. I am allowed no time to consolidate. I must assault the dyke at once. I do not like being hurried, Mughal."

"The Sultan is impatient. Since you gave him Aekir he thinks you can work miracles."

"Perhaps, but I do not appreciate meddling. I am to launch an assault on the dyke as soon as sufficient troops have come up. I am not allowed to probe the Torunnan flanks because of the time it will waste. I am to throw my men at this fortress as though they were the waves of the sea assaulting a rock."

Mughal frowned. "Do you have doubts about this campaign, Khedive?"

"I am not my own man since Aekir, my friend. Aurungzeb, may the sun shine on him, has appointed *commissioners* to oversee my movements. And to make sure I take my Sultan's tactical advice. If I do not attack and take the dyke speedily enough to suit them I have a feeling there will be another general commanding this army."

"I cannot believe that."

"That is because you – and I – are not creatures of the court, Mughal. I have taken Aekir, accomplished the impossible. Everything that follows is easy. So thinks Aurungzeb."

"But not you."

"Not I. I believe this dyke may give us more trouble even than Aekir, but my opinion does not count for much in Orkhan these days. The would-be generals are already lining up at court to fill my shoes."

"The dyke will fall," Mughal said, "and in no time. It cannot resist this army – nothing can. Their John Mogen is dead, and they have no general alive of his calibre, not even this Martellus."

"I hope you are right. Perhaps I am getting too old; perhaps Aurungzeb is right. I see things with an old man's caution, not the optimism of youth."

"Ask the troops if they would prefer the optimism or the caution. They pay for our mistakes with their blood. Sometimes even sultans forget that."

"Hush, my friend, it is not good to say such things where there are ears to hear. Come, let us ride to the camp. My tents have been set up and there is good wine waiting. A glass or two may sweeten our outlook."

The banner-bright knot of officers and mounted bodyguards took off towards the west, scattering clods of mud from the hooves of their horses. And all the while, the Merduk host continued its march upon the face of the land like a huge, integral beast crawling infinitesimally across the earth, as unstoppable as the approach of night.

HERIA WAS IN his dreams again, and her screams brought him bolt upright in the narrow bunk, as they always did.

Corfe pressed his hands against his eyes until the lights spangled in the darkness there and the vision was gone. She was dead. She was beyond that. It was not happening.

He looked up at the narrow windows high above his head. A faint light was turning the black sky into velvet blue. It would be dawn soon. No point in lying back and trying to burrow down into sleep again. Another day had begun.

He pulled on his boots, yawning. Around him other sleepers snored and tossed and grumbled on their rickety beds. He was in one of the great warehouses which surrounded the citadel in the southern end of Ormann Dyke, but many of the warehouses, built to house the provisions of the garrison, were empty and had been turned into dormitories so that the least hardy of the refugees might sleep out of the rain.

But he was a refugee no longer. He wore the old blood and bruises again, an ensign's sash under his belt and a set of heavy half-armour under his bed. He had been attached to Pieter Martellus's staff as a kind of adviser. That was promotion of a sort, and the thought made his mouth twist into a bitter smile.

He hauled on the armour and made his clinking way out to one of the battlements to sniff the air and see what the day had in store.

Dawn. The sun was rising steadily into an unsullied sky. If he turned his back to the light in the east he could almost make out the white line on the horizon that was the Cimbric

Range, eighty leagues to the south-west. Beyond the Cimbrics was Perigraine, beyond Perigraine the Malvennor Mountains, beyond them Fimbria and finally the Hebrian Sea. Normannia, the Land of the Faith as the clerics had sometimes called it. It did not seem so large when one thought of it like that, when a man might fancy he saw clear across the Kingdom of Torunna at a glance one morning in the early dawn.

He brought his gaze closer to home, staring down on the sun-kindled length of the Searil river and the sprawling expanse of the fortress that ran alongside it. Miles of wall and dyke and stockade and artillery-proof revetments. The walls zigzagged so that the gunners might criss-cross the approaches with converging fire were any enemy to cross the Searil and assault the dyke itself. They looked strange, unnatural in the growing light of the morning, and the sharp-angled towers that broke their length every three hundred yards seemed like monuments to the fallen from some lost, titanic battle.

To the east, across the Searil, the eastern barbican lay on the land like a dark star. Its walls were flung out in sharp points and within them the fires of the Aekirian refugees were beginning to flicker and stipple the shadows there. Behind it the bridge barbican, a collection of walls and towers less strong and high, guarded the approach to the main bridge, and on the other side of the Searil was the island, so-called because it was surrounded by the river on the east and the dyke to the west. Another miniature fortress rose there, connecting the Searil bridge with the main crossing of the dyke. There were two other, smaller bridges of rickety wood, easily demolished, which crossed the dyke to north and south of the main bridge. These were to aid the deployment of sorties or to let the defenders of the island retreat on a broad front were it to be overwhelmed.

To the west of the dyke was the fortress proper. The Long Walls stretched for a league between the crags and cliffs of the ridges that hemmed in the Searil north and south. The citadel on which Corfe stood was built on an out-thrust crag on one of those ridges. In it Martellus had his headquarters. A general standing here would have a view of the entire battlefield and could move his men like pieces on a gaming board, watching them march and countermarch under his feet.

Finally, further west, beyond the buildings and complexes of the fortress, the dark shadow of the main refugee camp covered the land, a mist rising from it like the body heat of a slumbering animal. Almost two hundred thousand people were encamped there, even though thousands had been leaving day by day to trek further west. Martellus had managed to round up a motley force of four thousand volunteers from among the younger men of the multitude, but they were untrained and dispirited. He would not place much reliance on them.

One man for every foot of wall to be defended, the military manuals said. Though one man would actually occupy a yard of wall, the second would act as a reserve and the third would be set aside for a possible sortie force. Martellus had not the numbers to afford those luxuries.

Three thousand men in the eastern barbican. Two thousand manning the island. Four thousand manning the Long Walls. One thousand in the citadel. Two thousand set aside for a possible sortie. The four thousand civilian volunteers were in readiness behind the western walls. They would be fed on to the battlements as soon as the assault began to eat defenders.

It was impossible. Ormann Dyke was widely recognized as the strongest fortress in the world, but it needed to be garrisoned adequately. What they had here was a skeleton, a caretaker force, no more. With a general like Shahr Baraz commanding the attackers, there could be little doubt about the outcome of the forthcoming battle.

But this time, Corfe thought to himself, *I will not run away. I will go down with the dyke, doing my duty as I ought to have done at Aekir.*

CORFE BROKE HIS fast in one of the refectories, a meagre meal of army biscuit, hard cheese and watered beer. There were no problems with the dyke's supply lines – the route to Torunn was still open – but Martellus was also having to feed the refugees as well as he could. It was, Corfe considered, the reason why so many of them remained in the environs of the fortress. Had he been in command he would have stopped doling out rations to them days ago

and sent them packing, but then he no longer responded to
the same impulses as he had before Aekir's fall. Martellus
the Lion was a man of compassion, despite his hard exterior.

As well for me he is, Corfe thought. *The other officers
would as soon have hung me on the spot for desertion.*

He joined his general on the Long Walls, where he was
standing amid a knot of staff officers and aides, all of them
in half-armour, all looking east to the Searil and the land
beyond. There was a table littered with maps and lists,
stones weighing down the parchment against the breeze. It
was a fine morning, and sunlight was gilding the old stone
of the battlements and casting long shadows from their far
sides. It caught the many puddles that were strewn about
the land and lit them up like coins.

"There," Martellus said, pointing out beyond the river.

Corfe stared. He could see a line of horsemen coming down
the slopes of one of the further hills, pennons snapping and
outriders out to flanks and rear. Perhaps two hundred of them.

"The insolent dog," one of the other officers said hotly.

"Yes. He is happy to ride around under our very noses. A
flamboyant character, this Merduk commander. But this is
only a scouting force. Light cavalry, you see? Not a glint of
plate or mail among them, and unarmoured horses. He is
here to take a look at us."

There was a hollow boom that startled the morning,
a puff of white smoke from the eastern barbican, and a
moment later the eruption of a fiery flower on the hillside
below the horsemen. They halted. Martellus was grinning
like a cat sighting the mouse.

"That's young Andruw. He was always a restless dog."

"Shall we assemble a sortie and chase them away?" one
of the officers asked.

"Yes. I've no wish to make their intelligence-gathering
easy. Tell Ranafast to saddle up two squadrons, no more.
And see if he can take some prisoners. We need information
as much as they."

"I'll tell him," Corfe said at once, and before anyone
could respond he ran down from the battlements.

Ranafast was commander of the five hundred cavalry
that the garrison possessed. A quarter of an hour after

Corfe reached him they were riding out of the eastern barbican at the head of two squadrons: eightscore men in half-armour carrying lances and matchlock pistols. They were mounted on the barrel-chested Torunnan warhorses that were most often black or dark bay in colour, much larger than the beasts of the Merduk horsemen who preferred the smaller ponies of the steppes and mountains for their light cavalry.

The two squadrons shook out into line abreast, cheered on by the occupants of the eastern barbican, and thundered up the slopes beyond the river at a fast, bone-shaking trot.

It had been a long time since Corfe had been on a horse. He had originally been a heavy cavalryman in the days before the Merduk siege of Aekir had rendered the city's cavalry superfluous. It took him back to his former life to be part of a moving squadron again, the lance pennons of the troopers whipping about his head.

"Stick close to me, Ensign," Ranafast shouted. He was an emaciated-looking, oldish man whose hawk-like face was now almost entirely hidden by the Torunnan horse helm.

"Out matchlocks!" the cavalry commander ordered, and the lances were settled in their saddle and stirrup sockets. The men drew the already smoking pistols from their saddle holsters.

"East, lads! Close in on them first. Make sure we get the range."

The line of horsemen advanced steadily, the horses labouring a bit to fight the gradient. Ribbons of powder-smoke eddied downhill in countless lines from the glowing slow-match of the pistols. The Merduk cavalry seemed to be somewhat disordered. Knots of them rode this way and that as though uncertain as to their course of action.

The Torunnans clattered and thumped closer, heavy men on heavy horses, a mass of iron and muscle. Ranafast raised his voice.

"Bugler, sound the charge!"

The bugler raised the short instrument to his lips and blew a seven-note blast that rose until it had the hair on the back of Corfe's neck rising with it. The squadrons quickened into a canter.

Up on the hilltop the Merduks were still milling around with what looked to Corfe to be inexplicable confusion until he heard the booms over the noise of the Torunnan advance, and caught sight of the shell-bursts which were peppering the slopes behind the enemy. The gunners in the fortress had the Merduks' range and were deliberately overshooting, keeping the fast-moving horsemen from fleeing the approach of the Torunnan cavalry.

Corfe drew his sabre, possessing no lance or pistols, and leant low in the saddle to avoid the wicked Merduk lances.

They were at the hilltop. The Merduks were streaming away in disorder, the ground littered with smoking holes, dead horses, crawling men. The fort gunners were walking the barrage away eastwards, following their flight.

And then the Torunnans were upon them. The cannon had held back the enemy long enough for the heavier horses to close. The Torunnans fired their matchlocks, a great noise and smoke and riot of spouting flame, and then they were at full gallop, lances out and levelled.

There was no sense of impact, no rolling crash. The Torunnans melted into the rear of the fleeing Merduks and began spearing them from behind. Corfe picked a man on an injured horse, galloped up past him and took off most of his head with one satisfying, brutal blow of his sabre. He laughed aloud, searching for more quarry, but his horse was already tiring. He managed to slash the hindquarters of a fleeing Merduk pony, and then hack its rider from the saddle, but when he looked around again he saw that the Torunnan squadrons were over the hill. The fortress was out of sight and the cavalry was widely scattered, every man absorbed in his private pursuit. Ranafast and his bugler had halted and were blowing the *reform* but the excited men on blown horses were slow to respond. It was the first chance many of them had had to inflict damage on the enemy in weeks, and they had made the most of it.

A line of Merduk cavalry, five hundred strong, came boiling up over the crest of the next hill.

"Saint's blood!" Corfe breathed.

The furthest out of the pursuing Torunnans were engulfed in small groups as the Merduk line came on at an easy canter. The bugler was blowing the retreat frantically and dots of horsemen were turning and fleeing back the way they had come.

"A fucking ambush!" Ranafast was yelling. He had lost his helm and looked almost demented with rage.

"If we get back over the hill the gunners in the fort can cover our retreat," Corfe told him.

"We won't make it – not as a body. It's every man for himself. Get you on back to the river, Ensign. This is not your fight."

Corfe bridled. "It's mine as much as anyone else's!"

"Then save your hide so you can fight again. There's no shame in running away from this battle."

They gathered up what they could of the two squadrons and fought a rearguard action back up the slope they had galloped down a few minutes before. Luckily the Merduks did not possess firearms, so the Torunnans were able to turn in the saddle and loosen off a volley from their pistols every so often to rattle the enemy and stall his pursuit. As soon as Ormann Dyke was in sight once more, they galloped in earnest for the eastern gate whilst the gunners opened up on the Merduk cavalry behind them. It had been a close thing, and Ranafast brought back scarcely a hundred men through the gate, a loss the dyke could ill afford. As soon as the Merduks saw that the Torunnan cavalry were back within the walls of the dyke they called off the pursuit and retreated out of cannon range.

Ranafast and Corfe dismounted once they had clattered across the two bridges to the Long Walls. The surviving Torunnans were subdued, made thoughtful by their narrow escape.

"Well, now we know the strength of the enemy scout force," Ranafast growled. "Caught like a green first-campaigner, damn it. What's your name, Ensign?"

"Corfe."

"Part of Martellus's staff, are you? Well, if ever you want back in the saddle, let me know. You did all right out there, and I'm short of officers." Then the cavalry commander stumped off, leading his lathered horse. Corfe stared after him.

THE LEONINE MARTELLUS bent his knee and kissed the old man's ring reverently.

"Your Holiness."

Macrobius inclined his head absently. They covered his ragged and empty eye-sockets with a snow-white band of linen these days, so that he looked like a venerable blindman's-buff player. Or a hostage. But he was dressed in robes of lustrous black, and a Saint's symbol of silver inset with lapis lazuli hung on his breast. His ring had been Martellus's own, a gift from the Prelate of Torunna before the general had set out for the dyke. Perhaps there had been an element of prescience in the gift, because it fitted the High Pontiff's bony finger almost as well as it had Martellus's.

"They tell me there was a battle today," Macrobius said.

"A skirmish merely. The Merduks managed to stage an ambush of sorts. We came off worst, it's true, but no great damage was done. Your erstwhile bodyguard Corfe did well."

Macrobius's head lifted. "Ah, I am glad, but I never doubted that he would not. My other companion, Brother Ribeiro, died today, General."

"I am sorry to hear it."

"The infection had settled in the very bones of his face. I gave him his last absolution. He died raving, but I pray his soul will take itself swiftly to the Company of the Saints."

"Undoubtedly," Martellus said stoutly. "But I have something else I would discuss with you, Your Holiness."

"My public appearances, or lack of them."

Martellus seemed put out. "Why, yes. You must understand the situation, Holiness. The Merduks are finally closing in. Our intelligence puts their vanguard scarcely eight leagues away and, as you know, the skirmishes with their light troops go on daily. The men need something to hearten them, to raise their spirits. They know you are alive and in the fortress and that is to the good, but if you were to appear before them, preach a sermon and give them your blessing, it would be a wonderful thing for their morale. How could they not fight well, knowing they were safeguarding the representative of Ramusio on earth?"

"They knew that at Aekir," Macrobius said harshly. "It did not help them."

Martellus stifled his exasperation. His pale eyes flashed in the hirsute countenance.

"I command an army outnumbered by more than ten to one, yet they remain here at the dyke despite the knowledge that it would take a miracle to withstand the storm that is upon us. In less than a week we will see a host to our front whose size has not even been imagined since the days of the Religious Wars. A host with one great victory already under its belt. If I cannot give my men something to believe in, to hope for – no matter how intangible – we'd be as well to abandon Ormann Dyke here and now."

"Do you really believe that I can provide that thing they need to believe in, my son?" Macrobius asked. "I, who played the coward at Aekir?"

"That story is almost unknown here. All they know is that by some miracle you escaped the ruin of the Holy City and are here, with them. You have evidenced no desire to go south to Torunn or west to Charibon. You have chosen to remain here. That in itself is heartening for them."

"I could not play the coward again," Macrobius said. "If the dyke falls, I fall with it."

"Then help it stand! Appear before them. Give them your blessing, I beg you."

Eyeless though he was, Macrobius seemed to be studying the earnest soldier before him.

"I am not worthy of the station any more, General," he said softly. "Were I to give the men a Pontiff's blessing, it would be false. In my heart my faith wavers. I am no longer fit for this high office."

Martellus leapt up and began striding about the simply furnished apartments that were Macrobius's quarters in the citadel.

"Old man, I'll be blunt. I don't give a damn about your theological haverings. I care about my men and the fate of my country. This fortress is the gateway to the west. If it falls it will take a generation to push the Merduk back to the Ostian river, if we ever can. You will get up on the speakers' dais tomorrow and you will address my men, and you will put heart in them even if it means perjuring yourself. The greater good will be served, don't you see?

After this battle is over you can do whatever you like, if you still live; but for now you will do this thing for me."

Macrobius smiled gently. "You are a blunt man, General. I applaud your concern for your men."

"Then you will do as I ask?"

"No, but I will do as you demand. I cannot promise a rousing oration, an uplifting sermon. My own soul stands sadly in need of uplifting these days, but I will bless these worthy men, these soldiers of Ramusio. They deserve at least that."

"They do," Martellus echoed heartily. "It's not every soldier can go into battle with the blessing of the High Pontiff upon him."

"If you are so very sure I am yet High Pontiff, my son."

Martellus frowned. "What do you mean?"

"It has been some weeks since my disappearance. A Synod of the Prelates will have been convened, and if they have not received word of my abrupt reappearance, they may well have chosen a new Pontiff already, as is their right and duty."

Martellus flapped one large hand. "Messengers have been sent both to Torunn and Charibon. Rest your mind on that score, Your Holiness. The whole world should know by now that Macrobius the Third lives and is well in the fortress of Ormann Dyke."

THE ADDRESS OF the High Pontiff to the assembled troops took place the next day in the marshalling yards of the fortress. The garrison knelt as one, their ranks swelled by thousands upon thousands of refugees who had come to look upon the most important survivor of Aekir. They saw an old man with a white bandage where his eyes had been, and bowed their heads to receive his blessing. There was silence throughout the fortress for a few moments as Macrobius made the Sign of the Saint over the crowds and prayed to Ramusio and the Company of Saints for victory in the forthcoming ordeal.

Scant hours later, the lead elements of the Merduk army came into view on the hills overlooking Ormann Dyke.

Corfe was there on the parapets of the eastern barbican along with Martellus and a collection of senior officers.

They saw the enemy van spread out with smooth discipline, the long lines of elephant-drawn drays in their midst and regiments of heavy cavalry – the famed *Ferinai* – spread out on the flanks. Horsehair standards were lifted by the wind and on a knoll overlooking the deployment of the army Corfe could see a group of horsemen thick with standards and banners. Shahr Baraz himself and his generals.

"Those are the *Hraibadar*," Corfe told Martellus. "They spearhead the assaults. Sometimes the *Ferinai* dismount and aid them, for they are heavily armoured also. They are the only troops who are issued wholesale with firearms. The rest make do with crossbows."

"How far behind the van should the main body be?" asked Martellus.

"The main levy moves more slowly, keeping pace with the baggage and siege trains. They are probably three or four miles back down the road. They will be here by nightfall."

"He keeps his men well out of culverin range," Andruw, the young ordnance officer in charge of the barbican's heavy guns said, disgruntled.

"His light cavalry found out their ranges for him in that skirmish the other day," Martellus said. "He will not have to waste good troops by inching forward to test those ranges. A thoughtful man, this Shahr Baraz. Ensign, what kind of siege works did he use before Aekir?"

"Fairly standard. His guns in six-weapon batteries protected by gabion-strengthed revetments. A ditch and ramp surmounted by a stockade with many sally-ports. And a rearward stockade in case of any attempt to raise the siege."

"No need for him to worry about that here," someone said darkly.

"How long did he spend in preparation before the first assault?" Martellus asked, ignoring the comment.

"Three weeks. But this was Aekir, remember, a vast city."

"I remember, Ensign. What about mines, siege towers and the like?"

"We countermined, and he gave up on that. He used enormous siege towers a hundred feet high and with five or six tercios in each. And heavy onagers to break down the gates. That's how he forced entry to the eastern bastion: a bombardment of both guns and onagers accompanied by a ladder-borne assault."

"He must have lost thousands," someone said incredulously.

"He did," Corfe went on, his eyes never leaving the group of Merduk horsemen that looked down on the rest out in the hills. "But he could afford to. He lost maybe eight or nine thousand in every assault, but we lost heavily too."

"Attrition then," Martellus said grimly. "If he cannot be subtle, he will simply attack head on. He may find it difficult here, with the dyke and the river to cross."

"I think he will assault with little preparation," Corfe informed them. "He knows our strength by now, and he has lost much time in the passage of the Western Road. I think he will come at us with everything he has as soon as his host is assembled. He will want to be in possession of the dyke before the worst of winter."

"Ho, the grand strategist," one of the senior officers said. "Someone after your job there, General."

Martellus the Lion grinned, but there was little humour in the gesture. His canines were too long, the set of his face too cat-like.

"Corfe is the only one of us who has experienced a full-scale Merduk assault at first hand. He has a right to air his views."

There were some dark murmurings.

"Did the Aekir garrison sortie?" Martellus asked Corfe.

"In the beginning, yes. They harassed the enemy while he dug his siege lines, but there was always a large counterattack ready to be launched – mainly by *Ferinai*. We lost so many men in the sorties and they did so little damage that in the end Mogen gave up on them. We concentrated on counter-battery work, and mining. They are not so skilful with their heavy guns as we are, but they had more of them. We counted eighty-two six-gun batteries around the city."

"Sweet Saints!" Andruw the gunner exclaimed. "Here at the dyke we have less than sixty pieces, light and heavy, and we thought we were overgunned!"

"What about mortars?" Martellus asked. Everyone hated the huge, squat weapons that could throw a heavy shell almost vertically into the air. They rendered the stoutest protecting wall useless, firing over it.

"None. At least they used none at Aekir. They are too heavy, perhaps, to bring over the Thurians."

"That is something at least," Martellus conceded. "Direct-fire weapons only, so we will be able to rely on the thickness of our walls and the refugee camps cannot be bombarded while the wall stands."

"They should be herded out of the defences at once," Corfe blurted out. "It is madness to have a crowd of civilians in the fortress at a time like this."

Martellus blinked. "Among those civilians are would-be nurses and healers, powder and shot carriers, fire-fighters, labourers and perhaps a few more soldiers. I will not cast them out wholesale before seeing what I can get out of them."

"So that's why you have tolerated their presence for so long."

"Tomorrow they will be given orders to march west once more, except for those who are willing to place themselves in the aforementioned categories. I am willing to take help from any quarter, Ensign." Martellus's senior officers did not look too pleased at the news, but no one dared say anything.

"Yes, sir."

The group of men stared out at the deploying Merduk army again. The elephants looked like richly painted towers moving among the press of soldiers and horses, and the huge, many-wheeled wains they pulled were being unloaded with brisk efficiency. More of the animals were advancing with heavy-wheeled culverins behind them, drawing them up in batteries, and Merduk engineers were hurrying hither and thither marking out the hillsides with white ribbon and marker-flags. For fully three miles to their front, the hills were covered with men and animals and waggons. It was as if someone had kicked open a termite mound and the inhabitants had come pouring out searching for their tormentor.

"He will attack in the morning," Martellus said with cold certainty. "We can expect the first assault with the dawn. He will feel his way at first, feeding in his lesser troops as they come up. And the first blow will be here, on the eastern barbican."

"I'd have thought he'd at least spend a day or two setting up camp," one gruff officer said.

"No, Isak. That is what he expects us to think. I agree with our young strategist here. Shahr Baraz will hit us at once, to knock us off balance. If he can take the barbican in that first assault, then so much the better. But the Merduks love armed reconnaissances; this will be one such. He will watch our defence and the way we respond to his attack, and he will note our weaknesses and our strengths. When he knows those, he will commit his best troops and attempt to wipe us off the face of the earth in one massive assault."

Martellus paused and smiled. "That is how I see it, gentlemen. Ensign, you seem to have a head on your shoulders. I hereby promote you to haptman. Remain here in the barbican and stay close to Andruw. I want a full report on the first assault, so don't get yourself killed."

Corfe found it unexpectedly difficult to speak. He nodded at the tall, feline-swift general.

The senior officers left the parapet. Corfe remained behind with Andruw, a man not much older than himself. Short hair the colour of old brass, and two dancing blue eyes. They shook hands.

"To us the honour of first blood, then, in this petty struggle," Andruw said cheerfully. "Come below with me, Haptman, and we'll celebrate your promotion with a bottle of Gaderian. If our esteemed general is right, there'll be little time for drinking after today."

SEVENTEEN

12TH DAY OF Midorion, year of the Saint 551.

Wind nor'-nor'-east by north on the starboard quarter, veering and strengthening. White-tops and six-foot swell. Course due west at seven knots, though we are making leeway I estimate at one league in twelve.

Now three weeks out of Abrusio, by dead-reckoning some 268 leagues west of North Cape in the Hebrionese. Aevil Matusian, common soldier, lost overboard in the forenoon watch, washed out of the beakhead by a green sea. May the Saints preserve his soul. Father Ortelius preached in the afternoon watch. In the first dog-watch I had hands send up extra preventer-stays and bring in the ship's boats. Shipped hawse bags over the cable-holes and tarpaulins over all the hatches. Dirty weather on the way. The Grace of God is drawing ahead despite all Haukal does. Lost sight of her in the first dog-watch. I pray that both our vessels may survive the storm I feel is coming.

There was so much that the bald entries in the ship's log could not convey, Hawkwood thought, as he stood on the quarterdeck of the *Osprey* with his arm wrapped round the mizzen backstay.

They could not get across the mood of a ship's company, the indefinable tensions and comradeships that pulled it together or apart. Every ship had a personality of its own – it was one of the reasons that he loved his willing, striving carrack as she breasted the white-flecked ocean and slipped ever further westwards into the unknown. But every ship's company also had a personality of its own once it had been at sea for a while, and it was this which occupied his thoughts.

Bad feeling on board. The sailors and the soldiers seemed to have divided into the equivalent of two armed camps. It had started with the damned Inceptine, Ortelius. He had complained to Hawkwood that though the soldiers attended his sermons regularly – even the officers – the sailors did not, but went about their business as though he were not there. Hawkwood had tried to explain to him that the sailors had their work to do, that the running of the ship could not stop for a sermon and that those mariners not on duty were seizing four hours of well-earned rest – the most they ever had at one time, because of the watch system. Ortelius could not see the point, however. He had ended up calling Hawkwood impious, lacking in respect for the cloth. And all this at Murad's dinner-table whilst the scar-faced nobleman looked on in obvious amusement.

There were other things. Some of the sailors had gone to several of the passengers on board for cures to minor ailments – rope-burns, chilblains and the like – and the oldwives had been happy to cure them with the Dweomer they possessed. Friendships had sprung up between sailors and passengers as a result; after all, a large proportion of the crew were, so to speak, in the same boat as the Dweomer-folk: frowned upon by the Church and the authorities. Again Ortelius had protested, and this time Murad had backed him up, more out of devilry than for any real motive, Hawkwood suspected. No good could come to a ship which tolerated the use of Dweomer on board, the priest had said. And sailors being the superstitious lot they were, it had cast a pall over the entire crew. For many of them, however, the Ramusian faith was just another brand of Dweomer, and they did not stop their fraternization with the passengers.

There was a weather-worker aboard, Billerand had informed Hawkwood, one of those rare Dweomer-folk who could influence the wind. He was a mousy little man named Pernicus and had offered his services to the ship's master, but Hawkwood had not dared to use his abilities. There was enough trouble with the priest and the soldiery already. And besides, now that the wind had veered and was screaming in over the quarter, the ship was sailing more freely. They were logging over twenty-five leagues a day, no mean feat for an overloaded carrack. If, God forbid, the *Osprey* found herself on a lee shore, then Hawkwood would not hesitate to call on Pernicus's services, but for now he felt it was better to let well alone.

Especially considering what had happened today – that damned stupid soldier having a shit in the beakhead while the waves were breaking over the forecastle. He had been washed out of his perch by a foaming green sea, and they could not heave-to to pick him up, not with a quartering wind roaring over the side. Murad had been furious, especially when he had learned how many ribald jokes the incident had given rise to in the crew's quarters.

There was a change about the lean nobleman that Hawkwood could not quite define. He gave fewer dinners and left the drilling of the soldiers to his ensigns. He spent much of the time in his cabin. It was impossible to keep a secret on board a ship less than thirty yards long, and Hawkwood knew that Murad had taken two young girls from among the passengers to his bed. Apart from anything else, the noises coming through the bulkhead that separated their cabins were confirmation enough of that. But he had heard the soldiers' gossip: that Murad was somehow enamoured of one of the girls. Certainly, the man had all the symptoms of one lost in love, if one believed the bards. He was snappish, distracted, and his already pale face was as white as bone. Dark rings were spreading like stains below his eyes and when he compressed his thin lips it was possible to see the very shape of the teeth behind them.

A packet of spray came aboard and drenched Hawkwood's shoulders but he hardly noticed. The wind was still freshening and there was an ugly cross-sea getting up. The waves were running contrary to the direction of the wind and streamers of spray were tearing off them like smoke. The ship staggered slightly as she hit one of them; she was rolling as well as pitching now. No doubt the gundeck was covered with prostrate, puking passengers.

Billerand hauled himself up the ladder to the quarterdeck and staggered over to his captain.

"We'll have to take in topsails if this keeps up!" he shouted over the rising wind.

Hawkwood nodded, looking overhead to where the topsails were bellying out as tight as drumskins. The masts were creaking and complaining, but he thought they would hold for a time yet. He wanted to make the most of this glorious speed; he reckoned the carrack was tearing along at nine knots at least – nine long sea miles further west with every two turns of the glass.

"There's a bucketful on the way, too," Billerand said, glancing at the lowering sky. The clouds had thickened and darkened until they were great rolling masses of heavy vapour that seemed to be tumbling along just above the mastheads. It might have been raining already; they could not tell because of the spray that was being hurled through the air by the wind and the swift cleavage of the ship's passage.

"Rouse out the watch," Hawkwood said to him. "Get one of the spare topsails out across the waist. If we have a downpour I'd like to try and save some of it."

"Aye, sir," Billerand said, and wove his way back across the pitching quarterdeck.

The watch were prised from their sheltered corners by Billerand's hoarse shouts and a sail was brought out of the locker below. The seamen made it fast across the waist just as the clouds broke open above their heads. Within a minute, the ship was engulfed in a torrential downpour of warm rain, so thick it was hard to breathe. It struck the deck with hammer-force and rebounded up again. The sail filled up almost at once, and the sailors began filling small kegs and casks from it. Noisome water, polluted by the tar and shakings on the sail itself, but they might be glad of it some day soon, and if they were not it could be used to soak clothes made harsh and rasping by being washed in seawater.

The wind picked up as the crew were unfastening the sail and sent it flapping and booming across the waist like some huge, frightened bird. The ship gave a lurch, staggering Hawkwood at his station. He looked over the side to see that the waves were transforming themselves into vast, slate-grey monsters with fringes of roaring foam at their tops. The *Osprey* was plunging into a great water-sided abyss every few seconds, then rising up and up and up the side of the next wave, the green seas choking her forecastle and pouring in a torrent all the way down her waist. And the light failed. The clouds seemed to close in overhead, bringing on an early twilight. The storm Hawkwood had expected and feared was almost upon them.

"All hands!" Hawkwood roared above the screaming wind. "All hands on deck!"

The order was echoed down in the waist by Billerand, thigh-deep in coursing water. They had the sail in a bundle and were dragging it belowdecks. A forgotten keg rolled back and forth in the scuppers, crashing off the upper-deck guns. Hawkwood fought his way over to the hatch in the quarterdeck that opened on the tiller-deck below.

"Tiller there! How does she handle?"

The men were choked with the water that was rushing aft, struggling to contain the manic wrenchings of the tiller.

"She's a point off, sir! We need more hands here."

"You shall have them. Rig relieving tackles as soon as you are able, and bring her round to larboard three points. We have to get her before the wind."

"Aye, sir!"

Men were pouring out of the companionways, looking for orders.

"All hands to reduce sail!" Hawkwood shouted. "Take in those topsails, lads. Billerand, I want four more men on the tiller. Velasca, send a party belowdecks to make sure the guns are bowsed up tight. I don't want any of them coming loose."

The crew splintered into fragments, each intent on his duty.

Soon the rigging was black with men climbing the shrouds to the topmasts. Hawkwood squinted through the rain and the flying spray, trying to make out how much strain the topmasts were taking. He would put the ship before the wind and scud along under bare poles. It would mean they would lose leagues of their westering and be blown to the south-west, off their latitude, but that could not be helped.

A tearing rip, as violent as the crack of a gun. The foretopsail had split from top to bottom. A moment later the two halves were blasted out of their bolt-holes and were flying in rags from the yard. Hawkwood cursed.

A man who was nothing but a screaming dark blur plunged from the rigging and vanished into the heaving turmoil of the sea.

"Man overboard!" someone yelled, uselessly. There was no way they could heave-to to pick someone up, not in this wind. For the men on the yards, a foot put wrong would mean instant death.

The men eased themselves out on the topsail yards, leaning over to grasp fistful after fistful of the madly billowing canvas. The masts themselves were describing great arcs as the ship plunged and came up again, one moment flattening the sailor's bellies against the wood of the yards, the next threatening to fling them clear of the ship and into the murderous, cliff-like waves.

The wind picked up further. It became a scream in the rigging and the spray hitting Hawkwood's face seemed as solid as sand. The ship's head came round slowly as the men on the tiller brought her to larboard, trying to put the wind behind them. Hawkwood shouted down into the waist:

"You there! Mateo, get aft and make sure the deadlights are shipped in the great cabins."

"Aye, sir." The boy disappeared.

They would have to shutter the stern windows or else a following sea might burst through them, flooding the aft portion of the ship. Hawkwood railed at himself. So many things he had left undone. He had not expected the onset of the storm to be so sudden.

The waves around seemed almost as high as the mastheads, sliding mountains of water determined to swamp the carrack as though she were a rowing boat. The pitching of the ship staggered even Hawkwood's sea-legs, and he had to grasp the quarterdeck rail to steady himself. They had the topsails in now, and men were inching back down the shrouds a few feet at a time, clinging to the rough hemp with all the strength they possessed.

"Lifelines, Billerand!" Hawkwood shouted. "Get them rigged fore and aft."

The burly first mate went to and fro in the waist, shouting in men's ears. The noise of the wind was such that it was hard to make himself heard.

She was still coming round. This was the most dangerous part. For a few minutes the carrack would be broadside on to the wind and if a wave hit her then she might well capsize and take them all to the bottom.

Hawkwood wiped the spray out of his eyes and saw what he had dreaded – a glassy cliff of water roaring directly at the ship's side. He leaned down to the tiller-deck hatch.

"Hard a-port!" he screamed.

The men below threw their weight on the length of the tiller, fighting the seas that swirled around the ship's rudder. Too slowly. The wave was going to hit.

"Sweet Ramusio, his blessed Saints," Hawkwood breathed in the instant before the great wave struck the ship broadside on.

The *Osprey* was still turning to port when the enormous shock ran clear through the hull. Hawkwood saw the wave break on the starboard side and then keep going, engulfing the entire waist with water, swirling up to the quarterdeck rail where he stood. One of the ship's boats was battered loose and went over the side, a man clinging to it and screaming soundlessly in that chaos of wind and water. He saw Billerand swept clear across the deck and smashed into the larboard rail like a leaf caught in a gale. Other men clung to the guns with the water foaming about their heads, their legs swept out behind them. But even as Hawkwood watched the wave caught one of the guns and tore it loose from the side, sending the ton of metal careering across the waist, devastation in its wake. The gun went over the larboard side, shattering the rail and tearing a hole in the ship's upper hull. Even above the roaring torrent of the water, Hawkwood thought he could hear the rending timbers shriek, as though the carrack were crying out in her maimed agony.

They were almost swamped. Hawkwood could feel the sluggishness of the carrack, as though she were doubly ballasted with water. The deck began to cant under his feet like the sloping roof of a house.

There was a tearing crack from above. An instant later the main topmast went by the board, the entire mast with its spars and yards and cordage coming crashing down on the larboard side. Blocks and tackle and fragments of shattered wood were hurled down round Hawkwood's ears. Something thudded into the side of his head and knocked him off his feet. He slid along the sloping deck and ended up in the lee scuppers, entangled with rope. The falling mast had crashed through the sterncastle and was hanging over the side, dragging the carrack further over. He was dimly aware that he could hear horses screaming somewhere down in the belly of the ship, a wailing like a multitude in pain. He shook his head, blood pouring down across his eyes and temples, and reached for one of the axes which were stowed on the decks. He began to swing at the mass of broken wood and tangled cordage that was threatening to pull the ship over on to her side.

"Axemen here!" he shrieked. "Get this thing cut away or it'll take us all with it!"

Men were labouring up out of the foaming chaos of the waist with boarding axes in their hands. He saw Velasca there, but no sign of Billerand.

They began chopping at the fallen topmast like men possessed. The carrack rose on the breast of another gargantuan swell of water, tilting ever further. She would capsize with the next wave.

The topmast shifted as they hacked at it. Then there was a cracking and wrenching of wood, audible above the wind and the roaring waves and the sharp concussions of the biting axes. The mass of wreckage moved, tilted, and then slithered over the ship's side into the sea, taking a fiferail with it.

The carrack, freed of the unbalancing weight, began to right herself. The deck became momentarily horizontal again. Then it began to slant once more, but from fore to aft this time. She had turned. The ship was before the wind. Hawkwood looked aft over the taffrail and saw the next wave, like a looming mountain, rear up over the stern as if it meant to crush them out of existence. But the ship rose higher and higher as the bulk of water slid under the hull, lifting the carrack into the air. Then they were descending again – thank God for the high sterncastle to prevent them being pooped – and the ship was behaving like a rational thing once more, riding the huge waves like a child's toy.

"Velasca!" Hawkwood called, wiping blood out of his eyes.

"See to the foremast backstays. I think the topmast destroyed one. We don't want the foremast going as well." He glanced around. "Where's Billerand?"

"Took him below," one of the men said. "Had his shoulder broke."

"All right, then. Velasca, you are acting first mate. Phipio, second mate." Hawkwood looked at the battered wreckage, the shattered rails, the stump of the mainmast like an amputated limb. "The ship is badly hurt, lads. She'll swim, but only with our help. Phipio, get a party down below to check for leaks, and have men working on the pumps as soon as you can. Velasca, I want all other hands sending up extra stays. We can't get the topmasts down, not in this, so we'll have to try and strengthen the masts. This is no passing squall. We're in for a long run."

The crowd of men split up. Hawkwood left them to their work for the moment – Velasca was a competent seaman – clambered down the broken remnants of the ladders to the waist and entered the companionway to the aft part of the ship.

The heaving of the carrack threw him against one bulkhead and then another, and there was water swirling in the companionway, washing around his calves. He made his way to the tiller-house where six men were battling to bring the tiller under control as it fought their grip in the monstrous battering of the waves.

"What's our course, lads?" he shouted. Even here the wind was deafening, and there was also the creaking and groaning of the carrack's hull. The ship was moaning like a thing in pain, and there was the horse still neighing madly somewhere below and people wailing on the gundeck. But that was not his problem now.

"Sou'-sou'-west, sir, directly before the wind," one of the struggling helmsmen answered.

"Very well, keep her thus. I'll try and have you relieved at the turn of the watch, but you may be in for a long spell."

Masudi, the senior helmsman and an ex-corsair, gave a grin that was as brilliant as chalk in his dark face.

"Don't you worry about us, sir. You keep the old girl swimming and we'll keep her on course."

Hawkwood grinned back, suddenly cheered, then bent over the binnacle. The compass was housed in a glass case, and to one side within it a small oil lamp burned so the helmsmen might see the compass needle at all times of the day or night. It was one of Hawkwood's own inventions, and he had been inordinately proud of it. As he bent over the yellow-lit glass his blood fell upon it, becoming shining ruby like wine with candlelight behind it. He wiped the glass clean irritably. Sou'-sou'-west all right, and with this storm his dead-reckoning was shot to pieces. They were going to be far off course when this thing blew itself out, and if they wanted to get back on their old latitude they would have to beat for weeks into the teeth of the wind: an agonizing, snail's-pace labour.

He swore viciously and fluently under his breath, and then straightened. How was the *Grace of God* faring? Had Haukal been caught as unprepared as he? The caravel was a sound, weatherly little vessel, but he knew for a fact that it had never before encountered seas as high as these.

He waved to the helmsmen and left the tiller-house, lurching with the dip and rise of the ship. He slid down a ladder and then kept going forward until he was through into the gundeck. There he halted, looking up the long length of the ship.

The place was a shambles. The sailors had lashed the guns tight so they were crouched up against the gunports like great, chained beasts, and in between them a mass of humanity cowered and writhed in a foot of water that came surging up and down the deck with every dip of the carrack's bow. Hawkwood saw bodies floating face-down in the water, the pathetic rag-tag possessions of the passengers drifting and abandoned. There was a collective wailing of women while men cursed. The lanterns had been put out, which was just as well. The deck resembled the dark, fevered nightmare of a visionary hermit, a picture of some subterranean hell.

Someone staggered over to him and took his arm.

"Well, Captain, are we sinking yet?"

There was no panic in the voice, perhaps even a kind of irony. In the almost dark Hawkwood thought he could make out a roughly broken nose, short-cropped hair, the square carriage of a soldier.

"Are you Bardolin, the girl Griella's guardian?"

"Aye."

"Well, we've no fear of sinking, though it was touch and go for a moment or two there. This storm may last some time so you had best get the passengers to make themselves as comfortable as they can."

The man Bardolin glanced back down the heaving length of the gundeck.

"How many hours do you think it will last?"

"Hours? More than that, it'll be. We're in for a blow of some days, if I'm any judge. I'll try and get the ship's cook to serve out some food as soon as we have things more settled. It'll be cold, mind. There will be no galley fires lit whilst the storm lasts."

He could see the dismay, instantly mastered, on the older man's face.

"Do you need any help?" Bardolin asked.

Hawkwood smiled. "No, this is a job for mariners alone. You see to your own people. Calm them down and make them more comfortable. As I say, this storm will last a while."

"Have you seen Griella? Is she all right?" Bardolin demanded.

"She'll be with Lord Murad, I expect."

As soon as he had said the words Hawkwood wished he had not. Bardolin's face had become like stone, his eyes two shards of winking glass.

"Thank you, Captain. I'll see what I can do here."

"One more thing." Hawkwood laid a hand on Bardolin's arm as he turned away. "The weather-worker, Pernicus. We may need him in the days to come. How is he?"

"Prostrate with fear and seasickness, but otherwise he is hale."

"Good. Look after him for me."

"Our ship's chaplain will not be happy at the thought of a Dweomer-propelled vessel."

"You let me worry about the Raven," Hawkwood growled and, slapping Bardolin on the arm, he left the gundeck with real relief.

Deeper he went, into the bowels of the ship. The *Osprey* was a roomy vessel, despite her lower than usual sterncastle. Below the gundeck was the main hold, and below that again the bilge. The hold itself was divided up into large compartments. One for the cable tiers, where the anchor cables were coiled down, one for the water and provisions, a small cubbyhole that was the powder store and then the newly created compartment that housed the damned horses and other livestock.

There was water everywhere, dripping from the deckhead above, sloshing around his feet, trickling down the sides of the hull. Hawkwood found himself a ship's lantern and fought it alight after a few aggravating minutes of fumbling in the dark with damp tinder. Then he made his way deeper below.

Here it was possible to hear more clearly the sound of the hull itself. The wood of the carrack's timbers was creaking and groaning with every pitch of her beakhead, and the sound of the wind was muted. The horses had gone silent, which was a blessing of sorts. Hawkwood wondered if any of them had survived.

He found a working party of mariners sent down by Velasca to secure the cargo. There was four feet of water in the hold, and the men were labouring waist-deep among the jumbled casks and sacks and boxes, lashing down anything that had come loose in the carrack's wild battle with the monster waves.

"How much water is she making?" Hawkwood asked their leader, a master's mate named Mihal, Gabrionese like himself.

"Maybe a foot with every two turns of the glass, sir. Most of it came down from above with those green seas we shipped, but her timbers are strained, too, and there's some coming in at the seams."

"Show me."

Mihal took him to the side of the hull, and there Hawkwood could see the timbers of the ship's side quivering and twisting. Every time the carrack moved with the waves, the timbers opened a little and more water forced itself in.

"We're not holed anywhere?"

"Not so far as I can see, sir. I've had men in the cable tiers and in the stockpens aft – a bloody mess down there, by the by. No, she's just taking the strain, is all, but I hope Velasca has strong men on the pumps."

"Report to him when you've finished here, Mihal. The pump crews and the helmsmen will need relieving soon."

"Aye, sir."

Hawkwood moved on, wading through the cold water. He struggled aft against the movement of the ship and passed through the bulkhead hatch that separated the hold from the stockpens nearer the stern.

Lanterns here, the terrified bleating of a few sheep, straw and dung turning the water into a kind of soup. Animal corpses were bobbing and drifting. Hawkwood approached the group of men who were working there in leather gambesons – soldiers, then, not members of his crew.

"Who's that?" a voice snapped.

"The Captain. Is that you, Sequero?"

"Hawkwood. Yes, it's me."

Hawkwood saw the pale ovals of faces in the lantern light, the shining flanks of a horse.

"How bad is it?"

Sequero splashed towards him. "What kind of ship's master are you, Hawkwood? No one was told to secure the horses, and then the ship went on its damned side. They never had a chance. Why could you not have warned my people?"

Sequero was standing before him, filthy and dripping. Something had laid open his forehead so that a flap of skin glistened there, but the blood had slowed to an ooze. The ensign's eyes were bright with fury.

"We had no time," Hawkwood said hotly. "As it was we almost lost the ship, and I've lost some of my men putting her to rights. We had no time to worry about your damned horses."

He thought for a second that Sequero was going to fly at him and tensed into a crouch, but then the ensign sagged, obviously worn out.

"I am no sailor. I cannot say whether you are in the right of it or not. Will the ship survive?"

"Probably. How many did you lose?"

"One of the stallions and another mare. They broke their legs when the ship went to one side."

"What about the other livestock?"

Sequero shrugged. It was not his concern.

"Well, get what stock have survived and secure them in their stalls. Lash them to the pens if you have to. This could be a long blow." Hawkwood was beginning to feel like a parrot, repeating his litany to everyone he met.

Sequero nodded dully.

"What about the soldiers? How are they faring?"

"Drunk, most of them. Some of the older ones have been saving their wine rations. They thought they were going to die, and so decided to drown whilst drunk."

Hawkwood laughed. "I've heard of worse ideas. What of Lord Murad?"

"What of him? He's closeted with his peasant whore as usual."

A violent lurch of the ship pitched them both into the stinking water. They struggled out of it spitting and cursing.

"Are you sure this thing won't sink, Captain?" Sequero sneered.

But Hawkwood was already retracing his steps forward. Time to get back on deck and take up his proper place. He was blind down here.

IT HAD BECOME a little lighter and the clouds seemed to have lifted above the level of the mastheads. The seas were just as mountainous though, great hills of water with troughs a quarter of a mile apart and crests as high as the carrack's topmasts. They were running before the wind now, and the waves were rising around the ship's stern, lifting her high into the air and then passing under her, leaving her almost becalmed in their lee. There seemed to be little danger of her being pooped, thanks to her construction, but they would have to ride the storm out, letting it blow them where it willed.

Velasca had had hawsers sent up to the mastheads and there were men working in the tops, struggling to secure them. Others were double lashing the upper-deck guns and the two ship's boats that had survived, though the passage of the runaway gun had smashed chunks out of both their sides. And to both larboard and starboard thick jets of white water were spewing out of the pumps as men bent up and down over them, trying to lighten the ship.

"Tiller there!" Hawkwood shouted down the hatch. "How's she steering?"

"Easier, sir," Masudi called back. "But the men are tiring."

"Mihal and his mess will be up to relieve you soon. Steady as she goes, Masudi."

"Aye, sir."

For hour after hour the carrack rode the vast waves and careered before the wind roughly south-west, away off their course and into seas unknown even to Tyrenius Cobrian. Despite the fact that the yards were bare, her speed was very great as she was shunted forward on the shining backs of the enormous breakers.

The watch changed. Exhausted seamen were relieved by others scarcely less exhausted, but the hands remained on deck for hour after hour, pumping, splicing, repairing or simply remaining in readiness for the next crisis.

It grew colder. When Hawkwood estimated that their storm-driven run had taken them some forty leagues off course the balminess in the air vanished and the water took on a grey, chill aspect in the sunless dawn of the next day. All that day they continued to run before the wind, eating bread and raw salt pork when they could, feeling the salt in their clothing rasp their saturated skin and continuing the unending repairs.

After a second night and a second day they began to feel that they had never been warm or dry, and had never really known sleep before. They lost another man off one of the yards who had slackened his grip out of sheer weariness, and they threw overboard the bodies of three passengers who had died of the injuries sustained in the first, savage squall. And they continued south-west across the titanic, illimitable Western Ocean, like a stick of wood adrift in a millrace with a knot of frenzied ants clinging to it. There was nothing else to do.

EIGHTEEN

THEY CAME WITH the dawn, as Martellus had said they would. Had it not been for the vigilance of the pickets they might have swarmed up to the very walls, so sudden was their onset; for the Merduks had elected to forgo a preliminary bombardment, preferring to gamble on achieving surprise. But the watching sentries set light to the signal rockets and flares, and suddenly the eastern barbican and the river were lit up with smoking red lights that described bright parabolas across the lightening sky and illuminated the bristling phalanxes of advancing troops below.

The garrison of the barbican rushed out to their stations. All along the walls, slow-match was lit and set to one side, men shouldered their arquebuses and powder and shot-carriers hurried up to the parapets with their vital loads.

The Merduk host, discovered, came on with a mighty roar, a rush of shouting and thumping feet that set the hair crawling on Corfe's head. Once again, he beheld the teeming mass of a Merduk army assaulting walls, like a seaweed-thick tide lapping at a cliff face.

The sun was coming up. More powder rockets were launched, this time to help the gunners aim their culverins. The swarming mob of Merduks was perhaps two hundred yards from the walls when Andruw stabbed the slow-match into the touch-hole of the first cannon.

It jumped back with a roar and an exploding fog of smoke. At the signal, the other big guns of the fortress began to bark out also until the entire barbican was a massive reeking smoke cloud stabbed through and through with red and yellow flame.

Corfe was able to see the result of the first few salvoes before the smoke hid the advancing hordes. The Torunnans were using delayed-fuse shells that exploded in midair and scattered jagged metal in a deadly radius beneath them. He saw swathes of the enemy fall or be tossed into the air and ripped to pieces, like crops flattened by an invisible wind. Then they came on again, dressing their broken lines and screaming their hoarse battlecries. There were hundreds of ladders in their midst, carried shoulder-high.

"What of their numbers, Corfe?" Andruw shouted. "What do you make them?"

How to set a figure to that broiling mass of humanity? But Corfe was a soldier, a professional. His mind played with figures in his head.

"Nine or ten thousand in the first wave," he shouted back, the smoke aching his throat already. "But that's just the first wave."

Andruw grinned out of a blackened face. "Plenty for everyone then."

They were at the foot of the walls now, a roaring multitude horned with scaling ladders and baying like animals. The rising sun lit up the further hills, shafted through the billowing powder smoke and made something ethereal and beautiful out of it, the defenders seeming to be flat silhouettes in the fiery reek. The gunners of the lighter pieces depressed their guns to maximum and began firing down into the packed masses below, whilst the arquebusiers were holding fire, waiting for Andruw's order.

Scaling ladders thumping against the battlements. Grapnels, ropes and a shower of crossbow bolts that knocked down half a dozen men in Corfe's vision alone. The ladders began to quiver as the enemy climbed up them.

"Hold your fire, arquebusiers!" Andruw shouted. A few nervous men were already letting loose.

Faces at the top of the ladders, black as fiends from Hell.

"Fire!"

A rippling series of explosions as two thousand arquebuses went off almost as one. Many ladders crashed back down in the press below, unbalanced by the death throes of the men at their tops. Others remained, and more of the enemy continued their climb.

"Fork-men, to the front!" the order went out, and Torunnans came forward bearing objects shaped like long-handled pitchforks. Two or three of the defenders would push these against the scaling ladders and send them out in a slow, graceful arc, packed with men, to swing down into red ruin in the massed ranks at the foot of the walls.

The assault paused, checked. The noise of men shouting and shrieking, the boom of cannon and crack of arquebus were deafening.

"Have they no strategy at all?" Andruw was asking Corfe. "They're like a ram butting a gate. Do they reckon nothing of casualties?"

"They don't have to," Corfe told him. "Remember what Martellus said? Attrition. They are losing men by the thousand, we by the score. But they can afford to lose their thousands. They are as numberless as the sand of a beach."

They stood near the gate that was the main entrance to this part of the fortress. The sun was rising rapidly and a rosy-gold light was playing over the scene. They could see through gaps in the smoke to where fresh forces were already being marshalled on the hills beyond. The Merduk guns were being brought into play now, but they were firing high. Most of their shots seemed to be falling into the Searil, raising fountains of white, shattered water.

"So they use explosive shells, too," Andruw said, surprised. It was something the Ramusians had invented only twenty years ago.

"Yes, and incendiaries. I hope we have enough firefighters."

"Fire is the last thing we have to worry about. Here they come again."

A fresh surge at the foot of the walls. Crossbow bolts came clinking and cracking against the battlements in a dark hail. Men fell screaming from the catwalks.

Another assault, the ladders lifted up and thrown down once more. The ground at the bottom of the fortifications was piled with corpses and wreckage.

"I don't like it," Corfe said. "This is too easy."

"Too easy!"

"Yes. There is no thought behind these assaults. I think they are a cover for something else. Even Shahr Baraz does not throw his men's lives away for no gain."

There was an earth-shuddering concussion that seemed to come from beneath their very feet. Almost the entire gatehouse was enveloped in thick smoke through which flame speared and flapped.

"They've blown the gate!" Andruw cried.

"I'll see to it. Stay here. They'll make another assault to cover the breaching party."

Corfe ran down the wide stairs to the courtyards and squares below. Torunnan soldiers and refugee civilians were running about carrying powder, shot, wounded men, match and water. He seized on a group of a dozen who possessed arquebuses and led them into the shadow of the gatehouse.

There in the arch a fierce fire was burning, and the massive gates were askew on their hinges, white scars marking the shattered wood. Already the Merduk engineers were swarming through the gaps and a hundred more were clustered behind them. It was like watching dark maggots writhing in a wound.

"Present pieces!" Corfe yelled to his motley command, and the arquebuses were levelled.

"Give fire!"

The volley flung back a score of Merduks who were clambering through the wrecked gates.

"Out swords. Follow me!" Corfe cried, and led the Torunnans at a run.

They stepped over wriggling, maimed men and began slashing and hewing in the burning gloom of the arch like things possessed. In a few moments there were no Merduks left alive inside the gatehouse, and those trying to force their way through the battered portals had limbs and heads lopped off by the defenders.

The fire spread. Corfe was dimly aware of men with water buckets. He hacked the fingers off a hand that was pulling at the broken gate. Then someone was tugging him away.

"The murder-holes! They're going to use them. Out of the gateway!"

He allowed himself to be hauled away, half blind with sweat and smoke. The Torunnans fell back.

Immediately the Merduks were squirming through the gates again. In seconds a score of them were on the inside and more of their fellows were joining them by the moment.

"*Now!*" a voice yelled somewhere.

A golden torrent poured down on the hapless Merduks from holes in the ceiling of the gatehouse. It was not liquid, but as soon as it struck the men below they screamed horribly, tearing at their armour and dropping their swords. They flailed around in agony for long minutes whilst their comrades halted outside, watching in helpless fury.

"What is it?" Corfe asked. "It looks like –"

"Sand," he was told by a grinning soldier. "Heated sand. It gets inside the armour and fries them to a cinder. More economical than lead, wouldn't you say?"

"Make way, there!" A gunnery officer and a horde of blackened figures were man-hauling two broad-muzzled falcons into position before the gate. As the torrent of sand faltered the Merduks outside began clambering inside again with what seemed to Corfe to be arrant stupidity or maniac courage.

The falcons went off. Loaded with scrap metal, they did the remains of the gates little damage, but the Merduks in the archway were blown to shreds. Blood and fragments of flesh, bone and viscera plastered the interior of the archway.

"They're falling back!" someone yelled.

It was true. The attack on the gate was being abandoned for the moment. The Merduks were drawing away.

"Keep these pieces posted here, and get engineers to work on these gates," Corfe commanded the gunnery officer, not caring what his rank might be. "I'll send men down from the wall to reinforce you as soon as I can."

Without waiting for a reply, he ran for the catwalk stairs to rejoin the men on the battlements.

Another assault – the cover for the breaching party – had just been thrown back. Men were reloading the cannons frantically, charging their arquebuses, doctoring minor wounds. The dead were tossed off the parapet like sacks; time for the solemnities later.

Andruw's sabre was bloody and his eyes startlingly white in a filthy face. "What about the gate?"

"It's holding, for the moment. They're persistent bastards. I'll give them that. We sent half a hundred of them to join their prophet before they drew back."

Andruw laughed heartily. "By sweet Ramusio's blessed blood, they'll not walk over us without a stumble or two. Was it as tight as this at Aekir, Corfe?"

Corfe turned away, face flat and ugly.

"It was different," he said.

MARTELLUS WATCHED THE failure of the assault from his station on the heights of the citadel. His officers were clustered about him, grave but somehow jubilant. The Merduk host was drawing back like a snarling dog that has been struck on the muzzle. All over the eastern barbican on the far side of the river a vast turmoil of rising smoke shifted and eddied, shot through with flame. Even here, over a mile away, it was possible to hear the hoarse roar of a multitude in extremity, a formless, surf-like sound that served as background to the rolling thunder of the guns.

"He's lost thousands," one of the senior officers was saying. "What is he thinking of, to throw troops bare-handed against prepared fortifications like that?"

A messenger arrived from the eastern bank, his face grimed and his chest heaving. Martellus read the dispatch with thin lips, then dismissed him.

"The gate is damaged. We would have lost it, were it not for the efforts of my new aide. Andruw puts his own casualties at less than three hundred."

Some of the other officers grinned and stamped. Others looked merely thoughtful. They eyed the retreat of the attacking Merduk regiments – orderly despite the barrage that the Torunnan guns were laying down – then their gazes moved up the hillsides, to where the main host was encamped in its teeming thousands and the Merduk batteries squatted silent and ominous.

"He's playing with us," someone said. "He could have continued that attack all day, and not blinked an eye at the casualties."

"Yes," Martellus said. The early light filled his eyes with tawny fire and made a glitter out of the white lines in his hair. "This was an armed reconnaissance, no more, as I said it would be. He now knows the location of our guns and the dispositions of the eastern garrison. Tomorrow he will attack again, but this time it will not be a sudden rush, unsupported and ill-disciplined. Tomorrow we will see Shahr Baraz assault in earnest."

HUNDREDS OF MILES away to the west. Follow the Torrin river northwards to where the gap between the Cimbric Mountains and the Thurians opens out. Pass over the glittering Sea of Tor with its dark fleets of fishing boats and its straggling coastal towns. There, in the foothills of the western Cimbrics, see the majestic profile of Charibon, where the bells of the cathedral are tolling for Vespers and the evening air is thickening into an early night in the shadow of the towering peaks.

In the apartments that had been made over to the new High Pontiff Himerius, the great man himself and Betanza, Vicar-General of the Inceptine Order sat alone, the attending clerics dismissed. The muddy, travel-worn man who had been with them minutes before had been led away to a well-earned bath and bed.

"Well?" Betanza asked.

Himerius's eyes were hooded, his face a maze of crannied bone dominated by the eagle nose. As High Pontiff he wore robes of rich purple, the only man in the world entitled to do so unless the Fimbrian emperors were to come again.

"Absurd nonsense, all of it."

"Are you so sure, Holiness?"

"Of course! Macrobius died in Aekir. Do you think the Merduks would have missed such a prize? This eyeless fellow is an impostor. The general at the dyke, this Martellus, he has obviously circulated this story in order to raise the morale of his troops. I cannot say I blame the man entirely – he must be under enormous pressure – but this really is inexcusable. If he survives the attack on the dyke I will see to it that he is brought before a religious court on charges of heresy."

Betanza sat back in his thickly upholstered chair. They were both by the massive fireplace, and broad logs were burning merrily on the hearth, the only light in the tall-ceilinged room.

"According to this messenger," Betanza said carefully, "Torunn was informed also. Eighteen days he says it took to get here, and four dead horses. Torunn will have had the news for nigh on a fortnight."

"So? We will send our own messengers denying the validity of the man's claim. It is too absurd, Betanza."

The Vicar-General's high-coloured face was dark as he leaned back out of the firelight.

"How can you be so sure that Macrobius is dead?" he asked.

Himerius's eyes glittered. "*He is dead*. Let there be no question about it. I am High Pontiff, and no Torunnan captain of arms will gainsay me."

"What are you going to do?"

Himerius steepled his fingers together before his face.

"We will send out riders at once – tonight – to every court in Normannia – all the Five monarchies. They will bear a Pontifical bull in which I will denounce this impostor and the man who is behind him – this Martellus, the Lion of Ormann Dyke."

Himerius smiled. "I will also send a private letter to King Lofantyr of Torunna, expressing my outrage at this heretical occurrence and telling him of my reluctance to commit our Knights Militant to the defence of his kingdom whilst that same kingdom harbours a pretender to my own position, an affront against the Holy Office I occupy, a stink in the nostrils of God."

"So you will withhold the troops you promised Brother Heyn," Betanza said. He sounded tired.

"Yes. Until this thing is dealt with Torunna shall receive no material aid from the Church."

"And Ormann Dyke?"

"What of it?"

"The dyke needs those men, Holiness. Without them it will surely fall."

"Then so be it. Its commander should have thought of that before he started elevating blind old men to the position of High Pontiff."

Betanza was silent. As the Knights Militant were quartered in Charibon they were nominally under the command of the head of the Inceptine Order. But never in living memory had a Vicar-General flouted the wishes of his Pontiff.

"The men are already on the march," Betanza said. "They must be halfway to Torunna by now."

"Then recall them," Himerius snapped. "Torunna shall receive nothing from me until it extirpates this impostor."

"I beg you to consider, Holiness... What if this man is who he says he is?"

"Impossible, I tell you. Are you questioning my judgement, Brother?"

"No. It is just that I do not want you to make a mistake."

"I am directly inspired by the Blessed Saint, as his representative on earth. Trust me. I know."

"By rights we should reassemble the Synod and put this to the convened Colleges and Prelates."

"They're happily trekking homewards by now. It would waste too much time. They will be informed in due course. What is the matter with you, Brother Betanza? Do you doubt the word of your Pontiff?"

One of the powers inherent in the Pontifical office was the nomination or removal of the Vicar-General of the Inceptines. Betanza looked his superior in the eye.

"Of course not, Holiness. I only seek to cover every contingency."

"I am glad to hear it. It is always better when the Vicar-General and the Pontiff have a good working relationship. It can be disastrous if they do not. Think of old Baliaeus."

Baliaeus had been a Pontiff of the last century who had quarrelled with his Vicar-General, removed the man from office and assumed the position himself in addition to his Pontiffship. The event had scandalized the entire Ramusian world, but none had attempted to reinstate the unfortunate head of the Inceptines. The man had died a reclusive hermit in a cell up in the Cimbrics.

"But you are no Baliaeus, Holiness," Betanza said, smiling.

"I am not. Old friend, we have worked too hard and striven too long to see what we laboured for torn away from us."

"Indeed." So if Himerius went, Betanza went. That much was clear at least.

"In any case," Himerius went on suavely, "we may be worrying over nothing. You have said yourself that the dyke must fall. If it does, the impostor will fall with it and all those who believe in him there. Our problems will be at an end."

Betanza stared at him, open-mouthed.

"That will do, my lord Vicar-General. Have the scribes sent to me when you leave. I will dictate the dispatches this evening. We must strike whilst the iron is hot."

Betanza got up, bowed and kissed his Pontiff's ring. He left the room without another word.

Brother Rogien was waiting for him as he exited. He strode along the wide corridors of Charibon with Rogien silent at his side. He could hear Vespers being sung from half a dozen college chapels and smell the enticing aromas from the kitchens of the monastery.

Rogien was an older man, broad-shouldered and stooped, with hair as white and fine as the down on a day-old chick. He was Betanza's deputy, experienced in the ways of Inceptine intrigue.

"He will not even investigate it!" Betanza raged at last, striding along at a swift, angry pace.

"What did you think, that he would tamely lie down and accept it?" Rogien asked caustically. "All his life he has coveted the position he now occupies. He is more powerful than any king. It is not a thing to be abandoned lightly."

"But the way he goes about it! He will recall the Knights promised to Torunna; he will alienate Heyn and the Torunnan king. He will gladly see Ormann Dyke fall rather than risk his own position!"

"So? We knew that was what would happen."

"I have been a soldier of sorts, Rogien. I commanded men in my youth and maybe that gives me a different outlook. But I tell you that this man will see the west riven by fire and ruin if he thinks it will advance his own cause one jot."

"You have attached yourself to him," Rogien said implacably. "His fortunes are yours. You worked with him to gain the Pontiffship; he helped vote you into your position. You cannot turn around now and forsake him. It will ruin you."

"Yes, I know!"

They reached the Vicar-General's quarters, dismissed the Knights at the door and went inside, lighting candles as they did so.

"You would never have become head of the order were it not for him," Rogien went on. "Your age and your late vocation counted against you. It was Himerius's lobbying that swung the Colleges. You are his creature, Betanza."

The Vicar-General poured himself wine from a crystal decanter, made the Sign of the Saint with a clenched fist and drank the wine at a gulp.

"Yes, his creature. Is that what they will say in the history books? That Betanza stood by whilst his Pontiff brought down the west? Can the man be so blinkered that he is unable to see what he is doing? By all means, denounce the impostor; but withhold the Torunnan reinforcements as well? That smacks of paranoia."

Rogien shrugged. "He is willing to take no risks. He knows it will bring Lofantyr to heel quicker than anything else. And you have to admit it would look odd were the High Pontiff to send troops to bolster the garrison of a fortress which has raised up a rival High Pontiff."

"Yes, there is that, I suppose." Betanza smiled wryly and poured his colleague and himself more wine. "Mayhap I am losing my skill at the Inceptine game."

"You bring to it the wisdom of a man who has not worn a black habit his whole life. You were a nobleman once, a lay-leader. But that is in the past. If you are to survive and to prosper, you must learn to think wholly as an Inceptine. The order must retain its pre-eminence. Let the kings worry about the defence of the west; it is their province. We must concern ourselves with the spiritual welfare of the Ramusian world – and what would happen to it were there to be two Pontiffs? Chaos, anarchy, a schism that might take years to heal. Think on that, Brother."

Betanza regarded his subordinate with sour humour.

"I think sometimes that you would be better off sitting in my chair and I in a soldier's harness before Ormann Dyke, Rogien."

"As you are Himerius's creature, I am yours, lord."

"Yes," the Vicar-General said quietly. "You are."

He threw back his wine. "Send a half-dozen of our quickest scribes to the High Pontiff's chambers. He will be wanting to dictate his dispatches at once. And warn off a squad of our dispatch-riders to be ready for a long journey."

Rogien bowed. "Will there be anything else? Shall I have your meal sent up, or will you eat in hall?"

"I am not hungry. I must be alone for a while. I must think, and pray. That will be all, Rogien."

"Very well, my lord." The older man left.

Betanza moved to the window and threw back the heavy shutters. A keen air smelling of snow wafted into the dim room. He could see where the majestic Cimbrics loomed right at the shores of the Sea of Tor, the last light of the sun touching their white peaks while the rest of the world was sinking into shadow. Eighteen days the messenger had been on the road. The dyke had most likely already fallen and his worries were academic. The largest army yet seen could be even now resuming its march westwards, and he remained here splitting hairs with an egocentric Churchman.

He smiled. What Inceptine was not egocentric, ambitious, imperious? Even the novices behaved like princes when they walked the streets of the fisher villages.

It would cause trouble. He could feel it in his bones. It was not just the Merduk war; there were other straws in the wind tonight. The Conclave of Kings would be convening very soon; he would know more then. He had his informants in place.

A time of change was approaching. Attitudes were shifting, not just among the common people but among kings and princes. Himerius already had the aspect of a man on the defensive. But perhaps his efforts would be no more effectual than the efforts of those few unfortunates who were fighting and dying along the Searil River at this very moment. The mood of the age could not be turned around by a few ambitious men, even ones as powerful as the High Pontiff.

He wondered if Macrobius were truly alive. There was little chance of it, of course, and the likeliest explanation for the dispatch they had received that afternoon was the one proffered by Himerius. But if the impostor were the old Pontiff, Betanza doubted very much whether Himerius would step down. There would be a schism: two Pontiffs, a divided Ramusian continent with the Merduks baying at its borders. Such a scenario did not bear thinking about.

He left the window, shutting out the cold air and the sunset-tinted mountains. Then he knelt on the stone floor and began to pray.

NINETEEN

AN UNENDING EXPANSE of ocean, blue as the cerulean vault which arced down to meet it, unbroken on every horizon. Limitless as the space between stars.

And on that unruffled ocean a minuscule speck, a tiny piece of flotsam overlooked by the elements. A ship, and the souls contained within its wooden walls.

THE *OSPREY* WAS becalmed. After three days and nights the storm had veered off to the north-west, having had its diversion and driven the carrack uncounted leagues off her course. Then the wind had died, leaving the sea as glassily calm as the water in a millpond on a still summer's day. The ship's company had watched the black towering banners of the storm billow off into the distance, taking the darkness and the cold with them, and they had been left with an eerie silence, an absence of noise that they could not quite account for until they remembered the absence of the wind.

The ship was a battered hulk, a relic of the proud vessel which had sailed out of Abrusio harbour a scant month before. The main topmast had gone, and its passing had torn chunks out of the larboard sterncastle. The gun that had been wrenched overboard had also ripped a hole in the ship's side so that the carrack looked as though some immense monster had been chewing on it. Rags and loose ends of rigging dangled everywhere and the normally smooth lines of the ropes which formed the rigging itself were bunched and untidy after being knotted and spliced countless times throughout the storm.

The ship was floating in a greasy pool of her own filth. Around the hull floated human waste and detritus, fragments of wood and hemp, and even the bloated corpses of a pair of sheep. The miasma of the stagnant surroundings stank out the ship along with the familiar reek of her bilge, now somewhat sluiced out by the tons of seawater the ship had made and pumped away throughout the tempest. The ship's boats were full of holes so the crew could not even tow the carrack out of the area. And the heat battered down relentlessly from a sun that seemed made of beaten brass. The pitch bubbled in the seams and, as the upper deck dried, so the planking opened and let water drip down through the ship, soaking everything. The ship's company became accustomed to finding mould and strange fungi sprouting in the unlikeliest of dark corners throughout the carrack.

19th day of Midorion, year of the Saint 551.

Flat calm. The fourth day with no wind. The ship is still in the doldrums. By my estimate we have been blown some one hundred and eighty leagues off our course to the south-west or sou'-sou'-west. From cross-staff observations I believe that we are on the approximate latitude of Gabrion, but my calculations must needs be largely guesswork. In the middle of the worst of the storm the glass was neglected for almost half a watch, and so our timings must begin anew and dead-reckoning becomes ever more unreliable.

There is only one recourse that I can see to help us make up our lost northing, and that is Pernicus, the weather-worker. If he can be prevailed upon to conjure up a favourable wind then we may yet make landfall ere the winter storms begin. But I know what prejudices such a line of action would evoke. I must talk to the man Bardolin, who seems to have become a spokesman of sorts for the passengers since the storm, and, of course, Murad. But I will be damned to the bottom if I will endanger my ship any further for the religious fanaticism of a cursed Raven whom no one wanted on this ship in the first place.

Hawkwood looked over what he had written and then, cursing under his breath, he scored out the last sentence heavily and retrimmed his quill.

Ortelius will surely see reason. It may be a choice between utilizing the abilities of the weather-worker or, at best, extending the voyage by a good two months. At worst it could mean our deaths.

Crew employed about the ship on repairs. We will be swaying up a new topmast in the first dog-watch, and then working on the ship's boats. I must report the deaths of Rad Misson, Essen Maratas and Heirun Japara, all able seamen. May the Company of the Saints find a place for their benighted souls, and may the Prophet Ahrimuz welcome Heirun to his garden.

Four men, including First Mate Billerand, confined to their hammocks with injuries sustained in the storm. Velasca Ormino acting first mate for the duration.

I must report also the deaths of three passengers, who were consigned to the sea during the storm itself. They were Geraldina Durado, Ohen Durado and Cabrallo Schema. May God have mercy on their souls. Brother Ortelius today conducted a ceremony to mark their passing and preached a sermon about the consequences of heresy and disbelief.

"The bastard," Hawkwood said aloud.

Of Haukal and The Grace of God *there is no sign. I cannot believe that such a well-found ship under such a captain could have foundered, even in the blow that we went through.*

Unless, Hawkwood thought with that persistent hollow feeling in his stomach, they had been pooped and broached-to whilst running before those enormous waves. The *Grace*'s stern was not as high as the carrack's, and a wave might have overwhelmed her whilst Haukal had been putting her before the wind. And those lateen yards were less handy than the square-rigged ones of the carrack. Frequently sail was taken in by lowering the yards to the deck, and in such a sea there might not have been time to do that.

He had a man in the foretop round the clock, and from up there the lookout could survey at least seven leagues in any direction, despite the haze that was beginning to cloud the horizon with the growing heat. There was just no telling.

Hawkwood looked up from his desk. Beyond the stern windows he could see the glittering, unmoving sea, and the darkness on the northern horizon that was the last of the storm. The windows were open to try and get some air circulating, but it was a fruitless gesture. The heat and the stench were hanging in the throats of every soul on the ship, and the hold was a shattering wooden oven, humid as the jungles of Macassar. He must get the animals out of there for a while, and rig up a wind sail to get some air belowdecks. If there were any wind to fill it.

There was a knock at the cabin door.

"Enter."

He was startled to see Ortelius the Inceptine standing there when he turned.

"Captain, do you have a moment?"

He was half inclined to say "no," but he merely nodded and gestured to the stool behind the door. He closed the ship's log, feeling absurdly shifty as he did so.

The cleric pulled out the stool and sat down. He was obviously uncomfortable with the low perch.

"What is it you would say to me, Father? I cannot give you long, I am afraid. We'll be swaying up the new topmast in a few minutes."

Ortelius had lost weight. His cheeks seemed to have sunk in on themselves and the channels at the corners of his nose were as deep as scars.

"It is the voyage, my son."

"What of it?" Hawkwood asked, surprised.

"It is cursed. It is an offense against God and the Holy Saint. The smaller vessel is already lost and soon this one will be also if we do not turn back and set sail for the lands that are lit by the light of the Faith."

"Now wait a moment –" Hawkwood began hotly.

"I know you are Gabrionese, Captain, not from one of the five Ramusian bastions that are the Monarchies of God, but I say this to you: if you have any piety about you whatsoever, you will heed my words and turn the ship around."

Hawkwood could have sworn that the man was sincere – more, that he was genuinely afraid. The sweat was pouring off him in drops as big as pearls, and his chin quivered.

There was an odd glitter to his eyes that somehow made Hawkwood uneasy, as though they had something lurking behind them. For an instant he was inclined to agree with the distressed priest, but then he dismissed the notion and shook his head.

"Father, what reasons can you give for this, beyond the usual disquiet of a landsman at being far out to sea? It affects all of us at one time or another – the absence of land on any horizon, the limitless appearance of the ocean. But you will grow used to it, believe me. And there is no reason to think the caravel is lost. It is as fine a vessel as this one, and I'll be surprised if we ever have to weather a worse storm than the last in our crossing of the Western Ocean."

"Even if we are upon it when winter comes?" the Inceptine asked. He had one hand white-knuckled round his Saint's symbol.

"What makes you think we will still be at sea by then?" Hawkwood asked lightly.

"We have been blown far off our course. Any fool can see that. Can you even tell us where we are, Captain? Could any man? It could be we will be sailing until our provisions run out." His hand tightened further on the symbol at his breast until Hawkwood fancied he could hear the fine gold creak. "And we will thirst or starve to death, becoming a floating graveyard upon this accursed sea. I tell you, Captain, it is rank impiety to suppose that any man can cross the Western Ocean. It is a border of the world set there by the hand of God, and no man may breach it."

Here he looked away, and Hawkwood could have sworn that the priest knew these words were false.

"I cannot authorize the abandonment of the voyage," Hawkwood said in measured tones, hiding the exasperation he felt. "For it is not I who bears the ultimate responsibility. While the ship floats and is in a condition to carry on, the broader decisions are left to Lord Murad. I can only override him if I feel that my technical knowledge renders my decisions more valid than his. The ship can go on, once we have made our repairs, so the decision to turn back is not mine to make, but Murad's. So you see, Father, you have come to the wrong man."

Let Murad muzzle this priest, not I, he was thinking. *The pious dastard thinks of me as common scum, to obey the orders of the Church nobility without question. Well, I will not disabuse him of that notion. Let him go to Murad for his refusal. He may take it more easily from one of his station.*

"I see," the priest said, bowing his head so that Hawkwood might not see his eyes.

They could hear the shouts of the sailors out on deck, the creak of rope and squeak of pulleys. The crew must have been hauling the new topmast out of the hold. Hawkwood chafed to be away, but the Inceptine continued to sit with his head bowed.

"Father –" Hawkwood began.

"I tell you there is a curse on this ship and those aboard her!" the priest blurted out. "We will leave our bones upon her decks ere we ever sight any mythical Western Continent!"

"Calm down, man! Making wild claims like these will help no one. Do you want to panic the passengers?"

"The passengers!" Ortelius spat. "Dweomer-folk! The world would be better rid of them. Do they even know where they are headed? They are like cattle being driven to the slaughter!"

With that he leapt up off his stool and, throwing open the cabin door, launched out into the companionway. He barked his shin on the storm sill and went sprawling, then gathered himself up and billowed off, out to the glaring brightness of the deck. Hawkwood stared after his black flapping form in wonder and disquiet. He had the strangest idea that the Inceptine knew more of the ship's destination than he did himself.

"The old Raven is going mad," he said, slamming the bulkhead door and laughing a little uneasily.

Another knock at the just-closed door, but before Hawkwood could say anything it had opened and Murad was standing there.

"I heard," the nobleman said.

"Thin bulkheads. There are few secrets on board ship," Hawkwood said, annoyed.

"Just as well. Forewarned is forearmed, as they say." Murad perched on the edge of Hawkwood's desk nonchalantly. He had taken off his leathers and was in a loose linen shirt and breeches. A scabbarded poniard hung from his belt.

"Do you believe him?" Murad asked.

"No. Seamen may be superstitious, but they are not fools."

"Will we be at sea through the winter then, trying to regain our course?"

"Not necessarily," Hawkwood admitted. Murad looked terrible. They all did in the aftermath of the storm. Most of the crew were like badly animated zombies, but Murad was as lean as a well-gnawed bone and there were muddy puddles under his eyes, red lines breaking across his corneas. He was like a man who had forgotten how to sleep.

"There is a weather-worker on board. I suppose you've heard."

"The soldiers speak of it."

"Well, we have two choices. Either we whistle for a wind and then try beating north-west, which according to Tyrenius's rutter – or what you have allowed me to read of it – would be right into the teeth of the prevailing north-westerlies."

"What would that mean?" Murad snapped.

"It would mean extra months at sea. Half-rations, the loss of your remaining horses. Probably the deaths of the weakest passengers."

"And the other alternative?"

"We ask the weather-worker to utilize his skills."

"His sorcery," Murad sneered.

"Whatever. And he blows us back on course as easy as you please."

"Have you sailed with a weather-worker before, Hawkwood?"

"Only once, in the Levangore. The Merduks employ them in their galley squadrons to bring down calms when they are attacking sailing ships. The one I met was chief pilot in the port of Alcaras in Calmar. Their magic works, Murad."

"Their magic, yes." The nobleman seemed deep in thought.

"Do you realize that Ortelius is a spy, sent to observe the voyage for his master the Prelate of Hebrion?"

"The thought had crossed my mind."

"It will be bad enough that our crew are half-Merduk and our passengers a parcel of sorcerers. Now we are to use sorcery to propel the very ship itself."

"Surely the voyage comes under the King's protection. The Prelate would not dare –"

"It is the colony I am thinking of. It is a new Hebrian province we will be seeking to establish in the west, Hawkwood, but if the Prelate of Hebrion sets his face against it, it may become simply a place of exile for undesirables."

Hawkwood laughed at that. "I can see it now: Murad, lord of witches and thieves."

"And Hawkwood, admiral of prison hulks," Murad countered.

They glared at one another, tension sizzling in the air between them.

"It is your decision to make," Hawkwood said stiffly at last. "But as master of the *Osprey* I feel bound to tell you that if we do not use sorcery to fill our sails then we will be drinking our own piss ere we sight land."

"I will think on it a while," Murad told him, and moved towards the door.

"One more thing," Hawkwood said, feeling reckless.

"Yes?"

"That fellow Bardolin. He asked me to have a word with you about the girl Griella."

Murad spun on his heel. "What about her?"

"I suppose he wants you to leave her alone. Perhaps she does not relish your attentions, my lord."

Before Hawkwood could even flinch, Murad's poniard was naked and shining at his throat.

"My affairs of the heart are not a basis for discussion, Captain, at any time."

Hawkwood's eyes were aflame. "The passengers are my responsibility, along with the running of the ship."

"What's the matter, Captain? Are you jealous? Have you lost your taste for boys, perhaps?"

The poniard broke the skin.

"I do not hold with rape, Murad," Hawkwood said

steadily. "Bardolin is rumoured to be a mage, not a man to cross lightly."

"Neither am I, Captain." The blade left Hawkwood's throat, was scabbarded again. "Find this weather-worker, and let him ply his trade," Murad said casually. "We can't let a man like our good priest end up drinking his own piss."

"What will you tell him?"

"Nothing. He is worn-looking, don't you think? Maybe he has a streak of madness in him induced by the strain of the past days. It would be a shame were something to happen to him ere we sight land."

Hawkwood said nothing, but rubbed his throat where the poniard tip had pricked it.

PERNICUS WAS A small man, red-haired and weak-eyed. His nose was long enough to overhang his upper lip and he was as pale as parchment, a bruise on his high forehead lingering evidence of the passage of the storm.

He stood on the quarterdeck as though it were the scaffold, licking dry lips and glancing at Hawkwood and Murad like a dog searching for its master. Hawkwood smiled reassuringly at him.

"Come, Master Pernicus. Show us your skill."

The waist was crowded with people. Most of the passengers had learned of what was happening and had dragged themselves out of the fetid gundeck. Bardolin was there, as stern as a sergeant-at-arms, and beside him was Griella. Most of the ship's crew were in the shrouds or were standing ready at the lifts and braces, waiting to trim the yards when the wind appeared. Soldiers lined the forecastle and the gangways, slow-match lit and sending ribands of smoke out to hang in the limpid air. Sequero and di Souza had their swords drawn.

But at the forefront of them all, at the foot of the quarterdeck ladder, stood Ortelius, his eyes fixed on the diminutive weather-worker above. His face was skull-like in the harsh sunlight, his eyes two deep glitters in sunken sockets.

"Get to it, man!" Murad barked impatiently. Pernicus jumped like a frog, and there was a rattle of laughter from the soldiers on the forecastle. Then silence again as the two ensigns glared round and sergeant Mensurado administered a discreet kick. The sails flapped idly overhead and the ship was motionless under the blazing sun, like an insect impaled upon a pin. Pernicus closed his eyes.

Minutes went past, and the soldiers stirred restlessly. Three bells in the afternoon watch was struck, the ship's bell as loud as a gunshot in the quiet. Pernicus's lips moved silently.

The main topsail swayed and flapped once, twice. Hawkwood thought he felt the faintest zephyr on his cheek, though it might have been his hopeful imagination. Pernicus spoke at last, in a choked murmur:

"It is hard. There is nothing to work for for leagues, but I think I have found it. Yes. I think it will do."

"It had better," Murad said in a low, ominous voice.

The sun was unrelenting. It baked the decks and made tar drip from the rigging on to those below, spotting the painfully bright armour of the soldiers. Finally Pernicus sighed and rubbed his eyes. He turned to face Hawkwood.

"I have done it, Captain. You shall have your wind. It is on its way."

Then he left the quarterdeck, gaped at by those who had never seen a weather-worker perform before, and went below.

"Is that it?" Murad snapped. "I'll have the little mountebank flogged up and down the ship."

"Wait," Hawkwood said.

"Nothing happened, Captain."

"Wait, damn you!"

The crowd in the waist was already dispersing, buzzing with talk. The soldiers were filing down off the gangways, beating out their slow-match on the ship's rail and guffawing at their own jokes. Ortelius remained motionless, as did Bardolin.

A breeze ruffled Hawkwood's hair and made the sails crack and fill.

"Ready, lads!" he called to the crew, who were waiting patiently at their stations.

The light faded. The ship's company looked up as one to see outrider clouds moving across the face of the sun. The surface of the sea to the south-east of the ship wrinkled like folded silk.

"Here she comes. Steady on the braces. Tiller there, course nor'-nor'-west."

"Aye, sir."

The breeze strengthened, and suddenly the sails were full and straining, the masts creaking as they took the strain. The carrack tilted and her bow dipped as the wind took her on the stern. She began to move, slowly at first and then picking up speed.

"Brace that foresail round, you damned fools! You're spilling the wind. Velasca, more men to the foremast. And set bonnets on the courses."

"Aye, sir!"

"We're moving!" someone shouted from the waist, and as the carrack began to slide swiftly through the water the passengers broke out into laughter and cheers. "Good old Pernicus!"

"Leadsman to the forechains!" Hawkwood shouted, grinning. "Let's see what she's doing."

The carrack was alive again, no longer the stranded, battered creature she had been in the past days. Hawkwood experienced a jet of sheer joy as he felt the ship stirring under his feet and saw her wake beginning to foam astern.

"So we have our wind," Murad said, sounding a little bemused. "I have never seen anything like it, I must say."

"I have," said Brother Ortelius. He had climbed up to the quarterdeck, his face like granite. "May God forgive you both – and that wretched creature of Dweomer – for what you have done here today."

"Easy, Father –" Hawkwood began.

"Brother Ortelius," Murad said coldly, "you will kindly refrain from making comments which might be construed as detrimental to the morale of the ship's company. If you have opinions you may seek to air them in private with either myself or the captain; otherwise you will keep them to yourself. You are not well, obviously. I would not like to have to confine a man of your dignity to his hammock, but I will if need be. Good day, sir."

Ortelius looked as though a blood vessel might burst. His face went scarlet and his mouth worked soundlessly. Some of Hawkwood's crew turned aside to hide their exultant smiles.

"You cannot muzzle me, sir," Ortelius said at last, dripping venom. "I am a noble of the Church, subject to no authority save my spiritual superiors. I answer to them and to no one else."

"You answer to me and to Captain Hawkwood as long as you are aboard this ship. Ours is the ultimate responsibility, and the ultimate authority. Priest or no, if I hear you have been preaching any more superstitious claptrap I'll have you put in irons in the bilge. Now go below, sir, before I do something I may regret."

"You have already done that, sir, believe me," Ortelius hissed out of a mottled countenance. His eyes glittered like a snake and he made the Sign of the Saint as though flinging a curse at the lean nobleman.

"I said go below. Or will I have a pair of soldiers escort you?"

The black-garbed priest left the quarterdeck. There was a hoot of laughter, quickly smothered, from one of the sailors on the yards.

"That may not have been wise," Hawkwood said quietly.

"Indeed. But by all the saints in God's heaven, Hawkwood, I enjoyed it. Those black vultures think they have the world in their pocket; it is good to disabuse them of the notion now and again." Murad was smiling, and for a moment Hawkwood almost liked him; he knew he could never have stood up to the Inceptine in the same manner. No matter how much he hated the Ravens, their authority was deeply ingrained in his mind, as it was in the mind of every commoner. Perhaps one had to be a noble to see the man behind the symbol.

"There is something I cannot account for, though," Murad said thoughtfully.

"What is that?"

"Ortelius. He was angry, yes; furious, even. But I could have sworn his outrage was founded on more than that. On fear. It is strange. Inexplicable."

"I think he knows more than he seems to," Hawkwood said in a low voice. As one, he and Murad moved to the larboard rail to be out of earshot of the crew.

"My thought also," the scarred nobleman agreed.

"You're sure he was sent by the Prelate of Hebrion?"

"Almost, yes. I have not encountered him before, though, and I know most of the clerics who hang about Abeleyn's court and the Prelate's."

"There is no clue as to his background?"

"Oh, he'll be a scion of some minor noble family – the Inceptines always are. There will probably be a plum post or other waiting for him in return for his services on the voyage."

"You do not seem too concerned about what he may report back to the Church in Abrusio."

Murad stared at Hawkwood, face expressionless. "There are many long leagues of sailing before us yet, Captain, and an unknown continent awaiting our feet. Many things could happen before any of us sees Hebrion once more. Hazardous things. Dangerous things."

"You cannot do that, Murad! He is a priest."

"He is a man, and his blood is the same colour as my own. When he chose to set his will against mine he fixed his own fate. There is nothing more to be said."

Murad's matter-of-fact tone chilled Hawkwood. He had seen battle, ship-to-ship actions with the corsairs where blood had washed the decks and men had been mangled by shot and blade, but this cold, calculated dismissal of another man's life unsettled him. He wondered what he would have to do to earn the same treatment from the scheming nobleman.

He left the larboard rail and stood at the break of the quarterdeck, wishing to put distance between himself and Murad. The carrack was flying along and spray was coming aboard to cool his brow. The third of the leadsmen, the one stationed by the taffrail, was holding the dripping, knotted rope with the thick faggot of wood fastened to the end.

"Six knots, sir, and she's still gathering way!"

Hawkwood forced himself to respond to the leadsman's gaiety, though whatever joy he had in the ship's progress had been dampened by Murad.

"Try her again, Borim. See if she won't get up to eight when the bonnets are on."

"Aye, sir!"

Murad left the quarterdeck without another word. Hawkwood watched him go, knowing that the nobleman was plotting murder on his ship.

BARDOLIN LEANED ON the forecastle rail and stared down into the breaking foam of the carrack's bow. They were clipping along at a wonderful rate and the cool moving air was like a benison after the unmoving furnace of the doldrums.

The soldiers had hauled the remaining horses up out of the waist hatches and were exercising them, leading them round and round the deck. The poor brutes were covered in sores and their ribs stood out like the hoops on a barrel. Bardolin wondered if they would ever live to set foot on the new continent that awaited them in the west.

A good man, that Pernicus. It had been Bardolin who had convinced him to use his powers and call in a wind. He was below now, concentrating. There were few suitable systems of air in the region, and he was having constantly to maintain the one that propelled the ship. Usually a weather-worker selected a suitable system nearby and manoeuvred it into a position where it could do his work for him, but here Pernicus was having to keep at it to make sure the sorcerous wind did not fade away.

A desolate ocean, this. They were too far from land to sight any birds, and the only sea-life Bardolin had glimpsed were a few shoals of wingfish flitting over the surface of the waves. He had seen a deep-sea jellyfish, too, which the sailors called devil's toadstools. This one had been twenty feet across, trailing tentacles half as long as the ship and glowing down in the dimmer water as it pulsed its obscure way through the depths.

The imp chirruped with excitement. It was peeking out of his robe, its eyes shining as it watched the water break under the keel and felt the swift breeze of the ship's passage. It was growing steadily more restless at having to keep out of sight. The only time Bardolin set it free was in the night, when it hunted rats up and down the ship.

He had wondered about sending it into Murad's cabin, to observe him and Griella, but the very thought had shamed him.

As though conjured up by his preoccupations, Griella appeared at his side. She leant on the rail beside him and scratched the ear of the imp, which gurgled with pleasure.

"We have our wind, then," she said.

"So it would seem."

"How long can Pernicus keep it going?"

"Some days. By then we should have picked up one of the prevailing winds beyond the area of the doldrums."

"You're beginning to sound like a sailor, Bardolin. You'll be talking of decks and companionways and ports next... Why have you been avoiding me?"

"I have not," Bardolin said, keeping his gaze anchored in the leaping waves.

"Are you jealous of the nobleman?"

The mage said nothing.

"I thought I told you: I sleep with him to protect us. His word is law, remember? I could not refuse."

"I know that," Bardolin said testily. "I am not your keeper in any case."

"You *are* jealous."

"I am afraid."

"Of what? That he might make me his duchess? I think not."

"It is common knowledge amongst the crew and the soldiers that he is... besotted with you. And I look at his face every day, and see the changes being wrought in it. What are you doing, Griella?"

She smiled. "I think I give him bad dreams."

"You are playing with a hot coal. You will get burned."

"I know what it is I do. I make him pay for his nobility."

"Take care, child. If you are discovered for what you are, your life is forfeit – especially with that rabid priest on board. And even the Dweomer-folk have no love for shifters. You would be alone."

"Alone, Bardolin? Would you not stand by me?"

The mage sighed heavily. "You know I would, though much good it would do us."

"But you don't like killing. How would you defend me?" she asked playfully.

"Enough, Griella. I am not in the mood for your games." He paused, then, hating himself, asked: "Do you *like* going to his bed?"

She tossed her head. "Perhaps, sometimes. I am in a position of power, Bardolin, for the first time in my life. He loves me." She laughed, and the imp grinned at her until the corners of its mouth reached its long ears.

"He will be viceroy of this colony we are to found in the west, and he loves me."

"It sounds as though you *do* expect to be a duchess."

"I will be something, not just a peasant girl with the black disease. I will be something more, duchess or no."

"I spoke to the captain about you."

"What?" She was aghast. "Why? What did you say?"

Bardolin's voice grew savage. "At that time I thought you were not so willing to be bedded by this man. I asked the captain to intercede. He did, but he tells me that Murad would hear none of it."

Griella giggled. "I have him in thrall, the poor man."

"No good will come of it, girl. Leave it."

"No. You are like a mother hen clucking over an egg, Bardolin. Leave off me." There was a touch of violence in her voice. Bardolin turned and looked into her face.

It was almost four bells in the last dog-watch, and the sky was darkening. Already the lanterns at the stern and mastheads had been lit in the hope that the other ship would see them and the little fleet would be reunited. Griella's face was a livid oval in the failing light and her tawny hair seemed sable-dark. But her eyes had a shine to them, a luminosity that Bardolin did not like.

"Dusk and dawn, they are the two hardest times, are they not?" he asked quietly. "Traditionally the time of the hunt. The longer we are at sea, Griella, the harder it will become to control. Do not let your tormenting of this man get out of hand, or the change will be upon you ere you know it."

"I can control it," she said, and her voice seemed deeper than it had been.

"Yes. But one time, in the last light of the day or in the dark hour before the dawn, it will get the better of you. The beast seeks always to be free, but you must not let it out, Griella."

She turned her face away from him. Four bells rang out, and the watch changed, a crowd of sailors coming up yawning from belowdecks, those on duty leaving their posts for the swaying hammocks below.

"I am not a child any more, Bardolin. I do not need your advice. I sought to help you."

"Help yourself first," he said.

"I will. I can make my own way."

Without looking at him again she left the forecastle. He watched her small, upright figure traverse the waist – the sailors knew better than to molest her now – and enter the sterncastle where the officers' cabins were.

Bardolin resumed his watching of the waters whilst the imp cheeped interrogatively from his breast. It was hungry, and wanted to be off on its nightly search for rats.

"Soon, my little comrade, soon," he soothed it.

He leaned on the rail and watched the sun sink down slowly into the Western Ocean, a great saffron disc touched with a burning wrack of cloud. It gave the sea on the western horizon the aspect of just-spilled blood.

The carrack forged on willingly, propelled by the sorcerous wind. Her sails were pyramids of rose-tinted canvas in the last light of the sunset and the lanterns about her gleamed like earthbound stars. The ship was alone on the face of the waters; as far as any man might see, there was no other speck of life moving under the gleam of the rising moon.

TWENTY

ORMANN DYKE.

The tumbling thunder of the bombardment went on relentlessly, but they had grown used to it and no longer commented upon it.

"We are more or less blind to what goes on over the brow of the nearest hill," Martellus told his assembled officers. "I have sent out three different scouting missions, but none has returned. The Merduks' security is excellent. All we know therefore is what we see: a minimum of siegeworks, the deployment of the batteries to the front –"

"And a hive of activity to the rear," old Isak finished.

"Just so. The eastern barbican has taken a pasting, and the gunnery battle is all but over. He will assault very soon."

"How many guns do we have still firing across the river?" one man asked.

"Less than half a dozen, and those are the masked ones that Andruw has been saving for the end."

"We cannot let the eastern side of the bridge go without a struggle," one officer said.

"I agree." Martellus looked round at his fellow Torunnans. "The engineers have been working through the night. They have planted charges under the remaining supports. The Searil bridge can be blown in a matter of moments, but first I want to bloody their nose again. I want them to assault the barbican."

"What's left of it," someone murmured.

Three days had passed since the first, headlong assault of the Merduk army. In those three days there had, contrary to Martellus's prediction, been no direct attack on the eastern fortifications. Instead Shahr Baraz had brought up his heavy guns, emplaced them behind stout revetments and begun an artillery duel with the guns in the eastern barbican. He had lost heavily in men and material in the first deployment, but once his pieces were secure the more numerous Merduk heavy culverins had begun to pound the Torunnan fort on the eastern bank to rubble. The bombardment had continued unabated for thirty-six hours. Most of Andruw's guns were silenced, and the eastern barbican was holed and breached in several places. Only a scratch garrison remained there. The rest had been withdrawn back over the river to the island, that long strip of land between the river and the dyke.

"The heavy charges are in place. When they occupy the eastern fort they are in for a shock, but we must make them occupy it – we must make them pay for it. And to do that we must keep troops there, to tempt them in," Martellus said relentlessly.

"Who commands this forlorn hope?" an officer asked.

"Young Corfe, my aide, the one who was at Aekir. Andruw will have his hands full directing the remaining artillery. The rest of the skeleton garrison is under Corfe."

"Let us hope he will not turn tail like he did at Aekir," someone muttered.

Martellus's eyes turned that pale, inhuman shade which always silenced his subordinates.

"He will do his duty."

JAN BAFFARIN, THE chief engineer, came scuttling like a crab through the low-ceilinged bomb-proof towards Corfe and Andruw.

"We've repaired the powder lines. There should be no problem now."

He was shouting without realizing it, as they all had been for the past day and night. The huge tumult of the bombardment overhead had ceased to seem unusual and was now part of the accepted order of things.

The bomb-proof was large, low and massively buttressed. Five hundred men crouched within it as the shell and shot rained down on the fortress above their heads. Dust and fragments of loose stone came drifting down when there was a particularly close hit, and the air seemed to shake and shimmer in the light of the shuddering oil lamps. "The Catacombs," the troops had wryly labelled their shelter, and it seemed apt. All around the bodies of men sprawled and lolled, some asleep despite the unending noise and vibration. They looked like the aftermath of the plague, a scene from some febrile nightmare.

Corfe roused himself from the concussed stupor he had been in.

"What of the guns?"

"The casemates are intact, but Saint's love, those are the heaviest calibre shells I've ever seen. The gatehouse is a pile of rubble, and the walls are in pieces. They don't have to attack. If they keep this up they'll reduce Ormann Dyke to powder without ever setting foot in it."

Andruw shook his head. "They can't have the ammunition and powder, not with their supply line as long as it is. I'll wager a good bottle of Candelarian that they're running low right now. This bombardment is for show as much as anything else. They want to stun us into surrender, perhaps."

A particularly close explosion made them wince and duck instinctively. The granite ceiling seemed to groan under the assault.

"Some show," Baffarin said dubiously.

"Your men know the drill," Corfe said. "As soon as the rearguard is across the bridge you touch off the charges, both on the bridge itself and in the barbican. We'll send the whole damn lot of them flying into the Thurians. There's a show for you."

The engineer chuckled. The bombardment stopped.

There were a few tardy detonations from late-falling shells, and then a silence came down which was so profound that Corfe was alarmed, for a second believing that he had gone deaf. Someone coughed, and the noise seemed abnormally loud in the sudden stillness. The sleeping men began rousing themselves, staring around and shaking each other.

"On your feet!" Corfe shouted. "Gunners to your pieces, arquebusiers to your stations. They're on their way, lads!"

The catacombs dissolved into a shadowy chaos of moving men. Baffarin grasped Corfe's arm.

"See you on the other side of the river," he said, and then was gone.

THE DEVASTATION WAS awe-inspiring. The eastern barbican was like a castle of sand which had been undermined by the tide. There were yawning gaps in the walls, mounds of stone and rubble everywhere, burning timber crackling and shimmering in the dust-laden air. Corfe's meagre command fanned out to their prearranged positions whilst Andruw's gunners began wheeling the surviving culverins into firing positions.

Corfe clambered up the ruin of the gatehouse and surveyed the Merduk dispositions. Their batteries were smoke-shrouded, though a cold breeze from the north was shredding the powder fog moment by moment. He glimpsed great bodies of men on the move, elephants, regiments of horsemen and lumbering, heavy-laden waggons. The hills were crawling with orderly and disorderly movement.

A gun went off, as flat as a hand-clap after the thunder of the heavy-calibre cannons, and a sort of shudder went through the columns behind the smoke. They began to move, and soon it was possible to make out three armies marching towards the line of the river. One was aimed at the ruin of the barbican, the other two to the north and south, their goal apparently the Searil River itself. They were oddly burdened, and waggons rolled along in their midst, hauled by elephants.

The five hundred Torunnans who were the barbican's last defenders spread out along the tattered battlements, their arquebuses levelled. Their orders were to make a demonstration, to draw as many of the enemy as possible into the fortifications and then withdraw slowly, finally escaping over the Searil bridge. It would be a difficult thing to control, this fighting retreat. Corfe felt no fear at the thought of the coming assault or the possibility of injury and death, but he was mortally afraid of making a hash of things. These five hundred were his command, his first since the fall of Aekir; and he knew he was still regarded by many of his fellow Torunnans as the man who had deserted John Mogen. He was coldly determined to do well today.

The warmth of the sun was bright and welcome. Men wriggled fingers in their ears to let out the ringing aftermath of the artillery, then sighted down their weapons at the advancing enemy.

"Easy!" Corfe called out. "Wait 'til I give the word."

A gun barked from one of the upper casemates, and a second later a blossom of blasted earth appeared on the slope before the Merduk formations. Andruw testing the range.

They came on at a slow walk, the high-sided waggons trundling in their midst. The northern and southern hosts had more of these elephant-drawn vehicles than the one which was aimed at the barbican. Corfe strained his eyes to make out the strange loads, then whistled.

"Boats!" The waggons were loaded with shallow-hulled, punt-like craft piled one on top of the other. They were going to try and cross the Searil to north and south whilst engaging the garrison on the east bank at the same time.

"They'll be lucky," a nearby soldier said, and spat over the battered wall. "The Searil's swollen after the rain. It's running along like a bolting horse. I hope they have strong arms, or they'll be washed all the way down to the Kardian."

There was a spatter of brief laughter along the ramparts.

Andruw's guns began to sing out one by one. The young gunnery officer had kept his five most accurate pieces this side of the river, and was adjusting their traverse and elevation personally. They began to lob explosive shells into the forefront of the central enemy formation, blasting them into red ruin. Corfe saw an elephant lifted half off its feet as a shell exploded squarely under it. Another hit one of the high-laden wains and sent slivers of deadly wood spraying like spears through its escort. There was confusion, men milling about, panic-stricken beasts trampling and trumpeting madly. The Torunnans watched with a high sense of glee, happy to be repaying the Merduks in kind for the relentless bombardment of the past days.

But the ranks reformed, and the Merduks came on again faster, loping along at a brisk trot, leaving the waggons behind. Corfe could see that the lead elements of these men were in shining half-armour and mail. They were the *Hraibadar*, the shock-troops of Shahr Baraz.

The formation splintered and spread out so that the shellbursts took a lesser toll. As they jogged ever closer Corfe rapped out orders, pitching his voice to carry over the rippling booms of the Torunnan artillery.

"Ready your pieces!"

The men fitted the smouldering slow-match into the serpentine-locks of their arquebuses.

"Present your pieces!"

He raised his sabre. He could see individual faces in the ranks of the approaching enemy, horsehair plumes, panting mouths underneath the tall helms.

He swept his sabre down. "Give fire!"

The walls erupted in a line of smoke and flame as nigh on five hundred arquebuses went off in a single volley. The enemy, scarcely a hundred yards away, were thrown back as if by a sudden gale of wind. The front ranks dissolved into a mass of wriggling, crawling men, and those behind faltered a moment, then came on again.

"Reload!" Corfe shouted. It was Andruw's turn now.

The five guns of the remaining Torunnan battery waited until the Merduks were within fifty yards, and then fired as one. They were loaded with deadly canister: hollow cans of thin metal containing thousands of arquebus bullets. Five jets of smoke spurted out, and the Merduks were flattened once more in a dreadful slaughter.

The smoke was too thick for aiming. Corfe shouted at the top of his voice, waving his sabre: "Back off the walls! Second position, lads! Back on me!"

The Torunnans ran down from the ruined battlements and formed a swift two-deep line below. Their sergeants and ensigns pushed them into position and then stood ready.

The gunners were leaving their pieces, having spiked the touch-holes. Corfe saw Andruw there, laughing as he ran. When the last artillerymen were behind the line of arquebusiers he gave the order.

"Ready your pieces!"

A line of figures pouring through the gaps in the walls now, hundreds of them, screaming as they came.

"Front rank, present your pieces!"

Thirty yards away. Could they be stopped? It seemed impossible.

"Give fire!"

A shattering volley that hid the enemy in clouds of dark smoke.

"First rank, fall back. Second rank, give fire!"

The first rank were running back through the fortress to the bridge, where Baffarin and his engineers waited. It would be very close.

The second volley staggered the smoke, flattened more of the oncoming enemy, but Corfe's men were falling now for the Merduks had arquebusiers up on the battlements firing blindly into the Torunnan ranks.

A shrieking line of figures issued out of the powder cloud like friends catapulted out of Hell.

A few weapons were fired, a ragged volley. And then it was hand-to-hand down the line. The arquebusiers dropped their weapons and drew their sabres, if they had time. Others flailed about them with the butts of their firearms.

Corfe gutted a howling Merduk, swept the heavy sabre across the face of another, punched the spiked hilt into the jaw of a third.

"Fall back! Fall back to the bridge!"

They were being overwhelmed. The enemy was pouring in – thousands of them, perhaps. All across the rubble-strewn and pitted drill square Corfe saw his line dissolve into knots and groups of isolated men as the Merduks punched into it. Those who could were retreating; others went down under the flashing scimitars still swinging their weapons.

He clanged aside a scimitar, elbowed the man off-balance, thrust at another, then spun round at the first man and slashed open his arm. They were all around him. He whirled and hacked and thrust without conscious volition. The knot broke apart. There was space again, a moving turmoil of figures running past, shouting; there was flashing murder every instant and so much blood it seemed some other element spilling everywhere.

Someone was pulling frantically at his arm. He swung round and almost decapitated Andruw. The gunner officer had a slash across his face which had left a flap of flesh hanging over one eye.

"Time to go, Corfe. We can't hold them any longer."

"How many at the bridge?"

"Enough. You've done your duty, so come. They're preparing to blow the charges."

Corfe allowed himself to be tugged away and followed Andruw's lead out of the fortress, calling the last of his men with him as he went.

The bridge was standing on a few stone supports. The rest had been chiselled and blasted away. Baffarin was there, grinning. "Glad to see you, Haptman. We thought you had got lost. You're among the last."

Corfe and Andruw ran across the long, empty bridge. The lead elements of the enemy were a scant fifty yards behind, and arquebus balls were kicking up splinters of stone around their feet as they made the western bank. The survivors of Corfe's command were crouched there among the revetments of the island. Those who still possessed their firearms were firing methodically into the press of the advancing enemy. As they saw Corfe and Andruw a hoarse cheer went up.

Baffarin's engineers were touching off ribbons of bound rags with slow-match. A culverin was firing canister across the bridge, stalling the Merduk advance. Corfe sank to his knees in the shelter of the earthworks behind the bridge, chest heaving. He felt as though someone had lit a fire inside his armour and the black metal seemed insufferably heavy, though when running he had not even noticed its weight.

"Only a few seconds now," Baffarin said. He was still grinning, but there was no humour on his face; it was like a rictus. Sweat carved runnels down his black temples.

Then the charges went off.

Not a noise, just a flash, an immense... impression. A sense of a huge happening that the brain could not quite grasp. Corfe felt the air sucked out of his lungs. He shut his eyes and buried his face in his arms, but he heard the secondary explosions distantly, as though he were separated from them by thick glass. Then there was the rain of rubble and wood and more terrible things falling all around him. Something heavy clanged off his backplate. Something else hit his hand as it gripped the back of his head, hard enough to numb. Rolling concussions, a swift-moving thunder. Water raining, men moaning. The echoes of the detonations reverberated off the face of the hills, faceted thunder, at last dwindling.

Corfe looked up. The bridge was gone, and the very earth seemed changed. Of the eastern barbican, that great, high-walled fortress, there was little left. Only stumps and mounds of smoking stone amid a huge series of craters. The catacombs laid bare to the sky. Fire flickering – the smell of powder and blood and broken soil, a reek heavier and more solid than any he had ever experienced before, even at Aekir.

"Holy God!" Andruw said beside him.

The slopes leading down to the site of the barbican were black with men, some alive and cowering, others turned into corpses. It was as if they had simultaneously experienced a vision, witnessed an apparition of their prophet, perhaps. The carcasses of elephants lay like outcrops of grey rock, except where they had been mutilated into something else. The entire battlefield seemed frozen in shock.

"I'll bet they heard that in Torunn," Baffarin said, the end of the slow-match still gripped in an ivory-knuckled hand.

"I'll bet they heard it in fucking Hebrion," a nearby trooper said, and there were automatic chuckles, empty humour. They were too shocked.

The air clicked in Corfe's throat. He found his voice, and surprised himself with its steadiness. "Who have we got here? Tove, Marsen, good. Get the men spread out along the earthworks. I want weapons primed. Ridal, get you to the citadel and report to Martellus. Tell him – tell him the eastern barbican and bridge are blown –"

"In case he hadn't noticed," someone put in.

"– And tell him I have some..." He glanced around. Sweet Saints in heaven! So few? "I have some tenscore men at my disposal."

The survivors of Corfe's first command busied themselves carrying out his orders.

"They're fighting along the river," someone said, standing and peering to the north. The boom of artillery and crackle of arquebus fire had shattered the momentary silence.

"That's their fight. We've a job to do here," Corfe said harshly. Then he sat down quickly with his back to a revetment, lest his rubber legs turn traitor and buckle under him.

MARTELLUS WATCHED THE climax of the battle from his usual vantage point on the heights of the citadel. Not for him the hurly-burly of trying to command his men from the thick of things. John Mogen had been the man for that. No, he liked to stand back and study the layout of the developing conflict, base his decisions on logic and the dispatches that he received minute by minute, borne by grimed and bloody couriers. A general could direct things best from afar, distanced from the shouting turmoil of his battle. Some men, it was true, could command an army whilst fighting almost in the front rank, but they were rare geniuses. Inevitably Mogen came to mind again.

The roar of the explosion was a distant echo of thunder rolling back and forth between hills ever further away. A huge plume of smoke rose up from the centre of the battlefield where the eastern barbican had once been. The assault had been blunted there, perhaps even crippled. Young Corfe had done a good job. He was someone to watch, despite the cloud hanging over his past.

But to north and south of the smoke two fresh Merduk formations, each perhaps twenty-five thousand strong, had closed on the river. The artillery on the Long Walls and the island had peppered their ranks unceasingly with shells, but they came on regardless. Now they were unloading the flat punt-like boats from the elephant wains and preparing to brave the foaming current of the swollen Searil River.

Once they cross the river in force, Martellus thought, *it is only a matter of time. We may destroy them in their thousands as they cross the dyke, but cross it they will. The river is our best defence, at least while it is running this full.*

He turned to an aide.

"Is Ranafast standing ready with the sortie force?"

"Yes, sir."

"Then go to him. Give him my compliments and tell him he is to take his command out to the island at once. He can also strip the walls of every fourth man except for gunners, and all are to be arquebus-armed. He is to contest the crossing of the river. Is that clear?"

"Yes, sir."

A scribe nearby had been scrawling furiously. The written order was entrusted to the aide after Martellus had flashed his signature across it, and then the aide was gone, running down to the Long Walls.

There was not much time for Ranafast to scratch together his command and get into position. Martellus cursed himself. Why had he never envisaged a mass boat crossing? They had been busy, the Merduk engineers, in the weeks they had been stalled at Aekir.

The first of the boats were already being shoved down the eastern bank and into the water. They were massive, crude affairs, propelled by the paddles of their passengers. Fourscore men at least manned each one, and Martellus counted over a hundred of them lining the eastern bank like southern river lizards basking in a tropical sun. Shellbursts were sprouting up in their midst like momentary fungi, shattering boats, sending men flying, panicking the elephants.

The Searil was three hundred yards across at the dyke, a wide brown river that was churning wild and white in many places and was thick with debris from its headwaters. No easy task to paddle across it at the best of times. To do it under shellfire, though... These men excited Martellus's admiration even as he plotted their destruction.

The first wave was setting out. To north and south of the ruined bridge the Searil suddenly became thick with the large, flat boats, like a stream clogged with autumn leaves near its banks.

A thunder of hooves, and Ranafast was leading his horsemen – the vanguard of his command – across the dyke bridges to the island. A column of marching men followed on after the cavalry. With luck, there would be over seven thousand on the western bank to contest the crossing, supported by artillery from the walls.

And yet when he looked at the size, the teeming numbers, of those who clogged the eastern bank, Martellus could not help but feel despair. For miles the edge of the Searil was crawling with enemy soldiers, boats, elephants, horses and waggons. And that was only the assaulting force. On the hills beyond the reserves, the cavalry, the artillery, the countless camp-followers darkened the face of the land like some vast blight. It was inconceivable that the collective will of such a multitude should be thwarted.

And yet he must do it – he *would* do it. He would defy the gloom-mongers and amateur generals and all the rest. He would hold this fortress to his last breath, and he would bleed the Merduk armies white upon it.

Globes of smoke, tiny with distance, appeared along the length of the walls. After a few seconds the boom of the cannon salvoes came drifting up to the citadel, and soon the guns of the citadel itself were firing. The noise was everywhere, together with the blood-quickening smell of gunpowder.

White fountains of exploding water began to burst amid the Merduk boats. Martellus could make out the men in the craft straining like maniacs at their paddles, but remaining in time. They had their heads bowed and shoulders hunched forward as though they were braving a heavy shower of rain. Martellus had seen the same position assumed by most men advancing against heavy fire; it was a kind of instinct.

One, two, then three of the boats were struck in quick succession as the Torunnan artillery began to range in on their targets. Martellus had the best gunners in the world here at the dyke, and now they were fulfilling his faith in them.

The men in the shattered boats sank out of sight at once, weighed down by armour. Even had they worn none, they had no chance in the rushing current.

Ranafast was deploying his men along the western bank whilst his own shells whistled over his head. He had a couple of galloper-guns with him also. But the men were spread perilously thin, and Martellus could see now that the central Merduk column was staging an attack on Corfe's position, manhandling boats amid the debris of the bridge, all the time under heavy fire from Corfe's surviving command and the other defenders who were posted there. Ranafast should see the danger, though.

Sure enough, the cavalry commander brought his two light guns down to Corfe's position, and soon they were barking canister at close range into the Merduks trying to cross there. An ugly little fight, but the main struggle was still going on along the flanks.

The waterborne Merduks were in trouble. More boats were being struck by Torunnan shells, and when these did not sink at once they began to roar downstream like sticks caught in a millrace, crashing into their fellows and sending them downriver in their turn. Soon there were scores of boats whirling and drifting in the middle of the river, wreckage and bodies bobbing up and down, the geysers of shellbursts exploding everywhere.

Some boats reached the western bank, only to receive a hail of arquebus bullets. Their complements straggled ashore to be cut down by Ranafast's men. A tidemark of bodies built up there on the western bank while the Torunnans reloaded methodically and fired volley after volley into the wretches floundering ashore.

The battle had quickly degenerated into a one-sided slaughter. Signal guns began to sound from the Merduk lines calling off the attack, and those on the eastern bank halted as they were about to push a fresh wave of craft into the water. The unfortunates already on the river tried to come about and retrace their course, but it was impossible in that maelstrom of shot, shell and white water. They perished almost to a man.

The assault ground to a bloody and fruitless halt. Some of the Merduks remained on the edge of the river to try and help those labouring in the water, but most began a sullen retreat to their camps on the hillsides above. And all the while, Torunnan artillery lobbed vindictive and jubilant shells at their retreating backs. The attack had not just failed; it had been destroyed before it could even start.

"I want another battery of gallopers detached from the walls and sent to Corfe's position," Martellus said crisply. "Send him another three tercios also; he is closest to the enemy. He must hold the island."

An aide ran off with the order. Martellus's brother officers were laughing and grinning, scarcely able to believe their eyes.

For miles along the line of the river powder smoke hung in the air in thick clouds, and strewn along both banks was the wreck of an army. Men, boats, animals, weapons. It was awesome to behold. They dotted the land like the fallen fruit in an untended orchard, and the river itself was thick with boats half awash, a few figures clinging desperately to the wreckage. They were coursing downstream out of sight, helpless.

"He's lost ten thousand at least," old Isak was saying. "And some of his best troops, too. Sweet Saints, I've never seen carnage like it. He throws away his men as though they were chaff."

"He miscalculated," Martellus said. "Had the river been less full, he would have been at the dyke by now. This attack was intended to see him to the very walls on which we stand. Its repulse will give him pause for thought, but let us not forget that he still has fifty thousand men on those hills who have not yet been under fire. He will try again."

"Then the same thing will happen again," Isak said stubbornly.

"Possibly. We have exhausted our surprises, I think. Now he knows what we have and will be searching his mind for openings, gaps in our defences."

"He cannot mean to assault again for a while, not after that debacle."

"Perhaps not, but do not underestimate Shahr Baraz. He was profligate with his men's lives at Aekir because of the prize that was at stake. I had thought he would be more careful here, if only because of the natural strength of the dyke. It may be that someone in higher authority is urging him on into less well-judged assaults. But we cannot become overconfident. We must look to our flanks. After today he will be probing the upper and lower stretches of the Searil, looking for a crossing point."

"He won't find one. The Searil is running as fast as a riptide and apart from here, at the dyke, the banks are treacherous, mostly cliffs and gorges."

"We know that, but he does not." Martellus sagged suddenly. "I think we have won, for the moment. There will be no more headlong assaults. We have gained a breathing space. It is now up to the kings of the world to aid us. The Saints know we deserve some help after the defence we have made."

"Young Corfe did well."

"Yes, he did. I intend to give him a larger command. He is able enough for it, and he and Andruw work well together."

A few desultory cannon shots spurted out from the Torunnan lines, but a calm was descending over the Searil valley. As though by common consent, the armies had broken off from each other. The Merduks rescued the pathetically few survivors of the river assault without further molestation and loaded them on carts to be driven back within the confines of the camps. A few abandoned boats burned merrily on the eastern bank. The guns fell silent.

THE INDABA OF officers had broken up less than an hour before, and Shahr Baraz was alone in the darkened tent. It was as sparsely furnished as a monk's cell. There was a low wooden cot strewn with army blankets, a folding desk piled with papers, a chair and some stands for the lamps.

And one other thing. The old general set it on the desk and drew the curtain from around it. A small cage. Something inside it chittered and flapped irritably.

"Well, Goleg," Shahr Baraz said in a low voice. He tapped the bars of the cage and regarded its occupant with weary disgust.

"Ha! Man's flesh is too tough for Goleg. Wants a child, a young, sweet thing just out of the cradle."

"Summon your master. I must make my report."

"I want sweet flesh!"

"Do as you are told, abomination, or I'll leave you to rot in that cage."

Two tiny dots of light blinked malevolently from the shadows behind the bars. Two minuscule clawed hands gripped them and shook the metal.

"I know you. You are too old. Soon you will be carrion for Goleg."

"Summon your master."

The two lights dimmed. There was a momentary quiet, broken only by the camp noises outside, the neighing of horses in the cavalry lines. Shahr Baraz sat as if graven in stone.

At last a deep voice said: "Well, General?"

"I must make my report, Orkh. Relay me to the Sultan."

"Good tidings, I trust."

"That is for him to judge."

"Did the assault fail, then?"

"It failed. I would speak to my ruler. No doubt you will be able to eavesdrop."

"Indeed. My little creatures all answer to me – but you and Aurungzeb know that, of course." Another pause. "He is busy with one of his new concubines, the raven-haired Ramusian beauty. Ah, she is exquisite. I envy him. Here he is, my Khedive. The luck of the Prophet be with you."

And with that mild blasphemy, Orkh's voice died. Aurungzeb's impatient tones echoed through the tent in its place.

"Shahr Baraz, my Khedive! General of generals! I am afire. Tell me quickly. What happened?"

"The assault failed, Majesty."

"*What?* How? How did this happen?"

The old soldier seemed to stiffen in his chair, as though anticipating a blow.

"The attack was hasty, ill-judged and ill-prepared. We took the eastern barbican of the fortress, but it was mined and I lost two thousand men when the Ramusians touched it off. The river, also, was flowing too fast for our boats to make a swift crossing. They were cut to pieces whilst still in the water. Those who made it to the western bank died under the muzzles of Torunnan guns."

"How many?"

"We lost some six thousand of the *Hraibadar* – half of those who remained – and another five thousand of the levy."

"And the –/the enemy?"

"I doubt he lost more than a thousand."

The Sultan's voice, when it came again, had changed; the shock had gone and it was as hard as Thurian granite.

"You said the attack was ill-judged. Explain yourself."

"Majesty, if you will remember, I did not want to make this assault. I asked you for more time, time to throw up siegeworks, to look over our options more thoroughly –"

"Time! You have had time. You dawdled in Aekir for weeks. You would have done the same here had I not enjoined you to hasten. This is a paltry place. You said yourself the garrison is less than twenty thousand strong. This is not Aekir, Shahr Baraz. The army should be able to roll over it like an elephant stepping on a frog."

"It is the strongest fortification I have ever seen, including the walls of Aekir," Shahr Baraz said. "I cannot throw my army at it as if it were the log hut of some bandit chieftain. This campaign could prove as difficult as the last –"

"It could if the famed Khedive of my army – *my* army, General – has lost his zest for campaigning."

Baraz's face hardened. "I attacked on your orders, and against my own judgement. That mistake has cost us eleven thousand men dead or too maimed ever to fight again. I will not repeat that mistake."

"How dare you speak to me thus? I am your Sultan, old man. You will obey me or I will find someone else who will."

"So be it, my Sultan. But I will be a party to no more amateur strategy. You can either replace me or leave me to conduct this campaign unhindered. Yours is the choice, and the responsibility."

A long silence. The homunculus's eyes blinked in the shadow of its cage. Shahr Baraz was impassive. *I am too old for diplomacy*, he thought. *I will end what I have always been – a soldier. But I will not see my men slaughtered in my name. Let them know who ordered the attack. Let them see how their Sultan values their lives.*

"My friend," Aurungzeb said finally, and his voice was as smooth as melted chocolate. "We have both spoken hastily. Our concern for the men and our country does us credit, but it leads us into passionate utterances which might later be regretted."

"I agree, Majesty."

"So I will give you another opportunity to prove your loyalty to my house, a loyalty which has never faltered since the days of my grandsire. You will renew the attack on Ormann Dyke at once, and with all the forces at your disposal. You will overwhelm the dyke and then push on south to the Torunnan capital."

"I regret that I cannot comply with your wishes, Majesty."

"Wishes? Who is talking about wishes? You will obey my *orders*, old man."

"I regret that I cannot."

"And why not?"

"Because to do so would wreck this army from top to bottom, and I will not permit that."

"Eyes of the Prophet! Will you defy me?"

"Yes, Majesty."

"Consider yourself my Khedive no longer, then. As the Lord of Victories rules in Paradise, I have suffered your ancient insolence for the last time! Hand over your command to Mughal. He can expect orders from me in writing – and a new Khedive!"

"And I, Majesty?"

"You? Consider yourself under arrest, Shahr Baraz. You will await the arrival of my officers from Orkhan."

"Is that all?"

"By the Lord of Battles, yes – that is all!"

"Fare thee well then, Majesty," Shahr Baraz said calmly. He stood, lifted the cage with its monstrous occupant, and then dashed it to the ground. The homunculus screamed, and in its scream Shahr Baraz heard the agony of Orkh, its sorcerous master. Smiling grimly, he stamped his booted foot on the structure, crunching metal and bone in a morass of ichor and foul-stinking flesh. Then he clapped his hands for his attendants.

"Take this abomination away and burn it," he said, and they flinched from the fire in his eyes.

TWENTY-ONE

IT WAS A scream that brought Murad bolt upright in his hanging cot. He remained stock-still, listening. Nothing but the creak of the ship's timbers, the lap of the water against the hull, the tiny thumps and slaps that were part of being at sea. Nothing.

A dream. He relaxed, lying down again. The girl had disappeared as she always did, and she had left him with a hideous dream – as she always did. The same dream. He preferred to put it out of his mind.

But could not. She was a witch, that was clear – otherwise she would not be a passenger aboard this ship. Maybe she was the man Bardolin's apprentice. He was a wizard of sorts. No doubt she was putting a black spell on him, perhaps ensnaring him with some kind of love magic.

But he doubted it. Their love-making was too real, too solid and genuine to be the product of any spell. It was almost as though she had been dry tinder waiting for a spark. She came to life in his arms, and their coupling was like a nightly battle, a duel for mastery. He had her mastered, he was sure of that. Smiling up at the deckhead he relived the satisfaction of plunging into her and feeling her body heave up in answer. She was a delightful little animal. He would find a position for her when the colony was established, keep her by him. He could never marry her – the idea was absurd enough to make him chuckle aloud – but he would see her decently provided for.

He must keep her. He needed her. He craved that nightly battle, and wondered sometimes if any other woman would interest him again.

Why did she always leave just before the dawn? And that old man – what was she to him? Not a lover, surely.

His mouth tightened and he clenched his fists on the coverlet. *She is mine*, he thought. *I will allow her to have no others. I must keep her.*

But the dreams: they came every night, and every night they were the same. That suffocating heat, the weight and prickling fur of the beast on top of him. Those eyes regarding him with unblinking malevolence. What could it mean?

He was always tired these days, always weary. He had been a fool to put down the Inceptine like that – the man would have to die now. He was too powerful an enemy. Abeleyn would see the necessity of it.

He rubbed the dark orbits of his eyes, feeling as though he could never entirely grind the tiredness out of them. He wanted her here, warm and writhing in his arms. For a second the intensity of that desire unnerved him.

He sat up again. There was something strange about the ship, something he had to consider for a moment before realizing. Then it struck him.

The carrack was no longer moving.

He leapt from the hanging cot so that it swung and banged against the bulkhead, pulled on his clothes hurriedly and grabbed the rapier with its baldric. As he reached the door, it was knocked on loudly. He yanked it open to find the ship's boy, Mateo, standing there with a white face.

"Captain Hawkwood's compliments, sir, and he asks would you join him in the hold? There is something you ought to see."

"What is it? Why have we stopped moving?"

"He said to... You have to see, sir." The boy looked as though he was about to be sick.

"Lead on then, damn you. It had better be important."

THE WHOLE SHIP was astir, the passengers milling on the gundeck and soldiers posted at every hatch and companionway with their slow-match lit and swords drawn. In their journey into the bowels of the carrack Murad ran into a prowling Sergeant Mensurado.

"Sergeant, by whose orders are these sentries posted?"

"Ensign Sequero, sir. He's down in the hold. We've orders to let none but the ship's officers pass."

Murad was about to ask him what had happened, but that would reflect poorly on his own grasp of the situation. He merely nodded and said, "Carry on, then," and followed Mateo down the dark hatches towards the hold.

Some water washing about among the high stacks of casks and crates and sacks. Rats skipping underfoot. It was pitch black but for the small hand lantern Mateo carried, but as they came through one of the compartment bulkheads Murad saw another clot of light flickering ahead and men gathered in a knot within its radiance.

"Lord Murad," Hawkwood said, straightening from a crouch. Sequero was there, and di Souza, and the injured first mate, Billerand, his arm strapped to his side and his face puffed with pain.

They drew back, and he saw the shape lying in the water, the dark gleam of blood and viscera, the limbs contorted beyond life.

"Who is it?"

"Pernicus. Billerand found him half a glass ago."

"I was mooching around," the mustachioed first mate said, "checking the cargo. It's all I'm up to these days."

Murad knelt and examined the corpse. Pernicus's eyes were wide open, the mouth agape in a last scream.

Had he heard it? Or had that been part of his dream?

The man's neck had been almost entirely bitten through; Murad could see the clammy tube of the windpipe, the ragged ends of arteries, a white-shard of vertebra.

Lower down the intestines had spilled out like a coil of greasy rope. There were chunks missing from the body. The marks of teeth were plain to see.

"Sweet Ramusio!" Murad whispered. "What did this?"

"A beast of some kind," Hawkwood said firmly. "Something came down here in the middle watch – one of the crew thought he glimpsed it. Pernicus liked to work his magic from the hold because it was more peaceful than the gundeck or the waist. It came down here after him."

"Did the man say what it was like?" Murad asked.

"Big and black. That's all he could say. He thought he

had imagined it. There is nothing like that aboard the ship."

A dream or nightmare of a great, black-furred weight atop him. Could it have been real?

Murad mastered his confusion and straightened up out of the foul water.

"Is it still aboard, do you think?"

"I don't know. I want a thorough search of the ship. If whatever did this is on board, we'll find it and kill it."

Murad remembered the log of the *Cartigellan Faulcon*. It could not be. The same thing could not be happening again. Such things were not possible.

"I have sent for the mage, Bardolin. He may be able to enlighten us," Hawkwood added.

"Do the passengers know what has happened?"

"They know Pernicus is dead. I could not stop that from leaking out, what with the loss of the wind, and all. But they don't know the manner of his death."

"Keep it that way. We don't want a panic on board."

The four of them stood round the corpse in silence for a moment. It occurred to all of them in the same instant that the beast could be here with them now, lurking among the shadows. Di Souza was shifting uneasily, his drawn sword winking in the lantern light.

"Someone's coming," he said. Another globe of light was approaching and two men were clambering over the cargo towards them.

'That's far enough, Masudi!" Hawkwood called. "Go back. Bardolin, you come forward alone."

The mage splashed towards him, and they could make out Masudi's lantern growing smaller as he returned the way he had come.

"Well, gentlemen," Bardolin began, and bent to the corpse much as Murad had done.

"Well, Mage?" Murad asked coolly, having regained his poise.

Bardolin's face was as pale as Mateo's had been. "When did this happen?"

"Sometime before the dawn, we think," Billerand told him gruffly. "I found him here, as he lies."

"What did it?" Murad demanded.

The mage turned the limbs, examining the lacerated flesh with an intensity that was disturbing to the more squeamish among them. Sequero looked away.

"How were the horses last night?" Bardolin asked.

Sequero frowned. "A bit restless. They took a long time to quieten down."

"They smelled it," the mage said. He got to his feet with a low groan.

"Smelled what?" Murad demanded impatiently. "What did this, Bardolin? What manner of beast? It was not a man, that's plain."

Bardolin seemed reluctant to speak. He was staring at the mangled corpse with his face as grim as a gravestone.

"It was not a man, and yet it was. It was both, and neither."

"What gibberish is this?"

"It was a werewolf, Lord Murad. There is a shape-shifter aboard this ship."

"Saint's preserve us!" di Souza said into the shocked silence.

"Are you sure?" Hawkwood asked.

"Yes, Captain. I have seen such wounds before." Bardolin seemed downcast and strangely bitter, Murad thought. And not as shocked as he ought to be.

"So it is not just an animal," Hawkwood was saying. "It changes back and forth. It could be anyone, anyone of the ship's company."

"Yes, Captain."

"What are we to do?" di Souza asked plaintively. No one answered him.

"Speak to us, Mage," Murad grated. "What can we do to find the beast and kill it?"

"There is nothing you can do, Lord Murad."

"What do you mean?"

"It will be wearing its human face again now. We will simply have to be watchful, to wait for it to strike again."

"What kind of plan is that?" Sequero snapped. "Are we cattle, to wait for the slaughter?"

"Yes, Lord Sequero, we are. That is exactly what we are to this thing."

"Is there no way of telling who is the werewolf?" Billerand asked.

"Not that I know of. We will simply have to be vigilant, and there are certain precautions we can take also."

"Meanwhile we are becalmed once more," Hawkwood said.

"Pernicus's wind died with him. The ship is in the doldrums again."

They stood in silence, looking down at the wreck of the weather-worker.

"I do not think this a chance murder," Bardolin said eventually. "Pernicus was singled out for slaughter. Whatever other motives this thing has, it does not want this expedition to reach the west."

"It is rational then, even when in beast form?" Hawkwood asked, startled.

"Oh, yes. Werewolves retain the identity of their human form. It is just that their... impulses are naked, uncontrollable."

"Bardolin, Captain, I wish to confer with you both in my cabin," Murad said abruptly. "Ensigns, between you you will dispose of Pernicus's body. Make sure no one else sees it. The man was murdered, that is all the rest of the folk aboard need to know. Sequero, keep the guards posted on every hatch leading down into the hold. It may still be down here."

"Have you any iron balls for the arquebuses?" Bardolin asked.

"No, we use lead. Why?"

"Iron and silver are what harm it most. Even the steel of your sword will do but little damage. Best get some iron bullets moulded as fast as you can."

"I'll get the ship's smith on to it," Billerand said.

They left Sequero and di Souza to their grisly work and made their way back up through the ship.

"Are you sure you should be out of your hammock?" Hawkwood asked Billerand. The first mate was groaning and puffing as he progressed up the companionways.

"It'll take more than a few cracked bones to keep me from my duty, Captain. And besides, I have a feeling that soon we'll be needing all the ship's officers we can get."

"Aye. See the gunner, Billerand. I want every man issued with a weapon. Arquebuses, boarding axes, cutlasses, anything. If anyone gets overly curious, spin them a tale of pirates."

Billerand grinned ferociously under his shaggy moustache. "And won't they wish it were true!"

"You'd best beat to quarters as well, to complete the picture. If we can make everyone think the danger we face is external, human, then there's less chance of a panic."

"Let slip that there's some kind of spy on board," Bardolin put in, "and that is who murdered Pernicus."

Murad laughed sourly. "There *is* a spy on board."

HAWKWOOD, BARDOLIN AND Murad assembled in the nobleman's cabin, whilst behind them the ship went into an uproar. The decks were filled with thunder as the guns were run out, the sailors issued with arms and the passengers shepherded into spare corners. It would be easy for Murad's officers to quietly splash Pernicus's body over the side in the turmoil.

"Have a seat, gentlemen," Murad said sombrely, gesturing to the cot and the stool that were spare. The heat was beginning to build up belowdecks now that the wind had dropped, and their faces were shining with sweat. But Murad did not open the stern windows.

"The noise will cover our conversation," he said, jerking a thumb at the din beyond the cabin. "Just as well."

He opened a desk drawer and brought out an oilskin-wrapped package. It was rectangular, the covering much worn. He unwrapped it and revealed a thick, battered book.

"The rutter," Hawkwood breathed.

"Yes. I have deemed it time to reveal its contents to you, Captain, and to you, Bardolin, since I feel you probably have an expertise in these matters."

"I don't understand," the mage said. The imp squirmed in his robe, but went unnoticed.

"We are not the first expedition to search for the Western Continent. There was one – in fact there were two – who went before us, and both ended in disaster; the second because the ship had a werewolf on board."

There was a pause. The racket and clamour of the carrack went on heedlessly outside.

"I was never informed of this," Hawkwood said coldly.

"I did not think it necessary, but I do now with things the way they are. It would seem that western expeditions have a way of coming to grief that is similar."

"Explain, please," Bardolin said. Sweat was trickling down his temples and dripping off his battered nose.

Briefly, Murad informed them both of the fate of the *Cartigellan Faulcon*, over a century before. He also told them of the references in the rutter to an even earlier voyage west, one undertaken by a group of mages fleeing persecution in the Ramusian kingdoms.

"The information is fragmentary, and obscure, but I have tried to glean what I can from it," he said. "What disturbs me are the similarities between the three voyages. Werewolves, Dweomer-folk. Murders on board ship."

"And ultimate disaster," Hawkwood added. "We should turn back for Abrusio, get the boats out and tow the ship's head into a wind. That Inceptine is right: this voyage is cursed."

Murad brought a fist down on the desk with a startling thump. Dust rose from the pages of the ancient book.

"There will be no turning back. Whatever demon has taken ship with us wants precisely that. You heard what Bardolin said. Someone or something has been sabotaging westward voyages for three centuries or more. I intend to find out why."

"Do you think the Western Continent is inhabited, then?" Bardolin enquired.

"Yes, I do."

"What about the *Grace of God*?" Hawkwood asked suddenly. "Could her disappearance be the result of some kind of sabotage also?"

"Perhaps. Who can say?" Hawkwood cursed bitterly.

"If the caravel is lost, Captain, don't you want to find out how or why? And who it was that destroyed your ship and killed your crew?" Murad's voice was low, but as hard as frost.

"Not at the expense of this ship and the lives of her company," Hawkwood said.

"That may not be necessary, if we are vigilant enough. We have been warned by the fate of the previous ships; we need not go the same way."

"Then how do we track this thing down? You heard Bardolin – there is no telling which man on this ship is the shifter."

"Perhaps the priest can tell. I have heard it rumoured that the clergy can somehow sniff out these things."

"No," Bardolin put in quickly. "That is a fallacy. The only way to weed out a shifter is to wait until it changes and be ready for it."

"What makes it change?" Hawkwood asked. "You said it was rational after a fashion, even in its beast form."

"Yes. And I also said it is impulsive, uncontrollable. But if we turn back it will, I believe, have got what it wants and may not find the need to shift again. On the other hand, if we announce that we are sticking to our course it may feel forced to persuade us otherwise."

"Excellent," Murad said. "There you are, Captain. We must continue westwards if we want to hunt this thing out into the open."

"Continue westwards!" Hawkwood laughed. "We are not continuing anywhere at the moment. The sails are as slack as a beggar's purse. The ship is becalmed."

"There must be something we can do," Murad said irritably. "Bardolin, you are supposed to be a mage. Can't you whistle up a wind?"

"A mage is master of only four of the Seven Disciplines," Bardolin replied. "Weather-working is not one of mine."

"What about the other passengers? They're mages and witches to a man, else they would not be here. Surely one of them could do something?"

Bardolin smiled wryly. "Pernicus was the only one gifted in that particular field. Perhaps you should ask Brother Ortelius to pray for a wind, my lord."

"Do not be insolent," Murad snapped.

"I only point out that the dregs of Ramusian society have suddenly become sought-after in a crisis."

"Only because one of those dregs jeopardizes the entire ship's safety with his own accursed brand of hellish sorcery," Murad said icily. "Set a thief to catch a thief, it is said."

Bardolin's eyes glinted in his old-soldier face. "I will catch your thief for you, then, but I will not do it for nothing."

"Aha! Here's the rub. And what would you like in way of payment, Mage?"

"I will let you know that at the appropriate time. For now, let us just say that you will owe me a favour."

"The damn thing isn't caught yet," Hawkwood said quietly. "Worry about obligations after we have its head on a pike."

"Well said, Captain," Murad agreed. "And here" – he threw the rutter into Hawkwood's lap – "peruse that at your leisure. It may be of use."

"I doubt it. We are far off our course, Murad. The rutter is no longer any use to me. From now on, unless we regain our former latitude – which is well-nigh impossible without a Dweomer wind – we are sailing uncharted seas. From what you have told me, it seems that the *Faulcon* never came this far south. My intent now is to set a course due west, parallel to our old one. There is no point in trying to beat up towards our former latitude."

"What if we miss the Western Continent altogether and sail to the south of it?" Murad asked.

"If it is even half the size of Normannia it will be there on this latitude. In any case, to try and sail back north would be almost suicidal, as I told you before we enlisted Pernicus's services."

Murad shrugged. "It is all one to me, so long as we sight land in the end and are in a fit state to walk ashore."

"Let me worry about that. Your concern is this beast that haunts the ship."

BY THE END of the morning watch the guns had been run back in and the rumour had circulated round the ship like a fast-spreading pestilence: Pernicus had been murdered by a stowaway spy, and the murderer lurked aboard, unknown. The carrack began to take on some of the aspects of a besieged fortress, with soldiers everywhere asking people their business, the crew armed and the ship's officers barking orders left and right. The patched-up boats were swung out from the yardarms and crews of sailors began hauling the carrack westwards, out of the doldrums; a killing labour in the stock-still heat of the day.

In the midst of the militant uneasiness the last of the storm's damage was rectified and the ship began to look more like her old self, with new timber about the sterncastle and waist and new cable sent up to the tops. But the sails remained flaccid and empty, and the surface of the sea was as obstinately flat as the surface of a green mirror, whilst the sun glared down out of a cloudless sky.

It was in the foretop that Bardolin and Griella finally found the peace to speak without being overheard. They sat in the low-walled platform with the bulk of the topmast at their backs and a spider tracery of rigging all about them.

Still red-faced from clambering up the shrouds in this heat, Bardolin released the imp. With a squeak of pleasure it darted around the top, gazing down at the deck far below and peering out at the haze-dim horizon.

"You've heard, I suppose?" Bardolin asked curtly.

"About Pernicus? Yes. Why would anyone have done such a thing? He was a harmless enough little man." Griella was dressed in her habitual breeches and a thin linen shirt that Bardolin suspected was a cast-off of Murad's. Fragments of lace clung to its neck and she had rolled the voluminous sleeves up to her elbows, exposing brown forearms with tiny golden hairs freckling them.

"He was killed by a shifter, Griella," the mage said in a flint-hard voice.

The pale eyes widened until he could see the strange yellow-golden circle around the pupils. "Bardolin! Are you sure?"

"I have seen shifters kill before, remember."

She stared at him. Her mouth opened. Finally she said:

"But you don't think – you *do*! You think it was me!"

"Not you, but the beast that inhabits you."

The eyes flared; the yellow grew in them until they were scarcely human any longer. "We are the same, the beast and I, and I tell you that it was not I who slew Pernicus."

"Are you expecting me to believe there are two shifters on board this ship?"

"There must be, or else you are mistaken. Maybe someone killed him in such a way as to make it look as though it was done by a beast."

"I am not a fool, Griella. I warned you about this many times. Now it has happened."

"I did not do it! Please, Bardolin, you must believe me!" The glow in the eyes had retreated and there was only the light of the pitiless sun setting the tears in them afire. She was a small girl again, tugging at his knee. The imp looked on, aghast.

"Why should I?" Bardolin said harshly, though he longed to take her in his arms, to say that he did, to make it all right.

"Is there nothing I can do to convince you?"

"What could you do, Griella?"

"I could let you see into my mind, the way you did before when I was about to change into the beast and you stopped me. You saw into me then, Bardolin. You can do it again."

"I –"

He was not so sure of himself now. He had thought to extract a confession from her, but he had not considered beyond that. He knew he would never have turned her over to Murad – there would have been some bargain made, some deal done. But now he no longer knew what to do.

Because he did believe her.

"Let me see your eyes, Griella. Look at me."

She tilted up her head obediently. The sun was behind him and his shadow fell upon her. He looked deep, deep into the sea-change of the eyes, and the top, the mast, the ship and the vast ocean disappeared.

A heartbeat, huge and regular. But as he listened the rhythm changed. It became erratic, slipping out of time. It took him a moment to realize that he was listening to two hearts beating not quite in tune with each other.

Pictures and images flickering like a shower of varicoloured leaves. He saw himself there, but shied away from that. He saw the ragged brown peaks of the Hebros Mountains that must have been her home. He saw swift, red-tinted images of wanton slaughter flitting past.

Too far back. He had gone too deep with his impatience. He must pull out a little.

The other heartbeat grew louder, drowning out the first. He thought he could feel the heat of the beast and the prickle of its harsh fur against his skin.

There! A ship upon a limitless ocean, and in the dark hours aboard a vision of white limbs intertwined, linen sheets in crumples of light and dark. An ecstatic, lean face he knew to be Murad's hovering over him in the night.

The beast again, very close this time. He felt its anger, its hunger. The unrelenting rage it felt at being confined.

Except it was not. It was free and lying beside the naked man in the swaying cot, the stout supporting ropes creaking under the weight. It wanted to kill, to rip the night apart with scarlet carnage. But did not. It lay beside the sleeping, nightmare-ridden nobleman and watched over him in the night.

It wanted to kill, but could not. There was something that prevented it, something the beast could not understand but could not disregard.

Nothing else. A few spangled images. Himself, the imp, the terrible glory of the storm. Nothing more. No memory of murder, not on the ship, not since Abrusio. She had told the truth.

Bardolin lingered a moment, peering round the tangled interstices of Griella's mind, noting the linkages here and there between the wolf and the woman, the areas where they were pulling apart, where control was weakest. He withdrew with a sense both of relief and of mourning. She did love Murad, in some perverse manner that even the beast could recognize. And in loving him, she was doing some violence to herself that Bardolin could not quite fathom.

She loved himself, old Bardolin, also – but not in the same way, not at all. He scourged himself for the unexpectedly acute sense of grief at the discovery.

The sun was beating down on them. Griella's eyes were glassy. He tapped her lightly on the cheek and she blinked, smiled.

"Well?"

"You told the truth," he said heavily.

"You don't sound too overjoyed."

"You may not have killed Pernicus, but you play a dangerous game with Murad, child."

"That is my business."

"All right, but it seems that the impossible is true: there is another shifter aboard the ship."

"Another shifter? How can that be?"

"I have no idea. You have not sensed anything, have you? You do not have any suspicions?"

"Why, no. I have never in my life met another sufferer of the black disease, though folk said the Hebros were full of them."

"Then it seems there is nothing we can do until he chooses to reveal himself."

"Why would another shifter take ship with us?"

"To cause the abortion of the voyage, perhaps. That would be his motive for killing Pernicus. Murad told me something today which intrigues me. I must go down and consult my books."

"Tell me, Bardolin! What is going on?"

"I don't yet know myself. Keep your eyes open. And Griella: do not let the beast free for a while, not even in the privacy of Murad's cabin."

She flushed. "You saw that! You pried on us."

"I had no choice. The man is bad for you, child, and you for him. Remember that."

"I am not a child, Bardolin. You had best not treat me like one."

He stroked her satin cheek gently, fingers touching the tawny freckles there, the sun-brown skin.

"Do not think ill of me, Griella. I am an old man, and I worry about you."

"You are not so old, and I am sorry you worry." But her eyes were unrelenting.

Bardolin turned away and scooped up the watching imp. "Come. Let us see if this not-so-old man can make his way down this labyrinth of ropes without cracking open his grey-haired skull on the deck."

THE CARRACK INCHED westwards painfully, towed by the labouring men in the ship's boats. They made scarcely two leagues a day, and the sailors became exhausted though the boat crews changed every hour. Hawkwood began to ration the water as though it were gold, and soldiers with iron bullets in their arquebuses guarded the water casks in the forward part of the hold day and night. The ship's company became subdued and apprehensive. Salt sores began to appear on everyone's bodies as the allowance of fresh water for washing was cut and the salt in garments began to abrade the skin. And still the sun blasted down out of a flawless sky, and in the clear green water below the keel the shadow of hanging weed grew longer as it built up on the carrack's hull.

The sailors trolled for fish to eke out the shipboard provisions. They hauled in herrin on their westward migration, wingfish, huge tub-bodied feluna, and sometimes the writhing, entangled sliminess of large octopuses, some of them almost big enough to swamp the smaller of the longboats.

Weed began to be sighted in matted expanses across the surface of the sea, and on the weed itself colonies of pink and scarlet crabs scuttled about seeking carrion. The weed beds stank to high heaven and were infested with sealice and other vermin. Inevitably some made their way aboard, and soon most of the ship's company had their share of irritating red bites and unwelcome itches on scalp and in groin.

In the dark of one middle watch a great glistening back rose like a birthing hill out of the sea alongside the carrack, and for half a glass it rose and sank there, a bulk that rivalled the ship in size. A long-necked head with a horny beak regarded the astonished ship's watch before diving below the surface again in a flurry of white foam. A knollback turtle. The sailors had heard of them in old maritime tales and legends. They were supposed to have been mistaken for islands by land-hungry mariners far from home. The crew made the Sign of the Saint at their breasts, and the next day Brother Ortelius's sermon was better attended than it had ever been before, affording the Inceptine a grim kind of pleasure. He called the voyage a flight in the face of God, and with Murad looking on declared that God's servants could not be muzzled by threats or fear. God's will would be done, in the end.

The same evening Hawkwood had two men flogged for questioning the orders of the ship's officers.

The men in the boats rowed on through the humid nights, watch on watch, their oars struggling through the stinking, matted weed with its population of crabs and mites. And on the gun deck the talk was turned to Pernicus's death and its possible author. Wild theories were hatched and did the rounds and it was all Bardolin could do to keep the Dweomer-folk calm. As it was, there were more manifestations of magic now. Some of the old wives were able to purify small amounts of salt water whilst others worked to heal the salt sores everyone bore, and still more ignited white were-lights and left them burning through the night for fear of what would creep about the decks in the dark hours.

And then, eight tense, airless, back-breaking days after Pernicus had met his end, a wind came ruffling over the surface of the undisturbed sea. A north-easter that gathered in strength through the morning watch until the carrack's sails were drawing full again and the white foam broke beneath her bow. The ship's company drew a collective sigh of relief as the wake began to extend ever further behind her and she set her bowsprit squarely towards the west once more.

It was then that the killing began.

TWENTY-TWO

VOL EPHRIR, CAPITAL of Perigraine. A city considered by many to be the most beautiful in the world.

It sat on an island in the midst of the mighty Ephron river. Here, three hundred miles from its headwaters, the Ephron was a glittering blue expanse of water over a mile wide. Ephrir island was a long, low piece of land that curved with the meanders of the Ephron for almost three leagues. Centuries ago the Fimbrians had walled it in against the constant flooding of the river water and they had reared up an artificial hill a hundred feet high in its midst so that a citadel might be built there. The city had grown around the fortress, fisher villages coalescing into towns, merchant wharves taking up more and more of the riverfront, fine houses and towers springing up in the island's interior – until one day the entire island had been built over, a sprawl of houses and villas and warehouses and taverns and shops and markets with no discipline, no order. A long-ago king of Perigraine had decreed that the city must be better regulated. The fisher slums were demolished, the streets widened and paved, the harbours rebuilt and dredged out to accommodate the deep-bellied grain lighters that came upriver from Candelaria.

The city had been reconstructed along the lines of an architectural ideal, and had become a marvel for most of the western world: the perfect city. And Vol Ephrir had never known war or been besieged, unlike many of the other Ramusian capitals.

There was something peculiarly innocent about the place, Abeleyn mused as he rode along its wide streets and inhaled the fragrance of its gardens. Perhaps it was the balminess of the climate. Although a man might look east and see the Cimbrics thirty leagues away, white with early snow, here in the Vale of Perigraine the air was neither warm nor cold. It could be bitter in the winter, but this slow slide into autumn suited the city, as did the millions of red and yellow leaves that floated in the city's ponds and upon the surface of the mighty Ephron, having fallen from the birch and maple woods that were flaming everywhere. The drifting leaves heightened the impression of quietude, for though Vol Ephrir was a busy, thriving place, it was nonetheless sedate, dignified. Somehow ornamental. The population of the place, at a quarter of a million, was almost as great as that of Abrusio, but there was something about Abeleyn's home city that was more frantic. Its teeming colour, perhaps, its vibrant cheek-by-jowl disorder. If Vol Ephrir was a dignified lady who welcomed guests with regal stateliness, then Abrusio was a bawdy old whore who opened her legs for the world.

King Abeleyn of Hebrion had been two days in the Perigrainian capital. Already he had been feasted by young King Cadamost and had tried his hand at hunting vareg, the vicious, tusked herbivore which haunted the riverside forests. Now he was impatient for the conclave to convene. The major rulers had arrived: himself and Mark of Astarac, their alliance a secret between the pair of them; white-haired, irascible Haukir of Almark, Inceptine advisers flapping around him like vultures eyeing a lame old warhorse; Skarpathin of Finnmark, a young man who had assumed his throne in rather murky, murderous circumstances; Duke Adamir of Gabrion, the very picture of a grizzled sea-dog; and Lofantyr of Torunna, looking harried and older than his thirty-two years.

There were others, of course. The dukes of the Border Fiefs were here: Gardiac, Tarber, and even isolated Kardikia had sent an envoy, though Duke Comorin could not come in person. Since the fall of Aekir, Kardikia was cut off from the rest of the Ramusian world; the only links it had with the other western powers now were by sea.

The Duke of Touron and the self-styled Prince of Fulk were present also, and in Abeleyn' s own entourage, but not seated at the council table, was a representative of Narbukir, that Fimbrian electorate which had broken away from its fellows almost eighty years ago. The Narbukan envoy was to be revealed at the proper time. From the Fimbrian Electorates proper Abeleyn had had no news, no response to his overtures. He had expected as much, for all Golophin's optimism.

The rulers of the Ramusian kingdoms of the world were young men in the main. It seemed that a generation of older kings had relinquished their hold on power within a few years of each other, and the sons had taken their father's thrones whilst in their twenties or early thirties.

There were three Prelates present in the city also, newly arrived from the recent Synod at Charibon. Escriban of Perigraine, who was Prelate of the kingdom itself, Heyn of Torunna, who had spent hours closeted with King Lofantÿr, and Merion of Astarac, who had spent the time likewise with Mark. Old Marat, the Prelate of Almark, had taken the quickest route home, but his monarch, Haukir, was so hemmed in by clerical advisers that he had probably deduced his presence unnecessary; so Abeleyn thought sourly.

The first meeting of the conclave was convened amid a buzz of rumour and speculation. There were reports that the first assaults on Ormann Dyke had taken place, and though part of the fortress complex had fallen the rest was standing, defying a Merduk horde half a million strong. Thanks to Golophin's gyrfalcon, Abeleyn was more accurately informed. Though it had taken place only days ago, and was almost a month's travel away, he knew of the failed river assault and the current enemy lethargy. He was at a loss to account for it, however.

But the miracle had been granted: the dyke still stood. It might be possible to reinforce it now. Five thousand Knights Militant were purportedly riding to the relief of the fortress from Charibon even as the kings took council in Vol Ephrir.

But there was another item of news which only Abeleyn and a few others were privy to. It had been confirmed that Macrobius was alive and well at the dyke, blinded but in possession of his senses. Himerius's elevation to the Pontiffship was therefore null and void. It was the best news Abeleyn had heard in weeks. He settled back in his leather-padded chair at the council table in the King's Hall of Vol Ephrir in a better mood than might otherwise be expected.

King Cadamost of Perigraine, as befitted his status as host, called the meeting to order.

The most powerful men in the western world were in a circular chamber in the highest tower of the palace. The floor upon which their chairs scraped was exquisitely mosaicked with the arms and flags of the Royal houses of Normannia. Tall windows of coloured glass tinted the flooding sunlight twenty feet above the heads of the assembled kings, and Perigrainian war banners hung limp from the rafters. There were no guards in the great chamber; they were posted on the staircases below. The round table at which everyone sat was littered with quills and papers. Those who disdained to read or write themselves had brought scribes along with them.

Courtesies were exchanged, greetings bandied about, protocol satisfied with an interminable series of speeches expressing the gratitude of the visiting kings to their host. As a matter of fact, hosting the conclave was no mean feat, even for the spacious city of Vol Ephrir. Every ruler present had brought several hundred retainers with him, and these had to be accommodated in a certain style, as did the monarchs themselves. Entertainments had to be laid on, banquets and tourneys to keep the crowned heads diverted when they were not in the council chamber, delicacies to whet their appetites, beer and wine and other liqueurs to help them relax. All in all, Abeleyn thought petulantly, Cadamost could have raised and equipped a sizeable army with the money he had spent playing the gracious host to his fellow monarchs. But that was the way the world worked.

Once the preliminaries were over, Cadamost rose from his seat to address the men about the table. They awaited his words with interest. Some of the seats among them were empty, and they were keen to know whether or not they would be filled, and by whom.

"This is a time of trial for the Ramusian states of the world," Cadamost said. He was a slim man of medium height, and he had the aspect of a scholar rather than that of a king. Some ocular complaint had ringed his eyes with red. He blinked painfully, but in compensation his voice was as musical as a bard's.

"In the past, conclaves have been called to deal with a crisis affecting the kingdoms and principalities of Normannia. They are convened to offer a place of arbitration and settlement. All the kingdoms represented here have at one time warred upon one another – and yet their monarchs sit now in peace beside each other, united by a common crisis, a foe who threatens us all.

"In the past there has been one power upon the continent that has always gone unrepresented at our meetings, and has refused to join in our councils. This power was once supreme across Normannia, but of late it has withdrawn into itself. It has become isolated, cut off from the concourse of normal diplomacy and international relations. I am glad to say that this state of affairs has changed. Only this morning, envoys arrived from that state. I ask you, my fellow rulers, to bid welcome to the envoys of Fimbria."

On cue, a pair of doors opened in the wall and two men stood there, dressed wholly in black.

"I bid you welcome, gentlemen," Cadamost said in his lilting voice.

The men marched into the chamber and took seats at the council table without a word. The doors boomed shut as if to emphasize the finality of their entrance.

"I give you Marshals Jonakait and Markus of Neyr and Gaderia, authorized in this instance to speak also for the electorates of Tulm and Amarlaine. In effect, they are the voice of Fimbria."

The other monarchs sat stunned, none more so than Abeleyn. His own envoys had returned empty-handed from the enigmatic Electors of Fimbria. But the four electorates had combined to send two representatives to the conclave. It was unprecedented. One of the reasons for the fall of the Fimbrian Hegemony had been the bitter rivalries between the electorates. What had caused this change of heart?

Cadamost looked rather smug. Regarded as a political lightweight by the other monarchs, he had nevertheless pulled off a massive diplomatic coup. Abeleyn glanced at the red-rimmed eyes, the unimpressive exterior of Perigraine's king. There was more to him than a singer's voice.

The Fimbrians sat impassively. They were square men, their hair shorn brutally short and their hollow-cheeked faces speaking of great physical endurance. They wore traditional Fimbrian black, the garb of all men of any rank in the electorates since the fall of their Hegemony and the death of the last emperor. Torunnan black and scarlet, the dress of Lofantyr, was a derivative of Fimbrian sable, and it was the Torunnans who had inherited the mantle of foremost military power upon the continent. But who knew how the Fimbrians would fare these days? Narbukan Fimbria, it was true, had opened itself to the outside world after the schism with the rest of the electorates, but as a result it was no longer seen as truly Fimbrian.

"We are here at the behest of two kings," Jonakait said. "We of the electorates recognize that the west is facing its greatest threat since the time of the Religious Wars. Fimbria, once the foremost power in the world, will no longer isolate itself from the normal run of diplomatic contact. I am here, authorized to enter into agreements and treaties with the other monarchs of Normannia, and authorized also to promise military aid if that is what is required."

"Why didn't your Electors come in person?" Lofantyr asked sharply, clearly resenting the "foremost power" bit.

Jonakait blinked. "Markus and I are authorized to act on their behalf. We have been invested with Electoral Imperium. We sit here as the de facto rulers of Fimbria, and are able to authorize any course of action we see fit."

Things had been changing in Fimbria then, and no one had even noticed, Abeleyn thought. The Electorates had somehow patched up their squabbles and acted in unison. He wondered just how much authority these two men truly possessed.

"Can you sanction the commitment of Fimbrian troops?" Lofantyr asked, his eagerness transparent.

"We can."

The Torunnan king leaned back. "You may be held to that promise, Marshal."

The Fimbrian shrugged ever so slightly.

Abeleyn wondered, though, who else among the men seated around the table would truly tolerate Fimbrian tercios on the march again across Normannia. He had thought himself open-minded, devoid of any prejudices springing from the past, but even he felt a cold shiver at the thought. The memories ran deep. No wonder many of the faces around the table looked outraged as well as astonished.

Cadamost took the floor again, striving to push the meeting past the sensational entrance of the two marshals.

"Urgent questions lie before us at this time, and it is imperative that the issues behind them be addressed. If the west is to have any kind of concerted policy towards the eastern crisis – and other happenings – then we must, as the heads of our nations, come to some decisions within the walls of this chamber."

"Do we work on the basis of rumours or of fact, cousin?" Haukir asked. His white beard bristled. It was said that he and his Prelate, Marat, were related, and more closely than might be supposed. The Almarkan Prelate, gossip had it, was born into the Royal house, but on the wrong side of the blanket. Certainly the two men were as similarly gruff and obstinate as to be twins.

"What do you mean, cousin?" Cadamost shot back.

"These rumours that Macrobius is alive and at Ormann Dyke, for instance. They must be quashed before they do harm."

"I agree," Abeleyn spoke up. "They should be thoroughly investigated, in case there is some germ of substance at their heart."

"Pieter Martellus at the dyke insists that Macrobius is there," Lofantyr said.

Haukir snorted. "Do you believe him? He's just trying to inject a little backbone into his garrison, is all."

"I have never heard that Torunnan soldiers lacked backbone," Lofantyr flared. "I thought perhaps their conduct at Aekir would have been testimony enough to their courage. My countrymen have been dying in their tens of thousands so that the kingdoms which shelter behind their bucklers might rest easy at night. So do not prate to me of backbone, cousin."

Bravo! Abeleyn thought gleefully as Haukir's face darkened and he began to sputter with wrath.

But Lofantyr was not yet done.

"It has been brought to my attention that the five thousand Knights Militant promised to my Prelate by the Vicar-General of the Inceptines have turned around in their march to the dyke and are retracing their steps to Charibon. So much for the help of the Church. Himerius takes the same line as you, Haukir: he condemns out of hand without waiting to hear the evidence for or against. Myself, I vow to keep an open mind. If Macrobius is truly alive, then surely it is a sign from God that the Merduk tide is on the turn. The news from the dyke confirms this."

Abeleyn shared a look with Mark of Astarac. So that was it. Lofantyr had found the strength to defy the new Pontiff because of the successes at the dyke. But also, Abeleyn suspected, because there were Fimbrians at the table making promises of troops. The Torunnan king did not feel he had to rely on Church forces any longer. Lofantyr was his own man again, and that was all to the good.

"Accusations and recriminations have no place at this assembly," Cadamost said, holding up a hand to forestall Haukir's explosion.

"Do we defy the Pontifical bull of the new spiritual leader of the Ramusian world, then?" Skarpathin of Finnmark asked easily, his killer's face creased by a sardonic smile.

Cadamost paused, and Abeleyn spoke quickly into the silence.

"The Pontiff may not be adequately informed. He acted as he thought best to prevent disorder, confusion – even schism – within the Church at this vital time. But though we can abide by the letter of the bull, I yet believe that we can conduct ourselves as just men, and await the result of further investigations with an open mind."

There were rumbles at this, but no open disagreement. Everyone knew that the Hebriate King and his one-time Prelate had always been at odds with one another. Haukir glared at Abeleyn suspiciously. He was the irreligious boy-king, the trickster. He must be up to something. Abeleyn kept his own face carefully bland.

Cadamost flicked a look of gratitude at Abeleyn. Clearly, his role of referee was a wearing one.

"The subjects for discussion have most of them been raised, then," he said. "This rumour of Macrobius's survival, the defence of Ormann Dyke and the other eastern marches, and the advent of our new colleagues, the Fimbrians."

"There are others, cousin," Mark of Astarac said.

"Such as?"

"Such as these damned burnings that have been going on in Hebrion and which seem set to be extended to every Ramusian state on the continent."

"That is an issue for the Church alone to decide," Haukir said.

"It is an infringement of the authority of the crown, and as such will be debated by this assembly," Abeleyn said. There was nothing of the boy about him now. His dark eyes flashed like glass catching the sun.

The other rulers stared at Mark and Abeleyn, sensing something there, some secret agreement. Time enough yet, though, before revealing the Hebro-Astaran Treaty of Alliance. Abeleyn and Mark had copies of it lurking in their suites, ready to be brought out at the right moment.

"Very well," Cadamost said. "The issue of the purges will be tabled also, though I do not see what lay rulers are able to do about it; it seems to me to be the Province of the Church alone."

"Let us say that I have my doubts as to the motives behind it," Abeleyn said.

"Are you questioning the judgement of the Holy Pontiff?" Lofantyr asked, ignoring the fact that he had done that very thing himself moments ago.

"He was not Pontiff when this decision was made. He was Prelate of Hebrion, and thus his actions come under the purlieu of the Hebriate crown."

"Lawyer's niceties!" Haukir snorted.

"Those lawyer's niceties may have some import if the case is brought before a Royal commission," Abeleyn said.

"You cannot put the High Pontiff on trial," Skarpathin of Finnmark said, a conservative despite his youth and the bloody steps he had taken to secure his throne.

"No, but perhaps he is not the High Pontiff, if Macrobius yet lives. Also the purges were initiated by a Prelate, not a Pontiff. We have yet to read a Pontifical bull extending them formally."

"I hear that two thousand of the Knights are almost on Hebrion's borders, cousin. That would not have anything to do with your haste to table this issue?" Haukir said, smiling unpleasantly.

"I rejoice that the resources of the Church are so lavished on my kingdom, but like Lofantyr I think they could be better employed elsewhere."

"You need men to fight the Merduks, not words," Markus, the Fimbrian marshal said suddenly, his bluntness disconcerting. "You can no longer rely on the troops of the Church, that is plain. The Pontiff and his Prelates are playing their own game; they do not care about the fate of Ormann Dyke. They may even be glad to see it fall, if it rids them of this rival Pontiff at the same time."

It was unforgivable to speak the truth so openly. *Isolation has atrophied any kind of diplomatic subtleties the Fimbrians might once have possessed*, Abeleyn thought.

Haukir seemed to be on the verge of another explosion, but the Fimbrian continued speaking in his level, toneless voice.

"The Fimbrian Electorates have decided to put their forces at the disposal of the west. There are six hundred tercios under arms in Fimbir itself. These troops have been set aside for possible employment beyond the borders of the electorates. Any monarch who needs them may have them."

The table sat stunned in silence. Six hundred tercios! Over seventy thousand men. They had had a chimera in their midst and had not known it.

"Who will these tercios serve under?" Lofantyr asked.

"They will have their own officers, and any expeditionary force will be commanded by a Fimbrian marshal who will in turn accept orders from whichever ruler employs him."

"*Employs?*" Cadamost asked, his red eyes narrowing. "Tell me, Marshal, who will pay the wages of these soldiers?"

For the first time Markus looked less than impassive. "Their costs will have to be met by the monarch they serve under, of course."

So that was it. The Fimbrians were killing two birds with the same stone. Now that the electorates had seemingly patched up their differences they no doubt had a wealth of unemployed soldiers on their hands. What to do with them, these peerless fighters? Farm them out to the other western states, relieve a no-doubt strained economy – and extend Fimbrian influence at the same time. The Fimbrian crutch might well transform into a club one day. It was a neat policy. Abeleyn wondered if Lofantyr were desperate enough to take the bait. Surely he must see the ramifications.

"I would speak to you privately after this day's meeting is concluded, Marshal," the Torunnan king said at last.

Markus bowed slightly, but not before Abeleyn had caught the gleam of triumph in his eye.

"THE DAMN FOOL!" Mark raged. "Can't he see what he is doing? The Fimbrians will put a leash about his throat and lead him around like a dog."

"He is in a tight corner," Abeleyn said, sipping his wine and rolling a black olive round and round the table to catch the sunlight. "He has been baulked of his reinforcements by the Church, so he must have men from somewhere. The Fimbrian intelligence service must be quite efficient. The timing of this offer is perfect."

"Do you think they hanker after empire again?"

"Of course. What else could have persuaded the electorates to cease their internal strife? My ploy of bringing the Narbukan envoy here has fallen flatter than a pricked bladder. It is strange. Golophin must have suspected that there was something afoot in Fimbria, for it was he who advised me to sound out the electorates. I do not think he imagined this, though, not in his wildest dreams."

"Or nightmares. Our alliance looks like pretty small beer compared with this news."

"On the contrary, Mark. It is more important than ever. Cadamost has come to some secret arrangement with the marshals, of that I am sure. They accepted his invitation, not mine. And Torunna needs troops. How does one get to Torunna from Fimbria? Via Perigraine! Cadamost has been playing a very deep game. Who would have believed him capable of that?"

They were seated at a roadside tavern in one of the main thoroughfares of the city. Waggons and carts trundled past unendingly, and around them was the red-gold shade of the turning trees, avenues of which lined almost every street in Vol Ephrir. Scarlet and amber leaves dotted the ground like a crunching carpet, and there was a cool breeze blowing. If they looked up, past the well-constructed buildings on the other side of the street, they could see the palace towers of Vol Ephrir shining white with marble. Abeleyn raised his glass to them and drank. It was Candelarian. Fully half of Candelaria's exports were to Perigraine.

"We must speak with Lofantyr," Abeleyn said. "He must be made to see what he is doing. We will not dissuade him from utilizing Fimbrian troops, but he must at least be frugal in their deployment. One good thing about this: it has secured his independence from the Church, and it may ensure the recognition of Macrobius as Pontiff once again. Lofantyr will back him all the way. He has nothing to lose and much to gain from a Pontiff who might well become a Torunnan puppet."

"If Himerius steps down," Mark said sombrely.

"A very interesting *if*, cousin. Who would support him if he did not? Almark, of course, and Finnmark – most of the Border Duchies."

"Perigraine, maybe."

"Maybe. I am all at sea when thinking of this kingdom. Cadamost has rattled me – most unpleasant."

A third person joined them at their table, appearing out of the throng of people who coursed up and down the street. She bowed to both kings and then drank some wine from Abeleyn's glass.

"My lady Jemilla," the Hebrian monarch said easily. "I trust you have been enjoying your trip about the city?"

"It is a wondrous place, sire, so different from our crowded old Abrusio. Like something from one of the old courtly tales."

"You look pale. Are you well?"

Jemilla was wearing a loose robe of deep scarlet encrusted with pearls and gold thread. Her dark hair was bound up on her head with more pearl-headed pins, and her face was as white as sea-scoured bone.

"Quite well, sire. I am a little tired, perhaps."

Mark ignored her. He had been rather scandalized by Abeleyn's bringing her to the conclave, especially since the Hebrian king was officially, if secretly, betrothed to his sister.

"You should keep out of the sun. It is very bright on the eye in this part of the world. There is no dust to blunt its passage."

"I am waiting for my barouche, sire. Will you walk me to the corner? My maids seem to have deserted me for the moment."

"By all means, my lady. Cousin, you will await my return?" Mark flapped a hand affably enough and buried his nose in his glass.

"He doesn't like me," Jemilla said when they were out of earshot.

"He is attracted to you, but Mark is an austere sort of fellow at times. He loves his wife, and is prone to guilt."

"You and he behave like a pair of 'prentice ensigns out on the town. Have you no attendants with you?"

Abeleyn laughed. "My bodyguards – and Mark's – are very discreet, and Cadamost no doubt has people watching us also. You need not fear for my safety in Vol Ephrir. If anything happened here it would reflect badly on Perigraine's king."

Jemilla leaned on his arm. She was walking more slowly than her usual brisk pace.

"Is anything the matter, my lady?"

She leaned close to him, spoke into his ear. "I am with child."

They halted in the street, curious folk glancing at the pair as they passed by.

"Are you sure?" Abeleyn asked in a voice gone toneless and cold.

"Yes, sire. It is yours. There has been no one else in the time we have been together."

Abeleyn stared at her. The bright sunlight brought out the lines at the corners of her eyes, accentuated the whiteness of her skin, the shadows under her cheekbones.

"You are not well, lady," he murmured.

"I can keep nothing down. It is a passing thing."

"Does anyone else know?"

"My maid will have guessed." Jemilla caressed her stomach through the thick, loose robe. "It is hardly noticeable as yet, but my flow has been –"

"All right, all right! I don't want to hear about your woman's mechanisms!" Like most men, Abeleyn knew little and cared less about that particular subject. It was bad luck to couple with a woman at that time, an offence against God. That was as far as he cared to enquire.

"You're sure it's mine, Jemilla?" he demanded in a low voice, taking her by the arms.

Her eyes filled with tears. "Yes, sire." She bent her head and began to sob quietly.

"Saint's teeth! Where is that blasted cart? Dry your eyes, woman, for God's sake!"

The covered carriage came trundling along the street and Abeleyn hailed it.

"Will you be all right?" he asked as he helped her inside. He had never seen her weep before and it disconcerted him.

"Yes, sire, I will be fine. But I cannot – I cannot perform the same services that I have undertaken up until now."

Abeleyn coloured. "Never mind that. We'll get you back to Hebrion by sea. You won't be climbing the Malvennors in your state. There are a few things I must arrange. You will be looked after, Jemilla."

"Sire, I have to say – I want to keep this child. I will not have it... disposed of."

Abeleyn stiffened. For a second he bore an uncanny resemblance to his severe, rigidly pious father.

"That is one notion that never entered my mind, Jemilla. As I said, you will be looked after, and the child also."

"Thank you, sire. I never doubted it."

He closed the door and the carriage sped away to the palace where she had a suite of her own. He followed its departure with a grim set to his mouth.

A bastard child, and not by some strumpet either. By a lady from a noble house. That could cause problems. He would have to be careful.

"Anything wrong?" Mark asked when Abeleyn rejoined him.

"No. Women's inquisitiveness. I sent her on her way."

"A handsome woman, if rather on the mature side."

"Yes. She's a widow."

"And nobly born," Mark noted unsmilingly.

Abeleyn gave him a piercing look. "Not nobly enough, cousin, believe me. Not nobly enough. Order some more wine, will you? I'm as dry as a summer lane."

IN THE CLOSED carriage, the lady Jemilla's face was bright and hard, the tears dried. The carriage was well-sprung, the motion easy, for which she was grateful. She had never borne a child full-term before. She was not entirely sure about what awaited her. But that was not important.

He had believed her – that was the main thing. What would he do now? What prospects had a bastard son of Hebrion's king? It remained to be seen. She did not like the way Abeleyn was so friendly with Mark of Astarac. As a bachelor he might secretly welcome a son, even one from the wrong side of the blanket, but were he to marry and make an Astaran princess his queen...

It was not Abeleyn's child, of course; it was Richard Hawk-wood's. And it would be a boy – she could feel it in her marrow. But Hawkwood was no doubt dead by now, fathoms deep in the waters of some unending ocean. And even if he were not, he was not nobly born. He must never know that he had a son. No, this child of hers would grow up a king's son, and one day she would see that he claimed what he was owed. He would not be cheated of his birthright, and when he claimed it his mother would be there to guide him.

TWENTY-THREE

THEY FOUND BILLERAND halfway through the middle watch, down in the cable tiers in the fore part of the hold. He had gone below to check on the eight-inch cables that served the anchors. The boy Mateo had been with him; of his body there was no trace. The soldiers said they had heard nothing.

A file of arquebusiers fired a volley as what remained of his corpse was slipped over the side in recognition of the soldier he had once been, then they went back to their posts, in fours now instead of pairs, and with lanterns burning throughout the hold to try and keep the shadows at bay.

Hawkwood and Murad spent what was left of the night drinking good brandy in the nobleman's quarters and racking their tired brains for something to do, some course of action that would help. Hawkwood even suggested asking Ortelius for aid, but Murad vetoed him. Bad enough that the priest seemed to be winning more and more influence among the soldiers and the sailors, but for the ship's officers to go running to him for help was intolerable.

Bardolin joined them, bad news written all over his face. "Ortelius is addressing a meeting of sorts on the gundeck,' he told them.

"The gundeck!" Murad exclaimed.

"Yes. It would seem he has made it his mission to win over the poor lost souls of the Dweomer-folk to his way of thinking. There are many of the soldiers there, and some of the mariners too."

"I'll get Sequero to break up their little party," Murad said, beginning to rise from his chair.

"No, Lord Murad, I beg you do not. It can only do harm. Most of your men are still at their posts, and the majority of your sailors, Captain, but I noticed one of your ship's officers, Velasca. He was there with the rest."

"Velasca?" Hawkwood exploded. "The mutinous dog!"

"It would seem," Murad drawled, "that our subordinates are evolving minds of their own. Have some brandy, Mage. And take that thing out of the front of your robe for the Saint's sake. I have seen familiars before."

Bardolin released the imp. It hopped on to the table and sniffed at the neck of the brandy decanter, then grinned as Murad chucked it gently under the chin.

"Good luck, an imp aboard ship," Hawkwood said quietly.

"Yes," Bardolin said. "I remember Billerand telling me once, back in Abrusio."

There was a heavy silence. Hawkwood downed his brandy as though it were water. "What have you found out?" he asked the wizard at last, eyes watering from the strong spirit.

"I have been doing some reading. On werewolves. My collection of thaumaturgical works is pitifully inadequate – my home was ransacked ere we left Hebrion – and I have had to be discreet in enquiring as to whether any of the other passengers have similar works in their possession, you understand. But according to what meagre researches I have been able to carry out, shifters do not like confinement of two kinds. Gregory of Touron reckons that the longer the man who is the shifter retains his human form, the more violent the actions of the beast once he transforms. Hence if shifters do not intend to run entirely amok once in animal form, they must change back and forth regularly, even if the beast form only lies motionless. It is like lancing a boil. The pus must be let out occasionally. The beast must breathe."

"What's the other form of confinement?" Murad asked impatiently.

"That is simple. Any prolonged period of incarceration in close quarters, such as a house, a cave –"

"Or a ship," Hawkwood interrupted.

"Just so, Captain."

"Brilliant," Murad said caustically, flourishing his glass. "What good do these priceless nuggets do us, old man?"

"They tell us that this shifter is suffering on two counts. First because he is in the confined space of a ship, and second because he cannot change back and forth with the frequency he might desire. And so the pressure builds up, and the frustration."

"You're hoping he will make a mistake, lose control," Hawkwood said.

"Yes. He has been very careful so far. He has murdered our weather-worker and left us becalmed, thinking perhaps that will be enough. But the wind has struck up again and still the ship is pointed west, so he strikes again – at a ship's officer this time. He is starting to sow the seeds of panic."

"They know it was a shifter that killed Pernicus," Murad said, his eyes two slits in his white-skinned face. "It's hard to say who are the most terrified, the soldiers or the passengers."

"He hopes to ignite a mutiny, perhaps," Hawkwood said thoughtfully.

"Yes. There is one other thing Gregory tells us, however. It is that the shifter who has recently killed is not sated – quite the reverse, in fact. Often he finds he must kill again and again, especially when he is in these confined conditions I have mentioned. He loses more control with every murder until in the end the rational part of him recedes and the mindless beast gains control."

"Which perhaps is what happened to the shifter aboard the *Faulcon*," Hawkwood put in.

"Yes, I am afraid so."

"The *Faulcon* did not carry a complement of Hebrian soldiers, nor arquebuses with iron bullets," Murad said stoutly. "No, this thing is becoming afraid, is my guess. If the wizard is correct then the shifter is beginning to succumb to his more bestial impulses. It may work to our advantage."

"And in the meantime we await another death?" Hawkwood asked.

"Yes, Captain, I think we do," Bardolin said.

"I don't think much of your strategy, Mage. It is like that of the sheep as the wolf closes in."

"I can think of nothing else."

"There is no mark, no sign by which the beasts can be recognized in human form?"

"Some old wives say there is something odd about the eyes. They are often strange-looking, not quite human."

"That's not much to go on."

"It is all I have."

"Where will he strike next, do you think?" Murad asked.

"I think it will be at what he perceives to be the centre of resistance and the source of authority. I think that next he will strike at one of those sitting about this table."

Murad and Hawkwood stared blankly at one another. Finally the scarred nobleman managed a strangled laugh.

"You have a sure way of ruining good brandy, Mage. It might be vinegar in my mouth."

"Be prepared," Bardolin insisted. "Do not let yourselves be found alone at any time, and always carry a weapon that will bite its black flesh."

THE CARRACK SAILED on with its twin cargoes of fear and discontent. Velasca, Hawkwood noted, was slow to obey orders and seemed perpetually ill at ease, even when the splendid north-easter continued steadily, breezing in over the starboard quarter and propelling the ship along at a good six knots. Two leagues run off with every two turns of the glass, one hundred and forty-four sea miles with every full day of sailing. And west, always due west. The carrack's beakhead bisected the sinking disc of every flaming sunset as though it meant to sail into its very heart. Hawkwood loved his ship more than ever then, as she responded to his attentions, his cajolings, his lashing on of sail after sail. She seemed unaffected by the feelings on board, and leapt over the waves like a willing horse scenting home in the air ahead.

2nd day of Endorion, year of the Saint 551.

Wind north-east, fresh and steady. Course due west. Speed six knots with the breeze on the starboard quarter. Courses, topsails and bonnets.

Six weeks out of Abrusio harbour, by my estimate over eight hundred leagues west of North Cape in the Hebrionese, on the approximate latitude of Gabrion, which we will follow until we find land in the west.

In the forenoon watch Lord Murad had three soldiers strappadoed from the main yardarm for insubordination. As I write they are being attended on the gundeck by Brother Ortelius and some of the oldwives aboard. Strange bedfellows.

Hawkwood looked over the entry, frowning, then shrugged as he sat and dipped his quill in the inkwell again.

In the five days since First Mate Billerand and Ship's Boy Mateo were lost there have been no further deaths on board, though the mood of the ship's company has not improved. I have had words with Acting First Mate Velasca; it seems he is not happy with our course and the voyage as a whole. I told him that I expect to sight land within three weeks, which seemed to improve his temper and that of the crew. The soldiers, however, are growing more restless by the day, and despite the efforts of Murad's junior officers, they refuse to man their posts down in the hold. There is something down there, they say, and they will only guard working parties hauling up provisions.
Billerand is sorely missed.

Hawkwood rubbed his tired eyes as the flickering table lantern played over the pages of his log. On the desk by the lantern Bardolin's imp squatted cross-legged and watched the scrawling quill with fascination. The little creature was covered with ink; it seemed to love daubing itself with it.

On a chair by the door of the cabin his master slumped, asleep. The mage had an iron spike loosely gripped in one hand and his head had fallen forward on to his chest. He was snoring softly.

They had taken Bardolin's advice to heart. None of them remained alone any more, especially at night.

If Hawkwood paused to listen, he could hear the creak and groan of the ship's timbers, the rush and hiss of the sea as the carrack's bow went up and down, the voices of men on the deck above his head. And from the other side of the thin bulkhead, dark moans and thumps from Murad's cabin. He was not alone either. He had the girl in there with him, Griella.

It was late. Hawkwood felt he had neglected the log; he felt he should pad out the bald entries more fully, leave something for posterity perhaps. The thought made him smile wryly. Perhaps some fisherman might find it one day, grasped in his skeletal hand.

He looked again at the last sentence he had written, and his face fell.

Billerand is sorely missed.

Aye. He had not truly realized how much he had depended on the bald, mustachioed ex-soldier. He and Julius Albak had been the two indomitable pillars aboard ship. Good shipmates, fine friends.

Now they were both gone, Julius at the hands of the Inceptines – they had killed him, no matter that it was a marine's arquebus which had stopped his heart – and Billerand under the muzzle of a werewolf. Hawkwood felt strangely alone. On him rested the entire responsibility for the expedition, especially if the *Grace of God* had foundered, which he was beginning to believe had happened. He and he alone could point the *Osprey*'s beakhead in the right direction.

The knowledge weighed on him sorely. He had told Velasca that three weeks would see landfall, but that had been a mere sop to the man's fear. Hawkwood had no idea how long they had to go before the fabled Western Continent would loom up out of the horizon.

He heard the ship's bell struck twice. Two bells in the middle watch, an hour past midnight. He would take a last sniff of air up on deck, check the trim of the sails and then retire to his bunk.

He placed a sea cloak over the gently snoring Bardolin and went to the door. The imp chirruped wheedlingly at him and he turned.

"What is it, little one?"

With a bound, it launched itself off the desktop and landed on his shoulder. It nuzzled his ear, and he laughed.

"All right, then. You want some fresh air too?"

He left, reasoning that Bardolin would be all right for

a moment or two, and climbed up to the quarterdeck. Mihal had the watch, a good, steady fellow who was also Hawkwood's countryman. Two soldiers, ostensibly on guard duty, leaned at the break of the deck smoking pipes and spitting over the ship's rail. Hawkwood scowled. Discipline had gone to the wall these past days.

Mihal stared at the imp momentarily and then recited:

"Steady nor'-west, sir. Course due west under everything she can bear."

"Good. You might want to furl the courses in a glass or two. We don't want to run smack into the Western Continent in the middle of the night."

"Aye, sir."

"Where's the rest of the watch?"

"On the forecastle, mostly. I've two men on the tiller. She's steering easily enough."

"Very good, Mihal."

Hawkwood leaned on the windward rail gazing out at the night sea. It was as dark as the ink on his desk. The sky was almost clear, and great bands of speckled stars were arching from horizon to horizon. Most he knew and had steered by for twenty years. They were old friends, the only familiar things on this unending ocean.

The imp made a noise, and he looked down into the waist to see a black-robed figure disappearing into the sterncastle. Ortelius, most likely. What would he want at this time of night?

"Wake me if the wind shifts," he told Mihal, and made his way back down the companionway.

The imp was whimpering and shifting around on his shoulder, clearly upset. He shushed it and then, stepping into the deeper dark of the sterncastle, he knew something was wrong.

A golden bar of lantern light was coming from the door to his cabin – but he had closed it after him.

He drew his dirk and pushed through the door quickly. Bardolin was still asleep in his chair but the sea cloak had fallen to the floor. The imp hopped from Hawkwood's shoulder to his master's, still chittering urgently.

The door was pushed shut behind Hawkwood.

He spun round and his mouth dropped with shock. "Mateo!"

"Well met, Captain," the figure said with a ghastly smile.

The ship's boy was filthy and bloody, his hair crawling with lice and his nails long and black. His eyes had a light in them that made the hair on the back of Hawkwood's neck stand up like wire.

"Mateo, we thought you were dead!"

"Aye, and so did I, Captain." The voice which had been on the verge of breaking before he disappeared was as deep and full as a man's. "And didn't you wish I was dead – the bumboy you were so ashamed of having used? Didn't you, Captain? But I wasn't and I'm back again, different but the same."

"What in the world are you talking about, Mateo?" Hawkwood asked. The boy was circling like a prowling cat. Now he was between Hawkwood and the sleeping mage. The imp was frozen, utterly petrified. It eyed Mateo as though he were a fiend incarnate. Then the horrible thought occurred to Hawkwood.

"It was you," he breathed. "You are the werewolf. You killed Pernicus and Billerand." His voice shook as he said it. He wondered how many would hear his shout, how much time he would have.

Mateo grinned, and Hawkwood could see the lengthening canines, the black flush of hair that was breaking out like a rash down the sides of his face.

"Wrong, Captain, it was not me. It was my new master, a man who appreciates me as you never did."

"Your – ? Who is he?"

"A man high up in his society, and high up in other things too. He has promised me much and given me much already. But I am tired of rats and what he gave me of Billerand. I want a fresh kill. You, whom I loved and who discarded me like a spent horse. You, Richard."

"*Bardolin!*" Hawkwood screamed in the same instant as Mateo launched himself at him.

MURAD SAT UP to find Griella awake beside him, her eyes shining in the dark, something strange about her profile.

Another dream?

"I thought I –"

She shook her head and nodded towards the door of the cabin. Standing hunched in the doorway was a vast, black shape, its ears as tall as horns and its eyes two burning yellow lights. Around its feet in a puddle of shadow were a set of black robes.

"My Lord Murad," the beast said, its long teeth gleaming. "Time for you to die."

In the same moment, Murad heard Hawkwood scream out Bardolin's name on the other side of the partition. There was a thump and crash. The beast cocked its massive head.

"He has much to learn," it said, seemingly amused. Then it leapt.

THE THING WAS on top of him, its fetid breath wreathing about his face. It was recognizable as Mateo, but the face was changing even as Hawkwood grappled with it, the nose broadening and pushing out into a snout. The eyes flared with saffron light and the heat of it made him choke.

It dipped its forming muzzle and bit deep.

Hawkwood shrieked in agony as the jaws met in his flesh. The dirk glanced off the thick fur that now covered the boy's body and slipped out of his nerveless hand. The pair of them rolled across the deck of the cabin, blood jetting from Hawkwood's mangled shoulder. They knocked against the table and it came down. Ink splattered them; the loose pages of the log flew about like pale birds and the table lantern crashed to the ground with a spatter of burning oil.

The heat, the awful heat. It was wholly beast-like now and it covered him like a choking carpet. He lay still, strength ebbing away with the thick ropes of blood that were pulsing out of his ripped veins.

"I love you, Richard," the werewolf said, its insane eyes glaring at him over its blood-soaked muzzle. The maw descended again.

Then it had thrown itself back off him, howling in agony and fury. The cabin was a thrashing, flickering chaos of shadows and flames. The wood of the deck and bulkhead were on fire, and the werewolf was wrenching a black spike out of its neck, still howling.

Bardolin stood there, the flames illuminating his face, filling the imp's eyes with light as it perched on his shoulder. Dimly Hawkwood was aware of other voices shouting in the ship, and a turmoil of snarling and violence on the other side of the bulkhead, Murad's voice raised in fear.

"Get you gone," Bardolin said quietly, almost conversationally, and he pointed one large hand at the writhing beast.

Blue fire left his fingers, crackled like lightning and sank into the black fur to disappear.

The werewolf shrieked. Its head snapped up and down. It retreated to where the flames were climbing the wall of the cabin and blue fire sparked out of its mouth. There was the smell of burning flesh.

Then the entire cabin wall disintegrated beside it.

Two huge black figures smashed clear through the bulkhead and fell on to the floor entangled in each other's arms. Hawkwood crawled feebly away from the flames and the thrashing beasts, slumping at the further wall. He watched the scene with utter amazement.

Murad was standing in the gap of the shattered partition wall with a long knife in his hand, whilst on the deck three werewolves fought and howled amid the rising flames. Hawkwood saw one detach itself from the melee, azure light spurting from its eyes and nostrils. It hurled itself at the stern windows and they gave way, glass, frame, planking and all. It flew out into the dark night beyond and splashed into the carrack's foaming wake. There was a flash of aquamarine, so bright it dimmed the fire on board ship, and then a concussion that shook the entire stern and sent the sea into an insane turmoil of explosions and geysers brilliantly lit from below.

The entire aft end of the cabin was a gaping, blazing hole with two firelit silhouettes battling there, their fur on fire and their eyes glaring the same colour as the flames. The violence of their battle made the entire ship quiver and the blackened planking screeched and groaned under their clawed feet whilst their howls hurt Hawkwood's ears.

The cabin door was flung open to reveal Ensign Sequero, behind him a crowd of soldiers with smoking arquebuses. He stared blankly at the hellish scene for a second, then shouted a command. The soldiers levelled their weapons through the doorway.

"No!" Bardolin yelled.

A volley of shots, plumes of smoke and fire spurting from the weapons. Hawkwood saw fur lifted from the grappling beasts, blood erupting over the walls and deckhead.

One of the werewolves broke free and came roaring towards the soldiers, its fur blazing and gore spurting from its wounds.

It batted Sequero aside, wrenched an arquebus from a terrified soldier and clubbed another so brutally that the weapon's stock shattered. For a moment it seemed that it would succeed in getting away.

But then the second werewolf leapt on to its back. Hawkwood saw the thing's jaws sink deep into fur and flesh, then wrench free with a gobbet of bleeding meat between the teeth.

Someone hauled him out of the way. It was Murad. He dragged Hawkwood out of the cabin and into the companionway.

"Griella, it's Griella," he was saying. "She's one of them. She's a shifter too."

"The fire," Hawkwood croaked. "Put out the fire, or the ship is lost." But Murad had gone again.

There were more soldiers there, crowding the sterncastle, and then some sailors.

"Velasca!" Hawkwood managed to shout.

"Captain! What in the world –"

"The ship's afire. Leave the soldiers to their work and organize fire-fighting parties."

"Captain – your shoulder –"

"Do it, you insubordinate bastard, or I'll see you marooned!"

"Aye, sir." Velasca disappeared, chalk-faced.

Hawkwood heard Bardolin's voice raised in fury, telling the soldiers to hold fire. He struggled to his feet, his one working hand clutching the bloody mess of his shoulder. He could feel the ends of his collar-bone under his hands, and splinters of bone pricked his palm like needles.

"Sweet Ramusio," he groaned.

He staggered back into the wreck of the stern cabin, pushing aside the arquebusiers. The place was thick with smoke and the reek of blood and powder. The flickering radiance of the fire played about the deck and bulkheads.

Hawkwood sank down on the storm sill, light-headed but as yet not in much pain. He could no longer remain on his feet.

Men shouting, a shower of water coming down past the gaping hole in the stern of the ship, the flames eating into the precious wood. His poor *Osprey*.

Bardolin and Murad standing like statues, the nobleman's iron knife dangling from one hand. The imp had buried its little face in its master's neck.

And lying amid the flames two hulking, broken shapes with the blood bubbling in their wounds and swathes of bare, blistered flesh shining where the fur had been burnt off.

One werewolf had a paw clutched to its chest much as Hawkwood nursed his shoulder. The black lips drew back from the teeth in a parody of a smile.

"Your iron has done for me, after all," it sneered. "Who'd have thought it? The maid a fellow sufferer. Little lady, we could have talked, you and I."

The other beast was barely conscious. It growled feebly, the light in its eyes becoming fainter moment by moment.

More water cascaded down from above. They had rigged the hand-pumps and were frenziedly pumping seawater over the burning ship.

"You will never find the west," the werewolf said to Hawkwood, whose eyes were stinging and blurred with smoke and pain. To him the beast that had been Ortelius was nothing but a looming shadow backlit by sputtering flames and brightly lit cascades of seawater. "Better for you and yours that you do not. There are things there best left alone by the men of Normannia. Turn your ship around if it remains afloat, Captain. I am only a messenger; there are others more powerful than I whose faces are set against you. You cannot survive."

The werewolf hauled itself with startling speed to its feet.

At the fore end of the cabin the crowd by the door watched transfixed as it hurled itself, laughing, from the shattered stern and disappeared into the sea beyond.

A volley of shots followed it down into the water, stitching the sea with foam. It was gone.

"Griella," Murad groaned, and started forward into the fire. Bardolin stopped him.

"Better to let her burn," he said with great gentleness. "She cannot live."

The men watched as the shape in the flames became smaller and paler. The ears shrank, the fur withered away and the eyes dulled. In seconds there was a naked girl lying there in the fire, her body ravaged with terrible wounds. She turned her head to them before the end, and Hawkwood thought she smiled. Then her body blackened, as though some preserving forces had suddenly failed, and the flames were licking around a charred corpse.

Murad's face was as bleak as a skull.

"She saved my life. She did that for me. She loved me, Bardolin."

"Get more water in here," Hawkwood said calmly, "or we'll lose the ship. Do you hear me there? Don't just stand around."

Murad shot him a look of pure hatred and stormed out past the staring soldiers.

"The ship. You must save the ship," Hawkwood insisted, but the fire and the bulkheads and the faces were retreating down a soundless tunnel away from him. He could not hold the scene in focus. Men were coming and going, and he was being lifted. He thought Bardolin's face was close to his, lips moving soundlessly. But his tunnel continued to lengthen. Finally it grew so long that it blotted out the light, and all the pictures faded. The faces and the mounting pain dimmed with growing distance. He held on as long as he could, until he could hear the pumps sluicing water all around him. His poor ship.

Then the shadows swooped in on his tired mind, and bore it off with them to some howling place of darkness.

TWENTY-FOUR

"SHAHR INDUN JOHOR," the vizier announced.

Aurungzeb the Golden waved a hand. "Send him in."

He kissed the nipple of the raven-haired Ramusian concubine one last time then threw a silk sheet over her naked limbs.

"You will remain," he said in her barbaric tongue, "but you will be a statue. Do you hear me?"

Heria nodded and bowed her head. He tugged the sheet up until she was entirely covered, then pulled his robe about him and sashed it tight. He thrust his plain-hilted dagger into the sash and when he looked up again Shahr Johor was there, kneeling with his eyes fixed floorwards.

"Up, up," he said impatiently, and gestured to a low stool while he himself took his place on a silk-upholstered divan by one wall.

They could hear the birds singing in the gardens beyond the seraglio, the bubble of water in the fountains. This room was one of the most private in the entire palace, where Aurungzeb perused the most exquisite of his treasures – such as the girl cowering on the bed by the other wall, the sheet that cloaked her quivering as she breathed. The chamber was thick-walled, isolated from the labyrinth of the rest of the complex. One might scream to the depths of one's lungs within its confines and yet go unheard.

"Do you know why you are here?" the Sultan of Ostrabar and Aekir asked.

Shahr Johor was a young man with a fine black beard and eyes as dark as polished ebony.

"Yes, Majesty."

"Good. What think you of your new appointment?"

"I shall try to fulfil your wishes and ambitions to the best extent of my abilities, Majesty. I am yours to command."

"That's right," the Sultan grunted emphatically. "Your predecessor, the esteemed Shahr Baraz, is unfortunately rendered infirm due to the weight of his years. A magnificent soldier, but I am told his faculties are not what they once were – hence our failure before this absurd Ramusian fortress. You will carry on where Baraz left off. You will take Ormann Dyke, but first you will reorganize the army. My sources report that it is somewhat demoralized. Winter is coming on, the Thurian passes are closed and your only supply line is the Ostian river. When you reach the dyke you will put the army into winter quarters, and attack again once the weather has improved. In the meantime the accursed Ramusians will have to contend with coastal raids from our new allies, the Sultanates of Nalbeni and Danrimir. They will be prevented from reinforcing the dyke, and you will storm it when the winter snows abate."

"Then I am not to attack at once, Majesty?"

"No. As I said, the army is in need of some... reorganization. This present campaign is over. You will see that communications between the camps and the supply depots in Aekir are improved. Baraz was building a road, I believe; one of the last of his more coherent plans. Everything must be made ready so that in the spring the army is ready to move again. The dyke will be crushed and you will march on Torunn. A fresh levy will be made available to you then. Have you any questions?"

Shahr Johor, new supreme commander of the Merduk armies of Ostrabar, hesitated a moment and then said:

"One question, Majesty. Why was I selected for this particular honour? Shahr Baraz's second-in-command Mughal is surely better qualified."

Aurungzeb's florid face darkened. His fingers toyed with the hilt of his dagger.

"Mughal has a certain absurd attachment to Shahr Baraz. It would not do to leave him in command. He is being transferred elsewhere, as are most of the previous staff officers. I want a new beginning. We have been shackled by the old *Hraib* for too long; the world is entering a new age, when such outdated codes are a hindrance rather than a help. You are young and you have studied the new modes of warfare. I want you to apply your knowledge to the coming campaigns. There is a shipment of forty thousand arquebuses travelling down the Ostian River even as we speak. You will equip the best troops with them, and train them in the tactics that the Torunnans have used against us in the past. We will no longer face firearms with steel and muscle and raw courage. War has become a scientific thing. You will be the first general of my people to wage it according to the new rules."

Shahr Johor flung himself to the floor.

"You honour me too much, my Sultan. My life is yours. I will send you the spoils of all the Ramusian kingdoms. The west shall be brought into the fold of the True Faith, if Ahrimuz wills it."

"He wills it," Aurungzeb said sharply. "And so do I. Do not forget that." He waved a hand. "You may go."

Shahr Johor backed away, bowing as he went. Aurungzeb stood motionless long after he had gone, then: "Sit up!" he said abruptly.

Heria straightened, the silk sliding like water from her shoulders.

"Raise your head."

She did so, staring at a point on the ornate ceiling.

Aurungzeb sidled over to her. He was as silent as a cat in his movements, despite being a big man on the edge of corpulence. His eyes drank her in. One brown ring-encrusted hand slid along her torso. She remained as motionless as marble, a lovely statue sculpted by some genius.

"I shall give you a name," the Sultan breathed. "You must have a name. I know. I shall call you Ahara. It is the old name for the wind that every year sweeps westward across the steppes of Kambaksk and Kurasan. My people followed that wind, and with them went the Faith. Ahara. Say it."

She stared at him dumbly. He cursed and began speaking in the halting Normannic that was the common language of the western kingdoms.

"Your name is Ahara. Say it."

"*Ahara.*"

He grinned hugely, his teeth a white gleam in his beard.

"I will have you taught our tongue, Ahara. I want to hear you speak it to me on our wedding night."

Still her eyes revealed nothing. He laughed.

"I talk to myself, do I not? You Ramusians... You will have to be consecrated into the Prophet's worship, of course. And you are too thin, the marks of the journey are upon you yet. I will feed you up, put flesh on those bones of yours. You will bear me fine sons in the time to come, and they will spend so much time killing each other that their sire will be left in peace in his old age." He pulled the sheet up around her. "Wife number twenty-six, you will be. I should have had more, but I am an abstemious man."

He flung an arm out towards the doorway. "Go," he said in Normannic.

She scampered from the chamber, the silk billowing from her shoulders like a pair of wings. Her feet could be heard pattering on the marble and porphyry of the floors beyond. Aurungzeb smiled into the empty room. He was in a good mood. He had found himself a superb new wife – he would marry her, despite the inevitable objections. She was too rare a jewel to keep as a mere concubine.

And he had rid himself of that relic from the past, Shahr Baraz. The orders had gone out by special courier, a picked squad of the palace guard journeying with them to carry them out. Soon the old man's head would be carted towards Orkhan in a jar, pickled in vinegar. He had been a faithful servant, a superb soldier, but now that Aekir had fallen and the impossible had been achieved, he was no longer needed. And besides, he was growing dangerously insubordinate. Shahr Johor was different. He was forward-looking for one thing, and after the example of Baraz he would know better than to disobey his Sultan.

Aurungzeb lay back on the rumpled, sex-smelling bed.

A pity they would not take the dyke in the same campaigning season as they had taken Aekir. That would have been a feat indeed. But it was of no great import that they would have to wait out the winter. It would give him a chance to cement the new alliances with Nalbeni and Danrimir.

The Ramusians, he knew, mostly thought of the Seven Sultanates as one Merduk power-bloc, but the reality was different. There were rivalries and intrigues, even minor wars between this sultanate and that. Danrimir was virtually an Ostrabarian client state, so closely tied to Orkhan had she become in the last months, but Nalbeni was a different matter.

The oldest of the Merduk countries, Nalbeni had been founded before even the Fimbrian-Hegemony had fallen. It was primarily a sea power and its capital, Nalben, was supposed to be the largest port in the world, save perhaps for Abrusio of Hebrion in the west. It did not trust this upstart state from the north of the Kardian Sea, so naturally had allied with it to keep a closer eye on its progress. It was a good way of insinuating Nalbenic diplomats into Aurungzeb's court. Diplomats with flapping ears and heavy purses. But such was the way of the world. Ostrabar needed Nalbeni to keep up the pressure on Torunna from a different direction, so that when Shahr Johor moved against the dyke in the spring he would not find it manned by all the armies of Torunna.

This war was not coming to a close; it was only beginning. *Before I am done*, Aurungzeb thought, *I will have all the Seven Sultanates doing my bidding, and Merduk armies will be marching to the very brim of the Western Ocean. Charibon I will set afire, and its black priests I shall crucify by the thousands. Temples of the True Faith shall be reared up over the whole continent. If the Prophet wills it.*

A shadow fell through the doorway. Aurungzeb sat up at once.

"Akran?"

"No, Sultan. It is I, Orkh."

"You were not announced."

"I was not seen."

The shadow glided into the room and was nothing more than that: an absence of light, a mere shape.

"What do you want?"

"To speak with you."

"Speak, then. And let me see you. I am sick of this ghost business."

"You might not like what you see, Sultan."

"Show yourself. I command it."

The shadow took on substance, another dimension. In a moment a man stood there in long dun-coloured robes. Or what had once been a man.

"Beard of the Prophet!" Aurungzeb breathed.

The thing smiled, and the lights that were its eyes became two glowing slots.

"Is this what happened to you when – ?"

"When Baraz slew my homunculus? Yes. I was relaying your own voice through it, acting as a conductor; thus I could not defend myself against the... consequences until it was too late."

"But why has it done this to you?"

"The surge of power was like the explosion of a gun when the barrel is blocked. Something of the Dweomer that went into making the homunculus was blasted back through me, and I had no barriers up because of my role in the communication. It changed me. I am working on a remedy for the unfortunate effects."

"I see now why you haunt the palace like a shadow."

"I have no wish to frighten your concubines – especially one so delicious as just passed me in the corridor."

"What did you want, Orkh? I am meeting the Nalbenic ambassadors soon."

"I am your eyes and ears, Majesty, despite the malady which afflicts me. I have agents in every city in the west. It is partly because of my network of information gatherers that this sultanate has risen to the prominence it now enjoys. Is that not true?"

"There may be something in what you say," Aurungzeb admitted, scowling. He did not like to be reminded of his reliance on the sorcerer, or on anyone else for that matter.

"Well, I have a very interesting piece of information I would like to impart to you. It does not concern the present war, but an occurrence much further west in one of the Ramusian states."

"Go on."

"It seems there is a purge in progress in the kingdom of Hebrion, which seeks to rid the land of its exotic elements. I lost two of my best agents to their damned pyres, but the chief targets of the purge seem to be oldwives, herbalists, weatherworkers, thaumaturgists and cantrimers – in short, anyone who has an inkling of the Dweomer."

"Interesting."

"My sources – those who survived – tell me, however, that this purge was initiated by the accursed Inceptines – the Black Priests of the west – and has not found favour with King Abeleyn."

"Why does he not command it stopped then?" Aurungzeb asked gruffly. "Is a king not King in his own land?"

"Not in the west, sire. Their Church has a great say in the running of every kingdom."

"Fools! What kind of rulers are they? But I interrupt. Continue, Orkh."

"Abeleyn hired a small fleet, I am told, filled it to the brim with fleeing sorcerers and the like and commissioned the fleet to sail west."

"To where? Hebrion is the westernmost kingdom of the world."

"Exactly, sire. To where? They did not touch upon any of the other Ramusian states as far as I know. It may be they made landfall in the Brenn Isles or the Hebrionese, but there are rumours flying round the Hebrian capital."

"Rumours of what?"

"It is said that the fleet sailed with a Royal warrant for the setting up of a new colony, and it carried in addition to its passengers and a complement of soldiers everything that might be needed when starting a settlement in a hitherto uninhabited land."

"Orkh! Are you saying – ?"

"Yes, my Sultan. The Ramusians have discovered a land in the far west, somewhere in the Great Western Ocean, and they are claiming it for themselves."

Aurungzeb sank back on the bed. Orkh let his Sultan sit in silence for a few moments; he could see the wheels turning.

"How reliable is this information, Orkh?" the Sultan asked at last.

"I am not a peddler of hearsay, sire. My informants know that to feed me false news is the best way to ensure a swift end. The rumours have been investigated, and they have substance."

Another pause.

"We cannot let it be, of course," the Sultan said thoughtfully. "We must test the veracity of your rumours, and if they possess the substance you say they do we shall outfit our own expedition and stake our claim. But Ostrabar is not a sea power. We have no ships."

"Nalbeni?"

"I trust them less than I do Ramusians. No, this must be done further from home. The Sea-Merduks of Calmar. Yes. I will commission them to send a fleet into the west, commanded by my own officers of course."

"It will be expensive, my Sultan."

"After Aekir, my credit is good anywhere," Aurungzeb said with a chuckle. "You have agents in Alcaras. See to it, Orkh. I will select the officers of this expedition personally."

"As my Sultan wishes. I have one boon to ask of him, however."

"Ask! Your information merits reward."

"I wish to be included in this expedition. I wish to sail west."

Aurungzeb stared closely at the hideously inhuman face of his court mage. "I need you here."

"My apprentice Batak, whom you know, is well able to take my place, and he does not have the same disability that afflicts me."

"Are you seeking a cure in the west, or oblivion, Orkh?"

"A cure if I can find one – oblivion if I cannot."

"Very well. You shall sail with the expedition."

Orkh faded back into misty shadow as the vizier came into the room, bent low, eyes averted.

"My Sultan, the Nalbenic ambassadors are here. They await your inimitable presence."

Aurungzeb waved a hand. "I'll be there directly."

The vizier left, still bowed. Aurungzeb stared around the chamber.

"Orkh? Are you there, Orkh?" But there was no answer. The mage had gone.

THE FIRST SNOWS had come to the Searil valley. Shahr Baraz had felt them in his tired old bones before he had even thrown off the furs. His head ached. It had been too long since he had slept out under the stars like his forebears, the chieftains of the eastern steppes.

Mughal already had the fire going. It was almost colourless in the bright morning light and the snow glare. Melted slush sizzled around the burning wood.

"Winter arrives early this year," Mughal said.

Shahr Baraz climbed to his feet. Darkness danced at the corners of his vision until he blinked it away. He was almost eighty-four years old.

"Pass me the skin, Mughal. My blood needs some heat in it."

He drank three gulps of searing mare's-milk spirit, and his limbs stopped shuddering. Warmth again.

"I had a look over the hill as the sun came up," Mughal said. "They have pulled back the camps to the reverse slopes and are busy entrenching there."

"A winter camp," Shahr Baraz said. "Campaigning is finished for this year. Nothing else will happen until the spring."

"Jaffan's loyalty is to you, my Khedive."

"Jaffan will obey the orders of Orkhan or he will find his head atop a spear before too long. He will not be left in command for he was too close to me. No, another khedive will be sent out. I hope, though, that Jaffan will not suffer for letting two old men slip away into the night."

"Who will the new khedive be, you think?"

"Who knows? Some creature of Aurungzeb's who is more malleable than I. One who will put his own ambitions above the lives of his men. The Searil will flow scarlet ere we take that fortress, Mughal."

"But it will fall in the spring. It will fall. And where will we be then?"

"Eating yoghurt in a felt hut on the steppes."

Mughal guffawed, then bent his face to the fire and nudged the kettle into the flames. They would have steaming *kava* to warm them before they broke camp and continued their journey.

"Will you turn your back on it so easily?" he asked.

Shahr Baraz was silent for a long time.

"I am of the old *Hraib*," he said at last. "This war which we have begun will usher the world into a new age. Men like myself and John Mogen were not destined to be leaders in the times to come. The world has changed, and is changing yet. The Merduk people are no longer the fierce steppe horsemen of my youth; their blood is mixed with many who were once Ramusian, and the old nomadic times are only a memory.

"Even the way of the warrior itself is changing. Gunpowder counts for more than courage. Arquebus balls take no heed of rank. Honour counts for less and less. Soon generals will be artisans and engineers rather than soldiers, and war will be a thing of equations and mathematics. That is not the way I have waged it, or ever will.

"So yes: I will turn my back on it, Mughal. I will leave it to the younger men who come after me. I have seen a Merduk host march through the streets of Aekir; my place in the story is assured. I have that to take with me. Now I will ride east to the land of my fathers, there to see the limitless plains of Kambaksk and Kolchuk, the birthplace of our nation, and there I will leave my bones."

"I would come with you, if I may," Mughal said.

The terrible old man smiled beneath the twin tusks of his moustache.

"I would like that. A companion shortens a journey, it is said. And it will be a long journey."

"But it is the last journey," Mughal murmured, and poured steaming *kava* for them both.

"Tell me what you see," Macrobius said.

They stood on the battlements of the citadel of Ormann Dyke, a cluster of officers and soldiers and one old man who was missing his eyes. Corfe stared out at the white, empty, snow-shrouded land beyond the flinty torrent of the Searil river.

"There is nothing there. The camps have been abandoned. Even the trenches and walls they delved and reared are hard to see under the snow; mere shadows running across the face of the hills. Here and there is the remnant of a tent, a strew of wreckage covered with snow. They have gone, Holiness."

"What is that smell on the air, then?"

"They gathered their dead under the terms of the burial truce, and burned them on a pyre in one of the further valleys. It is smoking yet, a hill of ashes."

"Where have they gone, Corfe? Where did that great host go to?"

Corfe looked at his commander. Martellus shrugged. "They have retreated into winter camp, a league or more from the walls."

"Then they are defeated. The dyke is safe."

"For now, yes. They will be back in the spring, when the snows melt. But we will be ready for them. We will hurl them back beyond the Ostian river and cleanse Aekir once more."

The High Pontiff bent his ravaged head, his white hair flickering in the chill breeze. "Thanks to God and the Blessed Saint."

"And you, Your Holiness, have done your duty here and done it well," Martellus said. "It is time you left to take up your proper place."

"My proper place?" Macrobius said. "Perhaps. I am no longer sure. Has there been no word from Charibon?"

"No," Martellus lied. "King Lofantyr will be returning from Vol Ephrir very soon; it is best you are in Torunn to meet him. There will be much for you and he to discuss. Corfe will go with you. He is a colonel now; he has done well. He is the only Torunnan to have survived Aekir and he will be able to answer the King's questions."

"Are you so sure the Merduks will not attack again, General?"

"I am. They have abandoned their artillery emplacements and will have to fight to rehouse their batteries again. No – my scouts tell me that they are completing a great new road between here and Aekir for the passage of supplies. And they have small parties sniffing the upper and lower stretches of the Searil, searching for a way to outflank the Dyke. They will not find it. The Fimbrians did well to build their fortress here. The campaign is finished for this year. You will spend a more comfortable winter in Torunn than you would here, Holiness, and you will be of more service to us there."

"Meaning?" Macrobius asked.

"Meaning I want you and Corfe to work on King Lofantyr. The dyke must be reinforced ere the snow melts. The Merduks have been having command difficulties – one of the reasons we are still here. But come spring they will be at our throats again under a new general. So it is rumoured."

Macrobius started. "Is Shahr Baraz dead then?"

"Dead or replaced – it makes little difference. But the Ostian is reputed to be thick with supply barges, many of them carrying firearms. The tactics will be different when they come again, and we have lost the eastern barbican. We hang on here by a thread, despite the fools who are celebrating in the refugee camps – another subject that Corfe will bring up when he meets the King."

Macrobius smiled wryly, looked blindly at Corfe.

"You have come far, my friend, since we shared burnt turnip on the Western Road. You have become a man who consorts with kings and Pontiffs, and your star has not finished rising yet; I can feel it."

"You will have thirty of Ranafast's troopers to escort you," Martellus said, a little put out. "It is all we can spare, but it should be enough. The road south is still open, but you should leave as soon as you can."

"I travel in state no longer, General," Macrobius said. "All I own I wear on my back. I can go whenever you wish."

"It is time the world saw Macrobius again, and heard of the things that have been done here. We have done well, but it is only the first battle of a long war."

THE YEAR WAS turning. Even in Vol Ephrir the balminess was vanishing from the air and the flaming trees were growing barer by the day. The Conclave of Kings ground on interminably as the land settled into an early winter, a bitter winter that was already rendering the mountains impassable. This dark season would be long and hard, harder still for those lands which were under the shadow of invasion and war.

The High Pontiff in Charibon, Himerius II, issued a Pontifical bull denouncing the old blind man rumoured to be Macrobius and housed in Ormann Dyke as an impostor and a heretic. His sponsor, the Torunnan general Pieter Martellus, who had successfully defended the dyke against the army of Shahr Baraz, was indicted on charges of heresy in his absence, and couriers were sent to Torunna to demand his removal and punishment.

A second bull authorized clerical authorities in the Five Ramusian Kingdoms of the West, as well as the duchies and principalities, to seize and detain any person or persons who were users of black magic, who were natives of a state not within the Ramusian fold or who publicly objected to the seizure of any of the above. These persons' property was to be considered confiscate and divided between the Church and the secular authorities of the region, and they were to be detained pending a Religious Trial.

At roughly the same time two thousand Knights Militant reached Abrusio in the Kingdom of Hebrion and were met by representatives of the Inceptine Order. The city of Abrusio was put under Theocratic Law and governed by a body of Inceptines and nobles answerable only to the High Pontiff and to the Hebrian king – who unfortunately was far away in Vol Ephrir. The first day of the new rule was marked by the burning of seven hundred and thirty people, thus emptying the catacombs for the influx of fresh heretics and foreigners the Knights were rounding up throughout the city and the kingdom beyond.

But the crisis that would do most to affect the shape of the world in the times to come occurred in Vol Ephrir, where the assembled kings met to discuss the bulls of Himerius and the dilemmas facing the west.

"To ALL APPEARANCES, we have two Pontiffs," Cadamost said simply. "That is a situation which cannot be allowed to continue. If it does, then anarchy will ensue."

"Anarchy is already alive and well throughout the Five Kingdoms, thanks to Himerius," Abeleyn snarled. He had been apprised of the situation in Hebrion by Golophin's gyrfalcon, and now he burned to be away, to take back his kingdom and halt the atrocities.

"You verge on the edge of heresy, cousin," Skarpathin of Finnmark said, smiling unpleasantly.

"I teeter on the abyss of common sense, whilst you fools dance arguments on the heads of pins. Can't you see what is happening? Himerius realizes he is the impostor – the wrongly elected High Pontiff – so he strikes first, stamping his authority across the continent in fire and blood –"

"And rightly so," said Haukir of Almark resoundingly. "It is time the Church governed with a strong hand. Macrobius, who is undoubtedly dead, was an old woman who let things slide. Himerius is the kind of man we need on the Pontifical throne: a man unafraid to act. A strong hand on the tiller."

"Spare me the eulogy, cousin," Abeleyn sneered. "Everyone knows that the Inceptines have had Almark in the pocket of their habits for years."

Haukir went white. "Even kings have limits," he said in an unusually subdued voice. "Even kings can transgress. Your words will condemn you, boy. Already the Church governs your capital. If you do not take care it will end up governing your kingdom and you will die an excommunicate."

"I will die my own man then, and not a puppet of power-hungry Ravens!" Abeleyn cried.

The chamber went silent, the heads of state appalled at this exchange. The Fimbrians, however, looked only distantly interested, as if this were nothing to do with them.

"I will not obey the bulls of Himerius," Abeleyn said in a calmer voice. "I do not recognize him as Pontiff, but call him impostor and usurper. The true Pontiff is Macrobius. I repudiate the authority of Charibon, based as it is on a falsehood, and I will not see my kingdom torn apart by avaricious murderers who happen to be in the guise of clerics!"

Cadamost started to speak, but Abeleyn quelled him with a look. He was on his feet now, and every eye in the room was turned to him. In the silence it was possible to hear the birds singing in the tallest of the trees that surrounded the palace towers.

"I hereby withdraw Hebrion from the company of Ramusian Kingdoms which recognize the Prelate Himerius as High Pontiff. His inhumane edicts I will ignore, his servants I will banish from my borders. I stand here and say to you: who else is with me in this thing? Who else recognizes Macrobius as the true head of the Church?"

There was a pause, and then Mark of Astarac stood up slowly, heavily. His reluctance was obvious, but he faced the other rulers squarely.

"Astarac is allied to Hebrion in this thing; Abeleyn is betrothed to my sister. I will stand by him. I also repudiate Himerius the usurper."

A buzz of talk swept the room. It was silenced by the scraping of another chair on the beautifully ornate floor.

Lofantyr of Torunna was on his feet.

"Torunna has stood alone against the threat from the east. No succour have we had from any western state, and as Pontiff, Himerius has denied us the aid which is our right. I believe my general, Martellus the Lion of Ormann Dyke. Macrobius is alive and is Pontiff. I will stand with Hebrion and Astarac in this thing."

That was all. No one else stood up, no one else spoke. The Ramusian Kingdoms were irrevocably split down the middle, and the continent possessed two High Pontiffs, perhaps two Churches. The air in the chamber was pregnant with foreboding, a sense of the destiny of the moment.

Cadamost cleared his throat and when he spoke was as hoarse as a crow, his singer's voice crushed.

"I beg you, think of what you are doing. You lead three of the great kingdoms of the west. At a time when the enemy howls on our borders, we cannot afford to be riven apart like this. We cannot let the faith that sustains us be the weapon which cleaves our ranks apart."

"You are Heretics, all three of you," old Haukir said with scarcely concealed satisfaction. "No aid will you receive now, Lofantyr; you have signed the death warrant of your kingdom. And Hebrion and Astarac cannot stand alone against the other states of the west."

Abeleyn looked at them as they sat there: kings, dukes and princes. Almark and Perigraine, Finnmark and Candelaria, Tarber and Gardiac, Touron and Fulk. Even Gabrion, long known for its tradition of independence. But what of the two men in black who sat silent in their midst? What of the Fimbrians?

"Do the electorates have anything to say about this, or will they follow the lead of others?" he asked.

Marshal Jonakait raised his eyebrows slightly.

"Fimbria has never recognized the authority of any power outside its borders, including that of the Pontiff. We too are a Ramusian country, and the Inceptines live and work within our borders, but the electors are not bound by the bulls or edicts of the head of the Church."

Hope sprang up in Abeleyn. "Then your offer of troops still stands?"

Something like a smile crossed the marshal's hard face and then was gone.

"We will not contribute soldiers to any fellow-Ramusian state which wars upon another, but we will make them available to fight the Merduks."

Cadamost started up. "You cannot! You will be aiding heretics whose souls are as damned as the Merduks' are!"

Jonakait shrugged. "Only in certain eyes. The struggle in the east takes precedence over all else in the eyes of our superiors. If others disagree, then they will have to make their arguments known and we will consider them. But no Fimbrian will be farmed out as a mercenary in a fratricidal religious war."

"That is absurd!" Haukir cried. "Not long ago you were promising troops to whoever wanted them. What is that if not farming your soldiers out as mercenaries?"

"Each and every case will be considered on its merits. I can promise no more."

The Fimbrians naturally could not commit themselves here and now. The west had split down the middle. In honour, the electorates would have to send troops to Lofantyr – he had already asked for them, Abeleyn knew that. But they would wait and see what happened before committing them anywhere else. No doubt the marshals were secretly hugging themselves with glee at the thought of a divided west, the Five Kingdoms at each other's throats. It augured well for any Fimbrian attempt to re-establish the Hegemony she had lost centuries before. But for the moment, more important was the fact that Lofantyr would have his reinforcements – though they would have a long journey ahead of them were they not to traverse Perigraine to reach Ormann Dyke.

The gamble had paid off. Mark and Lofantyr had played their roles well, but then Abeleyn had had them well-rehearsed in the days following the news from Charibon.

Haukir glared at the three renegade monarchs.

"I will personally see that the High Pontiff excommunicates you, and it will mean war – Ramusian versus Ramusian. May God forgive you for what you have done this day."

Abeleyn leaned forward on to the table. His eyes were like two black holes.

"What we have done today is lift our heads out of the Inceptine yoke that has been tightening on the throat of every land in the west for decades. We have delivered our kingdoms from the terror of the pyre."

"You have plunged the west into war at a time when she is already fighting for her life," Cadamost said.

"No," Lofantyr told him hotly. "Torunna is fighting for her life. My kingdom, my people – we are the ones who are dying on the frontier. You here know nothing of what we have suffered, and you have cared less. The true Pontiff resides in Ormann Dyke at the heart of the struggle to defend the west. He is not sitting in Charibon issuing edicts that will send thousands to the pyre. I tell you this: before I am done, I will see this Himerius burned on the same pyre he has already burned so many innocents upon."

There was a shocked stillness. The men sitting at the table had an air of disbelief about them, as though they could not quite credit what they had heard.

"Leave this city," Cadamost said finally, his face white as paper and his eyes two red-limned orbs. "Leave it as kings in due state, for once Charibon hears of this you will be beyond the Church and every right-thinking man's hand will be turned against you. Your anointed right to rule will be stripped from you and your kingdoms declared outlaw states. No orthodox ruler need fear retribution if he invades your borders. Our faces are turned against you. Go."

The three kings left their places and stood together. Before they started for the door, Abeleyn turned round one last time.

"It is Himerius we defy. We harbour no ill-will towards any other state or ruler –"

Haukir snorted derisively.

"– but if any seek to injure us without good cause, then I swear this to all of you: our armies will seek redress in the blood of your subjects, our fleets will make unending infernos of your coasts and we will show less pity to our foes than the blackest Merduk sultan. You will rue the day and hour you crossed swords with Hebrion, or Astarac, or Torunna. And so, gentlemen, we bid you good day."

The three young men, all kings, turned and left the chamber together. In the silence that followed, the Himerian kings, as they would come to be known, stared at the round table which had witnessed their conclave and the dissolution of the Five Kingdoms. The path of history had been set; all they could do now was follow it and pray to God and the blessed Ramusio for guidance on their journey.

TWENTY-FIVE

THE NORTH-EASTER STAYED with them, as steady and as welcome as the Hebrian trade. Hawkwood could feel the constant thrumming of its power on the ship as though it were acting on the marrow of his very bones. The *Osprey* was alive, afloat, running before the wind. His mind relaxed and wandered off to that other place once more.

HE WAS A boy again, at sea for the first time on the clumsy caravel which had been the first Hawkwood-owned ship. His father was there, shouting obscenities at the straining seamen, and the white spray was coming aboard in packets as the vessel ran before the wind on the peridot-green swells of the Levangore. If he looked aft he could see the pale, dust-coloured coast of Gabrion with the darker rises of forests among the inland hills; and to larboard were the first islands of the Malacar Archipelago, floating like insubstantial ghosts in the haze of heat that had settled on the horizon.

Up and down, up and down the bow of the caravel went, the green waves like shimmering walls looming up and retreating again, the gulls screeching and calling and dropping guano over the deck, the rigging straining and creaking in time to the working timbers of the ship, and the blessed wind they had harnessed bellying out the booming and flapping sails.

This, he had thought, *is the sea*. And he had never questioned his right to be on it; rather he had welcomed his craft as a man would his wife.

HAWKWOOD COULD NOT move. He was drenched in sweat and as immobile as a marble caryatid. There was an unfamiliar smell in his nostrils. Burning.

A VAST SHUDDER as the ships came together, their hulls crunching and colliding.

"Fire!" Hawkwood yelled, and along the deck the men whipped the smoking slow-match across the touch-holes of the guns. Like a rippling thunder they exploded in sequence, leaping back on their carriages like startled bulls. There was an enormous noise, unlike any other. Louder than a storm-surf striking a rocky shore or a tempest in the heights of the Hebros. The whole starboard side of the ship disappeared in smoke and fire. Only men's screams and the shrieking of the blasted timbers carried above the roar.

The corsairs fired their own broadside, the muzzles of their culverins touching the very side of the carrack. They elevated the muzzles so the shot plunged upwards through the deck. The air exploded, became full of jagged shards of wood which ripped men apart, flung them clear across the deck or tossed them overboard like gutted fish. Hawkwood clambered on to the starboard quarterdeck rail and raised the heavy cutlass above his head. "*Now*, lads, at them. Boarding parties away!"

And then he leapt on to the crowded slaughterhouse of the enemy ship.

"RICHARD!" SHE CRIED as he pushed into her, expending himself, driving her backbone into the stuffed softness of the bed. The sweat dripped off his face to land on her collarbone and trickled between her breasts. Jemilla grinned fiercely up at him, her body answering his, struggling against him. The sweat was a slick glue between them so their skins sucked and slid as they moved together and apart, like a ship breasting a heavy swell, the keel burying itself in each wave.

BUT THE HEAT. His body was on fire, lying in a pool of liquid metal, every movement a torment, every pore oozing his life's fluid. The heat squeezed the water out of him until he was as dry and withered as the salted fish they had barrelled in the hold. If he moved he would crackle and creak and break apart into fragments as fine and desiccated as ash.

"*Richard.*"

He opened his eyes.

Bardolin smiled. "So you have returned from your voyaging at last."

The ship moved about him, a lulling presence. He sensed that the wind was fine and steady on the quarter, a fresh breeze pushing them ever westwards. In the almost-quiet he heard the ship's bell struck three times, and the noise was incredibly comforting, like hearing the sound of a familiar voice.

He turned his face to one side and immediately the pain began, a molten glow that was centred deep in his right shoulder. He groaned involuntarily.

"Easy." The mage's strong fingers steadied his head, grasping his chin.

"The fire," he croaked.

"We got it under control. The ship is safe, Captain, and we are making good progress."

"Help me sit up."

"No. You –"

"Help me up!"

The pain came and went in sobbing waves, but he blinked and ground his teeth until it was a bearable presence, something he could live with.

Their surroundings were unfamiliar to him. A small cabin, with a culverin squatting against one wall.

"Where is this?"

"The gundeck. The carpenter rigged up some partitions for you. You needed the peace."

So. He recognized it now, but it was strangely silent, as though the deck were almost deserted. He could hear many feet thumping above his head, and voices murmuring.

"The fire. The stern cabin –"

"More or less patched up. Chips has been working like a man possessed. We have no new glass for the stern windows though, so they must be shuttered most of the time."

"The log. Bardolin, did the log survive?"

The mage looked grim. "No. It went in the fire, as did most of your charts and the old rutter."

"Griella?"

"She is at peace. I was wrong ever to bring her on this

voyage, and yet she saved our lives, I think. Murad's, anyway. It is hard to know. A hard thing to have done."

"She loved him." It could have been question or statement.

"In her own way, yes. But no good would have come of it. They would have destroyed each other in the end and it is better, perhaps, that it has come about this way." The mage's arm, unexpectedly strong, steadied Hawkwood as he swayed. "Be careful, Captain. We don't want anything springing its seams again."

"Ortelius," Hawkwood was saying, ignoring him. "I can't believe it."

"Yes, who would have? An Inceptine cleric also a werewolf! That raises many questions, Captain, both for us on board ship and for the great and the good back home. I have this feeling that we have overlooked something, in our pride and our wisdom. There is something deep down in our society which we had not thought to find. Something abominable."

"Mateo, ere he changed, said his master was high in a society. I don't think he meant the one we know."

"We may find some answers in the west, I suppose. I do not see this as a voyage of discovery any longer, Captain, or an attempt at colonization. It is more of an armed reconnaissance. Murad concurs."

"The west. You think – ?"

"That it is inhabited? Yes, but by what manner of men or beasts or both I know not."

Hawkwood swung his legs off the hanging cot. He could manage the pain now. It came and went like a tide. His right arm was strapped tightly to the side of his chest, unbalancing him.

"How bad is this?"

"The thing bit your collar-bone clean through, and mangled the ends of the bone. I have been cleaning the wound, removing the splinters. A couple of the oldwives have sat with me and kept wound-sickness at bay. It smells sweet enough and I think we have brought it off, but you will have a terrible scar and a lump, and your right arm will never be as strong again."

But I'm alive, Hawkwood thought. *That is something. And my ship is afloat; that is something more.*

He was wearing only a clout of linen about his loins and his legs seemed oddly pale to him, the feet a long distance away. He stared at them absently, and then a jet of fear thrilled him.

"Bardolin, the beast bit me. Does that mean I have its disease? Will I change?"

"The black disease is not contagious in the way people think. It is not carried in a bite."

"But Ortelius made a werewolf of Mateo."

"Yes. That intrigues me, I must admit. Fear not, Captain, whatever arcane and bloody initiation turned the ship's boy into a shifter was not practised on you. Men do not catch lycanthropy from a bite, no matter what the superstitions say. Gregory confirms it, and my old master, Golophin, believed it also. There is something more at work which we cannot yet understand."

Relieved somewhat, Hawkwood relaxed. "Why did he do it? Why did he do that to poor Mateo?"

"My guess is he needed help. He had seen how determined we were to continue west and was set on wiping out the three of us – you, Murad and I. To do that swiftly and in one swoop, he would need a fellow conspirator. He may also have been... lonely. Who knows? I cannot lay claim to any great insights into the souls of shifters, for all that I knew Griella better than most. There is a mystery in them that has to do with the relationship between the man – or the woman – and the beast." He halted and smiled wryly. "My apologies. I had not intended to confront you with a treatise."

"You knew – you knew what she was before ever she came aboard."

"I knew, may God forgive me. I was a little in love with her also, you see. I thought I could control her. I even had wild ideas of curing her. But that is done with. I will have it on my conscience."

"It's all right. It's over with anyway – for the best, maybe. Tell me, how long has it been since the fire and the rest? How long have I been on my back?"

"Eight days."

"Eight days! Sweet Saints in heaven! Help me to my feet, Bardolin. I must talk to Velasca. I must check our course."

Bardolin pushed him gently but inexorably back on to the cot.

"Velasca, it seems, knows how to sail due west, and the wind has been as steady as you please. I will send him down to you if you desire, but you are not going anywhere. Not for a while yet."

Hawkwood sank on to the blankets once more. His head was spinning.

"Very well. Send him down at once, and get someone to help me dress, will you? And send Chips, too. I want to talk to him about the repairs."

"All right, Captain. I'll get them down as soon as I may." Bardolin left him, frowning.

Eight days. They might be within a sennight of reaching land, if Velasca had kept to his course. They were going to do it. Hawkwood could feel it in his mangled bones. He could feel the land, bulking somewhere on some unconscious horizon illuminated only by a mariner's intuition. It was there, and they were closing on it with every hour the carrack ploughed on before the kindly wind.

MURAD STOOD AT the break of the quarterdeck with his officers on either side, his stance adjusting itself automatically to the roll of the ship. His long lank hair was flying free and he was dressed in his black riding leathers. His rapier hung scabbarded by his side. Though his face was white as chalk, the scar that furrowed one hollow cheek seemed to have been kindled by the wind into a blazing carmine and his eyes were as dark as sloes.

The waist was packed with people, the gangways lined with watching soldiers. Nearly all the ship's company were present for punishment.

"Carry on, Sequero," Murad said tonelessly.

Sequero stepped forward to the rail. "Sergeant Mensurado, bring the man forward."

There was a boil of activity in the waist. Mensurado and two other soldiers thrust through the throng with a fourth man whose hands were tied behind his back.

"Read the charges, Ensign."

Sequero called out in a clear voice so the assembled company could hear:

"Gabriello Habrar, you are charged that on the eleventh day of Endorion in the year of the Saint five hundred and fifty-one, you did in the forecastle of the carrack *Gabrian Osprey* utter remarks detrimental to the morale and determination of a crown-sponsored expedition and thus did revile and denigrate the authority of our commander and his lord, our sovereign King, Abeleyn of Hebrion and Imerdon."

Sequero paused and glanced at Murad. The lean nobleman nodded curtly.

"You are therefore sentenced to the strappado. Sergeant Mensurado, carry on. Drummer."

A harsh, dry drumming began as one of the soldiers started to ply the goatskin of his instrument. A sailor perched on the main yardarm let down a rope which Mensurado and his comrades fastened to the wrists of the accused man. The other end of the rope was thrown to the soldiers on the gangway.

Murad lifted a hand.

The bound man was hauled into the air by the wrists, his hands at a horrible angle up his back and his shoulder-blades protruding grotesquely. He screamed in agony, but the rasping drum-roll smothered the sound. Then he dangled, kicking and twisting. After a few minutes the screaming stopped and he swayed on the end of the rope like a sack of meat, his eyes bulging, blood trickling from his bitten tongue.

"Cut him down," Murad ordered, and turned away from the sight to a contemplation of the carrack's wake. Sequero and di Souza went to him.

"I will have discipline," Murad said coldly. "You, gentlemen, have not been doing your job. The men are muttering and mutinous. I will have that out of them if I have to flog and strappado every last one of the dastards. Is that clear?"

Di Souza mumbled an agreement. Sequero did not speak, but his eyes were blazing.

"Have you something you wish to say, Ensign?" Murad demanded, turning on his aristocratic subordinate.

"Only that if you strappado every man in the tercio we'll have damned few fit to shoulder an arquebus when finally we hit land," Sequero said, not one whit intimidated by the snakeblank eyes of his superior officer.

Murad stared at him for a long moment, and the ensign blenched but stood his ground. Finally a smile twisted the older man's face.

"I would sooner have a maimed man who is loyal than a fit one who is not," he said quietly. "It would seem, Sequero, that you are developing some regard for your fellow men, scum from the bottom of the heap though they might be. Perhaps this voyage is teaching you the compassion of a commoner or a Mendicant Friar. If at any stage your burgeoning sympathy for the common soldiery interferes with your duty and your loyalty to your superior and your king, you will, I am sure, be the first to let me know."

Sequero said nothing, but he looked at his senior officer with open hatred. Murad smiled again, that dead, cold smile which was worse than an angry glare.

"You may go, both of you. See to Habrar, di Souza. Get one of these witches on board to have a look at him. Sequero, we will have small-arms practice this evening after the meal."

They both saluted, then turned on their heels and left the quarterdeck. The crowd in the waist was already dispersing, many black looks being thrown at the nobleman who lounged at the carrack's taffrail.

Murad did not care. He knew that his vision of a colony in the west governed by himself was a pipe-dream, morning mist to be burned away by the sun. Talking to Bardolin, he had found himself agreeing with the mage that there must be something in the west, something Ortelius had been charged to keep them from discovering. But by whom had he been charged? Either the shape-shifting cleric had been sent on his mission by a Ramusian monarch, which was unlikely – none of the western kings would willingly use both an Inceptine and a werewolf as an agent – or he was working for someone already in the west. Murad's undiscovered continent had already been claimed.

But by whom?

Werewolves. Shifters. Mages. He was sick to death of

the lot of them. They made him shudder. And the memory of his dreams – what he had thought were dreams – still caused him to lie open-eyed and sweating in the night. He had shared a bed with the beast, had felt its heat and the baleful regard of its eyes.

He remembered Griella's body taut as cord under him, the tawny smoothness of her skin. And he turned his face to the carrack's wake once more so that none of the scum below might see the burning brightness that flooded his expressionless black eyes.

THE CARRACK WAS regularly running off sixty leagues a day, the north-easter propelling her along at a smooth seven knots. Four hundred and eighty leagues, perhaps, since Hawkwood had been confined to his bunk. They had travelled the distance from the southern Calmaric deserts to the far frozen north of Yazdegard; the extent of the known world. And still it seemed there was no sign of an end to the ocean.

The fire on board had caught the mizzen course and burned away the mizzen backstays and a fair portion of the shrouds. If a squall had hit them then they would have lost the mast, but the sea had been kind to them. The flames had been doused with Dweomer-pumped seawater, some of the sorcerers on board lifting hundred-gallon packets of the stuff out of the waves and dumping it over the mizzen, the quarterdeck and the stern. Whilst Hawkwood had been unconscious the repairs had gone on apace, and the carrack was whole again with only a few black charred scars to mark how close to disaster she had come. But as the carpenter informed Hawkwood that afternoon, they had used up the last of their timber stores to put right the damage and could now do no more. If the ship was damaged again they would have nothing to repair her with. They had no spare cordage or cable, either. It would be knotting and splicing until they made landfall.

Velasca made his report also. He had kept a tolerably legible log in the days he had conned the ship alone, but he was obviously relieved to have his captain conscious and clearheaded. He knew little of the nuances of navigation, being just about able to take a cross-staff reading and keep the ship on a compass bearing. As soon as he was able, Hawkwood was up on deck, taking sightings from the Pole Star and checking his dead-reckoning over and over. He had a man in the forechains day and night with the deep-sea lead, sounding for the bottom, and he shortened sail at night despite the protests of Murad, who wanted them to tear along under every scrap of canvas the carrack possessed. He could not convince the nobleman of his own conviction that they were nearing land at last. It was a mariner's guess, something in the smell of the air, perhaps, or the appearance of the ocean, but Hawkwood was sure that the Western Continent was not far away.

IN THE TWENTIETH day of Endorion, nine days after Hawkwood had woken to find Bardolin leaning over him, the leadsman in the forechains raised his voice into a strangled shout that made every man and woman on board look up. For days he had been chanting monotonously: "No bottom. No bottom here with this line." But now he yelled excitedly:

"Eighty fathoms! Eighty fathoms with this line!" Hawkwood and Murad were on the quarterdeck, Hawkwood bending over the table they had brought up from below, writing laboriously and painfully with his left hand into his new log.

"Seventy-five! Seventy-five fathoms!" the leadsman called. And the ship was swept with a buzz of excited talk. The companionways thundered as passengers and soldiers clambered out on deck to see what was going on.

"Seventy fathoms! White sand and seashells in the lead!"

"Keep sounding!" Hawkwood bellowed forward. "All hands! All hands to shorten sail!"

Eight bells in the last dog-watch had just been struck and the watch had changed, but the whole ship's crew came scampering out into the waist and forecastle.

"Velasca!" Hawkwood roared over the soft thudding of feet and the rising babble. "Topsails alone! Keep her braced round there!"

"Is it land?" Murad was asking, his eyes glittering. "Is that it? I can see nothing."

Hawkwood ignored him and peered up at the foretop where the lookout was stationed.

"In the foretop there! What do you see?" There was a pause.

"Nothing but haze out to six or seven leagues, sir."

"Keep a good eye out, then."

"What is happening?" Murad demanded, his face puce with anger.

"We are on a shelving shore, Lord Murad," Hawkwood said calmly. "The sea is shallowing."

"Does that mean we are approaching landfall?"

"Possibly, yes."

"How far away is it?" Murad scanned the horizon as though he fully expected the Western Continent to pop up over it at that very second.

"I have no way of knowing, but we're shortening sail so we don't run full-tilt on to any reefs."

"Saints in heaven!" Murad said hoarsely. "It's really out there, isn't it?"

Hawkwood allowed himself to grin. "Yes, Murad, it really is."

On into the evening the carrack ran smoothly with the wind on her quarter and most of the ship's company on deck, their faces turned towards the west. When the first stars came out in the towering blue-black vault of the night sky the passengers retired below to eat, but Hawkwood kept both watches on deck, chewing salt pork and ship's biscuit. And the leadsman continued his chant from the forechains:

"Sixty fathoms. Sixty fathoms with this line."

There was a different quality to the air. The sailors could feel it. There was something more humid and cloying about it that was entirely at odds with the usual keen nature of the open sea, and Hawkwood thought he could smell something now; that growing smell like a breath of a summer garden. It was not far away.

"White foam! White foam dead ahead two cables!" the lookout screamed.

Hawkwood bent to call down the tiller-hatch. "Tiller there! Larboard by two points. West-sou'-west."

"Aye, sir."

The carrack moved smoothly round, the wind coming right aft now. The crew rushed to the braces to trim the yards. Hawkwood saw the white flicker and rush of foam breaking on black rocks off on the starboard side.

"Leadsman! What's our depth?"

There was a splash, a long waiting minute, then the leadsman declared, "Forty fathoms, sir, and white sand!"

"Take in topsails!" Hawkwood shouted.

The crew raced up the shrouds, bent over the topsail yards and began folding in the pale expanses of canvas. The ship lost speed.

"Why are we slowing down, Captain?" It was Murad, coming up the quarterdeck ladder almost at a run.

"Breakers ahead!" the lookout shrieked. "Starboard and larboard. Three cables from the bow!"

"God almighty!" Hawkwood exclaimed, startled. "Let go anchor!"

A seaman knocked loose the heavy sea anchor from the bows with the blow of a mallet. There was an enormous splash that lit up the black sea and the ship lost way, coming gradually to a full stop. She began to yaw as the wind pushed her stern around.

"Get a bower anchor out from the stern, Velasca," Hawkwood told his first mate. "And pray it holds in this ground."

He could see them himself – a broken line of white water barely visible off in the night – and there was a new sound, the distant roar of surf. Hawkwood found he was trembling, his shoulder a scarlet flame of pain and the sweat sour and slick about him. But for the vigilance of the lookout, the ship would still be sailing towards the distant rocks.

"Is that it?" Murad asked in a breath, gazing out at the white foam which sliced open the darkness.

"Maybe. It might be a reef. We can't take any chances. I've dropped anchor. I don't like the ground, but there's no way I'm going any further in at night. We'll have to wait for daylight."

They both listened, watched. Hard to imagine what might be out there in the night; what manner of country lay beyond the humid darkness and the line of treacherous breakers.

"Stern anchor out and holding, sir," Velasca reported.

"Very good. Send down the larboard watch, and have the starboards haul the boats out over the side. They need a wetting, or they'll leak like sieves in the morning."

"Aye, sir."

Hawkwood stared out into the darkness, feeling the ship roll and pitch beneath his feet like a tethered animal bucking the halter. The heat of the night seemed more intense now, and he thought he saw the tiny bodies of insects flickering about the stern lantern. Not an isolated reef, then, but something ~ more substantial. It was hard to believe after all this time that their destination was most likely out there in the darkness, under their lee.

He wondered what Haukal would have made of it, and for a moment pondered the disappearance of his other ship, the graceful little caravel and the good seamen who had manned her. Were they sailing still, on some distant latitude? Or were the fishes gnawing at their bones? He might never know.

Murad had gone. Hawkwood could hear the nobleman shouting orders down in the waist, calling for his officers and sergeants. He must have everything polished and shining; they would be claiming a new world for their king in the morning.

THAT LAST NIGHT, Hawkwood, Murad and Bardolin shared a bottle of Candelarian wine in the stern cabin, the shutters open to let in some air. A moth flew in the glassless windows and flapped about the table lantern like a thing entranced, and they, equally entranced, watched it avidly until it ventured too close to the flame and fell to the table, blackened. They let it lie there like some sort of mocking talisman, a promise of things to come, perhaps. And they toasted the voyage and whatever the morning might bring in the good wine, saving the last drops for a libation to be poured into the sea in a ritual far older than any vision of Ramusio's. They drank to those whose souls had been lost in their passage of the ocean and to whatever future might appear to them out of the sunrise.

In the morning the sun came up out of a belt of molten cloud, like the product of some vast furnace housed below the eastern horizon. Every member of the ship's company was on deck dressed in their best; Hawkwood was even wearing a sword. They could hear clearly the thunder of breaking surf, feel the damp, heavy air of the land. There were birds perched in the rigging, little dun sparrow-like creatures that twittered and sang with the rising of the sun. It was a sound that had the crew staring and smiling with wonder. Birdsong – something from a former life.

There was a mist, honeyed by the sunrise. The lookout in the foretop was the first man to be clear of it, and he yelled out to the depth of his lungs:

"Land ho! Abaft the starboard beam there – hills and trees. Great God!"

There was a spasm of cheering which Murad and his officers silenced. The mist thinned moment by moment.

And there it was. A green country of thick vegetation solidifying out of the veils of morning. Mountains rearing up into a clear sky, and the gathering sunrise gilding it.

"Man the boats," Hawkwood said hoarsely.

The crews of the two ship's boats that had survived scrambled down the ship's side, the soldiers clumsy with armour and weapons, the seamen agile as apes.

"Cast off!" Hawkwood shouted as soon as they were seated on the thwarts. There was no need to say anything else; all the crew had been well briefed, and Velasca knew his duty.

The lines were flung clear of the gunwales and the oars were lowered. The men began to row steadily, the exertion squeezing sweat out of their pores despite the youth of the morning. The ship grew smaller behind them.

There was a long gap in the breakers which would have accommodated the *Osprey* the night before, had there been the light to see it. The two boats powered through, lifted and tossed by the breaking waves. Within the reefs the water was calmer and they could see a ribbon of white sand fringing the unbroken curtain of jungle ahead.

"Captain!" one of the men cried. "Captain, look aft, on the landward side of the reef!"

Hawkwood and Murad turned as one to squint into the morning sun.

"I can't –" Murad began, and then was silent.

There on the westward side of the reef was the fragment of a ship. It was a beakhead, part of a keel and a few other skeletal timbers. It looked as though the ship had run full tilt upon the reef, the fore part of the hull riding over it, the rest smashed away and sunk.

It was the *Grace of God*.

Men made the Sign of the Saint at their breasts, murmuring. Hawkwood's eyes were stinging as though in sympathy with his aching shoulder. To have come so far only to fail. So many good men.

"God have mercy on them," he murmured.

"Could any have survived?" Murad asked.

He shook his head slowly, studying the fragmented wreck and the booming surf, the jagged reef. It was sheer fluke that a portion of the ship had remained caught on the reef; it had been wedged there by the explosive force of the breakers. Only a miracle could have preserved those aboard.

"We are alone, then," Murad said. "We are alone," Hawkwood agreed.

The water shallowed. They could feel the heat of the land like a wall. The men raised their oars and a few seconds later the bottom of the boats kissed the sand.

Richard Hawkwood splashed out of the first boat, closely followed by Murad. Through the noise of the breakers out on the reef a glimmer of strange birdsong could be heard from the wall of jungle ahead.

They walked up out of the shallows and stood in hot white sand with the early sun heating their backs. The crews hauled the boats out of the water and stood panting. Soldiers held their arquebuses at the ready.

Murad turned to look at Hawkwood, and without a word they both began walking up the blazing beach, to where the jungle of the Western Continent gleamed dark and impenetrable before them.

The HERETIC KINGS

This is the century of the soldier.

– Fulvio Testi, 1641

For my brothers,
Sean and James Kearney

PROLOGUE

ALWAYS, MEN MOVE WEST. Is it something to do with the path of the sun? They are drawn to it like moths to the flame of a taper.

Many long turning years have slipped by, and still I remain: the last of the founders, my body scarcely my own at the end. I have seen four centuries of the waking world trickle past, their passage scarcely marked by any change in the land I have made my home. Men change, and they like to think that the world changes with them. It does not; it merely tolerates them, and continues to follow its own, arcane revolutions.

And yet there is something in the air, like a whisper of winter in this country which knows no seasons. I feel a change coming.

THEY CAME TREADING the saffron and scarlet course of the sinking sun, as we had always known they would, with their tall ships trailing streamers of weed from worm-eaten hulls.

We watched them from the jungle. Men in salt-encrusted armour with scurvy-swollen faces bearing swords and pikes, and, later, reeking arquebuses, the slow-match glowing and hissing in the wind. Gaunt men of Hebrion, or Astarac, or Gabrion; the sea-rovers of the Old World. Hard-handed buccaneers with the greed dazzling their eyes.

We had come here fleeing something; they had come seeking. We gave them fear to fill their bellies and night-dark terror to plump out their purses. We made of them the hunted, and took from them whatever we desired.

Their ships rotted slowly at their moorings, untenanted and filled with ghosts. A few, a very few, we let live, to take the tale of us back east to the Monarchies of God. In this way, the myth was created. We hid our country behind a curtain of tall tales and dark rumours. We laced the truth with the hyperbole of madness; we beat out a legend as though it were the blade of a sword on a smith's anvil. And we quenched it in blood.

But the change is coming. Four centuries have we lingered here, and our people have slowly filtered back to the east in accordance with the plan. They are everywhere now in Normannia. They command soldiers, they preach to multitudes, they watch over cradles. Some of them have the ear of kings.

The time is come for our keels to recross the Western Ocean, and claim what is ours. The beast will out, in the end. Every wolf will have its day.

PART ONE

SCHISM

ONE

YEAR OF THE SAINT 551

VESPERS HAD LONG since been rung, but Brother Albrec had affected not to hear. He chewed the end of his quill so that damp bits of feather dropped on to the bench, but he did not notice. His face, squinting in the dim light of the dip, was akin to that of a near-sighted vole, pointed and inquisitive. His hand shook as he turned the page of an ancient parchment which lay before him. When once a corner crumbled at the touch of his nimble fingers he whined a little back in his throat, for all the world like a dog seeing its master leave the room without it.

The words on the parchment were beautifully inscribed, but the ink had faded. It was a strange document, he thought. There were none of the illuminations which had always been thought so necessary an adornment to the holy texts of Ramusio. Only words, stark and bare and elegantly written, but fading under the weight of so many years.

The parchment itself was poor quality. Had the scribe of the time possessed no vellum? He wondered, for this was hand-enscribed, not churned out on one of the famous presses of Charibon. This was old.

And yet it was almost as though the author had not wanted to draw too much attention to the work. And indeed the manuscript had been found, a rolled-up wad of untidy fragments, stuffed into a crack in the wall of one of the lowest of the library levels. Brother Columbar had brought it to Albrec. He had thought perhaps to use the parchment as blotting for the scriptorium, for Charibon still produced hand-written books, even now. But the faint, perfect writing visible upon it had made him hesitate, and bring it to the attention of the Assistant Librarian. Albrec's natural curiosity had done the rest.

Almost he halted, rose from his seat to tell the Chief Librarian Brother Commodius. But something kept the little monk rooted there, reading on in fascination while the other brothers were no doubt sitting down to their evening meal.

The scrap of parchment was five centuries old. Almost as old as Charibon itself, holiest of all the university-monasteries on the continent now that Aekir was gone. When the unknown author had been writing, the Blessed Ramusio had only just been assumed into heaven – conceivably, that great event had happened within the lifetime of the writer.

Albrec held his breath as the petal-thin parchment stuck to his sweating fingers. He was afraid to breathe on it for fear that the ancient, irreplaceable text might somehow blur and run, or blow away like sand under some sudden zephyr.

...and we begged him not to leave us alone and bereft in such a darkening world. But the Blessed Saint only smiled. "I am an old man now," he said. "What I have begun I leave to you to continue; my time here is finished. You are all men of faith; if you believe in the things which I have taught you and place your lives in the hand of God, then there is no need to be afraid. The world is a darkening place, yes, but it darkens because of the will of man, not of God. It is possible to turn the tide of history – we have proved that. Remember, in the years ahead, that we do not merely suffer history, we create it. Every man has in him the ability to change the world. Every man has a voice to speak out with; and if that voice is silenced by those who will not listen, then another will speak out, and another. The truth can be silenced for a time, yes, but not for ever...

The rest of the page was missing, torn away. Albrec leafed through the indecipherable fragments that followed. Tears rose in his eyes and he blinked them away as he realized that the parts which were missing were indeed lost beyond recall. It was as if someone had given a thirsting man in a desert a drop of water to soothe his parched mouth, and then poured away a quart into the sand.

Finally, the little cleric got off his hard bench and knelt on the stone floor to pray.

The life of the Saint, an original text which had never been seen before. It told the story of a man named Ramusio, who had been born and who had lived and grown old, who had laughed and wept and spent sleepless nights awake. The story of the central figure in the faith of the western world, written by a contemporary – possibly even someone who had known him personally...

Even if so much of it had been lost, there was still so much gained. It was a miracle, and it had been granted to him. He thanked God there on his knees for revealing it to him. And he prayed to Ramusio, the Blessed Saint whom he was now beginning to see as a man, a human being like himself – though infinitely superior, of course. Not the iconic image the Church had made him out to be, but a man. And it was thanks to this incredibly precious document before him.

He regained his seat, blowing his nose on the sleeve of his habit, kissing his humble Saint's symbol of bog-oak. The tattered text was beyond price; it was comparable to the *Book of Deeds* compiled by St. Bonneval in the first century. But how much of it was here? How much was legible?

He bent over it again, ignoring the pains that were shooting through his cramped neck and shoulders.

No title page or covering, nothing that might hint at the identity of the author or his patron. Five centuries ago, Albrec knew, the Church had not possessed the virtual monopoly on learning that it did now. In those days many parts of the world had not yet been converted to the True Faith, and rich noblemen had sponsored scribes and artists in a hundred cities to copy old pagan texts or even invent new ones. Literacy had been more widespread. It was only with the rise to prominence of the Inceptines in the last two hundred years or so that literacy had declined again, becoming a preserve of professionals. It was said that all the Fimbrian emperors could both read and write, whereas until recently no western king could so much as spell his own name. That had changed with the new generation of kings that was coming to the fore, but the older rulers still preferred a seal to a signature.

His eyes stung, and Albrec rubbed them, sparking lights

out of the darkness under their closed lids. His friend Avila would have missed him at dinner, and might even try to seek him out. He often scolded Albrec for missing meals. No matter. Once he saw this rediscovered jewel...

The quiet thump of a door shutting. Albrec blinked, looking about him. One hand pulled a sheaf of loose papers over the old document while the other reached for the lamp.

"Hello?"

No answer. The archive room was long and cluttered, shelves piled high with books and scrolls dividing it up into compartments. It was also utterly dark, save where Albrec's trembling lamp flame flickered in a warm circle of yellow light.

Nothing.

The library had its share of ghosts, of course; what ancient building did not? Working late sometimes, clerics had felt cold breath on their cheeks, or sensed a watching presence. Once the Senior Librarian, Commodius, had spent a night in vigil in the library praying to Garaso, the saint for whom it was named, because some novices had become terrified by the shadows they swore gathered there after dark. Nothing had come of it, and the novices had been ribbed for weeks afterwards.

A sliding scrape in the blackness beyond the light of the lamp. Albrec got to his feet, gripping his A-shaped Saint's symbol.

> *Sweet Saint that watches over me*
> *In all the lightless spaces of the night*

he prayed the ancient prayer of travellers and pilgrims.

> *Be thou my lamp and guide and staff*
> *And keep me from the anger of the beast.*

Two yellow lights blinked in the darkness. Albrec received a momentary impression of something huge hulking in the shadow. The hint of an animal stink which lasted only a second, and then was gone.

Someone sneezed, and Albrec's start rocked the table behind him. The lamplight fluttered and the wick hissed as oil spilled upon it. Shadows swooped in as the illumination guttered. Albrec felt the hard oak of the symbol creak under the white bones of his fingers. He could not speak.

A door again, and the pad of naked feet on the bare stone of the floor. A shape loomed up out of the darkness.

"You've missed dinner again, Brother Albrec," a voice said.

The figure came into the light. A tall, gaunt, almost hairless head with huge ears and fantastically winged eyebrows on either side of a drooping nose. The eyes were bright and kindly.

Albrec let out a shuddering breath. "Brother Commodius!"

One eyebrow quirked upward. "Who else were you expecting? Brother Avila asked me if I would look in on you. He is doing penance again – the Vicar-General will tolerate only so many bread fights of an evening, and Avila's aim is none so good. Have you been digging in the dust for gold, Albrec?"

The Senior Librarian approached the table. He always walked barefoot, winter and summer, and his feet, splayed and black-nailed, were in proportion to his nose.

Albrec's breathing was under control again.

"Yes, Brother." Suddenly the idea of telling the Senior Librarian about the rediscovered text did not appeal to Albrec. He began to babble.

"One day I hope to find something wonderful down here. Do you know that almost half the texts in the lower archives have never been catalogued? Who knows what may await me?"

Commodius smiled, becoming a tall, comical goblin. "I applaud your industry, Albrec. You have a true love of the written word. But do not forget that books are only the thoughts of men made visible, and not all those thoughts are to be tolerated. Many of the uncatalogued works of which you speak are no doubt heretical; thousands of scrolls and books were brought here from all over Normannia in the days of the Religious Wars so that the Inceptines might appraise them. Most were burned, but it is said that a good number were laid in corners and forgotten. So you must be careful what you read, Albrec. The merest whiff of unorthodoxy in a text, and you must bring it to me. Is that clear?"

Albrec nodded. He was sweating. Somewhere in his mind he was wondering if withholding facts would be construed as a sin. He remembered his own private store of scrolls and manuscripts that he had hoarded away to save from the fire, and his unease deepened.

"You look as white as paper, Albrec. What's wrong?"

"I – I thought there was something else in here, before you came."

This time both eyebrows shot up the hairless head. "The library has been playing its tricks again, eh? What was it this time, a whisper in your ear? A hand on your shoulder?"

"It was... a feeling, no more."

Commodius laid a massive, knot-knuckled fist on Albrec's shoulder and shook him affectionately. "The faith is strong in you, Albrec. You have nothing to worry about. Whatever ghosts this library is home to cannot touch you. You are girded with the armour of true belief; your faith is both a beacon to light the darkness and a sword to cleave the beasts which lurk therein. Fear cannot conquer the heart of a true believer in the Saint. Now come: I mean to rescue you for a while from the dust and the prowling ghosts. Avila has saved some supper for you and insists you be made to eat it."

One great hand propelled Albrec irresistibly away from his work table, whilst the other scooped up the lamp. Brother Commodius paused to sneeze again. "Ah, the unsettled dust of the years. It settles in the chest you know."

When they had exited the darkened room Commodius produced a key from his habit and locked the door behind them. Then the pair continued up through the library to the light and noise of the refectories beyond.

FAR TO THE west of Charibon's cloisters, across the ice-glittering heights of the Malvennor Mountains. There is a broad land there between the mountains and the sea beyond, an ancient land: the birthplace of an empire.

The city of Fimbir had been built without walls. The Electors had said that their capital was fortified by the shields of the Fimbrian soldiery; they needed no other defence.

And there was truth in their boast. Almost uniquely among the capitals of Normannia, Fimbir had never been besieged. No foreign warrior had ever entered the massively constructed City of the Electors unless he came bearing tribute, or seeking aid. The Hegemony of the Fimbrians had ended centuries before, but their city still bore the marks of empire. Abrusio was more populous, Vol Ephrir more beautiful, but Fimbir had been built to impress. Were it ever to become deserted, the poets said, men of later generations might suppose that it had been reared by the hands of giants.

East of the city were the parade grounds and training fields of the Fimbrian army. Hundreds of acres had been cleared and flattened to provide a gaming board of war upon which the Electors might learn to move their pieces. A hill south of the fields had been artificially heightened to provide a vantage point for generals to regard the results of their tactics and strategy. Nothing that ever occurred in battle, it was said, had not already been replicated and studied upon the training fields of Fimbir. Such were the tales that the tercios of the conquerors had engendered over the years and across the continent.

A cluster of men stood now on the vantage point of the hill overlooking the fields. Generals and junior officers alike, they were clad in black half-armour, their rank marked only by the scarlet sashes that some wore wrapped beneath their sword belts. A stone table that was a permanent fixture here stood in their midst, covered with maps and counters. Coprenius Kuln himself, the first Fimbrian emperor, had set it here eight hundred years previously.

Horses were hobbled off to one side, to mount order-bearing couriers. The Fimbrians did not believe in cavalry, and this was the only use they had for the animals.

On the training fields below, formations of men marched and counter-marched. Fifteen thousand of them, perhaps, their feet a deep thunder on the ground that had hardened with the first frosts. A cold early morning sunlight sparked off the glinting heads of their pikes and the barrels of shouldered arquebuses. They looked like the massed playthings of a god left lying on a nursery floor and come to sudden, beetling life.

Two men strolled away from the cluster of officers on the hill and stood apart, looking down on the panoply and magnificence of the formations below. They were in middle age, of medium height, broad-shouldered, hollow-cheeked. They might have been brothers save that one wore a black hole where his left eye should have been, and the hair on that side of his head had become silver.

"The courier, Caehir, died at his own hand last night," the one-eyed man said.

The other nodded. "His legs?"

"They took them off at the knee; there was no saving them. The rot had gone too far, and he had no wish to live as a cripple."

"A good man. Pity to lose one's life because of frostbite, no more."

"He did his duty. The message got through. By now, Jonakait and Merkus will be in the passes of the mountains also. We must hope they meet with better luck."

"Indeed. So the Five Kingdoms have split. We have two Pontiffs and a religious war in the offing. And all this while the Merduks howl at the gates of the west."

"The men at Ormann Dyke; they must be soldiers."

"Yes. That was a fight. The Torunnans are no mean warriors."

"But they are not Fimbrians."

"No, they are not Fimbrians. How many of our people are we to send to their aid?"

"A grand tercio, no more. We must be cautious, and see how this division of the kingdoms goes."

The Fimbrian with the unmutilated face nodded fractionally. A grand tercio comprised some five thousand men – three thousand pike and two thousand arquebusiers – plus the assorted gunsmiths, armourers, cooks, muleteers, pioneers and staff officers who went with them. Perhaps six thousand in all.

"Will that be enough to save the dyke?"

"Possibly. But our priority is not so much to save Ormann Dyke as to establish a military presence in Torunna, remember."

"I find I am in danger of thinking like a general instead of a politician, Briscus."

The one-eyed man named Briscus grinned, showing a range of teeth with smashed gaps between them. "Kyriel, you are an old soldier who sniffs powder-smoke in the wind. I am the same. For the first time in living memory our people will leave the bounds of the electorates to do battle with the heathen. It is an event to quicken the blood, but we must not let it cloud our judgement."

"I do not altogether like farming our men out as mercenaries."

"Neither do I; but when a state has seventy thousand unemployed soldiers on hand, what else can one do with them? If Marshal Barbius and his contingent impress the Torunnans sufficiently, then we will have all the Ramusian kingdoms crying out for our tercios. The time will come when every capital will have its contingent of Fimbrian troops, and then –"

"And then?"

"We will see what we can make out of it, if it happens."

They turned to look down on the training fields once more. The pair were dressed no differently from the other senior officers on the hill, but they were Fimbrian Electors and represented half the ruling body of their peculiar country. A word from them, and this army of thousands would march off the training fields and into the cauldron of war wherever they saw fit to wage it.

"We live in an age where everything will change," one-eyed Briscus said quietly. "The world of our forefathers is on the brink of dissolution. I feel it in my bones."

"An age of opportunity, also," Kyriel reminded him.

"Of course. But I think that before the end all the politicians will have to think like soldiers and the soldiers like politicians. It reminds me of the last battle by the Habrir river. The army knew the Electors had already signed away the Duchy of Imerdon, and yet we deployed that morning and fought for it nonetheless. We won, and threw the Hebrians in disorder back across the fords. Then we gathered up our dead and marched away from Imerdon for ever. It is the same feeling: that our armies can win any battle they choose to fight, and yet in the end it will make no difference to the outcome of things."

"You wax philosophical this morning, Briscus. That is unlike you."

"You must forgive me. It is a hazard of advancing years."

From the formations below, lines of smoke puffed out and seconds later the clattering rumble of arquebus fire reached them on the hill. Regiments of arquebusiers were competing against each other to see who could reload the fastest, shooting down lines of straw figures that had been set up on the plain. Volley followed volley, until it seemed that a high-pitched thunder was being generated by the very earth and was clawing up to heaven. The plain below became obscured by toiling clouds of powder-smoke, the fog of war in its most literal sense. The heady smell of it drifted up to the two Electors on the hillside and they snuffed it in like hounds scenting a hare on a winter's morning.

A third figure left the gaggle of officers around the stone table and stood to attention behind the Electors until the pair had noticed him. He was a square man; what he lacked in height he made up for in width. Even his chin was as regular as the blade of a shovel, his mouth a lipless gash above it partially obscured by a thick red moustache. His hair was cut so short as to stand up like the cropped mane of a horse; the mark of a man who often wore a helm.

"Well, Barbius?" Briscus asked the man. "How do they fare?"

Barbius stared straight ahead. "They're about as handy as a bunch of seamstresses on a cold morning, sir."

Briscus snorted with laughter. "But will they pass?"

"I'll work them up a little more before we go, sir. Three rounds a minute, that's our goal."

"The Torunnans think themselves well-drilled if they can get off two in that time," Kyriel said quietly.

"They're not Torunnans, sir – with respect."

"Damn right, by God!" Briscus said fervently. His one eye flashed. "I want your command to be as perfect as you can make it, Barbius. This will be the first Fimbrian army the rest of the kingdoms have seen in action for twenty-five years. We want to impress."

"Yes, sir." Barbius's face had all the animation of a closed helm.

"Your baggage train?"

"Fifty carts, eight hundred mules. We travel light, sir."

"And you're happy with the route?"

Here Barbius allowed himself the merest sliver of a smile. "Through the Narian Hills by way of Tulm, and so to Charibon for the Pontifical blessing. Along the south-eastern shore of the Sea of Tor and down into Torunna by way of the Torrin Gap."

"And another Pontifical blessing from the other Pontiff," Kyriel added, his eyes dancing.

"You've been briefed on your behaviour and that of your men?" Briscus said, serious now.

"Yes, sir. We are to be as respectful as possible to the Pontiff and the Church authorities, but we are not to be deflected from our line of march."

"There is nothing on that line which has the remotest chance of stopping a Fimbrian grand tercio," Briscus said, his eye narrowing. "But you are to avoid the slightest friction with anyone, especially Almarkans. That is clear, Marshal? You are a nameless functionary; you are obeying orders. All complaints, protests and similar are to be directed to Fimbir, and you are not to delay your march for anything."

"Of course, sir."

"Let them think you are a mindless soldier whose job is to do as he is told. If you pause to argue with them just once, then they will wrap you up in coils of Inceptine law and hamstring you. This army must get through, Marshal."

Barbius looked the Elector in the eye for the first time. "I know, sir."

"Very well. Good luck. You are dismissed."

Barbius slapped a forearm against his cuirass and left them. Kyriel watched him go, pulling at his lower lip with one restless hand.

"We are walking a rope here, Briscus."

"Don't I know it. Himerius must accept that we are going to help Torunna, heretic king or no; but we cannot afford to alienate him completely."

"I see what you mean, about soldiers and politicians."

"Yes. We live in a complicated world, Kyriel, but of late it's become even more interesting than it was before."

TWO

THE KING WAS gone, and there were those who said that he would never be coming back.

Abrusio.

Capital of the Kingdom of Hebrion, greatest port of the western world – indeed, some would say of the entire world. Only ancient Nalbeni might vie with Abrusio for the title.

For centuries the Royal House of the Hibrusids had ruled in Hebrion and their palace had frowned down over the raucous old port. There had of course been dynastic squabbles, internecine warfare, obscure marital entanglements; but in all that time the Royal house had never relaxed its grip on the throne.

Things had changed.

Winter had come to the west, propelled on the wings of war. The armies that battled on the eastern frontiers of the continent had withdrawn to their winter quarters and it seemed that the ships which plied the western seas had followed their example. The trade lanes of nations grew emptier as the waning year grew colder.

In Abrusio the Great Harbour, the Inner and Outer Roads as the other harbours were named, the sea itself, were whipped into a broken swell of tumultuous waves, white-tops gilding their tips. A steady roar of surf pounded the huge man-made moles that sheltered the harbours from the worst of the winter storms, and the beacon towers were lit along their length, gleaming flames battling the wind to warn approaching ships of the shallows and mark the harbour entrances.

The wind had backed as it freshened; the season for the Hebrian Trade had long ended, and now it howled in from the south-west, shoving Hebrion-bound vessels landwards and making the teeth of ship-masters grate as they fought to avoid that worst nightmare of any mariner, a lee shore.

Abrusio was not at its best at this time of year. It was not a city that relished winter. It housed too many pavement taverns, open-air markets and the like. It was a place which needed sunshine. In the summer its inhabitants might curse the unwavering heat that set the buildings shimmering and brought almost to an art form the stink of the sewers and tanneries, but the city was more alive, more crowded – like a termite-mound with a broken shell. In winter it closed in on itself; the harbours saw only a tithe of the trade they were accustomed to, and the waterside inns and brothels and ships suffered as a result. In winter the city tightened its belt, turned its face from the sea and grumbled to itself, awaiting spring.

A spring without a king, perhaps. For months King Abeleyn of Hebrion had been absent from his capital, away at the Conclave of Kings in Perigraine. In his absence the new High Pontiff of the west, Himerius – one-time Prelate of Hebrion – had ordered an army of the Church's secular arm, the Knights Militant, into Abrusio to check the rising tide of sorcery and heresy in the old city. The King no longer ruled in Hebrion. Some said he would pick up the reins as soon as he returned from his travels. Others said that when the Church manages to worm its way into the chambers of government, it is not so easy to eject it.

SASTRO DI CARRERA let the wind water his eyes and stood with his doublet billowing about him on the wide balcony. A tall man, his black beard oiled to a curling point and a ruby the size of a caper set in one ear, he had the hands of a lutist and the easy carriage of one accustomed to having his own way. And that was only natural, for he was the head of one of the great houses of Hebrion and, at present, one of the de facto rulers of the kingdom.

He stared out and down across the city. Below were the prosperous quarters of the merchants and the lesser nobility, the halls of some of the more prestigious guilds, the gardens of the rich denizens of the Upper City. Farther down the hills, the teeming slums and tenements of the poorer, low-born people; thousands of ochre-tiled roofs with hardly a gap between them. A sea of humble dwellings that bloomed out in the drizzle and wind of the day down to the harbours and the waterfronts, what some called the bowels of Hebrion. He could pick out the looming, stone-built massiveness of the arsenals and barracks in the western arm of the Lower City. Down there were the sinews of war, the culverins and powder and laid-up arquebuses and swords of the Crown. And the men: the soldiers who comprised the Hebrian tercios, some eight thousand of them. The mailed fist of Abrusio.

Looking farther out still, he fixed his gaze where the city ended in a maze of quays and jetties and warehouses, and a huge tangled forest of masts. Three enormous harbours crammed with miles of ship berths, an uncountable myriad of vessels from every port and kingdom in the known world. The bloodstream of trade, which kept Abrusio's leathery old heart beating.

And there, over half a league away, Admiral's Tower with its scarlet pennant snaking and snapping in the wind, hardly to be seen but for the glint of gold upon it. In the state shipyards rested galleys, galleasses, caravels and war-carracks by the hundred. The fleet of the most powerful seafaring nation west of the Cimbric Mountains. There, that was what power looked like. It was a gleam of iron on the barrel of a cannon; the glitter of steel at the head of a lance. It was the oak of a warship's hull. These things were not the trappings, but the essence of power, and those who thought themselves in positions of authority often forgot that, to their lasting regret. Power in this day and age was in the muzzle of a gun.

"Sastro, for the Saint's sake close the screen, will you? We'll perish in here of the cold before we're done."

The tall nobleman smiled out at the wintry metropolis, cast his glance left, to the east, and he saw there something to brighten the dullness of the day. On a cleared patch of ground near the summit of the city, perhaps some four acres in extent, was what appeared to be a conflagration, a carpet of fire which lit up the afternoon. On closer inspection it might be seen that the inferno was not one single blaze, but a huge number of lesser bonfires grouped closely together.

They were silent; the wind carried the hungry roar of the flames away from him. But he could just make out the dark stick-figure at the heart of every tiny, discrete fire. Every one a heretic, yielding up his spirit in a saffron halo of unimaginable agony. Over six hundred of them.

That, Sastro thought, *is power also. The ability to withhold life.*

He stepped in off the balcony and shut the intricately carved screen behind him. He found himself in a tall stone room, the walls hung with tapestries depicting scenes from the lives of various saints. Braziers burned everywhere, generating a warm fug, a charcoal smell. Only above the long table where the others sat did oil lamps burn, hanging from the ceiling on silver chains. The day outside, with the screen closed, was dark enough to make it seem nocturnal in here. The three men seated around the table, elbow-deep in papers and decanters, did not seem to notice, however. Sastro took his seat among them again. The headache which had occasioned his stepping out on to the balcony was still with him and he rubbed his throbbing temples as he regarded the others in silence.

The rulers of the kingdom, no less. The dispatch-runner had put in only that afternoon, a sleek galleass which had almost foundered in its haste to reach Abrusio. It had set out from Touron a scant nineteen days ago, spent a fortnight pulling against the wind to get clear of the Tulmian Gulf, and then had spread its wings before the wind all the way south along the Hebrian coast, running off eighty leagues a day at times. It bore a messenger from Vol Ephrir who was now a month on the road, who had hurtled north through Perigraine killing a dozen horses on the way, who had stopped at Charibon a night and then had hurtled on again until he had taken ship with the galleass in Touron. The messenger bore news of the excommunication of the Hebrian monarch.

Quirion of Fulk, Presbyter of the Knights Militant, an Inceptine cleric who bore a sword, leaned back from the table with a sigh. The chair cracked under his weight. He was a corpulent man, the muscle of youth melting into fat, but still formidable. His head was shaved in the fashion of the Knights, and his fingernails were broken by years

of donning mail gauntlets. His eyes were like two gimlets
set deep within a furrowed pink crag, and his cheekbones
thrust out farther than his oft-broken nose. Sastro had seen
prize-fighters with less brutal countenances.

The Presbyter gestured with one large hand towards the
document they had been perusing.

"There you have it. Abeleyn is finished. The letter is
signed by the High Pontiff himself."

"It is hastily written, and the seal is blurred," one of the
other men said, the same one who had complained of the cold.
Astolvo di Sequero was perhaps the most nobly born man in
the kingdom after King Abeleyn himself. The Sequeros had
once been candidates for the throne, way back in the murky
past which followed the fall of the Fimbrian Hegemony some
four centuries ago, but the Hibrusids had won that particular
battle. Astolvo was an old man with lungs that wheezed like
a punctured wineskin. His ambitions had been extinguished
by age and infirmity. He did not want to be a player in the
game, not at this stage of his life; all he wanted of the world
now were a few tranquil years and a good death.

Which suited Sastro perfectly.

The third man at the table was hewn out of the same rock as
Presbyter Quirion, though younger and with violence written
less obviously across his face. Colonel Jochen Freiss was
adjutant of the City Tercios of Abrusio. He was a Finnmarkan,
a native of that far northern country whose ruler, Skarpathin,
called himself a king though he was not counted among the
Five Monarchs of the West. Freiss had lived thirty years in
Hebrion and his accent was no different from Sastro's own,
but the shock of straw-coloured hair which topped his burly
frame would always mark him out as a foreigner.

"His Holiness the High Pontiff was obviously pressed
for time," Presbyter Quirion said. He had a voice like a
saw. "What is important is that the seal and signature are
genuine. What say you, Sastro?"

"Undoubtedly," Sastro agreed, playing with the hooked
end of his beard. His temples throbbed damnably, but his
face was impassive. "Abeleyn is king no more; every law
of Church and State militates against him. Gentlemen,
we have just been recognized by the holy Church as the

legitimate rulers of Hebrion, and a heavy burden it is – but we must endeavour to bear it as best we may."

"Indeed," Quirion said approvingly. This changes matters entirely. We must get this document to General Mercado and Admiral Rovero at once; they will see the legitimacy of our position and the untenable nature of their own. The army and the fleet will finally repent of this foolish stubbornness, this misplaced loyalty to a king who is no more. Do you agree, Freiss?"

Colonel Freiss grimaced. "In principle, yes. But these two men, Mercado and Rovero, are of the old school. They are pious, no doubt of that, but they have a soldier's loyalty towards their sovereign, as have the common troops. I think it will be no easy task to overturn that attachment, Pontifical bull or no."

"And what happened to your soldier's loyalty, Freiss?" Sastro asked, smiling unpleasantly.

The Finnmarkan flushed. "My faith and my eternal soul are more important. I swore an oath to the King of Hebrion, but that king is no more my sovereign now than a Merduk sham. My conscience is clear, my lord."

Sastro bowed slightly in his chair, still smiling. Quirion flapped one blunt hand impatiently.

"We are not here to spar with one another. Colonel Freiss, your convictions do you credit. Lord Carrera, I suggest you could exercise your wit more profitably in consideration of our changed circumstances."

Sastro raised an eyebrow. "Our circumstances have changed? I thought the bull merely confirmed what was already reality. This council rules Hebrion."

"For the moment, yes, but the legal position is unclear."

"What do you mean?" Astolvo asked, wheezing. He seemed faintly alarmed.

"What I mean," Quirion said carefully, "is that the situation is without precedent. We rule here, in the name of the Blessed Saint and the High Pontiff, but is that a permanent state of affairs? Now that Abeleyn is finished, and is without issue, who wears the Hebrian crown? Do we continue to rule as we have done these past weeks, or are we to cast about for a legitimate claimant to the throne, one nearest the Royal line?"

The man has a conscience, Sastro marvelled to himself. He had never heard an Inceptine cleric talk about legality before when it might undermine his own authority. It was a revelation which did away with his headache and set the wheels turning furiously in his skull.

"Is it one of our tasks, then, to hunt out a successor to our heretical monarch?" he asked incredulously.

"Perhaps," Quirion grunted. "It depends on what my superiors in the order have to say. No doubt the High Pontiff will have a more detailed set of commands on its way to us already."

"If we put it that way, it may make clerical rule easier to swallow for the soldiery," Freiss said. "The men are not happy at the thought of being ruled by priests."

Quirion's gimlet eyes flashed deep in their sockets. "The soldiery will do as they are told, or they will find pyres awaiting them on Abrusio Hill along with the Dweomer-folk."

"Of course," Freiss went on hastily. "I only point out that fighting men prefer to see a king at their head. It is what they are used to, after all, and soldiers are nothing if not conservative."

Quirion rapped the table, setting the decanters dancing. "Very well then," he barked. "Two things. First, we present this Pontifical bull to the admiral and the general. If they choose to ignore it, then they are guilty of heresy themselves. As Presbyter I am endowed with prelatial authority here, since the office is vacant; I can thus excommunicate these men if I have to. Charibon will support me.

"Two. We begin enquiries among the noble houses of the kingdom. Who is of the most Royal blood and untainted by any hint of heresy? Who, in fact, is next in line to the throne?"

As far as Sastro knew that privilege was old Astolvo's, but the head of the Sequero family, if he knew it himself, was saying nothing. Whoever ruled would be a puppet of the Church. With two thousand Knights Militant in the city and the regular tercios hamstrung into impotence by the delicate consciences of their commanders, the new king of Hebrion, whoever he might turn out to be, would have no real power – whatever appearances might suggest. Power as Sastro had defined it to himself earlier. The kingship was not necessarily to be coveted, whatever prestige it might bring with it. Not unless the king were a man of remarkable abilities, at any rate. Clearly, the High Pontiff meant the Church to control Hebrion.

"The situation requires much thought," Sastro said aloud with perfect honesty. "The Royal scribes will have to look through the genealogical archives to trace the bloodlines. It may take some time."

Astolvo stared at him. The old nobleman's eyes were watering. He did not want to be king and thus said nothing; but no doubt there were young bloods aplenty in his house who would jump at the chance. Could Astolvo keep them in check? It was doubtful. Sastro did not have much time. He must arrange a private meeting with this Finnmarkan mercenary, Freiss. He needed power. He needed the muzzles of guns.

A TRUE NORTHERLY, one that the old salts liked to call the Candelan Heave, had blown down as steady and pure as an arrow's flight to take them out of the gulf of the Ephron estuary and into the Levangore. South-south-east had been their course, the mizzen brailed up and the square courses bonneted and full before the stiff stern wind.

On reaching the latitude of Azbakir, they had turned to the west, taking the wind on the starboard beam. Slower going after that, as they forged through the Malacar Straits with their guns run out and the soldiers lining the ship's side in case the Macassians cared to indulge in a little piracy. But the straits had been quiet, the shallow-bellied galleys and feluccas of the corsairs beached for the winter. The northerly had veered after that, and they had had it on their starboard quarter ever since: the best point of sail for a square-rigged vessel like a carrack. They had entered the Hebrian Sea without incident, passing the winter fishing yawls of Astarac and pointing their bows towards the Fimbrian Gulf and the coast of Hebrion beyond, three quarters of their homeward voyage safely behind them. The northerly had failed them then, and a succession of lesser breezes had veered round to east-south-east, right aft. Now the wind showed signs of backing again, and the ship's company were kept busy trying to anticipate its next move.

Forgist had begun, that dark month which heralded the ending of the year. One month, followed by the five Saint's Days which were for the purification of the old year and the welcoming in of the new, and then the year 551 would have slipped irrevocably into the annals of history. The unreachable past would have claimed it.

King Abeleyn of Hebrion, excommunicate, stood on the windward side of the quarterdeck and let the following spray settle rime on the fur collar of his cloak. Dietl, the master of the swift carrack beneath his feet, kept to the leeward rail, studying his mariners as they braced the yards round and occasionally barking out an order which was relayed by the mates. The northerly was showing signs of reappearing as the wind continued to back; soon they would have it broad on the starboard beam.

A young man, his curly black hair unspeckled with grey as yet, the Hebrian King had been five years on his throne. Five years which had seen the fall of Aekir, the imminent ruin of the west at the hands of the Merduk hordes and the schism of the holy Church of God. He was a heretic: when he died his soul would howl away the eons in the uttermost reaches of Hell. He was as damned as any heathen Merduk, though he had done what he had done for the good of his country – indeed, for the good of the western kingdoms as a whole.

Abeleyn was no simpleton, but the faith of his rigidly pious father had settled deep in his marrow and he felt the thin, cold fear of what he had done worming there. Not fear for his kingdom, or for the west. He would always do what was best for them and let no qualm of conscience tug at the hem of his cloak. No – fear for himself. He felt a sudden terror at the thought of his deathbed, the demons which would gather round the spent body to drag away his screaming spirit when the time came for him to quit the world at last...

"Grim thoughts, sire?"

Abeleyn turned, seeing again the bright swells of the Hebrian Sea, feeling the rhythm of the living ship under his feet. There was no one near him, but a tattered-looking gyrfalcon sat perched on the ship's weather-rail regarding him with one yellow, inhuman eye.

"Grim enough, Golophin."

"No regrets, I trust."

"None of any import."

"How is the lady Jemilla?"

Abeleyn scowled. His mistress was pregnant, scheming, and very seasick. His early departure from the Conclave of Kings had meant that she could take ship with him back to Hebrion instead of finding her own way.

"She is below, no doubt still puking."

"Good enough. It will occupy her mind wonderfully."

"Indeed. What news, old friend? Your bird looks more battered than ever. His errands are wearing him out."

"I know. I will grow a new one soon. For now, I can tell you that your fellow heretics are both well on their way back to their respective kingdoms. Mark is headed south, to cross the Malvennors in southern Astarac where they are passable. Lofantyr is in the Cimbrics, having a hard time of it, it seems. I fear it will be a bitter winter, sire."

"I could have told you that, Golophin."

"Perhaps. The Fimbrian marshals are made of sterner stuff. Their party is forcing the Narboskim passes of the Malvennors. They are waist deep already, but I think they will do it. They have no horses."

Abeleyn grunted. "The Fimbrians were never an equestrian people. Sometimes I think that is why they have never bred an aristocracy. They walk everywhere. Even their emperors tramped about the provinces as though they were infantrymen. What else? What news of home?"

There was a pause. The bird preened one wing for several seconds before the old wizard's voice issued eerily from its beak once more.

"They burned six hundred today, lad. The Knights Militant have more or less purged Abrusio of the Dweomer-folk now. They are sending parties out into the surrounding fiefs to hunt for more."

Abeleyn went very still. "Who rules in Abrusio?"

"The Presbyter Quirion, formerly Bishop of Fulk."

"And the lay leaders?"

"Sastro di Carrera for one. The Sequeros, of course. Between them they have carved up the kingdom very nicely, with the Church in overall authority, naturally."

"And the diocesan bishops? I always thought Lembian of Feramuno was a reasonable man."

"A reasonable man, but still a cleric. No, lad: their faces are all set against you."

"What of the army, the fleet?"

"Ah, there you have the bright spot. General Mercado has refused to put his men at the disposal of the council, as these usurpers style themselves. The tercios are confined to barracks, and Admiral Rovero has the fleet well in hand also. The Lower City of Abrusio, the barracks and the harbours are no-go areas for the Knights."

Abeleyn let out a long breath. "So we can make landfall. There is hope, Golophin."

"Yes, sire. But Mercado is an old man, and a pious one. The Inceptines are working on him. He is as loyal as a hound, but he is also intolerant of heresy. We cannot afford to lose any time, or we may find the army arraigned against us when we reach Hebrion."

"You think a Pontifical bull could have arrived there already?"

"I do. Himerius will waste no time once he hears the news from Vol Ephrir. And therein lies your danger, sire. Refusing to obey the will of a few trumped-up, would-be princes is one thing, but remaining loyal to an absent heretic is quite another. The bull may be enough to sway the army and the fleet. You must prepare yourself for that."

"If that happens I am finished, Golophin."

"Nearly, but not quite. You will still have your own lands, your own personal retainers. With Astarac's help you could reclaim the throne."

"Plunging Hebrion into civil war while I do."

"No one ever said this course would be an easy one, sire. I could wish that we had made better time in our journey, though."

"I need agitators, Golophin. I need trusted men who will enter the city before me and spread the truth of the matter. Abrusio is not cut out to be ruled by priests. When the city hears that Macrobius is alive and well, that Himerius is an imposter and that Astarac and Torunna are with me in this thing, then it will be different."

"I will see what I can do, lad, but my contacts in the city are growing thinner on the ground day by day. Most of them are ashes, friends of fifty years. May the lord God rest their souls. They died good men, whatever the Ravens might think."

"And you, Golophin. Are you safe?"

Something in the yellow gleam of the bird's eye chilled Abeleyn as it replied in the old mage's voice.

"I will be all right, Abeleyn. The day they try to take me will be one to remember, I promise you."

Abeleyn turned and stared back over the taffrail. Astarac was out of sight over the brim of the horizon, but he could just make out the white glimmer of the Hebros Mountains ahead, to the north-west.

Astarac, far astern of them: the kingdom of King Mark, soon to be his brother-in-law. If there were ever time for weddings again after all this. What was waiting for Mark in Astarac? More of the same, perhaps. Ambitious clerics, nobles leaping at the opportunity to rule. War.

A sea mile astern of Abeleyn's vessel two wide-bellied *nefs*, the old-fashioned trading ships of the Levangore, were making heavy going of the swell. Within them was the bulk of Abeleyn's entourage, four hundred strong; the only subjects whose obedience he still commanded. It was because of them he had taken the longer sea route home instead of trying to chance the snowbound passes of the mountains. He would need every loyal sword in the months to come; he could not afford to abandon them.

"Golophin, I want you to do something."

The gyrfalcon cocked its head to one side. "I am yours to command, my boy."

"You must procure a meeting with Rovero and Mercado. You must let the army and the fleet know the truth of things. If the Hebrian navy is against me, then we will never get to within fifty leagues of Abrusio."

"It will not be easy, sire."

"Nothing ever is, my friend. Nothing ever is."

"I will do my best. Rovero, being a mariner, has always had a more open mind than Mercado."

"If you must choose one, then let it be Rovero. The fleet is the most important."

"Very well, sire."

"Sail ho!" the lookout cried from the maintop. "I see five
– no, six – sail abaft the larboard beam!"

Dietl, the master, squinted up at the maintop. "What are
they, Tasso?"

"Lateen-rigged, sir. Galleasses by my bet. Corsairs maybe."

Dietl blinked, then turned to Abeleyn.

"Corsairs, sire. A whole squadron, perhaps. Shall I put
her about?"

"Let me see for myself," Abeleyn snapped. He clambered
over the ship's rail and began climbing the shrouds. In
seconds he was up in the maintop with Tasso, the lookout.
The sailor looked both amazed and terrified at finding
himself on such close terms with a king.

"Point them out to me," Abeleyn commanded.

"There, sire. They're almost hull up now. They have the
wind on the starboard beam, but you can see their oars are
out too. There's a flash of foam along every hull, regular as
a waterclock."

Abeleyn peered across the unending expanse of white-
streaked sea while the maintop described lazy arcs under
him with the pitch and roll of the carrack. There: six sails
like the wings of great waterborne birds, and the regular
splash of the oars as well.

"How do you know they're corsairs?" he asked Tasso.

"Lateen-rigged on all three masts, sir, like a xebec.
Astaran and Perigrainian galleasses are square-rigged on
fore and main. Those are corsairs, sir, no doubt about it,
and they're on a closing course."

Abeleyn studied the oncoming ships in silence. It was too
much of a coincidence. These vessels knew what they were
after.

He slapped Tasso on the shoulder and sidled down the
backstay to the deck. The whole crew was standing staring,
even the Hebrian soldiers and marines of his entourage. He
joined Dietl on the quarterdeck, smiling.

"You had best beat to quarters, Captain. I believe we
have a fight on our hands."

THREE

AT TIMES IT seemed as though the whole world were on the move.

From Ormann Dyke the road curved round to arrow almost due south through the low hills of northern Torunna. A fine road, built by the Fimbrians in the days when Aekir had been the easternmost trading post of their empire. The Torunnan kings had kept it in good repair, but in their own road-building they had never been able to match the stubborn Fimbrian disregard for natural obstacles, and thus the secondary roads which branched off it curved and wound their way about the shoulders of the hills like rivulets of water finding their natural level.

All the roads were clogged with people.

Corfe had seen it before, on the retreat from Aekir, but the other troopers of the escort had not. They were shocked by the scale of the thing.

The troop had passed through empty villages, deserted hamlets, and even a couple of towns where the doors of the houses had been left ajar by their fleeing occupants. And now the occupants of all northern Torunna were on the move, it seemed.

Most of them were actually from Aekir. With the onset of winter, General Martellus of Ormann Dyke had ordered the refugee camps about the fortress broken up. Those living there had been told to go south, to Torunn itself. They were too big a drain on the meagre resources of the dyke's defenders, and with winter swooping in – a hard winter too, by the looks of it – they would not survive long in the shanty towns which had sprung up in the shadow of the dyke. Hundreds of thousands of them were moving south, trekking along the roads in the teeth of the bitter wind. Their passage had had a catastrophic effect on the inhabitants of the region. There had been looting, killing, even pitched battles between Aekirians and Torunnans. The panic had spread, and now the natives of the country were heading south also. A rumour had begun that the Merduks would not remain long in winter quarters, but were planning a sudden onslaught on the dyke, a swift sweep south to the Torunnan capital before the heaviest of the snows set in. There was no truth to it. Corfe had reconnoitred the Merduk winter camps himself, and he knew that the enemy was regrouping and resupplying, and would be for months. But reason was not something a terrified mob hearkened to very easily, hence the exodus.

The troop of thirty Torunnan heavy cavalry were escorting a clumsy, springless carriage over the crowded roads, battering a way through the crowds with the armoured bodies of their warhorses and warning shots from their matchlocks. Inside the carriage Macrobius III, High Pontiff of the Western World, sat with blind patience clutching the Saint's symbol of silver and lapis lazuli General Martellus had given him. Nowhere in Ormann Dyke could there be found material of the right shade to clothe a Pontiff, so instead of purple Macrobius wore robes of black. Perhaps it was an omen, Corfe thought. Perhaps he would not be recognized as Pontiff again, now that Himerius had been elected to the position by the Prelates and the Colleges of Bishops in Charibon. Macrobius himself did not seem to care whether he was Pontiff or not. The Merduks had carved something vital out of his spirit when they gouged the eyes from his head in Aekir.

Unbidden, her face was in Corfe's mind again, as clear as lamplight. That raven-dark hair, and the way one corner of her mouth had tilted upward when she smiled. His Heria was dead, a burnt corpse in Aekir. That part of him, the part which had loved her, was nothing but ash now also. Perhaps the Merduks had carved something out of his own spirit when they had taken the Holy City: something of the capacity for laughter and loving. But that hardly mattered now.

And yet, and yet. He found himself scanning the face of every woman in the teeming multitude, hoping and praying despite himself that he might see her. That she might have survived by some miracle. He knew it was the merest foolishness; the

Merduks had snatched the youngest and most presentable of Aekir's female population on the city's fall to be reserved for their field brothels. Corfe's Heria had died in the great conflagration which had engulfed the stricken city.

Sweet blood of the holy Saint, he hoped she had died.

The outrider Corfe had dispatched an hour before came cantering back up the side of the road, scattering trudging refugees like a wolf exploding a flock of sheep. He reined in his exhausted horse and flung a hurried salute, his vambrace clanging against the breast of his cuirass in the age-old gesture.

"Torunn is just over the hill, Colonel. Barely a league to the outskirts."

"Are we expected?" Corfe asked.

"Yes. There is a small reception party outside the walls, though they're having a hell of a time with the refugees."

"Very good," Corfe said curtly. "Get back in the ranks, Surian, and go easier on your mount next time."

"Yes, sir." Abashed, the youthful trooper rode on down the line. Corfe followed him until he had reached the bumping carriage.

"Holiness."

The curtains twitched back. "Yes, my son?"

"We'll be in Torunn within the hour. I thought you might like to know."

The mutilated face of Macrobius stared blindly up at Corfe. He did not seem to relish the prospect.

"It starts again, then," he said, his voice barely audible over the creak and thump of the moving carriage, the hoofbeats of horses on the paved road.

"What do you mean?"

Macrobius smiled. "The great game, Corfe. For a time I was off the board, but now I find myself being moved on it again."

"Then it is God's will, Father."

"No. God does not move the pieces; the game is an invention of man alone."

Corfe straightened in the saddle. "We do what we must, Holy Father. We do our duty."

"Which means that we do as we are told, my son."

The wreck of a smile once more. Then the curtain fell back into place.

TORUNNA WAS ONE of the later-founded provinces of the Fimbrian Empire. Six centuries previously, it had consisted of a string of fortified towns along the western coast of the Kardian Sea, all of them virtually isolated from one another by the wild Felimbric tribesmen of the interior. As the tribes became pacified Torunn itself, built athwart the Torrin river, became an important port and a major fortress against the marauding steppe nomads who infested the lands about the Kardian Gulf. Eventually the Fimbrians settled the land between the Torrin and Searil rivers by planting eighty tercios of retired soldiers there with their families to provide a tough buffer state between the prospering province to the south and the savages beyond.

Marshal Kaile Ormann, commander of the Eastern Field Army, dug a huge dyke at the only crossing point of the swift, gorge-cutting Searil river and for forty years it was the easternmost outpost of the Fimbrians, until the founding of Aekir on the Ostian river still farther east. The Torunnans themselves were thus direct descendants of the first Fimbrian soldier-settlers, and the great families of the kingdom all traced their origins back to the most senior officers from among those first tercios. The Royal family of Torunn was descended from the house of Kaile Ormann, the builder of Ormann Dyke.

It was one of the ironies of the world that Torunna was the first province to rebel against Fimbria and declare its independence from the Electors. It snatched Aekir for itself and was recognized by the then High Pontiff, Ammianus, as a legitimate state in return for four thousand volunteer troops, who were to become the forerunners of the Knights Militant.

Torunna was thus a cockpit of momentous history in the west, and during the long years of Fimbrian isolation following the empire's collapse it had become the foremost military power among the new monarchies, the guardian-state both of the Pontiff and the eastern frontier.

A man coming upon Torunn for the first time – especially from the north – might see in it uncanny similarities to the layout and construction of Fimbir. The old city walls had long ago been enlarged and changed so that they bristled with ravelins, bastions, crownworks and hornworks designed for a later age of warfare, when gunpowder counted for more than sword blades; but there was a certain brutal massiveness about the place which was wholly Fimbrian.

It brought back memories for Corfe as his troop of horsemen and their trundling charge came over the final slopes before the city. A tangled riot of later building meant that Torunn was surrounded by unwalled suburbs beyond which the grey stone of the walls could be seen lying like the flanks of a great snake amid the roofs and towers of the Outer City. This was the place where he had joined the tercios, where he had been trained, where his adolescence had been roughly hewn into manhood. He was a native of Staed, one of the southern coastal cities of the kingdom. To him, Torunn had seemed like a miracle when first he had seen it. But he had seen Aekir since, and knew what a truly huge city looked like. Torunn housed some fifth of a million people, and that same number were now on the roads leading towards it, seeking sanctuary. The enormity of the problem defeated his imagination.

In the suburbs the press of people was worse. There were Torunnan cavalry there, struggling to keep order, and open-air kitchens had been set up in all the market places. The noise and the stink were incredible. Torunn had the aspect of one of those apocalyptic religious paintings which depicted the last days of the world. Though Aekir at its fall, Corfe thought bitterly, had been even closer.

Before the new, low-built city gates a tercio of pikemen had been drawn up in ranks and a pair of demi-culverins flanked them. Slow-match burned in lazy blue streamers. Corfe was not sure if the show of force was to receive the High Pontiff or to keep the teeming refugees out of the Inner City, but as the carriage was spotted the culverins went off in salute, blank charges roaring out in clouds of smoke and spitting flame. From the towers above, other guns began to fire until the walls seemed to ripple with smoke and the thunderous sound recalled for Corfe the Merduk bombardment at Ormann Dyke.

The Torunnans presented arms, an officer flourished his sabre, and the High Pontiff was welcomed through the gates of Torunn.

KING LOFANTYR HEARD the salute echoing across the city, and paused in his pacing to look out of the tower windows. He pushed aside the iron grilles and stepped out on to the broad balcony. The city was a serried sea of roofs reaching out to the north, but he could glimpse the puffing smoke clouds from the casemates on the walls.

"Here at last," he said. The relief in his voice was a palpable thing.

"Perhaps now you will sit a while," a woman's voice said.

"Sit! How can I sit? How will I ever take my ease again, mother? I should never have listened to Abeleyn; his tongue is too renowned for its persuasiveness. The kingdom is on the brink of ruin, and I brought it there."

"Pah! You have your father's gift for drama, Lofantyr. Was it you who brought the Merduks to the gates of Aekir?" the woman retorted sharply behind him. "The kingdom won a great battle of late and is holding the line of the east. You are Torunnan, and a king. It is not seemly to voice the doubts of your heart so."

Lofantyr turned with a twisted smile. "If I cannot voice them to you, then where shall I utter them?"

The woman was seated at the far end of the tall tower chamber in a cloud of lace and brocade. An embroidery board was perched on a stand before her, and her nimble hands worked upon it without pause, the needle flashing busily. Her eyes flicked up at her son the King and down to her work, up and down. Her fingers never hesitated.

Her face was surrounded by a deviously worked halo of hair that was stabbed through with pearl-headed pins and hung with jewels. Golden hair, shot through with silver. Earrings of the brightest lapis lazuli. Her face was fine-boned, but somehow drawn; it was possible to see that she had been a beautiful woman in her youth, and even now her charms were not to be lightly dismissed, but there was a fragility to the flesh which clothed those beautiful bones, a system of tiny lines which proclaimed her age despite the stunning green magnificence of her eyes.

"You have won the battle, my lord King – the fight against time. Now you have a Pontiff to parade before the council and quell these murmurings of heresy." She caught her tongue between her teeth for a second as the needle bored in a particularly fine stitch. "Unlike the other kings, you can show your people that Macrobius truly lives. That, and the storm which approaches from the east, should suffice to unite most of them under you."

She set aside her needle at last. "Enough for today. I am tired."

She stared keenly at Lofantyr. "You look tired also, son. The journey from Vol Ephrir was a hard one."

Lofantyr shrugged. "Snow and bandit tribesmen – the usual irritants. There is more to my tiredness than the aftermath of a journey, mother. Macrobius is here, yes; but beyond the city walls thousands upon thousands of Aekirians and northern Torunnans are screaming for succour, and I cannot give it to them. Martellus wants the city garrisons moved to the dyke, and the Knights Militant promised to me will now never arrive. I need every man I can spare across the country to hold down the nobles. They are straining at the leash despite the fact that I promised them the true Pontiff. Already there are reports of minor rebellions in Rone and Gebrar. I need trusted commanders who do not see opportunity in the monarch's difficulties."

"Loyalty and ambition: those two irreconcilable qualities without which a man is nothing. It is a rare individual who can balance both of them in his breast," the woman said.

"John Mogen could."

"John Mogen is dead, may God keep him. You need another war leader, Lofantyr, someone who can lead men like Mogen did. Martellus may be a good general, but he does not inspire his men in the right way."

"And neither do I," Lofantyr added with bitter humour.

"No, you do not. You will never be a general, my son; but then you do not have to be. Being King is trial enough."

Lofantyr nodded, still with a sour smile upon his face. He was a young man like his fellow heretics, Abeleyn of Hebrion and Mark of Astarac. His wife, a Perigrainian princess and niece of King Cadamost, had already left for Vol Ephrir, vowing never to lie with a heretic. But then she was only thirteen years old. There were no children, and a severed dynastic tie meant little at the moment with the west struck asunder by religious schism.

His mother, the Queen Dowager Odelia, pushed aside her embroidery board and rose to her feet, ignoring her son's hurriedly proffered arm.

"The day I cannot rise from a chair unaided you can bury me in it," she snapped, and then: "Arach!"

Lofantyr flinched as a black spider dropped from the rafters on a shining thread and landed on his mother's shoulder. It was thickly furred, and bigger than his hand. Its ruby eyes glistened. Odelia petted it for a moment and it uttered a sound like a cat's purr.

"Be discreet, Arach. We go to meet a Pontiff," the woman said. At once, the spider disappeared into the mass of lace that rose up at the back of Odelia's neck. It could barely be glimpsed there, a dark hump nestled in the fabric which transformed her upright carriage into something of a stoop. The purring settled into a barely audible hum.

"He is getting old," the Queen Dowager said, smiling. "He likes the warmth." She took her son's arm now, and they proceeded to the doors in the rear of the chamber.

"As well I became a heretic," Lofantyr said.

"Why is that, son?"

"Because otherwise I'd have to burn my own mother as a witch."

THE AUDIENCE CHAMBERS were filling rapidly. In his eagerness to show the living Macrobius to the world, Lofantyr had allowed His Holiness only a few hours to recover from his journey before requesting humbly that he bestow his blessing upon a gathering of the foremost nobles of the kingdom. There were hundreds of people congregating in the palace, all clad in the brightest finery they possessed. The ladies of the court had emulated Perigrainian fashions with the King's marriage to the young Balsia of Vol Ephrir, and they looked like a cloud of marvellous butterflies with wings of stiff lace and shimmering jewels, their faces painted and their fans fluttering – for the audience chambers were hot with the press of people and the huge logs blazing merrily in the fireplaces. It was a far cry from the austere days of Lofantyr's father, Vanatyr, when the nobles wore only the black and scarlet of the military and the ladies simple, form-fitting gowns without headdresses.

Corfe and his troop had quartered their mounts in the palace stables and tried to spruce themselves up as best they could, but they were muddy and worn from the travelling and many of them wore the armour they had spent weeks fighting in during the battles at the dyke. His men made a dismal showing, Corfe admitted to himself, but every one of them was a veteran, a survivor. That made a difference.

The court chamberlain had hurriedly procured a set of purple robes for Macrobius, but the old man had refused them. He had also refused to be carried into the audience chamber in a sedan-chair, and to let anyone but Corfe take his arm and guide him up the long length of the crowded hall.

"You have guided me on a harder road than this," he said as they waited in an antechamber for the trumpet blasts that would announce their entry. "I would ask you one last time to be my eyes for me, Corfe."

The doors were swung open by liveried attendants, and the vast, gleaming length of marble that was the floor of the audience chamber shone before them, whilst on either side hundreds of people – nobles, retainers, courtiers, hangers-on – craned their necks to see the Pontiff they had thought dead. At the end of the hall, hundreds of yards away it seemed to Corfe, the thrones of Torunna glittered with silver and gilt. Lofantyr the King and his mother the Queen Dowager sat there. A third throne, that of the young Queen, was empty.

The trumpet notes died away. Macrobius smiled. "Come, Corfe. Our audience awaits."

The tramp of his military boots and the slap of Macrobius's sandals were the only sound. Perhaps there was a faint murmuring as the crowd took in the soldier in the battered armour and the hideously mutilated old man. Out of the corner of his eye, Corfe glimpsed some of the spectators looking hopefully back at the end of the hall, as if they expected the real Pontiff and his guide to come issuing out of the end doors in a sweep of state and ceremony.

They walked on. Corfe was sweating. He took in the immense height of the building, the arched roof with its buttresses of stone and rafters of black cedar, the huge hanging lamps... then he saw the galleries there, packed with watching faces, brilliant with liveries of every rainbow hue. He cursed to himself. This was not his province, this august ceremonial, this painted game of politics and etiquette.

Macrobius squeezed his arm. The old man seemed amused by something, which unsettled Corfe even more. His hand slithered round the hilt of his sabre, the one he had taken off a dead Torunnan trooper on the Western Road.

And he remembered. He remembered the inferno of Aekir, a roaring chaos like the very end of the world. He remembered the long, vicious nights in the retreat west. He remembered the battles at Ormann Dyke, the desperate fury of the Merduk assaults, the ear-numbing roar of the enemy guns. He remembered the endless killing, the thousands of corpses which had clogged the Searil river.

He remembered his wife's face as she left him for the last time. They had reached the end of the hall. On the dais before them the King of Torunna regarded them with mild astonishment. His mother's gaze was a calculating green appraisal. Corfe saluted them. Macrobius stood silent.

There was a cough somewhere, and then the chamberlain banged his staff on the floor three times and called out in a practised, ringing voice which filled the entire hall.

"His Holiness the High Pontiff of the Western Kingdoms and Prelate of Aekir, the head of the holy Church, Macrobius the Third..." The chamberlain looked at Corfe then with incipient panic. Obviously he had no idea who the Pontiff's battered companion might be.

"Corfe Cear-Inaf, colonel in the garrison at Ormann Dyke, formerly under the command of John Mogen at Aekir." It was Macrobius, in a voice clearer and stronger than Corfe had ever heard him use before, even when he had preached at the dyke.

"Greetings, my son." This was to Lofantyr.

The Torunnan King hesitated a moment, and then descended from the dais in a sweep of scarlet and sable, his circlet catching the light of the overhead lamps. He knelt before Macrobius, and kissed the old man's ring – another gift from Martellus; the Pontifical ring had been lost long before.

"You are welcome to Torunna, Holiness," he said, a little stiffly, Corfe thought. Then he recalled his own manners, and as Lofantyr straightened he bowed. "Your Majesty."

Lofantyr nodded briefly to him and then took Macrobius's arm.

He led the blind old man up to the dais and placed him on the vacant Queen's throne. Corfe stood alone and uncertain until he caught the eye of the chamberlain, who was beckoning discreetly to him. He marched over into the whispering press of people who were gathered on either side of the dais.

"Stay out of the way," the chamberlain hissed into his ear, and he banged his staff on the floor again.

Lofantyr had risen from his throne to speak. A hush fell on the hall once more. The King's voice was less impressive than his chamberlain's but it carried well enough.

"We welcome here at our court today the living embodiment of the faith that sustains us all. The rightful High Pontiff of the world has been delivered by a miracle out of the cauldron of war in the east. Macrobius the Third lives and is well in Torunn, and with his presence here this city of ours has become the buckler of the Church – the true Church. With the Holy Father's prayers to sustain us, and the knowledge that right is on our side and God watches over our ranks, we are sure that the armies of Torunna, greatest and most disciplined in the world, will continue the work begun in the past few weeks at Ormann Dyke. Other victories will be stitched upon the battle flags of our tercios, and it will not be long ere our standard is reared up once again on the battlements of Aekir and the heathen foe is flung back across the Ostian river into the wilderness of unbelief and savagery from whence he came..."

There was more of this. It passed over Corfe's head unheeded.

He was tired, and the rush of adrenalin which had carried him up the hall had washed out of him, leaving him as drained as a flaccid wineskin. Why had Martellus insisted he come here?

"So I say to the usurper in Charibon," Lofantyr went on, "there is no heresy in recognizing the true spiritual head of the Church, in fighting to hold the eastern frontier safe for the kingdoms behind us. Torunna and Hebrion and Astarac represent the kingdoms of the True Faith, not the diocese of an imposter who must in his turn be branded heretic."

The speech ended at last, and the hall boiled with talk. The people within began to spread out across the bare central space in knots of conversation, whilst from side doors up and down the chamber attendants came bearing silver salvers upon which decanters of wine and spirits gleamed. The King poured for Macrobius, and the hall hushed again as the Pontiff stood up with the wineglass blood-full in his hand.

"I am blind."

And the silence became absolute.

"Yes, I am Macrobius. I escaped from the ruin of Aekir when so many did not. But I am not the man I once was. I stand before you –" He paused and looked sightlessly to one side, where the Queen Dowager had risen from her seat and taken his arm.

"In our haste to welcome the Holy Father into the city, we did not take account of his weariness. He must rest. But before he leaves us for the chambers we have appointed for him, we would beg him for his blessing, the blessing of the true head of the Church."

Some of the people near the dais took up the cry. "A blessing! A blessing, Your Holiness!"

Macrobius stood irresolute for a moment, and Corfe had the weirdest feeling that the old man was somehow in danger. He pushed through the clots of people towards the dais, but when he got to its foot he found his way blocked by a line of halberd-bearing guards. The chamberlain appeared at his elbow as if by magic. "No farther, soldier."

Corfe looked up at the figures on the dais. Macrobius stood stock still for several moments, whilst the smile on the Queen Dowager's face grew ever thinner. Finally, he raised his hand in the well-known gesture, and everyone in the hall bowed their heads.

Except for the flint-eyed guards facing Corfe.

The blessing took a matter of seconds, and then attendants in scarlet doublets helped the Pontiff off the dais by a door at the rear of the thrones. Lofantyr and Odelia resumed their seats, and the room seemed to relax. Talk blossomed, punctuated by the clink of glasses. From the galleries floated the soft sounds of lutes and mandolins. A woman's alto began singing a song of the Levangore, about tall ships and lost islands or some other romantic rubbish.

A tray-bearing attendant offered Corfe wine, but he shook his head. The air was thick with perfume; it seemed to rise from the white throats of the ladies like incense. Everyone was talking with unusual animation; obviously Macrobius's appearance had ramifications beyond Corfe's guessing.

"What am I to do?" he asked the chamberlain harshly. A red anger was building in him, and he was not sure as to its source.

The chamberlain gazed at him as though surprised to see he was still there. He was a tall man, but thin as a reed. Corfe could have snapped him in two over his knee.

"Drink some wine, talk to the ladies. Enjoy a taste of civilization, soldier."

"I am 'Colonel,' to you."

The chamberlain blinked, then smiled with no trace of humour.

He looked Corfe in the eye, an unflinching stare which seemed to be memorizing his features. Then he turned away and became lost in the mingling crowd. Corfe swore under his breath.

"Did you dress especially for the audience, or are you always so trim?" a woman's voice asked.

Corfe turned to find a foursome at his elbow. Two young men in dandified versions of Torunnan military dress, and two ladies on their arms. The men seemed a curious mixture of condescension and wariness; the women were merely amused.

"We travelled in haste," the remnants of politeness made Corfe say.

"I think it made for a very touching scene." The other woman giggled. "The ageing Pontiff in the garb of a beggar and his travelworn bodyguard, neither sure as to who should lean on whom."

"Or who was leading whom," the first woman added, and the four of them laughed together.

"But it is a relief to know our king is no longer a heretic," the first woman went on. "I imagine the nobles of the kingdom are thanking God while we speak." This also produced a tinkle of laughter.

"We forget our manners," one of the men said. He bowed. "I am Ensign Ebro of His Majesty's guard, and this is Ensign Callan. Our fair companions are the ladies Moriale and Brienne of the court."

"Colonel Corfe Cear-Inaf," Corfe grated. "You may call me 'sir.'"

Something in his tone cut short the mirth. The two young officers snapped to attention. "I beg pardon, sir," Callan said. "We meant no offence. It is just that, within the court, one becomes rather informal."

"I am not of the court," Corfe told him coldly.

A sixth person joined the group, an older man with the sabres of a colonel on his cuirass and a huge moustache which fell past his chin. His scalp was as bald as a cannonball and he carried a staff officer's baton under one arm.

"Fresh from Ormann Dyke, eh?" he barked in a voice better suited to a parade ground than a palace. "Rather stiff up there at times, was it not? Let's hear of it, man. Don't be shy. About time these palace heroes heard news of a real war."

"Colonel Menin, also of the palace," Ebro said, jerking his head towards the newcomer.

It seemed suddenly that there was a crowd of faces about Corfe, a horde of expectant eyes awaiting entertainment. The sweat was soaking his armpits, and he was absurdly conscious of the mud on his clothing, the dints and scrapes on his armour. The very toes of his boots were dark with old blood where he had splashed in it during the height of the fighting.

"And you were at Aekir, too, it seems," Menin went on. "How is that? I thought that none of Mogen's men survived. Rather odd, wouldn't you say?"

They waited. Corfe could almost feel their gazes crawl up and down his face.

"Excuse me," he said, and he turned away, leaving them. He elbowed his way through the crowd feeling their stares shift, astonished, to his back, and then he left the hall.

Kitchens, startled attendants with laden trays. A courtier who tried to redirect him and was brushed aside. And then the fresh air of an early evening, and the blue dark of a star-spattered twilit sky. Corfe found himself on one of the bewildering series of long balconies which circled the central towers of the palace. He could hear the clatter of the kitchens behind him, the humming din of a multitude. Below him all of Torunn fanned out in a carpet of lights to the north. To the east the unbroken darkness of the Kardian Sea. Somewhere far to the north Ormann Dyke with its weary garrison, and beyond that the sprawling winter camps of the enemy.

The starlit world seemed vast and cold and somehow alien. The only home that Corfe had ever truly known was a blackened shell lost in that darkness. Utterly gone. Strangely enough, the only person he thought he might have spoken to of it was Macrobius. He, too, knew something of loss and shame.

"Sweet Lord," Corfe whispered, and the hot tears scalded his throat and seared his eyes though he would not let them fall. "Sweet Lord, I wish I had died in Aekir."

The music started up again from within. Tabors and flutes joined the mandolins to produce a lively military march, one for soldiers to swing their arms to.

Corfe bent his head to the cold iron of the balcony rail, and squeezed shut his burning eyes on the memories.

FOUR

THE FIRST SHOT sent the seabirds of the gulf wailing in distracted circles about the ships and puffed up a plume of spray barely a cable from the larboard bow.

"Good practice," Dietl, the carrack's master, admitted grudgingly, "but then we are broadside-on to them, as plump a target as you could wish, and the galleasses of the corsairs carry nothing but chasers. No broadside guns, see, because of the oars. They'll close and board soon, I shouldn't wonder."

"We can't outrun them then?" Abeleyn asked. He was a competent enough sailor, as Hebrion's king should be, but this was Dietl's ship and the master knew her like no one else ever could.

"No, sire. With those oars of theirs, they effectively have the weather gauge of us. They can close any time they wish, even into the wind if they have to. And as for those pig-slow *nefs* your men are in, a one-armed man in a rowboat could overtake them. No, it's a fight they're looking for, and that's what they're going to get." Dietl's earlier diffidence to the King on his quarterdeck seemed to have evaporated with the proximity of action. He spoke now as one professional to another.

All along the decks of the carrack the guns had been run out and their crews were stationed about them holding sponges, wads, wormers and lint-stocks – the paraphernalia of artillery, whether land or naval. The thin crew of the merchant carrack that Abeleyn had hired in Candelaria was supplemented by the soldiers of his retinue, most of them well used to gunnery of one sort or another. The deck had been strewn with sand so the men would not slip in their own blood once the action began, and the coiled slow-match was burning away happily to itself in the tub beside every gun. Already the more responsible of the gun captains were sighting down the barrels of the metal monsters, eyeing the slender profiles of the approaching vessels. Six sleek galleasses with lateen sails as full and white as the wings of a flock of swans.

The carrack was heavily armed, one of the reasons why Abeleyn had hired her. On the main deck were a dozen demiculverins, bronze guns whose slim barrels were eleven feet long and which fired a nine-pound shot. On the poop deck were six sakers, five-pounders with nine-foot barrels, and ranged about the forecastle and up in the tops were a series of falconets, two-pounder swivel guns which were to be used against enemy boarders.

The sluggish *nefs* a mile behind on the choppy sea were less well armed, but they carried the bulk of Abeleyn's men: over a hundred and fifty trained Hebrian soldiers in each. It would take a stubborn enemy to board them with any hope of success. Abeleyn knew that a galleass might have a crew of three hundred, but they were not of the same calibre as his men. And besides, he knew that he was the prize the enemy vessels were after. The corsairs were out king-hunting this bright morning in the Fimbrian Gulf, that was certain. He would have given a lot to know who had hired them.

Another shot ploughed into the sea just short of the carrack, and then another. Then one clipped the waves like a stone sent skimming by a boy at play and crashed into the side of the ship with a rending of timbers. Dietl went purple. He turned to Abeleyn.

"By your leave, sire, I believe it's time we heated up the guns."

Abeleyn grinned. "By all means, Captain."

Dietl leaned over the quarterdeck rail. "Fire as they bear!" he shouted.

The culverins leaped back on their carriages with explosions of smoke and flame erupting from their muzzles. The main-deck almost disappeared in a tower of smoke, but the northerly sent it forward over the forecastle. The crews were already reloading, not waiting to see the fall of shot. Some of the more experienced gunners clambered over the

side of the ship to gauge their aim. Abeleyn stared eastwards.
The six galleasses appeared unhurt by the broadside. Even as
he watched, little globes of smoke appeared on their bows as
the chasers fired again. A moment later came the retorts, and
the high whine of shot cutting the air overhead. The King
saw holes appear in the maincourse and foretopsail. A few
fragments of rigging fell to the deck.

"They have us bracketed," Dietl said grimly. "There's hot
work approaching, sire."

Abeleyn's reply was cut off by the roar of the carrack's
second broadside. He glimpsed a storm of pulverized water
about the enemy vessels and the flap of white canvas gone
mad as the topmast of one galleass went by the board and
crashed over her bow. The carrack's crew cheered hoarsely,
but did not pause in their reloading for an instant.

From the maintop the lookout yelled down: "Deck there!
The northerly squadron is veering off. They're going after
the *nefs*!"

Abeleyn bounded to the taffrail. Sure enough, the farther
squadron of vessels was turning into the wind. They already
had their sails in. Under oar power alone, they changed course
to west-nor'-west on an intercept course with the two *nefs*. At
the same time, the remaining three galleasses seemed to put on
a spurt of speed and their oars dipped and rose at a fantastic
rate. All three of their bows were pointed at the carrack.

Another broadside. The galleasses were half a mile off the
larboard bow and closing rapidly. Abeleyn saw an oarbank
burst to pieces as some of the carrack's shots went home.
The injured galleass at once went before the wind. There
were men struggling like ants on the lateen yards, trying to
brace them round.

The whine of shot again, some of it going home. The fight
seemed to intensify within minutes. The crew of the carrack
laboured at the guns like acolytes serving the needs of brutal
gods. Broadside after broadside stabbed out from the hull
of the great ship until it seemed that the noise and flame
and sour smoke were intrinsic to some alien atmosphere,
an unholy storm which they had blundered blindly into.
The deck shook and canted below Abeleyn's feet as the guns
leapt inboard and then were loaded and run out again. The

regular broadsides disintegrated as the crews found their own rhythms, and the battle became one unending tempest of light and tumult as the vessels of the corsairs closed in to arquebus range and, closer still, to pistol range.

But then a series of enemy rounds struck home in quick succession. There were crashes and screams from the waist of the carrack and in the smoking chaos Abeleyn saw the monster shape of one of the culverins upended and hurled away from the ship's side. It tumbled across the deck and the entire ship shuddered. There was a shriek of overburdened wood, and then a portion of the deck gave way and the metal beast plunged out of sight, dragging several screaming men with it. The deck was a shattered wreck that glistened with blood and was littered with fragments of wood and hemp. But still the gun crews hauled their charges into position and stabbed the glowing match into the touch-holes. A continuous thunder, ear-aching, a hellish flickering light. Some fool had discharged his culverin without hauling it tight up to the bulwark, and the detonation of the gun had set the shrouds on fire. Teams of fire-fighters were instantly at work hauling up wooden tubs of seawater to douse the flames.

The ship's carpenter staggered to the quarterdeck.

"How does she swim, Burian?" Dietl asked out of a powder-grimed face.

"We've plugged two holes below the waterline and we've secured that rogue gun, but we've four feet in the well and it's gaining on us. There must be a leak in the hold that I can't get at. I need men, Captain, to shift the cargo and come at it, otherwise she'll go down in half a watch."

Dietl nodded. "You shall have them. Take half the crews from the poop guns – but work fast, Burian; we'll need those men back on deck soon enough. I'm thinking they're closing to try and board."

"You're sure they won't try ramming?" Abeleyn asked him, surprised.

Another broadside. They had to howl in one another's ears to be heard.

"No, sire. If you're the prize they're after, they'll try and take you alive, and a rammed ship can go to the bottom in seconds. And besides, they're a mite too close to get up the speed for ramming. They'll board, all right. They have the men for it. There's damn near a thousand of the bastards in those three galleasses; we can muster maybe a tenth of that. They'll board, by God."

"Then I must have my men from your gun crews, Captain."

"Sire, I –"

"Now, Captain. There's no time to lose."

Abeleyn went round the guns in person collecting the soldiers who had taken ship with him. The men dropped their gun tools, picked up their arquebuses and began priming them, ready to repel boarders. Abeleyn glimpsed the enemy vessels over the ship's side, incredibly close now, their decks black with men, the sails taken in and the chase-guns roaring. Some of the sailors had left their culverins and were also reaching for arquebuses and cutlasses and boarding-pikes. From the tops a heavy fire came from the falconets and swivels, knocking figures off the bows of the galleasses.

A crash from aft which knocked Abeleyn off his feet. One of the galleasses had grappled alongside and corsairs were climbing up the side of the carrack from the lower enemy vessel, scores of them clinging to the wales and waving cutlasses, shrieking as they came. Abeleyn got up and ran to a deserted culverin.

"Here!" he yelled. "To me! Give me a hand here!"

A dozen men ran to help him, some of them canvas-clad mariners, others in the gambesons of his own soldiers.

"Heave her up, depress the muzzle! Quick there! Don't bother worming her out – load her."

A crowd of faces at the gunport, one broken open by the thrust of a soldier's halberd. A press of men wriggling over the ship's side to be met by a hedge of flailing blades. The carrack's crew defended her as though they were the garrison of a castle standing siege. There was another shuddering crash as a second galleass grappled with the tall ship. Men on the enemy vessel's yards cast lines and grappling irons, entangling the rigging of the struggling vessels, binding them together, whilst in the carrack's top the falconets fired hails of smallshot and fought to cut the connecting lines.

"Lift her – lift her, you bastards!" Abeleyn shouted, and the men with him lifted the rear of the culverin's barrel whilst he wedged it clear of its carriage with bits of wood and discarded cutlasses.

A wave of enemy boarders overwhelmed the carrack's defenders in the waist. The men around Abeleyn found themselves in a vicious melee with scarcely room to swing their swords. When men went down they were trampled and stabbed on the deck. A few arquebus shots were fired but most of the fighting was with steel alone. Abeleyn ignored it. He grasped the slow-match that lay smouldering on the deck, was knocked to his knees in the slaughterous scrum, stabbed his rapier into a howling face and had the weapon wrenched out of his hand as the man fell backwards. Then he thumped the slow-match into the culverin's touch-hole.

A flash, and a frenzied roar as it went off, flying back off its precarious perch. It fell over, crushing half a dozen of the enemy boarders. Abeleyn's own men surged forward, cheering hoarsely. A hellish cacophony of shouts and screams came from over the ship's side. Abeleyn struggled to the carrack's larboard rail and looked down.

The galleass had been directly below and the heavy shot had struck home. The deck was closer to the water already, and men were diving off it into the foam-ripped sea. The vessel was finished; the cannonball must have blasted clear through her hull.

But the boarders from the second galleass were clambering into the waist in droves. Abeleyn's defenders were outnumbered five to one. He seized a broken pike, raising it into the air.

"To the castles!" he shouted, waving his pike. "Fall back to the castles. Leave the waist!"

His men understood, and began to fight their way inch by murderous inch towards the high fore- and sterncastles of the carrack which dominated the waist like the towers of a fortress. A bloody rearguard action was fought on the ladders there as the corsairs sought to follow them, but they were held. Abeleyn found himself back on the quarterdeck. Dietl was standing there holding a rope tourniquet about one elbow. His hand had been lopped off at the wrist.

"Arquebusiers, form ranks!" Abeleyn screamed. He could see none of his officers present and shoved his men about as though he were the merest sergeant. "Come on, you God-damned whoresons! Present your pieces! You sailors – get a couple of those guns pointing down into the waist; load them with canister. Quickly now!"

The Hebrian soldiers formed up in two ragged ranks at the break of the quarterdeck and aimed their arquebuses into the raging press of men below.

"Give fire!"

A line of stabbing flames staggered the front ranks of the boarders down below. Men were flung back off the ladders, tumbling down on those behind them. The waist was a toiling mass of limbs and faces.

"Fire!" Dietl yelled, and the two canister-loaded sakers which his mariners had manhandled round erupted a few seconds later. Two groups of shrieking corsairs were levelled where they stood, and the bulwarks of the carrack were intagliated with gore and viscera as the thousands of balls in the canister shot tore through their bodies. On the forecastle, another rank of arquebusiers was firing, dropping more of the enemy, whilst the men in the tops were blasting almost vertically downwards with the little falconets. The corsairs who had boarded were thus surrounded on all sides by a murderous fire. Some of them ducked into the shattered hatches of the carrack, seeking shelter in the hold below, but most of them dived overboard. Scores of them left their bodies, or what was left of them, strewn across the reeking deck.

The gunfire petered out. Farther to the north they could hear broadsides booming as the *nefs* fought for their lives against the other squadron, but here the corsairs were drawing off. One galleass was already awash, the sea up to her scuppers and her bow half submerged. Another was drifting slowly away from the carrack, the men in the tops having cut her grappling lines. The third was circling just out of arquebus range like a wary hound padding round a cornered stag. The water about the four vessels was crammed with swimming men and limp bodies, pieces of wreckage and fragments of yards.

"They'll ram us now, if they can," Dietl panted, his face as white as paper under the blood and filth that streaked it. He was holding his stump upright with his good hand. Bone glinted there, and thin jets of blood spat from the severed arteries despite the tourniquet. "They'll draw off to gain speed and pick up their men. We have to hit them while they're at close range."

"Stand by the starboard guns!" Abeleyn shouted. "Sergeant Orsini, take six men and secure any enemy still on board. Load the starboard culverins, lads, and we'll give them something to remember us by!" He bent to speak through the connecting hatch to the tillermen below, who all this time had been at their station keeping the carrack on course through the storm of the fighting. "Bring us round to due south."

"Aye, sir! I mean Majesty."

Abeleyn laughed. He was strangely happy. Happy to be alive, to be in command of men, to hold his life in the palm of his own hand and tackle problems that were immediate, visible, final.

The gun crews had rushed back down into the waist and were loading the starboard batteries, unfired as yet. The enemy galleass was struggling to brace round the huge lateen yards; both vessels had the wind right aft now, but the square-rigged carrack was better built to take advantage of it than the fore-and-aft yards of the galleass. She was overtaking her foe.

"Tiller there!" Dietl shouted, somehow making his failing voice carry. "Wait for my word and then bring her round to sou'-west."

"Aye, sir!"

Dietl was going to cut around the bow of the galleass and then rake her from stem to stern with his full broadside. Abeleyn spared a look for the other enemy vessels. One was visible only as a solitary mast sticking above the packed sea. The other was taking on survivors of the failed boarding action and reducing sail at the same time. The sea was still stubbled with the bobbing heads of men.

The carrack gained on her enemy, sliding ahead. The gun crews, or what was left of them, crouched like statues by their weapons, the slow-match smoke drifting from the hands of the gun captains as they awaited the order to fire.

"If we bow-rake her, can't she ram us amidships?" Abeleyn asked Dietl.

"Aye, sire, but she hasn't enough way on her yet to do us any real damage. Her oarbanks are shot to hell and she's not too happy with this stern wind. We'll rake her until she strikes."

The galleass was on the starboard quarter now. A few arquebus shots came cracking overhead from her, but mostly she seemed intent on putting her oarsmen and her yards in order. "Bring her round to sou'-west!" Dietl shouted down the tillerhatch.

The carrack curved to starboard in a beautiful arc, turning so her starboard broadside faced the beakhead of the oncoming galleass. Abeleyn glimpsed the wicked-looking ram on the enemy vessel, only just awash, and then Dietl screamed "*Fire!*" with what seemed to be the last of his strength.

The air was shattered as the unholy noise began again and the culverins resumed their deadly dance. The crews had depressed the muzzles of the guns as much as they could to compensate for the larboard roll of the ship as she turned. At this range and angle the heavy balls would hit the bow and rip through the length of the enemy vessel. The carnage on her would be unbelievable. Abeleyn saw heavy timbers blasted from her hull and flung high in the air. The mainmast swayed as shot punched through its base, and then toppled into the sea, smashing a gap in the galleass's side. The vessel lurched to larboard, but kept coming, her ram gleaming like a spearhead.

And struck. She collided amidships with the carrack and the concussion of the impact staggered Abeleyn and toppled Dietl off his feet. The gun crews of the carrack were still reloading and firing, pouring shot into the helpless hull of the galleass at point-blank range. The decks of the enemy vessel were running with blood and it poured from her scuppers in scarlet streams. Men were leaping overboard to escape the murderous barrage, and a desperate party of them came swarming up the carrack's side but were beaten back and flung into the sea.

"Port your helm!" Abeleyn yelled to the tillermen. Dietl was unconscious in a pool of his own blood on the deck.

There was a grating noise, a deep, grinding shudder as the wind worked on the carrack and tore her free of the stricken galleass. She was sluggish, like a tired prize-fighter who knows he has thrown his best punch, but finally she was free of the wrecked enemy vessel. There were half a dozen fires raging on board the corsairs' craft and she was no longer under command. She drifted downwind, burning steadily as the carrack edged away.

The third galleass was already in flight, having picked up as many of the corsairs as she could. She spread her sails and set off to the south-east like a startled bird, leaving scores of helpless men struggling in the water behind her.

An explosion that sent timbers and yards a hundred feet into the air as the crippled galleass which remained burned unchecked. Abeleyn had to shout himself even hoarser as flaming wreckage fell among the carrack's rigging and started minor fires. The exhausted crew climbed the shrouds and doused the flames. The carpenter, Burian, appeared on the quarterdeck looking like a dripping rat.

"Sire, where's the master?"

"He's indisposed," Abeleyn told him in a croak. "Make your report to me."

"We've six feet of water in the hold and it's still gaining on us. She'll settle in a watch or two; the breach the ram made is too big to plug."

Abeleyn nodded. "Very well. Get back below and do what you can. I'll set a course for the Hebrian coast. We might just make it."

Suddenly Dietl was there, staggering like a drunk man but upright. Abeleyn helped him keep his feet.

"Set a course for the Habrir river. West-sou'-west. We'll be there in half a watch. She'll bring us to shore, by God. She's not done yet, and neither am I."

"Take him below," Abeleyn said to the carpenter as the master's eyes rolled back in his head. Burian threw Dietl over his shoulder as though he were a sack, and disappeared down the companionway to his task of keeping the ship afloat.

"Sire," a voice said. Sergeant Orsini, looking like some bloody harbinger of war.

"Yes, Sergeant?"

"The *nefs*, sire – the bloody bastards sank them both."

"*What?*" Abeleyn ran to the starboard rail. Up to the north he made out the smoke and cloud of the other action. He could see two galleasses and two burning hulks, one unrecognizable, the other definitely one of the wide-bellied *nefs* of his retinue. As he watched, a globe of flame rose from it and seconds later the boom of the explosion drifted down the wind.

"They're lost then," he said. The weariness and grief were slipping into place now. The battle joy had faded. Three hundred of his best men gone. Even if the carrack had been undamaged, they would take hours to beat up to windwards and look for survivors, and the two galleasses that remained would find her easy prey. It was time for flight. The monarch in Abeleyn accepted that, but the soldier loathed it.

"Someone will pay for this," he said, his voice low and calm. But the tone of it set the hair crawling on Orsini's head. Then the King turned back to the task in hand.

"Come," he said in a more human voice. "We have a ship to get to shore."

FIVE

BROTHER COLUMBAR COUGHED again and wiped his mouth on the sleeve of his habit. "Saint's blood, Albrec, to think you've been thirteen years down in these warrens. How can you bear it?"

Albrec ignored him and raised the dip higher so that it illuminated the rough stone of the wall. Columbar was an Antillian like himself, clad in brown. His usual station was with Brother Philip in the herb gardens, but a cold had laid him low this past week and he was on lighter duties in the scriptorium. He had come down here two days ago, hunting old manuscript or parchment that might serve as blotting for the scribes above. And had found the precious document which had been consuming most of Albrec's time ever since.

"There have been shelves here at one time," Albrec said, running his fingers across the deep grooves in the wall. "And the stonework is rough, as though built in haste or without regard for appearances."

"Who's going to see it down here?" Columbar asked. He had a pendulous nose that was red and dripping and his tonsure had left him with black feathers of hair about his ears and little else. He was a man of the soil, he was proud of saying, a farmer's son from the little duchy of Touron. He could grow anything given the right plot, and thus had ended up in Charibon producing thyme and mint and parsley for the table of the Vicar-General and the poultices of the infirmary. Albrec had a suspicion that he was unable to read anything beyond a few well-worn phrases of the Clerical Catechism and his own name, but that was not uncommon among the lesser orders of the Church.

"And where's the gap where you found it?" Albrec asked.

"Here – no, over here, with the mortar crumbling. A wonder the library hasn't tumbled to the ground if the foundations are in this state."

"We're far below the library's foundations," Albrec said absently, poking into the crevice like a rabbit enlarging a burrow. "These chambers have been hewn from solid rock; those buttresses were left standing while the rest was cleared away. The place is all of a piece. So why do we have mortared blocks here?"

"It was the Fimbrians built Charibon, like they built everything else," Columbar said, as if to prove that he was not entirely ignorant.

"Yes. And it was a secular fortress at first. These catacombs were most probably used for the stores of the garrison."

"I wish you would not call them catacombs, Albrec. They're grim enough as it is." Columbar's breath was a pale fog about his face as he spoke.

Albrec straightened. "What was that?"

"What? I heard nothing."

They paused to listen in the little sanctuary of light maintained by the dip.

To call the chambers they were in catacombs was not such a bad description. The place was low, the roof uneven, the floor, walls and roof sculpted out of raw granite by some unimaginable labour of the long-ago empire. One stairway led down here from the lower levels of the library above, also hewn out of the living gutrock. Charibon had been built on the bones of the mountains, it was said.

These subterranean chambers seemed to have been used to house the accumulated junk of several centuries. Old furniture, mouldering drapes and tapestries, even the rusted remains of weapons and armour, quietly decayed in the dark peace. Few of the inhabitants of the monastery-city came down here; there were two levels of rooms above them and then the stolid magnificence of the Library of St. Garaso. The bottom levels of the monastery had not been fully explored since the days of the emperors; there might even be levels below the one on which the two men now stood.

"If you hate the dark so much, I'm blessed if I know what you were doing down here in the first place," Albrec whispered, his head still cocked to listen.

"When Monsignor Gambio wants something you find it quick, no matter where you have to look," Columbar said in the same low tone. "There wasn't a scrap of blotting left in the whole scriptorium, and he told me not to poke my scarlet proboscis back round the door until I had found some."

Albrec smiled. Monsignor Gambio was a Finnmarkan, a crusty, bearded old man who looked as though he would have been more at home on the deck of a longship than in the calm industry of a scriptorium. But he had been one of the finest scribes Charibon possessed until the lengthening years had made crooked mockeries of his hands.

"I should be grateful you put scholarly curiosity over the needs of the moment," Albrec said.

"I suffered for it, believe me."

"There! There it is again. Do you hear it?"

They paused again to listen. Somewhere off in the cluttered darkness there was a crash, the sound of things striking the stone floor, a clink of metal. Then they heard someone cursing in a low, irritated and very unclerical manner.

"Avila." Albrec said with relief. He cupped a hand about his mouth. "Avila! We're over here, by the north wall!"

"And which way is north in this lightless pit? I swear, Albrec..."

A light came into view, flickering and bobbing over the piles of rubbish. Gradually it neared their own until Brother Avila stood before them, his face smeared with dust, his black Inceptine habit grimed with mould.

"This had better be good, Albrec. I'm supposed to be face-down in the Penitential Chapel, as I was all yesterday. Never throw a roll at the Vicar-General if you've buttered it first. Hello, Columbar. Still running errands for Gambio?"

Avila was tall, slim and fair-haired, an aristocrat to his fingertips. Naturally, he was an Inceptine, and if he refrained from flinging too many more bread rolls he could be assured of a high place in the order ere he died. He was the best friend, perhaps the only one, that Albrec had ever known.

"Did anyone see you come down here?" Albrec asked him.

"What's this? Are we a conspiracy then?"

"We are discreet. Think about that concept, Avila."

"Discretion – there's a novel quality. I'll have to consider it. What have you dragged me down here for, my diminutive friend? Poor Columbar looks on the verge of a seizure. Have the ghosts been leaning over his shoulder?"

"Don't say such things, Avila," Columbar said with a shiver.

"We're looking for more of the document that Columbar unearthed, as you know very well," Albrec put in.

"Ah, *that* document: the precious papers you've been so secretive about."

"I must be going," Columbar said. He seemed more uneasy by the moment. "Gambio will be looking for me. Albrec, you know that if –"

"If the thing turns out to be heretical you had nothing to do with it, whereas if it is as rare and wonderful as Albrec hopes you'll be clamouring for your sliver of fame. We know, Columbar." Avila smiled sweetly.

Brother Columbar glared at him. "*Inceptines*," he said, a wealth of comment in the word. Then he stomped away into the darkness, taking one of the dips with him. They heard him blundering through the tumbled rubbish as his light grew ever fainter and then disappeared.

"You had no call to be so hard on him, Avila," Albrec said.

"He's an ignorant peasant who wouldn't know the value of literature if it sat up and winked at him. I'm surprised he didn't take your discovery to the latrines and wipe his arse with it."

"He has a good heart. He ran a risk for my sake."

"Indeed? So what is this thing that has got you so excited, Albrec?"

"I'll tell you later. For now, I want to see if we can find any more of it down here."

"A man might think you had discovered gold."

"Perhaps I have. Hold the lamp."

Albrec began to poke and pry at the crevice wherein Columbar had discovered the document. There were a few scraps of parchment left in it, as broken and brittle as dried autumn leaves. Almost as fragile was the mortar which held the rough stones surrounding it together. Albrec was able to lever some of them loose and widen the gap. He pushed his hand in farther, trying to feel for the back of the crevice. It seemed to run deep into the stonework. When he had pushed and scraped his arm in as far as his elbow, he found to his shock that his hand was in an empty space beyond. He flapped his fingers about, but the space seemed large. Another room?

"Avila!"

But Avila's strong hand was across his mouth, silencing him, and the dip was blown out to leave them in utter night.

Something was moving on the other side of the subterranean chamber.

The two clerics froze, Albrec still with one arm disappearing into the gap in the wall.

A light flickered as it was held aloft and under its radiance the pair could see the grotesque shadow-etched features of Brother Commodius scanning the contents of the chamber. The knuckles which were wrapped about the lamp handle brushed the stone ceiling; the light and dark of its effulgence made his form seem distorted and huge, his ears almost pointed; and his eyes shone weirdly, almost as though they possessed a light of their own. Albrec had worked under Commodius for over a dozen years, but this night he was almost unrecognizable, and there was something about his appearance which filled Albrec with terror. He suddenly knew that it was vitally important he and Avila should not be seen.

The Senior Librarian glared around for a few moments more, then lowered his lamp. The pair of quaking clerics by the north wall heard his bare feet slapping on the stone, diminishing into silence. They were left in impenetrable pitch-blackness.

"Sweet Saint!" Avila breathed, and Albrec knew that he, too, had sensed the difference in Commodius, the menace which had been in the chamber with his presence.

"Did you see that? Did you feel it?" Albrec whispered to his companion.

"I – What was he doing here? Albrec, he looked like –"

"They say that great evil can be sensed, like the smell of death," Albrec said in a rush.

"I don't – I don't know, Albrec. Commodius, he's a *priest*, in the name of God! It was the lamplight. The shadows tricked us."

"It was more than shadows," Albrec said. He withdrew his hand from the wall crevice, and as he did something came out along with it and clinked as it struck the stone floor below.

"Can you rekindle the light, Avila? We'll be here all night else, and he's gone now. The place feels different."

"I know. Hold on."

There was a rustling of robes, and then the click and flare of sparks as Avila struck flint and steel on the floor. The spark caught the dry lichen of the tinder almost at once and with infinite care he transferred the minute leaf of flame to the lamp wick. He picked up the object that had fallen and straightened.

"What is this?"

It soaked up the light, black metal curiously wrought. Avila wiped the dust and dirt from it and suddenly it was shining silver.

"What in the world –?" the young Inceptine murmured, turning it over in his slender fingers.

A dagger of silver barely six inches long. The tiny hilt had at its base a wrought pentagram within a circle.

"God's blood, Albrec, look at this thing!"

"Let me see." The blade was covered in runes which meant nothing to Albrec. Within the pentagram was the likeness of a beast's face, the ears filling two horns of the star, the long muzzle in the centre.

"This is an unholy thing," Avila said quietly. "We should go to the Vicar-General with it."

"What would it be doing down here?" Albrec asked.

Avila put the lamp against the black hole in the wall. "This has been blocked off. There's a room beyond these stones, Albrec, and the Saint only knows what kind of horrors have been walled up in it."

"Avila, the document I found."

"What about it? Is it a treatise on witchery?"

"No, nothing like that." Briefly Albrec told his friend about the precious manuscript, the only copy in the world perhaps of the Saint's life, written by a contemporary.

"*That was here?*" Avila asked incredulously.

"Yes. And there may be more of it, perhaps other manuscripts – all behind this wall, Avila."

"What was it doing lying hidden with this?" Avila held up the dagger by the blade. The beast's face was uncannily lifelike, the dirt rubbed into the crevices in its features giving it an extra dimension.

"I don't know, but I intend to find out. I can't take this to the Vicar-General, Avila, not yet. I haven't finished reading the document for one thing. What if they deem it heretical and have it burned?"

"Then it's heretical, and for the best. Your curiosity is overcoming rationality, Albrec."

"No! I have seen too many books burned. This one I intend to save, Avila, whatever it takes."

"You're a damn fool. You'll get yourself burned along with it."

"I'm asking you as a friend: say nothing to anyone of this."

"What about Commodius? Obviously he suspects something, else he would not have been here."

They were both silent, remembering the unnerving aspect of the Senior Librarian's appearance a few minutes ago. Taken together with the artefact they had found, it seemed to shake their knowledge of the everyday ordinariness of things.

"Something is wrong," Avila murmured. "Something is most definitely wrong in Charibon. I think you are right. We were not frightened by shadows alone, Albrec. I think Commodius was... different, somehow."

"I agree. So give me a chance to see if I can get to the bottom of this. If there is indeed something wrong, and Commodius has something to do with it, then part of it is here, behind this wall."

"What are you going to do, knock it down?"

"If I have to."

"And to think I likened you to a mouse when first I met you. You have the heart of a lion, Albrec. And the stubbornness of a goat. And I am a fool for listening to you."

"Come, Avila, you are not an Inceptine completely – at least not yet."

"I am starting to share the Inceptine fear of the unknown, though. If we're caught there will be a host of questions asked, and the wrong answers could send us both to the pyre."

"Give me the dagger, then. I have no wish to see you embroiled in my mischief."

"Mischief! Mischief is throwing rolls at the Vicar-General's table. You are flirting with heresy, Albrec. And worse, perhaps."

"I am only preserving knowledge, and seeking after more."

"Whatever. In any case, I am loath to let an ugly misshapen little Antillian upstage me, an Inceptine of noble birth. I'll join you in your private crusade, Brother Conspiracy. But what of Columbar?"

"He knows only that he found a manuscript of interest to me. I'll have a talk with him and secure his discretion."

"There are more brains in the turnips he raises. I hope he knows the value of the word."

"I'll impress it upon him."

They paused as if by common consent to listen again. Nothing but the soundlessness of the deep earth, the drip of water from ancient bedrock.

"This place predates the faith," Avila said in an undertone. "The Horned One had a shrine on the site of Charibon until the Fimbrians tore it down, it is said."

"Time to go," Albrec told him. "We'll be missed. You have your penance to finish. We'll come back some other time, and we'll have that wall down if I have to scrape it away with a spoon."

Avila tucked the pentagram dagger into the pocket of his habit without a word. They set off through the dark together towards the stairs beyond, the tall Inceptine and the squat Antillian. In a few short minutes it seemed that their world had become less knowable, full of sudden shadows.

The lightless spaces of the catacombs watched them go in silence.

TWELVE THOUSAND OF the Knights Militant had died fighting at Aekir, almost half of their total strength throughout

Normannia. Their institution was a strange one; some said a sinister, anachronistic one also. They were the secular arm of the Church, at least in theory, but their senior officers were clerics, Inceptines to a man. The "Ravens' Beaks" they were sometimes called.

They were feared across the continent by the commoners of every kingdom, their actions sanctioned by the Pontiff, their authority vaguely defined but indisputable. Kings disliked them for what they represented: the all-pervading power and influence of the Church. The nobility saw in them a threat to their own authority, for the word of a Knight Presbyter might not be gainsaid by any man of lower rank than a duke. Across the breadth of the continent, men with their noses in their beer might jocularly lament the fact that Macrobius had gathered only half of the Knights in Aekir before its fall, but they did so with one eye cocked at the door, and in undertones.

Golophin hated them. He loathed the very sight of their sombre cavalcades as they trooped through the streets of Abrusio on their destriers. They wore three-quarter armour, and over it the long sable surcoats with the triangular Saint's symbol worked in malachite green at breast and back. They bore poniards, longswords and lances, having disdained the new technology of gunpowder. More often than not, folk muttered, the only weapon they needed or utilized was the torch.

The pyres were still ablaze up on the hill. Two hundred today for the Knights were beginning to run short of victims. All the Dweomer-folk of the city and the surrounding districts had fled – those who survived. Most of them were freezing in the snowbound heights of the Hebros. Some Golophin and his friends had procured berths for on outbound ships. The Thaumaturgists' Guild had been decimated by the purges; most of its members were too prominent, too well known in the city to have had any chance of escaping. But a few, including Golophin, survived, scuttling like vermin in the underbelly of Abrusio, doing what they could for their people.

His face was a blurred shadow under his wide-brimmed hat. Anyone who looked at him would find it strangely difficult to remember any of its features. A simple spell, but one hard to maintain in the bustle of the Lower City. Speech negated it, and anyone who looked long and hard enough might just see through it. So Golophin moved quickly, a tall, incredibly lean figure of economic movements in a long winter mantle with a bag slung over one bony shoulder. He looked like a pilgrim journeying in haste to the site of a shrine.

The Lower City was still virtually off-limits to the Knights Militant, the common people bolstered in their defiance by the stand that General Mercado and Admiral Rovero were making. But already whispers were abroad that a messenger had brought news of the King's excommunication to the newly established Theocratic Council which technically ruled Abrusio. Abeleyn had been named a heretic, it was said, and his kingship was annulled. The general and the admiral must soon acknowledge the rule of the council or face the same fate themselves. And after that, the pyres would be kept stocked for years as the Knights went through the Lower City cleansing it of all who had defied them.

Admiral's Tower reared up over the rooftops ahead like a brooding megalith. It housed the headquarters of Hebrion's navy, the administrative offices of the State Shipyards and the halls of the fleet nobility. Golophin knew the place well, an outdated, labyrinthine fortress which butted on to the waters of the Inner Roads. The masts of the fleet rose like a forest in the docks at its foot and the old walls were whitened by the guano of a hundred generations of seabirds.

It was busy down here. The ships of the fleet required constant overhaul and their crews were kept eternally occupied by vigilant officers. Between eight and ten thousand mariners in all, they were volunteers to a man. Less than half their vessels were in port at the moment, however.

Ships of the Hebrian fleet were continually occupied with guarding the sea lanes which constituted the life's blood of Abrusio, even in winter. There were squadrons maintained in the Malacar Straits, the Hebrionese, even as far north as the Tulmian Gulf. They kept the trade routes free of the corsairs and the northern Reivers, and often exacted a discreet toll from passing merchantmen in return.

The sentries at the gates of Admiral's Tower never noticed the man in dun robes and wide-brimmed hat. Momentarily they both found the flight of a gull overhead utterly engrossing, and when they had blinked and looked at each other in mild puzzlement, he was past them, wending his undisturbed way through the darkened passages of the old fortress.

"YOU CAME THEN," Admiral Jaime Rovero said. "I was not sure if you would, especially in daylight, but then I suppose a man like you has his ways and means."

Golophin swept off his hat and rubbed an entirely bald scalp that gleamed with perspiration despite the raw coldness of the day.

"I came, Admiral, as I said I would. Is Mercado here yet?"

"He awaits us within. He is not happy, Golophin, and neither am I," Admiral Rovero was a burly, heavily bearded man whose face spoke of long years of exposure to the elements. His eyes seemed permanently slitted against some contrary wind and when he spoke only one corner of his mouth opened, the lips remaining obstinately shut on the other side. It was as if he were making some sardonic aside to an invisible listener at his elbow. The voice which issued from his lopsided mouth was deep enough to rattle glass.

"Who is happy in these times, Jaime? Come, let's go in."

They left the small anteroom and went through a pair of thick double doors which led to the state apartments of the Admiral of the Fleet. The short day was already winding down towards a winter twilight, as grey and cheerless as a northern sea, but there was a fire burning in the vast fireplace which occupied one wall. It made the daylight beyond the balcony screens seem blue and threw the far end of the long room into shadow.

The rams from fourteen Astaran galleys were set in the stone near the ceiling like the trophy heads of a hunter; they testified to the years of naval rivalry with Astarac. The curved scimitars of corsairs and Sea-Merduks criss-crossed the walls in patterns of flickering steel, and immensely detailed models of ships stood on stone pedestals below them. On the walls also, vellum maps of the Hebrian coast, the Malacar Straits and the Levangore hung like pale tapestries between the weapons. The room was a lesson in Hebrian naval history.

Another man stood with his back to the fire so that the flames threw his shadow across the flagged floor like a cape. He turned his head as Admiral Rovero and the old mage entered and Golophin saw the familiar shine of silver from the battered face.

"Good to see you again, General," he said.

General Mercado bowed. His visage was something of a marvel, created by Golophin himself, As a colonel in the bodyguard of Bleyn the Pious, he had taken a scimitar blow in the face. The blade had slashed away his nose, his cheekbone and part of his temple. Golophin had been on hand to save his sight and his life, and he had grafted a mask of silver on the injury. One half of Mercado's face was thus the bearded countenance of a veteran soldier, the other was an inhuman facade of glittering metal from which a bloodshot eye glared, lidless and tearless, but sustained by pure theurgy, a spell of permanence whose casting had cost Golophin the last of the scanty hair on his scalp. That had been twenty years ago.

"Have a seat, Golophin," the General said. The metal half of his face made his voice resound oddly, as though he were speaking from out of a tin cup.

"You've heard the rumours, I suppose," the old mage said, seating himself comfortably not far from the fire and rummaging through his robes for his tobacco pouch.

"Not rumours, not any more. The Papal bull of excommunication arrived two days ago. Rovero and I have been summoned to the palace tomorrow to view it and reconsider our positions."

"So the pair of you will walk tamely into the palace."

The human part of Mercado's face quirked upwards in a smile. "Not tamely, no. I intend to take an honour guard of two hundred arquebusiers, and Rovero will have a hundred marines. It will be public, no chance of a dagger in the back."

Golophin thumbed leaf into the bowl of his long-stemmed pipe. "It is not my place to preach to you about security," he conceded. "What will you do if you are satisfied the bull is genuine?"

Mercado paused. He and Rovero looked at one another. "First tell us what you have to say on the matter."

"Then your minds are not made up?"

"Damn it, Golophin, stop playing games!" Admiral Rovero burst out. "What of Abeleyn? Where is he and how does he fare?"

The old wizard lit his pipe with a spill caught from the flames of the fire. He puffed in silence for a few seconds, filling the room with the scents of Calmar and Ridawan.

"Abeleyn has just fought a battle," he said calmly at last.

"*What?*" Mercado cried, horrified. "Where? With whom?"

"Two squadrons of corsairs ambushed his ships as they were sailing south through the Fimbrian Gulf. He beat them off, but lost three-quarters of his men and two of his own vessels. He had to beach his remaining ship on the coast of Imerdon. He is intending to march overland the rest of the way to Hebrion."

Rovero was grinding one fist into a palm, striding back and forth restlessly and spitting words out of the corner of his mouth as though he were unwilling to let them go.

"Corsairs that far north. In the gulf! Two squadrons, you say. Now there's a happy chance, a synchronicity of fate. Someone tried to take the King, that's clear. But who? Who hired them?"

"Why Admiral," Golophin said with mild surprise, "you almost sound as though you care about the fate of our heretical ex-monarch."

Rovero stopped his pacing and glared at Golophin. "Beat them off, eh? Then at least he hasn't forgotten all I've taught him. Ex-monarch, my arse! Assault the person of the King, would they, the Goddamned heathen piratical dastards..."

"He sank three of them," Golophin went on. "They were in galleasses, the older sort with no broadsides, only chasers."

"How were the King's vessels armed?" Rovero demanded, his face alight with professional interest.

"Culverins, sakers. But that was only on the carrack. The two *nefs* had falcons alone. The corsairs sank one and burned the other to the waterline."

"Abeleyn's bodyguard?" Mercado asked abruptly.

"Almost all lost. Most were in the *nefs*. They gave a good account of themselves, though. Abeleyn has barely a hundred men left to him."

"They were good men," Mercado murmured. "The best of the Abrusio garrison."

"Where has he beached? How long will he take to get here?" Admiral Rovero asked, his eyes as narrow as the edge of a blade.

"That I don't know for sure, alas, and neither did the King when... when I communicated with him last. He is in the coastal marshes, close to the border with Imerdon, south-west of the mouth of the Habrir river. That is all I know."

The admiral and the general were silent, conflicting emotions flitting across their faces. "Is Abeleyn still your liege-lord, gentlemen?" Golophin asked. "He needs you now as he never has before."

Rovero grimaced as though he had bitten into a lemon. "God forgive me if I do wrong, but I am the King's man, Golophin. The lad is a fighter, always has been. He is a worthy successor to his father, whatever the Ravens might say."

Only someone watching Golophin with particular care could have seen the tiny whistle of breath that escaped his lips, the imperceptible sag of relief which relaxed his hitherto rigid shoulder blades.

"General," he said quietly to Mercado, "it would seem that Admiral Rovero still has a king. What say you in this matter?"

Mercado turned his face from Golophin so that the mage could see only the expressionless metal side.

"Abeleyn is my king too, Golophin, God knows. But can a king rule if his soul is damned? Who would gainsay the word of the Pontiff, the successor to Ramusio? Maybe the Inceptines are right. The Merduk War is God's punishment. We all have a penance to do before the world can be set to rights."

"The innocent are burning, Albio," Golophin said, using the general's first name. "A heretic sits on the throne of the Pontiff whilst its true occupant is in the east. Macrobius lives, and he is aiding the Torunnans in their battles to maintain the frontier. He helped them save Ormann Dyke when the world thought it irredeemably lost. The faith is with him. He is our spiritual head, not this usurper who sits in Charibon."

Mercado twisted to meet Golophin's eyes. "Are you so sure?"

Golophin raised an eyebrow. "I have my ways. How else do you think I stay abreast of Abeleyn's adventures?"

The fire cracked and spat. A gun began to boom out the evening salute somewhere on the battlements beyond. They would be lighting the ship beacons along the harbours of the city. The men of the ships would be changing watch, half of them trooping into the messes for the evening meal.

Faint and far-off amid the nearer noises, Golophin thought he could hear the cathedral bells tolling Vespers up on Abrusio Hill, nearly two miles away. He knew that if he stepped outside and looked that way he would be able to make out the dying glow of the pyres, finally fading. The dwindling reminder of another day's genocide. He stifled the bitter fury which always arose when he thought of it.

"We must play for time," Mercado said at last. "Rovero and I must not see this bull of theirs. We must hold them off as long as we are able, and get Abeleyn into the city safely. Once he is back in Abrusio, the task is simpler."

Golophin rose and gripped the general's hand. "Thank you, Albio. You have done the right thing. With you and Rovero behind him, Abeleyn can retake Abrusio with ease."

Mercado did not seem to share Golophin's happiness.

"There is something else," he said. He sounded troubled, almost embarrassed.

"What?"

"I cannot be sure of all my men."

Golophin was shocked. "What do you mean?"

"I mean that my adjutant, Colonel Jochen Freiss, has been conducting secret negotiations with a member of the council, Sastro di Carrera. I believe he has suborned a significant number of the garrison."

"Can you not relieve him of his post?" Golophin demanded.

"That would be tipping our hand too soon. I have yet to plumb the depths of his support, but I believe some of the junior officers may have joined him in conspiracy."

"It will mean war," Admiral Rovero said ominously. His voice sounded like the rumble of surf on a far-off strand.

"How can you sound out the loyalty of your men?" Golophin asked sharply.

"I have my ways and means, even as you have, Mage," Mercado retorted. "But I need time. For now we will continue to hold the Lower City. Some of the lesser guilds are on our side, though the Merchants' Guild is waiting to see which way the wind blows before committing itself."

"Merchants," Rovero said with all the contempt of the nobility for those in trade.

"We need the merchants on our side," Golophin told them. "The council is sitting on the treasury. If we are to finance a war then the merchants are our best source of money. Abeleyn will grant them any concessions they wish, within reason, in return for a regular flow of gold."

"No doubt the council will be putting the same proposition to them," Mercado said.

"Then we must be sure it is our proposition they accept!" Golophin snapped. He stared into the ashen bowl of his pipe. "My apologies, gentlemen. I am a little tired."

"No matter," Rovero assured him. "My ships may tip the scales. If the worst comes to the worst I can threaten them with a naval blockade of the city. That'll soon loosen their purse-strings."

Golophin nodded. He tucked his pipe back into a pocket which was scorched from similar use. "I must be going. I have some people to see."

"Tell the King, when next you speak to him, that we are his men – that we always have been, Golophin," Mercado said haltingly.

"I will, though he has always known it," the wizard replied with a smile.

Six

THE CHAMBER WAS small and circular. Its roof was domed and in the dome was a bewildering array of small beams, too slender to provide any architectural support. Corfe could not guess at their purpose, unless it were mere ornamentation. They were hung with cobwebs.

Large windows covered half the circumference of the walls, some of stained glass, predominantly Torunnan scarlet which lent a rosy hue to the place despite the greyness of the weather outside. Inside, the furnishings were rich and comfortable. Velvet-upholstered divans whose lines curved with the walls. Intricately embroidered cushions. A miniature library, the shelves untidy with added scrolls and papers. A tiny desk with a quill springing out of an inkwell. A bronze figurine of a young woman, nude, the face laughing exquisitely. An embroidery stand with rolls of thread tumbled about its foot. The room of an educated, affluent woman.

Corfe had no idea why he was here.

A palace flunkey, all lace cuffs and buckled shoes, had shown him the way soon after he had received the summons. He stood alone now in the private tower of the Queen Dowager, utterly at a loss.

There was a click, and a part of the wall opened to admit the Queen Dowager Odelia. It shut behind her and she stood serenely looking Corfe up and down, a slight smile on her face.

Corfe remembered his manners and bowed hurriedly; he was not of sufficient rank to kiss her hand. Odelia inclined her head graciously in response.

"Sit, Colonel."

He found himself a stool, absurdly conscious of the contrast between his appearance and the lady's. He still looked rather as though he had just trudged off a battlefield, though he had been in Torunn for two days. He had no money, no way to improve his wardrobe, and no one had offered him any advice or help in the matter. Macrobius had been borne away on wings of policy and state, and Corfe had had it brought home to him exactly how insignificant he was. He longed to be back at the dyke with his men doing the only job he had ever been fit for, but could not leave until he had the King's permission, and getting to see the King was well-nigh impossible. He was baffled, therefore, by the Queen Dowager's summons; he had thought himself entirely forgotten.

She was watching him patiently, a glint of what might have been humour in the marvellous green eyes. Carnelian pins secured her golden hair in a stately column atop her head, emphasizing the fine line of her neck. Corfe had heard the rumours; the Queen Dowager was a sorceress who preserved her looks through judicious use of thaumaturgy, sacrifices of new-born babes and the like. It was true she looked a good deal younger than her years. She might have been Lofantyr's elder sister rather than his mother, but Corfe could see the blue veins on the backs of her hands, the slightly swollen knuckles, the faint creases at the corners of her eyes and on her brow. She was attractive, but the signs were there.

"Do you believe me a witch, Colonel?" she asked, startling him. It was almost as though she had followed his train of thought.

"No," he said. "At least, not as the rumours have it. I don't believe you slay black cockerels at midnight or some such nonsense... your Majesty." He was not sure of the right way to address her.

Something black scuttled along one of the beams above his head, too quickly for him to catch more than a glimpse of it. So they have rats even in palaces, he thought.

"Lofantyr is 'Majesty,'" the Queen Dowager said. "To you I am just 'lady,' unless there is some other epithet you would prefer." She seemed to be deliberately trying to disconcert him. The realization irritated him. He had no time for the games of the Torunnan court.

"Why did you summon me here?" he asked bluntly.

She cocked her head to one side. "Ah, directness. I like that. You would be amazed how little of it there is in Torunn. Or perhaps you would not. You are a soldier pure and simple, are you not, Colonel? You are not at ease here in the intricacies of the court. You would rather be hip-deep in gore at Ormann Dyke."

"Yes," he said, "I would." There was nothing else he could say. He had never been any use at dissembling, and he sensed it would do him no good here.

"Would you like some wine?"

He nodded, totally at sea.

She clapped her hands and the door through which Corfe had entered opened. A willowy girl with the almond-shaped eyes and high cheekbones of the steppe peoples – a household slave – entered bearing a tray. She set out a decanter and two glasses in silence and then left as noiselessly as she had come. The Queen Dowager poured two generous glassfuls of ruby liquid.

"Ronian," she said. "Little known, but as good as Gaderian if it is well cared for. Our southern fiefs have fine vineyards, but they don't export much."

Corfe sipped at the wine. It might have been gun oil for all he tasted it.

"General Pieter Martellus thinks highly of you, Colonel. In his dispatches he says you made an excellent defence of Ormann Dyke's eastern bastion ere it fell. He also adds that you seem to work best as an independent commander."

"The general flatters me," Corfe said. He had not known that the dispatches he carried from the dyke had included a report on himself.

"You are also the only Torunnan officer to have survived Aekir's fall. You must be a man of luck."

Corfe's face became a stiff mask. "I don't much believe in luck, my lady."

"But it exists. It is that indefinable element which in war or peace – but especially in war – sets a man apart from his fellows."

"If you say so."

She smiled. "Aekir has marked you, Corfe. Before the siege you were an ensign, a junior officer. In the months since you have soared to the rank of colonel purely on merit. Aekir's fall may have been the counterweight to your ascent."

"I would give all my rank, and more besides, to have Aekir back again," Corfe said with some heat. *And to have Heria again*, his soul cried out.

"Of course," she said soothingly. "But now you are here in Torunn, friendless and penniless, an officer without a command. Merit is not always enough in this world. You must have something else."

"What?"

"A... sponsor, perhaps. A patron."

Corfe paused, frowning. At last he said: "Is that why I am here? Am I to become your client, lady?"

She sipped her wine. "Loyalty is more precious than gold at court, for if it is to be real it cannot be bought. I want a man whom gold cannot buy."

"Why? For what purpose?"

"For my own purposes, and those of the state. You know that Lofantyr has been excommunicated by the rival Pontiff Himerius. His nobles know Macrobius is alive – they have seen him with their own eyes. But some do not choose to believe what they see, because it suits them. Torunna is boiling with rebellion; men of rank never need much in the way of an excuse to repudiate their liege-lord. If nothing else, Corfe, I think Aekir and Ormann Dyke have burnt loyalty into you, whether you like it or not. That kind of loyalty, when it is accompanied with real ability, is a rare thing."

"There must be some men loyal to the King in the kingdom," Corfe growled.

"Men tend to have families; they put that loyalty first. If they serve the crown well, it is because they want advancement not only for themselves but for their families also. Thus are the great houses of the nobility created. It is a necessary but dangerous exchange."

"What do you want of me, lady?" Corfe asked wearily.

"I have spoken to the Pontiff of you, Corfe. He also thinks highly of you. He tells me you have no family, no roots now that the Holy City is no more."

Corfe bent his head. "Perhaps."

She rose from her chair and came over to him. Her hands encircled his face, the fingertips just touching his cheekbones. He could smell the lavender her dress had been

stored in, the more subtle perfume that rose off her skin.
The brilliant eyes held his.

"There is pain in you, a rawness that may never scab over
entirely," she said in a low voice. "It is this that drives you
on. You are a man without peace, Corfe, without hope of
peace. Was it Aekir?"

"My wife," he said, his voice half strangled in his throat.
"She died."

The fingertips brushed his face as lightly as a bee nuzzling
a flower. Her eyes seemed enormous: viridian orbs with
utter black at their core.

"I will help you," she said.

"Why?"

She leaned down. Her face seemed almost to glow. Her
breath stirred his forelock.

"Because I am only a woman, and I need a soldier to do
my killing for me." Her voice was as low as the bass note of
a lute, dark as heather honey. Her lips brushed his temple
and the hair on the back of his neck rose like the pelt of a
cat caught in a thunderstorm. They remained like that for
an endless second, breathing each other's breath.

Then she straightened, releasing him.

"I will procure a command for you," she said, suddenly
brisk. "A flying column. You will take it wherever I wish
to send it. You will do whatever it is I want you to do.
In return –" She hesitated and her smile made her seem
much younger. "In return, I will protect you, and I will
see that the intrigues of the court do not hamstring your
every move."

Corfe looked up at her from his stool. He was not tall;
even had he been standing their eyes would just have been
level with each other.

"I still don't understand."

"You will. One day you will. Go to the court chamberlain.
Tell him you have need of funds; if he objects, tell him to
come to me. Procure for yourself a more fitting wardrobe."

"What of the King?" Corfe asked.

"The King will do as he is told." she snapped, and he saw
the iron in her, the hidden strength. "That is all, Colonel.
You may go."

Corfe was bewildered. As he stood up she did not move away at once and he brushed against her. Then she turned away from him.

He bowed to her slender backbone, and left the chamber without another word.

It was a featureless, windswept land. Flat salt marshes spread out for miles in every direction but the sea. The only sounds were the piping of marsh birds and the hissing of the wind in the reeds. Off to the north-west the Hebros Mountains loomed, their knees already pale with snow.

The longboats were ferrying the last of the stores from the ship. The soldiers had lit fires on the firmer of the reed islands and were busy constructing shelters to keep out the searching wind. Abeleyn stood by one of the fires and stared out at the skewed hulk of the beached carrack. Dietl was beside him, his eyes red-rimmed with grief and pain. They had sealed his stump with boiling pitch, but the agony of seeing his ship in such a pass seemed to have affected him more than the loss of his hand.

"When I come into my kingdom again, you shall have the best carrack in the state fleet, Captain," Abeleyn told him gently.

Dietl shook his head. "Never was there such a ship. She broke my heart, faithful to the last."

They had heaved the guns overboard as the ship took on more and more water, then the heavier of the stores and finally the fresh water casks. The carrack had grounded upon a sandbar with the sea swirling around her hatches, and there had settled, canting to one side as the tide went out. It was a narrow bar, and as the supporting water withdrew her back had broken with an agonized screeching and groaning that seemed almost sentient.

Abeleyn clapped Dietl on his good shoulder and walked away from the fire. "Orsini!"

"Yes, sire." Sergeant Orsini was immediately on hand. He was the only soldier of any rank remaining with Abeleyn's company: the officers had gone down fighting in the two *nefs*.

"What have we got, Sergeant? How many and how much?"

Orsini blinked, his mind turning it over.

"Some sixty soldiers, sire, maybe a dozen of your own household attendants, and the remaining crew of the carrack numbers near thirty. But of that total, maybe twenty are wounded. There's two or three won't last out the night."

"Horses?" Abeleyn asked tersely.

"Drowned in the hold, most of 'em, sire, or shot through with splinters in the battle. We managed to get out your own gelding and three mules. It's all there is."

"Stores?"

Orsini looked at the mounds of waterlogged sacks, crates and casks that were piling up on the little island and its neighbours, half hidden in the yellow reed beds.

"Not much, sire, not for a hundred men. Supplies for a week if we're easy on 'em. Ten days at a pinch."

"Thank you, Sergeant. You'll have a guard rota set up, of course."

"Yes, sire. Nearly every man salvaged his arquebus, though the powder'll take a while to dry."

"Good work, Orsini. That's all."

The sergeant went back to his work. Abeleyn's mouth tightened as he watched the parties of soaked, bloodied and exhausted men setting up their makeshift camp on the soggy reed islands. They had fought a battle, struggled to bring a dying ship to shore, and now they would have to scrabble for survival on this remote coast. He had heard not a word of dissension or complaint. It humbled him.

He knew that they had beached somewhere south of the Habrir river; technically they were in Hebrion, the river marking the border between the kingdom and its attached duchy. This was a desolate portion of Abeleyn's dominions though, an extensive marshland which reached far inland and was crossed by only one or two causeway-raised Royal roads. There would be villages within a day's march, but no town of any significance for fifteen leagues – and that the city of Pontifidad, back to the north-east. Abrusio was over fifty leagues away, and to get to it overland they would have to cross the lower passes of the Hebros, where the mountains that were the backbone of Hebrion plunged precipitously into the sea.

A swoop of wings, and he turned to find Golophin's gyrfalcon perched on a thick reed behind him.

"Where have you been?" he asked shortly.

"The bird or I, sire? The bird has been resting, and well-earned the rest has been. I have been busy, though."

"Well?"

"Rovero and Mercado are ours, thank the Blessed Saints."

Abeleyn muttered a quiet prayer of thanks himself. "Then I can do it."

"Yes. There are other ramifications, though –"

"Talking to birds again, sire?" a woman's voice said. Golophin's familiar took off at once, leaving a barred feather circling in the air behind it.

The lady Jemilla was dressed in a long, fur-trimmed mantle of wool the colour of a cooling ember. She had let her thick mane of ebony hair tumble down about her face, emphasizing the paleness of her skin, and her lips were rouged. Of her pregnancy, some three months gone, there was as yet no visible sign.

Abeleyn's temper flickered a moment, but he mastered it. "You look well, lady."

"Last time you saw me, sire, I was prostrate, retching and green in the face. I should hope that I look well now, by contrast if nothing else." She came closer.

"I trust my men have made you comfortable?"

"Oh, yes," she replied, smiling. "They are such gallants at heart, your soldiers. They have built me a lovely shelter of canvas and driftwood, with a fire to warm it. I feel like the Queen of the Beachcombers."

"And the – the child?"

One hand went immediately to her still-flat belly. "Yet within me, as far as I can tell. My maid was convinced that the seasickness would put paid to it, but the child seems to be a fighter. As a king's child should be."

She was verging on insolence and Abeleyn knew it, but he had ignored her lately and the last few days must have been hard on her. So he merely bowed slightly in acknowledgement, not quite trusting himself to retort with civility.

Her voice changed; it lost its hard edge. "Sire, I apologize if I disturbed you in your... meditations. It is only that I have missed your company of late. My maid has set a skillet of wine on the fire to heat. Will you not join me in a glass?"

There were a million and one things he should be doing, and he was with child himself to hear Golophin's news; but the offer of hot wine was tempting, as was the other, unspoken offer in her eyes. Abeleyn was exhausted to the marrow. The thought of relaxing for a little while decided him. His men could do without him for an hour.

"Very well," he said, and he took the slim hand she extended and let himself be led away.

From its perch on a nearby bulrush, the gyrfalcon watched with cold, unblinking eyes.

HER SHELTER WAS cosy indeed, if a timber-framed canvas hut could be cosy. She had salvaged a couple of chests and some cloaks from the wreck; these did duty as furnishings.

She dismissed the maid and hauled off Abeleyn's bloody, salt-cracked boots with her own hands, tipping a trickle of water out of each; then she ladled out a pewter tankard of the steaming wine. Abeleyn sat and watched the flames of the fire turn from pale transparency to solid saffron as the day darkened. So short, the daylight hours at this time of year. A reminder that this was not the campaigning season, not the proper season for war.

The wine was good. He could almost feel it coursing through his veins and warming his chilled flesh. He recalled Jemilla's maid and ordered her to take the rest of it to the tents of the wounded. He saw Jemilla's lips thin as he did, and smiled to himself. The lady had her own ideas of worthy and unworthy, expendable and indispensable.

"Are you hurt, sire?" she asked. "Your doublet is bespattered with gore."

"Other men's, not mine," Abeleyn told her, sipping his wine.

"It was magnificent – all the soldiers say so. A battle worthy of Myrnius Kuln himself. Of course, I only heard it. Consuella and I were crouched in the stink of the lower hold under sacks; hardly a good post to observe the ebb and flow, the glory of it."

"It was a skirmish, no more," Abeleyn said. "I was careless to think we would get away so easily from Perigraine."

"The corsairs were in league with the other kings, then?" she asked, shocked.

"Yes, lady. I am a heretic. They want me dead – it is that simple. Using corsairs to kidnap or assassinate me rather than national troops was merely to utilize a certain discretion."

"Discretion!"

"Diplomacy has always been a mixture of cunning, courtesy and murder."

She placed a hand on her stomach, seemingly unaware of the gesture. "What of King Mark and King Lofantyr? Were attempts made on their lives?"

"I don't know. Possibly. In any case, when they arrive home they will face men of power who intend to take advantage of the situation. As I will."

"It is rumoured that Abrusio is in the control of the Church and the nobles," Jemilla said.

"Is it? Rumours are unreliable things."

"Are we still travelling to Abrusio, sire?"

"Of course. Where else?"

"I – I had thought –" She collected herself, squaring her shoulders like a woman determined to face bad news. "Are you to be married, sire?"

Abeleyn rubbed his eyes with one hand. "One day I hope to be, yes."

"To the sister of King Mark of Astarac?"

"More rumours?"

"It was the talk of Vol Ephrir when we left."

Abeleyn stared at her. "That rumour happens to be true, yes."

She dropped her eyes. There were also rumours that the lady Jemilla had had a low-born lover ere Abeleyn had taken her into his bed. She was not sure if the King had heard them.

"Then what of... what of the child I bear?" she asked pitifully.

Abeleyn knew his mistress to be one of the most calculating and accomplished women of his court, the widow of one of his father's best generals; but with his death, she was unrelated to any of the great families of Hebrion. That was one reason why he had allowed himself to be seduced by her: she was alone in this world, and did not belong to any of the power blocs which wrangled in the shadow of the Hebrian throne. She rose or fell on Abeleyn's whim. He could call in Orsini and have her run through here and now, and no one would raise a hand to defend her.

"The child will be looked after," he said. "If it happens to be a boy, and shows promise, then the lad will never lack for anything, I swear to you."

Her eyes were fixed on his, black stabs of colour in her ivory-pale face. Her hand alighted upon his knee.

"Thank you, sire. I have never been blessed with a child before. I hope only that he will grow up to serve you."

"Or she," Abeleyn added.

"It is a boy." She smiled, the first genuine smile Abeleyn had seen from her since leaving Hebrion. "He feels like a boy. I see him curled in my womb with his fists clenched, growing."

Abeleyn did not reply. He stared into the fire again, remembering the flame and wreck of the battle lately fought. A skirmish, he had called it, honestly enough. There was worse awaiting them in Abrusio. The Knights Militant would not vacate the city without a fight, and no doubt the personal retainers of the Sequeros and Carreras would stand shoulder to shoulder with them. But he would win, in the end. He had the army and the fleet at his back.

Jemilla's hand slid slowly upwards from the King's knee, bringing him out of his reverie. It began to stroke him intimately. "I thought in your condition..." he began.

She smiled. "There are many things a man and a woman can do together, your Majesty, even in my condition, and I have not taught you a tithe of them yet."

It was this quality in her that both pricked his pride and fascinated him. She was older, experienced, the tutor of his bed. But he was too weary. He lifted her hand away gently.

"There are things to do, lady. I do not have the time, even if the inclination is there."

Her eyes flared for a second: another thing about her which aroused him; she was unaccustomed to not getting her own way – even with a king, it seemed. It took an effort of will for Abeleyn to stand up. Her hand caressed his ankle, the fish-white skin which had not been wholly dry for days.

"Later, perhaps," she said.

"Perhaps. There will not be much time for it in the days to come, however."

He hauled on the clammy boots and kissed her.

She turned her cheek aside so his lips met her mouth. Then her tongue was questing like a warm snake over his teeth. She drew away with an arch smile. Abeleyn stumbled out of the hut into the firelit darkness beyond, feeling that once again she had somehow had the last word.

SEVEN

THE BARRICADES HAD gone up overnight.

When the deacon led his demi-troop out on their regular patrol of the city in the blue murk of the dawn, they found that the streets were occupied. Carts had been overturned, sacks and crates from the docks piled up and roped together. Even the narrowest of alleys had its obstacle, manned by citizens who had lit braziers against the cold and were standing round them rubbing their hands and chatting good-naturedly. Every street, roadway, avenue and alley which led down into the western half of the Lower City of Abrusio had been blocked off. The place had been sealed as tight as the neck of a stoppered bottle.

The deacon of the Knights Militant and his nine serving brethren sat their heavy horses and watched the Abrusian citizens and their makeshift fortifications with a mixture of anger and uncertainty. True, over the past weeks the Lower City had been an unfriendly place and any Knight who ventured down there was liable to have a chamber pot emptied over his head from an upper window. The Presbyter, Quirion, had ordered his men to stay away from the region whilst the delicate negotiations went on with the Abrusio garrison commanders. But this, this was different. This was open rebellion against the powers which had been ordained by the High Pontiff to rule the city.

The quiet horses with their heavy loads of steel and flesh stood their ground on the cobbles of the street, breathing out spumes of steam into the cold dawn air. It was a narrow place, the closely packed timber-framed houses of this part of the city leaning together overhead so that it seemed their terracotta tiles almost met to form an arch over the thoroughfare below. The citizens behind the barricade left their braziers to stare at the Knights. They were of both sexes, old and young. They carried makeshift weapons fashioned from agricultural implements, or simply hefted the tools of their trades: hammers and picks, scythes, pitchforks, butcher's cleavers. A weaponry as diverse as the colourful citizenry of Abrusio.

The shape of the city was like a horseshoe, within which was the trefoil outline of a cloverleaf. The horseshoe represented the confining outer walls, curving round to end on the northern and southern shores of the Southern Gulf, or the Gulf of Hebrion as it was sometimes called. The cloverleaf represented the three harbours within the walls. The northernmost blade of the leaf was the Inner Roads which extended into the heart of the city, the wharves and docks lapping at the very foot of Abrusio Hill. To left and right of it, and not so far inland, were the Outer Roads, two later-built harbours which had been improved by the addition of man-made moles. The western Inner Roads housed the shipyards and dry docks of the Hebrian navy and were frowned over by the bulk of Admiral's Tower. On a promontory to their north, another ageing fortress stood. This was the Arsenal, the barracks and magazines of Abrusio's garrison. Both fleet and army were therefore quartered in the western arm of the Lower City, and it was this area which had been blocked off by the barricades of the citizens.

But the earnest young deacon was not deliberating on that as he sat his horse in the early morning and wondered what to do. He knew only that a group of rabble had seen fit to deny passage to a demi-troop of the Knights Militant, the secular defenders of the Church on earth. It was an insult to the authority of the Pontiff himself.

"Out swords!" he ordered his men. They obeyed at once. Their lances had been left in their billets as they were inconveniently long to carry when traversing the narrow, packed streets of Lower Abrusio.

"Charge!"

The ten horsemen burst into a trot, then worked into a canter, the shoes of their mounts striking sparks off the cobbles. Two abreast, they thundered down the narrow street like avenging angels, if angels might be so laden with iron and mounted on steaming, wide-nostrilled warhorses.

The citizens stared at the approaching apocalypse for one moment, and then scattered. The barricades were deserted as people took to their heels, fleeing down the street or shouldering in the closed doors of houses on either side.

The deacon's mount struck the piled oddments which blocked the street and reared up, armour, rider and all, then scrambled over the barricade, tearing half of it down as it did so. The other Knights followed suit. The street became full of the din of nickering animals and the clang of steel. The up-ended cart fell back on to its wheels with a crash. They were through, urging their gasping mounts into a trot again, screaming "Ramusio!" at the top of their purpling lungs.

They clattered onwards. People were trying to dodge the heavy swords and the hooves of the destriers. The deacon clipped one fellow on the back of the head and took a chunk out of the base of his skull. When he went down, the horses trampled him into a steaming pulp.

Others too slow to hide or get away were smashed off their feet and suffered the same fate. There were no side alleyways, no way out. Several men and women were hacked as they thumped closed doors frantically with their fists, seeking sanctuary in the adjoining houses. The horses reared as they were trained to do, splintering bone and rending flesh with their ironshod forehooves. The street became a charnel house.

But it opened out. The streams of survivors scattered as the street became one arm of a three-way junction. There was a little square there.

The deacon was hoarse from yelling the Knights' battlecry, grinning as he swung and hacked at the fleeing mob. Sweat dripped off his nose and slicked his young body inside his armour. This was sport indeed.

But there was something in the air. An odd smell. He paused in his slaughter, puzzled. His men gathered about him panting, the gore dripping from their swords in viscous ribbons. The clattering chaos of a few moments before stilled.

Powder-smoke.

The end of the street had emptied of people. Standing there now were two ranks of Hebrian soldiers with streams of smoke eddying from the lighted match in their arquebuses.

Still the deacon did not fully understand. He kicked his mount forward, meaning to have a word with these fellows. They were in the way.

An officer at the end of the front rank lifted his sword. A pale winter sun was rising over the rooftops of the houses. It caught the steel of his rapier and turned it into a blaze.

"Ready your pieces!"

The arquebusiers cocked back the serpentine locks which held the glowing match.

"Front rank, kneel!"

The front rank did so.

"Wait!" the deacon shouted angrily. What did these men think they were doing? Behind him, his brother Knights looked on in alarm. One or two began kicking their tired horses into life.

"Front rank, give fire!"

"*No!*" the deacon yelled.

An eruption of flame and smoke, a furious rolling crackle. The deacon was blasted off his horse. His men staggered in the saddle. Horses were screaming as the balls ripped through their iron armour and into their flesh. The massive animals tumbled to the ground, crushing their riders beneath them. A fog of smoke toiled in the air, filling the breadth of the street.

In the powder-smoke, the surviving Knights heard the officer's voice again.

"Rear rank, present your pieces."

The surviving Knights turned as one to the enemy and savagely urged their terrified horses into a canter. Shrieking like fiends they charged down the street into the smoke, determined to avenge their fallen brethren.

They were met by a second storm of gunfire.

All of them went down. The momentum of the two lead riders carried them into the ranks of the arquebusiers, and the horses collapsed through the formation scattering the Hebrian soldiers like skittles. One of the Knights was flung clear, clanging across the cobbles. As he struggled to his feet in the heavy armour that the Knights wore, two Hebrian soldiers flipped him on his back again, as though he were a monstrous beetle. They stood on his wrists, pinioning him, then ripped off his casque and cut his throat.

A final shot as a moaning horse was put out of its pain. From the doors of the houses the people emerged. A ragged cheer went up as they saw the riddled corpses which littered the roadway, though some went to their knees in the clotted gore, cradling the head of a butchered friend or relative. The keening cries of women replaced the cheering.

The citizens of Abrusio rebuilt their barricades whilst the Hebrian soldiers methodically reloaded their weapons and resumed their hidden stations once more.

"I DON'T BELIEVE it!" Presbyter Quirion said. Abrusio stretched out, mist-shrouded and sun-gilded, in the morning light. He blinked as the sound of arquebus fire came again, echoing over the packed rooftops to the monastery-tower wherein he stood.

"So far three of our patrols have been ambushed," the Knight-Abbot said. "Skirmishing goes on even as we speak. Our casualties have been serious. We are cavalry, without firearms. We are not equipped to fight street battles with foes who possess arquebuses."

"And you are sure it is the Hebrian soldiery who are involved, not civilians with guns?"

"Yes, your Excellency. All our brothers report the same thing: when they try to force the barricades, they are met with disciplined gunnery. It has to be the garrison troops; there can be no other explanation."

Quirion's eyes were blue fires.

"Recall our brethren. There is no profit in them throwing themselves under the guns of rebels and heretics."

"Yes, your Excellency."

"And have all officers above the rank of deacon assemble in the speech-hall at noon. I'll address them myself."

"At once, your Excellency." The Knight-Abbot made the Sign of the Saint on his armoured breast and left.

"What does this mean?" the Presbyter asked.

"Would you like me to find out for you?" Sastro di Carrera said, one hand fiddling with the ruby set in his earlobe.

Quirion turned to face his companion squarely. They were the only occupants of the high-ceilinged room.

"No."

"You don't like me, your Excellency. Why is that?"

"You are a man without much faith, Lord Carrera. You care only for your own advantage."

"Doesn't everyone?" Sastro asked smiling.

"Not everyone. Not my brothers... *Do* you know anything about these developments then?"

Sastro yawned, stretching out his long arms. "I can deduce as well or better than the next man. My bet is that Rovero and Mercado have somehow had a communication from our ex-King Abeleyn. They have come down on his side at last – another reason why they postponed the viewing of the Pontifical bull scheduled yesterday. The army and the fleet will hold the Lower City against us until Abeleyn arrives in person, then go over on to the offensive. It is also my guess that your Knights were not meant to be slain; they pressed too hard. Obviously the general and the admiral meant this to look like a popular uprising, but they had to use national troops to defend their perimeter when your brethren tested it."

"Then we know where we stand," Quirion snarled. His face looked as though invisible strings had pulled chin and forehead towards each other; fury had clenched it as it might a fist. "They will be excommunicated," he went on. "I will see them burn. But first we must crush this uprising."

"That may not be so easy."

"What of your friend Freiss?" And when Sastro seemed genuinely surprised, Quirion's bass gravelled out a harsh laugh. "You think I did not know of your meetings with him? I will not let you play a private game in this city, my Lord Carrera. You will pull alongside the rest of us, or you will not be a player at all."

Sastro regained his composure, shrugging. His hand toyed now with the gleaming, scented point of his beard. He needed to toy with his features constantly, it seemed to Quirion. An irritating habit. The man was probably a pederast; he smelled like a sultan's harem. But he was the most effective of the nobles, and a necessary ally.

"Very well," Sastro said casually. "My friend Freiss, as you put it, says he has won over several hundred men of the garrison, men who cannot stomach heresy and who expect to be rewarded for their loyalty once the Church has assumed full control of Abrusio."

"Where are they?"

"In barracks. Mercado has his suspicions and has segregated them from the other tercios. He is probably having them watched also."

"Then they are of little use to us."

"They could stage a diversion while your brethren assault these absurd barricades."

"My brethren are not equipped for street fighting, as you have already heard. No, there must be another way."

Sastro regarded the ornate plasterwork of the ceiling with some interest. "There are, of course, my personal retainers..."

"How many?"

"I could muster maybe eight hundred if I called out some of the lesser client houses as well."

"Their arms?"

"Arquebuses and sword-and-buckler men. No pikes, but then pikes are no better at street fighting than cavalry."

"That would be ideal. They could cover an assault by my brethren. How long would it take to muster them?"

"A few days."

The two men looked at each other like a pair of prize-fighters weighing up each other's strengths and weaknesses in the ring. "You realize I would be risking my house, my followers, ultimately my fortune," Sastro drawled.

"The Hebrian treasury is in the possession of the council. You would be amply compensated," Quirion growled.

"That is not what I was thinking of," Sastro said. "No, money is not my main concern. It is just that my men like to fight for the betterment of their lord's situation as well as their own."

"They would be defending the True Faith of the Ramusian kingdoms. Is that not reward enough?"

"It should be, I know, my dear Presbyter. But not all men are as... single-minded, you might say, as your brethren."

"What do you want, Lord Carrera?" Quirion asked, though he thought he already knew.

"You are looking through the archives, are you not, trying to establish who should take the throne now that the Hibrusid line is finished?"

"I have Inceptine archivists working on it, yes."

"You will find, I think, that Astolvo di Sequero is the most eligible candidate. But he is an old man. He does not want the kingship with all that it entails. He will refuse it."

"Are you so sure?"

"Oh, yes. And his sons are flighty, vicious young things. Hardly Royal material. You will need the next king of Hebrion to be a mature man, a man of abilities, a man who is happy to work hand in gauntlet with the holy Church. Otherwise the other noble houses might get restless, mutinous even, at the idea of one of Astolvo's brats ruling."

"Where might we find such a man?" Quirion asked guardedly. He had not missed the threat in Sastro's words.

"I am not sure, but if your archivists delve deep enough I believe they may find the house of Carrera closer to the throne than you think."

Quirion laughed his coarse laugh – the guffaw of a commoner, Sastro thought with disgust, though nothing of his feelings showed on his face.

"The kingship in return for your men, my lord?" the Presbyter said.

Sastro raised his carefully trimmed eyebrows. "Why not? No one else will make you a similar offer, I'll warrant."

"Not even the Sequeros?"

"Astolvo will not. He knows that were he to do so his life would be hanging by a thread. His sons are champing at the bit beneath him; he would not last a year. How would that look? The Church-sponsored monarchy of Hebrion embroiled in murderous intrigue, perhaps even parricide, within months of its establishment."

Quirion looked thoughtful, gauging. "Such decisions of moment must be referred to Himerius in Charibon. The Pontiff will have the final word."

"The Pontiff, may the Saints be good to him, will no doubt follow the recommendations of his representative on the spot."

Quirion repaired to the table on which sat a host of decanters.

He poured himself a dribble of wine and drank it off, grimacing. He did not imbibe as a rule, but he felt the need of the warming liquid; there was a chill in the room.

"Get word to your co-conspirator, Freiss," he said. "Tell him to prepare his men for action. And start gathering your own followers together, Lord Carrera. We must work on a combined plan."

"Will there then be a messenger sent to Charibon with your recommendations?" Sastro asked.

"There will. I will... advise my archivists to look into the genealogy of your house."

"A wise decision, Presbyter. You are obviously a man of sagacity."

"Perhaps. Now that the bargaining is done, can we attend to the more mundane details? I want rosters, equipment lists."

The man has no style, Sastro thought. *No sense of the moment*. But that was by-the-by. He had secured the kingship for himself; that was the main thing. He had negotiated a path to power. But he had not arrived at its threshold, not yet. There remained much to be done.

"I will have everything ready for you to peruse this afternoon," he said smoothly. "And I will have couriers sent to my estates and those of my vassals. The men will begin assembling directly."

"Good. This thing must be done quickly. If we cannot storm the Lower City before Abeleyn arrives, it will be the work of several campaigns to secure Abrusio, with all the destruction that entails."

"Indeed. I have no wish to rule over a hill of ashes."

Quirion stared at his aristocratic companion. "The new king will rule in conjunction with the Church. I have no doubt that the Pontiff will wish to maintain a garrison of the Knights here, even after the rebels are extinguished."

"They will be an inestimable help, a valued adjunct to Royal authority."

Quirion nodded. "Just so we understand each other. Now if you will excuse me, my Lord Carrera, I must prepare to address my brethren. And there are wounded to visit."

"By all means. Will you give me your blessing before I go, Excellency?"

Sastro rose, then knelt before the Presbyter with his head bowed. Quirion's face spasmed. He grated out the words of the blessing as though they were a curse. The nobleman regained his feet, made the Sign of the Saint with mocking flamboyance and left the room.

OVER FIVE HUNDRED leagues away, the Thurian Mountains were thick and white with midwinter snows. The last of the passes had been closed and the sultanate of Ostrabar was sealed off to the west and the south by the mountain barrier, itself merely an outlying range of the fearsome Jafrar Mountains farther east.

The tower had once been part of the upland castle of a Ramusian noble, one of the hundreds which had dotted the rich vales of Ostiber in the days when it had been a Ramusian kingdom. But it was different now. For sixty years the Merduk overlords had possessed the rich eastern region. Its ruler was Aurungzeb the Golden, the Stormer of Aekir, and the people he ruled had come to accept the Merduk yoke, as it was called in the west. They tilled their fields as they had always done and by and large they were no worse off under their Merduk lords than they had been under the Ramusian ones.

True, their sons must needs serve a stint in the Sultan's armies, but for the most talented of them there was no bar to ambition. If a man had ability, he might rise very high in the service of the Sultan no matter how low his birth. It was one of the cunning ways in which the Merduks had reconciled the people to their rule, and it brought continual new blood into the army and the administration. The grandfathers of the men who had fought under the banners of Ahrimuz the Prophet at Aekir and Ormann Dyke had struggled against those same banners two generations before. For the peasantry it was a pragmatic choice. They were tied to their land and when it changed owners they would change masters as a matter of course.

Most of the upland castle was in ruins, but one wing with its tall tower remained intact and it gave a fine view of the valleys below. On a clear day it was even possible to see Orkhan, the capital of the Sultan, glittering with minarets in the distance. But the castle was isolated. Built too high in the Thurian foothills, it had been deserted even before the Merduks came, its occupants forced out by the severity of the upland winters.

Sometimes the local inhabitants lower in the valley would remark upon the dark tower standing alone on the wintry heights above. It was rumoured that strange lights could be seen flashing in its windows after dark, and there were tales of inhuman beasts which roamed the fells around it in nights of moon. Sheep had gone missing, and a boy herder had disappeared. No one dared to approach the old ruin, though, and it was left to its malignant contemplation of the dales below.

THE BEAST TURNED from the window and its monochrome world of white snow and black trees and distant lights. It shuffled across the circular tower chamber and sank into a padded chair before the fire with a sigh. The endless wind was moaning about the gaps in the roof and occasional confettis of snow would flutter in the glassless window.

A beast was dressed in human robes, and its head was like some grotesque marriage of humanity and reptile. The body was awkward and bent, and talons scraped the flagged floor in place of toes. Only the hands remained recognizably human, though they were treble-jointed and slightly scaled, reflecting back the firelight with a green tint.

Other things reflected back the firelight also. Arranged around the walls on shelves were great glass carboys full of liquid, the light of the flames kindling answering shines from their depths. In some floated the small grey corpses of newborn babies, eyes shut as though they were still dreaming in the womb. In others were the coiled bodies of large snakes, their sides flattened against the glass. And in three of the fat-bellied jars, dark bipedal shapes stood gazing down into the room with eyes that were the merest gleeds of bright incarnadine. They moved restlessly in the surrounding liquid, as though impatient at their confinement.

The room was full of a sour smell, like clothes left lying out in the rain. On a small table in front of the hearth was a silver salver upon which smoked the dying ashes of a tiny fire. There were small bones in the ashes, the miniature egg-sized remnant of a fanged skull.

The thing in the chair leaned forward and poked at the ashes with one long forefinger. Its eyes glittered. With a furious gesture it sent ashes, salver and all flying into the fire. Then it leaned back in the chair, hissing.

From a niche near the ceiling the winged shape of a homunculus fluttered down like a gargoyle in miniature. It settled on the beast's shoulder and nuzzled the wattled neck.

"Easy, Olov. It is no matter," the beast said, patting the distressed little creature. And then: "Batak!"

A door opened at the rear of the chamber and a man dressed in travelling clothes of fur-lined cape and high boots entered. He was young, his eyes coal-black, earlobes heavy with gold rings. His face was as pale as plaster and he was sweating despite the season.

"Master?"

"It failed again – as you can see. I merely destroyed another homunculus."

The young man came forward. "I am sorry."

"Yes, you are. Pour me some wine, will you, Batak?"

The young man did so silently. His hand was shaking and he mopped spilt liquid with one corner of his sleeve, darting frightened glances at the thing in the chair as he did so.

The beast took the proffered wine and threw it back, tilting its head like a chicken to drink. The crystal of the goblet cracked within its digits. The beast regarded the object with a weary irritation, then threw the flawed thing to shatter in the fire.

"The whole world is new to me," it muttered.

"What will you do now, master? Are you going to undertake the journey?"

The beast looked at him with bright, fulvid eyes. The air around it seemed to shimmer for a second and the homunculus took off for the rafters with a squeak. When the air steadied once more there was a man sitting there in place of the beast, a lean, dark-skinned man with a face as fine-boned as that of a woman. Only the eyes remained of the former monster, lemon-bright and astonishing in the handsome visage.

"Does this make you less nervous, Batak?"

"It is good to see your face again, master."

"I can only hold this form for a few hours at a time, and the eyes resist any change. Perhaps because they are the windows of the soul, as it is said." The man smiled without the slightest trace of humour. "But in answer to your question: yes, I will undertake the journey. The Sultan's agents are already in Alcaras hiring ships – big, ocean-going ships, not the galleys of the Levangore. I have an escort and a carriage billeted down in the village; the Sultan means to be sure I go where I say I am going."

"Into the uttermost west. Why?"

The man stood and put his back to the fire, splaying his hands out against the heat. There was a flickering blur, like a ripple of shadow around his silhouette. Dweomer-born illusions were always unstable in bright light.

"There is something out there, in the west. I know it. In my research I have come across legends, myths, rumours. They all point to the same conclusion: there is land in the west, and something else. Someone, perhaps. Besides, I am little use to the Sultan as I am. When Shahr Baraz – may he rot in a Ramusian hell – destroyed the homunculus which was my conductor he not only warped my body, he crippled the Dweomer within me. I am still powerful, still Orkh the master-mage, but my powers are not what they were. I would not have that come to light, Batak."

"Of course. I –"

"You will be discreet. I know. You are a good apprentice. In a few years you will have mastered the Fourth Discipline and you will be a mage yourself. I have left you enough of my library and materials for you to continue your studies even without my guidance."

"It is the court, master, the harem. They unsettle me. There is more to being the Sultan's sorcerer than Dweomer."

Orkh smiled, this time with some real warmth. "I know, but that is something else you must learn. Do not cross the vizier, Akran. And court the eunuchs of the harem. They know everything. And never reveal to the Sultan the limits of your power – never say you cannot do something. Prevaricate, obfuscate, but do not admit to any weakness. Men think mages all-powerful. We want to keep it that way."

"Yes, master. I will miss you. You have been a good teacher."

"And you a good pupil."

"Do you hope to be healed in the west? Is that it? Or are you merely removing yourself from the sight of men?"

"Aurungzeb asked me the same thing. I do not know, Batak. I weary of being a monster, that much I do know. Even a leper does not know the isolation I have suffered, the loneliness. Olov has been my only companion; he is the only creature which looks upon me without fear or disgust."

"Master, I –"

"It is all right, Batak. There is no need to pretend. In my research, I have discovered that several times in the past centuries ships have sailed for the west and have not returned. They carried passengers – sorcerers fleeing persecution in the Ramusian states. I do not believe that all those ships were lost. I believe there may be survivors or descendants of survivors out there still."

Batak's eyes grew round. "And you think they will be able to heal you?"

"I don't know. But I weary of the intrigues at court. I want to see a new horizon appear with every dawn. And it suits Aurungzeb's policies. The Ramusians have already sent a flotilla westwards; it left Abrusio months ago under a Gabrionese captain named Richard Hawkwood. They should be in the west now. The Merduk sultanates cannot allow this new world to be claimed by our enemies. I concur with Aurungzeb in that."

"You know that Shahr Baraz is not dead? He disappeared along with his pasha, Mughal. It is said they rode off eastwards, back into the steppes."

"I know. My revenge may never happen. He will leave his pious old bones in the Jafrar, or on the endless plains of Kambaksk. It matters not. Other things concern me now."

Orkh left the fire and strode over to a nearby table which supported an iron-bound chest. He opened the lid, looked in, nodded, then turned to his apprentice once more.

"In here you will find the details of my intelligence network. Names of agents, cyphers, dates of payments – everything. It is up to you to run it, Batak. I have men in every kingdom in the west, most of them risking their lives each day. That is a responsibility which I do not hand over lightly. No one else must ever see the contents of this chest. You will secure it with your most potent spells, and destroy it if there is a possibility of it falling into any other hands except your own – even Aurungzeb's. Do you understand?"

Batak nodded dumbly.

"There is also a more select network of homunculi, some dormant, some active. I have them planted everywhere, even in the harem. They are the eyes and ears you can trust most, for they are without bias or self-interest. When their bellies are full, at any rate. Use them well; and be discreet. They can be a useful cross-reference to back up the reports of your agents. When you are ready for a familiar, I would advise you to choose a homunculus. They can be wayward, but the ability to fly is always a help and their night vision is invaluable." Here Orkh's mouth tilted upwards. "Olov has shown me some rare sights in his nocturnal patrols of the harem. The most recent Ramusian concubine is a delight to behold. Aurungzeb takes her twice nightly, as eagerly as a boy. He has little notion of subtlety, though."

The mage collected himself.

"At any rate, there is amusement to be had if you use your resources properly, but if you gain information which you should not know I do not have to tell you to keep it to yourself, no matter how useful it might prove. The network must be safeguarded at all costs."

"Yes, master."

Orkh stepped away from the chest. "It is yours, then. Use it wisely."

Batak took the chest in his arms as though it were made of glass.

"You may go. I find the maintenance of this appearance wearisome. When you ride through the village, tell the escort rissaldar that I will be ready to leave at moonrise tomorrow night. I have some final packing to do."

Batak bowed awkwardly. As he went out of the door he turned. "Thank you, master."

"When you see me again – if you do – it will be as a mage, a master of four of the Seven Disciplines. On that day you shall take me by the hand and call me Orkh."

Batak smiled uncertainly. "I shall look forward to that."

Then he left.

THE SNOW WAS as crisp as biscuit underfoot and the taloned feet of the beast cracked the surface crust, but the widespread toes stopped it from sinking any deeper. Naked and scaled, its tail whipping back and forth restlessly, it prowled the streets of the sleeping village. The moon glittered from its skin as though it were armoured in many-faceted silver. The glowing eyes blinked as it eased open the shutter of a cottage with inhuman, silent strength. A dark room within, a tiny shape blanket-wrapped in the cradle.

It took the bundle out into the hills, and there it fed, dipping its snout into the steaming, broken body. Sated at last, it raised its head and stared up at the savage, snow-gleaming peaks of the encircling mountains. West, where the sun had set. Where a new life awaited it, perhaps.

It cleaned its snout in the snow. With a bestial form came bestial appetites. But it saved a morsel of the child for Olov.

EIGHT

THEY WERE INTONING the Glory to God, the *terdiel* which brought Matins to a close. For centuries, the monks and clerics of Charibon had sung it in the early hours of every new day, and the simple yet infinitely beautiful melody was taken up by half a thousand voices to echo into the beams and rafters of the cathedral.

The benches of the monks lined the walls of the triangular cathedral's base. Monsignors, presbyters and bishops had their own individual seats at the back with ornately carved armrests and kneeling boards. The Inceptines assembled on the right, the other orders – mostly Antillian, but with a few Mercurians – on the left. As the monks sang, an old Inceptine with a candle lantern went up and down the rows, nudging any of the brethren who had nodded off. If they happened to wear the white hoods of novices they would receive a kick and a glare rather than a shake of their shoulder.

Himerius the High Pontiff had joined his fellow clerics for Matins this morning, something he rarely did. He was seated facing his brethren, his Saint's symbol glittering in the light of a thousand beeswax candles. His hawk's profile was clearly picked out by the candlelight as he sang.

Elsewhere in Charibon, the thousands of other clerics were also awake and paying homage to their God. At this time in the morning Charibon was a city of voices, it was said, and fishermen in their boats out on the Sea of Tor would hear the ghostly plainchant drifting out from shore, a massed prayer which was rumoured to still the waves and bring the fish to the surface to listen.

Matins ended, and there was a clamour of scraping benches and shuffling feet as the singers rose to their feet row by row. The High Pontiff left the cathedral first in the company of the Inceptine Vicar-General, Betanza. Then the senior churchmen filed out, and then the Inceptines. Last in the orderly throng to leave would be the novices, their stomachs rumbling, their noses red with early morning chill. The crowds would splinter as the clerics made their way to the various refectories of the orders for bread and buttermilk, the unchanging breakfast of Charibon's inhabitants.

HIMERIUS AND BETANZA had not far to go to the Pontifical apartments, but they took a turn around the cloisters first, their hands tucked in their habits, their hoods pulled up over their heads. The cloisters were deserted at this time of the morning as everyone trooped into the refectories for breakfast.

It was dark, the winter morning some time away as yet. The moon had set, though, and the predawn stars were bright as pins in a sky of unsullied aquamarine. The breath of the two senior clerics was a white mist about their hoods as they walked the serene, arched circuit of the cloisters. There was snow in the air; it was thick in the mountains but Charibon had as yet received only a tithe of its usual share. The heavy falls would come within days, and the shores of the Sea of Tor would grow beards of ice upon which the novices would skate and skylark in the little free time they had. It was a ritual, a routine as old as the monastery-city itself, and absurdly comforting to both the men who now walked in slow silence about the empty cloisters.

Betanza, the bluff ex-duke from Astarac, threw back his hood and paused to stare out across the starlit gardens within the cloisters. Trees there, ungainly oaks purportedly planted before the empire fell. In the spring the brown grass would explode with snowdrops, then daffodils and primroses as the year turned. They were dormant now, sleeping out the winter under the frozen earth.

"The purges have begun across the continent," he said quietly. "In Almark and Perigraine and Finnmark. In the duchies and the principalities they are herding them by the thousand."

"A new beginning," the High Pontiff said, his nose protruding like a raptor's beak from his hood. "The faith has been in need of this. A rejuvenation. Sometimes it takes an upheaval, a crisis, to breathe new life into our beliefs. We are never so sure of them as we are when they are threatened."

Betanza smiled sourly. "We have our crisis. Religious schism on a vast scale, and a war with the unbelievers of the east which threatens the very existence of the Ramusian kingdoms."

"Torunna is no longer Ramusian," Himerius corrected him quickly. "Nor is Astarac. They have heretics on their thrones. Hebrion, thank God, is coming under the sway of the true Church once more. The bull will have reached Abrusio by now, unlike its heretical king. Abeleyn is finished. Hebrion is ours."

"And Fimbria?" Betanza asked.

"What of it?"

"More rumours. It is said that a Fimbrian army is on the march eastwards to the relief of Ormann Dyke."

Himerius waved a hand. "Talk is a farthing a yard. Have we any more word of the Almarkan king's condition?"

Haukir, the aged and irascible monarch of Almark, was laid low by a fever. The winter journey homewards from the Conclave of Kings had started it. He was bedridden, without issue, and more foul-tempered than ever.

"The commander of the Almarkan garrisons here received word yesterday. He is dying. By now he may even be dead."

"We have people on hand?"

"Prelate Marat is at his bedside; the two are said to be natural brothers on the father's side."

"Whatever. Marat must be present at the end, and the will with him."

"You truly believe that Haukir may leave his kingdom to the Church?"

"He has no one else save a clutch of sister-sons who amount to nothing. And he has always been a staunch ally of the Inceptine Order. He would have entered it himself had he not been born Royal; he said as much to Marat before the conclave."

Betanza was silent, thoughtful. Were the Church to inherit the resources of Almark, one of the most powerful kingdoms in the west, it would be unassailable. The anti-Pontiff, or imposter rather, Macrobius, and those monarchs who had recognized him, would face a Church which had become overnight a great secular state.

"Quite an empire we are building up for ourselves," Betanza said mildly.

"The empire of Ramusio on earth. We are witnessing the symmetry of history, Betanza. The Fimbrian empire was secular, and was brought down by religious wars which established the True Faith across the continent. Now is the time of the second empire, a religious hegemony which will raise up the Kingdom of God on earth. That is my mission. It is why I became Pontiff."

Himerius's eyes were shining in the depths of his hood. Betanza remembered the wheeling and dealing which had secured Himerius the Pontiffship, the bargaining. Perhaps he was naive. Though head of the Inceptine Order, he had been a lay nobleman until quite late in life. It gave him a different outlook on things which at times made him oddly uncomfortable.

"Dawn comes," he said, watching the glow of the approaching sun in the east. He felt an obscure urge to throw himself face down on the ground and pray; a dread and apprehension the like of which he had never experienced before rose in him like a breeding darkness.

"Do you recall *The Book of Honorius*, Holy Father? How does it go?

"'And the Beast shall come upon the earth in the days of the second empire of the world. And he shall rise up out of the west, the light in his eyes terrible to behold. With him shall come the Age of the Wolf, when brother will slay brother. And all men shall fall down and worship him.'"

"Honorius was a crazed hermit, a Friar Mendicant. His ravings verge on the heretical."

"And yet he knew Ramusio, and was one of his closest followers."

"The Blessed Saint had many followers, Betanza, among them a proportion of lunatics and mystics. Keep your mind on the present. We go to meet the Arch-Presbyter of the Knights Militant this morning to talk to him about recruiting. The Church needs a strong right arm, not a perusal of ancient apocalyptic hallucinations."

"Yes, Holy Father," Betanza said.

The two resumed their walk around the quiet cloisters of Charibon while the silent dawn broke open the sky above them.

ALBREC HAD MISSED Matins, and he did not go down to breakfast. His stomach was as closed as a stone and he was kneeling in prayer on the hard stone floor of his frigid little cell. The dawn light was slanting in through the narrow window making the lit candle he had been reading by seem dim and yellow. On the table before him the pages of the old document had been laid out in orderly piles.

He rose at last, his pointed face deeply troubled, and sat before the table where he had spent most of the night. One hand snuffed out the candle as the rising sunlight stole into the room, and the smoke from the extinguished wick writhed back and forth in front of his eyes in grey wires and strings. The eyes were rimmed in scarlet.

He turned over the leaves of the document yet again, and his movements were as ginger as if he expected the pages to explode into flame at any second.

"The winter of a man's life," said the Saint, *"is the time when all those around him take the measure of all he has done and sought to do. And all that he has failed to accomplish. My brothers, I have set in this soil a garden, a thing which is pleasing in the sight of God. It is yours to tend now. Nothing can uproot it, for it grows in men's hearts also: that one place where a tyrant's fist can never reach. The Empire is failing and a New Order begins, one based on the truth of things, and the compassion of God's own plans.*

"But for myself, my work here is done. Others will do the teaching and the preaching now. I am only a man, and an old one at that."

"What will you do?" we asked him.

The Saint lifted his head in the morning light which was breaking over this hillside in the province of Ostiber; for we had talked and prayed the night away.

"I go to plant the garden elsewhere."

"But the faith is spread across all Normannia," we said. "Even the Emperor has begun to see that it can no longer be suppressed. Where else is there to go?" And we begged him to remain with us and live in peace and honour among his followers, who would revere him all the remaining days of his life.

"That is the way of pride," he said, shaking his head. And then he laughed. "Would you set me up as a wrinkled idol to be venerated as the tribes of old worshipped their gods? No, friends. I must go. I have seen the road stretching ahead of me. It goes on a long way from here yet."

"There is nowhere to go," we protested, for we were afraid of losing his leadership in the great trials which still awaited us. But also we loved this old man. Ramusio had become father to us and the world without him would seem a drear and empty place.

"There is a far country which the truth has not yet reached," he told us. And then he pointed eastwards, to where the Ostian river foamed sunlit and brilliant between its banks, and farther away the black heights of the Jafrar which mark the beginning of the wilderness beyond. "Out there it is night still, but I may yet use the years remaining to me to usher in the morning in the land beyond yon mountains."

A teardrop dripped off Albrec's nose to land on the precious page below, and he blotted it at once, angry with himself.

He could see the sunshine of that long-ago morning, when the Blessed Saint had stood in the twilight of his life on a hillside in Ostiber – or Ostrabar as it was now – and had talked with the closest of his followers, themselves grown old in their travels with him. St. Bonneval was there, who was to become the first Pontiff of the holy Church, and St. Ubaldius of Neyr, who would be the first Vicar-General of the Inceptine Order. The men who watched that sunrise break over the eastern mountains would become the founding fathers of the Ramusian faith, canonized and revered by later generations, prayed to by the common people, immortalized in a thousand statues and tapestries across the world.

But that morning, in the early light of a day gone by these five centuries and more, they were merely a group of men afraid and grieved by the thought of losing he who had been their mentor, their leader, the mainstay of their lives.

And who was the mysterious narrator? Who was the writer of this precious document? Had he really been there, one of the chosen few who had accompanied the Blessed Saint through the provinces of the empire, spreading the faith?

Albrec turned through the crumbling pages, mourning the lost leaves, the illegible paragraphs.

That morning in Ostrabar was a day sacred to the Church and all Ramusians. It was the last day of the Saint's life on earth. He had been assumed into heaven from the hillside, his followers watching as God took to his bosom this the most faithful of his servants. Until Ostiber had fallen to the Merduks and become Ostrabar, the hilltop had been a holy place of pilgrimage for the Ramusians of the continent, and a church had been built there within a few years of the miraculous event.

At least, that was what Albrec and every other member of the Ramusian faith had been taught. But the document told an entirely different story.

He took no companion and would accept no company, and he forbade those he was to leave behind ever to follow him. On a mule he left us, his face towards the east, from whence the morning comes. And the last we saw of him, he was in the lower passes of the mountains, the mule bearing him ever higher. So he was lost to the west for ever.

It was this and the succeeding pages which had kept Albrec up all night, reading and praying until his eyes smarted and his knees were cold and sore from the flags of the floor. Nothing here of an assumption into heaven, a glorious vision of the Saint entering God's kingdom. Ramusio had last been seen as a tiny figure on a mule headed into the heights of the most terrible mountains in the world. The implications of that made Albrec tremble.

But the story did not end there. There was more.

Among the folk who went to and fro across the borders of the empire at that time, there was a merchant named Ochali, a Merduk who every year braved the passes of the Jafrar with his camel trains, bringing silks and furs and steppe ivory to trade from the lands of Kurasan and Kambaksk beyond the mountains. He was a worshipper of the Horned One, like all those who lived beyond the Ostian river. Kerunnos was the forbidden name he and his people gave to their God, and when he reached the provinces of the empire every summer he would give sacrifice at the roadside shrines of the tribes for a safe passage of the Jafrar. But one summer, some eight years after Ramusio had journeyed east, he neglected to make his usual sacrifices to the Horned One.

Men who knew him asked why, and he told them that he had found a new faith, a true faith which owed nothing to sacrifices or idols. An old man, he said, had been preaching in the camps of the steppe peoples for several years now, and his words had gained him many followers. A new religion was birthing in the far lands of the Merduks, and even the horse chieftains had taken it to heart.

When Ochali's acquaintances in the province of Ostiber pressed him further he refused to elaborate, saying only that the Merduk peoples had found a prophet, a holy leader who was taking them out of the darkness and putting an end to the interminable clan wars which had always racked his people. Merduk no longer slew Merduk in the distant steppes beyond the Jafrar, and the men who abode there lived in harmony and brotherhood. The Prophet Ahrimuz had shown his people the one true path to salvation.

There was a thumping at Albrec's door and he jumped like a startled hare. He had time to cover the ancient document with his catechism before the door opened and Brother Commodius walked in, his big bare feet slapping on the stone floor.

"Albrec! You were missed at Matins. Is everything all right?" The Senior Librarian looked his normal ugly self; the face regarding Albrec with concern and curiosity was the same one the monk had worked with for nearly thirteen years. The same huge beak of a nose, out-thrust ears and unruly fringe of hair about the bald tonsure. But Albrec would never again see it as just another face, not after the night in the lowest levels of the library.

"I – I'm fine," he stammered. "I didn't feel well, Brother. I have a bit of a flux so I thought it better to stay away. I'm going to the privy every few minutes." Lies, lies and sins. But that could not be helped. It was in a greater cause.

"You should see the Brother Infirmiar then, Albrec. It's no good sitting here and reading your catechism, waiting for it to go away. Come, I'll take you."

"No, brother – it's all right. You go and open the library, I've made you late enough as it is."

"Nonsense!"

"No, truly, Brother Commodius, I can't keep you from your duties. I'll visit him myself. Perhaps I'll see you after Compline. I'm sure an infusion of arrowroot will set me up."

The Senior Librarian shrugged his immense, bony shoulders. "Very well, Albrec, have it your own way." He turned to go, then hesitated on the threshold. "Brother Columbar tells me that you and he were down in the catacombs beneath the library."

Albrec opened his mouth, but no sound came out.

"Seeking blotting for the scriptorium, it seems. And I dare say you were doing a little ferreting around on your own account, eh, Albrec?" Commodius's eyes twinkled. "You want to be careful down there. A man might have an accident among all that accumulated rubbish. There's a warren of tunnels and chambers that have not been disturbed since the days of the empire. They're best left that way, eh?"

Albrec nodded, still speechless.

"I know you, Albrec. You would mine knowledge as though it were gold. But the possession of knowledge is not always good; some things are better left undiscovered... Did you find Gambio's blotting paper?"

"Some, Brother. We found some."

"Good. Then you will not need to go down there again, will you? Well, I must go. As you say, I am late. There will be a huddle of scholar-monks congregated round the door of St. Garaso thinking uncharitable thoughts about me. I hope your bowels clear up soon, Brother. There is work to be done." And Commodius left, closing the door of Albrec's cell behind him.

Albrec was shaking, and sweat had chilled his brow. So Columbar could not keep his mouth shut. Commodius must have questioned him; he had seen Albrec and Avila that night, perhaps.

Albrec had joined the Antillian Order for many reasons: hatred of the open sea which had been his fisherman father's daily bread; a love of books; but also a desire for security, for peace. He had found it in Charibon, and had never regretted his thirteen years in the confines of the St. Garaso Library. But now he felt that the earth had shifted from under his feet. His safe world was no longer so tranquil. There was an old saying among the clerics of Charibon that it was but a short step from the pulpit to the pyre. For the first time Albrec appreciated the truth behind the dark humour of it.

He uncovered the document, glancing fearfully at the door as he did so, as though Commodius might leap out with his face a devil's mask again.

He should destroy it. He should burn it, or lose it somewhere. Let someone else discover it a hundred years hence, perhaps. Why should it be he who must shoulder this burden?

It is my belief, the narrative went on, *that the Blessed Saint did indeed succeed in crossing the Jafrar. He was a man in the seventh decade of his life, but he was still strong and vigorous, and the missionary flame burned hotly in him. He was like a captain of a ship who can never rest until he has found an uncharted shore, and then another, and another. There was a restlessness to him which I and others believed to be the spirit of God.*

As the greatest conquerors can never sit at peace and reflect upon their past victories but must always move on, fighting fresh battles, chancing their lives and their fortunes until the end of their strength, so Ramusio could never be content to cease his proselytizing, his unending work of spreading the truth. His fire was not suited to the administration of an organized church. He inspired men

and then moved on, leaving it to his followers to write rules
and catechisms, to make into formulas and commandments
the tenets of his faith.

He was the gentlest man I have ever known, and yet
his will was adamantine. There was a puissance to his
determination which was not of this world, and which
awed all those who knew him.

I do not doubt that he reached the steppes beyond the
mountains, and that he awed the Merduks as he had
the men of the west. Ramusio the Blessed Saint became
Ahrimuz the Prophet, and the faith which sustains us here
in the west is the same as that which inspires the Merduks
who have become our mortal enemies. That is the pity of it.

There it was. Once he had read it, Albrec's world
changed irrevocably. He knew the document was genuine,
that the author had lived and breathed in the same long-
lost world which the Blessed Saint had known, a world
five hundred years distant. He spoke of Ramusio as a
man, a teacher, and as a friend, and the authenticity of his
recollections convinced Albrec of the truth of what he was
reading. Ramusio and Ahrimuz were one and the same,
and the Church, the kingdoms, the entire edifices of two
civilizations which spanned the known world were founded
on a misconception. On a lie.

He bent his head and prayed until the cold sweat was
rolling down his temples in agonized drops. He prayed for
courage, for strength, for some morsel of the determination
which had possessed the holy Saint himself.

The last section of the document was missing entirely, the
rotted threads which bound the work having given way to
time and abuse. He did not know the name of the author
or the date of the work, but there was no doubt why it had
been hidden away.

He had to find out more. He had to go back to the
catacombs.

NINE

CORFE HATED THE new clothes, but the tailor had assured
him that they were typical court wear for officers of the
Torunnan army. There was a narrow ruff which encircled his
neck, below which glittered a tiny mock breastplate of silver
suspended by a neck chain and engraved with the triple sabres
of his rank. The doublet was black embroidered with gold,
heavily padded in the shoulders and with voluminous slashed
sleeves through which the fine cambric of his shirt fluttered.
He wore tight black hose beneath, and buckled shoes. Shoes!
He had not worn shoes for years. He felt ridiculous.

"You will do very well," the Queen Dowager had said to
him when she had looked him over, with the tailor bowing
and hovering like a blowfly behind him.

"I feel like a dressmaker's mannequin," he snapped back.

She smiled at that and, folding her fan, she chucked him
under the chin with it.

"Now, now, Colonel. We must remember where we are.
The King has expressed a wish to see you in the company
of his senior officers. We cannot let you march into their
council of war looking like a serf dragged in from the fields.
And besides, this becomes you. You have the build for it,
even if your legs are a little on the short side. It comes of
being a cavalryman, I suppose."

Corfe did not reply. The Queen Dowager Odelia was
gliding round him as though she were admiring a statue,
her long skirts whispering on the marble floor.

"But this thing" – her fan rapped against Corfe's scabbarded
sabre – "this is out of place. We must find you a more fitting
weapon. Something elegant. This is a butcher's tool."

Corfe's fist tightened on the pommel of the sword. "By
your leave, lady, I'd prefer to keep it with me."

"Why?"

She had glided in front of him. Their eyes met.

"It helps remind me of who I am."

They stared at each other for a long moment. Corfe could sense the tailor's presence behind him, uneasy and fascinated.

"You must be in the chambers of the war council by the fifth hour," Odelia said, turning away abruptly. "Do not be late. The King has something for you, I believe."

She was gone, the end of her skirts trailing round the doorway like the tail of a departing snake.

AS THE PALACE bells sounded the fifth hour, Corfe was ushered into the council chambers by a haughty footman. He was reminded a little of his arrival at Ormann Dyke, when he had walked in on General Pieter Martellus's council of war. But that had been different. The officers at the dyke had been dressed like soldiers on campaign, and they had been planning for a battle which was already at their door. What Corfe walked into in the palace of Torunn was more like a parody, a game of war.

A crowd of gorgeously dressed officers. Infantry in black, cavalry in burgundy, artillery in deepest blue. Silver and gold gleamed everywhere with the pale accompaniment of lace and the bobbing magnificence of feathers from the caps some of the men retained. King Lofantyr was resplendent in sable and silver slashed hose and the crimson sash of a general. The light from a dozen lamps glittered off silver-buckled shoes, rings, gem-studded badges of rank and chivalric orders. Corfe made his deepest bow. He had refused cavalry burgundy, preferring infantry black though he belonged to the mounted arm. He was glad.

"Ah, Colonel," the King said, and gestured with one hand. "Come in, come in. It is all informality here. Gentlemen, Colonel Corfe Cear-Inaf, late of John Mogen's field army and the garrison of Ormann Dyke."

There was a murmur of greetings. Corfe was subjected to a dozen stares of frank appraisal. His skin crawled.

The other officers turned back to the long table which dominated the room. It was scattered with papers, but what occupied its shining length principally was a large map of Torunna and its environs. Corfe went closer, but his way was blocked. Irritably he looked up and found himself face to face with one of the dandies of the palace audience.

"Ensign Ebro, sir," the officer said, smiling. "We've met, I believe, though one would hardly recognize you out of your fighting gear."

Corfe nodded coldly. There was an awkward pause, and then Ebro stepped aside. "Pardon me, sir."

His sabre was unwieldy, harder to handle than the slim rapiers the other officers sported. He found himself peering over shoulders to see the rolled-out map. Figurines of Torunnan pikemen cast in silver had been placed at the four corners to stop the stiff paper from curling up. There were decanters on the table, crystal glasses, a blunt dagger of intricate workmanship which King Lofantyr picked up and used as a pointer.

"This is where they are now," he said, tapping a point on the map some eighty leagues west of Charibon. "In the Narian Hills."

"How many, sire?" a voice asked. It was the crusty, mustachioed Colonel Menin, whom Corfe had also encountered the evening of the audience.

"A grand tercio, plus supporting artisans. Five thousand fighting men."

A series of whispers swept the chamber.

"They will be a great help, of course," Menin said, but the doubt was audible in his voice.

"Fimbrians on the march again across Normannia," someone muttered. "Who'd have thought it?"

"Does Martellus know yet, sire?" another officer asked.

"Couriers went off to the dyke yesterday," King Lofantyr told them. "I am sure that Martellus will be glad of five thousand reinforcements, no matter where they are from. Marshal Barbius and his command are travelling light. They intend to be at the Searil river in six weeks, if all goes well. Plenty of time for his men to settle in before the beginning of the next campaigning season."

Lofantyr turned aside so that an older man in the livery

of a court official could whisper in his ear. He was holding a sheaf of papers.

"We have commanded General Martellus to send out winter scouting patrols to ascertain the state of readiness of the Merduks at all times. At the moment it seems they are secure in their winter camps, and have even detached sizable bodies of men eastwards to improve their supply lines. The elephants and cavalry, also, have been billeted further east where they will be nearer to the supply depots on the Ostian river. There is no reason to fear a winter assault."

Corfe recognized the papers in the court official's hands; they were the dispatches he had brought from the dyke.

"What of the Pontifical bull demanding Martellus's removal, sire?" Menin asked gruffly.

"We will ignore it. We do not recognize the imposter Himerius as Pontiff. Macrobius, rightful head of the Church, resides here in Torunn; you have all seen him. Edicts from Charibon will be ignored."

"Then what of the south, sire?" an officer with a general's sash about his middle, but who looked to be in his seventies, asked.

"Ah – these reports we've been getting of insurrections in the coastal cities to the south of the kingdom," Lofantyr said airily. "They are of little account. Ambitious nobles such as the Duke of Rone and the Landgrave of Staed have seen fit to recognize Himerius as Pontiff and our Royal self as a heretic. They will be dealt with."

The talk went on. Military talk, hard-edged and assured. *Councils of war love to talk*, John Mogen had once said. *But they hate to fight*. Most of the conversations seemed to Corfe to be less about tactics and strategy and more about the winning of personal advantage, the catching of the King's eye.

He had forgotten how different the Torunnan military of the capital and the home fiefs was from the field armies which defended the frontiers. The difference depressed him. These did not seem to him to be the same kind of men with whom he had fought at Aekir and Ormann Dyke. They were not of the calibre of John Mogen's command. But perhaps that was just an impression; he had not mixed much with the rank and file of the capital. And besides, he lashed himself, he was not such a great one to judge. He had deserted his regiment in the final stages of Aekir's agony, and while his comrades had fought and died in a heroic rearguard action on the Western Road, he had been slinking away in the midst of the civilian refugees. He must never forget that.

There was no mention of the refugee problem at this meeting, however, which puzzled Corfe extremely. The camps on the outskirts of the capital were swelling by the day with the despairing survivors of Aekir who had first fled the Holy City itself and had then been moved on from Ormann Dyke in the wake of the battles there. If he were the King, he would be concerned with feeding and housing the hopeless multitudes. It was all very well for them to camp outside the walls by the hundred thousand in winter, but when the weather warmed again there would be the near certainty of disease, that enemy more deadly to an army than any Merduk host.

They were discussing the scattered risings of the nobles in the south of the kingdom again. Apparently Perigraine was giving the disaffected aristocrats surreptitious support, and there were vague tales of Nalbenic galleys landing weapons for the rebels. The risings were localized and isolated as yet, but if they could be welded together by any one leader they would pose a serious threat. Swift and severe action was called for. Some of the officers at the council volunteered to go south and bring back the heads of the rebels on platters and there were many protestations of loyalty to Lofantyr, which the King accepted graciously. Corfe remained silent. He did not like the complacent way the King and his staff regarded the situation at the dyke. They seemed to think that the main effort of the Merduks was past and the danger was over except for some minor skirmishing to come in the spring. But Corfe had been there; he had seen the teeming thousands of the Merduk formations, the massed batteries of their artillery, the living walls of war elephants. He knew that the main assault had yet to come, and it would come in the spring. Five thousand Fimbrians would be a welcome addition to the dyke's defenders – if they would fight happily alongside their old foes the Torunnans – but they would not be enough. Surely Lofantyr and his advisors realized that?

The talk was wearisome, about people whose names meant nothing to Corfe, towns to the south, far away from the Merduk war. As members of Mogen's command, Corfe and his comrades had always seen the true danger in the east. The Merduks were the only real foes the west faced. Everything else was a distraction. But it was different here. In Torunn the eastern frontier was only one among a series of other problems and priorities. The knowledge made Corfe impatient. He wanted to get back to the dyke, back to the real battlefields.

"We need an expedition to clamp down on these traitorous bastards in the south, that's plain," Colonel Menin rasped. "With your permission, sire, I'd be happy to take a few tercios and teach them some loyalty."

"Very good of you, I'm sure, Colonel Menin," Lofantyr said smoothly. "But I need your talents employed here, in the capital. No, I have another officer in mind for the mission."

The more junior officers about the table eyed each other a little askance, wondering who the lucky man would be.

"Colonel Cear-Inaf, I have decided to give you the command," the King said briskly.

Corfe was jerked out of his reverie. "What?"

The King paused, and then stated in a harder voice: "I said, Colonel, that I am giving you this command."

All eyes were on Corfe. He was both astonished and dismayed. A command that would take him south, away from the dyke? He did not want it.

But could not refuse it. This, then, was what the Queen Dowager had been referring to earlier. This was her doing.

Corfe bowed deeply whilst his mind fought free of its turmoil.

"Your Majesty is very gracious. I only hope that I can justify your faith in my abilities."

Lofantyr seemed mollified, but there was something in his regard that Corfe did not like, a covert amusement, perhaps. "Your troop awaits you in the Northern Marshalling Yard, Colonel. And you shall have an aide, of course. Ensign Ebro will be joining you –"

Corfe found Ebro at his side, bowing stiffly, his face a mask. Clearly, this was not a post he had coveted.

"– And I shall see what I can do about releasing a few more officers to you."

"My thanks, your Majesty. Might I enquire as to my orders?"

"They will be forwarded to you in due course. For now I suggest, Colonel, that you and your new aide acquaint yourselves with your command."

Another pause. Corfe bowed yet again and turned and left the chamber with Ebro close behind him.

As soon as they were outside, striding along the palace corridors, Corfe reached up and savagely ripped the lace ruff from his throat, flinging it aside.

"Lead me to this Northern Marshalling Yard," he snapped to his aide. "I've never heard of it."

NO ONE HAD, it seemed. They scoured the barracks and armouries in the northern portion of the city, but none of the assorted quartermasters, sergeants and ensigns they spoke to had heard of it. Corfe was beginning to believe that it was all a monstrous joke when a fawning clerk in one of the city arsenals told them that there had been a draft of men brought in only the day before who were bivouacked in one of the city squares close to the northern wall; that might be their goal.

They set off on foot, Corfe's shiny buckled shoes becoming spattered with the filth of the winter streets. Ebro followed him in dumb misery, picking his way through the puddles and mudslimed cobbles. It began to rain, and his court finery took on a resemblance to the sodden plumage of a brilliant bird. Corfe was grimly satisfied by the transformation.

They emerged at last from the stinking press and crowd of the streets into a wide open space surrounded on all sides by timber-framed buildings. Beyond, the sombre heights of the battlemented city walls loomed like a hillside in the rain-cloud. Corfe wiped water out of his eyes, hardly able to credit what he saw.

"This can't be it – this cannot be them!" Ebro sputtered. But Corfe was suddenly sure it was, and he realized that the joke was indeed on him.

Torunnan sentries paced the edges of the square with halberds resting on their shoulders. In the shop doorways all around arquebusiers stood yawning, keeping their weapons and powder out of the rain. As Corfe and Ebro appeared, a young ensign with a muddy cloak about his shoulders approached them, saluting as soon as he caught sight of the badge on Corfe's absurd little breastplate.

"Good day, sir. Might you be Colonel Cear-Inaf, by any chance?"

Corfe's heart sank. There was no mistake then. "I am, Ensign. What is this we have here?"

The officer glanced back to the scene in the square. The open space was full of men, five hundred of them, perhaps. They were seated in crowds on the filthy cobbles as though battered down by the chill rain. They were in rags, and collectively they stank to high heaven. There were manacles about every ankle, and their faces were obscured by wild tangles of matted hair.

"Half a thousand galley slaves from the Royal fleet," the ensign said cheerily. "Tribesmen from the Felimbri, most of them, worshippers of the Horned One. Black-hearted devils, they are. I'd mind your back, sir, when you're near them. They tried to brain one of my men last night and we had to shoot a couple."

A dull anger began to rise in Corfe.

"This cannot be right, sir. We must be mistaken. The King must be in jest," Ebro was protesting.

"I don't think so," Corfe murmured. He stared at the packed throng of miserable humanity in the square. Many of them were staring back, glowering at him from under thatches of verminous hair. The men were brawny, well-muscled, as might be expected of galley slaves, but their skin was a sodden white, and many of them were coughing. A few had lain down on their sides, oblivious to the stone cobbles, the pouring rain.

So this was his first independent command. A crowd of mutinous slaves from the savage tribes of the interior. For a moment Corfe considered returning to the palace and refusing the command. The Queen Dowager had obtained the position for him, but clearly Lofantyr had resented her interference. He was supposed to refuse it, Corfe realized. And when he did, there would never be another. That decided him.

He stepped forward. "Are there any among you who can speak for the rest, in Normannic?"

The men muttered amongst themselves, and finally one rose and shuffled to the fore, his chains clinking.

"I speak your tongue, Torunnan."

He was huge, with hands as wide as dinner plates and the scars of old lashings about his limbs. His tawny beard fell on to his chest, but bright blue eyes glinted out of the brutish face and met Corfe's stare squarely.

"What's your name?" Corfe asked him.

"I am called the Eagle in my own tongue. You would say my name was Marsch."

"Can you speak for your fellows, Marsch?"

The slave shrugged his massive shoulders. "Perhaps."

"Do you know why you were taken from the galleys?"

"No."

"Then I will tell you. And you will translate what I say to your comrades, without misinterpretation. Is that clear?"

Marsch glared at him, but he was obviously curious. "All right."

"All right, *sir*," Ebro hissed at him, but Corfe held up a hand. He pitched his voice to carry across the square.

"You are no longer slaves of the Torunnan state," he called out. "From this moment on you are free men." That caused a stir, when Marsch had translated it, a lifting of the apathy. But there was no lessening of the mistrust in the eyes which were fixed on him. Corfe ground on.

"But that does not yet mean that you are free to do as you please. I am Corfe. From this moment on you will obey me as you would one of your own chieftains, for it is I who have procured your freedom. You are tribesmen of the Cimbrics. You were once warriors, and now you have the chance to be so again, but only under my command."

Marsch's deep voice was following Corfe's in the guttural language of the mountain tribes. His eyes never left Corfe's face.

"I need soldiers, and you are what I have been given. You are not to fight your own peoples, but are to battle

Torunnans and Merduks. I give you my word on that. Serve me faithfully, and you will have honour and employment. Betray me, and you will be killed out of hand. I do not care which God you worship or which tongue you speak as long as you fight for me. Obey my orders, and I will see that you are treated like warriors. Any who do not choose to do so can go back to the galleys."

Marsch finished translating, and the square was filled with low talk.

"Sir," Ebro said urgently, "no one gave you authority to free these men."

"They are my men," Corfe growled. "I will not be a general of slaves."

Marsch had heard the exchange. He clinked forward until he was towering over Corfe.

"You mean what you say, Torunnan?"

"I would not have said it otherwise."

"And you will give us our freedom, in exchange for our swords?"

"Yes."

"Why do you choose us as your men? To your kind we are savages and unbelievers."

"Because you are all I have got," Corfe said truthfully. "I don't take you because I want to, but because I have to. But if you will take service under me, then I swear I will speak for you in everything as though I were speaking for myself."

The hulking savage considered this a moment.

"Then I am your man." And Marsch touched his fist to his forehead in the salute of his people.

Others in the square saw the gesture. Men began to struggle to their feet and repeat it.

"If we break faith with you," Marsch said, "then may the seas rise up and drown us, may the green hills open up and swallow us, may the stars of heaven fall on us and crush us out of life for ever."

It was the old, wild oath of the tribes, the pagan pledge of fealty. Corfe blinked, and said:

"By the same oath, I bind myself to keep faith with you."

The men in the square were all on their feet now, repeating Marsch's oath in their own tongue.

Corfe heard them out. He had the oddest feeling that this was the beginning of something he could not yet grasp: something momentous that would affect the remaining course of his life.

The feeling passed, and he was facing five hundred men standing manacled in the rain.

He turned to the young ensign, who was open-mouthed. "Strike the chains from these men."

"Sir, I –"

"*Do it!*"

The ensign paled, saluted quickly, and ran off to get the keys. Ebro looked entirely at a loss.

"Ensign," Corfe snapped, and his aide came to attention. "You will find a warm billet for these men. If there are no military quarters available, you will procure a private warehouse. I want them out of the rain."

"Yes, sir."

Corfe addressed Marsch once more. "When did you last eat?"

The giant shrugged again. "Two, three days ago. Sir."

"Ensign Ebro, you will also procure rations for five hundred from the city stores, on my authority. If anyone questions you, refer them to – to the Queen Dowager. She will endorse my orders."

"Yes, sir. Sir, I –"

"Go. I want no more time wasted."

Ebro sped off without another word. Torunnan guards were already walking through the crowd of tribesmen unlocking their ankle chains. The arquebusiers had lit their match and were holding their firearms at the ready. As the tribesmen were freed, they trooped over to stand behind Marsch.

This is my command, Corfe thought.

They were starved, half naked, weaponless, without armour or equipment; and Corfe knew he could not hope to obtain anything for them through the regular military channels. They were on their own. But they were his men.

PART TWO

The WESTERN CONTINENT

TEN

THE AIR WAS different, somehow heavy. It trickled down
their throats and through the interstices in their armour
and lodged there, a solid, unyielding presence. It ballooned
their lungs and crimsoned their faces. It brought the sweat
winking out in glassy beads on their foreheads. It made the
soldiers pause to tug at the neck of their cuirasses as though
they were trying to loosen a constricting collar.

The white sand clung to their boots. They screwed up
their eyes against its brightness and slogged onwards. In
a few steps, the boom of the surf out on the reef became
distant, separate. The sun faded as the jungle enfolded
them, and the heat became a wetter, danker thing.

The Western Continent.

Sand gave way to leaf mulch underfoot. They slashed
aside creepers and the lower boughs of the trees, sharp palm
fronds, huge ferns.

The noise of the sea, their universe for so long, faded
away. It was as if they had entered some different
kingdom, a place which had nothing to do with anything
they had known before. It was a twilit world enshadowed
by the canopy of the immense trees which soared up on
all sides. Naked root systems like the tangled limbs of
corpses on a battlefield tripped them up and plucked at
their feet. Tree trunks two fathoms in diameter had discs
of fungi embedded in their flanks. A bewildering tangle of
living things, the very atmosphere full of buzzing, biting
mites so that they drew them into their mouths when they
breathed. And the stink of decay and damp and mould,
overpowering, all-pervading.

They stumbled across a stream which must have had its
outlet on the beach. Here the vegetation was less frenetic

and they could make a path of sorts, slashing with cutlass and poniard.

When they halted to rest and catch their breath – so hard to do that here, so hard to draw the thick air into greedy lungs – they could hear the sound of this new world all around them. Screeches and wails and twitterings and warblings and hoots of human-sounding laughter off in the trees. A symphony of invisible, utterly unknown life cackling away to itself, indifferent to their presence or intentions.

Several of the soldiers made the Sign of the Saint. There were things moving far up in the canopy, where the world had light and colour and perhaps a breeze. Half-glimpsed leaping shadows and flutterings.

"The whole place is alive," Hawkwood muttered.

They had found a tiny clearing wherein the stream burbled happily to itself, clear as crystal in a shaft of sunlight which had somehow contrived to survive to the forest floor.

"This will do," Murad said, wiping sweat from his face. "Sergeant Mensurado, the flag."

Mensurado stepped forward, his face half hidden in the shade of his casque, and stabbed the flagpole he had been bearing into the humus by the stream.

Murad produced a scroll from his belt pouch and unrolled it carefully as Mensurado's bark brought the file of soldiers to attention.

"'In this year of the Blessed Saint five hundred and fifty-one, on this the twenty-first day of Endorion, I, Lord Murad of Galiapeno do hereby claim this land on behalf of our noble and gracious sovereign, King Abeleyn the Fourth of Hebrion and Imerdon. From this moment on it shall be known as –'" he looked up at the cackling jungle, the towering trees – "'as New Hebrion. And henceforth as is my right, I assume the titles of viceroy and governor of this, the westernmost of the possessions of the Hebriate crown.'

"Sergeant, the salute."

Mensurado's parade-ground bellow put the jungle cacophony to shame.

"Present your pieces! Ready your pieces! Fire!"

A thunderous volley of shots went off as one. The clearing

was filled with toiling grey smoke which hung like cotton in the airless space.

The forest had gone entirely silent.

The men stood looking up at the crowded vegetation, the huge absence of sound. Instinctively, everyone stepped closer together.

A crashing of undergrowth, and Ensign di Souza appeared, scarlet face and yellow hair above his cuirass, with a pair of sailors and Bardolin the mage labouring in his wake. The wizard's imp rode on his shoulder, agog.

"Sir, we heard shooting," he panted.

"We have seen off the enemy," Murad drawled. He loosened the drawstrings on the Hebrian flag and it fell open, a limp gold and crimson rag.

"Report, Ensign," he said sharply, waving powder-smoke from in front of his face.

"The second wave of boats are ashore, and the mariners are off-loading the water casks as we speak. Sequero asks your permission, sir, to get the surviving horses ashore and start hunting up fodder for them."

"Permission denied," Murad said crisply. "The horses are not a priority here. We must secure a campsite for the landing party first, and investigate the surrounding area. Who knows what may be lurking in this devil's brush about us?"

Several of the soldiers glanced round uneasily, until Mensurado, with shouts and kicks, got them to reloading their arquebuses.

Murad considered the little clearing. The forest noises had started up again. Already they were becoming used to them, a background irritation, not a thing to fear.

"We'll throw up a camp here," he said. "It's as good a place as any, and we'll have fresh water. Captain Hawkwood, your men can refill their water casks here also."

Hawkwood looked at the knee-deep stream, already muddied by the boots of the soldiers, and said nothing.

Bardolin joined him. The old wizard mopped his streaming face with his sleeve and gestured at the surrounding jungle. "Have you ever seen anything like this before? Such trees!"

Hawkwood shook his head. "I've been to Macassar, the jungles inland from the Malacars, after ivory and hides and river-gold, but this is different. This has never been cleared; it is the original forest, a country where man has never made a mark. These trees might have stood here since the Creation."

"Dreaming their strange dreams," Bardolin said absently, caressing his imp with one hand. "There is power in this place, Hawkwood. Dweomer, and something else. Something to do with the very nature of the land, perhaps. It has not yet noticed us, I think, but it will, in its slow way."

"We've always said the place might be inhabited."

"I am not talking about inhabitants, I am talking about the land itself. Normannia has been scoured and gouged and raped for too long; we own it now. We are its blood. But here the land belongs only to itself."

"I never took you for a mystic, Bardolin," Hawkwood said with some irritation. His injured shoulder was paining him.

"Nor am I one." The mage seemed to come awake. He smiled. "Maybe I'm just getting old."

"Old! You're more hale than I am."

Two seamen appeared: Mihal and Masudi, one bearing a wooden box.

"Velasca wants to know if he can let the men have a run ashore, sir," Masudi said, his black face gleaming.

"Not yet. This isn't a blasted pleasure trip. Tell him to concentrate on getting the ship rewatered."

"Aye, sir." Masudi said. "Here's the box you wanted from the cabin."

"Put it down."

Murad joined them. "I'm taking a party on a reconnaissance of the area. I want you two to come with us. Maybe you can sniff out things for us, Mage. And Hawkwood, you said –"

"I have it here," Hawkwood interrupted him.

He bent to open the box at his feet. Inside was a brass bowl and an iron sliver which had been pasted on to a wafer of cork. Hawkwood filled the bowl from the stream. Some of the soldiers crowded round to look and he barked angrily: "Stand aside! I can't have any metal around when I do this. Give me some space."

The men retreated as he set the iron to bob on the water. He crouched for a long minute staring at it, and then said to Murad: "The stream heads off to nor'-nor'-west. If we followed it – and it's the easiest passage – then we'd be coming back east-southeast."

He poured the water off, put everything back in the box and straightened.

"A portable compass," Bardolin said. "So simple! But then the principle remains the same. I should have realized."

"We'll move out and follow the line of the stream," Murad said. He turned to di Souza. "We'll fire three shots if there's any trouble. When you hear them, pack up and get back to the ship. Do not try to come after us, Ensign. We'll make our own way. The same procedure follows if anything occurs here while we're gone. But I intend to return well before dark anyway."

Di Souza saluted.

THE PARTY SET out: Murad, Hawkwood, Bardolin and ten of the soldiers.

They tramped through the stream, as it was the path of least resistance, and it seemed to them that they were travelling through a green tunnel lit by some radiance far above. It was dusk down here, with occasional shafts of bright sun lancing through gaps in the canopy to provide a dazzling contrast to the pervading gloom.

They ducked under hanging limbs, skirted sprawling roots as thick as a man's thigh which lolled in the water like torpid animals come to drink. They slashed aside hanging veils of moss and creeper, and staggered hurriedly away from the sudden brilliance of gem-bright snakes which slithered through the mulch of the forest floor, intent on their own business.

It grew hotter. The noise of the sea died away, the fading of a once-vivid memory. They were in a raucous cathedral whose columns were the titanic bulk of the great trees, whose roof sparkled with distant light and movement, the mocking cries of weird birdlife.

The ground rose under their feet and stones began to rear up out of the earth like the bones of the land come poking through its decaying hide. Their progress grew more laboured, the soldiers with their heads down and arquebuses on their shoulders puffing like fractured bellows. A cloud of tiny, iridescent birds swept through the company like airborne jewels. They flickered one way and then another, turning in unison like a shoal of twisting fish, their fleetness almost derisory. A few of the soldiers batted at them half-heartedly with gunstock and sword but they whispered away again in a spray of lapis lazuli and amethyst before swooping into the canopy overhead.

The stream disappeared into a tangle of boulders and bush, and the forest closed in on them completely. The ground was rising more steeply now, making every step an effort. The men scooped up handfuls and helmetfuls of the water, gulping it down and sluicing their faces. It was as warm as a wet nurse's milk, and hardly seemed to moisten their mouths. Murad led them onwards, hacking with a seaman's cutlass at the barrier of vegetation ahead, his feet slipping and turning on the mossy stones, boots squelching in mud.

They came across ants the size of a man's little finger which carried bright green leaves like the mainsail of a schooner on their backs. They found beetles busily winking in the earth, their wingcases as broad as an apple, horns adorning their armoured heads. Wattle-necked lizards regarded them silently from overhead branches, the colours of their skin pulsing from emerald through to turquoise.

They took a new bearing from the source of the stream and headed north-west this time, as the way seemed easiest on that course. Murad detailed one of the soldiers to blaze a tree every twenty yards, so thick was the undergrowth. They stumbled onwards in the wake of the gaunt nobleman as though he were some kind of demented prophet leading them to paradise, and Sergeant Mensurado, his voice hoarsened to a croak with overuse, hurried the stragglers along with shoves and blows and venomous whispers.

The jungle began to open out a fraction. The trees were more widely spaced and the ground between them was littered with rocks, some as long as a ship's culverin. The ground changed texture and became dark and gritty, almost like black sand. It filled their boots and rasped between their toes.

Then Murad stopped dead in his tracks.

Hawkwood and Bardolin were farther back in the file. He called them forward in a low hiss.

"What?" Hawkwood asked.

Murad pointed, his eyes not moving from whatever drew them. Up in the tree, maybe forty feet off the ground. The canopy was broken there, bright with dappled sunlight. Hawkwood squinted in the-unaccustomed glare.

"Holy God," Bardolin said beside him.

Then Hawkwood saw it too.

It stood on a huge level branch, and had flattened itself against the trunk which spawned its perch. It was almost the same shade as the butternut-coloured tree bark, which was why Hawkwood had not seen it at first. But then the head turned, and the movement caught his eye.

A monstrous bird of some sort. Its wings were like those of a bat, only more leathery. They hugged the tree trunk: there were claws at the end of the skeletal frame. It was hard to be precisely sure as to where they began and the skin of the tree itself ended, so good was the beast's camouflage, but the thing was big. Its wrinkled, featherless and hairless body was as tall as a man's, and the span of the wings must have been three fathoms or more. The long neck supported a skull-like head, eyes surprisingly small, both set to the front of the face like an owl, and a wicked, black beak between them.

The eyes blinked slowly. They were yellow, slitted. The creature did not appear alarmed at the sight of the party, but regarded them with grave interest; almost, they might have said, with intelligence.

Bardolin stepped forward, and with his right hand he inscribed a little glimmer on the air. The creature stared at him, unafraid, seemingly intrigued.

There was a loud crack, a spurt of flame and billow of smoke. "Hold your fire, God-damn you!" Murad cried.

The bird thing detached itself from the tree and seemed to fall backwards. It flipped in mid-fall with incredible speed and grace, then the great wings opened and flapped twice in huge whooshes of air which staggered the smoke and blew the plastered hair off Hawkwood's brow. The wings boomed and cracked like sails. The thing wheeled up into the canopy, and then was a shape against the blue sky beyond, dwindling to a speck and disappearing.

"Who fired?" Murad demanded. "Whose weapon was that?" He was quivering with rage. A soldier whose arquebus was leaking smoke quailed visibly as Murad advanced on him.

Sergeant Mensurado stepped between them.

"My fault, sir. I told the men to keep their serpentines back, the match burning. Glabrio here, he tripped, sir. Must have been the sight of that monster. It won't happen again. I'll see to him myself when we get back."

Murad glared at his sergeant, but at last only nodded. "See that you do, Mensurado. A pity the fool missed, since he had to fire a shot. I'd like to have had a closer look at that."

Several of the soldiers were making the Sign of the Saint discreetly. They did not seem to share their commander's wish.

"What was it, Bardolin?" Murad asked the wizard. "Any ideas?"

The old mage's face was unusually troubled.

"I've never seen anything remotely like it, except perhaps in the pages of a bestiary. It was a warped, unnatural thing. Did you see its eyes? There was a mind behind them, Murad. And it stank of Dweomer."

"It was a magical creature, then?" Hawkwood said.

"Yes. More than that, a created creature: not fashioned by the hand of God, but by the sorcery of men. But the power it would take to bring such a thing into the world, and then give it permanence... it is staggering. I had not thought that any mage living could have such power. It would kill me, were I to attempt a similar thing."

"What did you make glow in the air?" Murad demanded.

"A glyph. Feralism is one of my disciplines. I was trying to read the heart of the beast."

"And could you?"

"No... No, I could not."

"Blast that whoreson idiot and his itchy trigger finger!"

"No, it was not that. I could not read the thing's heart because it was not truly a beast."

"What is this you're saying, Mage?"

"I am not sure. What I think I am saying is that there was humanity there, in the beast. A soul, if you will."

Murad and Hawkwood regarded the wizard in silence. The imp looked around and then cautiously took its fingers from out of its ears. It hated loud noises.

Murad realized that the soldiers were crowded around, listening. His face hardened.

"We'll move on. We can discuss this later. Sergeant Mensurado, lead off and make sure the men have their pieces uncocked. I want no more discharges, or we will have Ensign di Souza evacuating the camp behind us."

That raised a nervous laugh. The men shook out into file again, and set off. Bardolin trudged along wordlessly, the frown lines biting deep between his brows.

THE GROUND CONTINUED to rise. It seemed that they were on the slopes of a hill or small mountain. It was hard going for all of them, because the black sand-like stuff of the forest floor sank under their boots. It was as if they were walking up the side of an enormous dune, their feet slipping back a yard for every yard advanced.

"What is this stuff?" Murad asked. He slapped a sucking insect off his scarred cheek, grimacing.

"Ash, I think," Hawkwood said. "There has been a great burning here. The stuff must be half a fathom deep."

There were boulders, black and almost glassy in places. The trees were slowly splitting them apart and shifting them down-slope. And such trees! Nowhere in the world, Hawkwood thought, even in Gabrion, could there be trees like these, straight as lances, hard as bronze. A shipwright might fashion a mainmast from a single trunk, or a vessel's keel from two. But the labour – the work of hewing down these forest giants. In this heat, it would kill a man.

A gasping, endless time in which they put down their heads and forgot everything but the next step in front of them. Several of the soldiers paused in their travails to vomit, their eyes popping. Murad gave them permission to take off their helmets and loosen their cuirasses, but they gave the impression that they were slowly being boiled alive inside the heavy armour.

At last there was a clear light ahead, an open space. The trees ended. There was a short stretch of bare rock and ash and gravel before them, and then nothing but blue, unclouded heaven.

They bent over to grasp their knees, their guts churning, the sunlight making them blink and scowl. Several of the soldiers collapsed on to their backs and lay there like bright, immobilized beetles, unable to do anything but suck in lungfuls of steaming air.

When Hawkwood finally straightened, the sight before them made him cry out in wonder.

They were above the jungle and on top of this world, it seemed. They had reached the summit of what proved to be a razor-backed ridge which was circular in shape, an eerily perfect symmetry.

Hawkwood could see for uncounted leagues in all directions. If he turned round he could see the Western Ocean stretching off to the horizon. There was the *Osprey* riding at anchor, distant as a child's toy. A line of white surf up and down the coast marked the reefs, and there was a series of little, conical islands off to the north, eight leagues away perhaps.

Inland, to the west, the jungle rolled in an endless viridian carpet, lurid, garish, secretive. Its mass was broken by more formations identical to the one upon which they stood: circles of bare rock amid the greenery, barren as gravestones, unnatural-looking. They pocked the forest like crusted sores, and beyond them, far off and almost invisible in the heat shimmer and haze, were high mountains as blue as woodsmoke.

To the north and west was something else. Clouds were building up there, tall thunderheads and anvils and horsetails of angry vapour, grey and heavy in the underbelly. A shadow dominated that horizon, rearing up and up until its head was lost in the cloud. A mountain, a perfect cone. It was taller than any of the granite giants in the Hebros. Fifteen thousand feet, maybe, though it was hard to tell with its summit lost in billowing vapour.

"Craters," Bardolin said, appearing beside him.

"What?"

"Saffarac of Cartigella, a friend of mine, once had a viewing device, an oracular constructed of two finely ground lenses mounted in a tube of leather. He was hoping to find evidence for his theory that the earth moved around the sun, not the other way round. He looked at the moon, the nearest body in heaven, and he saw there formations like these. Craters. He postulated two causes; one, fiery rock had erupted out of the moon in a series of vast explosions –"

"Like gunpowder, you mean?"

"Yes. Or two, they were caused by vast stones falling to the surface, like the one that fell in Fulk some ten years back. Big as a horse it was, and glowing red when it hit the ground. You see them on clear nights, streaks of light falling to earth. Dying stars giving out their last breath in a streak of light and beauty."

"And that's what made this landscape?" Murad said, coming up behind them.

"It is one theory."

"I have heard that in the southern latitudes there are mountains such as this one," Hawkwood volunteered. "Some of them leak smoke and sulphurous gases."

"Mariners' stories," Murad sneered. "You are not in some Abrusian pothouse trying to impress the lowly, Hawkwood." Hawkwood said nothing. His gaze did not shift from the panorama before them.

"Not fifty years ago a man might be burnt at the stake for daring to venture that the world was round, and not flat like a buckler," Bardolin said mildly. "And yet now, even in Charibon, they accept that we are spinning on a sphere, as Terenius of Orfor suggests."

"I do not care what shape the world is, so long as my feet can bear me across it," Murad snapped.

They looked down into the bowl which their ridge contained. It was perfectly round, a circle of jungle. They stood at a height of some three thousand feet, Hawkwood estimated, but the air did not seem any less dense.

"*Heyeran Spinero*," Murad said. "Circle Ridge. I will put it on the map. This is as far as we will go today. It looks like rain is coming in from the north, and I wish to be back at the camp before dark."

None of them mentioned it, but they were all thinking of the monstrous bird which had studied them so nonchalantly. The thought of a night spent away from the rest of their comrades in a forest populated by such things was not tolerable.

Mensurado's croak attracted their attention. The sergeant was pointing down at the land below.

"What is it, Sergeant?" Murad asked harshly. He seemed to be fighting off exhaustion with bile alone.

Mensurado could only point and whisper, his parade-ground bellow hoarsened out of existence. "There, sir, to the right of that weird hill, just above its flank. You see?"

They peered whilst the rest of the soldiers sat listlessly, slugging the last of their water and mopping their faces.

"Sweet Blessed Saint!" Murad said softly. "Do you see it, gentlemen?"

A space in the jungle, a tiny clearing wherein a patch of beaten earth could be glimpsed.

"A road, or track," Bardolin said, sketching out a farseeing cantrip to aid his tired eyes.

"Hawkwood, get out that contraption of yours and take its bearing," the nobleman said peremptorily.

Frowning, Hawkwood did as he was told, filling the bowl with some of his own drinking water. He studied it, then looked up, gauging, and said: "West-nor'-west of here. I'd put it at fifteen leagues. It's a broad road, to be seen at that distance."

"That, gentlemen, is our destination," Murad said. "Once we have ourselves organized, I am taking an expedition into the interior. You will both accompany me, naturally. We will make for that road, and see if we can't meet up with whoever built it."

Sergeant Mensurado was as motionless as a block of wood. Murad turned on him.

"The fewer folk who hear of this the better, for now. You understand me, Sergeant?"

"Yes, sir."

"Good. Rouse the men. It's time we were getting back."

"Yes, sir."

In minutes they were off again, downhill this time, trudging in the hollows their feet had made on the way up. Hawkwood and Bardolin remained behind for a few minutes, watching the gathering clouds about the shoulders of the great mountain to the north.

"I'll kill him before we leave this land," Hawkwood said. "He will goad me one time too often."

"It is his way," Bardolin said. "He knows no other. He looks to you and me for answers, and hates the necessity for it. He is as lost as any of us."

"Lost! Is that how you see us?"

"We are on a dark continent which those who were here before us did not mean us to see. There is Dweomer here, everywhere, and there is such a teeming life. I have never felt anything like it. Power, Hawkwood, the power to create warped grotesqueries such as that winged creature. I did not say so before because I was not sure, but I am now. That bird was once a man like you or me. There was the remnant of a man's mind in the beast's skull. Not as it is in a shifter, but different. Permanent. There is someone or something in this land who is committing monstrous deeds, things which offend the very fabric of nature's laws. Murad may be eager to meet them, but I am not, if only because I can to some extent understand the motive behind the act. Power allied to irresponsibility. It is the most dangerous thing in the world, the most seductive of temptations. It is evil, pure and simple."

They followed off after the last of the soldiers without another word, the jungle creatures calling out mockingly all around them.

ELEVEN

IT RAINED ON the way back, as Murad had predicted, and, like everything else in this land, the rain was strange. The sky clouded over in minutes, and the dimness beneath the tops of the trees became a twilight they stumbled through half-blind, eyes fixed on the man in front. There was a roaring noise above, and they looked up in time to catch the first drops cascading down from the ceiling of vegetation.

The roar intensified until they could hardly hear each other's voices. The rain was torrential, maniac, awesome. It was as warm as bath water and thick as wine. The canopy broke most of its force and it tumbled in waterfalls down the trunks of the trees, creating rivers which gurgled around their boots, battering plants to the forest floor and submerging them in mud and slime. The company huddled in the shelter of one of the forest leviathans whilst their dimly lit world became a storm of smashing rain, a blinding, water-choked quagmire.

They glimpsed the dark shapes of little twisting animals falling to earth, washed off their perches higher in the trees. The rain coming down the tree boles became a soup of bark and insects, pouring down the necks of the soldiers' armour, soaking the arquebuses and waterlogging the powder-horns beyond hope of drying.

An hour or more they crouched there and watched the storming elements in fear and bewilderment. And then the rain stopped. Within the space of a dozen heartbeats, the roaring thunder of it faded, the torrents dwindled and the light grew.

They stood, blinking, tipping water out of gun barrels and helmets, wiping their faces. The forest came to life again. The birds and other unknown fauna took up their endless chorus once more. The water about their feet soaked into the spongy soil and disappeared, and the last of the rain dripped in streams from the leaves of the great trees, lit up like tumbling gems by the sunlight above. The jungle stank and steamed.

Murad shook his lank hair from his face, wrinkling his nose. "The place stinks worse than a tannery in high summer. Bardolin, you're our resident expert on the world. Was that rain normal for here, do you think?"

The wizard shrugged, dripping.

"In Macassar they have sudden rains like that, but they come in the rainy season only," Hawkwood volunteered.

"We've arrived here in the midst of the rainy season then?"

"I don't know," the mariner said wearily. "I've heard merchants of Calmar say that to the south of Punt there are jungles where it rains like this every day, and there is no winter, no summer; no seasons at all. It never changes from one month to the next."

"God save us," one of the soldiers muttered.

"That is ridiculous," Murad snapped. "Every country in the world has its seasons; it must have. What is a world without spring, or winter? When would one harvest crops, or sow seeds? When will you cease spinning your travellers' tales with me, Hawkwood?"

Hawkwood's face darkened, but he said nothing.

They moved on without further talk, and had it not been for Hawkwood's compass they would never have got their bearings again, for the little stream which they had followed that morning had become one of many muddy rivulets. They retraced their course like mariners at sea, by compass bearing alone, and by the time they heard the voices of the men back at the makeshift camp there was a transparency, a frailty to the light in the sky which suggested that sundown was very near.

The camp was a shambles. Murad stood with his fists resting on his lean hips and surveyed it with skull-like intensity. The stream which had run through it had overflowed its soggy banks and the men were sucking through a veritable swamp of mud and decaying vegetation, steam rising like fog from the saturated earth. They had chopped down a score of saplings and tried to fashion a rude palisade, but the wood would not stand up in the soft soil; the stakes sagged and wobbled like rotten teeth.

Ensign di Souza forced his way over to his superior, his boots heavy with mud.

"Sir, I mean your Excellency – the rain. It washed out the camp. We managed to keep some of the powder dry..." He tailed off.

"Move off to one side, away from the stream," Murad barked. "Get the men to it at once. There's not much light left."

A new shape in the gathering gloom and Ensign Sequero, di Souza's more aristocratic fellow officer, appeared, amazingly clean and tidy, having just come from the ship.

"What are you doing ashore, Ensign?" Murad asked. He looked like a man being slowly bent into some quivering new shape, the tension in him a palpable thing. The soldiers went to their work with a will; they knew Murad's displeasure was a thing to avoid.

"Your Excellency," Sequero said with a smile, hovering just below insolence. "The passengers are wondering when they'll be let ashore, and there is the livestock also. The horses especially need a run on dry land, and fresh fodder."

"They will have to wait," Murad said with dangerous quietness. "Now get you back to the ship, Ensign."

Even as he spoke, the light died. It grew dark so quickly that some of the soldiers and sailors stared around fearfully, making the Sign of the Saint at their breasts. A twilight measured in moments followed by pitch blackness, a weight of dark which was broken only by the spatters of stars visible through gaps in the canopy overhead.

"Sweet Ramusio!" someone said. "What a country."

No one spoke for a few minutes. The men stood frozen as the jungle disappeared into the night and became one with it. The noises of the forest changed tone, but did not decrease their volume one whit. The company was in the midst of an invisible bedlam.

"Strike a light, someone, for God's sake," Murad's voice cracked, and the stillness in the camp was broken. Men fumbling in the dark, the sucking squelch of feet in mud. A rattle of sparks. "The tinder's soaked through..."

"Use any dry powder you have, then," Hawkwood's voice said. A sulphuric flare in the night, like a far-off eruption.

"Burn a couple of the stakes. They're the only things which are near-dry."

For perhaps the space of half an hour, the inhabitants of the crown's new colony in the west huddled about a single soldier who was striving to create fire. They might have been men at the dawn of the world, crouched in the terrifying and unknowable dark, their eyes craving the light to see what was coming at them out of the night.

The flames caught at last. They saw themselves; a circle of faces around a tiny fire. The jungle towered off on all sides, the night creatures laughing and croaking at their fear. They were in an alien world, as lost and alone as forgotten children.

HAWKWOOD AND BARDOLIN sat by one of the fires later in the night. There were thirty men ashore, lying around half a dozen campfires which spat and hissed in the surrounding mud. A dozen men stood guard with halberd and sword whilst a few others were methodically and cautiously turning a pile of gunpowder off to one side, trying to dry it out without blowing themselves to kingdom come. The arquebuses were useless for the moment.

"We don't belong here," Hawkwood said quietly, chucking Bardolin's imp under the chin so that it gurgled and grinned at him, its eyes two little lamps in the firelight.

"Maybe the first Fimbrians to venture east of the Malvennors said the same thing," Bardolin replied. "New countries, unexplored lands, are always strange at first."

"No, Bardolin, it's more than that and you know it. This country's very nature is different. Inimical. Alien. Murad thought he could wade ashore and start building his own kingdom here, but it won't be that way."

"You wrong him there," the mage said. "After what happened on the ship, I think he knew better than to expect it to be easy. He is feeling his way, but he is hidebound by the conventions of his class and his training. He is thinking like a soldier, a nobleman."

"Are we commoners so much more flexible in our thinking, then?" Hawkwood asked, grinning weakly.

"Maybe. We do not have so much at stake."

"I have a ship – I had two ships. My life is gambled on this throw also," Hawkwood reminded him.

"And I have no other home; this continent is the only place in the world, perhaps, where I and my like can be free of prejudice, make a new beginning," Bardolin retorted. "That, at least, was the theory."

"And yet tonight you were too tired even to conjure up a glimmer of werelight. What kind of omen is that for your new beginning?"

The wizard was silent, listening to the jungle noises.

"What is out there, Bardolin?" Hawkwood persisted. "What manner of men or beasts have claimed this place before us?"

The old mage poked at the fire, then slapped his cheek suddenly, wincing. He peeled an engorged, many-legged thing from his face, eyed it with mild curiosity for a second and then threw it into the flames.

"As I said, there is Dweomer here, more than I have ever sensed in any other place," he said. "The land we saw before us today is thick with it."

"Was that truly a road? Are we to stumble across another civilization here?"

"I think so. I think something exists on this continent which we in the Ramusian west have never even guessed at. I keep thinking of Ortelius, our stowaway Inceptine and werewolf. He was charged with making sure your ships never made it this far, that much is clear. Perhaps he had a fellow on your other vessel, the one that was lost. In any case, his mission was entrusted to him by someone in this land, this strange country upon which we have made landfall. And there is Dweomer running through it all, the work of mages. Hawkwood, I do not think we will leave this continent alive, any of us."

The mariner stared at him across the fire. "Rather soon to be making such predictions of doom, isn't it?" he managed at last.

"Soothsaying is one of the Seven Disciplines, but it is not one of mine, along with weather-working and the Black Change. Yet I feel we have no future here. I know it, and for all Murad's claims and posturings, I think he knows it too."

IT WAS A clammy, muddy campsite that presented itself to the shore party with the dawn, but Murad began issuing orders immediately and the soldiers were harangued out of their torpor by Sergeant Mensurado. Nothing had happened during the night, though few of them had slept. Hawkwood for one had missed the lulling rock of his ship beneath him, the waves lapping at the hull. His *Osprey* now seemed to him to be the most secure place in the world.

They staggered down to the brightness of the beach, the heat already being flung at their faces from its reflected glare. The carrack rode at anchor beyond the reef, an incredibly comforting sight for soldier and sailor alike.

Breakfast was ship's biscuit and wood-hard salt pork, eaten cold on the beach. All manner of fruit was hanging within easy reach, but Murad had forbidden anyone to touch the stuff so they ate as if they were still at sea.

Throughout the morning the longboats plied the passage of the reef and brought across stores and equipment. The surviving horses were too weak to swim ashore behind the boats so they were trussed up and lowered into the larger of the vessels like carcasses. Released on dry land for the first time in months, they stood like emaciated caricatures of the fine animals they had once been and Sequero put half a dozen men to finding fodder for them.

The water casks were replenished by Hawkwood's sailors and towed back out to the carrack in bobbing skeins. Another party led by Hawkwood himself rowed out to that part of the reef upon which the wreck of the *Grace of God* rested.

The surf was too rough for them to go close, but they could see a desiccated body wedged in the timbers of the beakhead, unrecognizable, the seabirds and the elements having done their work too well.

Further up the coast there was more wreckage, fragments mostly. The caravel had been shattered by its impact on the reef as if by an explosion. Hawkwood's crew found the shredded remnants of another corpse a mile to the north and some threads of clothing, but nothing more. The caravel's crew and passengers had perished to a man, it seemed.

The passengers aboard the carrack were rowed ashore at last, over eighty of them. They stood on the beach of this new land like folk cast adrift. Which in a way was what they were.

Back in Hebrion it was winter, and the old year was almost over. There would be snow thick upon the Hebros, the winter storms thrashing the swells of the Fimbrian Gulf and the Hebrian Sea. Here the heat was relentless and choking, a miasma of humid jungle stink hanging in their throats like a fog. It sapped their strength, weighed them down like chainmail. And yet the work did not cease, the orders continued to be issued, the activity went on without let-up.

They moved in off the beach a quarter of a mile, perhaps, abandoning the campsite of the night before. Murad set soldiers, civilians and sailors alike to clearing a space between the trunks of the huge trees. Many of the younger trees were felled, and the would-be colonists burned off what vegetation they could, slashing and uprooting that which was too wet to catch fire. They erected shelters of wood and canvas and thatched leaves, and built a palisade as high as a man's head, loopholed for firearms and with crude wooden watch-towers at each corner.

Almost every afternoon the work was halted by the titanic, thunderous rainstorms which came and went like the rage of a petulant god. Some of the colonists fell sick almost at once – the older ones, mostly, and one squalling toddler. Two died raving in fever, the rigours of the voyage and this new land too much for them. Thus the fledgling colony acquired a cemetery within its first week.

THEY NAMED THE settlement Fort Abeleius after their young king. One hundred and fifty-seven souls lived within its perimeter, for Murad would allow none of the colonists to forge off on their own in search of suitable plots of land. For the moment, Hebrion's newest colony was nothing more than an armed camp, ready to repel attack at short notice. No one knew who the attackers might be, or even what they might be, but there were no complaints. The story of the warped bird had spread quickly, and no one was keen to venture into the jungle alone.

Titles were distributed like sweetmeats. Sequero became a *haptman*, military commander of the colony, now that Murad was governor. In reality, Murad still commanded the soldiers personally, but it amused him to see Sequero lording it over his subordinate, di Souza.

Hawkwood became head of the Merchants' Guild, which as yet did not exist, but true to his word Murad had procured monopolies for him and he had them in writing, heavy with seals and ribbons, the signature at the bottom none other than that of Abeleyn himself. They were beginning to grow mould with the damp heat, and he had to keep them tightly wrapped in oilskin packets.

And Hawkwood was ennobled. Plain Richard Hawkwood had become Lord Hawkwood, albeit lord of nothing and nowhere. But it was a hereditary title. Hawkwood had ennobled his family for ever, if he managed to return to Hebrion and raise a family. Old Johann, his rascally father, would have been uproariously delighted, but to Hawkwood it seemed an empty gesture, meaningless in the midst of this steaming jungle.

He sat in his crude hut sorting through what documents he had brought from the ship. Velasca was on the carrack with a skeleton crew. The vessel had been rewatered and they had also taken on board several hundredweight of coconuts, one of the few fruits growing here which Hawkwood recognized.

His original ship's log was gone, lost in the fire which had come close to destroying his ship, and with it the ancient rutter of Tyrenius Cobrian, the only other record of a voyage into the west. Hawkwood had started a new log, of course, but flipping through it he realized with a cold start that there was no sure way he could ever find his way back to Fort Abeleius or this anchorage were he to undertake a second voyage in the wake of the first. The storm which had driven them off course had upset his calculations, and the loss of the log had made things worse for he could not remember every change of course and tack since then. The best he might do was to hit upon the Western Continent at the approximate latitude his cross-staff told him this was and then cruise up and down until he rediscovered the place.

He thought of telling Murad, but decided against it. The scarred nobleman was like a spring being compressed too tightly these days, more haughty and savage than ever. It would do no good.

It was dimming outside, and Hawkwood immediately struck himself a light, a precious candle from their dwindling store. Scarcely had he done so when the dark came, a settling of deep shadow which at some indefinable point became true night.

He dipped his nub of a quill in the inkwell and began to write his log.

26th day of Endorion, ashore Fort Abeleius, year of the Saint 551 – though only a few sennights remain of the old year, and soon we will be into the Saint's days which denote the turning of the calendar.

The palisade was finished today, and we have begun the task of felling some of the huge trees which stand within its perimeter. Murad's plan is to lop them a little at a time and use them for construction and firewood. He will never uproot them; I think such trees must have roots running to the core of the earth.

The building work proceeds apace. We have a governor's residence – the only building with a floor, though it has an old topsail for its back wall. I dine there tonight. Civilization comes to the wilderness.

Hawkwood reread his entry. He was becoming loquacious now that he no longer had to write of winds and courses and sailing arrangements. His log was turning into a journal.

At last we have dry powder, though keeping it so in this climate has tried the wits of every soldier among us. It was Bardolin who suggested sealing the powder-horns with wax. He has become a little odd, our resident mage. Murad regards him as the leader of the colonists, the scientific problem-solver, but also as something of a fraud. Whether this last attitude of his is assumed or not I do not know. Since his peasant lover turned out to be a shifter, Murad has been different – at once less sure of himself and more autocratic. But then who among us was not changed by that weird voyage and its horrors?

I would that Billerand were here, or Julius Albak, my shipmates of old. Our company is the poorer without them, and I am not entirely happy with Velasca as first mate. His navigation leaves a lot to be desired.

"Captain?" a voice said beyond the sailcloth flap that served as Hawkwood's door.

"Come in, Bardolin."

The mage entered, stooping. He looked older, Hawkwood thought. His carriage had always been so upright, his face so battered and grizzled that he seemed made out of some enduring stone; but the years were beginning to tell on him now. His forehead shone with sweat, and like everyone else's his neck and arms were blotched with insect bites. The imp that rode on his shoulder seemed as sprightly as ever, though. It leapt on to the crate which Hawkwood used as a desk and he had gently to pry the inkwell out of its tiny hands.

"What cheer, comrade wizard?" Hawkwood asked the old mage.

Bardolin collapsed on the heap of leaves and seacloak which had been piled into a bed.

"I have been purifying water for the invalids among us. I am tired, Captain."

Hawkwood produced a rotund bottle from behind his crate and offered it. "Drink?"

They both had a gulp straight from the neck, and spluttered over the good brandy.

"That calms the bones," Bardolin said appreciatively, and nodded towards the open log. "Writing for posterity?"

"Yes. The habit of a master-mariner's lifetime, though I am in danger of becoming a chronicler." Hawkwood shut the heavily bound book and rewrapped it in its oilcloth. "Ready for tomorrow?"

Bardolin rubbed the shadows under his eyes. "I suppose... How does it feel to be a lord?"

"I still sweat, the mosquitoes still feed off me. It is not so different. "

Bardolin smiled. "What conceit we have, we men. We throw up a squalid camp like this and name it a colony. We distribute titles amongst ourselves, we lay claim to a country which has existed without us since time's dawn; we impose our rules upon things we are utterly ignorant of."

"It is how society is made," Hawkwood said.

"Yes. How did the Fimbrians feel, do you think, when they came together in their tribes nine centuries ago and made themselves into one people? Was there a shadow of their empire flickering about them, even then? History. Give it a hundred years and it will make heroes and villains out of every one of us – if it remembers us."

"The world rolls on. It is for us to make what we can of it."

The old mage stretched. "Of course. And tomorrow we will see a little more of it. Tomorrow the governor sets out to explore this place he has claimed."

"Would you rather be playing hide-and-seek with the Inceptines back in Abrusio?"

"Yes. Yes, I would. I am afraid, Captain, truly afraid. I am frightened of what we will find here in the west. But curious also. I would not stay behind tomorrow for all the world. It is man's insufferable curiosity which makes him set sail across unknown seas; it is a more potent force even than greed or ambition – you know that, I think, better than anyone."

"I'm as ambitious and greedy as the next man."

"But curiosity drove you here."

"That, and Murad's blackmail."

"Aha! Our noble governor again! He has brought us all into the tangle of his own machinations. We are flies trembling in his web. Well, even spiders have their predators. He is beginning to realize that, in spite of his bluster and arrogance."

"Do you hate him then?"

"I hate what he represents: the blind bigotry and pride of his caste. But he is not as bad as some; he is not stupid, nor does he wilfully ignore the truth, no matter what he says."

"You have too many new ideas, Bardolin, I too find it hard to accommodate some of them. Your hills which spout flames and ash – those I can believe. I have heard men talk of them before. But this *smell* of magic from the trees and soil; from the land itself. An earth which circles the sun. A moon bombarded by stones from beyond the sky... Everyone knows that our world is at the heart of God's creation, even the Merduks."

"That is the Church talking."

"I am no blind son of the Church, you know that."

"You are a product of its culture."

Hawkwood threw up his hands. Bardolin exasperated him, but he could not dislike the man. "Drink some more brandy, and stop trying to right the wrongs of society for a while."

Bardolin laughed, and complied.

THEY WERE TO venture into the interior again in the morning, and Murad's dinner was both a social event and a planning conference. He had killed the last of the chickens, as if to prove to the world that he had no fears for the future, and one of the soldiers had shot a tiny deer, no bigger than a lamb, which was the centrepiece of the table. Bardolin examined its bones as if they were the stuff of an augury. Beside the meat courses there was the last of the dried fruit, nuts, pickled olives, and a tiny scrap of Hebrion sea cheese as hard as soap. They drank Candelarian which was as warm as blood in the humid night, and finished with Fimbrian brandy.

Hawkwood, Murad, Bardolin, Sequero and di Souza: the hierarchy of the colony. Murad's exclusive guestlist had antagonized half a dozen of the more prominent of the colonists, who felt they should have been drinking his brandy also.

The lucky few talked civilly enough amongst themselves, with the light of the precious ship's candles playing on their glistening faces. Sequero was mourning his horses; they were deteriorating fast in this foreign climate, and no fodder the men could find seemed to suit them. Not that a horse could bear a man anywhere in the jungle, Hawkwood thought; but from now on the nobility would walk like the meanest trooper. Perhaps that was what grieved the aristocratic young officer most.

Huge moths circled the candles, some as big as Hawkwood's hand, and fizzling around them were the tinier insects which were nevertheless the more irritating. Despite the attempts Murad had made to make the gathering a gracious affair, with a couple of the female colonists as maidservants, the men around the rough board table and mould-spattered linen tablecloth were none too clean and tidy. Leather rotted here with incredible swiftness, they had found, and many of the soldiers were already securing their armour with twisted lengths of creeper or ship's rope. Soon they would be a crowd of savages dressed in rags.

The colonists were experimenting with the fruits which hung in profusion from almost every tree, Bardolin told them. Some were very good, others smelled like corruption the minute they were opened. A few birds had been trapped with greenlime smeared on branches. There was food here for all, if only they could learn how to use it, prepare it, recognize it.

"Food for savages," Sequero sneered. "I for one would prefer to trust to the ship's salt pork and biscuit."

"The ship's stores will not last for ever," Hawkwood said. "And most of them will have to be reserved for the homeward voyage. I have men trying to extract salt from the shallower pools on the shore, but we must assume that we have no way of preserving food. The barrelled stores must be kept intact."

"I agree," Murad said unexpectedly. "This is our country and we must learn to use it. From tomorrow onwards, the exploring party will be living off the land. It would be absurd to try and carry our food with us."

Sequero held up a glass of the ruby Candelarian. "We will miss many things ere long, I suppose. It is the price we pay for being pioneers. Sir, how long do you expect to be gone?" He was to be in command of the colony while Murad was away.

"A month or five weeks, not more. I expect progress in my absence, Haptman. You can start clearing plots for those families with able-bodied men, and I want the coast surveyed up and down for several leagues and accurate charts made. Hawkwood's people will help you in that."

Sequero bowed slightly in his seat. He did not seem unduly burdened by his new responsibilities. Di Souza sat opposite him, his big red face expressionless. He was a noble only by adoption; he could not have hoped for Sequero's promotion. But he had hoped, all the same.

They lifted the sailcloth wall of Murad's residence to let air flow in and out. Around the fort the rude huts of the other colonists squatted, some of them lit by campfires, others illuminated by the bobbing globes of werelight kindled by those who knew some cantrimy. They were like outsized fireflies hovering fascinated in the darkness, an eldritch sight with the forest moths circling them. Little flapping planets in erratic orbits about miniature suns, Hawkwood thought, remembering Bardolin's beliefs.

"They say that Ramusio tramped every road and track in Normannia in his spreading of the faith," Bardolin said quietly. "But the Saint's foot never trod this earth. It is a dark continent we have discovered. I wonder if we shall ever bring any light to it save for fire and werelight."

"And gunfire," Murad added. "That we have brought also. Where faith does not sustain us, arquebuses will. And the determination of men."

"Let us hope it is enough," the old wizard said, and swallowed the last of the wine.

TWELVE

THERE WAS A mist in the morning which hung no higher than a man's waist. It seemed to have seeped out of the very ground, and to those moving about the fort it was as if they were wading through a monochrome sea.

The expedition set off soon after dawn, Murad in the lead with Sergeant Mensurado at his side, followed by Hawkwood, Bardolin and two of the *Osprey*'s crew, the huge black helmsman Masudi and master's mate Mihal, a Gabrionese like Hawkwood himself. After them came twelve Hebrian soldiers in half-armour bearing arquebuses and swords, their helmets slung at their hips and clanking as they walked. The expedition sounded like a pedlar's caravan, Hawkwood thought irritably. He and Bardolin had tried to persuade Murad to leave the heavy body armour behind, but the lean nobleman had refused point-blank. So the sweating soldiers had an extra fifty pounds on their backs.

The remaining score or so of the demi-tercio turned out to see them off, along with most of the colonists. They fired a volley in salute which sent the birds screaming and flapping for miles around and made Bardolin roll his eyes. Then Fort Abeleius was left behind, and the company was alone with the jungle.

They took a bearing with Hawkwood's bowl-compass, and set off as close as they could to due west. One of the soldiers was detailed to blaze a tree every hundred yards or so, though their path would have been easy to retrace since it looked like the blundering tunnel a stubborn bull might have made in the vegetation.

Slow going, the unceasing noise of hacking cutlasses, men gasping for breath, cursing the rabid undergrowth.

The day spun round, and they sheltered in the lee of the trees as the customary afternoon tempest battered down, making their surroundings into a dripping, sodden, steaming bathhouse. Then they crashed onwards again, nursing their dry gunpowder as though it were gold dust.

They found the rocky flank of the hill they had climbed on their first day, and at Murad's insistence they climbed it again with an agony of effort. Once at the top they paused to feel the freer air and have a look at a wider world. They divided into pairs and divested each other of the fat leeches which crept up their legs and down the back of their necks, then they started to parallel the contours of the hollow hill, following the line of the ridge round to the north-east, coming up almost to due north. It was a farther hike, but faster since they had no jungle to hack through.

Night came as they were finally on the descent, and they made a rough camp amid the rocks of the ridge, piling up stones into platforms to sleep upon. The mist came down to sour their tongues and bead the rocks, and the soldiers bickered over the lighting of the campfires until Mensurado silenced them. They stood watch three at a time, and it was about the middle of the graveyard watch when Hawkwood was roughly shaken awake by Murad.

"Look, down in the jungle. They've just appeared."

Hawkwood rubbed his swollen eyes and peered out into the noisy darkness below. Hard to see if he concentrated. Better to let his vision unfocus. There: a tiny blur of brightness far off in the night.

"Lights?"

"Yes, and they're not blasted glow-worms either."

"How far, do you think?" They were talking in whispers. The sentries were awake and alert, but Murad had woken no one else.

"Hard to say," the nobleman said. "Six or eight leagues, anyway. They must be above the trees. On the flank of one of these weird hills, perhaps."

"Above the trees, you say?"

"Keep your voice down. Yes, otherwise how could we see them? I noted no clearings within sight on the way down the ridge."

"What do we do?" Hawkwood asked.

"You get out your contraption and take a bearing on those lights. That is our route for tomorrow."

Hawkwood did as he was told, fumbling with bowl and water and needle in the firelight.

"North-west or thereabouts."

"Good. Now we have something to aim for. I was not happy at the thought of simply wandering into the interior until we struck that road."

"I don't suppose it's occurred to you that we were *meant* to see those lights, Murad?"

The nobleman's face twisted in a rictus-like smile. "Does it matter? Whatever dwells on this continent, we will have to confront it – or them – at some point. Better to do it sooner."

There was a strange light in Murad's eyes, an eagerness which was disquieting. Hawkwood felt as though he were on a rudderless ship with a lee shore foaming off the bow. That sensation of helplessness, of being manipulated by forces he could do nothing about.

"Go back to sleep," Murad told him in an undertone. "It is hours yet until the dawn. I will take your watch; there's no sleep left in me tonight."

He looked like a creature which no longer needed sleep anyway. He had always been sparely built, but now he appeared gaunt to the point of emaciation, a pale creature of sinew and bone held together by the will which blazed out of the too-bright eyes. The beginnings of fever? Hawkwood would bring it up with Bardolin tomorrow. With any luck, the bastard might even expire.

Hawkwood returned to his stony bed and shut his eyes to await his own sleep, that coveted oblivion.

THE SIGHTS OF the night were not mentioned in the morning, and the party set off with rumbling stomachs. They had brought a little biscuit with them, but nothing else. If they were to live off the land, they would have to start doing so soon.

They left the crater-hill behind and plunged into dense forest once more, still descending. It was noon before the land levelled out, and the ground was boggy and wet with the run-off water from the ridge. Streams glittered everywhere, and the trees had put out great naked roots like buttresses from high on their trunks, so fantastical looking that it was hard to believe they had not been grafted on by some demented botanist. Masudi and Mensurado, slashing a path at the front, were sprayed with water when the creepers they sliced spouted like hoses.

They halted to rest, rubber-legged with fatigue and hunger. Bardolin and a few of the soldiers collected fruit from the surrounding branches, and the company sat down together to experiment. There was a buff-coloured circular fruit which when sliced open looked almost exactly like bread, and after a few cautious tastings the men wolfed it down, heedless of the old wizard's warnings. They found also a huge kind of pear, and curved green objects growing in clusters which Hawkwood had encountered before in the jungles of Macassar. He showed the men how to peel off the outer skin and eat the sweet yellow fruit within. But despite the bounty the soldiers craved meat, and several walked with slow-match lit, ready to shoulder arms and fire at any animal they might encounter.

Another afternoon downpour. This time they continued trudging through it, though they were almost blinded by the stinging rain. Men held their water bottles up as they marched to collect the liquid, but it was full of the detritus of the canopy above, alive with moving things, and they had to empty out what they had collected in disgust.

They were imperceptibly beginning to slip into the routine of the jungle. They had tied off their breech legs with strips of leather and cord to prevent the leeches climbing inside them, and they accepted the daily rain as a normal occurrence. They became more adept at picking their way through the dense vegetation, and learned to avoid the low-hanging branches from which snakes occasionally dropped down. They knew what to eat and what not to eat – to some extent – though those who had gorged themselves on fruit were soon dropping out of the column to perform their necessary functions with greater and greater frequency. And the incessant noise, the screechings and warblings and wailings of the forest denizens soon became a scarcely registered thing. Only when it stopped sometimes, inexplicably, would they pause without saying a word, and stand like men turned to stone in the midst of that vast, unnerving silence.

The second night they lit their fires with snatches of gun-powder, since they had no dry tinder remaining, and built beds of leaves and ferns to try and keep something between their tired bodies and the vermin of the forest floor. Then the soldiers sat cleaning equipment and drying their arquebuses whilst Masudi and Mihal collected fruit for the evening meal. There was little talk. The lights of the night before were common knowledge, but the soldiers did not seem too disturbed by what they might imply. Where there were lights there was civilization of a sort, and they seemed to think that it was theirs to claim by the sword if they had to. They had yet to strike upon any sign of civilization, such as the road they had glimpsed from the ridge, however.

Masudi's shout brought them to their feet, and they pelted off towards it, grabbing burning faggots from the campfires and hurriedly setting them to the slow-match. The jungle was a wheeling chiaroscuro of shadow and flame, looming blacknesses, whipping leaves. They splashed through a shallow stream. The torch taken by the two fruit hunters rippled faintly ahead.

"What is it? What happened?" Murad demanded.

Masudi's black face glistened with sweat, but he did not seem very afraid. Behind him Mihal stood with a shirtful of fruit.

"There, sir," the giant helmsman said, raising his hissing torch. "Look what we found."

The company peered into the flame-etched night. Something else there, bulkier even than the trees. They could see a snarling face, a muzzle zigzagged with fangs and two long ears arcing back from a great skull. It was half-bearded with creepers.

"A statue," Bardolin's voice said calmly.

"It made me shout, coming across it like that. I nearly dropped the torch. I'm sorry, sir," Masudi said to the quivering Murad.

"It's a werewolf," Hawkwood told them, staring at the monolith. The thing was fifteen feet tall and snarling as though it longed to be free of the creepers which bound it. The body was almost hidden in spade-shaped leaves. One taloned paw lay on the ground at its feet. The jungle was slowly working the hewn stone apart, breaking it down and absorbing it.

"A good likeness," Murad said with a forced jocularity that fooled no one.

Bardolin had lit the cold glow of a werelight, and was investigating the statue more closely, though most of the soldiers had hung back, their arquebuses pointed at the surrounding darkness as though they were expecting flesh-and-blood doppelgangers of the thing to leap into the torchlight.

A ripping of vegetation. The imp helped its master tear away the clinging leaves and stems.

"There's an inscription here I think I can read." The werelight sank down until it almost touched the wizard's lined forehead. "It's in Normannic, but an archaic dialect."

"*Normannic?*" Murad spat out the word incredulously. "What does it say?"

The mage rubbed moss away with his hand. Around them the jungle noise had died and the night was almost silent.

> *Be with us in this Change of Dark and Life*
> *That we may see the heart of living man,*
> *And know in hunger that which binds us all*
> *To this wide world awaiting us again.*

"Gibberish," Murad growled.

The mage straightened. "I know this from somewhere."

"You've read it before?" Hawkwood asked.

"No. But something similar, perhaps."

"We'll discuss the historical implications later. Back to camp, everyone," Murad ordered. "You sailors, bring what fruit you've gathered. It will suffice for tonight."

THERE WAS LITTLE sleep for anyone that night, because the jungle remained as silent as a tomb for hours and the silence was more disquieting by far than any din of nocturnal bird or beast. The company built their fires despite the fact that the sweat was dripping off their very fingertips. They needed the light, the reassurance that their comrades were around them. The fires had a claustrophobic effect, however, making the towers of the trees press ever closer in on them, emphasizing the huge, restless jungle which pursued its own arcane business off in the darkness as it had for eons before them. They were mere nomadic parasites lost in the pelt of a creature which was as big as a turning world. That night they were not afraid of unknown beasts or strange natives, but of the land itself, for it seemed to pulse and murmur with a beating life of its own, alien, unknowable, and utterly indifferent to them.

THEY HAD ANOTHER look at the statue when the sun rose. It seemed less impressive in daylight, more crudely sculpted than they had thought. Year by year, the jungle was comprehensively destroying it. They could only guess at its age.

Another day on the march. They followed the direction Hawkwood pointed out in the morning, keeping their route straight by checking and rechecking with the trail of blazed trees they left behind them. It was impossible to be sure, but Hawkwood reckoned that they had come some six leagues west of their first hill, the one Murad had named *Heyeran Spinero*. The soldiers quarrelled over this news, believing they had marched twice as far, but Hawkwood had averaged out his paces and even been generous in his reckoning. It seemed impossible that days of Herculean effort should have brought them such a small distance.

Murad alone seemed unconcerned, perhaps because he was counting on running into the natives of this country before they had trudged and hacked their way too many more miles.

Another hot night ensued, another pile of firewood to collect, another series of sweet, insubstantial fruits to wolf down in the light of the yellow flames. And then sleep. It came easy tonight, despite the heat and the marauding insects and the unknown things in the darkness.

BARDOLIN WOKE AT some dead hour in the night to find that the fires had sunk into red glows and the sentries were asleep. The jungle was silent and still.

He listened to that vast quiet, the loudest sound the faint rush of his own heartbeat in his mouth. He had the strangest impression... that someone was calling him, someone he knew.

"Griella?" he whispered, the night air invading his head.

He got up, leaving his imp asleep and whimpering, and picked his way over the snoring forms of his comrades, oddly unalarmed.

Blackness like the inside of a wolf's throat surrounded and enfolded him. He walked on, his feet hardly touching the detritus of the forest floor, his eyes wide and unseeing. The jungle soared to tenebrous heights above him, the night stars invisible beyond the shrouding canopy of the trees. Leaves caressed his face, dripping warm water over him. Creepers slid across his body like hairy snakes, both rough and soft. He felt that he had sloughed away a thicker skin, and was left with each of his nerve endings naked and pulsing in the night, quivering to every waft of air and drop of water.

A deeper shadow before him, a shape blacker even than the witch-dark forest. In it two yellow lights burned and blinked in unison. Still, he was not afraid.

I'm dreaming, he told himself, and the merciful thought kept terror at bay.

The lights moved, and he was conscious of a warmth that had nothing to do with the night air. His skin crawled as it approached him, a black sunlight.

The lights were eyes, bright saffron and slitted with black like those of a vast cat. It was standing before him. There was a noise, a low susurration like a continuous growl but in a lower key. He felt the sound with his new skin as much as heard it.

And felt the fur of the thing, as soft as crushed velvet. A sensual, wholly pleasurable sensation which made him want to bury his palms deep in its softness.

The world spun, and the breath had been knocked out of him. He was on the ground, on his back, and two huge paws were on his shoulders. He felt the prickle of whiskers, sharp as needles, the thing's breath on his face.

It sank down on him as though it meant to mould itself to his body. His hands felt the thickly muscled ribs under the fur and brushed a line of nipples along the taut belly.

He thought it groaned, an almost human sound. He was conscious of the throbbing warmth in his crotch, the heat of the thing as it pressed against him there.

And then it had reared up. A scratch of pain somewhere around his hipbone which made him cry out; his breeches were ripped off and it had plunged itself down on him, taking him inside.

A feverish heat and liquid grip of muscle. It pushed his buttocks into the moist humus, its head thrown back and the red mouth open so that he could see the long glint of fangs. He grabbed fistfuls of its fur as his climax came, and thought he screamed.

It was down on him again for a moment, and he could feel the teeth pressed against his neck. Then the crushing weight and heat were raised off him. He found himself sunk deep into the muck of the jungle floor, utterly spent.

He felt a kiss – a human kiss of laughing lips on his own. Then he knew he was alone again, back with his ageing body, the razor-awareness of everything gone. He wept like a struck child.

AND WOKE UP. Dawn had come, and the camp was stirring awake. The sour reek of old smoke hung heavy in the air.

Hawkwood handed him a waterbottle, looking ten years older in the grey morning, moss in his tawny beard.

"Another day, Bardolin. You look like you've had a hard night."

Bardolin swallowed a gulp of water. His mouth soaked it up and remained as dry as gunpowder. He swallowed more.

"Such a dream I had," he said. "Such a dream."

There were black hairs sweat-glued to his palms. He stared at them in curiosity, wondering where they could have come from.

THE COMPANY BROKE camp in morose silence, the men moving slowly in the gathering heat. They shook out into their accustomed file, some gnawing fruit, others pulling up their breeches, their faces drawn by the chaos of their bowels. More and more of them were succumbing to the inadequacies of their strange diet. The surrounds of the camp stank of ordure. Hollow-eyed, they started off on the day's journey.

On the afternoon of this, the fourth day, the rain came down with its weary regularity, and they plodded on under it like cattle oblivious to the drover's stick. Masudi and Cortona, one of the strongest soldiers, were at the front chopping a path blindly with one hand shielding their eyes as though from too-brilliant sunlight. Behind them the rest of the soldiers staggered onwards, their once-bright armour now coral coloured in places, green in others. Their rotting boots sank deep into the leaf litter and muck and they were sometimes obliged to bend over and pull their feet free of the sucking mud with their hands.

Then the two point-men stopped. The heavy vegetation had given way like a breached wall and there was a clearing in front of them, the far side of it misted by the pouring rain.

"Sir!" Cortona shouted above the downpour, and Murad was shoving everyone out of the way to get to the head of the file.

A figure was sitting in the middle of the clearing, cross-legged and head bowed in the wet. As far as they could tell, it was a woman, her dark hair bound up, dressed in leather with bare arms and legs. She did not look up at the gaping explorers, nor did she acknowledge their presence in any way, but they knew she was aware of them. And there were odd flickerings of movement along the edge of the clearing behind her.

The company stood like men stunned, water pouring down their faces and into their open mouths unheeded. At last Murad drew his rapier, ignoring Bardolin's urgent hiss.

The woman in the clearing looked up, but at the sky above, not at them. For an instant her eyes seemed blank and white in the rain, lacking iris or pupil. Then the rain stopped as swiftly as it always did in this country. Their job done, the clouds began to break up and the sun to filter down.

The woman smiled, as though it were all her handiwork and she was proud of it. Then she looked straight at the crowd of men who stood opposite, swords drawn, arquebuses levelled.

She smiled again, this time showing white, sharp teeth like those of a cat. Her eyes were very dark, her face pointed and delicate. She rose from her sitting position in one sinuous movement that made the breath catch in the throat of every man who watched her. A bare midriff, lines of muscle on either side of the navel. Unshod feet, slender limbs the colour of honey.

"I am Kersik," she said in Normannic that had a slight burr to it, an old-fashioned slowness. "Greetings and welcome."

Murad recovered more quickly than any of them, and, aristocratic to his fingertips, he bowed with a flourish of the winking rapier.

"Lord Murad of Galiapeno at your service, lady." Hawkwood noted wryly that he did not introduce himself as his Excellency the governor.

But the woman Kersik looked past him to where Bardolin stood with the imp perched, bedraggled and dripping, on his shoulder.

"And you, brother," she said. "You are doubly welcome. It is a long time since a Master of Disciplines came to our shores."

Bardolin merely nodded stiffly. For a moment they stared into each other's eyes, the battered old wizard and the slim young woman. Bardolin frowned, and she smiled as though in answer, eyes dancing.

There was a pause. The soldiers were drinking the woman in, but she seemed unperturbed by their hungry regard.

"You are bound for the city, I take it," she said lightly.

Murad and Hawkwood shared a glance, and the scarred nobleman bowed again. "Yes, lady, we are. But we are sadly puzzled as to how to get there."

"I thought as much. I will take you, then. It's a journey of many days."

"You have our thanks."

"Your men have been eating too much of the wrong kinds of fruit, Lord Murad of Galiapeno," Kersik said. "They have the air of the flux about them."

"We are unaccustomed as yet to your country and its ways, lady."

"Of course you are. Put your men into camp here in the clearing. I'll fetch them something to calm their stomachs. If they start the journey to Undi in this condition they might not finish it."

"*Undi.* Is that the name of your city?" Hawkwood asked. "What language might it be in?"

"In an old, forgotten language, Captain," the woman said. "This is an old continent. Man has been here a long time."

"And from whence did you come? I wonder," Hawkwood muttered, unsettled by being called "Captain." How had she known?

Kersik glanced at him sharply. She had heard his whispered comment.

"I'll return ere nightfall," she said then. And disappeared. The men blinked. They had seen a tan blur across the clearing, nothing more.

"A witch, by Ramusio's beard," Murad growled.

"Not a witch," Bardolin told him. "A mage. The Dweomer is thick about her. And something else as well." He rubbed his face as though trying to scrub the weariness from it.

"Sorcery, always sorcery," Murad said bitterly. "Maybe she has gone to collect a few cohorts of her fellow warlocks. Well, I wonder what they'll make of Hebrian steel."

"Steel will do you no good here, Murad," Bardolin said.

"Maybe. But we have iron bullets for the arquebuses. That may give them pause for thought. Sergeant Mensurado!"

"Sir."

"We'll make camp, do as we're told. But I want the slow-match lit, and every weapon loaded. I want the men ready to repel any attack."

"Yes, sir."

As THE LIGHT died and the night swooped in once more, the company gathered about three campfires, each big enough to roast an ox over. The soldiers stood watch with powder-smoke from the glowing match eddying about their cuirasses, stamping their feet and whistling to keep awake, or slapping at the incessant probing of the insects.

"Will she come back, do you think?" Hawkwood asked, grimacing as he kneaded his bad shoulder.

Murad shrugged. "Why not ask our resident expert in all things occult?" He nodded at Bardolin.

The mage seemed on the verge of sleep, his imp lying wide-eyed and watchful in his lap. His head jerked, and the silver stubble on his chin glistened in the firelight.

"She'll be back. And she'll take us to this city of hers. They want us there, Murad. If they didn't, we'd be dead by now."

"I thought they'd prefer us sunk somewhere in the Western Ocean," Hawkwood said. "Like the caravel's crew."

"They did, yes. But now that we're here, I believe they are interested in us." *Or in me*, the thought came, alarming and unwelcome.

"And just who are *they*, Mage?" Murad demanded. "You speak as though you knew."

"*They* are Dweomer-folk of some kind, obviously. Descendants of previous voyagers, perhaps. Or indigenous peoples maybe. But I doubt that, for they speak Normannic. Something has happened here in the west. It has been going on for centuries whilst we've been fighting our wars and spreading our faith oblivious to it. Something different. I'm not sure what, not yet."

"You're as vague as a fake seer, Bardolin," said Murad in disgust.

"You want answers; I cannot give them to you. You will have to wait. I've a feeling we'll know more than we ever wanted to before this thing is done."

They settled into an uncomfortable silence, the three of them. The fires cracked and spat like angry felines, and the jungle raved deliriously to itself, a wall of dark and sound.

"What bright fires," a voice said. "One might almost think you folk were afraid of the dark."

Their heads snapped up, and the woman Kersik was standing before them. She carried a small hide bag which stank like rancid sap. The tiny hairs on her thighs were golden in the firelight. As her mouth smiled its corners arced up almost to her ears and her eyes were light-filled slits.

Murad sprang to his feet and she stepped back, becoming human again. Mensurado was berating the sentries for having let her slip past them unseen.

"You do not need men to keep watch in the night," she said. "Not now I am here." She dumped the hide bag on the ground. "That is for those among you whose guts are churning. Eat a few of the leaves. They'll calm them."

"What are you, a forest apothecary?" Murad asked.

She regarded him, her head on one side. "I like this one. He has spirit." And while Murad considered this: "Best you should sleep. We will walk a long way tomorrow."

THEY SET SENTRIES, though she laughed at them for doing so. She sat cross-legged off at the edge of the firelight as she had been sitting when first they had seen her. Men made the Sign of the Saint when they thought she was not looking. They ate their meagre supper of gleaned fruit, not one of them trusting her enough to try the bag of leaves she had brought. Then they lay down on the wet ground with sword and arquebus close to hand.

Bardolin's imp could not settle. It would nestle against him in its accustomed sleeping position and then shift uneasily again and squirm out from beside him to take in the camp and the sleeping figures, the watchful sentries.

It nudged him awake some time before the dawn and in the half-sleeping state between unconsciousness and wakefulness he could have sworn that the camp was surrounded by a crowd of figures which stood motionless in the trees. But when he sat up, scraping at his gummed eyelids, they were gone and the Kersik woman was sitting cross-legged, not a particle of weariness in her appearance.

Murad sat with his back to a tree opposite, an arquebus in his hands with its slow-match burnt down almost to the clamp. His eyes were feverish with fatigue. He had watched her all night, it seemed. The woman rose and stretched, the muscles rippling under her golden skin.

"Well rested for the travel ahead?" she asked.

The nobleman looked at her through sunken eyes.

"I'm ready for anything," he said.

THIRTEEN

EIGHTEEN DAYS THEY travelled through the unchanging jungle. Eighteen days of heat and rain and mosquitoes and leeches and mud and snakes.

Looking back on it, Hawkwood found it remarkable how quickly the men had been worn down. These were hardened campaigners who had seen battle in the dust-choked furnaces of the summer Hebros valleys. On board ship they had seemed swaggering veterans, hard men with rough appetites and constitutions of iron. Here they sickened like kittens.

They buried the first six days after they had met their new guide, the woman Kersik.

Glabrio Feridas, soldier of Hebrion. He had crouched shakily in the jungle to ease his overworked bowels, and it seemed to those who came across his corpse that he had voided all the blood that the mosquitoes and leeches had left in him.

After that, men ate the leaves that Kersik had brought for them. They avoided the fruits she told them to avoid, and they boiled their water every evening in their rusting helmets. There was no more flux, but many of them continued to feel feverish and soon the stronger men were carrying the armour of those who could no longer support its weight.

On the tenth day, Murad was finally prevailed upon by Hawkwood and Bardolin to allow the soldiers to take off the armour and cache it. The men piled it up and covered it with fallen branches and leaves, blazed a dozen trees around it and marched on the lighter by fifty pounds, clad in their leather gambesons.

They made better time after that. Hawkwood calculated they were travelling roughly nor'-nor'-west, and they were covering perhaps four leagues a day.

On the twelfth day Timo Ferenice was the second man to die.

A snake had sidled up to his ankle as he stood nodding on sentry duty and bit quickly and efficiently. He had died in convulsions, spraying foamy spittle and calling on God, Ramusio and his mother.

The following day they hit upon a road, or track rather. It was just wide enough for two men to walk abreast, a tunnel of beaten earth and close-packed stones seemingly well cared for, which led them farther to the north. They had bypassed the cluster of lights Murad had seen from the Spinero and were travelling almost parallel to the far-off coast.

All the while they travelled, Kersik strode along easily at the front of the column, frequently pausing to let the gasping men behind her catch up. The land rose almost imperceptibly, and Bardolin hazarded that they were nearing the southern slopes of the great conelike mountain they had sighted on the first day of their landfall.

Their pace should have quickened upon hitting the road, but it seemed to the members of the company that their strength was ebbing. Lack of sleep and poor food were taking their toll, as was the unrelenting heat. By the seventeenth day, the twenty-first out of Fort Abeleius, the soldiers were stumbling along in linen undershirts, their leather gambesons too rotten and mouldering to be of any further use. And medicinal leaves or no, two of them were so far gone in fever they had to be carried in crudely thrown-together litters by their exhausted comrades.

"I BELIEVE I have yet to see her sweat," Hawkwood said to Bardolin as they sat in camp that night. Kersik was off to one side, her legs folded under her, face serene.

Bardolin had been nodding off. He started awake and caressed the chittering imp. The little creature ate better than any of them, for it happily gorged itself on all manner of crawling things it found in the leaf litter. It was just back from foraging and was contentedly grinning in Bardolin's lap, its belly as taut as a drum.

"Even wizards sweat," the old mage said, irritated because he had been on the verge of precious sleep.

"I know. That is why it's so odd. She doesn't seem real, somehow."

Bardolin lay back with a sigh. "None of it seems real. The dreams I have at night seem more real than this waking life."

"Good dreams?"

"Strange ones, unlike any I have known before. And yet there is an element of familiarity to them too. I keep feeling that everything here I have come across splices together somehow – that if I could but step back from it I would see the pattern in the whole. That inscription on the statue we found – it reminds me of something I once knew. The girl: she is Dweomer-folk, certainly, but there is something unknown at work in her also, something I cannot decipher. It is like trying to read a once-known book in too dim a light."

"Maybe there will be a brighter light for you once we hit upon this city. Tomorrow, she says, we'll arrive there. I wish I could say I was looking forward to it, but the discoverer in me has lost some of his relish for our expedition."

"*He* has not," Bardolin said, and he waved a hand to where Murad was doing his nightly rounds of the campfires, checking on his men.

"He cannot keep it up much longer," Hawkwood said. "I don't believe he's had more than an hour's sleep a night since we left the coast."

Murad looked less like an officer administering to his men than a ghoul preying on the sick. His lank hair fell in black strings across his face and the flesh had been pared away from nose and cheekbones and temples. His scar now seemed an extravagant curl of tissue, like an extra thin-lipped mouth on the side of his face. Even his fingers were skeletal.

"We have been ashore scarcely a month," Hawkwood said quietly. "We have buried five shipmates in that time – maybe more back at the fort by now – and the rest of us are close to breaking down. Do you really believe this land can ever be fit for civilized men, Bardolin?"

The mage shut his eyes and turned away. "I'll tell you after tomorrow."

THAT NIGHT THE dream came to Bardolin again.

But this time it was the woman Kersik who came to him in the night, nude, her skin a flawless bloom of honey. She was incandescently beautiful despite the two rows of nipples that lined her torso from pectoral to navel and the claws which curled at the tips of her fingers. Her eyes blazed like the sun behind leaves.

They made love on the yielding ground beyond the camp. This time Bardolin was atop her, grinding into her firm softness with the vigour of a young man. And all around the straining couple a masque of fantastic figures danced and capered madly, spindle-thin, cackling, with green slits for eyes and hornlike ears. Bardolin could feel their feet, light as leaves, dancing in the hollow of his back as he pushed into the woman below him.

But there was another presence there. He arched his head to see, despite the grip of her hand on the nape of his neck, a tall darkness towering above the frolics.

A shifter in wolf form.

NONE OF THEM had slept well. Bardolin ached as though someone had been kicking him all night. The company dragged themselves erect, Sergeant Mensurado hauling men to their feet. Kersik looked on like an indulgent parent.

Murad appeared from the trees. He had shaved, the blood on his chin testimony to the effort it had cost him. His straggling hair had been tied back and he had changed into a clean shirt which was nonetheless dotted with mould. He looked almost fresh, despite the sunken glitter of his eyes.

"So we are to see this city of yours today," he said to Kersik.

The woman seemed amused at some private joke, as she often did. "Why yes, Lord Murad, if your comrades are fit to march."

"They're fit. They're Hebrian soldiers," Murad drawled, and he turned away from her with such languid contempt that Hawkwood actually found himself admiring him. The woman's smile took on a fixed quality for a second, and then became pure sunshine again.

They set off after a frugal meal of the inevitable fruit. It was weeks since any of them had tasted meat, and they were becoming nostalgic even at the thought of the ship's salt pork.

Another day of labour. Though they were tramping a passable road, they still had to take it in turns to carry the two delirious soldiers. Even Murad did his share.

There was more life in the jungle here, if that were possible.

Not the squeakings and scurryings of before, but the crash and thump of larger beasts moving off in the vegetation. Kersik appeared oblivious to them, but the company travelled with loaded weapons and drawn swords. They were aware of a subtle change in their surroundings. The trees were smaller, the canopy less dense. Almost the forest here looked like secondary growth, a reclaiming of land once cleared.

To reinforce this opinion they came across the remains of huge stone-built buildings half hidden at the sides of the narrow road. Bardolin wanted to pause and examine them, for they seemed to be liberally dotted with carved writing, but Kersik would not allow it. When he asked her about them she seemed even more reluctant to give out information than she had throughout the journey.

"They are *Undwa-Zantu*," she said at last, surrendering to Bardolin's badgering.

"What does that mean?" the mage asked.

"They are old, from the earlier time, the first peoples."

With that one sentence she let loose a torrent of questions from both Bardolin and Hawkwood, but would answer none of them.

"You will learn more when we get to the city," was all she would say.

THEY HAD REACHED the foot of the mountain to the north of their anchorage. They could see it clearly, even through the canopy overhead. It reared up like a grey wall above the jungle, the forest struggling to maintain itself at its knees but gradually thinning and clearing all the same.

"How far do you think we have come?" Bardolin asked Hawkwood.

The mariner shrugged with one shoulder. He had taken bearings as often as he could – Kersik had been inordinately fascinated by the compass – and he'd had both Masudi and big Cortona pacing to check his own count, but in the day-to-day labour it was probable that major inaccuracies had crept in.

"We're walking almost due north now," he said. "Since we met the girl, I'd say we've come some sixty leagues, but we've changed course several times."

They were far back in the file. Kersik was twenty yards in front, Murad striding beside her like her consort. Bardolin lowered his voice. Her hearing was better than a beast's.

"She slips past questions like a snake. She knows everything, I'm sure of it – perhaps the whole history of this land, Captain. For it has a history, you can be sure of that. These ruins look as ancient as the crumbling Fimbrian watchtowers you can see up in the Hebros passes, and they are six centuries old and more."

"Maybe we'll find answers in this city she keeps talking about, though where it might be I'm sure I don't know. The way she talks it must be on the slope of this damned mountain; but how could one build a city on slopes so steep?"

"I don't know. It may be that if there is a city there somewhere we'll find more answers in it than we bargained for."

The file halted. Murad called for them at its head and the wizard and the mariner hurried past the line of soldiers.

The way was blocked by a trio of figures so fantastic that even Murad had momentarily lost his poise.

Two were inhumanly tall, eight feet perhaps. They were black-skinned, a black so dark that it made Masudi's skin appear yellowish. Their limbs were bare and they wore simple loincloths, but where their heads should have been were incredible masks. One was of a leopard-like creature, only heavier and more muscular. The other had the head of a great mandrill, with bright blue patches of ridged flesh on either side of the flaring nose.

But the masks were not masks. The leopard-head licked its teeth and the eyes moved. The mandrill sniffed the air, its nostrils quivering. In their human hands, the two creatures carried bronze-bladed spears twice the height of a man, wickedly barbed.

The third figure was tiny by comparison, shorter even than Hawkwood. He seemed entirely human and his skin, though deeply tanned, was as pale as a Ramusian's. He wore a shapeless bag of supple hide for a hat, and white linen robes which concealed his entire body except for small, broad-fingered hands. His face was pouchy and bejowled, eyes bright and black shining out of puffy sockets. Were it not for the strange garments, he might have passed for a well-to-do merchant of Abrusio with too many rich meals and too much good wine under his belt. His only ornament was a pendant of gold in the shape of a five-pointed star which enclosed a circle. It hung from his wattled neck on a gold chain whose links were as thick as a child's finger.

"Gosa," Kersik said, and she bowed. "I have brought the Oldworlders."

The leopard head growled deeply.

"Well done," the man in the linen robes said. "I thought I'd provide you with an escort into Undi. And my curiosity was consuming me. It's been a long time." His glance strayed to the members of the company who stood silent behind Kersik, even Murad at a loss for words.

"Greetings, brother," Gosa said to Bardolin.

The mage blinked, but did not reply. His imp uttered a single little yelp which sounded almost interrogative. The leopard head growled again.

Murad stepped forward, clearly angered by being left out of the exchanges. Immediately the mandrill head levelled his spear until it touched the noble's chest, stalling him.

A series of clicks. Sergeant Mensurado, Cortona and the other soldiers had their arquebuses in the shoulder, the serpentines cocked back, the muzzles pointed squarely at the exotic trio in the middle of the track. Powder-smoke eddied about the company. Gosa sniffed at it, and smiled to show yellow teeth, canines from which the gums had retreated.

"Ah, the very essence of the Old World," he said, not at all put out by the weapons pointed at his ample belly. "Put up your weapons, gentlemen; you will not need them here. Ilkwa – for shame – can't you see the man is merely trying to introduce himself?"

The tall spear swung back to the vertical. Murad nodded at Mensurado and the arquebuses were uncocked, though the men kept their slow-match lit.

"Murad of Galiapeno at your service," the nobleman said wryly.

"Gosa of Undi at yours," the plump, berobed man said, bowing slightly. "Will you follow me into our humble city, Lord Murad? There are refreshments waiting, and those who wish to can bathe."

Murad bowed in his turn. Gosa, Kersik and the two outlandish beast-men led off. The company fell in behind them, still hauling the two litters with the fever-ridden soldiers.

The world changed in a twinkling.

The jungle disappeared. One moment they were walking under the shadowed shelter of the forest, and the next it had vanished. Uninterrupted sunshine blinded them. The borderline between the riotous vegetation and barren emptiness was as clear-cut as if a giant razor had shaved the mountainside clean of all living things.

Now they could see the true size of the peak which soared above them. Its head was lost in cloud, and though from a distance it had seemed perfectly symmetrical, closer up they could decipher broken places in its cone, ragged tears in the flanks of stone, petrified waterfalls where long-cold lava had once gushed forth. The place was a wilderness, a desert leached of colour, defined only in greys and blacks. There were dunes of what looked like ebony sand, weird bubbles of basalt, outwellings and holes and the stumps of solidified geysers. A landscape, Bardolin thought, like that which he had glimpsed through Saffarac's viewing device long ago. Lunar, dead, otherworldly.

The going was harder, and the men puffed and panted as they laboured up the steep slopes. There was still a road of sorts here, a crude pavement of tufa blocks. Cairns marked its twistings and turnings as it zigzagged up the face of the mountain. The men gasped in the withering heat, choking on volcanic dust, their faces becoming black with what looked like soot and tasted like ash. It dried out their mouths and gritted between tongue and teeth.

"I see no city," Murad rasped to Kersik and Gosa. "Where are you taking us?"

"There is a city, trust me." Gosa beamed at him, a benevolent gnome with obsidian shards for eyes. "Undi is not so easily chanced across unless one is led there by one of its inhabitants. And this is Undabane whose knees we clamber across. The Sacred Mountain, heart of fire whose rages have been tamed." He stopped. "Have patience, Lord Murad. It is not much farther."

The company became strung out despite all that Murad and Mensurado could do. It was a line of antlike figures struggling up the monstrous mountainside, the soldiers pausing to catch their breaths, the litter-bearers changing every hundred yards. So it was Hawkwood and Bardolin, at the front, who saw it first.

A cleft in the mountain's conical top, a huge rent in its perfect shape. The summit was still some six or seven thousand feet above, but here they were working slowly around its western face, and the cleft was invisible from the northern approach. A glimpse of dark walls within shooting to incredible heights, and something else.

At the base of the cleft was a monumental statue weathered almost into shapelessness by the elements. It was perhaps a hundred and twenty feet high, and vaguely humanoid. A stump of a spear in one crumbling fist. Deep eyes visible in a face which had a snout for a nose. The impression of a powerful torso. The thing had been built out of tufa blocks bigger than the carrack's longboat and they were eroding at the joins so that it seemed to have a grid imposed upon it.

The rest of the party caught up as Gosa, Kersik and the two beast-men paused. There was only one litter.

"Forza died," Murad said to the questioning looks. "We don't know when – no one noticed. We built a cairn over him," He seemed angry with himself, as though it were his fault. "God curse this pestilent country."

Gosa pursed his lips disapprovingly, but did not comment. The company moved on again, the soldiers sullen and silent, even Mensurado cast down. The sick man's death seemed like an omen.

Rocks clattered under their feet, and their sodden boots were full of ash, blistering their heels and toes. They were down to their last swirl of water in the canteens, and Murad would let no one finish it.

Into the shade of the massive statue, their heads hardly reaching to its ankles.

The world contracted. They were trudging through a narrow place whose walls soared up hundreds, perhaps thousands, of feet on either side, a snake-thin gap in the wall of the mountain through which the wind whistled and hissed like a live thing. Water dripped in glittering fringes from the gorge sides, and the men stood under the drips with their tongues out, begging. Flat, iron-tasting water full of grit, it nonetheless enabled their tongues to move about inside their mouths again.

The world opened once more, or rather exploded upon them. Like the change from jungle to ashen desert on the slopes of the mountain, the transition was abrupt and astonishing.

They found themselves on a shelf of rock, maybe a thousand feet up *inside* the mountain. Undabane was hollow, a vaster version of the crater which Murad had named the Spinero. They could look up and see the walls of the mountain rearing on all sides, sheer as cliffs, unscalable. The blue unclouded sky was a semicircle of pure colour above the rock.

And below there was a disc of brilliant jungle, as though someone had lifted it whole, a small, flat world of it, and placed it inside Undabane after knocking the summit off the hollow mountain. The view stupefied them. There was a dark curve across the crater floor, the shadow of the mountain's lip dragging in the wake of the sun. Looking at it, Bardolin understood in an instant the phases of the moon.

There were buildings down there amid the trees: pylons of black basalt monumental in size but dwarfed to insignificance by their setting, flat-roofed houses built entirely of stone, a stepped pyramid as tall as Carcasson's spires, the step faces painfully bright with gold. Avenues and roads. A city, indeed. A place utterly alien to anything they had seen before or imagined. It took speech out of their parched mouths and left them gaping. Even Murad could find nothing to say.

"Behold Undi," Gosa said with quiet satisfaction. "The Hidden City of the Zantu and the Arueyn, the Heart of Fire, the Ancient Place. Worth a trek, is it not?"

"Who built this?" Bardolin asked at last. "Who are these people you name?"

"All questions will be answered in the end. For now, we have but a little descent and then you will be able to rest. Word of your coming has gone ahead of you. There is food and drink waiting, and succour for the sick amongst you."

"Take us down there, then," Murad said with brutal directness. "I'll have no more of my men die in this hellhole because you stand there preening yourself."

Gosa's eyes flared with an odd light, though his face did not change. He inclined his head slightly and led the party onwards, down a track which had been hewn out of the side of the mountain. Kersik shot the nobleman a look of pure venom, however.

They stumbled and stared and cursed their way down to the floor of the crater, which by this time was nearly all in shadow. There were dark clouds gathering in the circle of sky thousands of feet above them, the beginning of the daily downpour. They found themselves walking along a wide, well-paved road which had rain gutters on either side. It was a street of sorts, for there were more of the flat-roofed buildings set back from it amid the trees. As they hobbled deeper into the heart of the city the trees grew sparser and the buildings closer together. And there were people here.

They were tall, lean and black and were dressed in a white linen-like cloth. They were delicately featured, with sharply chiselled noses and thin lips. The women were as tall and stately as queens, their breasts bare, gold pendants ornamenting them. Many had their bodies decorated with some form of intricate ritual scarring which swirled in circles and currents around their torsos and on their cheeks. They regarded the company with interest, and many pointed especially at Masudi, who was like them and yet not like them. But they were restrained, dignified. The company passed through what could only be a market place, with stalls of fruit and meat set out, but there was little hubbub. The people there halted to stare at the ragged soldiers of Hebrion, and then went on about their business. To Hawkwood, who knew the crazed, chaotic bazaars of Ridawan and Calmar, the orderliness was unnerving. And there were no children anywhere to be seen. Neither were there any animals, not even a stray dog or lounging cat – if they had such things in this country.

The pyramid towered above the rest of the buildings, its gold dulled now as the sun was hidden and the afternoon rain began to tumble down inside the mountain. Gosa and his inhuman companions led the company to a tall, square house off the market place and thumped upon a hardwood door. It was opened by a tall old man whose hair was as white as his face was black.

"I have brought them, Faku," Gosa said. "See they are well cared for."

The old man bowed deeply, as inscrutable as a Merduk grand vizier, and the company trooped into the house.

"Rest, eat, bathe. Do whatever you wish, but do not leave the building," Gosa told them cheerfully. "I will be back this evening, and tomorrow... tomorrow we will see about answering some of those questions you have been harbouring for so long."

He left. The old man clapped his hands and two younger versions of himself appeared, shut the doors of the room – which the company saw was a kind of foyer – and stood expectantly.

Murad and his soldiers were glaring about them as if they expected an armed host to rush out of the walls. It was Hawkwood who smelled the cooking meat first. It brought the water springing into his mouth.

Kersik said something to the old man, Faku, and he clapped his hands again. His helpers swung open side doors in the big room, and there was the gurgle of running water. Marble pools with fountains. Clean linen. Earthenware bowls of fruit. Platters of steaming meat.

"Sweet Saints in heaven," Bardolin breathed. "A bath!"

"It might be a trick," Murad snarled, though he was swallowing painfully as the smell of the food obviously tantalized him.

"There is no trick." Kersik laughed, darted into the room and snatched a roasted rib of the meat, biting into it so the juices ran down her chin. She came over to Bardolin and stood close to him.

"Will you not try it, Brother Mage?" she asked, offering him the rib.

He hesitated, but she thrust it under his nose. That secret amusement was in her eyes. "Trust me," she said in a low voice, vixen grin on her face, mouth running with the meat juices. "Trust me, brother."

He bit into the rib, shredding meat from the bone. It seemed the most delicious thing he had ever tasted in his life.

She wiped the grease out of his silver beard, then spun from him. For an instant he could see her eyes in the air she had vacated, hanging as bright as solar after-images.

"You see?" she said, holding up the rib as though it were a trophy.

The men scattered, making for the piled platters and bowls. Faku and his colleagues stood impassively, looking on like sophisticates at a barbarian feast. Bardolin remained where he was. He swallowed the gobbet of meat and stared at Kersik as she danced about the gorging soldiers and laughed in Murad's livid face. Hawkwood remained also.

"What was it?" he asked Bardolin.

"What do you mean?"

"What kind of meat?"

Bardolin wiped his lips free of grease. "I don't know," he said. "I don't know." His ignorance suddenly seemed terrible to him.

"Well, I doubt they brought us this far to poison us." Hawkwood shrugged. "And by the Saints, it smells wholesome enough."

They gave in and joined the soldiers, wolfing down meat and slaking their thirst with pitchers of clear water. But they could not manage more than half a dozen mouthfuls ere their stomachs closed up. Bloated on nothing, they paused and saw that Kersik was gone. The heavy doors were shut and the attendants had disappeared.

Murad sprang up with a cry and threw himself at the

doors. They creaked, but would not move.

"Locked! By the Saints, they've locked us in!"

The tiny windows high in the walls, though open to the outside, were too small for a man to worm through.

"The guests have become prisoners, it would seem," Bardolin said. He did not seem outraged.

"You had an idea this would happen," Murad accused him.

"Perhaps." Even to himself, Bardolin's calm seemed odd. He wondered privately if something had indeed been slipped into the food.

"Did you think they would leave us free to wander about the city like pilgrims?" Bardolin asked the nobleman. The meat was like a ball of stone in his stomach. He was no longer used to such rich fare. But there was something else, something in his head which disquieted him and at the same time stole away his unease. It was like being drunk; that feeling of invulnerability.

"Are you all right Bardolin?" Hawkwood asked him, concerned.

"I – I –" Nothing. There was nothing to worry about. He was tired, was all, and needed to get himself some sleep.

"*Bardolin!*" they called. But he no longer heard them.

FOURTEEN

WHAT IS YOUR name?

"Bardolin, son of Carnolan, of Carreirida in the Kingdom of Hebrion." Was he speaking? It did not matter. He felt as safe as a babe in the womb. Nothing would touch him.

That's right. You will not be harmed. You are a rare bird, my boy. How many of the Disciplines?

"Four. Cantrimy, mindrhyming, feralism and true theurgy."

Is that what they call it now? Feralism – the ability to see into the hearts of beasts, and sometimes the craft to duplicate their like. You have mastered the most technical of the Seven Domains, my friend. You are to be congratulated. Many long hours in some wizard's tower poring over the manuals of Gramarye, eh? And yet you have none of the instinctive Disciplines – soothsaying, weather-working. Shifting.

A tiny prick in the bubble of well-being which enfolded Bardolin, like a sudden draught in a sturdy house, a breath of winter.

"Who are you?"

Kersik! She has much to learn of herbalism yet. Rest easy, brother of mine. All will come to light in the end. I find you interesting. There has not been much to seize my interest this last century and more. Did you know that when I was an apprentice there were nine disciplines? But that was a long time ago. Common witchery and herbalism. They were amalgamated, I believe, in the fifth century and brought under that umbrella term "true theurgy," to the profit of the Thaumaturgists' Guild and the loss of the lesser Dweomer-folk. But such is the way of things. You interest me greatly, Bardolin son of Carnolan. There is a smell about you that I know. Something there is of the beast in you. I find it intriguing... We will speak again. Rejoin your friends. They worry about you, worthy fellows that they are.

He opened his eyes. He was on the floor and they were clustered around him with alarm on their faces, even Murad. He felt an insane urge to giggle, like a schoolboy caught out in some misdeed, but fought down the impulse.

A wave of relief. He felt it as a tactile thing. The imp clung to his shoulder, whimpering and smiling at the same time. Of course. If he had been drugged it would have been left bereft, lost, the guiding light of his mind gone from it. He stroked it soothingly. He had put too much into his familiar, too much of himself. The things were meant to be expendable. He felt a thrill of fear as he caressed it and it clung to him. Much of his own life force had gone into the imp, giving it an existence beyond him. That might not be to the good any more.

Drugged? Where had that thought come from?

"What happened?" Hawkwood was asking. "Was it the food?"

It was an enormous effort to think, to speak with any sense.

"I – I don't know. Perhaps. How long was I gone?"

"A few minutes," Murad told him, frowning. "It happened to no one else."

"They are playing with us, I think," Bardolin said, getting to his feet rather unsteadily. Hawkwood supported him.

"Lock us up, drug one of us – what else do they have in store?" the mariner said.

The soldiers had retrieved their arms and lit their match; it stank out the room.

"We'll have that door down, and shoot our way out of here if we have to," Murad said grimly. "I'll not meet my end caught like some fox in a trap."

"No," Bardolin said. "If they are expecting anything, they are expecting that. We must do it another way."

"What? Await yonder wizard with a tercio of his beast-headed guards?"

"There is another way." Bardolin felt his heart sink as he said the words. He knew now what he would do. "The imp will go for us. It can get out of the window and see what is happening outside. It may even be able to open the door for us."

Murad appeared undecided for a moment; clearly, he had had his heart set on a fighting escape. He was still wound up too tightly; they all were. A spark would set them off and they would die here with the questions unanswered, and that was intolerable.

"All right, we'll let the imp go," Murad conceded at last.

Bardolin let out a sigh. He was utterly tired. He felt sometimes that this land had fastened on him like a succubus and would feed off him until there was nothing left but a withered husk that would blow away to ash in the wind. Soothsaying was not one of his Disciplines, and yet the presentiment had been upon him ever since they had made landfall that there was something deadly to the ship's company and to the world they had left behind, and it resided here, on this continent. If they escaped they would take it back to the old world with them like a disease which clung to their clothing and nestled in their blood. Like the rats which scurried in the darkness of the ship's hold.

He bent to the bewildered imp, stroking it.

"Time to go, my little friend." *Can you see the way out, up there in the wall? Up you go. Yes! That's it. Where the last of the daylight is coming through.*

The imp was peering through the narrow aperture in the wall. The entire company watched it in silence.

"I may leave you for some time," Bardolin told them. "But don't be alarmed. I am travelling with the imp. I will return. In the meantime, stand fast."

Murad said something in reply, but he was already gone. The world had become a vaster place in the wink of an eye, and the very quality of Bardolin's sight had changed. The imp's eyes operated in a different spectrum of colours: to it the world was a multivaried blend of greens and golds, some so bright they hurt to look at. Stone walls were not merely a blank facade, but their warmth and thickness produced different shadows, glowing outlines.

The imp looked back once, down at the silent room full of men, and then it was through the high, narrow window. It was hungry and would have liked to share in the meats that had been laid out for the company, but its master's will was working in it. It did as it was told.

Indeed, in some ways Bardolin *became* the imp. He felt its appetites and fears, he experienced the sensation of the rough tufa blocks under his hands and feet, he heard the noises of the city and the jungle with an enhanced clarity that was almost unbearable until he became used to it.

The rain had ended, and the city was a dripping, steam-shrouded place, fogged as a dawn riverbank. The light was dimmer than it should be; the crater sides would cut out much of the light in the later afternoon.

What to make of this hidden city? The volcanic stone of the buildings was dark and cold, but the lambent, upright figures of people were about – not many of them now – and a single crescent slice of sunshine glowed like molten silver way up on the side of the crater: the last of the departing sun. Soon night would settle. Best to wait a few minutes.

Something else, though. A... smell which seemed tantalizingly familiar.

The imp clambered down the side of the high wall like a fly, head-first. It reached the ground and scampered into a cooler place of deeper shadow, an alleyway it might have been called in Abrusio. There it crouched and breathed in the air of the dying day.

The daylight sank as though someone had slowly covered a great lamp somewhere beyond the horizon of the world. It was actually possible to see the growing of the night as a palpable thing. In minutes the city had sunk into darkness.

But not darkness to the imp. Its eyes began to glow in the murk of the alley and its vision grew sharper.

Still, that smell somewhere, hauntingly reminiscent of something from the past.

To our duty, my diminutive friend, Bardolin's mind gently prodded as the imp crouched puzzled and fascinated in the humid shadow.

It obeyed the urging of a mind that was moment by moment becoming one with it. Obediently it scuttled around the side of the house which imprisoned the company, looking for the front door, another window, any means of entry or egress.

There were things moving in the streets of the city. To the imp they were sudden dazzling brightnesses darting in and out of sight. It was the heat of their bodies that made them so luminous. The imp whimpered, wanted to hide. Bardolin had to sink more of his will into it in order to keep it under his command.

There – the door they had entered the place by. It was closed, but there was no sign of Kersik, Gosa or the beast-headed guards. The imp sidled over to it, listened and heard Murad's voice within. It chuckled to itself with an amusement that was part Bardolin's, and set one glowing eye to the crack at the door's foot. No lights, no warmth of a waiting body.

Push at the door, Bardolin told it, but before it could do as it was told it felt a growing heat behind it, the hot breath of some living thing. It spun around in alarm.

A man might have seen a tall, bulking shadow looming over him, with two yellow lights burning and blinking like eyes. But the imp saw a brightness like the sun, the effulgence of a huge, beating heart in the bony network of the chest. It saw the heat rising off the thing in shimmering waves of light. And as the mouth opened, it seemed to breathe fire, a smoking calefaction that scorched the imp's clammy skin.

"Well met, Brother Mage," a voice said, distorted, bestial but nonetheless recognizable. "You are ingenious, but predictable. I suppose you had no choice: that festering pustulence of a nobleman would have left you no other options."

The thing was a massively built ape, a mandrill, but it spoke with the voice of Gosa.

"Come. We have kept you waiting long enough. Time to meet the master."

A huge paw swept down and scooped up the imp even as it leapt for freedom. The were-ape that was Gosa laughed, a sound like the whooping beat of a monkey's cry but with a rationality behind it that was horrible to hear. The imp was crushed to the thing's shaggy breast, choking at the vile heat, the stench of the shifter which it had smelled but not quite recognized. It had been confused by memories of Griella, the girl who had been a werewolf and who had died before they had set foot on this continent. It had not recognized the peril close by.

The were-ape limbered off at speed, its free hand bounding it forward whilst the short back legs pushed out, a rocking movement which seemed to gather momentum. Bardolin saw that his familiar was being taken towards the stepped pyramid at the heart of the city.

They passed other creatures in the streets: shifters of all kinds, nightmarish beasts that reeked of Dweomer, warped animals and men. Undi at night was a masque of travesties, a theatre of the grotesque and the unholy. Bardolin was reminded of the paintings in the little houses of worship in the Hebros, where the folk were still pagan at heart. Pictures of Hell depicting the Devil as master of a monstrous circus, a carnival of the misshapen and the daemonic. The streets of Undi were full of capering fiends.

He should withdraw now, leave the imp to its fate and slip back into his own body, rejoin the others and warn them of what was waiting for them outside the walls of the house in which they were imprisoned. But somehow he could not, not yet. Two things kept him looking out of the imp's eyes and feeling its terror: one, he felt nothing but stark fear at the thought of abandoning his familiar, and with it a goodly portion of his own spirit and strength; the other was nothing more or less than sheer curiosity, which even in the midst of his fear kept him drinking in the sights of the nocturnal city through the imp's eyes. He was being taken to someone who perhaps knew all the answers, and as Murad hungered after power so Bardolin thirsted for information. He would remain in the imp's consciousness a little longer. He would see what was at the heart of this place. He would *know*.

"WHAT CAN HE be at?" Murad demanded, pacing back and forth. The room was lit only by a few tiny earthenware lamps they had found among the platters and dishes, but the burning match of the soldiers glowed in tiny points and the place was heavy with the reek of the powder-smoke. Bardolin lay with his eyes open, unseeing, as immobile as the tomb carving of a nobleman on his sarcophagus.

"Two foot of match we've burnt, sir," Mensurado said. "That's half an hour. Not so long."

"When I want your opinion, Sergeant, I'll be sure to ask you for it," Murad said icily.

Mensurado's eyes went as flat as flint. "Yes, sir."

"It's dark out," Hawkwood said. "It could be he's waiting for the right moment. There are probably guards and it's only an imp, after all."

"Sorcerers! Imps!" Murad spat. "I've had a belly-full of the lot of them. *Brother* Mage indeed! For all we know he could be in league with his fellow necromancers, plotting to turn us over to them."

"For God's sake, Murad," Hawkwood said wearily.

But the nobleman wasn't listening. "We've waited long enough. Either the mage has betrayed us or his familiar has met with some mishap. We must get out of here unaided, by ourselves. Sergeant Mensurado –"

"Sir."

"– I want that door down. Two men to carry our slumbering wizard – Hawkwood, your seamen will do. We'll want as many arquebuses ready as possible."

"What about Gerrera, sir?" one of the soldiers spoke up, pointing to their fever-struck comrade who lay on his litter on the floor, his face an ivory mask of sweat and bone-taut skin.

"All right. Two more of you take him. Hawkwood, lend a hand there. That leaves us with seven arquebuses free. It'll have to do. Sergeant, the door."

Mensurado and Cortona, the biggest men in the company except perhaps for Masudi, squared up to the hardwood double doors as if they were an opponent in a fight ring. The two men looked at each other, nodded sombrely and then charged, leading with their right shoulders.

They rebounded like balls bounced off a wall, paused a second, and then charged again.

The doors creaked and cracked. A white splinter line appeared near the hinges of one.

Three more times they charged, changing shoulders each time, and on the fifth attempt the doors sagged and broke, the beam which had closed them smashed in two, their bronze hinges half dragged out of the wall.

The company hesitated a moment as the echo of the crash died away. Cortona and Mensurado were breathing heavily, rubbing their bruised shoulders. Finally Hawkwood raised one of the earthenware lamps and peered out into the gloom of the foyer beyond, in which they had met the old man Faku and his helpers. The place was deserted, the door to the street closed. The night seemed eerily silent after the jungle noise they were used to.

"There's no one here, it seems," he told Murad. He lifted the lamp this way and that. There was a stone staircase at the back of the big room. The running water of the pools had stopped except for an occasional drip. Shadows wheeled and flitted everywhere like restless ghosts.

"Now what?"

"We'll search the other rooms," Murad said.

"Mensurado, see to it. It may be that the imp is lost somewhere upstairs or nearby. And that Kersik woman may still be around."

Mensurado led a trio of soldiers upstairs.

"I don't like it," Hawkwood said. "Why leave us unguarded? They must have guessed we were capable of breaking down the door."

"They are magicians and sorcerers, every one," Murad said. "Who knows how their minds work?"

They heard the boots of Mensurado and his comrades clumping above their heads, then snatches of talk, and finally a cry, not of fear, more of surprise.

Hawkwood and Murad glanced at one another. There was a flurry of voices above, the thumping of feet and heavy things scraping across the floor.

Mensurado came running down the stairs. "Sir – take a look at this." He was holding a handful of coins.

Normannic gold crowns. On one side was a depiction of the spires of burnt Carcasson, on the other a crude, stylized map of the continent. Bank-minted money belonging to no kingdom in particular, but used in the great transactions between kings and governments. Coins such as this bribed princes, bought mercenaries, forged cannons.

"There are chests and chests of the damned stuff up there, sir." Mensurado was saying. "A king's ransom, the hoard of a dozen lifetimes."

Murad bit into one of the coins. "Real, by God. There's chests of the stuff you say, Sergeant?"

"Hundredweights, sir. I've never seen anything like it. The treasury of a kingdom could not hold more."

Murad threw aside the coin; it fell with a sweet kiss of metal on stone. "Everyone upstairs. Leave Gerrera and the mage here for the moment. I want every pouch and pocket filled. You shall each have your share, never fear."

He and Mensurado had a glitter in their eyes that Hawkwood had not seen before. As they left the room Hawkwood bent down beside the motionless Bardolin and shook him.

"Bardolin, for God's sake wake up. Where are you?"

No answer. The old mage's eyes remained wide open, his face as immobile as that of a corpse.

It sounded as though cascades of coins were being poured over the floor upstairs. Sharp blows as someone attacked a chest, splintering wood. Hawkwood felt no urge to join in the greedy festival. He loved gold as much as the next man, but there was a time and a place for it. As Mihal left his side to chance his luck upstairs, Hawkwood curtly ordered him back. Both Mihal and Masudi looked at him imploringly, but he shook his head.

"You'll see, lads. Nothing good will come of this gold. Me, I'll be happy to get out of here with my skin intact. That's riches enough."

Masudi grinned ruefully. "You can't run with your pockets full of gold, I'll warrant."

"Nor eat it, neither," Mihal added, resigned.

The soldiers began staggering downstairs, pockets bulging. They had even stuffed coins down the front of their shirts, giving themselves rattling paunches. Four of them were bearing two wooden chests between them. Murad descended last, holding up a lamp and seeming a little dazed.

"We'll come back," he was saying in a low voice. "We'll come back with a dozen tercios one day."

"I'd rather we had the tercios now," Hawkwood rasped. "If you want to leave this place, we'd best be going at once. There's no telling when that Gosa and his creatures will be back."

"I am not unaware of the need for urgency, Captain,"

Murad snapped. "What we carry away with us here could outfit an entire flotilla of ships, and can you imagine the backing I could call on when it became known that the Western Continent was stuffed with gold? We could bring an army here, and extirpate these monsters and sorcerers from the land for good."

"It's gold, yes, but minted in the form of Normannic crowns, Murad," Hawkwood said. "Did you think of that? What are they using it for, if not to spend in the Old World? We know nothing about what is going on in this land, or how it affects the Ramusian states at home."

"We'll find out another time," the nobleman said. "For now, all I want is to get clear of this place. Mensurado, the door. You men, pick up Gerrera."

Lumbering, rattling and clinking, the soldiers gathered themselves and prepared to leave.

But the door opened before Mensurado got to it. A black-skinned figure dressed in white stood there. The old man, Faku. His mouth opened.

A shot, amazingly loud in the confined space. Faku was hurled back out of the doorway.

"One less sorcerer," Mensurado snarled, and reloaded his arquebus with practised speed.

"We must move quickly," Murad said. "That shot will rouse the city. Out! Bring the chests."

What with the chests and the limp forms of Bardolin and Gerrera, only Mensurado and two other soldiers had their hands free. The company filed out into the hot night, stepping over Faku's body as though it were a pothole in the road. Hawkwood closed the old man's eyes, cursing under his breath.

"This way. Quickly," Murad said, leading off. The company followed him at a jog-trot, sweating and gasping ere they had gone a hundred yards. Coins slipped out of the soldiers' pockets to clink at the roadside.

The city seemed deserted. Not a light to be seen anywhere, not a living soul on the streets. But Hawkwood was continually aware of movement, like a flickering at the corner of his eye. The place was so dark that it was impossible to be certain. He looked up to see a disc of star-filled sky above the crater-rim, and was almost sure he saw things moving in that sky, wheeling darknesses which stood out against the stars. He had the uncomfortable notion that the city was not quiet and empty at all, but teeming with invisible, capering life.

The company paused to rest in a narrow side street, the soldiers who carried the heavy chests massaging their bloodless hands. They had come half a mile maybe from the house in which they had been imprisoned, and there was still no sign of a pursuit. Even Murad seemed uneasy.

"I thought the entire city would have been about our ears by now," he said to Hawkwood.

"I know," the mariner replied. "Everything is wrong, strange. What happened to Bardolin's imp, and to Bardolin himself? Why can't he come back to us? Are we being allowed to escape because –"

"Because what?"

"Perhaps because they have what they want."

Murad was silent for a long minute. At last he said: "It is a pity about the mage, but if you are right then we may yet get away unscathed. And after all, we bear him with us. His mind may yet return." He would not meet Hawkwood's eye, but scanned the massiveness of the buildings, the trees which were beginning to rear up in their midst; they were not far from the crater wall, and the narrow gorge which was their only exit.

"Time to move on."

The soldiers shouldered their burdens once more, and the company staggered onwards. The attack came so suddenly that they were surrounded before they had seen their assailants. The night was sprinkled with raging eyes, and huge forms charged them. The quiet was broken by roars and screams and wails from a hundred bestial throats. The men at the rear died before they could even drop the chests that weighed them down.

FIFTEEN

AT THE TOP of Undi's pyramid was another building whose sides curved inwards towards its roof. The Gosa shifter took the imp inside, and then in a series of bounds it leapt up a narrow line of steps. They were on the roof of the structure, a square platform perhaps three fathoms to a side. There the imp was gently lowered to its feet, and the were-ape left. A grating of stone, and the opening in the platform closed behind it.

Bardolin looked up with the imp's eyes to see the encircling pitch-night of the crater walls, and above them a roundel of stars turning in the endless gyre of heaven. There were so many of them that they cast a faint, cold light down on the city. Many of them were recognizable – it was possible to glimpse Coranada's Scythe – but they seemed to be in the wrong positions. Even as Bardolin watched, a streak of silver lightninged across the welkin, a star dying in a last flare of beauty.

"Awe-inspiring, isn't it?" a voice said, and the imp jumped. Instinctively it looked for somewhere to hide, but the stone platform was stark and bare, and there was nothing beyond its edge but a long fall to the pyramid steps below.

Bardolin gripped the will of the creature in his own, steadied it, held it fast.

There was a man on the platform. He had come out of nowhere and stood with the starlight playing across his features. He seemed amused.

"An attractive little familiar. We in Undi do not use them any more. They are a weakness as well as an asset. Are they still as hard to cast through as I remember?"

Bardolin's voice issued out of the imp's mouth. The creature's eyes went dull as he dominated it completely.

"Hard enough, but we get by. Might I ask your name?"

The man bowed. "I am Aruan of Undi, formerly of Garmidalan in Astarac. You are Bardolin of Carreirida."

"Have we met before?"

"In a way. But here – let me spare your trembling familiar. Take my hand."

He extended one large, blunt-fingered hand to the imp. The creature took it and Aruan straightened, pulling. But the imp did not come with him. Instead a shimmering penumbra slid out of its tiny body as though he had dragged from it its soul. He was holding on to Bardolin's own hand, and Bardolin stood there on the platform, astonished, glimmering in the starlight like a phantom.

"What did you do?" he asked Aruan. The imp was blinking and rubbing its eyes.

"A simulacrum, nothing more. But it renders communication a little easier. You need not fear; your essence, or the bulk of it, is with your sleeping body down in the city."

Bardolin's shining image felt itself with trembling hands. "This is magic indeed."

"It is not so difficult, and it makes things more... civilized."

Bardolin folded his imaginary arms. "Why am I here?"

"Can't you answer that yourself? You are a creature of free will, as are all God's creations."

"You know what I mean. What is it you want of me?"

The man named Aruan turned away, paced to the edge of the platform and stared out over the city of Undi. He was tall, and dressed in voluminous, archaic robes that a noble might have worn in the days of the Fimbrian Hegemony. He was bald but for a fringe of raven hair about the base of his skull, for all the world like a monk's tonsure. He had a beaked nose and deep-set eyes under bristling, fantastic brows, high, jutting cheekbones strangely at odds with the rest of his rather aristocratic face, as if someone had melded the features of a Kolchuk tribesman and a Perigrainian Landgrave. Hauteur and savagery, Bardolin noted them both.

"This is how I once looked," Aruan said. "Were you to see my true form now you might be repelled. I am old, Bardolin. I remember the days of empire, the Religious Wars. I have known men whose fathers spoke with the Blessed Saint. I have seen centuries of the world come and go."

"No man is immortal," Bardolin said, fascinated and apprehensive at the same time. "Not even the most powerful mage."

Aruan turned away from the dark city, smiling. "True, too true. But there are ways and means of staving off death's debt collectors. You ask what it is I want of you, and I am wandering around the answer. Let me explain something.

"In all the years I have been here, we have seen many ships arrive from the Old World – more than you could ever have imagined. Most of them carried cargoes of gold-hungry vultures who simply wanted to claim this, the Zantu-Country, and rape it. They were adventurers, would-be conquerors, sometimes zealots filled with missionary zeal. They died. But sometimes they were refugees, come fleeing the pyres of Normannia and the purges of the Inceptines. These people, for the most part, we welcomed. But we have never encountered an Oldworlder with your... potential."

"I don't understand," Bardolin said. "I am a common enough brand of mage."

"Technically, perhaps you are. But you possess a duality which no other mage who has come here from across the ocean has possessed, a duality which is the very key to our own thaumaturgical hierarchy here in the west."

Bardolin shook his head. "Your answers only provide the spur to further questions."

"Never mind. It will become plain enough in the time to come."

"I want you to tell me about this place – how you got here, how this began. What is happening."

Aruan laughed, a guffaw which made him sound like a hearty ruffian. "You want our history then, the centuries of it, laid before you like a woven tapestry for your eyes to drink in?"

"I want explanations."

"Oh – so little you think you are asking, eh? *Explanations*. Well, the night is fine. Give me your hand again, Brother Mage."

"A phantom hand."

"It will suffice. See? I can grasp it as though it were flesh and blood. In the other I will take your imp; it would not do to leave him alone here."

Something happened which Bardolin, for all his expertise in the field of Dweomer, could not quite catalogue. The platform disappeared, and they were thousands of feet up in the air and still rising. The air was cooler here, and a breeze ruffled Aruan's hair.

I can feel the breeze; I, a simulacrum, Bardolin thought with a start of fear. And then he realized that it was the imp's sensations he was feeling. Had to be. A simulacrum could not be given physical sensation.

Or could it? He could feel Aruan's hand in his own, warm and strong. Was that the sensation of the imp or himself?

They stopped rising. Bardolin could look down like a god. The moon had risen and was a bitten apple of silver which lit up the Western Ocean. The vault above Bardolin's head, strangely, did not feel any closer. The stars were clearer, but as far away as ever.

The incredible vastness of the world, night-dark and moonsilver, was staggering. The sky was a bright vault which spun endlessly above the sleeping earth, the Western Ocean a tissue of wrinkled silver strewn with the gossamer moonlight. And the Western Continent was a huge, bulking darkness in which only a few scattered lights burned. Bardolin could see the watchfires of Fort Abeleius on the coast, the tiny pricks of light that were the stern and masthead lanterns on the *Osprey* offshore, and inland red glows like scattered gleeds from an old fire.

"Restless forces of the world, at play amid the earth's foundations," Aruan said, sounding as though he were quoting something. "Volcanoes, Bardolin. This country is old and torn and troubled. It stirs uneasily in its sleep."

"The craters," Bardolin said.

"Yes. There was a great civilization here once, fully as sophisticated as that which exists upon Normannia. But the forces which create and destroy our world awoke here. They annihilated the works of the ancients, and created Undabane, the Holy Mountain, and a score of lesser cones.

The *Undwa-Zantu* died in a welter of flame and ash, and the survivors of the cataclysm reverted to barbarism."

"The dark, tall people who inhabit your city."

"Yes. When first I came upon them, in the year of the Saint one hundred and nine, they were savages and only legends and ruins remained of the noble culture they had once possessed. They called themselves *Zantu*, which in their tongue signifies the Remnant, and their ancestors they called *Undwa-Zantu*, the Elder Remnant. Their mages – for they had been a mighty folk of magic – had degenerated into tribal shamans, but they preserved much that was worth knowing. They were a unique people, that elder race, possessed of singular gifts."

But Bardolin was gaping. "You've been here... how long? Four and a half centuries?"

Aruan grinned. "In the Old World I was a mage at the court of King Fontinac the Third of Astarac. I sailed into the west in a leaky little caravel called the *Godspeed*, whose captain was named Pinarro Albayero, may God rest his unhappy soul."

"But how – ?"

"I told you: the shamans of the Zantu preserved some of the lore of their ancestors, theurgy of a potency to make what we called Dweomer in the Old World look like the pranks of a child. There is power in this country, Bardolin; you will have noticed it yourself. The mountains of fire spewed out raw theurgy as well as molten rock in their eruptions. And Undabane is the fountainhead, the source. The place is virtually alive. And the power can be tapped. It is why I am still here, when my poor frame should be dust and dry bone long since."

Bardolin could not speak. His mind was busy taking in the enormity of what Aruan was saying.

"I came here fleeing the purges of the High Pontiff Willardius – may he rot in a Ramusian hell for ever. With some of my comrades, I took ship with a desperate man, Albayero of Abrusio. He was nothing more or less than a common pirate, and he needed to quit the shore of Normannia as badly as we did." Aruan paused for a moment, and his eyes became vacant, as if looking back on that awful expanse of centuries, all gone to ash now.

"Every century or so," he went on, "there is a convulsion in the Faith of the Ramusians, and they must renew their beliefs. They do so with a festival of slaughter. And always their victims are the same.

"We fled one such bloodbath, my colleagues and I. Most of the Thaumaturgists' Guilds of Garmidalan and Cartigella became fugitives, for as I am sure you know, brother, the more prominent you are in our order, the less chance you have of being overlooked when the Ravens are wetting their beaks.

"So we took ship, some score of us with our families, those who had them, in the cranky little vessel of Pinarro Albayero.

"Albayero had intended to make landfall in the Brenn Isles, but a northerly hit us, taking us down to North Cape in the Hebrionese. We rounded the point with the help of the weather-workers amongst us, but not even they could help us make up our lost northing. The storms we rode would brook no interference, even from the master-mages amongst us. So we rode them out in our little ship, the weather-workers having to labour merely to keep us afloat. We were driven into the limitless wilderness of the Western Ocean, and there we despaired, thinking that we would topple off the edge of the world and plummet through the gaps between the stars.

"But we did not. We had hoped to find an uninhabited island among the archipelago of the Brenn Isles – for there were still such things, back in the second century – but now we had no idea where we might be cast ashore. The winds were too strong. It seemed almost as though God Himself had set His face against us, and was bent on driving us off the face of His creation.

"I know better now. God was at hand, watching over us, guiding our ship on the one true road to our salvation. We made landfall seventy-eight days after rounding North Cape, ninety-four after our departure from Cartigella.

"We landed on a continent which was utterly alien to anything we had experienced before. A place which was to become our home."

Aruan paused, chin sunk on breast. Bardolin could imagine the amazement, the joy and the fear which those first exiles must have felt upon walking up the blazing beach to see the impenetrable dark of the jungle beyond. For them there had never been any question of turning back.

"Half of us were dead within six months," Aruan went on, his voice flat, mechanical. "Albayero abandoned us, weighed anchor one night and was across the horizon before we had realized he was gone. He sold his knowledge to the nobility of Astarac, I afterwards found, enabling others to attempt the voyage in times of desperation. A good thing, as it turned out, for it meant that once or twice in the long, long years and decades and centuries following we had injections of new blood.

"We tamed the Zantu with feats of sorcery, and they came to serve and worship us. We lifted them out of savagery, made them into the more refined people you see today. But it was a long time before we truly appreciated their wisdom and learned to leave behind the prejudices of our Ramusian upbringing. We cleared Undi, which was an overgrown ruin lost in the belly of Undabane, and made it our capital. We made a life, a kingdom of sorts if you like, here in the wilderness. And we were not persecuted. You will never smell a pyre's stink in this country, Bardolin."

"But you did something, didn't you? I have seen man-beasts here, monstrosities of Dweomer and warped flesh."

"Experiments," Aruan retorted quickly. "The new power we discovered had to be explored and contained. A new set of rules had to be written. Before they were, there were some regrettable... accidents. Some of us went too far, it is true."

"And this no longer goes on?"

"Not if I do not wish it," Aruan said without looking at him.

Bardolin frowned. "A society glued together by the Dweomer. Part of me rejoices, but part of me recoils also. There is such scope for abuse, for –"

"For evil. Yes, I know. We have had our internal struggles over the years, our petty civil wars, if I can dignify them with that title. Why else do you think that out of all the founders of our country I alone remain?"

"Because you are the strongest," Bardolin said.

Aruan laughed his full, boisterous laugh again. "True enough! Yes, I was strongest. But I was also wisest, I think. I had a vision which the others lacked."

"And what do you see with this vision of yours? What is it you want out of the world?"

Aruan turned and looked Bardolin in the eye, the moonlight crannying his features, kindling the liquid sheen of his eyes. Something strange there, something at once odd and familiar.

"I want to see your people and mine take their rightful place in the world, Bardolin. I want the Dweomer-folk to rise up and cast away their fears, their habits of servitude. I want them to claim their birthright."

"Not all the Dweomer-folk are men of education and power," Bardolin said warily. "Would you have the herbalists and hedge-witches, the cantrimers and crazed soothsayers have their say in some kind of sorcerous hegemony? Is that your aim, Aruan?"

"Listen to me for a moment, Bardolin. Listen to me without that dogged conservatism which marks you. Is the social order which permeates Normannia so fine and noble that it is worth saving? Is it just? Of course not!"

"Would the social order which you would erect in its place be any more just or fair?" Bardolin asked. "You would substitute one tyranny for another."

"I would liberate an abused people, and remove the cancer of the religious orders from our lives."

"For someone who has spent the centuries here in the wilderness you seem tolerably well informed," Bardolin told him.

"I have my sources, as every mage must. I keep a watch on the Old World, Bardolin; I always have. It is the home of my birth and childhood and young manhood. I have not given up on it yet."

"Are all your agents in Normannia shifters, then?"

"Ah, I wondered when we would get to that. Yes, Ortelius was one of mine, a valuable man."

"What was his mission?"

"To make you turn back, nothing more."

"Our ship carried the Dweomer-folk whom you would

like to redeem; they were fleeing persecution, and yet you would have sent them back to the waiting pyres."

"Your ship also carried an official representative of the Hebrian crown, and a contingent of soldiers," Aruan said dryly. "They I could do without."

"And the other vessel, which ran aground and was wrecked on these very shores? Did you have a hand in that?"

"No, upon mine honour, Bardolin. They were simply unlucky. It was not part of my plan to massacre whole ship's companies. I thought that if I made the carrack, the ship with the leaders aboard, turn back, the lesser vessel would follow."

"Am I then to thank you for your humanity, your restraint, when the beast you ordered aboard was responsible for the foul deaths of my shipmates?" Bardolin was angry now, but Aruan answered him calmly.

"The exigencies of the situation allowed no other recourse and besides, Ortelius was outside my control. I regret unnecessary death as much as the next man, but I had to safeguard what we have built here."

"In that case, Aruan, you will have to make sure that none of the members of this current expedition ever leave this continent alive, won't you?"

There was a small silence.

"Circumstances have changed."

"In what way?"

"Perhaps we are no longer so concerned with secrecy. Perhaps other things occupy our minds."

"And who are *we*? Creatures such as your were-ape Gosa? Why must you always choose shifters as your minions? Are there no decent, proper mages left to you here in the west?"

"Why Bardolin, you sound almost indignant. You surprise me, you of all people."

"What do you mean?"

"I told you earlier."

"You've told me nothing, nothing of importance. What have you been doing here for all these centuries? Playing God to the primitives, indulging in petty power plays amongst yourselves?"

Aruan came close to the sparkling phantom that was Bardolin's presence.

"Let me show you what we have been doing over these lost years, Brother Mage, what tricks we have been learning out here in the western wilderness."

There was a change, as swift as breath misting a cold pane of glass. Aruan had disappeared, and in his place there loomed the hulking figure of a full-blooded shifter, a werewolf with lemon-bright eyes and a long muzzle glimmering with fangs. Bardolin's imp whimpered and hid behind his master's translucent simulacrum.

"It's not possible," Bardolin whispered.

"Did I not tell you, Bardolin, that we had found new and powerful wisdom among the inhabitants of this continent?" Aruan's voice said, the beast's muzzle contorting around the words, dripping ropes of saliva which glistened in the moonlight.

"It's an illusion," Bardolin said.

"Touch the illusion then, Brother illusion."

Of course – Bardolin at this moment was no more than an apparition himself, a copy of his true self, conjured up by the incredible power of this man, this beast before him.

"I am no simulacrum, I assure you," Aruan's voice said.

"It is impossible. Sufferers of the black disease cannot learn any of the other six disciplines. It is against the very nature of things. Shifters cannot also be mages."

The Aruan shifter drew close. "They can here. We all are, friend Bardolin. We all partake of the beast in this country; and now so do you."

Something in Bardolin quailed before the werewolf's calm certainty.

"Not I."

"But you do. You have looked into the very heart and mind of a shifter at the moment of its transformation. More, you have loved one of our kind. I can read this in you as though it were inked across the parchment of your very soul." The beast laughed horribly.

"Griella."

"Yes – that was the name. The memory of that moment is burned within you. There is a part of you, deep in the black spaces of your heart, which would gladly have joined her in her suffering, could she but have loved you in return...

"Your imp is a poor sort of buffer against probing, Bardolin. Where you yourself might hold out against me, he is a free conduit to the heart of your fears and emotions. You are a book lying open to be read any time I have a desire to read."

"You monster!" Bardolin snarled, but fear was edging an icicle of dread into his flesh.

The werewolf came closer until the heat and stink of it were all around him and the great head blotted out the stars. They stood on the pyramid once more: Bardolin's image could feel the stone of it under its soles.

"Do you know how we make shifters in this country, Bardolin?"

"Tell me," Bardolin croaked. Unable to help himself, he retreated a step.

"For a person to be infected with the black disease, he must do two things. Firstly, he, or she, must have physical relations with a full-blooded shape-shifter. Secondly, he or she must eat a portion of that shifter's kill. It's that simple. We have not yet divined why certain people become certain beasts – that is a complex field which would reward more study. A question of personal style, perhaps. But the basic process is well known to us. We are a race of shape-shifters, Bardolin, and now you are one of us as you once secretly wished to be."

"No," Bardolin whispered, aghast. He remembered a kind of lovemaking, a sweating half-dreamt battle in the night. And he remembered Kersik offering him the rib of meat to bite into. "Oh, lord God, no!"

He felt a grip on his shoulder as he stood there with his hands covering his face, and Aruan the man was back again, the beast gone. His face was both kindly and triumphant.

"You belong to us, my friend. We are brothers in truth, bound together by the Dweomer and by the malady which lurks in our very flesh."

"To Hell with you!" Bardolin cried. "My soul is my own."

"Not any more," Aruan said implacably. "You are mine, as much a creature in my keeping as Gosa or Kersik are.

You will do my bidding even when you are unaware that the will which rules you is not your own. I have hundreds like you across the entire reach of the Old World. But you are special, Bardolin. You are a man who might in a former time have been a friend. For that reason I will leave you be for a while. Think on this at our parting: the race whose blood runs in you and me, in the veins of the herbalists and the hedge-witches and the petty cantrimers – it came from here, in the west. We are an ancient people, the oldest race in the world, and yet for centuries we have bled and died to satisfy the prejudices of lesser men. That will change. We will meet again, you and I, and when we do you will know me as your lord, and as your friend."

The wraith that was Bardolin began to fade. The imp screamed thinly and tried to run towards the spectre of its vanishing master, but Aruan caught it in his arms. It writhed there pitiably, but could not get free.

"You have no further need of your familiar, Brother Mage. He is a weakness you can do without, and I have already mapped the road from his mind to yours. Say goodbye."

With a flick of his powerful arms, Aruan wrenched round the imp's head on its slim neck. There was a sharp crack, and the little creature flopped lifelessly.

Bardolin shrieked in grief and agony, and it seemed to him as though the jungle night dissolved in a sun-brightness, a scalding holocaust which seared the interstices of his mind and soul. The world funnelled past him like a plummeting star, and he saw the city, the mountain, the black jungle of the Western Continent swoop away as though he were riding the molten halo of a blasted cannonball into the sky.

His shriek became the tail of the comet he had become. He fell to earth again, a raging meteor intent on burying itself at the heart of the world.

And struck, passing through a terrible burning and light into utter darkness.

Sixteen

There was at once too much and too little to take in. Hawkwood was absurdly reminded of a festival he had attended once in southern Torunna, when the effigies of the old gods had been displayed to public ridicule: huge constructions of wicker and cloth and wood in every grotesque shape and form dancing madly with the teams of men who lurked inside their colourful carcasses, until it was impossible to tell one warped form from another and they had dissolved into a whirling confusion of monstrous faces and limbs.

Here, it was dark. There were no colours, simply a monochrome nightmare. Shadows with blazing eyes which seemed to shoot up out of the very ground, the heat from their raging darknesses a palpable thing even in the depths of the night. Forms rather than bodies. A picture here of an animal's head set upon a bipedal frame, the warm splash of blood, the screaming. It passed with the vivid unreality of a dream. A dark mirage. But it was real.

The men at the rear screamed horribly, the chest they bore torn out of their hands. A crash, and then a shower of tinkling gold across the roadway. Shadows lifted the two men high in the air and then something happened too quickly to make out, and they were in pieces, their viscera ribboning out like flung streamers, their bodies become meat and shattered bone which were flung away.

As the shadows closed in, the men at the front fired their arquebuses, flashes and plumes of smoke. There were howls of pain, despairing wails from the approaching shapes.

The rest of the soldiers had dropped the other chest, and also their sick comrade, Gerrera. They bunched together and levelled their own weapons. Gerrera screamed as the shadows came upon him and he was engulfed, torn apart. A volley of arquebus fire, the iron bullets tearing into the ranks of the half-glimpsed foe and the night was clawed apart by their screams. Huge bodies could be seen decorating the roadway, immobile but at the same time subtly changing in bulk and shape.

The attackers drew off for a moment, and Murad's soldiers reloaded their firearms feverishly.

"We must make a run for it," the nobleman said, his narrow chest heaving and the sweat standing out on his face. "It's not that far to the gorge: some of us might make it. We'll all die here, else."

"What about Bardolin?" Hawkwood asked.

"He'll have to take his chances. We can't carry him. Maybe the creatures will recognize him for one of their own sorcerous folk – who knows?"

"Bastard!" Hawkwood spat, but he was not sure who he was speaking of.

The things came roaring out of the night again. Seven arquebuses went off, felling about half a dozen of them, but the rest kept coming. They were amongst the surviving soldiers, biting and clawing and bellowing: apes and jaguars and wolves, and one snake with arms which Hawkwood slashed at viciously with his iron-bladed dirk so that it thrashed to the ground screaming thinly, its head becoming that of a beautiful woman even as its coils lashed in its death throes.

Cortona was smashed to the ground by a great were-ape and had his face ripped off with a twist of its fist. Murad seized the dead man's arquebus, slid out the rammer and jammed it into the creature's reeking maw. The iron of the rammer tore into the roof of its mouth and it fell. Something came at him from behind and raked his back with razor-sharp talons. He spun to find himself facing a huge black cat, and stabbed the rammer into its livid eye. He laughed as it shrieked and spun away, the gun tool protruding from its punctured pupil.

One of the soldiers was hoisted into the air by two of the beasts and torn asunder between them like a rotten sack, his innards exploding to shower the fray with stinking gore, the gold which he had stuffed in his shirt and pockets clinking out along with it. Another was pinioned whilst a werewolf bit through the back of his neck, his spine splintering in the tremendous jaws, his head lolling on a tenuous connection of windpipe and skin.

Mensurado had followed Murad's example and was stabbing out left and right with an iron arquebus rammer. He was roaring in a kind of battle frenzy, shouting obscenities and blasphemies, and the beasts actually made way for him. All he had to do with his crude weapon was break the skin, and the sorcery which maintained the beast form of the shifter would be broken. The iron would poison its system as surely as if a bullet had pierced its vitals.

Hawkwood grabbed Masudi. "Take Bardolin. We're going to run for it."

"Captain!" the big helmsman cried despairingly.

"Do as I say! Mihal, help him."

Masudi hoisted the unconscious mage on to his broad shoulders whilst around him the dwindling company fought for their lives. The three mariners had as secondary armament the cheaply made iron ship's knives which were more tool than weapon, but which were more valuable than gold in the melee, more effective than a battery of culverins could be. They slashed a way forward, the iron blades snicking back and forth in their hands as though they were threshing wheat. The beasts retreated before them: they knew that one nick from the knives meant death to them.

Behind the trio of desperate sailors the soldiers fought on with rammers and gunstocks and knives. But they had too many assailants. One by one they were enveloped, brought down and torn to pieces. The road was littered with gold coins and the fragments of bodies puddled with gore and entrails. Murad, Mensurado and a couple of others made a last effort, a combined charge. Hawkwood risked a glance back at them, but he could only see a crowd of monsters huddled together as if feeding at the same trough. They broke apart as Murad, his shirt torn from his back and his skin in strips, burst through them wielding a shard of an arquebus's serpentine. The nobleman sprinted away at unbelievable speed, a dozen shifters in pursuit, and disappeared into the night.

Hawkwood's group shuffled onwards, turning and spinning to keep their assailants at bay with lunges of their dirks. The wall of the volcano towered above them now and they were surrounded by trees and vegetation; they had left the main part of the city. The cleft in the crater wall could be seen as a wedge of stars ahead.

Mihal was too slow. As his arm snaked out to stab at a shifter it caught his wrist. He was yanked off into a scrum of snarling shadows and could not even scream before they had finished him. One knocked Masudi down from behind. Bardolin went sprawling and Hawkwood staggered, his dagger flying out of his hand.

He scrabbled off on hands and knees into the bushes, rolling and shoving himself forward into the vegetation like a fox intent on going to earth. Then he lay, utterly spent, the jungle teeming with howls, leaves brushing his face. He tried to summon a prayer, a last thought, something coherent out of the terror which washed across his brain, but his mind was blank. He lay there as dumb and senseless as a cornered animal, waiting for death to come ravening out of the darkness.

It came. He heard the bushes crackling, and there was a sensation of heat beside him, the impression of a hulking presence.

Nothing happened.

He opened his eyes, his heartbeat a red light that went on and off in his head, soughing through his throat like the ebb and flow of an unquiet sea. And he saw the yellow eyes of the beast that lay beside him, its breath stirring his sweat-soaked forelock.

"Sweet God, get it over with," he croaked, fear swamping him, robbing him of any last defiance.

The beast, an enormous werewolf, chuckled.

The sound was human, rational despite its author.

"Would I harm you, Captain, the navigator, the steerer of ships? I think not. I think not."

It was gone. The night was silent, the utter silence of the unquiet forest. Looking up, Hawkwood could see the stars shining in between the limbs of the trees.

He waited for the beast to return and finish him, but it did not. The night had become as peaceful as if the carnage had been imagined, a fever dream vivid on waking. He sat up cautiously, heard a groan nearby and struggled drunkenly to his feet.

Nothing was working. His mind was immobilized in shock, barely able to instruct the body which harboured it. He staggered out on to the roadway and the first thing he saw was the mocking sight of Masudi's head planted on the paving like a fallen fruit, dark and shining.

Hawkwood gagged and threw up a thin soup of scalding bile. Other things lay on the road, but he did not care to look at them. He heard the groan again and tottered over to its source.

Bardolin, moving feebly in a pool of Masudi's blood.

Hawkwood bent down to the mage and slapped the old man's face, hard. As if he were somehow to blame for the night's slaughter.

Bardolin opened his eyes.

"Captain."

Hawkwood could not speak, and he was shaking as though bitterly cold. He tried to help Bardolin up and slipped in the slick blood so that they were both lying in it like twins spat forth from some ruptured womb.

They lay there. Hawkwood felt that he had somehow lived through the end of the world. He could not be alive; he was in some manner of subtle hell.

Bardolin sat up rubbing his face, then fell back again. It took some minutes before finally they were both on their feet, looking like two intoxicated revellers who had splashed through a slaughterhouse. Bardolin saw Masudi's severed head and gaped.

"What is happening?"

But still Hawkwood could not speak. He dragged Bardolin away from the scene of the fighting, up the roadway to where the confining wall of the volcano reared up into the night cleft by its wedge of stars.

As HE WALKED, Hawkwood's strength returned and he was able to support the rubber-legged Bardolin. The mage was totally bewildered and did not seem to know where he was. He rambled on about pyramids and sea crossings and had philosophical arguments with himself about the Dweomer, reiterating its Seven Disciplines again and again until Hawkwood paused and shook him violently. That quietened him, but he seemed no less confused.

They reached the gorge which led outside the confining circle of the volcano's crater. In the darkness it was like the entrance to a primitive tomb, a megalithic burial place. It was unguarded, deserted. In fact, the entire circle of the city was dead and lightless, as though everything they had seen there had been delusion, the hallucinations of tired minds.

The pair stumbled through the cleft like sleepwalkers, tripping and rebounding off stone. They did not speak to one another, not even when they had finally come through to the other side and found themselves outside the hollow cone of Undabane with the barren slopes of the volcano stretching away below them in the moonlight, and beyond them the midnight sea of the jungle.

A shade rose out of the rocks before them and crunched through the tufa and ash until it was close enough to touch.

Murad.

Raw flesh glimmered over his naked torso, and sluggish blood welled from his wounds, black as tar. He was half bald where something had ripped his scalp from forehead to ear.

"Murad?" Hawkwood managed to ask. He could not believe that this human flotsam was the man he knew and detested.

"The very same. So they let you loose, did they? The mariner and the mage."

"We escaped," Hawkwood said, but knew that was a lie as the words passed his lips. The three of them stood as if they had not a care in the world, as if there were not a kingdom of monsters within the hollow mountain thirsting after their blood.

"They let us go," Murad said, his sneer still intact at least. "Or you, at any rate. Me I'm not so sure about. I may merely have been fortunate. How is the mage, anyway?"

"Alive."

"Alive." Suddenly Murad sagged. He had to squat down on his knees. "They killed them all," he whispered, "every last one. And such gold! Such... blood."

Hawkwood dragged him upright. "Come. We can't stay here. We've a long road ahead of us."

"We're walking dead men, Captain."

"No – we're alive. We were meant to stay alive, I believe, and at some point I want to find out why. Now take Bardolin's other arm. Take it, Murad."

The nobleman did as he was told. Together, the three of them stumbled down the slopes of the mountain, the ash burning in their wounds like salt.

By the time the dawn came lightening the sky they were almost at its foot, and the unchanging jungle whooped and wailed with weary familiarity before them. They plunged into it once more, becoming lost to the world of the dreaming trees, the shadowed twilight of the forest.

The hidden beast watched them as they disappeared, three wrecked pilgrims pursuing some cracked vision known only to themselves. Then it rose up out of its hiding place and followed them, as silent as a breath of air.

PART THREE

The WARS of the FAITH

...Whensoever he made any ostyng, or inroad,
into the enemies Countries, he killed manne,
woman and child, and spoiled, wasted and burned,
by the grounde, all that he might; leaving nothing
of the enemies in saffetie, which he could
possible waste or consume...

– Chronicle of Sir Humphrey Gilbert, 1570

SEVENTEEN

CHARIBON WAS A prisoner of winter.

The heavy snows had come at last, in a series of blizzards which roared down out of the heights of the Cimbric Mountains and engulfed the monastery-city in a storm of white. On the Narian Hills the snow drifted fathoms deep, burying roads and villages, isolating whole towns. The fishing boats which normally plied the Sea of Tor had been beached long since, and the margins of the sea itself were frozen for half a league from the shore, the ice thick enough to bear a marching army.

In Charibon a small army of labourers fought to keep the cloisters clear of snow. They were assisted by hundreds of novices who shovelled and dug until they were pink-cheeked and steaming, and yet had the energy for snowball fights and skating and other horseplay afterwards. Unlike the poor folk of the surrounding countryside, they did not have to worry whether they would have enough food to see them through the winter. It was one of the bonuses of the religious life, at least as Charibon's clerics lived it.

The monastery-city went about its business regardless of the weather, its rituals as changeless and predictable as the seasons themselves. In the scriptoria and refectories the fires were lit, fed with the wood which had been chopped and piled through the summer and autumn. Salted and smoked meat made more of an appearance at table, as did the contents of the vast root cellars. Enterprising ice fishermen hacked holes in the frozen sea to provide the Pontiff and Vicar-General's tables with fresh fish every now and again, but in the main Charibon was like a hibernating bear, living off what it had stored away throughout the preceding months and grumbling softly in its sleep. Except for the odd Pontifical courier determined (or well-paid) enough to brave the drifts and the blizzards, the city was cut off from the rest of Normannia, and would remain so for several weeks until the temperature dropped further and hardened the snow, making it into a crackling white highway for mule-drawn sledges.

The wolves came down out of the mountains, as they always did, and at night their melancholy moans could be heard echoing about the cathedral and the cloisters. In the worst of the weather they would sometimes even prowl the streets of Charibon itself, making it dangerous to walk them alone at night, and contingents of the Almarkan troops which garrisoned Charibon would periodically patrol the city to clear the beasts from its thoroughfares.

IT WAS AFTER Compline. Vespers had been sung two hours before, the monks had consumed their evening meal and most of them were in their cells preparing for bed. Charibon was settling down for the long midwinter night, and a bitter wind was hurling flurries of snow down from the Cimbrics, drowning out the howls of the wolves. The streets of the city were deserted and even the cathedral Justiciars were preparing for bed, having trimmed the votive lamps and shut the great doors of Charibon's main place of worship.

There was a soft rap at Albrec's door and he opened it, shivering in the cold wind which he admitted.

"Ready, Albrec?" Avila stood there, muffled in hood and scarf.

"No one saw you leave?"

"The whole dormitory have their heads under their blankets. It's a bitter night."

"You brought a lamp? We'll need two."

"A good one. It won't be missed until Matins. Are you sure you want to go through with this?"

"Yes. Are you?"

Avila sighed. "No, but I'm in it up to my neck now. And besides, curiosity is a terrible thing to live with, like an itch which cannot be scratched."

"Here's hoping we can scratch your itch tonight, Avila. Here, take this." The little monk handed his Inceptine friend something hard and angular and heavy.

"A mattock! Where did you pilfer this from?"

"Call it a loan, for the greater glory of God. I got it from the gardens. Come – it's time we were on our way."

The pair of them left Albrec's cell and whispered along the wide corridors of the chapter-house where Albrec slept. Due to his position as Assistant Librarian, he had a cell to himself, whereas Avila slept in a dormitory with a dozen other junior Inceptine clerics, for he had laid aside his novice's hood only three years before.

They crossed an arctic courtyard, their habits billowing in the biting wind. Scant minutes later, they found themselves outside the tall double doors of the Library of Saint Garaso. But Albrec led his friend around the side of the rime-white building, kicking his frozen, sandalled feet through piled snow and halting at a half-buried postern door. He poked his key into the hole and twisted it with a snap, then pushed the door open.

"More discreet here," he grunted, for the hinges were stiff. "No one will see us come and go."

But Avila was staring at the snowy ground about them. "Blast it, Albrec, what about our tracks? We've left a trail for the world to see."

"It can't be helped. With luck they'll be snowed over by morning. Come on, Avila."

Shaking his head, the tall Inceptine followed his diminutive friend into the musty, old-smelling darkness of the library. Albrec locked the door behind them and they stood silent for a second, alarmed by the quiet of massive masonry and waiting books, the wind a mere groaning in the rafters.

Avila struck a light and their shadows leaped at them from the walls as the lamp caught. They threw back their hoods and shook snow from their shoulders.

"We are alone," Albrec said.

"How do you know?"

"I know this place, winter and summer. I can feel when the library is empty – or as empty as it ever becomes, with its memories."

"Don't talk like that, Albrec. I'm as jumpy as a springtime hare already."

"Let's go then, and stay close. And don't touch anything."

"All right, all right. Lead on, master librarian."

They navigated the many rooms and halls and corridors of the library in silence, tall cases of books and scrolls looming over them like walls. Then they began to descend, taking to narrow staircases which to Avila seemed to have been built into the very walls of the building. Finally they hauled up a trapdoor of ironbound wood which had been concealed by a mat of threadbare hessian. Steep steps going down into uttermost dark. The catacombs.

They started down, the weight and bulk of the library hanging over and around them like a cloud. The fact that it was a winter-dark and wolf-haunted night outside should have made no difference to the darkness in here, but somehow it did. A sense of isolation stole over the pair as they stumbled through the accumulated rubbish in the catacombs and coughed at the dust they raised. It was as if they were explorers who had somehow chanced upon the ruins of a dead city, and were creeping through its bowels like maggots in the belly of a corpse.

"Which wall is the north one?" Avila asked.

"The one to your left. It's damper than the others. Keep to the sides and don't trip up."

They felt their way along the walls, lifting the lamp to peer at the stonework. Chiselled granite, the very gutrock of the mountains hewn and sculpted as though it were clay.

"The Fimbrians must have been twenty years carving out this place," Avila breathed. "Solid stone, and never a trace of mortar."

"They were a strange people, the builders of empire," Albrec said. "They seemed to feel the need to leave a mark on the world. Wherever they went, they built to last. Half the public buildings of the Five Kingdoms date from the Fimbrian Hegemony, and no one has ever built on the same scale since. Old Gambio reckons it was pride brought the empire down as much as anything else. God humbled them because they thought they could order the world as they saw fit."

"And so they did, for three centuries or so," Avila said dryly.

"Hush, Avila. Here we are." Albrec ranged the lamp about the wall where there were mortared blocks instead of the solid stone of the rest of the place. The light showed the crevice in which Albrec's precious document had been discovered.

"Light the other lamp," the little Antillian said, and he reached into the crevice with a lack of hesitation which made Avila shudder. There might be anything in that hole.

"There's a room on the other side of this, no doubt about it. A substantial space, at any rate."

Avila found a staved-in cask amid the wreckage and rubbish. He set it on its end and placed the lamps upon it. "What now? The mattock?"

"Yes. Give it here."

"No, Albrec. Valiant though you are, you haven't the build for it. Move aside, and keep a look out."

Avila hefted the heavy tool, eyed the wall for a second, and then swung the mattock in a short, savage arc against the poorly mortared stonework.

A sharp crack which seemed incredibly loud in their ears. Avila paused.

"Are you sure no one will hear this?"

"The library is deserted, and there are five floors of it above us. Trust me."

"Trust him," Avila said in a long-suffering voice. Then he began to swing the mattock in earnest.

The old mortar cracked and fell away in a shower. Avila hacked at the wall until the stones it held began to shift. He picked them out with the flat blade of the mattock and soon had a cavity perhaps six inches deep and two feet wide. He stopped and wiped his brow.

"Albrec, you are the only person I know who could cause me to break sweat in midwinter."

"Come on, Avila – you're nearly through!"

"All right, all right. Taskmaster."

A few more blows and then there was a sliding shower of stones and powder and dust which left them coughing in a cloud that swirled in the light of the lamps like a golden fog.

Albrec seized a lamp and got down on his knees, pushing the lamp into the hole which suddenly gaped there.

"Sweet Saints, Albrec!" Avila said in a horrified whisper. "Look what we've done. We'll never block up that hole again."

"We'll pile rubbish in front of it," Albrec said impatiently, and then, his voice suddenly hoarse: "Avila, we're through the wall. I can see what's on the other side."

"What – what is it?"

But Albrec was already crawling out of sight, his shoulders dislodging more stones and grit. He looked like a rotund rabbit burrowing its way into a hole too small for it.

He was able to stand. Hardly aware of Avila's urgent enquiries on the other side of the wall, Albrec straightened and held up his lamp.

The room – for such it was – was high-ceilinged. Like the catacombs he had just left, its walls were solid rock. But this chamber had not been carved by the hand of man. There were stalactites spearing down from the roof and the walls were uneven, rough. It was not a room but a cave, Albrec realized with a shock. A subterranean cavern which had been discovered by men untold centuries ago and which at some time in more recent history had been blocked off.

The walls were covered with paintings.

Some were savage and primitive, depicting animals Albrec had heard of but never seen: marmorills with curving tusks and gimlet eyes, unicorns with squat horns and wolves, some of which ran on four legs, some on two.

The paintings were crude but powerful, the flowing lines which delineated the animals drawn with smooth confidence. There was a naturalism about them which was totally at odds with the stylized illustrations in most modern-day manuscripts. In the flickering lamplight one might almost think they were moving, coursing along the walls in packs and herds and following long-lost migrations.

All this Albrec took in at a glance. What claimed his attention almost at once, however, was something different. A shape jumped out of the shadows at him and he almost dropped his lamp, then made the Sign of the Saint at his breast.

A statue, man high, standing at the far wall.

It was of a wolf-headed man, his arms raised, his beast's mouth agape. Behind him on the stone of the wall a pentagram within a circle had been etched and painted so that the lamplight threw it into vivid relief. Before the statue was a small altar, the surface of which had a deep groove cut in it. The stone of the altar was discoloured, stained as if by ancient, unforgivable sins.

There was a rattle of loose stone which made Albrec utter a squeak of fear, and then Avila was in the room brushing dust from his habit and looking both stern and amazed.

"Saint's blood, Albrec, why wouldn't you answer me?" And then: "Holy Father of us all! What is this?"

"A chapel," Albrec said, his voice as hoarse as a frog's.

"What?"

"A place of worship, Avila. Men paid homage here once, in some dark, lost time."

Avila was studying the hideous statue, holding his lamp close to its snarling muzzle.

"Old stonework, this. Crude. Which of the old gods might this one be, Albrec? It's not the Horned One, at any rate."

"I'm not sure if it was meant to be a god, but sacrifices were made here. Look at the altar."

"Blood, yes. Hell's teeth, Albrec, what about this?" And Avila produced from his habit the pentagram dagger they had found in their last visit to the catacombs.

"A sacrificial knife, probably. What made you bring it with you?"

Avila made a wry face. "To tell the truth I intended to lose it down here again. I don't want it anywhere near me."

"It might be important."

"It's more likely to be mischievous. And can you imagine me trying to explain it to the house Justiciar if it were found?"

"All right then." Albrec swung the lamp around to regard the other, darker corners of the cave. "We're forgetting what we came here for. Help me look for more of the document, Avila, and throw that thing away if you have to."

Avila tossed the dagger aside and helped Albrec sift through the rubbish which littered the floor of the cave. It seemed as if someone had tossed half the contents of a library down here a century ago and left it to rot. Their feet rested on the remains of manuscripts, and a jetsam of decaying vellum was piled against the walls like a tidemark. They knelt in it and brought the remnants to their noses, squinting at the faded and torn lettering in the light of the lamps.

"It's dry in here, or these would have been mushrooms long since," Avila said, discarding a page. "Strange – the wall beyond is damp, you said so yourself. What happened here, Albrec? What are these things, and why is this unholy chapel here in the bowels of Charibon?"

Albrec shrugged. "Men have lived on this site for thousands of years, rebuilding on the ruins of the settlements which went before them. It may be that this cave was nearer the surface once."

They found sections of texts written in the Merduk tongue with its graceful lettering and lack of illuminations. One group of pages had diagrams upon them which seemed to outline the courses of the stars. Another bore a line drawing of a human body, flayed so that the muscles and veins below the skin might be seen. The two monks made the Sign of the Saint as they stared at it.

"Heretical texts," Avila said. "Astrology, witchery. Now I know why they were walled up in here."

But Albrec was shaking his head. "Knowledge, Avila. They sealed up knowledge in here. They decided on behalf of all men what they might and might not know, and they destroyed anything which they disagreed with."

"Who are 'they,' Albrec?"

"Your brethren, my friend. The Inceptines."

"Maybe they acted for the best."

"Maybe. We will never know because the knowledge they destroyed is lost for ever. We will never be able to judge for ourselves."

"Not everyone is as learned as you, Albrec. Knowledge can be a dangerous thing in the hands of the ignorant."

Albrec smiled. "You sound like one of the monsignors, Avila."

Avila scowled. "You cannot change the way the world works, Albrec. No one man can. You can only do as you are told and make the best of it."

"I wonder if Ramusio would have agreed with that."

"And how many would-be Ramusios do you think they have sent to the pyre in the last five hundred years?" Avila said. "Striving to change the world seems to me to be a sure way of shortening one's tenure of it."

Albrec chuckled, then stiffened. "Avila! I think I have it!"

"Let me see."

Albrec was holding a few ragged pages, bound together by the remains of their cloth backing.

"The writing is the same, and the layout. And here's the title page!"

"Well? What does it say?"

Albrec paused, and finally spoke in a low, reverent voice. "'A true and faithful account of the life of the Blessed Saint Ramusio, as told by one who was his companion and his disciple from the earliest of days.'"

"Quite a title," Avila grunted. "But who wrote it?"

"It's by Honorius of Neyr, Avila. Saint Honorius."

"What? Like *The Book of Honorius*?"

"The very same. The man who inspired the Friar Mendicant Order, a founding father of the Church."

"Founding father of hallucinations," Avila muttered.

Albrec tucked the pages away in his habit. "Whatever. Let's get out of here. We've got what we came for."

They rose to their feet, brushing the detritus of the cave from their knees, and as they did there was a rattle of stone. They turned as one, the lamplight leaping in their hands, to find Brother Commodius appearing through the hole in the wall which led back to the catacombs.

The Senior Librarian dusted himself down much as Avila and Albrec had done whilst the pair stared at him in horror. The mattock they had left outside dangled from one of his huge hands. He smiled.

"We are well met, Albrec. And I see you have brought the beautiful Avila with you too. What joy."

"Brother, we – we were just –"

"No need, Albrec. We are beyond explanations. You have overreached yourself."

"We've done nothing wrong, Commodius," Avila said hotly. "No one is forbidden to come down here. You can't touch us."

"Be quiet, you young fool," Commodius snapped in return. "You understand nothing. Albrec does, though – don't you, my friend?" Commodius's face was hideous in its humour, the mien of a satisfied gargoyle, his ears seemingly too long to be real and his eyes reflecting the lamplight like those of a dog.

Albrec blinked as though trying to clear the dust from his eyes. Something in him seemed to calm, to accept the situation. "You knew this was here," he said. "You've always known."

"Yes, I have always known, as have all the Senior Librarians, all the custodians of this place. We pass down the information as we do the keys of the doors. In time, Albrec, it might have been passed on to you."

"Why would I want it?"

"Don't be obtuse with me, Albrec. Do you think this is the only secret chamber in these levels? There are scores of them, and mouldering away in the dark and the silence is the vanished knowledge of a dead age, lost generations of accumulated lore deemed too harmful or heretical or dangerous for men to know. How would you like to have that at your fingertips, Albrec?"

The little monk wet his dry lips. "Why?" he asked.

"Why what?"

"Why are you so afraid of knowledge?"

The mattock twitched in Commodius's fist. "Power, Brother. Power lies in knowledge, but also in ignorance. The Inceptines control the world with the information they know and that which they withhold. You cannot give mankind the freedom to know anything it wants; that is the merest anarchy. Take that document you found down here, the one you have hidden so inadequately in your cell along with the other heretical books you have been concealing: your pitiful attempt to save a kernel from the cleansing fire."

Albrec was as white as a winding sheet. "You know of it too?"

"I have read others like it, all of which I have had destroyed. Why else do you think there are no contemporary accounts of the Saint's life extant today? In that one document resides greater power than in any king. The old pages you discovered hold within them the potential to overturn our world. That will not happen. At least, not yet."

"But it's the *truth*," Albrec cried, almost weeping. "We are men of God. It is our duty –"

"Our duty is to the Church and its shepherdship of mankind. What do you think men would do if they discovered that Ahrimuz and Ramusio were one and the same? Or that Ramusio was not assumed into heaven, but was last seen riding a mule into oblivion? The Church would be riven to its very foundations. The basic tenets of our belief would be questioned. Men might begin to doubt the existence of God Himself."

"You've told us why you are going to do what you are about to do, Commodius," Avila said with the drawl of the nobleman. "Perhaps now you'll be good enough to do it without wearying our ears further."

Commodius gazed at the tall Inceptine, as haughty as a prince before him. "Ah, Avila, you are always the aristocrat, are you not? Whereas I am merely the son of a tanner, as humbly born as Albrec there, despite my black robe. How you would have graced our order. But it was not to be."

"What do you mean?" Albrec asked, and the tremor was back in his voice, fear rising over the grief.

"It's plain to see what has been happening here. Two clerics become victims of the unnatural urges which sometimes beset those of our calling. One lures the other into black magic, occult ritual" – Commodius gestured to the wolf-headed statue with the mattock – "and there is a falling-out, a fight. The lovers kill each other, their bodies laid out before the unholy altar which poisoned their minds. Not that the bodies will be found for a long time. I mean, who ever comes down here, and who will think to look beyond the rubble of a sealed wall?"

"Columbar knows we have been coming here –" Avila began.

"Alas, Brother Columbar died in his sleep this night, peacefully and in God's grace, his head resting on the pillow which stopped his breath."

"I don't believe you," Avila said, but his haughtiness was leaking away.

"It is immaterial to me what you choose to believe. You are carrion already, Brother."

"Take us both, then," Avila said, setting down his lamp as though preparing for battle. "Come, Commodius: are you so doughty that you can kill the pair of us?"

Commodius's face widened into a grin which seemed to split it in twain and displayed every gleaming tooth in his head. "I am doughty enough, I promise you."

The mattock clanked to the floor.

"The world is a strange place, Brothers," Commodius's voice said, but it sounded different, as though he were speaking into a glass. "There is more lurking under God's heaven than you have ever dreamed of, Albrec. I could have made you a glutton of knowledge. I could have sated your appetite and answered every question your mind ever had the wit to pose. It is your loss. And Avila – my sweet Avila – I could have enjoyed you and advanced you. Now it will have to be done a different way. Watch me, children, and experience the last and greatest revelation of all..."

Commodius had gone. In his place there loomed the brooding darkness of a great lycanthrope, a bright-eyed werewolf standing in a puddle of Inceptine robes.

"Make your peace with He who made you," the beast said. "I will show you the very face of God."

It leapt.

Albrec was shoved out of the way and hit the floor face-first. Avila had thrown himself to one side, scrabbling for the mattock. But the beast was too fast. It caught him in midair, its claws ripping his robe to shreds. A twist of its powerful arms, and Avila was flung across the cave, to strike the wall with a sickening slap of flesh. The werewolf laughed, and turned on Albrec.

"It will be quick, my little colleague, my tireless bookworm." It grasped Albrec by the neck and lifted him up as though he were made of straw. The vast jaws opened, bathing him in the stink of its breath.

But Avila was there again, his face a broken wound and something gleaming in his fist. He struck at the creature's back, trying to pierce the thick fur and failing. The beast spun round, dropping Albrec.

The Antillian watched in a daze as the werewolf that was Commodius smashed his friend across the breadth of the chamber once more. His own lamp had been broken and extinguished, and only Avila's light on the floor illuminated the struggle, making it seem a battle of shadowy titans amid the stalactites of the ceiling.

And kindling a glitter of something lying amid the detritus of the floor.

Albrec scrabbled over and grasped the pentagram dagger in his fist. He heard Avila give a last, despairing shout of defiance and hatred, and then he threw himself on the werewolf's back.

The creature straightened and the claws came reaching over its shoulders, raking the side of Albrec's neck. He felt no pain, no fear, only a clinical determination. He stabbed the pentagram dagger deep into the beast, the blade grating on the vertebrae as it shredded muscle and pierced flesh up to its hilt.

The werewolf's head snapped back, its skull cracking against Albrec's own with a force to explode bloody lights in his head and make him release his hold and tumble to the floor like a stringless puppet.

The beast gave an odd, gargling moan. It was Commodius again, shrunken, naked, bewildered, the pentagram hilt of the dagger protruding obscenely from his back.

The Senior Librarian looked at Albrec in disbelief, shaking his head as though circumstances had baffled him, and then he crumpled on top of Albrec, a dead weight which crushed the air out of the little monk's lungs. Albrec passed out.

Eighteen

THE BLIZZARD STRUCK as they were crossing the mountain divide. The pass disappeared in minutes and the world became a blank whiteness, featureless as a steamed-up window.

The column halted in confusion and the men fought to erect their crude canvas tents in the hammering wind. A numbing, aching time of struggle and pain, the fingers becoming blue and swollen as the blood inside them slowly crystallized, ice crackling in the nostrils and solidifying in men's beards. But at last Abeleyn and the remnant of his bodyguard were under shelter of a sort, the canvas cracking thunderously about their ears, the most accomplished fire starters amongst them striving to set light to the damp faggots they had carried all the way up from the lowlands.

It was a diminished band which accompanied the excommunicate King up into the Hebros. They had left the sailors and the wounded and the weaker of the soldiers behind to be tended by villagers in the foothills, along with an escort of unhurt veterans to guard them, for the folk in this part of the world, though Hebrian, were a hard, rapacious people who could not be trusted to treat helpless men with any charity. So it was with less than fifty men that Abeleyn had started the climb into the mountains that formed the backbone of his kingdom. He was afoot, like his subordinates, for he had put the lady Jemilla on the only horse which survived, and the dozen mules they had commandeered from the lowland villages were burdened with firewood and what meagre supplies they had been able to glean from the sullen population.

They had been eight days on the road. It was the eleventh day of Forgist, the darkest month of the year, and they were still twenty leagues from Abrusio.

THE LADY JEMILLA pulled her furs more closely about her and ordered her remaining maidservant to fetch her something to eat from one of the soldiers' fires. "And none of that accursed salt pork, either, or I'll have the hide flayed off you."

She was cold despite the fact that she had the best tent in the company and there was a fire burning by its entrance. She was beginning to regret her insistence that she accompany Abeleyn back to Abrusio, but she had been afraid to let the King out of her sight. She wondered what awaited them in the bawdy old city, which was under the sway of the Knights Militant and the nobles.

She bore Abeleyn's child – or so it would be believed. Were his attempt to reclaim his kingdom unsuccessful, her life would be forfeit. The present rulers of Hebrion could not allow a bastard heir of the former King to live. In carrying Abeleyn's issue she harboured her own death warrant within her very flesh.

If he failed.

He would not talk to her! Did he think that she was some empty-headed, high-born courtesan with no thoughts worth thinking beyond the bedroom? She had tried to wheedle infor-mation out of him, but he had remained as closed as an oyster.

The tattered raptor which was always coming and going was the familiar of the wizard, Golophin – everyone knew that. He was keeping the King informed as to events in his capital. But what were those events? Abeleyn was such a boy in many things – in sex most of all, perhaps – but he could suddenly go still and give that stare of his, as though he were awaiting an explanation for some offence. That was when the man, the King, came out, and Jemilla was afraid of him then, though she used all her skill at dissembling to conceal it. She dared not press him further than she already had, and the knowledge galled her immeasurably. She was as ignorant of his intentions as the basest soldier of his bodyguard.

Her thoughts wandered from the groove they had worn for themselves. The blizzard roared beyond the frail walls of the tent, and she found herself thinking of Richard Hawkwood, the mariner who had once been her lover and who had sailed away such a long time ago, it seemed. Where was he now, upon the sea or under it? Did he think of her as he paced his quarterdeck, or faced whatever perils he had to face in the unknown regions his ships had borne him to?

His child, this little presence in her belly, his son. He would have loved that: a son to carry on his name, something that whining bitch of a wife had never given him. But Jemilla had larger plans for this offspring of hers. He would not be the son of a sea captain, but the heir to a throne. She would one day be a king's mother.

If Abeleyn did not fail. If his betrothal to Astarac's princess could somehow be foiled. If.

Jemilla plotted on to herself, constructing a world of interconnecting conspiracies in her mind whilst the blizzard raged unheeded outside and the Hebros passes deepened with snow.

FOR TWO DAYS Abeleyn and his entourage cowered under canvas, waiting for the blizzard to abate. Finally the wind died and the snow stopped falling. They emerged from the half-buried shelters to find a transformed world, white and blinding, drifts in which the mules might disappear, mountain peaks glaring and powder-plumed against a brilliant cobalt blue sky.

They slogged onwards. The strongest men were put to the front to clear a way for the others, wading through the drifts and bludgeoning a path forward.

Two more days they travelled in this manner, the weather holding clear and bitterly cold. Four of the mules died on their feet in the freezing star-bright nights and one sentry was found hunched stiff and rime-brittle at his post in the early morning, his arquebus frosted to his grey hand and his eyes dead, glazed windows into nothing. But at last it seemed that the mountains were receding on either side of them. The pass was opening out, the ground descending beneath their feet. They had crossed the backbone of Hebrion and were travelling steadily down into the settled lands, the fiefs of the nobles and the wide farmlands with their olive groves and vineyards, their orchards and pastures. A kindlier world, where the people would welcome the coming of their rightful king. At least, such was Abeleyn's hope.

On their last night in the foothills they made camp and set to cooking the strips they had cut from the carcasses of the dead mules. There was still snow on the ground, but it was a thin, threadbare carpet beneath which sprouted tough clumps of brown upland grass which the surviving mules gorged themselves upon. Abeleyn climbed a nearby crag to look down on the bivouac, more the encampment of a band of refugees than the entourage of a king. He sat there in the cold wind to stare at this hard, sea-girt kingdom of his blooming out in the gathering twilight, the lights of the upland farms kindling below him, spangling the tired earth.

A rustle of pinions, and Golophin's bird had landed nearby and stood preening itself, trying to sort its ragged feathers into some kind of order. Had it been a purely natural creature, it could not have flown in the state it was in, but the Dweomer of its master kept it breathing, kept it airborne to run his errands for him.

"What tidings, my friend?" Abeleyn asked it.

"News, much news, sire. Sastro di Carrera has struck some sort of deal with the Presbyter Quirion. It is rumoured that he is to be named the next King of Hebrion."

Abeleyn gave a low whistle. In his worn travelling clothes he resembled a young shepherd come to seek a herd of errant goats up here on the stony knees of the mountain – except that he had too much care written into the darknesses below his eyes, and there was a growing hardness to the lines which coursed on either side of his nose to the corners of his mouth. He looked as though he had lately become accustomed to frowning.

"Rovero and Mercado. What are they doing?"

"They barricaded off the western arm of the Lower City as you ordered, and there have been clashes with the Knights but no general engagement. The troops Mercado considers unreliable have been segregated from the rest, but we were unable to arrest Freiss. He was too quick for us, and is with his tercios."

"They don't amount to much anyway," Abeleyn grunted.

"More troops have been coming into the city though, sire. Almost a thousand, most of them in Carreridan livery."

"Sastro's personal retainers. I dare say their deployment was the price of his kingship. Is there anything official yet about his elevation to the throne?"

"No, lad. It is a court rumour. The Sequeros are infuriated, of course. Old Astolvo is barely able to hold his young bloods in check. The kingship should have been his since he is next in line outside the Hibrusids, but he did not want it. Sastro's gold, it is said, is being showered about the city like rice at a wedding."

"He'll beggar himself to get the throne. But what does that matter, when he will control the treasury afterwards? Any news from my fiefs?"

"They are quiet. Your retainers dare not do anything at the moment. The Knights and the men at arms of the other great houses are watching them closely. The slightest excuse, and they will be wiped out."

Abeleyn had a couple of elderly aunts and a doddering granduncle. The Hibrusid house had become thin on the ground of late. These relics of its past had left all intrigue behind and preferred to stay away from court and live their vague lives in the peace of the extensive Royal estates north of Abrusio.

"We'll leave them out of it, then. We can do it with what we have anyway. Get back to the city, Golophin. Tell Rovero and Mercado that I will be approaching the city in four days, if God is willing. I want them to have a ship waiting ten miles up the coast from the Outer Roads. There is a cove there: Pendero's Landing. They can pick me up, and we'll sail into Abrusio with all honours, openly. That will give the population something to think about."

"You will have no problems with the common folk, Abeleyn," Golophin's falcon said. "It is only the nobles who want your head on a pike."

"So much the better," the young King said grimly. "Go now, Golophin. I want this thing set in train as soon as possible."

The bird took off at once, leaping into the air, its pinions shedding feathers as they flailed frantically.

"Farewell, my King," Golophin's voice said. "When next we meet it will be in the harbour of your capital."

Then the bird was labouring away across the foothills, lost in the star-filled night sky.

THE COMPANY SETTLED for the night, grateful for the fact that the worst of the winter weather had been left behind with the mountains. Abeleyn rolled himself in a boat-cloak and dozed by one of the soldiers' fires. He did not feel like sharing a tent with Jemilla tonight. It seemed somehow more wholesome to sleep under the stars with the firelight producing orange shadows beyond his tired eyelids.

He did not sleep for long, however. It was after midnight by the position of the Scythe when Sergeant Orsini shook him gently awake.

"Sire, pardon me, but there's something I think you should see."

Frowning, blinking, Abeleyn let himself be led out of the camp to the crag he had sat on earlier. Orsini, an efficient soldier, had placed a sentry there because it afforded a good view of the surrounding region. The sentry was there now, saluting quickly and then blowing on his cold hands.

"Well?" Abeleyn asked a little irritably.

Orsini pointed to the south-western horizon. "There, sir. What do you make of it?"

The world was dark, sleeping under its endless vault of stars. But there was something glowing at its edge. It might have been a mistimed sunset: the sky was red there, the clouds kindled with crimson light. A blush which lit up fully a quarter of the horizon glimmered silently.

"What do you think it is, sire?" Orsini asked.

Abeleyn watched the far-off flicker for a second. Finally he rubbed his eyes, squeezing the bridge of his nose as if trying to get rid of a bad dream.

"Abrusio is burning," he said.

ACROSS THE BREADTH of Normannia, over the two great ranges of the Malvennors and the Cimbrics, down to the coast of the Kardian Sea and the city of Torunn, capital of Lofantyr's kingdom.

Here it was already dawn; the sun which would not light up Hebrion's shores for hours yet was huge over the rooftops of the city, and the streets were already busy with the morning life of the markets. Carts and waggons clogged the roadways as farmers brought their produce in to sell, and herds of sheep and cattle were being driven to the stockpens which nestled below the city wall to the west. And beyond the walls to the north the steam and reek of the vast refugee camps sprawled over the land like a rash, whilst Torunnan soldiers manned the gates in that direction, vetting every entrant into the city. Once-prosperous citizens of Aekir had turned to beggary and brigandage in the past weeks, and the more disreputable of the refugees were denied entrance to the walled centre of Torunn. Convoys of crown waggons laden with victuals were waiting to be hauled out to the camps to satisfy the immediate needs of the unfortunates, but Torunna was a country at war and had little enough to spare.

THE MORNING HAD started badly for Corfe. He was striding along the stone corridors of Torunn's Main Arsenal with Ensign Ebro hurrying to keep up beside him. The men of his new command had been grudgingly set aside a few barrack blocks for their quarters and were crammed into them like apples in a barrel. Ebro had seen to it that they were issued rations and clothes from the city stores, but as of yet not one sword or arquebus or scrap of mail had been forthcoming. And then, last night, a note had been brought to him from the Queen Dowager by a lady-in-waiting.

I have done what I could, it said. *The rest is up to you.*

So he was on his own.

He had applied to have more officers seconded to him; he and Ebro alone could not effectively command five hundred men. And he had had Ebro indent three times for armour and weapons to outfit his force, but to no avail. Worst of all was the rumour running about the Garrison Quarters that Lofantyr was going to set aside twenty tercios of the regular army for the job of subjugating the rebellious nobles in the south – the task Corfe had been entrusted with. Clearly, the King did not expect the Queen Dowager's protégé to accomplish anything beyond his own discrediting.

He hammered on the door of the Quartermaster's department, wearing again the ragged uniform he had worn at Aekir.

The Quartermaster's department of the Third Torunnan Field Army was housed in a vast string of warehouses close to the waterfront in the east of the city. The warehouses held everything from boots to waggonwheels, cannon barrels to belts. Everything needed to equip and sustain an army could be found in them, but they were giving Corfe's men nothing more than the clothes on their backs and he wanted to know why.

The Quartermaster-General was Colonel Passifal, a veteran with a short, snow-white beard and a wooden stump in place of the leg he had lost fighting Merduks along the Ostian river before Corfe was born. His office was as bare as a monk's cell, and the papers which covered his desk were set in neat piles. Requisition orders, inspection sheets, inventories. The Torunnan army had a highly organized system of paperwork which it had copied from its one-time overlord, Fimbria.

"What do you want?" Passifal barked, not looking up from the scraping nib of his quill.

"I indented for five hundred sets of half-armour, five hundred arquebuses, five hundred sabres and all the necessary accoutrements days ago. I would like to know why the requisition has not been filled," Corfe said.

Passifal looked up, his quill losing its flickering animation.

"Ah, Colonel Corfe Cear-Inaf, I take it."

Corfe nodded curtly.

"Well, there's nothing I can do for you, son. My orders are to release stores only to regular Torunnan troops for the duration – Martellus is crying out for equipment up at the dyke, you know – and that rabble the King has given you to play with are officially classed as auxiliary militia, which means that the Torunnan military is not responsible for their fitting-out. I've stretched things as it is, giving you uniforms and a place for them to lay their heads. So don't bother me any more."

Corfe leant over the broad desk, resting his knuckles on the rim. "So how am I supposed to arm my men, Colonel?"

Passifal shrugged. "Auxiliary units are usually equipped by the private individual who has raised them. Are you rich, Cear-Inaf?"

Corfe laughed shortly. "All I possess is what I stand up in."

Passifal gazed at the ragged uniform. "You got those rents at Aekir, I hear."

"And at Ormann Dyke."

"So you've smelled powder." Passifal scratched his white beard for a moment and then gestured with sudden peevishness. "Oh, take a seat, for God's sake, and stop trying to stand there on top of your dignity."

Corfe drew up a chair. Ebro remained standing by the door.

"I hear the King has played a joke on you, Colonel," Passifal said, grinning now. "He does that sometimes. The old woman rides him hard, and every so often he kicks at the traces."

"The Queen Dowager."

"Yes. What a beauty that woman was in her day. Not bad now, as a matter of fact. It's the witchery keeps her young, they say. But Lofantyr gets tired of being told which pot to piss in. He's outfitting an expedition to bring the south to heel – a proper one, infantry, cavalry and horse artillery – but he's going to let you go south and make an arse of it first to show his mother she shouldn't force her favourites on him."

"I thought as much," Corfe said calmly, though his fists clenched on his knees.

"Yes. My orders are not to let you have so much as a brass button from our stores. Those savages you style a command will have to fight with their fists and teeth alone. I'm sorry for it, Colonel, but that's the way it is."

"Thank you for explaining it to me," Corfe said in a flat voice.

He rose to go.

Passifal stuck out a hand. "Not so fast! There's no hurry, is there? You served under Mogen, I take it."

"I did."

"So did I. I was a cavalryman in one of his flying columns in the days when we went out looking for the Merduks instead of waiting for them to march up to our walls."

"I also was cavalry," Corfe said, unbending a little. "But there was no need for horsemen in Aekir once the siege began."

"Yes, yes, I daresay... Old Mogen used to say that cavalry was the arm of the gentleman, and artillery the arm of the mechanic. How we used to love that cantankerous old bastard! He was the best man we've ever had..."

Passifal stared at Corfe for a long moment, as if weighing him up.

"There is a way to equip your men, after a fashion," he said at last.

"How?"

Passifal rose. "Come with me." His stump thumped hollowly on the floor as he came round from behind his desk and retrieved a set of keys from the hundreds hanging in rows along one wall of the office. "You won't like it, mind, and I'm not sure if it's right, but they're barbarians you're commanding so I doubt if they'll care. And besides, the stuff isn't doing any good where it is, and technically it's not part of the regular military stores..."

Corfe and Ebro followed the one-legged Quartermaster out of the office, completely baffled.

THIS SECTION OF the Main Arsenal resembled nothing so much as the great market squares in the middle of Torunn. There were carts, waggons and limbers everywhere. Men were shifting stores from warehouses or into warehouses, culverins were being drawn by teams of oxen, and everywhere there was the squeal of pulleys and cries of labouring men. Down at the waterfront a trio of deep-hulled *nefs* had put in from the wide Torrin Estuary and were unloading cargoes of powder and pig-iron on to the quays, and a slim dispatch-runner had just docked: bearing news from the east, no doubt.

Passifal led them away from the hubbub to an older building which was set back from the waterfront. It was an ageing stone structure, windowless and somehow deserted-looking, as though it had been long forgotten.

The Quartermaster turned a key in the screeching lock and shouldered the heavy door open with a grunt.

"Stay close behind," he told Corfe and Ebro. "It's dark as a witch's tit in here. I'll strike a light."

The crack of flint on steel, and Passifal was blowing gently on the tinder-covered wick of an oil lamp. The light grew and he slapped shut the glass case on the lengthening flame, then held it up so that the radiance of it flushed the interior of the building.

"What in the world – ?" Corfe said, startled despite himself.

The building was very long; it extended beyond the lamplight into darkness. And it was crowded.

Piles of armour lay all about, in places stacked until they almost reached the raftered ceiling. Helmets, gauntlets, breast- and back-plates, chainmail, vambraces, aventails, rusting and cobwebbed and dented by blows, holed by gunfire. Mixed in with the armour were weapons: scimitars, tulwars, rotten-shafted lances with remnants of silk still attached to their heads. Strange weapons, unlike any the Torunnans used – or any other western army, for that matter.

Corfe bent and picked up a helmet, turning it in his hands and wiping the dust away. It was high-crowned with a flaring neck-guard and long cheek-pieces. The helmet of one of the *Ferinai*, the elite cuirassiers of the Merduks.

"Merduk armour," he said as the realization smote him. "But what is it doing here?"

"Trophies of war," Passifal said. "Been here sixty years, since we threw back the Ostrabarian Merduks after they overran Ostiber. That was Gallican of Rone, if you remember your history. A good general. He beat them as they were approaching the Thurian Passes and sent twenty thousand of the black-hearted bastards to join their precious Prophet. The King staged a triumphal march for him here in Torunn, parades of prisoners and so on. And he shipped back a thousand sets of armour to display during it. When it was over they were dumped here and forgotten. Been here ever since. I had been meaning to get rid of them – we're pressed for warehouse space, you see..."

Corfe dropped the old helm with a clang. "You expect me to dress my men up as Merduks?"

"Seems to me you haven't a lot of choice, son. This is the best I can do. You'll not find a better offer in the city, unless you can persuade the Queen Dowager to stump up the necessary cash."

Corfe shook his head, thinking.

"It's not honourable, sir, dressing up as heathens," Ebro said passionately. "You should decline the command. It's what they want you to do."

"And what you want me to do also, Ensign?" Corfe asked without turning around.

"Sir, I –"

"We'll take the armour," Corfe said briskly to Passifal. "But we can't let the men wear it as it stands; folk will think we're the enemy. Have you any paint, Quartermaster?"

Passifal's white eyebrows shot up. "Paint? Aye, tons of it, but what for?"

Corfe retrieved the helm he had thrown down a moment before. "We'll paint this gear, to distinguish ourselves. Red, I think. Yes – a nice shade of scarlet so that the blood won't show. Excellent." He was smiling, but there was little humour in his face. "My men have no transport facilities. I'll have them here within the hour and they can pick out their armour themselves. Can you have the paint waiting by then, Quartermaster?"

Passifal looked as though he had been let in on an enormous joke. "Why not? Yes, Colonel, the paint will be here. It'll be worth it to see your five hundred savages dressed up in Merduk armour and splashed crimson."

Again, the mirthless smile. "Not only the savages, Quartermaster. Ebro and I will also be donning Merduk gear."

"But sir, we have our own," Ebro protested. "There's no need –"

"We'll wear what the men wear," Corfe interrupted him. "And I shall have to think up some sort of battle standard, since the regular Torunnan banners will, it seems, be denied to us. Good. All that remains now is to meet the General Staff and receive my specific orders. After that, we can begin to plan."

"No waggons or mules, no transport for our gear," Ensign Ebro said, a last-ditch effort.

Corfe grinned at him, unexpectedly good-humoured. "You forget, Ebro, that our command is composed of savage tribesmen from the mountains. What need have they of a baggage train? They can live off the country, and may God help the country."

Passifal was watching Corfe as though he had just that moment recognized him from somewhere. "I see you intend to pick up the King's gauntlet, Colonel."

"If I can, Quartermaster," Corfe said flatly, "I intend to throw it back in his face."

NINETEEN

"WHAT A PRETTY picture a burning city makes," Sastro di Carrera said, leaning on the iron balcony rail of the Royal palace. Abrusio spread out beyond his perch in a sea of buildings, ending almost two miles away downhill in the confusion of ships and buildings and docks which butted on to the true sea, the Western Ocean which girdled the known edges of the world. It was twilight, not because the day was near its long winter sleep, but because of the towers of smoke that shrouded the sun. Sastro's face was lit by the radiance of the burning, and he could hear it as a far thunder, the mutterings of the banished elder gods.

"May God forgive us," Presbyter Quirion said beside him, making the Sign of the Saint across his breastplate. Unlike Sastro, who was immaculately tailored, Quirion was grimed and filthy. He had lately come from the inferno below, in which men were fighting and dying by the thousand, their collective screaming drowned out by the hungry roar of the holocaust, the tearing rattles of volley-fire.

"'And now,'" he said quietly, "'is Hell come to earth, and in the ashes of its burning will totter all the schemes of greedy men. The Beast, in coming, will tread the cinders of their dreams.'"

"What in the world are you talking about, Quirion?" Sastro asked.

"I was quoting an old text which foretells the end of the world we know and the beginning of another."

"The end of the Hibrusid world, at any rate," Sastro said with satisfaction. "And think of the prime building land the fire will clear for us. It will be worth a fortune."

Quirion looked at his aristocratic companion with

unconcealed contempt. "You are not King yet, my lord Carrera."

"I will be. Nothing will stop me or you now, Presbyter. Abrusio will be ours very soon."

"If there's anything left of it."

"The important parts will be left," Sastro said, grinning. "What a blessed thing a wind is, to blow the flames out to sea and take with it those heretical traitors and rebel peasants in the Lower City who defy us. God's hand at work, Quirion. Surely you can see that?"

"I do not like to ask God to intervene on my behalf; it smacks of hubris to assume that the Creator of the universe will think me, out of all His creations, worthy of attention. I merely try to further what I believe to be His divine will. In this instance, I needed two hundred barrels of pitch to set the Lower City alight."

"A practical kind of faith you Knights profess," Sastro said, raising his scented handkerchief to his face so that his mouth was concealed.

"I find it answers well enough."

The handkerchief was tucked back inside a snowy sleeve. "So how goes the fighting then, my practical Presbyter?"

Quirion rasped a palm over the stubble on his scalp. "Severe enough at times. Your retainers have been acquitting themselves well since I stiffened their tercios with contingents of Knights. The trained Hebrian troops are better, of course, but they are distracted by Freiss's men in their rear. He has three or four hundred arquebusiers holed up in the western arm of the Lower City cheek by jowl with the Arsenal, and they have had to tie up almost a thousand troops to keep him bottled in his bolthole."

"What of the navy? There was a lot of activity in the Inner Roads this morning."

"They were merely warping their ships off the docks; by now the fire will have swept down to the water's edge. They tried a few ranging shots at the palace this afternoon, but the distance is too far. We have a boom across the Great Harbour covered by the forts on the moles; it should suffice to keep the navy at bay, and their guns out of range of the Upper City. Abrusio was built to be defended from a seaborne attack as well as from a landward one. That works in our favour. And the confined nature of the battlefield means that our disadvantages in numbers are not so apparent."

"How far has the fire advanced?"

"As far as the Crown Wharves in the Inner Roads. It should almost be licking at the walls of the Arsenal itself. Mercado has had to set aside over three thousand men as firefighters, and another dozen tercios are overseeing the evacuation of the Lower City's population. He is as hamstrung as a bull caught half over a gate."

"His concern for the little people is laudable, but it will prove his undoing," Sastro said.

"The little people are fighting side by side with the city garrison, Lord Carrera," Quirion reminded him. "The population of the Upper City has remained neutral, but I would not place much faith in the nobles."

"Oh, they'll bend with the wind, as they always do. There's not a great house in Hebrion – even the Sequeros – who will tangle with us now. And the Merchants' Guild is being rapidly won over also. Gold is a marvellous comforter, I find, and the concessions that a future king can grant."

"Yes..."

The steady roar of the flames mixed with furious exchanges of arquebus fire made a collective wailing which at a distance seemed like Abrusio herself crying out in agony because of the inferno gnawing at her bowels. Warfare on this scale had not been seen west of the Cimbrics for twenty years, but now the Five Monarchies were being ripped apart by internal dissension and religious struggle: civil war in everything but name.

There were rumours that Astarac was going the way of Hebrion, the nobles fighting to depose the heretic King Mark and elect one of their own to the throne, helped, of course, by the Inceptine Order and the Knights Militant. And Torunna, as well as being menaced by the vast Merduk army which had lately been stalled at Ormann Dyke, had uprisings of its own to contend with. And Almark's king was dying – perhaps dead already – and was said to be intent on leaving his kingdom to the Church.

Quirion sighed. He was at heart a pious man, and a profoundly conservative one. Deeply convinced though he was that the Church was in the right and had to snuff out heresy wherever it took root – even were it to sprout in the palaces of kings – he did not like to see what he considered to be the natural order of things so disrupted and torn apart. Sastro, now... he relished any anarchy which might further his own ambitions, but the Presbyter of the Knights in Abrusio would rather have been fighting heathens on the eastern frontiers than slaughtering folk who, at the end of the day, believed in the same God as he.

It was a feeling he kept to himself and scourged himself for at every opportunity, flying as it did in the face of the directives issued by the Pontiff in Charibon, God's direct representative on earth. He was here to obey orders which in the last analysis were equivalent to the will of God. There could be no shirking of such a burden.

THE FIRE HURTLED through the narrow streets of Lower Abrusio like a wave, a bright tsunami which exploded the wooden buildings of this part of the city into kindling and ate out the interiors and the supporting wooden beams of those structures which were composed of yellow Hebrian stone until they toppled also. A dozen massed batteries of heavy culverins could not have bettered the destructive work, and the efforts of the soldiers-turned-firefighters in General Mercado's command to stem the onset of the flames seemed pointless, drops of maniac effort swamped in a sea of fire.

They were busy demolishing a wide avenue of houses southwest of the front of the conflagration, hoping thereby to form a firebreak which would starve the flames of sustenance. Engineers had laid charges at the cornerstones of all the buildings and were busy detonating them in a series of explosions which blasted the smoke into concentric rings, like the ripples of a stone-pocked lake.

While this went on, the fighting continued, the streets clogged with frantic, murderous scrums of armoured men who were being rained with cinders and burning timbers. Here and there companies and demi-tercios of arquebusiers had space to form up in lines and the opposing forces fired and reloaded and fired again only yards away from each other, the formations melting away under the withering barrage like solder in a furnace, to be replaced by reinforcements from their rear until one side broke and ran.

Wherever the regular Hebrian troops made a stand, the retainers of the Carreras and the Knights Militant who were with them could make no headway, though the Knights, their heavy armour some protection against bullets at all but the closest ranges, would form wedges of flesh and steel which would try to spear through the enemy lines by brute force. But they were not numerous enough. The firing lines opened to let them through after discharging a volley at point-blank range and those of the Knights who remained on their feet were swamped by scores of sword-and-buckler men to the rear.

And yet there was more to the battle than the mere contest between fighting men. Often in the middle of the carnage the combatants would cease their warring and as a body would seek shelter from the approaching holocaust. Men feared being burnt alive more than any other death, and would run into the enemy lines and be cut down quickly rather than remain to be consumed by the flames in their irresistible advance.

And civilians were there in the midst of the battling tercios and companies and demi-platoons. They fled their houses as the flames approached and died by the hundred as they ran through deadly crossfires or were caught by toppling buildings. Had anyone been in Abrusio who had also been at Aekir, he would have found the former more horrifying, for in Aekir men had been intent only on escape, on evading the enemy and the fire. Here they fought in the midst of the blaze, grappling with each other whilst the flames licked at their heads. Streets which were aflame from top to bottom but which were strategically valuable were defended to the last. The soldiers of Hebrion knew that by opposing the Knights they were labelling themselves heretics, the retainers of an excommunicate king, and that if they were captured, the pyre awaited them anyway. So no quarter was asked or given. The battle was more bitter than any struggle against the heathen, for the Merduks would at least take prisoners, intending them to swell the ranks of their slaves.

GOLOPHIN STOOD ON the topmost column of Admiral's Tower, a walled platform which housed the iron framework of the signal beacon. With him was General Mercado, his half-silver face alight with the sliding crimson reflections of the burning city. On the stairs below a knot of aides was collected, ready to take orders out to the various bodies of soldiery about the Lower City.

A wall of flame hid the heights of Abrusio Hill, hid even the peaks of the Hebros beyond – a curtain whose topmost fringe dissolved into anvils and thunderheads of toiling smoke.

They started by burning books, Golophin thought. *Then it was people, now it is the cities of the kingdoms themselves. They will consume the world ere they are done. And they do it in the name of God.*

"I would curse them, but I have no Dweomer left," he said to Mercado. "All I had, I used to divert the fire from the waterfronts. I am as dry as a desert stone, General."

Mercado nodded. "Your work is appreciated, Golophin. You saved a score of the fleet's biggest ships."

"Much good they're doing us at the moment. When is Rovero to assault the boom?"

"Tonight. He will send in fireships to cover his gunboats, and the troopships last. With luck, by tomorrow he will be bombarding the Upper City."

"Bombarding our own city," Golophin said bitterly. His eyes had sunk so far into his head that they were mere glints answering the bloody light of the fire. His face was skull-like below the bald scalp. He had over-extended himself in his efforts to save the ships of the fleet, more than two dozen of which had been in dock when the flames had begun licking round the wharves. As it was, six of them had been destroyed and could be seen burning, alight from truck to waterline, black silhouettes of phantom ships surrounded by saffron light, their guns going off in chaotic sequence. Six great carracks with almost a thousand men on board, men who had been cut off from escape and had leaped into the waters of the Inner Roads to drown like rats. Sailors did not swim. It seemed ridiculous, farcical. Their bodies, some ablaze, floated in the Inner Roads by the hundred. Hundreds more were living yet, clinging to spare topmasts or anything else they had had the presence of mind to fling overboard as the flames came ravening towards their vessels. No one could get near them: the fires had cut them off from land.

An unbearably bright flash, and seconds later the enormous boom of an explosion. The powder magazine of one carrack had gone up and the ship, hundreds of tons of wood and metal, had erupted into the air and was raining its dismembered fragments down on the waters of the harbour, starting fires on the other ships which had managed to put off from the blazing wharves in time to avoid its fate.

"If Hell were a creation of man, it would be very like that picture below us," Golophin said, awed by the spectacle.

"God has certainly no hand in it," Mercado said.

An aide came with a grubby parchment message. Mercado read it through, his lips muttering the words.

"Freiss's men have attempted to stage a break-out. The fire is finally at the walls of the Arsenal. He is dead, and most of his traitors with him."

"The Arsenal?" Golophin asked. "What of the stores within it? My God, General – the powder and ammunition!"

"We've shifted maybe a quarter of it, but we cannot get at the rest. First Freiss and then the fires have cut it off."

"And if the fire detonates the powder stores?"

"The main stores are thirty feet below ground in stone cellars. They have pipes in them which let out to the harbour. If the worst comes to the worst I can order the pipes opened and the powder magazines flooded. They would take half the city with them when they went up. Don't worry, Golophin – I won't let that happen. But it will mean destroying our powder and ammunition reserves, leaving only the naval stores here in the tower."

"Do it," Golophin said grimly. "Abrusio is hurt badly enough as it is. We must preserve something of her for Abeleyn to reclaim."

"Agreed." Mercado called an aide and began dictating the necessary orders.

"Rovero has taken a squadron to Pendero's Landing," the General went on when the aide had left. "Two carracks, some caravels and a trio of *nefs* in which are three thousand marines and arquebusiers of the garrison. He is going to try and convince the King that a land assault over the city walls will be more effective than attempting to carry the Great Harbour. If we can break the boom tonight, then in a couple of days we will be assaulting from both land and sea and another squadron can give supporting fire to the overland force if they attack the walls near the coast. That is Abeleyn's best bet, in my opinion. They have us pinned down here, by the fire itself and the guns they can bring to bear on us from Abrusio Hill. Also they are thin on the ground, and will be hard put to it to see off two attacks at once."

"Whatever seems best," Golophin said. "I am no general or admiral. I'll keep Abeleyn informed, though."

"Can that bird of yours bear a burden, Golophin?"

"A light one, perhaps. What is it?"

Mercado produced a heavily sealed scroll from his doublet. The galley-prow emblem of Astarac could be clearly seen, melted into the crimson wax which fastened it shut.

"This came today by special courier from Cartigella. It bears King Mark's personal seal and therefore can be opened only by another monarch. I think it may be urgent."

Golophin took the scroll. He itched to open it himself. "Good news, let us hope."

"I doubt it. Rumours have been coming in for days of an attempted coup in Cartigella, and of fighting through the streets of the city itself."

"The world goes mad," Golophin said quietly, stuffing the scroll into a pocket of his over-large robe.

"The world we knew is no more," Mercado said crisply. "Nothing will ever bring it back again now. If we are to fashion a new one, then we must build it on blood and gunpowder. And on faith."

"No," Golophin snapped. "Faith can have nothing to do with it. If we rear up something new, then let it be built upon reason and keep the clerics and the Pontiffs out of it. They have meddled for far too long: that is what this war of ours is about."

"A man must believe in something, Golophin."

"Then let him believe in himself, and leave God out of it!"

IN THAT WINTER of war and slaughter there were still a few kingdoms untouched by the chaos which was sweeping across Normannia. In Alstadt, capital of mighty Almark on the icy shores of the Hardic Sea, the trade and business of the city went on much as usual, with one difference: the banners of the Royal palace were at half-mast and wheeled traffic had been barred from the streets surrounding the palace. Alstadt was a sprawling, disorganized city, the youngest of the Ramusian capitals. It was unwalled save for the citadel which held the arsenals and the palace itself. Almark was a wide kingdom, a land of open steppes and rolling hills which extended from the Tulmian Gulf in the west to the River Saeroth which marked its border with Finnmark in the east. And to the south the kingdom extended to the snowy Narian Hills and the Sea of Tor, on whose shores nestled the monastery-city of Charibon. It was for this reason that Almark maintained a small garrison in Charibon to supplement the Knights Militant usually based there. Almark was a staunch ally of the Church which Charibon and its inhabitants represented, and its ailing monarch, Haukir VII, had always been a faithful son of that Church.

But Haukir was on his deathbed and he had no heir to succeed him, only a clutch of dissolute sister-sons whom the Almarkan people would not have trusted with the running of a baker's shop, let alone the mightiest kingdom north of the Malvennors and the Cimbrics. So the banners flew at half-mast, and the streets around the palace were quiet but for the screams of the scavenging gulls which swooped inland from the grey Hardic. And the dying King lay breathing his last surrounded by his counsellors and the Inceptine Prelate of the kingdom, Marat, who would oversee his departure from the world and close his tired eyes when his spirit fled.

The bedchamber of the King was dark and stuffy, full of the reek of old flesh. The King lay in the middle of the canopied bed like a castaway thrown up on a pale-sanded shore, one voyage ended and another about to begin. The Prelate, whom some said was his natural brother on the father's side, wiped the spittle which coursed in a line from one corner of Haukir's mouth into his slush-white beard. Some said it had been the fever, caught whilst journeying back from the Conclave of Kings in Vol Ephrir. Some said in whispers it was a stroke brought on by the King's outrage at the heresy of his fellow monarchs. Whatever had caused it, he lay withered and immobile in that wasteland of fine linen, his breath a stertorous whistle in his throat.

The King waved his hand at the assembled lawyers and courtiers and clerics, dismissing them from the room until all who remained were Prelate Marat, the Privy Minister and an inkwell- and parchment-laden Royal clerk, who looked distinctly uneasy at being alone in such august company.

The seagulls shrieked outside, and the hum of the living city was far off and distant, another world heard through a mirror. Haukir beckoned them closer.

"My end is here at last," he croaked in a poor mockery of his bellowing voice. "And I am not afraid. I go to meet He who made me, and the company of the living Saints, with the Blessed Ramusio at their head. But there is something I must do ere I leave this world. I must provide for the future welfare of my kingdom, and must ensure that it endures within the protection of the One True Faith after I am gone. Almark must remain firm in this era of heresy and war. I wish to alter my will..."

He closed his eyes and swallowed painfully. The clerk was nudged by the Privy Minister and hurriedly dipped his quill in the inkwell which dangled from one buttonhole.

"The main provisions I made prior to this date I set aside. Only the secondary provisions of my previous will shall be honoured. I name Prelate Marat, Privy Minister Erland and –" He stopped and glared at the clerk. "What's your name, man?"

"F-Finnson of Glebir, if it please your Majesty."

"And Finnson of Glebir as my witnesses on this fifteenth day of Forgist, in the year of the Blessed Saint five hundred and fifty-one."

The ragged breathing began to quicken. The King coughed up a mass of phlegm which Marat wiped away as tenderly as a nurse.

"Having no heirs of my blood which I consider suitable for bearing the burden of this crown, and seeing around me the world at this time falling ever farther into anarchy and heresy, I hereby leave the Almarkan crown to the stewardship of the Holy Church. I name my revered confessor, Prelate Marat, as regent of the realm until the High Pontiff, His Holiness Himerius of Hebrion, may see fit to make his own provisions for the ruling of the kingdom. As I entrust my soul to God, so I entrust my country to the bosom of God's representatives on earth, and I trust they will watch over Almark as the Blessed Saint watches over my pilgrim spirit as it makes its way into the glories of heaven..."

Haukir's head seemed to sink heavily into the pillow. Sweat shone over his face and his lips were blue.

"Shrive me of my sins, Marat. Send me on my way," he whispered, and as the Prelate gave him the final blessing the Privy Minister turned to the Scribbling clerk and hissed in an undertone: "Did you get all that?"

The clerk nodded, still scribbling. Marat ended his blessing and then paused.

"Goodnight, brother," he said softly. He closed the staring eyes and laid the hands over the silent chest.

"The King is dead," he said.

"Are you sure?" the Privy Minister asked.

"Of course I'm sure! I've seen dead men before! Now get that fool to make a copy of the revised will. I want other copies of it made and posted in the market place. And set out the black flags. You know what to do."

The Privy Minister stared at the cleric for a second, some indefinable tension fizzling in the air between them. Then he got down on one knee and kissed the Prelate's ring. "I salute the new regent of Almark."

"And send me a courier, and another clerk. I must get a dispatch off to Charibon at once."

"The snows –" the Privy Minister began.

"Damn the snows, just do as you're told. And get this inky-fingered idiot out of here. I will meet the nobles and the garrison commander in the audience chamber in one hour."

"As you wish," the Privy Minister said tonelessly.

They exited, and the Prelate was left alone with the dead King.

Already he could hear the murmuring in the chambers below which the appearance of the pair had produced among the notables gathered there.

Marat bent his head and prayed in silence for a second, the gulls still calling in their savage forlornness beyond the shuttered windows of the chamber. Then he rose, went to one of the windows and opened the shutters so that the keen sea air might rush in and freshen the death-smelling room.

Alstadt: broad, crude, thriving port-capital of the north. It opened out before him misted in drizzle, hazed by woodsmoke fires, alive with humanity in its tens of thousands. And beyond it, the wide kingdom of Almark with its horse-rich plains, its armies of cuirassiers. Himerius would be pleased: things could not have worked out better. And others would be pleased also.

Marat turned from the cold window to gaze down on the corpse of the King, and his eyes shone with a saffron light that had nothing human in it at all.

TWENTY

THEY WERE AN unlikely looking crowd, Corfe had to admit to himself. They had never been taught to form ranks, present arms or stand at attention and they milled about in an amorphous mob, as unmilitary a formation as could be imagined.

They were clad in bruised, holed and rusty Merduk armour of every shape and type, but mostly they had picked out the war harness of the *Ferinai*, the heavy cuirassiers of the east, as it was the best quality. And perhaps it appealed to some savage sensibility within them, for it was the armour of horsemen and these men had once been horsemen. Their fathers and grandfathers had raided the coastal settlements of the Torunnans time out of mind, swooping out of the Cimbric foothills on their rangy black horses – horses which were the product of secret studs high in isolated valleys. Cavalry was what these men ought to be. Horse-soldiers. But Corfe could no more provide them with horses than he could with wings, so they must fight afoot in their outlandish armour.

Armour which had been rendered even more strange-looking by the liberal addition of red paint. The tribesmen seemed as happy as finger-painting children as they splashed it over their armour and hurled it at each other in gore-like gobbets. A crowd had gathered to watch, black-clad Torunnan soldiers lounging in the Quartermaster's yard and laughing fit to split their sides at the dressing up of the savages from the mountains, the ex-galley slaves.

As soon as the first Torunnan laughs were heard, however, the tribesmen went as silent as crags. A tulwar was scraped out of its threadbare scabbard and Corfe had to step in to prevent a fight which would quickly have turned into a full-scale battle. He called upon Marsch to calm his fellow tribesmen down and the hulking savage harangued his comrades in their own tongue. He was a frightening figure: somehow he had found a Merduk officer's helm which was decorated with a pair of back-sweeping horns and a beak-like nose-guard. Lathered with red paint, he looked like the apotheosis of some primitive god of slaughter come looking for acolytes.

"Someone to see you, sir," Ensign Ebro told Corfe as the latter doffed his heavy Merduk helm and wiped the sweat from his face. Ebro also wore the foreign harness, and he looked acutely uncomfortable in it.

"Who is it?" Corfe snapped, squeezing the acrid sweat from his eyes.

"Someone who has tasted gunsmoke with you, Colonel," another, familiar voice said. Corfe spun to find Andruw there, holding out a hand and grinning. He shouted aloud and pumped the proffered hand up and down. "Andruw! What in the hell are you doing here?"

"I ask myself the same question: what have I done to deserve this? But be that as it may, it would seem that I am to be your adjutant. For what misdeed I know not."

The pair of them laughed together while Ebro stood stiff and forgotten. Corfe mustered his manners.

"Ensign Ebro, permit me to introduce... what rank have they showered upon you, Andruw?"

"Haptman, for my sins."

"There you are. Haptman Andruw Cear-Adurhal, late of the artillery, who commanded the Barbican Batteries of Ormann Dyke."

Ebro glanced at Andruw with rather more respect, and bowed. "I am honoured."

"Likewise."

"But what are you doing away from the Dyke?" Corfe asked Andruw. "I thought they'd need every gunner they could lay their hands on up there."

"I was sent to Torunn with dispatches. You have been seeking officers, I hear, driving the muster clerks mad with your enquiries. Apparently they decided that by seconding me to your command they could shut you up."

"And how goes it at the Dyke? Can they spare you?"

Andruw's bright humour faded a little. "They are short of everything, Corfe. Martellus is half out of his mind with worry, though as always he hides it well. We have had no reinforcements to replace our losses, no resupply for weeks. We are a forgotten army."

Andruw's gaze flicked to the weirdly garbed savages of Corfe's command as he spoke. Corfe noticed the look and said wryly: "And we are the army they would like to forget."

There was a pause. Finally Andruw asked: "Have you had your orders yet? Whither are we bound with our garish warrior band?"

"South," Corfe told him, disgust seeping into his voice. "I had best warn you now, Andruw, that the King expects us to end in some kind of debacle, fighting these rebels in the south. We are of small account in his plans."

"Hence the quaint war harness."

"It's all they would let me have."

Andruw forced a grin. "What is it they say? The longer the odds, the greater the glory. We proved that at Ormann Dyke, Corfe. We'll do it again, by Ramusio's beard."

LATER THAT AFTERNOON, Corfe reported to the Staff Headquarters for the detailed orders that were to send his command into its first battle. The place was busy with sashed officers and bustling aides. Couriers were coming and going and the King was closeted in conference with his senior advisors. No one seemed to recall any orders for Colonel Cear-Inaf and his command, and it was a maddening half-hour before a clerk finally found them. One unsealed roll of parchment with a scrawling, illegible signature at the bottom and a hasty impression of the Royal signet in a cracked blob of scarlet wax. It was in the stilted language of military orders not written in the field.

You are hereby directed and obliged to take the troops under your command south to the town of Hedeby on the Kardian Sea, and there engage the retainers of the traitor

Duke Ordinac in open battle, destroying them and restoring
their master's fiefs to their rightful allegiance. You will
march with due haste and prudence, and on accomplishing
your mission you will occupy the town of Hedeby and
await further orders.

By command of the Torunnan war staff, for His Highness
King Lofantyr.

That was all. No mention of supporting troops, timings,
supplies, the hundred and one pieces of information which
any military enterprise needed to function smoothly. Not
even an estimate of the enemy's numbers or composition.
Corfe crumpled the order into a ball and thrust it inside
his breastplate. His look wiped the sniggers off the clerks'
faces. No doubt they had heard about his strange soldiers
and their stranger armour.

"I acknowledge receipt of my orders," he said, his voice
as cold as a winter peak. "Please inform the staff that my
command will march at daybreak."

He turned to go, and one of the clerks let him get as far
as the door before saying: "Sir – Colonel? Another message
for you here. Not part of your orders, you understand. It
was brought this afternoon by a lady-in-waiting."

He collected this second message without a word and
left with it bunched in his fist. As he closed the door he
heard the buzz of the clerks' talk and laughter, and his face
gnarled into a grimace of fury.

The note was from the Queen Dowager requesting his
presence in her chambers this evening at the eighth hour.
So he must dance attendance upon a scheming woman
whilst he was preparing to take an untried and ill-equipped
command into the field. His first independent command.
Dear God!

Better if I had died at Aekir, he thought. *With honour*
and in comradeship with my countrymen. My Heria would
have met me in the Saint's company and we would have
shared eternity together.

Oh, dear God.

On an impulse, he veered away from the path back to the
barracks where his men were stationed. He felt worn and

tired, as if every step was a fight against something. He was too weary of the struggle to continue.

He wandered through the city for a while with no clear aim in mind, but something in him must have known whither he was bound for he found himself at the Abbey of the Orders as it was called, though once it had been the headquarters of the Inceptine Order alone. But that was before Macrobius had come into the city, and the black-clad Ravens had taken wing for Charibon rather than kiss the ring of a man they saw as an imposter, a heresiarch. This was now the palace of the High Pontiff, or one of them.

Corfe was admitted by a novice Antillian with white hood and dun habit. When asked his business he replied that he was here to see the Pontiff. The Antillian scurried away.

An older monk of the same order popped out of a nearby doorway soon after. He was a tall, lean man with a sharp little beard and dirty bare feet slapping under his habit.

"I am told you wish to see the Pontiff," he said, politely enough. "Might I ask your business with him, soldier?"

Of course. Corfe could not expect to see the head of the Church on demand. Much water had flowed under many bridges since he and Macrobius had shared a turnip on the nightmarish retreat from Aekir. Macrobius had become one of the figureheads of the world since then.

"My name is Corfe," he said. "If you tell His Holiness that Corfe is here, he will see me, I am sure."

The monk looked both taken aback and amused. "I will see what I can do," he said. "Wait here." And off he went.

Corfe was left just within the gate of the abbey, kicking his heels like a beggar awaiting charity. A dull anger grew in him, a tired resentment that was becoming a familiar feeling.

The monk came back accompanied by an Inceptine, a plump, well-robed figure who must have stayed to take his chances with this new Pontiff when his fellows flew the coop. He had a mouth like a moist rose and his fleshy nose overhung it. His eyes were deep-set and dark-ringed. The face of a debauchee, Corfe thought sourly.

"His Holiness is too busy at the moment to see anyone," the Inceptine said. "I am Monsignor Alembord, head of the Pontifical household. If you have any petitions you wish to place before the Holy Father then you can place them through me. Now, what is your business?"

Corfe remembered a blind old man whose empty eye-sockets had been full of mud. A man whose life he had saved at risk to his own. He remembered sheltering under a wrecked cart and watching the rain pouring down on the displaced tens of thousands who walked the Western Road.

"Tell His Holiness that I hope he remembers the turnip."

The two clerics gaped at him, then closed their mouths and glared.

"Leave this place at once," Alembord said, his jowls quivering. "No one makes mockery of the head of the Holy Church. Leave or I shall call some Knights to eject you."

"Knights – so you are getting those together again, are you? The wheel comes round once more. Tell Macrobius that Corfe will not forget, and that he should never forget either."

The renegade Inceptine clapped his hands and shouted for the Knights, but Corfe had already turned on his heel and was walking through the gate, some small, odd sense of mourning twisting in him. Ridiculous though it was, it felt like the loss of a friend.

THE REST OF his day was spent in the fog and mire of administrative matters, problems which he could get his teeth into and worry until they stopped kicking. It helped. It filled in the time, and kept his mind from thinking of other things.

Corfe managed alternately to bully and wheedle the Commissariat into issuing his men a week's rations for the march south. He divided his men into five under-strength tercios, each under a man recommended by Marsch as a leader, or *rimarc* as it was named in their own language. Marsch he made into an ensign of sorts, to Ebro's glowering outrage, and Andruw as adjutant was entrusted with the rostering and organisation of the command.

Twelve men had to be rejected as unfit; the galleys had broken them too completely for them ever to undertake active service again. These men Corfe sent on their way, giving them their rations and telling them to go home, back to the mountains. They were reluctant to leave because, Marsch said, they had sworn the oath along with the rest and would be bound by it until death. So Corfe asked them to act as recruiting agents once they regained their native valleys, and to send word of how many other tribesmen would be willing to take service under his banner when the spring came. He knew now that Lofantyr would never give him regular Torunnan troops. His command would have to be self-supporting.

As for the banner they would fight under, it took some thought. The tribesmen were pagan, and would baulk at fighting under the holy images which dominated the banners of the Ramusian armies, even if such banners were allowed to them. Corfe finally solved the problem in his own way, and had a seamstress in the garrison run up a suitable gonfalon. It was hastily done, and somewhat crude in conception as a result, but it stood out well atop its twelve-foot staff. Bright scarlet-dyed linen, the colour of sunset, and in sable at its heart the horned outline of the cathedral of Carcasson in Aekir. It was as Corfe had last seen it, a stark shadow against a burning sky, and the tribesmen were happy with it because to them it seemed the representation of Kerunnos, their horned god whom they worshipped above all others. Torunnan soldiers who saw the banner as it twisted lazily in the breeze saw only the outline of the cathedral, however, not its other, heretical, interpretation, and in time Corfe's men would be given a name because of that banner. They would be called the "Cathedrallers."

Now this last day in Torunn was wheeling to a close. The sun had disappeared behind the white summits of the Cimbrics in the west and Andruw was seeing to the last details of the command's organization. Corfe set off for the Royal palace and his audience with the Queen Dowager, and so preoccupied was he with the events of the day and the planning for tomorrow that he did not take off the scarlet Merduk armour, but wore it through the corridors of the Royal apartments to the bafflement and dismay of footmen and courtiers.

"LEAVE US," THE Queen Dowager Odelia said sharply when Corfe was shown into her apartments by a gaping doorman.

They were not in the circular chamber this time, but in a broad hall-like room with a huge fireplace occupying one wall, logs the thickness of Corfe's thighs burning within it and iron firedogs silhouetted against the flames. The fire was the only light in the room. Corfe sensed rafters overhead, lost in the shadows. The walls were heavily curtained, as was the other end of the room. Rugs on the floor, soft under his boots after the stone of the palace corridors. The sweetness of a gleaming censer hanging by long chains from the ceiling. Crystal sparkling with firelight on a low table, comfortable divans drawn up to the fire. The place was how Corfe imagined a sultan's chambers might be, upholstered and draped and hidden, hardly any bare stonework visible. He took off his brutal helm and bowed to the golden-haired woman whose skin seemed to glow in the hearthlight.

"You look like a bogey-man destined for the terrifying of children, Corfe," Odelia said in that low tone of hers. A voice as dark as heather-honey, it could also cut like a switch.

"Take off the armour, for pity's sake. You need not fear assault here. Where in the world did you get it from anyway?"

"We must make do with what we can get, lady," Corfe said, frowning as his fingers sought the releasing straps and buckles. He was not yet familiar with the working of this harness, and he found himself twisting and turning in an effort to take it off.

The Queen Dowager began to laugh. "We had a contortionist come to amuse the court with his antics last spring. I swear, Colonel, you put him to shame. Here, let me help."

She rose to her feet with a whisper of skirts, and Corfe could have sworn he saw something black scuttle from beneath them into the shadows beyond the firelight. He paused in his struggles, but then Odelia was before him and her nimble fingers were searching his armour for the straps which would loosen it. She had his back- and breastplates off in a twinkling. They thumped dully on the rug, and after them in swift succession came the vambraces, the baldric which supported his sabre, his gorget, pauldrons, thigh-guards and gauntlets. He was left standing amid a pile of glinting metal, feeling oddly exposed. He realized he had enjoyed the sensation of her hands working about him and he was almost disappointed when she stepped back.

"There! Now you can sit and sup with me like a civilized man – if a badly dressed one. What happened to the fine clothes I had the tailor run up for you?"

"These are my campaigning clothes," Corfe said awkwardly. "I take my command out at dawn."

"Ah, I see. Have a seat then, and some wine. Stop standing there like a graven image."

She was different this time, almost coquettish, whereas before she had been intense, dangerous. In the kindly light of the fire she seemed a young woman, or would were it not for the veins thrown into vivid relief on the backs of her hands.

He sipped at the wine, hardly aware of it. The fire cracked and spat like a cat. He wondered if he dare ask her what he was doing here.

"The King knows of your... patronage," he said as she sat as if waiting for him to begin. Her gaze was alarmingly direct. It seemed to draw the words out of him. "I do not think he approves of it."

"Of course he does not. He resents what he sees as my interference in his affairs, though they were my affairs before he was born. I am not a figurehead or a cipher in this kingdom, Corfe, as you should know by now. But I am not the hidden power behind the throne, either. Lofantyr grows into his kingship at last, which is good. But he still needs someone to watch over his shoulder sometimes. That is the burden I have taken upon myself."

"You may have set me up for professional ruin, lady."

"Nonsense. I knew you would equip your men somehow, just as I know that you and your command will acquit yourselves admirably in the fighting to come. And if you do not, then you are not worth worrying about and I shall cast about until I find another promising soldier to bring under my eye."

"I see," Corfe said stiffly.

"We are all expendable, Corfe, even those of us who wear crowns. The good of Torunna, of the whole of the west, must come first. This kingdom needs capable officers, not sycophants who know how to nod at Lofantyr's every suggestion."

"I'm not sure exactly what I'll be able to accomplish with my five hundred savages in the south."

"You will do as you are told. Listen: Lofantyr has begun outfitting what he sees as the true expedition to bring the rebellious southern fiefs to heel. It will be under the command of one Colonel Aras and will march in a week or ten days. Two thousand foot, five hundred horse and a train of six guns."

Corfe scowled. "A goodly force."

"Yes. You are being sent to deal with Ordinac at Hedeby – not one of the most important rebels, but the king feels he will be more than capable of tying down your motley command; he can put over a thousand men into the field. By the time you have been trounced by him, Colonel Aras and his command will have arrived on the scene to pick up the pieces, send you back to the capital in disgrace and get on with the real work of the campaign, the defeat of Duke Narfintyr at Staed."

"I see the King has everything planned in advance," Corfe said. "Is there any hope for my men and me, then?"

"I can only tell you this: you must defeat Ordinac speedily and move on to Staed. Colonel Aras does not outrank you and thus cannot give you orders. If you both arrive together at Staed, you will have to share the conduct of the campaign between you and thus there will be a greater chance of success for you and your men."

"What do you think of my chances, lady?"

She smiled. "I told you once before, Corfe: I think you are a man of luck. You will need all your luck if you are to prosper in this particular venture."

"Is this a test you've had the King set for me?"

She leaned closer. The firelight made a garden of shadows out of her features, started up green fires in her eyes. Corfe could feel her breath on his skin.

"It is a test, yes. I promise you, Corfe, if you pass it, you will move on to better things."

Abruptly she grasped his worn tunic and pulled him close. She kissed him full on the lips, softly at first and then with gathering pressure. Her eyes were open, laughing at his shock, and that suddenly angered him. He buried his fists in the gathered hair at her nape and crushed her mouth against his.

They were on the thickly carpeted floor, and he had ripped open the bosom of her dress while her laughter rang in his ears. Buttons flew through the air like startled crickets. The heavy brocade resisted even his hardened fists and she leapt up and down in his grasp as he sought to tear it off her.

Suddenly, the maniac absurdity of his position struck him, and he desisted. They crouched on the carpet facing each other. Odelia's breasts were bared, the round breasts of a woman who has given suck. Her dress had ripped to the navel and her hair was in banners about her shoulders, shining like spun gold. She grinned at him like a lynx. She looked incredibly young, vibrant, alive. He craved the feel of her again.

This time she came to him, sliding the gown from her body as easily as if it were a silken shawl. She was surprisingly wide-hipped, but her belly was taut and her skin when his hands met it was like satin, a thing to be savoured, a sensation he had almost forgotten in the recent burning turmoil of his life.

He explored the hardness of her bones, the softness of the flesh that clothed her, and when they finally coupled it was with great gentleness. Afterwards he lay with his head on her breast and wept, remembering, remembering.

She stroked his hair and said nothing, and her silence was a comfort to him, an island of quiet in the raging waters of the world.

SHE SAID NOT a word to him when he rose and dressed, pulling his tunic on and buckling the strange armour. Dawnsong had begun, though it was not yet light. His men would be waiting for him.

Naked, she stood and kissed him, pressed against the hard iron of his armour as he slipped the sword baldric over his head. She seemed old again, though, her forehead lined, fans of tiny wrinkles spreading from the corners of her eyes and the soft flesh hanging from the bones of her forearms. He wondered what magic had been in the night to make her appear so young, and she seemed to catch the thought for she smiled that feral grin of hers.

"Everyone needs a smidgen of comfort, the feel of another against them every so often, Corfe. Even Queens. Even old Queens."

"You're not so old," he said, and he meant it.

She patted his cheek as an aunt might a favoured nephew. "Go. Go off to war and start earning a name for yourself."

He left her chambers feeling oddly rested, whole. As if she had plugged for a while the bleeding wounds he bore. When he strode his way down to the parade grounds he found his five hundred waiting for him beneath their sombre banner, silent in the pre-dawn light, standing like ranks of iron statues with only the plumes of their breathing giving them life in the cold air.

"Move out," he said to Andruw, and the long files started out for the battlegrounds of the south.

TWENTY-ONE

THE SQUADRON WAS a brave sight as it hove into view around the headland. War carracks with their banks of guns, *nefs* bristling with soldiers and marines, darting caravels with their wing-like lateen sails; and all flying the scarlet of the Hebrian flag at their mainmasts and the deeper burgundy of Admiral Rovero's pennant at the mizzens. As they caught sight of the party on the beach they started firing a salute. Twenty-six guns for the recognition of their king, every ship in the squadron surrounded with powder-smoke as the thunder of the broadsides boomed out. Abeleyn's throat tightened at the sight and sound. He was a king again, not a travelling vagabond or a hunted refugee. He still had subjects, and his word could still bring forth the bellowed anger of guns.

He and Rovero went below as soon as the longboats brought the King's party out to the ships. The squadron put about immediately, the ponderous carracks turning like stately floating castles in sequence, the smaller vessels clustering about them like anxious offspring.

Rovero went down on one knee as soon as he and Abeleyn were alone in the flagship's main cabin. Abeleyn raised him up.

"Don't worry about that, Rovero. If there's one thing I've learned in the past weeks, it's not to stand on ceremony. How long before we strike Abrusio?"

"Two days, sire, if this south-easter keeps up."

"I see. And what of the city when you left? How bad is it?"

"Sire, wouldn't you like to change and bathe? And I have a collation prepared –"

"No. Tell me of my kingdom, Rovero. What's been happening?"

The admiral looked grim, and hissed the words out of

his lopsided mouth as though they were a curse uttered to someone behind him.

"I had a visit from Golophin's bird yesterday. The thing is almost destroyed. We have it in the hold as it cannot fly any more. It bore news of Abrusio, and this." The admiral handed Abeleyn a scroll with Astarac's Royal seal upon it. "It was meant for you, of course, sire, but the bird could go no farther."

Abeleyn held the scroll as gingerly as if it might burst into flame any second. "And Abrusio?"

"The Arsenal is burning. The powder magazines have been flooded, so there is no worry on that score. And Freiss is dead, his men taken, burned or fled into the Carreridan lines."

"That is something, I suppose. Go on, Rovero."

"We are holding our own against the traitors and the Knights Militant, but with the fire and the press of the population we cannot bring our full strength to bear. Fully two thirds of our men are fighting fire not traitors, or else they are conducting the evacuation of the Lower City. We may be able to save part of the western arm of Abrusio – engineers have been blasting a firebreak clean across the city – but thousands of buildings are already in ash, including the fleet dry docks, the Arsenal, the naval storage yards and many of the emergency silos that were meant to feed the population in the event of a siege. Abrusio has become two cities, sire: the Lower, which is well-nigh destroyed and is, for what it's worth, in our hands, and the Upper, which is untouched and in the hands of the traitors."

Abeleyn thought of the teeming life of his capital in summer. The crowded, noisy, stinking vitality of the streets, the buildings and narrow alleys, the nooks and corners, the taverns and shops and market places of the Lower City. He had roved Abrusio's darker thoroughfares as a young man – or a younger one – out in search of adventure disguised as just another blade with money in his pocket. All gone now. All destroyed. It felt as though part of his life had been wiped away, only the memories retaining the picture of what once was.

"We'll discuss our plans later, Admiral," he said, his eyes unseeing, burning in their sockets as though they felt the heat of the inferno that was destroying his city. "Leave me for a while, if you please."

Rovero bowed and left.

He is older, the admiral thought as he closed the cabin door behind him. *He has aged ten years in as many weeks. The boy in him is gone. There is something in his look which recalls the father. I would not cross him now for all the world.*

He stomped out into the waist of the ship, his mouth a skewed scar in his face. That damned woman, the King's mistress, was on deck arguing about her quarters. She wanted more room, a window, fresher air. She looked green about the chops already, the meddlesome bitch. Well, older woman or no, she'd no longer be able to twist this king about her finger as it was rumoured she had in the past. Wasn't she getting rather stout, though?

THE KING OF Hebrion stepped out of the cabin on to the stern gallery of the flag carrack, which hung like a long balcony above the foaming turmoil of the ship's wake. He could see the other vessels of the squadron in line before him scarcely two cables away, plain sail set, their bows plunging up and down and spraying surf to either side of their beakheads. It was a heart-wrenching sight, power and beauty allied into a terrible puissance. Engines of war as awesome and glorious as man's hand had the capacity to make them.

Man's hand, not God's.

He broke open King Mark's letter and stood on the pitching gallery reading it.

My Dear Cousin, it began. *This is written in haste and without ceremony – the dispatch galley waits in the harbour with her anchor aweigh. Her destination is Abrusio, for I know not where else you can be reached. Despite the terrible stories which are coming out of Hebrion, I believe that you will arrive back in your capital in the end and eject the traitors and Ravens who are intent on ruining the west.*

But I must tell you my news. My party was ambushed in the foothills of the southern Malvennors by a sizable force of unknown origin, and we barely scraped through with our lives. An assassination attempt, of course, an effort to rid the world of yet another heretic. It can only have been arranged by Cadamost of Perigraine and the Inceptine Prelate of that kingdom. I fear other attempts have been made, on both you and Lofantyr, but obviously if you are scanning this missive you survived.

The old laws which governed conduct and guided men's actions are destroyed. I have had an uprising of the nobles in Astarac to deal with, and it is only in the last few days that I have been able to call Cartigella my own capital again. But the traitors were ill-led and ill-equipped – and they had no Knights Militant to back them up. The army, which remained loyal in the most part, thank God, is now scouring Astarac for the remaining pockets of the rebels. But there are rumours that Perigraine is mobilizing and I must guard my eastern frontiers, else you would have Astaran reinforcements to help you in the sorry task of regaining your own kingdom.

My sister will wed you, and if she is as plain as a frog she is nonetheless a woman of sense and intelligence. More than ever we heretic kings must stand together, Abeleyn. Hebrion and Astarac shall be allied, for if we remain separate then we will fall alone. I will not waste time on pomp and ceremony. As soon as I hear from you that you are safe in Abrusio she shall be sent to your side, the living proof of our bond.

(Do you remember her, Abeleyn? Isolla. You pulled her plaits as a boy and mocked her crooked nose.)

From Torunna I have tidings much the same as here. Macrobius has been properly received as the true Pontiff, but according to my sources he is not seen much abroad and may be ailing, may God forfend. He is all that stands between us and utter anarchy. Lofantyr is directing the Merduk war personally, and yet Ormann Dyke seems to be neglected and the refugees surround Torunn by the hundred thousand. He is not a general, our cousin of Torunna. Sometimes I am not even sure if he is a soldier.

I must scrawl ever more hastily, as the tide will soon be on the turn. A Fimbrian army, it is said, is on the march. Its destination is reported to be the dyke, which may explain Lofantyr's neglect if it does not excuse it. He has hired the

*old empire-builders to fight his wars for him, and thinks
he can leave it at that. But the hound brought in over the
threshold can prove to be a wolf if it is not watched and
given discipline. I do not trust Fimbrian open-handedness.*

*I end here. A pitiful missive, without grace or form to
recommend it. My old rhetorics tutor will be grumbling in
his grave. Maybe one day philosophers will once more have
the time to dance angels on the heads of pins, but for now
the world has too much need of soldiers and the quill must
yield to the sword.*

Fare thee well, cousin.
Mark

Abeleyn smiled as he finished reading. Mark had never
been much of a one for polish. It was good to know that
Hebrion did not stand alone in the world, and that Astarac
seemed fairly on the road back to her proper order. The news
of the Fimbrians was interesting, though. Did Lofantyr truly
expect them to fight and die for Torunna in the east without
wanting something more than coinage in exchange?

Isolla. They had all played together as children, at
conferences and conclaves as their fathers changed the
shape of the world. She was thin and russet-haired, with a
freckled face and a bend to her nose that had been evident
even then, when they were not yet into their teens. She was
only a year or two younger than himself – quite old to be
married for the first time. He remembered her as a quiet,
long-suffering child who liked to be left alone.

Such memories were beside the point. The important
thing was that the Hebro-Astaran alliance would be firmly
cemented by this marriage, and personal feelings did not
come into it.

(He thought of Jemilla and her swelling belly, and felt a
thrill of uneasy apprehension for a reason he could not fully
understand.)

The feeling passed. He went inside and shouted for
attendants to come and help him disrobe and wash.
He poured himself a flagon of wine from the gimballed
decanters on the cabin table, gulped it down, bit into a
chunk of herb bread, gulped more wine.

The cabin door opened and his personal steward and valet were standing there, still in their castaway clothes, one chewing.

"Sire?"

He felt ashamed. He had forgotten that these men had been through whatever he had, and were as hungry and thirsty and tired and filthy as he was himself.

"It's all right. You are dismissed. Clean yourselves up and get yourselves as much food and wine as your bellies will hold. And kindly ask Admiral Rovero to step back in here when he has a moment."

"Yes, sire. The sailors have heated water for you in one of their coppers in the galley. Shall we have a bath prepared?"

A bath! Sweet heavens above. But he shook his head. "Let the lady Jemilla use the water. I will do well enough."

The men bowed and left. Abeleyn could smell himself above the usual shipboard smells of pitch and wood and old water, but it did not seem to matter. Jemilla was carrying his child, and she would appreciate a bath above all things at the moment. Let her have one – it would keep her away from him for a while.

He realized suddenly that he did not much like his mistress. As a lover she was superb, and she was as witty and intelligent as a man could want. But he trusted her no more than he would trust an adder which slithered across his boot in the woods. The knowledge surprised him somewhat. He was aware that something in him had changed, but he was not yet sure what it was.

A knock on the door. Admiral Rovero, his eyebrows high on his sea-dog face. "You wanted to see me, sire?"

"Yes, Admiral. Let us go through this plan you have concocted, you and Mercado, for the retaking of Abrusio. Now is as good a time as any."

There was to be no rest, no chance to sit and stare out at the foaming wake and the mighty ships which coursed along astern, tall pyramids of canvas and wood and gleaming guns. No time to turn away from the care and the responsibilities. And Abeleyn did not mind.

Perhaps that is what has changed, he thought. *I am growing into my crown at last.*

TWENTY-TWO

ALBREC'S HEAD WAS full of blood, swollen and throbbing like a bone-pent heart. His face was rubbing against some form of material, cloth or the like, and his hands, also, felt swollen and full.

He was upside-down, he realized, dangling with his midriff being crushed by his own weight.

"Put me down," he gasped, feeling as though he might throw up if he did not straighten.

Avila set him down carefully. The young Inceptine had been carrying him slung over one broad shoulder. The pair of them were breathing heavily. Albrec's world dizzied and spun for a moment as the fluids of his body righted themselves. The lamp Avila had been carrying in his free hand guttered on the floor, almost out of oil.

"What are you doing?" Albrec managed at last. "Where are we?"

"In the catacombs. I couldn't bring you round, Albrec. You were dead to the world. So I piled up stone in front of the hole and tried to find a way out for us."

"Commodius!"

"Dead, and may his warped spirit howl the eons away in the pits of Hell."

"His body, Avila. We can't just leave it down here."

"Why not? He was a creature of the lightless dark, a shapeshifter, and he tried to kill us both to protect his precious version of the truth. Let his corpse rot here unburied."

Albrec held his aching head in his hands. "Where are we?"

"I was following the north wall – the damp one, as you said – trying to find the stairs, but I must have missed them somehow."

"An easy thing to do. I will find them, don't worry. How long has it been since...?"

"Maybe half an hour, not long."

"Great God, Avila, what are we going to do?"

"Do? I – I don't know, Albrec. I hadn't been thinking beyond getting out of this dungeon."

"We've killed the Senior Librarian."

"We've slain a werewolf."

"But he changed back into Commodius the librarian. It's the last thing I remember. Who will believe us? What signs are there on his body to tell anyone what he was in life?"

"What are you saying, Albrec? That we are in trouble for saving our own lives, for putting an end to that foul beast?"

"I don't know, I don't know what to think. How could it happen, Avila? How could a priest be a thing like that, all these years, all the years I have worked with him? It was he who haunted the library; I see that now. It was his unclean presence which gave it its atmosphere. Oh, lord God, what has been going on here?"

The pair were silent, their eyes fixed on the tiny lamp flame which did not have too many minutes of life left to it. But it did not seem important that they might soon be left here in impenetrable darkness. The place seemed different somehow. They had seen the true face of evil, and nothing else could frighten them.

"They know," Albrec went on in a rasping whisper. "Did you hear him? They know the truth of things, the real story of the Saint and the Prophet, and they have been suppressing it. The Church has been sitting on the truth for centuries, Avila, keeping it from the world to safeguard its own authority. Where is piety, where humility? They have behaved like princes determined to hold on to their power no matter what the cost."

Avila fingered his black Inceptine robe thoughtfully.

"You have claw marks down the sides of your face," he told Albrec, as though he had only just seen them.

"There's blood on yours, too."

"We can't hide our hurts, Albrec. Think, man! What are we to do? Columbar is dead at Commodius's hand and Commodius is dead at ours. How will it look? We cannot tell them we were trying to discover and preserve the truth of things. They'll put us out of the way as quickly as Commodius intended to."

"There are good men yet in the Church – there must be."

"But we don't know who they are. Who will listen to us or believe us? Sweet blood of the Blessed Saint, Albrec, we are finished."

The lamp guttered, flared, and then went out. The dark swooped in on them and they were blind.

Avila's voice came thick with grief through the lightlessness. "We must flee Charibon."

"No! Where would we go? How would we travel in the depth of winter, in the snows? We would not last a day."

"We'll not last much longer than that here once this gets out. When Commodius is missed they'll search the library. They'll find him in the end. And who is the only other person who has the keys to the library? You, Albrec."

The little monk touched the torn skin of his face and neck, the lump on his forehead where the werewolf had knocked him. Avila was right. They would question him first, for he was Commodius's closest colleague, and when they saw his wounds the inquisition would begin.

"So what are we to do, Avila?" he asked, near to tears. He knew, but he had to let someone else say it.

"We'll have a day of grace. We'll stay out of sight and gather together what we can to help us on our journey."

"Journey to where? Where in the world are we to go? The Church rules Normannia, her Knights and clerics are in every city and town of the west. Where shall we run to?"

"We are heretics once this gets out," Avila said. "They will excommunicate us when they find the body in that unholy chapel and note our disappearance. But there are other heretics in the world, Albrec, and there is a heresiarch to lead them. The man some say is Macrobius has been set up as an anti-Pontiff in Torunn. Charibon's writ has no authority in that kingdom, and anyone hostile to the Himerian Church will be welcome there. The Macrobian kings will listen to us. We would be a powerful weapon in their armoury. And besides, Charibon seems now to me like a sink of corruption. If Commodius was a werewolf, could there not be others like him within the ranks of my order?"

"It does not bear thinking about."

"It must be thought about, Albrec, if we are to puzzle out a way to save our lives."

They stood awhile, not speaking, listening to the drip of water and the enfolding silence of the gutrock, the bowels of the mountains. Finally Avila moved. Albrec heard him groan from the pain of his hurts.

"My robe is ripped to threads, and I think I have some ribs broken. It is like a knife thrust into my side every time I draw breath. We must get back to our beds before Matins."

"You sleep in a dormitory, Avila. Won't your colleagues notice?"

"There is a bolster under my blankets doing service as a sleeping monk, and I stole out as quiet as a mouse. But I'll not be so quiet returning. Damnation!"

"You can't go back. You must come to my cell. We'll get some things together and hole up somewhere tomorrow – or today, as I suppose it must be – and leave tomorrow night."

Avila was gasping in short, agonizing pants. "I fear I will not be a swift traveller, my little Antillian comrade. Albrec, must we leave? Is there no way we can brazen it out?"

The decision had been made, but it terrified both of them. It would be so much easier to go on as if nothing had happened, to step back into the ancient routine of the monastery-city. Albrec might have done it, the inertia of fear tying him to the only life he had known. But Avila had painted things too clearly. The Antillian knew that their lives had changed without hope of recovery. They had stepped beyond the Church and were on the outside, looking in.

"Come," Albrec said, trying not to move his neck. "We've a lot to do before dawn. This thing has been thrust on us as Honorius's visions were thrust upon him, that poor, mad seeker after the truth, God has given us a burden as heavy as his to bear. We cannot shirk it."

He took Avila's arm and began leading him along the wall of the catacombs, touching its rough surface every now and then with his shaking palm.

"He died in the mountains, you know, died alone as a discredited hermit whom no one would listen to, a holy madman. I wonder now if it is not the Church which has been mad. Mad with pride, with the lust for power. Who is to say that it has not suppressed every holy truth-seeker who has arisen over the centuries? How many men have found out about Ramusio's true fate, and have paid for that knowledge with their lives? That is the pity of it. Take a lie and make it into belief, and it rots the rest of the faith like a bad apple in a barrel. No one knows what to believe any more. The Church totters on its foundations, no matter how much of its structure may be sound, and those good men who are in its service are tainted with its lies."

Avila groaned out a wrecked laugh. "You never change, Albrec. Still philosophizing, even at a time like this."

"Our fate has become as important as the downfall of nations," Albrec retorted humourlessly. "We carry our knowledge like a weapon of the Apocalypse, Avila. We are more potent than any army."

"I wish I felt so," Avila grated, "but I feel more like a wounded rat."

They found the stairs and began to ascend them as gingerly as old men, hissing and grimacing at every step. It seemed an age before they reached the library proper, and for the last time in his life Albrec walked among the tiers of books and scrolls and breathed in the dry parchment smell. The title page of the old document crackled in the breast of his robe like a grizzling babe.

The air of the passing night was bitterly cold as they left the library, locking it behind them, and trudged through the wind-smoked snowdrifts to the cloisters. There were a few other monks abroad, preparing for Matins. Charibon was wrapped in pre-dawn peace, dark buildings and pale drifts, the warm gleam of candlelight at a few windows. It was different now. It no longer felt like home. Albrec was weeping silently as he helped Avila to his own cell. He knew that tonight whatever peace and happiness his plain life had known had been lost. Ahead lay nothing but struggle and danger and disputation, and a death which would occur beyond the ministrations of the Church. Death on a pyre perhaps, or in the snows, or in a strange land beyond all that was familiar.

He prayed to Ramusio, to Honorius the mad saint, to God Himself, but no light appeared before him, no voice spoke in his mind. His supplications withered into empty stillness, and try as he might he could not stop his faith from following them into that pit of loss. All he was left with was his knowledge of the truth, and there grew in him a resolve to see that truth spread and grow like a painful disease. He would infect the world with it ere he was done, and if the faith tottered under that affliction, then so be it.

CHARIBON CAME TO life before the sun broke the black sky into slate-grey cloud. Matins was sung, and the monks went to their breakfasts; Lauds, and then Terce followed. The accumulated snows of the night were swept away and the city stirred, as did the fisher-villages down on the frozen shore of the Sea of Tor.

After Terce a group of scholars went to one of the Justiciars and complained that the library was not yet open. The matter was investigated, and it was found that the doors were locked and there were no lights within. The Senior Librarian could not be found, nor could his assistant. The matter was pursued further, and despite the frigid air a crowd of monks gathered around the main doors of the Library of Saint Garaso when at Sext they were broken open by a deacon of the Knights Militant and his men using a wooden beam as a battering ram whilst Betanza, the Vicar-General himself, looked on. The library was searched by parties of senior monks. By that time the body of Columbar had been discovered, and despite searches of the dormitories and cloisters the two librarians were still nowhere to be found. Charibon began to buzz with speculation.

Commodius's body was discovered just before Vespers, after the upper levels of the library had been turned upside down. Monks searching the lower levels had come upon a discarded oil lamp, and a pile of broken masonry built up against a wall of the catacombs. It fell apart as soon as they began to investigate it, and a monsignor entered the little temple along with two armed Knights to discover the corpse of the Senior Librarian stark and staring, the silver pentagram dagger buried in its spine.

The circumstances of the discovery were not bruited abroad, but the story made its way about the monastery-city that the Senior Librarian had been foully murdered in horrible surroundings somewhere deep in the foundations of his own library, and his assistant, along with a young Inceptine who was known to be his special friend, was missing.

Patrols of the Knights Militant and squads of the Almarkan garrison soldiers prowled the streets of Charibon, and the monks at Vespers whispered up and down the long pews when they were not singing to God's glory. There was a murderer, or murderers, loose in Charibon. Heretics, perhaps, come spreading fear in the city at the behest of the heresiarch Macrobius who sat at the Devil's right hand in Torunn. The senior Justiciars were forming an investigative body to get to the bottom of the affair, and the Pontiff himself was overseeing them.

But late that evening, in the white fury of yet another snowstorm, two events went unremarked by the patrols which were watching the perimeters of Charibon. One was the arrival of a small party of men on foot, struggling through the drifts with their black uniforms frosted white. The other was the departure of two bent and labouring monks bowed under heavy sacks, feeling their way through the blizzard with stout pilgrim's staves and gasping in their pain and grief as they trudged along the frozen shores of the Sea of Tor, bypassing the bonfires of the sentry-posts by hiking far out on the frozen surface of the sea itself to where the pancake ice bunched and rippled under the wind like the unquiet contents of a white cauldron. Albrec and Avila struggled on with the ice gathering on their swollen faces and the blood in their hands and feet slowly solidifying in the intense depth of the raging cold. The snowstorm cloaked them entirely, so that they were not challenged once in their fumbling progress. But it also seemed to be fairly on the way to killing them before their flight had even got under way.

THE PARTY OF black-clad men demanded admittance to the suites of the High Pontiff Himerius, and the startled guards and clerical attendants were spun into a frenzy by their unexpected appearance. Finally they were billeted in a warm, if austere, anteroom whilst the Pontiff was notified of their arrival. It was the first time in four centuries that Fimbrian soldiers had come to Charibon.

The Pontiff was being robed by two ageing monks in his private apartments when the Vicar-General of the Inceptine Order entered. The monks were dismissed and the two Churchmen stood looking at one another, Himerius still fastening his purple robe about his thickening middle.

"Well?" he asked.

Betanza took a seat and could not stifle a yawn: it was very late, and he had had a trying day.

"No luck. The two monks remain missing. They are either dead, if they are innocent, or fled if they are not."

Himerius grunted, regarding his own reflection in the full-length mirror which graced the sombre opulence of his dressing chamber.

"They are guilty, Betanza: I feel it. Commodius was trying to stop them from committing heresy, and he died for it." A spasm of indefinable emotion crossed the Pontiff's aquiline features and then was gone. "May God have mercy on him, he was a loyal servant of the Church."

"What makes you so sure that was the way of it, Holiness?" Betanza asked, obviously curious. His big soldier's face was ruddy with the day he had spent, and scarlet lines intagliated the whites of his eyes.

"I know," Himerius snapped. "You will send out search parties of the Knights to find these two runaways as soon as the weather permits. I want them brought back to Charibon to undergo inquisition."

Betanza shrugged. "As you wish, Holiness. What of these Fimbrians closeted below? Will you see them tonight?"

"Yes. We must know if their arrival here at this time is a coincidence or part of a larger plan. I need not tell you, Betanza, that the events of today must not leave the city. No tales of murder in Charibon must trickle out to the kingdoms. This place must be unbesmirched, pure, unsullied by scandal or rumour."

"Of course, Holiness," Betanza said, at the same time wondering how he was supposed to muzzle a city of many thousands. Monks were worse than women for gossip. Still, the weather would help.

"A courier arrived here this afternoon, while you were occupied with other matters," Himerius said lightly, and there was a different air about him suddenly, a glittering triumph that he could not keep out of his eyes. The Pontiff turned and faced the Vicar-General squarely, his hands clasped on his breast. It looked as though a wild grin was fighting to break out over his face. For an instant, Betanza thought, he looked slightly mad.

"Good news, my friend," Himerius said, mastering himself. He was once more the sober cleric, weighed down with dignity and *gravitas*. "The courier came from Alstadt. It would seem that our devoted son of the Church, King Haukir of Almark, has died at last, may the Saints receive his flitting soul into their bosoms. This pious king, this paragon of dutiful faith, has left his kingdom to the Church."

Betanza gaped. "You're sure?"

"The courier carried a missive from Prelate Marat of Almark. He has been named regent of the kingdom until such time as I see fit to organize its governance. Almark is ours, Betanza."

"What of the nobles? Have they aught to say about it?"

"They will acquiesce. They must. Almark has a strong contingent of the Knights Militant in its capital, and the Royal armies are for the most part billeted further east, along the line of the Saeroth river. Almark is ours, truly."

"They say that events of moment are like nodes of history," Betanza mused. "Where one occurs, others are likely to happen at the same time, sometimes in the same place. You may face these Fimbrians with new confidence, Holiness. The timing could not have been more opportune."

"Precisely. It is why I will receive them now, though it is so late. I want the news to be a shock to them."

"What do you think they want?"

"What does anyone these days? The Church owns Almark, it controls Hebrion. It has become an empire. Accommodation must be sought with it. I have no doubt that these Fimbrians are come to test the waters of diplomatic exchange. The old imperial power is bending in the new wind. Come: we will go down and meet them together."

The Pontifical reception hall was full of shadows. Torches burned in cressets along the walls, and glowing braziers had been brought in to stand around the dais whereon rested the Pontiff's throne. Knights Militant stood like graven monuments every ten paces along the walls, blinking themselves awake and stiffening the moment the Pontiff entered and sat himself down. Betanza remained standing at his right hand, and a pair of scribes huddled in their dark robes like puddles of ebony ink at the foot of the dais, quills erect. To one side Rogien, the old Inceptine who was also the manager of the Pontifical court, stood ready, his bare scalp gleaming in the torchlight.

The Fimbrians had to walk the length of the flame-and-shadowed hall, their boots clumping on the basalt floor. Four of them, all in black, except for the scarlet sash that one wore about his waist.

Hard-faced men, wind-burn rouging their cheeks and foreheads, their hair cropped as short as the mane of a hogged horse. They bore no weapons, but the Knights who lined the walls on either side of them watched them intently and warily with fists clenched on sword-hilts.

"Barbius of Neyr, marshal and commander in the Fimbrian army," Rogien announced in a voice of brass.

Barbius inclined his head to Himerius. Fimbrians did not bend the knee to anyone save their emperor. Himerius knew this, yet the slight bow had so much of contempt in it that he shifted in his throne, his liver-spotted hands tightening on the armrests.

"Barbius of the electorate of Neyr, you are welcome in Charibon," the Pontiff said calmly. "The urgency of your errand is written in your face and those of your companions, and so we have deigned to grant you an audience despite the lateness of the hour. Quarters appropriate for your rank have been set aside for you and your comrades, and as soon as the audience is over there will be food and drink served to help sustain the flagging spirit."

Barbius made the slight bow again in acknowledgement of this graciousness. His voice when he spoke was the grate of sliding rock to Himerius's deep music.

"I thank His Holiness for his hospitality, but am grieved to say that I shall not be able to take advantage of it. I and my men are in haste: the main body of our force is encamped some five leagues from here and we hope to rejoin them ere the morning."

"Main body?" Himerius repeated.

"Yes, Holiness. I am here to reassure you that the troops under my command bear the monastery-city nothing but goodwill, and you need not fear – nor need Almark fear – any rapine on their behalf. We are merely passing through, obeying the orders of the Electors."

"I don't understand. Are you not an embassy come from the electorates?" Himerius asked.

"No, Holiness. I am merely the commander of an eastward-bound Fimbrian army come to pay my respects."

The statement fell in the room like a thunderclap.

"A *Fimbrian army* is encamped five leagues from Charibon?" Betanza said, incredulous.

"Yes, Excellency."

"Whither are you bound?" Himerius inquired, and the music was gone from his voice. He sounded as hoarse as an old crow.

"We are bound for the relief of Ormann Dyke."

"At whose behest?"

"I am ordered by my superiors, the Electors of Fimbria."

"But who has asked for your help? Lofantyr the heretic? It must be."

Barbius shrugged, his red-gold moustache concealing any expression his mouth might have conveyed. His eyes were as flat and hard as sea ice. "I am only following orders, Holiness. It is not for me to question the doings of high policy."

"Do you realize you are imperilling your immortal soul by succouring a heretic who has repudiated the validity of the holy Church?" Himerius snapped.

"As I said, Holiness, I am merely a soldier obeying orders. If I do not obey them my life is forfeit. I called in on you here as a courtesy, to ask your blessing."

"You march to the aid of he who shields the heresiarch of the west, and you ask my blessing?" Himerius said.

"My army marches east to stem the Merduk invasion. It is performing a service for every kingdom in the west, be they Himerian or Macrobian," Barbius said. "I ask you, Holiness, to look on it in that light. The dyke will fall in the spring if my forces do not reinforce it, and the Merduks will be hammering at the gates of Charibon within a year. It may be that King Lofantyr is paying our wages, but the service we render is of value to every free man in Normannia."

Himerius was silent, thinking. It was Betanza who spoke next. "So you are mercenaries, you Fimbrians. You hire yourselves out to kings in need and fight for the gold in their coffers. What if the Merduk sultans offered you a greater wage than the western kings, Marshal? Would you then fight under the banners of the Prophet?"

For the first time, emotion crossed the face of the Fimbrian marshal. His eyes flared and he took one step forward, which made every guard in the chamber tense on the balls of his feet.

"Who built Charibon?" he asked. "Who founded Aekir and hollowed out Ormann Dyke and reared the great moles of Abrusio Harbour? My people did. For centuries the Fimbrians were the buckler behind which the people of the west sheltered from the steppe hordes, the horse-tribes, the Merduk thousands. The Fimbrians made the western world what it is. You think we would betray the heritage of our forefathers, the legacy of our empire? Never! Once again we are in the foremost rank of those defending it. All we ask" – and here the marshal's tone softened – "is that you do not see our reinforcing of the dyke as an assault on the Himerian Church. We intend no heresy, and would keep on good terms with Charibon if we could."

Himerius rose and lifted his hand. The torchlight made his face into an eagle mask, eyes glittering blackly on either side of the aquiline nose.

"You have our blessing then, Marshal Barbius of Neyr. May your arms shine with glory, and may you hurl the Merduk heathen back from the gates of the west."

"WHY DID YOU do it?" Betanza demanded. "Why did you legitimize the farming out of Fimbrian troops to heretics? It is senseless!"

He and the Pontiff were sweeping along one of Charibon's starlit cloisters, utterly deserted at this time of night. Their hands were hidden in their sleeves and they had their hoods drawn up against the biting cold, but the blizzards had ended and the night air was as clear as the bleb of an icicle, sharp as a shard of flint. Novices had swept the cloister clear of snow before retiring to bed and the two clerics were able to stride along without interruption.

"Why should I not do it? Had I refused the blessing, alienated the man, then I would have done the Church no favours and possibly a great deal of harm. We cannot argue with an army of Fimbrians. Think of that, Betanza! Fimbrians on the march again across the continent. The imperial tercios on the move. It is enough to make a man shudder with apprehension. We knew after the Conclave of Kings that something like this was in the wind – but so *soon*. Lofantyr has stolen a march on us, quite literally."

"But why bless his enterprise? It is giving tacit recognition of the Torunnan kingdom, which is no longer within the Church's fold."

"No. I merely blessed the Fimbrians: I did not wish Godspeed to heretics. If the old imperial power is once again stirring and taking an interest in the world, then it would be as well for us to keep it on our side. The Fimbrians are still a Himerian state, remember. They have never formally recognized the anti-Pontiff Macrobius, and therefore they are technically in our camp. Let us keep it that way. The Fimbrians themselves obviously want to keep the Church in their corner, else that brutish marshal would have marched past Charibon without a pause and we would be none the wiser of his passing. No – despite the bequest of Almark we are not strong enough to antagonize the Electors."

Their sandals slapped on the frigid stone of the cloisters.

"I pity them, sleeping out on a night like this," Betanza said.

Himerius snorted. "They are soldiers, little better than animals. They hardly register any feeling except the most base. Let them shiver."

They took one more turn about the cloister, and then: "I will to bed now, Holiness," Betanza said, oddly subdued. "My investigations into the death of Commodius will recommence at dawn. I wish to pray awhile."

"By all means. Good night, Betanza."

The Pontiff stood alone in the clear night, his eyes glittering under his hood. In his mind he was marshalling armies and putting the cities of the heretics to the torch. A second empire there would be on earth, and as mad Honorius had said it would rise in an age of fire and the sword.

I am tired, Himerius thought, his savage exaltation flickering out as the freezing wind searched his frame. *I am old, and weary of the struggle. But soon my task will be fulfilled, and I will be able to rest. Someone else will take my place.*

He padded off to his bed as silently as a cat.

"ALBREC. WAKE UP, Albrec!"

A blow on Albrec's cheekbone snapped his head to one side and tore the scab of ice from around his nose. He moaned as the cold air bit into the exposed flesh and fought open his eyes as someone shook him as though he were a rat being worried by a dog.

He lay half-buried in snow and a frost-white shape was pummelling him.

"All right, all right! I'm awake."

Avila collapsed in a heap beside him, the air sobbing in and out of his fractured chest. "It's stopped snowing," he wheezed. "We should try to move on."

But they both remained prone in the drift which had come close to burying them. Their clothes had stiffened on their backs to the consistency of armour, and they no longer had any feeling left in their extremities. Worse, white patches of frostbite discoloured their faces and ears.

"We're finished," Albrec moaned. "God has abandoned us."

The wind had dropped, and they lay on their backs in the snow staring up at the vast vault of the star-crowded night sky. Beautiful and pitiless, the stars were so bright that they cast faint shadows, though the moon had not yet risen.

Far off the two clerics heard the forlorn howl of a solitary wolf, come down out of the terrible winter heights of the Cimbrics seeking food.

Another answered it, and then there were more. A pack of them off in the night, calling to one another in some unfathomable fellowship.

Albrec was strangely unafraid. *I am dying*, he thought, *and it does not matter*.

"Sailors believe that in oyvips live the souls of lost mariners who drowned in a state of sin," the little monk told Avila, remembering his childhood on the Hardic Sea.

"What's an oyvip?" Avila asked, his voice a light feather of a thing balanced on his lips, as though his lungs were too racked with pain to give it depth.

"A great, blunt-nosed fish with a kindly eye and a habit of following ships. A happy thing, always at play."

"Then I envy those lost souls," Avila breathed.

"And woodsmen," Albrec went on, his own voice becoming slurred and faint. "They believe that in wolves abide the souls of evil men, and, some think, of lost children. They think that in the heart of the wolf lies all the darkness and despair of mankind, which is why shifters usually manifest as wolves."

"You read too much, Albrec," Avila whispered. "Too many things. Wolves are animals, mindless and soulless. Man is the only true beast, because he has the capacity not to be."

They lay with the cold seeping into their bones like some slow, cancerous growth, staring up at the stark beauty of the stars. There was no longer any pain for them, or any hope of flight or life, but there was peace out here in the drifts, in the wild country of the Narian Hills where the Free Tribes had once roamed and worshipped their dark gods.

"No more philosophy," Albrec murmured. The stars were winking out one by one as his sight darkened.

"Good night, Avila."

But from his friend there was no reply.

THE FIMBRIAN PATROL came across them an hour later, drawn by the shadowed figures of the wolves who were gathering around them. The soldiers kicked away the beasts and found two clerics of Charibon lying stiff and cold in the snow with their faces turned up to the stars and their hands clasped together like those of two lost children. The soldiers had to chip them free of the frozen drift with their swords. The pair had on their bodies the marks of violence and rough travel, but their faces were peaceful, as serene as the countenance of a sculpted saint.

The sergeant in charge of the patrol ordered them wrapped in cloaks and carried back to camp. The patrol followed his orders, picked up the bodies and started at the double back to where the campfires of the Fimbrian army glimmered red and yellow in the starlight, less than a mile away.

The wolves watched them go in silence.

TWENTY-THREE

THEY HAD MADE good time, marching sixty leagues in eleven days. Corfe had never seen anything quite like his motley little army of savage tatterdemalions. They were eager, talkative, fiercely good-humoured. On leaving Torunn they had changed completely, and their column often rang out with tribal songs, ribald laughter. It was as if the city had placed some kind of sombre restraint on them, but now that they were out in open country, marching with swords slapping at their thighs and lances in their hands, something in them took wing. They were undisciplined, yes, but they were more enthusiastic than any other soldiers Corfe had known. It was as if they thought they were marching south to take part in some manner of festival.

He put his views to Marsch one evening as they sat by the campfire, shivering in their threadbare blankets and watching flurries of snow lit up by the flames wheeling feather-like out of the darkness beyond. Almost a third of the men were barefoot, and many had no adequate covering to keep out the cold, but the bristling crowds about the other campfires were humming with low talk, like a summer garden alive with bees.

"Why do they seem so happy?" Corfe asked his newest ensign.

The huge tribesman wiped his nose on his blanket, shrugging. "They are free. Is that not enough to make a man happy?"

"But they are marching south to fight a battle which has nothing to do with them. Why do they seem so eager to do it?"

Marsch looked at his commander strangely. "How often do the causes for which men fight mean anything to them? For my people, the Felimbri, war is our life. It is the means by which a man advances himself in the esteem of his comrades. There is no other way."

Ensign Ebro, who was sitting close by with a fur cape clutched about his shoulders, snorted with contempt.

"That is the reasoning of a primitive," he said.

"We are all primitives, and always will be," Marsch said with unusual mildness. "If men were civilized truly, then they would not kill each other. We are animals. Something in us needs to fight in order to prove we are alive. My men have been chattels, beasts harnessed for brute labour. But now they bear the weapons of free men, and they are to fight like free men, in open contest. It matters not who they fight or where, or for what."

"The philosopher savage," Ebro laughed.

"So there is no cause needed," Corfe said.

"No. A man advances himself by making subject other men, either by killing them or so dominating them that they will not dare to challenge his word. Thus are kings made – among my people, at least."

"And what were you before the galleys claimed you, Marsch?" Corfe asked quietly.

The huge savage smiled. "I was what I still am, a prince of my people."

Ebro guffawed, but Marsch ignored him as if he did not exist.

"You could kill your Torunnan officers here and now, and leave for home. No one could stop you," Corfe said.

Marsch shook his head. "We have sworn an oath which we will not break. There is honour involved. And besides" – here he actually grinned at Corfe, showing square yellow teeth whose canines had been filed to sharp points – "we are interested to see how this colonel of ours will fare in open battle, with his Torunnan ways and his plain speaking."

Then it was Corfe's turn to laugh.

THERE WAS NO chance of the column's approach remaining a secret. Their appearance was so outlandish and unique that entire villages turned out at the side of the mud-deep roads to stare at them as they trudged past. The last few days were spent on short commons, as the Quartermaster-issued rations had run out and the men had to subsist on what they could glean from the surrounding countryside. Several cattle were quietly appropriated from awe-struck owners, but in general Corfe prevented any large-scale foraging because this was Torunna they were marching through, his own country, and also he wanted to make the greatest speed he could.

The men were marvellously fast marchers. Though their time in the galleys had blunted the fine edge of their fitness, building brute strength up in place of stamina, they were able to crack along at a fearsome pace, unhindered by an artillery train or baggage of any kind. It was all the three Torunnan officers in the column could do to keep up with their subordinates as they strode along with their helms slung at their hips and their lances resting on their powerful shoulders. Corfe was privately amazed. He had been brought up to believe that the tribes of the Cimbrics were degenerate savages, hardly worthy of attention from civilized men except when they became a nuisance with their raiding and brigandage. But now he was learning the truth of the affair, which was that they were natural-born soldiers. All they needed was a little discipline and leadership and he was sure they would acquit themselves well against any foe in the world.

Andruw was similarly impressed. "Good men," he said, as they sucked along through the rutted mud of the winter roads towards Hedeby. "I don't think I've ever seen a pack of fellows so keen for a fight. I'd give my left ball for a good battery of culverins, though."

Corfe chuckled. Humour was coming with a strange ease to him lately. Perhaps it was being free, in the field, his own man. Perhaps it was the prospect of slaughter. At any rate, he did not care to examine the reasons too closely.

"They'd not get far in this mud, your culverins. Nor would cavalry. I'm starting to think it's as well this force of ours is all infantry. We may find it more mobile than we supposed."

"They march fast enough, no doubt of that," Andruw agreed ruefully. "I'll be a short man by the time we get to Hedeby. I've walked at least an inch off each heel."

They were half a day's march from Hedeby when they sighted a small group of armoured cavalry outlined against the horizon ahead, watching them. Their banners flapped in the cold wind that winnowed the hills on either side of the road.

"Ordinac, I'll bet," Corfe said on sighting the horsemen, "come to have a look at what he's up against. Unfurl the banner, Andruw."

Andruw had their standard-bearer, a massive-thewed tribesman named Kyrn, pull loose the cathedral banner and let it snap out atop its twelve-foot staff, a point of vivid colour in the monochrome winter afternoon. The rest of the men gave out a cry at the sight, a five-hundred-voiced inarticulate roar which made the skylined horses flinch and toss their heads.

"Line of battle," Corfe said calmly. "He's having a look, so we might as well give him something to see. Andruw, take the fifth tercio forward and chase those riders away as soon as the others have shaken out."

Andruw's boyish face lit up. "With pleasure, sir."

The five tercios of Corfe's command got into line. Five men deep, the line extended for a hundred yards. As soon as it was in place, the standard flapping with the colour party in the centre, Andruw led one tercio up the hill towards the watching riders.

There were less than a score of horsemen there, though they wore the heavy three-quarter armour of the old nobility. When the tercio was within fifty paces they turned their horses and trotted away, not liking the odds. Andruw placed his men on the hilltop and soon a gasping runner was jogging down from his position. He handed Corfe a note.

Enemy camp half a league ahead, some three leagues out of town, it read. *Looks like they are beginning to deploy.*

"Your orders, sir?" Ensign Ebro asked. Like everyone else's, his scarlet armour was so liberally plastered with muck that it had become a rust-brown colour.

"We'll join Andruw's tercio," Corfe said. "After that, we'll see."

"Yes, sir." Ebro's voice was throbbing like the wing-beat of a trapped bird and his face was pale under its spattering of mud.

"Is there anything wrong, Ensign?" Corfe asked him.

"No, sir. I – it's just that – I've never been in a battle before, sir."

Corfe stared at him for a moment, somehow liking him better for this admission. "You'll do all right, Ensign."

The rest of the formation joined Andruw's men on the hilltop and stared down to where the leather tents of the enemy camp dotted the land. Off to the left, perhaps a mile away, was the sea, as grey and solid as stone. Ordinac's castle at Hedeby could be made out as a dark pinnacle in the distance. Corfe examined the duke's men with a practised eye.

"A thousand maybe, as we were told. Perhaps a hundred cavalry – the duke's personal bodyguard – and mostly pikemen apart from that. I can't see too many arquebusiers. These are second-rate troops, no match for the regular army. His guns – he has two, see? Light falcons – are not even unlimbered yet. Holy Saints, I do believe he's going to offer us battle at once."

"You mean today, sir?" Ebro asked.

"I mean right now, Ensign."

Andruw came over. "Time to fight, I believe. He'll come to us if we wait for him, though look at the mobs down there: he'll be half the day getting them into formation."

Crowds of men were collecting their stacked arms and milling about whilst gesticulating officers tried to sort them into some kind of order. The only organized group seemed to be that of the duke's bodyguard, who were drawn up in a two-deep line on their heavy horses ahead of the other troops, acting as a screen until their deployment was complete.

Corfe took in the situation in a moment. He was outnumbered: he was expected to fight a defensive battle. He occupied the high ground and thus had a good position. But his men had no firearms. The enemy could close to within firing range and blast away at him half the day whilst the cavalry threatened to cave in his flanks if he tried to close.

"We will attack," he said crisply. "Andruw, Ebro, go to your tercios. Marsch, inform the men that we are to charge the enemy at once and throw them into disorder before they have time to deploy."

"But the cavalry –" Ebro said.

"Obey your orders, Ensign. Marsch, peel off the rear rank and keep it back as a tactical reserve. I'll call for it when it's needed. Understood?"

The big tribesman nodded and pushed his way through the men behind him.

"Are you sure about this, Corfe?" Andruw asked.

"I'm not going to sit here and wait for them, Andruw. This is our only chance. We must be quick. I want everything at the double. We have to catch them while they're trying to deploy."

"Half a league at the double in this armour?" Andruw said doubtfully.

"The men can do it. Come, let's get to work."

The colour party moved out first, whilst the ranks of men behind it retied their helmstrings and loosened their swords in the scabbards. Then the formation began to move. Corfe had taught them a few words of command in Normannic, and he shouted one now, emphasizing the order with a wave of his sabre.

"*Double!*"

The men broke into a lumbering trot, sounding like a moving ironmonger's stall. The formation began to coalesce as they slogged downhill through the soft ground, tearing it into a morass as they went. Behind the main body, Marsch had his hundred of the reserve in a more compact mass following in the wake of their comrades.

Tearing effort, at first quite easy because of the downhill slope, then getting harder as the feet began to drag, the lungs began to fight for air and the heavy armour crushed down on the shoulders. The men would be tired when they made contact, but the enemy would be disorganized and in disarray. It was an exchange Corfe was willing to make.

Half a mile gone by, and the formation ground on in silence except for the suck of boots or bare feet in the mud, the clank and crash of iron, and laboured, gasping breathing. There was no energy to spare for battlecries.

Hard to fight the head up and make the brain work, to keep thinking. But the furious thinking and planning kept the mind off the physical pain.

The screen of heavily armoured horsemen seemed at a loss. They had obviously not expected this move. A bugle call sounded, and the riders kicked their mounts into motion up the hill. The animals were heavily laden, moving in soft, mucky ground up a gradient. The best they could do was a fast trot, counting on their weight and momentum to break Corfe's formation; that, and the fear of coming to grips with lancers.

The tribesmen uttered a hoarse, tearing whoop as the two bodies of troops met with a ringing crash, the horses struggling uphill and the infantry running down to meet them. The line was staggered, the ranks intermingling as the horsemen drove wedges of iron and muscle into it. Corfe saw one of his men speared clean through by a lance, armour and all, and tossed aside like a gutted fish.

But the horsemen could not keep up their advance. Corfe's men seized their lances and dragged them out of the saddle, stabbed upwards into armpit and groin or slashed the tendons of the horses so the screaming creatures went down kicking madly, crushing their riders. And once a rider was on his back, it was impossible for him to get up again. The heavy armour kept him pinned in the muck until a gleeful tribesman ripped off his helm and cut his throat.

It was over quickly. The cavalry line was broken into knots of milling riders who were in turn engulfed and brought down. A score of pain-crazed horses galloped riderless down the hill along with a few lancers who had somehow kept in the saddle and flailed their mounts into a canter.

"Reform!" Corfe shouted. And his men paused in their looting of the dead to dress their ranks and straighten the line.

"Double!"

The formation jogged on again. Corfe had no idea how many casualties his little army had suffered, but that did not matter. What was important was that they catch the rest of the rebel forces before they deployed.

His armour seemed light now. He had not struck a blow during the swift, brutal skirmish, too busy trying to direct things, to keep an eye out for the larger picture, to gauge the need for the reserve under Marsch. Now the battle energy was flowing in him, the cold strength that entered into every man at the imminent prospect of death. The tribesmen advanced downhill at a flat run, and this time

Corfe heard them break out into the shrill, unearthly wail that was their battlecry.

A mob of men before them, some dressed in line, some crowded in a shapeless mass. There was the bristling array of a pike tercio, the long, wicked weapons swinging down to present a fence of spikes to the attackers. Corfe's command charged into the enemy.

The rebels were pushed into a tighter mass almost at once as the men at the forefront of the formation recoiled. Here and there a company got off a rattle of volley fire, but for the most part isolated arquebusiers were loading and firing at will. Maybe the duke had died in the cavalry battle, Corfe thought; there seemed to be no leadership beyond the officers of individual tercios.

Only the tercio of pikemen kept their ranks. The tribesmen beat down the long weapons with their swords and tried to pierce the formation and disrupt it, but rear ranks of the enemy brought their own pikes down over the shoulders of their comrades and impaled the impetuous attackers. Corfe's men were pushing back the disorganized mobs of rebels elsewhere, but were taking heavy losses against the pikes.

Corfe fought his way out of the scrum until he was at the rear of his men. Marsch was waiting there with the reserve, his eyes aflame with impatience.

"Come with me," Corfe shouted at them, and led them off at a sprint.

He took them along the back of the battlefront, around the enemy flank. They met a company of arquebusiers there, placed to guard against such a move, but they were among them before the enemy could let off a volley, hacking and stabbing like scarlet-clad fiends. The arquebusiers broke and fled into their camp. Corfe led his men onwards, through the outer tents of the rebel encampment, the tribesmen kicking through fires and slashing guy-ropes as they went.

They were in the enemy rear. Incredibly, no one had posted a reserve here. The pike phalanx bristled like a vast porcupine ahead of them, Corfe's men still throwing themselves on the pike points and striving to beat them down.

"Charge!" Corfe screamed, and led his hundred forward into the rear of the pikes.

The enemy had no chance. Impressive though pikemen might be in formation, once their ranks were broken they were impotent, their unwieldy weapons a handicap. Corfe's reserve tercio slaughtered them by the score, shredding their formation to pieces.

The battle was won. Corfe knew that even as the rebels were fighting to break away from this twofold assault. The rebel army had become a mob, losing any vestige of military organization. It was simply a crowd of men struggling to save themselves, with the scarlet demons of Corfe's warriors cutting them down like corn as they ran.

"I give you joy of your victory, Colonel," Andruw said, meeting Corfe in the midst of that mass of murder. "As pretty a move as I've ever seen, and these men of ours!" He grinned. "There must be a virtue in savagery."

Victory. It tasted sweet, even if it was over fellow-Torunnans. It was better than wine or women. It was an exaltation which burned away self-doubt.

"Keep up the scare," he told Andruw. "We'll pursue them all the way to Hedeby if we have to. They mustn't be given a rest, or a chance to reform. Keep at them, Andruw."

Andruw gestured to the howling, slaughtering tribesmen who were following the retreating army and turning their rout into a murderous nightmare.

"I don't think I could stop them if I tried, Corfe."

BY NIGHTFALL IT was over. Hedeby's citadel had been surrendered by the town headsman, the nobility of the place having been killed in the battle. Corfe billeted his troops in the castle itself. The remains of Duke Ordinac's forces were scattered refugees, lost somewhere in the surrounding countryside. Many had surrendered in the town square, too exhausted to flee any farther. These were imprisoned in the castle cells. The people of the town, in terror of the bloody, weirdly armoured barbarians in their midst, refused them nothing in the way of food, drink, or anything else they had a mind to take, though Corfe issued stark orders against any maltreatment of the citizens. He had seen too much of that at Aekir to countenance it from men under his own command.

Four hundred of the duke's men had died on the field, and another tenscore were bleeding and screaming wounded, most of whom would follow their dead comrades into eternity. Corfe's men had lost less than a hundred, most of the casualties being incurred by the tercio which had engaged the enemy pikes head on.

Ordinac kept a good larder, and there was a feast for those well enough to stomach it that night, the tribesmen drinking and eating at the long tables of the castle hall, waited on by terrified serving attendants – Corfe had seen to it that these were male – and recounting the stories of what they had personally done in the battle lately fought. It was like a scene from an earlier, cruder age, when men put glory in battle above all other things. Corfe did not greatly care for it, but he let the men have their fun. They had earned it. He was amused to see Ensign Ebro flushed and drinking in the midst of the rest, being slapped on the back and not resenting it. Clearly the relief of having seen out his first battle without disgrace had unbent him. He was roaring with laughter at jokes told in a language he could not understand.

Corfe went out of the smoky hall to stand on the old-fashioned battlements of Hedeby Castle and look down on the town and the land below, dark under the stars. Up on the hill overlooking the town there was a dull red glow. The townspeople had dragged the bodies of the slain there on Corfe's orders and made a pyre of them. There they lay, Torunnan men-at-arms and duke and Felimbric tribesmen, all burning together. Corfe thanked his luck that his men did not seem to require elaborate burial rites. As long as the corpse burned with a sword in its hand, they were happy. Such strange men; he had come close to loving them today as they followed him without question or hesitation. Such loyalty was beyond the fortunes of kings.

Footsteps behind him, and he found himself flanked by Andruw and Marsch, the tribesman clutching a flaccid wineskin.

"Drunk already?" Andruw asked, though he might have asked the same question of himself.

"I needed air," Corfe told him. "Why are you two out here missing the fun?"

"The men want to toast their commander," Marsch said gravely.

He had been drinking solidly the whole evening, but he was as steady as a rock. He offered the wineskin to his colonel, and Corfe took a squirt of the thin, acidic wine of southern Torunna into his mouth. The taste brought back memories of his youth. He had come from this part of the world, though he had been stationed so long in the east that he nearly forgot it. Had he not joined the army at a tender age he might have been burning on that pyre on the hilltop right now, killed fighting for his overlord in a war whose cause he knew little of and cared less for.

"Are the pickets posted?" he asked Andruw.

The younger officer blinked owlishly. "Yes, sir. Half a mile out of town, sober as monks, and mounted on the best horses the stables could provide. Corfe, Marsch and I have been meaning to talk to you," Andruw draped an arm about Corfe's shoulders. "Do you know what we've found here?"

"What?"

"Horses." It was Marsch who was speaking now. "We have found many horses, Colonel, big enough for destriers. It would seem that this duke of yours had a passion for breeding horses. There are over a thousand in studs scattered over the countryside to the south. Some of the castle attendants told us."

Corfe turned to look Marsch in the eye. "What are you saying, Ensign?"

"My people are natural born horsemen. It is the way we prefer to fight. And this armour we wear: most of it is the armour of heavy cavalrymen anyway..." Marsch trailed off, his eyebrows raised.

"Cavalry," Corfe breathed. "So that's it. I was a cavalry officer myself once."

Andruw was grinning at him. "The property of traitors is confiscate to the crown, you know. But I'm sure Lofantyr will not miss a few nags. He's been niggardly enough to us so far."

Corfe stared out at the fire-split night. The pyre of the slain was like a dull eye watching him.

"On horseback we'd have more mobility and striking power, but we'd also need a baggage train of sorts, a mobile forge, farriers."

"There are men among the tribe who can shoe horses and doctor them. The Felimbri value their horseflesh above their wives," Marsch said, with perfect seriousness. Andruw choked on a mouthful of wine and collapsed into laughter.

"You're drunk, Adjutant," Corfe said to him.

Andruw saluted. "Yes, Colonel, I am. My apologies, Marsch. Have a drink."

The wineskin did the rounds between the three of them as they leaned against the battlements and narrowed their eyes against the chill of the wind that came off the sea.

"We will equip the men with horses then," Corfe said at last. "That's eight squadrons of cavalry we'll have, plus spares for every man and a baggage train for forage and the forge. Mules to carry the grain – there's plenty about the town. And then –"

"And then?" Andruw and Marsch asked together.

"Then we march on Duke Narfintyr at Staed, get there before Lofantyr's other column and see what we can do."

"I've heard folk in the town say that Narfintyr has three thousand men," Andruw said, momentarily sobered.

"Numbers mean nothing. If they're of the same calibre as the ones we fought today we've nothing to worry about."

The moon was rising, a thin sliver, a horned thing of silver which Marsch bowed to.

"'Kerunnos's Face,' we call it," he said in answer to the questioning looks of the two Torunnans. "It is the light of the night, of the twilight, of a dwindling people. My tribe is almost finished. Of its warriors, who once numbered thousands, there are only we few hundred left and some boys and old men up in the mountains. We are the last."

"Our people have fought you for generations," Corfe said. "Before us it was the Fimbrians, and before that the Horse-Merduks."

"Yes. We have fought the world, we Felimbri, but our time is almost done. This is the right way to end it. It was a good fight, and there will be other good fights until the last of us dies a free man with sword in hand. We can ask for nothing more."

"You're wrong, you know," Andruw spoke up unexpectedly. "This isn't the end of things. Can't you feel it? The world is changing, Marsch. If we live to old age we will have seen it become something new, and what is more we will have been a part of the forces that did the changing of it. Today, in a small way, we began something which will one day be important..."

He trailed off. "I'm drunk, friends. Best ignore me."

Corfe slapped him on the shoulder. "You're right in a way. This is just the beginning of things. There's a long road ahead of us, if we're strong enough to walk it. God knows where it'll take us."

"To the road ahead," Marsch said, raising the almost empty wineskin.

"To the road ahead."

And they drank from it one by one like brothers.

TWENTY-FOUR

THE REEK OF the burning hung about Abrusio like a dark fog, stretching for miles out to sea. The great fires had been contained, and were burning themselves out in an area of the city which resembled the visionary's worst images of Hell. Deep in those bright, thundering patches of holocaust some of the sturdier stone buildings still stood, though roofless and gutted, but the poor clay brick of the rest of the dwellings had crumbled at the touch of the fire, and what had once been a series of thriving, densely populated districts was now a wasteland of rubble and ash over which the tides of flame swept back and forth with the wind, seeking something new to feed their hunger even as they began to die down for lack of sustenance.

Fighting within the city had also died down, the protagonists having retreated to their respective quarters with the fire-flattened expanses providing a clear-cut no-man's-land between them. Many of the King's troops were engaged in the business of conducting evacuees beyond the walls and yet others were still demolishing swathes of the Lower City, street by street, lest the flames flare up again and seek a new path down to the sea.

"We are holding our own rather nicely," Sastro di Carrera said with satisfaction. His perch on a balcony high in the Royal palace afforded him a fine view of Lower Abrusio, almost half of which lay in flickering ruin.

"I think we have exhausted the main effort of the enemy," Presbyter Quirion agreed. "But a part of the fleet, a strong squadron, has not been in sight for days. Rovero may have sent it off somewhere to create some devilment, and the main part of Hebrion's navy is at anchor beyond the Great Harbour. I fear they may assault the booms soon."

"Let them," Sastro said airily. "The mole forts house a score of heavy guns apiece. If Rovero sends in his ships to force the entrance to the harbour they will be cut to pieces by a deadly crossfire. No, I think we have them, Quirion. This is the time to see whether they will consider a negotiated surrender."

Quirion shook his round, close-cropped head. "They're in no mood for talking yet, unless I miss my guess. They still have a goodly force left to them, and our own men are thinly stretched. They will make another effort soon, by ship perhaps. We must remain vigilant."

"As you wish. Now, what of my coronation plans? I trust they are forging ahead?"

Quirion's face took on a look of twisted incredulity. "We are in the middle of a half-fought war, Lord Carrera. This is hardly the time to begin worrying about pomp and ceremony."

"The coronation is more than that, my dear Presbyter. Don't you think that the presence in Abrusio of an anointed king, blessed by the Church, will be a factor in persuading the rebels to lay down their arms?"

Quirion was silent for a moment. From the city below came the odd crack of arquebus fire where pickets were taking potshots at each other, but compared to the hellish chaos of the past days Abrusio seemed almost tranquil.

"There may be something in what you say," he admitted at last. "But we will not be able to stump up much in the way of pomp for a time yet. My men and yours are too busy fighting to keep what we have."

"Of course, but I ask you to bear it in mind. The sooner this vacuum is filled the better."

Quirion nodded and then turned away. He leaned on the balcony rail and stared out over the maimed city.

"They say that fifty thousand of the citizens perished in the fire, quite apart from the thousands who died in the fighting," he said. "I don't know about you, Lord Carrera, but for me that is a heavy load for conscience to bear."

"They were heretics, the scrapings of the sewers. Of no account," Sastro said scornfully. "Do not let your conscience grow tender on their behalf, Quirion. The state is better off without them."

"Perhaps."

"Well *perhaps* you would care to walk with me and show me your plans for the defence of the Upper City."

"Yes, Lord Carrera," Quirion said heavily. As he turned away from the balcony, however, he had a moment of agonizing doubt. What had he done here? What kind of creature was he making a king of?

The moment passed, and he followed Sastro into the planning chamber of the palace, where the senior officers of their forces were awaiting them.

THERE WAS NO beauty in ships for the lady Jemilla. To her they were little more than complicated instruments of torture, set to float on an element which might have been designed specifically to cause her discomfort.

But there were times when she could dimly see some of the reasons why men held them in such awe and reverenced them so. They were impressive, if nothing else.

She was taking a turn about the poop-deck of the *Providence*, the flagship of Rovero and Abeleyn's squadron. If she did not spend too much time looking at the gentle rise and fall of the horizon and concentrated instead on the cold wind which fanned her pale cheeks, then she might almost enjoy the motion. In any case, she would rather die than be sick here on deck, in front of five hundred sailors and marines and soldiers, all of whom were stealing privy glances up at her as she paced heavily to and fro from one bulwark to the other.

The flagship was a magnificent two-decker mounting some fifty guns, four-masted and with high-built fore- and sterncastles. Seen from aft, with her gold ornament and long galleries hanging over her wake, she looked like nothing so much as some baroque church front. But her decks presented an entirely different aspect. They had already been strewn with sand so that when the time came the gunners and sailors would not slip in their own blood. The guns had been run out, the firetubs set around the mast butts, and the slow-match which would set off the guns already lit and spreading its acrid reek about the ship. They were cleared for action.

Abrusio was just over a league away. The admiral had told her they were doing six knots, and would raise the city in less than half an hour. She would be confined when that happened in the dark belowdecks, in the murky stench of bilge and close-packed humanity which was the particular hallmark of every warship. So she was making the most of the fresh air, preparing herself for the ordeal ahead.

Abeleyn joined her on the poop. He was in half-armour, black-lacquered steel chased with silver and with a scarlet sash about his middle. He looked every inch the sovereign as he stood there with one hand resting on his sword hilt and the other cradling the open-faced helm which he would wear into battle. Jemilla found herself curtseying to him without conscious volition. He seemed to have grown in stature somehow, and she noticed for the first time the streaks of grey in his curly hair behind the temples.

"I trust you are enjoying your last moments of freedom, lady," he said, and something in the way he said it made her shiver. "Yes, sire. I am no sailor, as you know. I would stay up here throughout the battle if I could."

"I believe you would." Abeleyn smiled, his regal authority falling from him. He was a young man again. "I have seen seasick marines lift their heads and forget about their malady the moment the guns begin to roar. Human nature is a strange thing. But I will feel better knowing that you are safe below the waterline."

She bowed slightly. "I am selfish. I think only of myself, and sometimes forget the burden I bear, the King's child." She could not resist reminding him, though she knew he disliked her doing it.

Sure enough, his face hardened. The boy disappeared again. "You had best go below, lady. We will be within range of the city batteries in less than half a glass."

"As you wish, sire," she said humbly, but as she started for the companion ladder she paused and set her hand on his. "Be careful, Abeleyn," she whispered.

He gripped her hand briefly and smiled with his mouth alone. "I will."

The squadron went about, the sails on every ship flashing in and out as one, obedient to the signal pennants of the flagship. They were around the last headland and could see in the distance Abrusio Hill, the sprawl of the city itself and the fleet which stood ready beyond its harbours.

The sight was a shock for Abeleyn, no matter that he had tried to prepare himself for it. It seemed to him at first glance that his capital was entirely in ruins. Swathes of rubble-strewn wasteland stretched across the city, and fires were burning here and there. Only the western waterfront and the Upper City on the hillside seemed unchanged. But Old Abrusio was destroyed utterly.

As the squadron was sighted, the fleet began its salute, some four hundred vessels suddenly coming alive in clouds of smoke and flame, a thunder which echoed across the hills inland and carried for miles out to sea as the King was saluted and welcomed back to his kingdom. The salute was the signal for the battle to commence, and before its last echoes had died away the warships of Hebrion had unfurled their sails and were weighing anchor. The blank rounds of a moment before were replaced by real cannonballs, and the bombardment of the mole forts which protected the Great Harbour had begun.

The staggering noise of a fleet action was something which had to be experienced for anyone to believe it. Added to the guns of the ships now was the return fire of the batteries on the city walls and the harbour forts. As his squadron edged closer to the eastern half of the Lower City, where his forces would attempt their landing, Abeleyn saw the water about the leading squadrons of the fleet erupt in geysers of foam as the first rounds went home. Topmasts were shattered by high-ranging shells and came crashing down in tangles of rigging and wood and billowing canvas. The bulwarks of the leading ships were swept with deadly chain shot, splinters of oak spraying through the gun crews like charges of canister. But still the great ships in the vanguard sailed on, their chasers firing across their bows and producing puffs of rubble and flame from the casemates of the forts.

Abeleyn saw one tall carrack dismasted entirely, her towering yards shattered and crumpling over her side. She yawed as the fallen spars dragged her to one side and in a moment had collided with one of her sister-ships. But the battle for the mole forts and the boom was being obscured by rising clouds of pale powder-smoke. It seemed that the whole surface of Abrusio's Great Harbour, over a mile from one end of it to the other, was a seething cauldron which bubbled steam, amid which the masts of ships could be glimpsed as the smoke rolled and toiled in vast thunderheads across the broken face of the sea.

The *Providence*'s guns were roaring, softening up the waterfront where the marines and soldiers of the squadron would make their landing. On the formation's vessels the fighting men stood in unbroken ranks amidships, their lips moving in prayer, their hands checking armour and weapons one last time. Three thousand men to carry the eastern half of Abrusio and hack a way up to the palace. They seemed pitifully few to Abeleyn, but he had to remind himself that the fleet was doing its part in the Great Harbour, and Mercado's men would be assaulting across the burnt wasteland of the western city also. With luck, his own forces should not have too many of the enemy to contend with.

He could see the sea walls of eastern Abrusio now, scarcely three cables away. The water was deep here, seven fathoms at least, and even the carracks would be able to run in close to the walls to support the landing parties with point-blank fire.

The longboats and cutters of the squadron were already on the booms, and sailors and marines were hauling together in sweating crowds to swing them out over the ship's sides and down to the water so far below. All this while the guns bellowed out broadside after broadside and were answered by the wall batteries. Abeleyn had to hold himself upright, unflinching, as rounds began to whistle and crash home on the carrack. A longboat took a direct hit and exploded in a spray of jagged wood and gore, men flung in all directions, ropes flapping free. But the work went on, and the small boats were lowered down the sides of the ships one by one. There were scores of them, enough to carry over a thousand men in the first wave.

"Your boat is ready, sire," Admiral Rovero shouted over the noise, his lopsided mouth seemingly built to concentrate the force of his voice. Abeleyn nodded. He felt a touch of warmth as Sergeant Orsini fell into step beside him, and took a moment to grip the man's shoulder. Then he put one leg over the bulwarks and began climbing down the rope ladder hanging there while a yard away on the other side of him the culverins exploded and were reloaded, running in and out like monsters let loose and then restrained.

He was in the boat, his heart almost as loud as the gunfire in his head. The vessel was already packed with men, struggling with oars and arquebuses and swords and ladders. Abeleyn stepped over them to the prow, where the laddermen were squatting ready. He waved his hand at the helmsman, and they cast off from the looming carrack along with half a dozen other crowded boats. The men's oars dipped, and they began to move over the shot-stitched water.

An agonizing time of simply sitting there while they crawled forward towards the walls. There were scores of boats in the water, a mass of close-packed humanity crammed into them, dotting the deadly space between the hulls of the warships and the sea walls of the city. But they took few casualties in that choppy approach. The broadsides of the carracks were smothering the wall batteries with fire like mother hens protecting their chicks. Abeleyn felt that if he stuck up a hand into the air he could catch a cannonball, so thick was the volume of shot screaming overhead. To his own alarm, he had a momentary urge to throw up. Several of the men in the boat had already done so. It was the waiting, the drawing tight of the nerves to unbearable tautness. Abeleyn swallowed a mouthful of vomit that was searing his throat. Kings could not afford to show such weaknesses.

They were at the wall, the boat's bow bumping against the weathered stone. Showers of rock were falling down on them as the shells from the carracks ploughed into the defences above their heads. The naval gunners would elevate their fire at the last moment, giving their comrades as much cover as possible in that murderous time of grappling with the ungainly ladders.

The laddermen stood up with their bulky charge – a fifteen-foot ladder with hooks of steel at its top which were clanging against the stone. They swayed and lurched, their legs held steady by their comrades, until finally the ladder had hooked on to an embrasure above.

Abeleyn pushed them out of the way and climbed first. Golophin and Mercado would have railed at him for such foolishness, but he felt there was nothing else to do. The King must be seen to take the lead. If these men showed their willingness to die for him, then he too must illustrate it in return.

So intent, so utterly concentrated were his thoughts, that he did not even pause to wonder if any of the men would follow him. The spectre of his death was something which hovered gleefully, cackling at his shoulder. His feet were leaden in their boots. He pictured his precious body torn asunder, riddled with bullets, tossed down into the bloody water below. His life ended, his vision of the world, unique and unrecoverable, made extinct. The strain was so great that for a second the wall in front of his nose seemed to turn slightly red, echoing the thunder of blood through his booming arteries.

He drew his sword, awkward and heavy in his armour, and climbed one-handed, gulping for air that would not be sucked into his lungs fast enough.

A stone clanged off one shoulder, and he almost fell. Looking up, he saw a wild-eyed Knight Militant looking over the battlements at him. He froze, utterly helpless as he stared into the man's raging countenance. But then the Knight's face disintegrated as a volley of arquebus fire from the boat below hammered into him, throwing him back out of sight. Abeleyn climbed on.

He was at the top, on the walls. Men running, dismounted guns, rubble, gaping holes in the defences. Shot from the carracks whistling higher as the guns were elevated.

Someone running towards him. His own sword flicking out before he even thought of it, clashing aside the other man's blade. A boot to the midriff, and the man was gone, screaming off over the catwalk.

More of his own men behind him. They were clearing a stretch of wall, fighting the knots of the enemy who were rushing towards them, pushing them back. It was only then that Abeleyn realized how lightly the walls were defended.

I'm alive, he thought with keen surprise. *I'm still here. We are doing this thing.*

Something in him changed. Until now he had been so preoccupied by what he had to do, by the possibility of his own death or maiming, that he had been thinking like a private soldier obsessed with the precariousness of his own existence. But he was the King. These men were looking to him for orders. He had the responsibility.

He remembered the seaborne fight aboard Dietl's carrack, a hundred years ago it seemed. He remembered the delight in battle, the sheer excitement of it, and his own feeling of invincibility. And he realized in a tiny, flashing instant, that he would never feel that way again, not about this. That feeling had something to do with youth and exuberance and the joy at being alive. But he had seen his city burned to ashes. He had a child growing in a woman's belly. His crown had cost his people thousands of lives. He would never feel so untrammelled and unafraid again.

"Follow me!" he shouted to his men. The enemy were falling back off the walls as hundreds more of the landing forces struggled atop the battlements. He led his troops off the sea defences of Abrusio into the streets of the city itself and the bloody work which yet awaited them.

GOLOPHIN STARED AT the awesome spectacle. A city in torment, burned, bombarded and broken down. Perhaps in the east, with the fall of Aekir and the battles at Ormann Dyke, they could match this scale of destruction and carnage, but nothing he had ever seen before in his long life had prepared him for it.

He had seen the King's squadron assault the eastern sea walls as the main body of the fleet attacked the mole forts and the boom which protected Abrusio's widest harbour. But now he could see nothing, not even with his cantrips, for the entire enclosed trio of bays which formed the seaward side of the city was obscured by thundering smoke clouds. Three miles of shell-torn water from which a steady roar issued, as though some titanic, agonizing labour of birth were going on deep in that fog of war.

His familiar was dying somewhere aboard the King's flagship. He had worn it out with his errands and only a flicker of life remained within its breast, a last spark of the

Dweomer he had created it with. He could feel the ebbing of its loyal, savage mind, and with it was fading his own strength. No light thing, the death of a familiar. It was like losing a child whose umbilical had never been cut. Golophin felt as old and frail as a brittle leaf, and the Dweomer had sunk in him to a dull glow. It would be a long time ere he was ready to perform miracles again.

And yet he chafed at being here, on the summit of Admiral's Tower, while the young man who was his lord and his friend fought for his birthright and the life of the city they both loved. The bastard traitors and Knights had ripped the bowels out of raucous Lower Abrusio. It would never be the same again, not in what remained of this old man's lifetime anyway.

General Mercado joined him, leaving the aides and staff officers and couriers who were clustered about the map-littered table on the other side of the tower.

"He is over the walls," the general said, one side of his face crannied with worry, the other silver perfection.

"Well, that is something. And the attack on the boom?"

"Too soon to say." An especially severe series of broadsides from the harbour tumult meant he had to raise his voice to be heard. "We've lost at least four great ships and there's no chance for the crews in that maelstrom. And those who make it ashore are being killed out of hand by the lackeys of the Carreras. At least two thousand men already."

"What of your land assault?"

"Slow progress there. They've thrown up breastworks along their front and my men are having to charge them across the wasteground. There will be no sudden breakthrough, not in this half of the city. We are merely pinning down his troops."

"So the main effort will be with Abeleyn?"

"Yes. His is the only assault which is presently getting anywhere. But with scarcely four thousand men the Presbyter cannot hold on to all his lines indefinitely. He will crack in the end. It only remains to be seen how much blood we must spill before he does."

"Great God, General, this will ruin the kingdom."

Golophin felt faint, worn, useless. The burly soldier steadied him with a hand on his thin arm.

"You should be resting, Golophin. We cannot spare men such as you, either now or in the future."

The old wizard smiled wanly. "My life is not of such great account, not any more. We are each of us expendable, save one. Nothing must happen to the King, Albio, or this is all for nothing. The King must be made to realize that."

"I'm sure he will be prudent. He is no fool, despite his youth."

"He is not such a youth any more, either."

THE ENEMY LINES had broken, and those who could were retreating westwards, having spiked their guns and fired their magazines. The Carrera retainers led the rout, whilst the Knights Militant brought up the rear, fighting stubbornly the whole way. Abeleyn's men took heavy casualties as they followed up the retreat and stumbled into bitter hand-to-hand conflict with the Knights, who were well-trained and superbly armoured. It was only when the King halted the advance and reformed what men he could that the Knights were thrown back in disorder. Abeleyn's arquebusiers and sword-and-buckler men had become disorganized and intermingled. He separated them and led the advance with quick-firing ranks of arquebusiers alone, which cut down the stolid Knights Militant and sowed panic in the enemy forces. The streets were streaming with men, some intent on saving their own lives, others intent on cutting them down. It had become a running battle, one-sided and fast-moving.

A gasping courier found Abeleyn near the foot of Abrusio Hill, directing the pursuit of the fleeing traitors in person and jogging along with his advancing forces as he snapped out orders right and left. The courier had to tug at the King's arm before Abeleyn could be halted.

"What? What is it, damn it?"

"I am sent from General Rovero, sire," the man panted. "He presents his compliments —"

"Damn his compliments! What has he to say?"

"The fleet has broken the boom, sire. They're sailing into the Great Harbour and beginning to bombard the Upper City. They'll be landing their marines in minutes. Sire, the general and Golophin beg that you do not expose yourself unnecessarily."

"My thanks for their advice. Now run to the waterfront and hurry along those landing parties. I want the palace surrounded before the traitors can escape. Go!"

"Yes, your Majesty." And Abeleyn had disappeared into the midst of his jubilant, advancing troops.

"It is over," said Quirion.

Sastro's face was as pale as snow. "What do you mean, 'over'?"

They could hear the crackling of arquebus volleys as they stood in the high chambers of the palace's topmost tower. It and the thunder of heavy guns mingled with the crash and rumble of lacerated masonry. Shells were falling closer. Men's voices could be made out in individual screams rather than the far-off roar of battle which had been what they had heard from this eminence so far. A curtain of battle din was inexorably advancing towards them.

"Our lines are broken, Lord Carrera, and our forces – even my Knights – are in full retreat. The enemy ships have broken the boom and are in the Great Harbour trying the range for the palace. In a few minutes the bombardment of this very edifice will commence. We are defeated."

"But how is that possible? Only this morning we were ready to discuss terms with an exhausted enemy."

"You were ready. I never believed it would happen. Abeleyn is in the city as we speak, advancing on the palace. His men fight like fiends when he is at their head, and ours become discouraged. It may be we can draw together what troops of ours remain and make a stand here, perhaps sue for some terms other than those of unconditional surrender. I do not know. Your retainers are in utter rout, and even my people are much broken up. I have my senior officers in the streets trying to rally them, but I do not hold out much hope."

"Then we must escape," Sastro said in a strangled voice, his dreams and ambitions crumbling away before his eyes. But his life – it must be possible to survive. It was unthinkable that he would not.

"The palace is surrounded. There is no hope of escape, and especially not for you." Here a note of some subtle satisfaction crept into Quirion's voice. "If you are caught they will execute you out of hand for high treason. Myself and my men I believe they may let depart in peace – we are not Hebrionese, after all – but you and your men are traitors and will pay the ultimate penalty. I suggest, Lord Carrera, that to avoid public humiliation at the hands of Abeleyn's soldiery, you use this –" And here Quirion held out a long, wicked-looking knife.

"Suicide?" Sastro squawked. "Is that the only end for me? Take my own life?"

"It would be a kinder end than the one Abeleyn will permit you."

"And you – you will tamely submit to the dictates of a heretic king? What will the Pontiff think of that, Presbyter?"

"The Pontiff will not be pleased, naturally, but better that I bring him a thousand Knights out of this debacle than nothing. There is the future to think of. My men must live to fight again for the Church."

"The future," Sastro said bitterly. Tears were brimming in his eyes. "You must help me get away, Quirion, I am to be King of Hebrion. I am the only alternative to Abeleyn."

"You bought your nomination with your men's bodies," Quirion said harshly. "There are others whose blood is better. Make a good end of it, Lord Carrera. Show them that you died a man."

Sastro was weeping openly. "I cannot! How can I die, I, Sastro di Carrera? It cannot be. There must be something you can do."

He clutched at Quirion's armoured shoulders as if he were a drowning man reaching for his rescuer. A spasm of disgust crossed the Presbyter's face.

"Help me, Quirion! I am rich – I can give you anything."

"You whining cur!" Quirion spat. "You would send a hundred thousand men to their deaths without a thought, and yet you cringe at the prospect of your own. Great Gods, what a king you would have made for this unhappy realm! So you will give me anything?"

"Anything, for God's sake, man! Only name it."

"I will take your life, then," the Presbyter snarled, and he thrust the knife into the nobleman's stomach.

Sastro's eyes flared in disbelief. He staggered backwards.

"Sweet Saints," he gasped. "You have killed me."

"Aye," Quirion said shortly, "I have. Now get about your dying like a man. I go to surrender Abrusio to the heretic."

He turned on his heel and left the room without a backward glance.

Sastro fell to his knees, his face running with tears. "*Quirion!*"

He gripped the hilt of the knife and tried to pull it out of his belly, but only yelped at the pain of it, his fingers slipping on the slick blood. He fell to his side on the stone floor.

"Oh, sweet Blessed Saint, help me," he whispered. And then was silent. A bubble of blood formed over his open mouth, hovered, and finally popped as his spirit fled.

"THERE ARE WHITE flags all over the city, sire," Sergeant Orsini told Abeleyn. "The enemy are throwing down their arms – even the Knights. Abrusio is ours!"

"Ours," Abeleyn repeated. He was bloody, grimed and exhausted. He and Orsini walked up the steep street to where the abbey of the Inceptines glowered sombre and high-spired on the skyline ahead. His men were around him, weapons still at the shoulder, but the glee of victory was brightening their faces. Shells were falling, but they were being fired by the ships in the harbour. The enemy batteries had been silenced. Men sank into crouches as a shell demolished the side of a house barely fifty yards away. Streamers of oily smoke were rising from the abbey as it burned from a dozen direct hits.

"Courier," Abeleyn croaked. His mouth felt as though someone had filled it full of gunpowder.

"Sire?"

"Run down to the waterfront. Get a message to Admiral Rovero. The bombardment of the Upper City is to cease at once. The enemy has surrendered."

"Gladly, sire." The courier sped off.

"I wish you joy of your victory, sire," Orsini said, grinning.

Abeleyn found himself smiling, though he did not know why. He held out his hand, and after a moment's surprise Orsini took it. They shook as though they had just sealed a bargain. The men cheered at the sight.

More Royal soldiers were congregating as the news spread. Soon there was a crowd of several hundred about Abeleyn, shaking their swords and arquebuses in the air and cheering, heedless of the cannonballs which were arcing down not far away. They picked up Abeleyn and carried him in crude triumphal procession towards the burning abbey and the shell-pecked palace which belonged to him again. Abrusio, broken and smouldering, had been restored to her rightful sovereign.

"Long live the King!" they shouted, a hoarse roar of triumph and delight, and Abeleyn, borne aloft by the shoulders and the approbation of the men who had fought with him and for him, thought that it was for this, this feeling, that men became conquerors. It was more precious than gold, more difficult to earn than any other form of love. It was the essence of kingship.

The shouting, parading troops were almost at the walls of the abbey, their numbers swelled to thousands, when the last salvo from the ships in the harbour came screaming down among them.

The street erupted around Abeleyn. One moment he was being borne along on the shoulders of a victorious army, and then the world became a heaving nightmare of bursting shells and screaming men. His bearers were scattered under him and he fell heavily to the cobbles, cracking his head on the stone. Someone – he thought it was Orsini – had thrown his body across him, but Abeleyn would have none of that. He would not cower behind other men like a frightened woman. He was a king.

Thus he was fighting to get to his feet in the panicked crush, pushing men aside to right and left, when the last shell in the salvo exploded not two yards away, and his world disappeared.

TWENTY-FIVE

THE WOMAN WAS beautiful in the winter sunlight, tall and slim as a mountain birch, with something of the same starkness about her colouring. The officers on the galley quarterdeck directed quick, hungry glances at her as she stood by the starboard rail. She was veiled, of course, as all the Sultan's concubines were, but Aurungzeb was so proud of his Ramusian beauty that her veil was translucent, scandalous, as was her clothing. As the wind shifted the layered gauze about her body it was possible to see the momentary imprint of her nipples, the line of her thigh and calf. The stolen looks kept many of the Merduk sailors dreaming for weeks, while the slaves who toiled at the oars and who had once been free Ramusian citizens regarded her with pity and outrage. She was somehow more evocative of her people's enslavement than the chains that shackled them at wrist and ankle, a taunting display of Merduk prowess.

It seemed that she was staring out at one thing only, and saw nothing else: the monstrous central tower of what had once been the cathedral of Carcasson, horned, forbidding and black with the flames it had survived. It stood alone amid the rubble of what had once been the greatest city in the world and was now a desolate wasteland, save where the walls of the larger buildings stood like monuments to a lost people.

Aekir, the Holy City. Months had passed since its fall, but it was still a ruin. The Merduks had encamped by the thousand around the Square of Victories, where the statue of Myrnius Kuln stood yet, and their tents formed streets and villages in the middle of the desolation, but even their teeming thousands could not fill a tithe of the space within the broken circuit of the city's walls. They were like maggots come squirming in the long-dead corpse of a unicorn, and Carcasson was the dead beast's horn.

The woman called Ahara by her lord and master the Sultan Aurungzeb had once been someone else. A lifetime, a millennium, a nightmare ago, she had been named Heria and had been married to an ensign of cavalry named Corfe. Until Aekir fell.

Now she was the bed toy of the greatest conqueror in the east. She was a trophy of war as much as ruined Aekir was, and she stared out at Carcasson's lonely spire as if in communion with it.

Her grasp of Merduk was very good now, but the Sultan did not know that. She had been careful to appear slow in comprehension and muddled in her own efforts at conversation. Not that there was much conversation required when Aurungzeb blew into the harem like a gale, calling for his favourite bedmate. One had to be willing and uncaring, and submit to whatever the Sultan had in mind.

She had no hope of deliverance: that dream had been knocked out of her long ago. And since her Corfe, who had been her life, was dead it did not seem to matter in what manner she spun out her existence. She was like a ghost hovering on the fringe of life, with no expectations and no prospect of change.

But she kept a little corner of her soul to herself. It was for this reason that she pretended to be slow in learning the Merduk language. Aurungzeb would say things in front of her, or hold discussions in her presence which he was sure she could not understand. That was power of a sort, a tiny gesture towards the maintenance of some personality of her own.

And thus she stood here as the Sultan's galley was rowed down the broad expanse of the Ostian river, with ruined Aekir running along the banks on either side. And she listened.

The commander of the main field army of Ostrabar, Shahr Indun Johor, was deep in talk with the Sultan whilst the staff officers kept to the port side of the quarterdeck. Heria, or Ahara, was able to eavesdrop on them as the toiling slaves propelled the galley downriver towards the concentration of ships and men that waited farther downstream.

"The Nalbenic transports have already docked, Highness," Shahr Johor was saying. A tall, fine-featured young man, he was the successor to Shahr Baraz, the old khedive who had taken Aekir and made the first, fruitless assaults on Ormann Dyke.

"Excellent." Aurungzeb had a white-toothed grin that was somehow startling in the midst of that expanse of beard, like suddenly glimpsing the bared canines of a dark-furred dog. "And how soon will the fleet be ready to sail?"

"Within two days, Highness. The Prophet has blessed us with mild winds. The transports will be in the Kardian Gulf before the end of the week, and at their assigned stations on the Torunnan coast three days after that. In less than two sennights we will have an army on Torunnan soil south of the Searil river. We will have outflanked Ormann Dyke."

"Ah, Shahr Johor, you gladden my heart," Aurungzeb's grin broadened. He was a hearty man with a thickening middle and eyes as black and bright as shards of jet. "Your Excellency!" he called to the group of men on the other side of the quarterdeck. "I must congratulate your lord on his swift work. The treaty is only signed a week and already his galleys are at their station. I am most impressed."

One of the men came forward and bowed. He was of below medium height, dressed in rich embroidered silk and with a gold chain about his neck: the Merduk badge of an ambassador.

"My sultan, may he live for ever, will be gladdened by your confidence and pleasure, Highness. Nalbeni has never wanted anything else but that it and Ostrabar might work together, as brothers would, for the propagation of the faith and the defeat of the unbelievers."

Aurungzeb laughed. His high spirits were spilling out of him. "We shall have a banquet tonight to toast this new cooperation between our states, and the confusion of the enemy who will no longer be able to defy the might of our armies behind walls of stone, but will have to come out into the field and fight like men."

Ahara was forgotten. The Sultan and his staff went below with the Nalbenic ambassador to pore over the maps they had already been poring over for days and fix the last details of their joint plans in place.

Ahara remained by the galley's rail. Aekir slid by, and the river became busier. There were hundreds of ships here, moored at the remnants of old wharves. A mighty fleet flying the Nalbenic flag, and an army encamped on the riverbank beside it. A hundred thousand men they said it numbered. Some had been withdrawn from before the dyke, others were fresh levies gathered throughout the winter from the farms and towns of Ostrabar and Nalbeni. Soon Torunna would be overwhelmed, the fortifications of Ormann Dyke rendered useless by the amphibious invasion. This panorama of men and ships was the death knell of the Ramusian west.

And it did not matter. The world Ahara had known had died here, in a welter of slaughter and rape and burning. She was numb to the possibility that the rest of the continent might soon fare similarly. She was only glad, in the small portion of her that remained her own, that she was allowed to stand here in the sunlight and listen to the seagulls and smell the salt air of the Ostian estuary. She gloried in her solitude.

But it ended, as it always did, and she was called below to attend upon the Sultan and his guests. Her dancing had come on apace, and Aurungzeb loved to have her perform for an audience. It whetted his appetite, he said.

The galley sailed on, the slaves bending at the oars, the vast armada of men and ships and munitions sliding past on each side. It seemed that the whole world had been picked up and reconfigured. It was a different place now, impervious to the wishes of the men who inhabited it. Some dreadful engine had begun to turn in the hot darkness of its vitals and could not be stopped any more than the sun could be halted in its path. The force of history, a philosopher might name it, or a more practical man might simply call it war. Whatever its epithet, it was about to break apart the world men had known, and fashion from the pieces something terrible and new.

Acknowledgements:

To John McLaughlin, Richard Evans and
Jo Fletcher, for their patience and
hard work on my behalf.

COMING SOON FROM PAUL KEARNEY

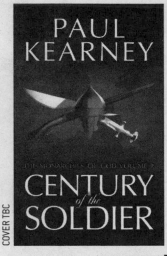

THE MONARCHIES OF GOD - VOLUME 2
CENTURY OF THE SOLDIER

UK: ISBN: 978 1 907519 08 6 • £8.99
US: ISBN: 978 1 907519 09 3 • $9.99

Hebrion's young King Abeleyn lies in a coma, his capital in ruins and his former lover conniving for the throne. Corfe Cear-Inaf is given a ragtag command of savages and sent on a mission he cannot hope to succeed. Richard Hawkwood finally returns to the Monarchies of God, bearing news of a wild new continent.

In the West the Himerian Church is extending its reach, while in the East the fortress of Ormann Dyke stands ready to fall to the Merduk horde. These are terrible times, and call for extraordinary people...

CORVUS

UK: ISBN: 978 1 906735 76 0 • £7.99
US: ISBN: 978 1 906735 77 7 • $7.99

It is twenty-three years since a Macht army fought its way home from the heart of the Asurian Empire. Rictus is now a hard-bitten mercenary captain, middle-aged and tired, and wants nothing more than to become the farmer that his father was. But fate has different ideas. A young warleader has risen in the very heartlands of the Macht, taking city after city, and reigning over them as king.

His name is Corvus, and the rumours say that he is not even fully human. He means to make himself absolute ruler of all the Macht. And he wants Rictus to help him.

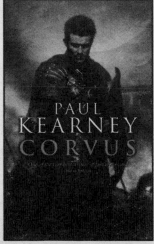

 WWW.SOLARISBOOKS.COM

Follow us on Twitter! www.twitter.com/solarisbooks